Archie's

BiG Book

VOLUME 4: FAIRY TALES

Publisher / Co-CEO: Jon Goldwater

Co-President / Editor-In-Chief: Victor Gorelick

Co-President: Mike Pellerito

Co-President: Alex Segura

Chief Creative Officer: Roberto Aguirre-Sacasa

Chief Operating Officer: William Mooar

Chief Financial Officer: Robert Wintle

Director of Book Sales & Operations: Jonathan Betancourt

Production Manager: Stephen Oswald

Lead Designer: Kari McLachlan

Associate Editor: Carlos Antunes

Production: Vincent Lovallo

Assistant Editor / Proofreader: Jamie Lee Rotante

Co-CEO: Nancy Silberkleit

Published by Archie Comic Publications, Inc. 629 Fifth Avenue, Suite 100, Pelham, NY 10803-1242

WRITTEN BY

Terry Collins, Frank Doyle, George Gladir, Al Hartley, Dan Parent, Mike Pellowski, and Kathleen Webb

ART BY

Mario Acquaviva, Jim Amash, Carlos Antunes, Janice Chiang, Teresa Davidson, Dan DeCarlo, Digikore Studios, Marty Epp, Stan Goldberg, Barry Grossman, Al Hartley, Rich Koslowski, Rudy Lapick, Rex Lindsey, Jack Morelli, Rod Ollerenshaw, Dan Parent, Henry Scarpelli, Samm Schwartz, Jeff Shultz, Joe Sinnott, Bob Smith, Dexter Taylor, Bill Vigoda, Bob White, Glenn Whitmore, and Bill Yoshida

COVER ART BY Dan Parent

Archie's® BiG

TABLE OF CONTENTS

CHAPTER ONE

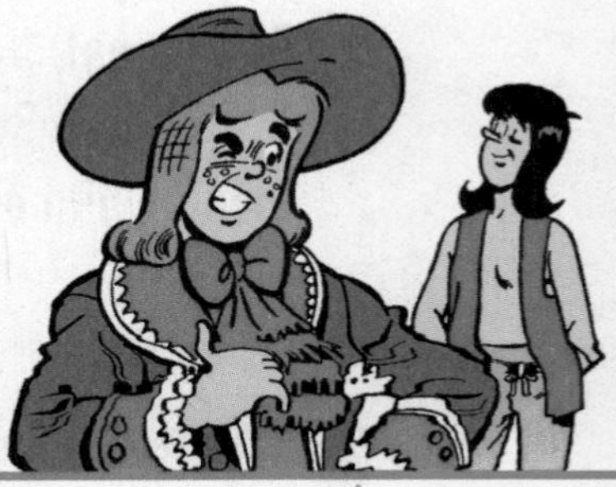

CHAPTER TWO

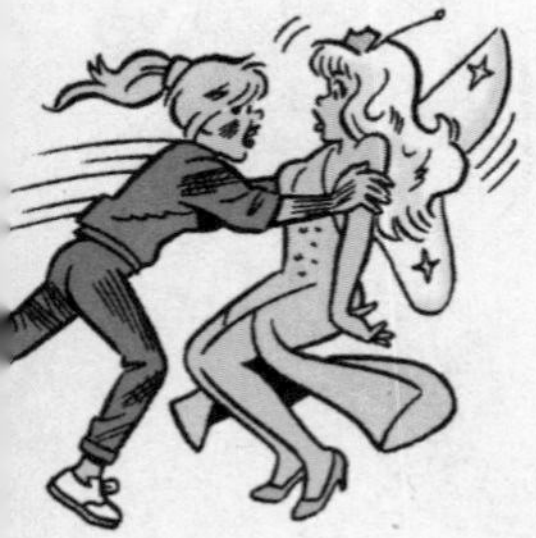

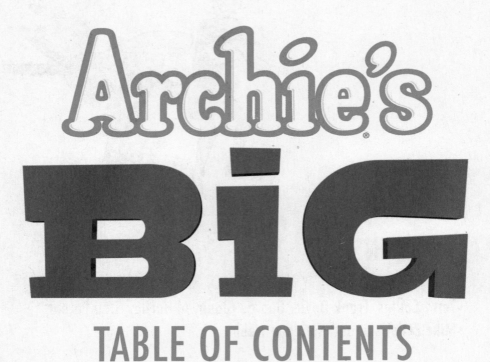

CHAPTER THREE

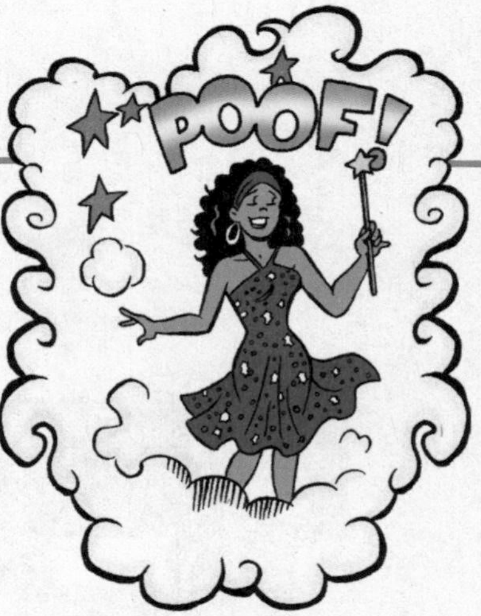
POOF!

CHAPTER FOUR

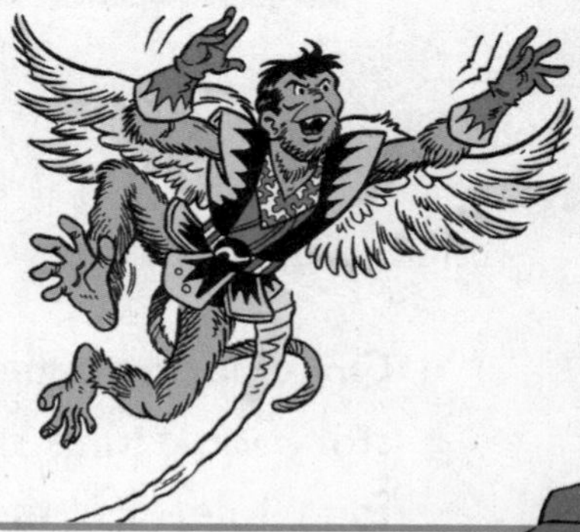

CHAPTER FIVE

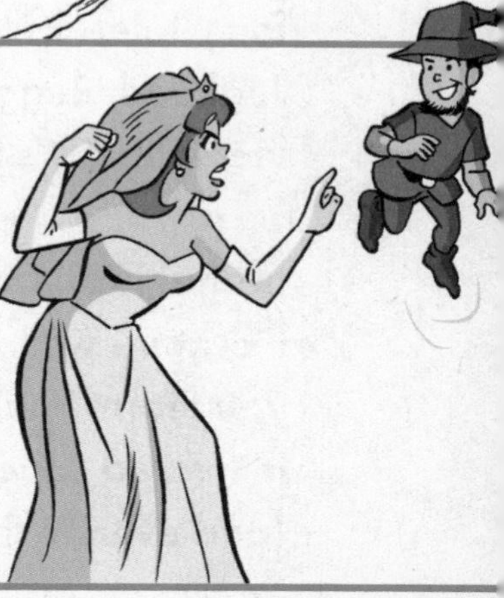

CHAPTER SIX

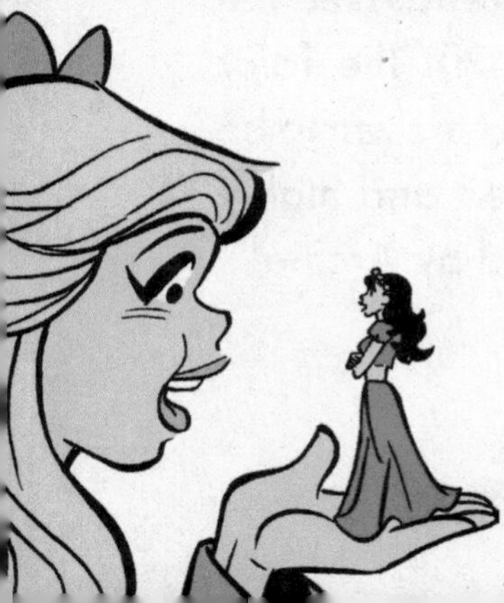

Archie's
BiG
INTRODUCTION

Once upon a time Archie took a walk down Riverdale's magical storybook lane and found himself the prince of his very own fairy tale—but that wasn't the first time Archie, Betty, Veronica, Jughead, Reggie and more found themselves living a fantastical life, in fact it's happened many times over the past six decades!

In the 1950s and 1960s a few short Archie stories combined literature with comics, applying a self-proclaimed "laugh while you learn" method for young readers. While we'd see this style mimicked especially in series like *The Mighty Archie Art Players* (and even in the multitudes of fantasy genre parodies, many of which you may have already seen in *Archie's Big Book Vol. 2!*), the fairy tale-inspired stories have proven to be some of the most beloved and highly praised comics published by Archie.

This Big Book collection aims to bring you some of the best and brightest of those very stories, spanning every decade from the 1950s to the present day—and there are still so many more yet to come!

So take a trip down the yellow brick road with Betty, dive under the sea with two BFF mermaids, watch as Archie's nose grows as he tells fibs, witness as Jughead turns mutant and find out why everyone wants to know Reggie's name!

What are you waiting for? Turn the page and let the fairy tale fun begin!

CHAPTER ONE

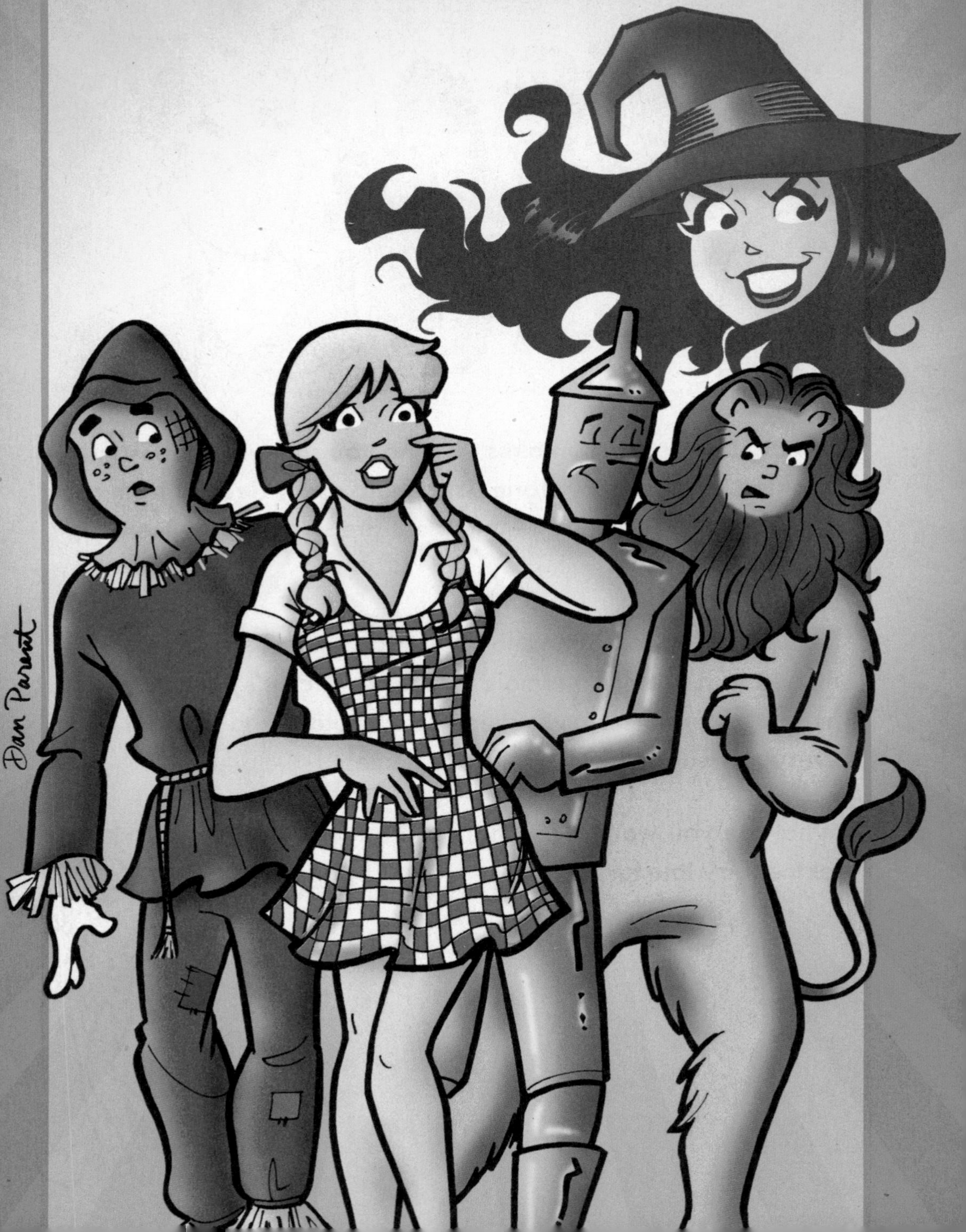
Dan Parent

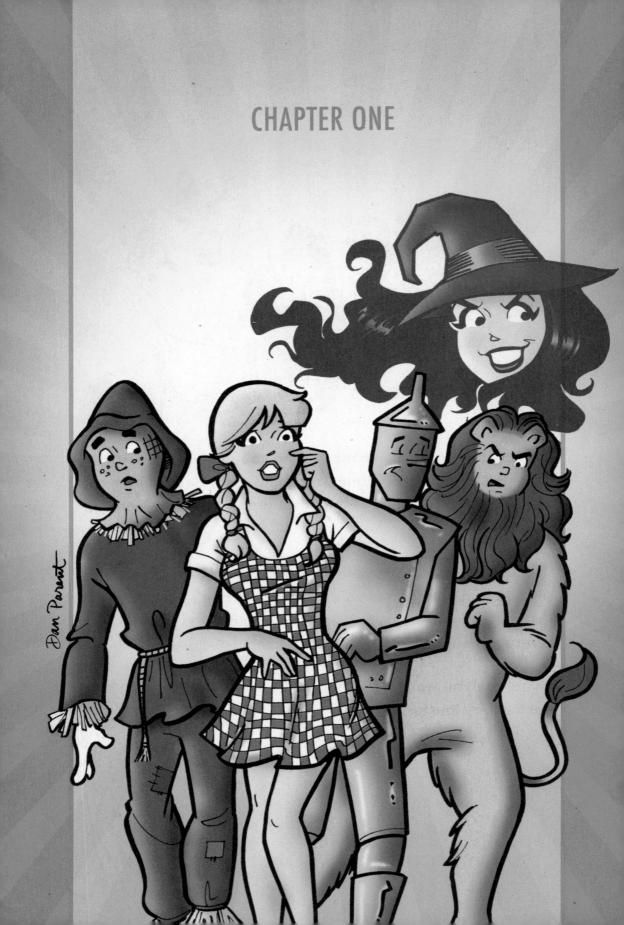

ARCHIE IN
ARCHIE'S FABLES
SEPTEMBER-OCTOBER 1954
PENCILS: SAMM SCHWARTZ   INKS: BILL VIGODA

BETTY IN
ARCHIE IN WONDERLAND
MAY 1960
SCRIPT: GEORGE GLADIR   PENCILS: BOB WHITE   INKS & LETTERS: MARTY EPP

ARCHIE & FRIENDS IN
THE PRINCESS AND THE PARTY POOPER
FEBRUARY 1972
SCRIPT & PENCILS: AL HARTLEY   INKS: JOE SINNOTT   LETTERS: BILL YOSHIDA

ARCHIE IN
LITTLE WOODENHEAD
APRIL 1972
**SCRIPT: FRANK DOYLE   PENCILS: BILL VIGODA   INKS: MARIO ACQUAVIVA
LETTERS: BILL YOSHIDA   COLORS: CARLOS ANTUNES**

LITTLE SABRINA IN
THE WITCHES OF OZ
APRIL 1972
**SCRIPT & PENCILS: DEXTER TAYLOR   INKS: RUDY LAPICK
LETTERS: BILL YOSHIDA   COLORS: BARRY GROSSMAN**

Archie's Fables

OLD FAVORITES RETOLD IN TEEN AGE TEMPO!!

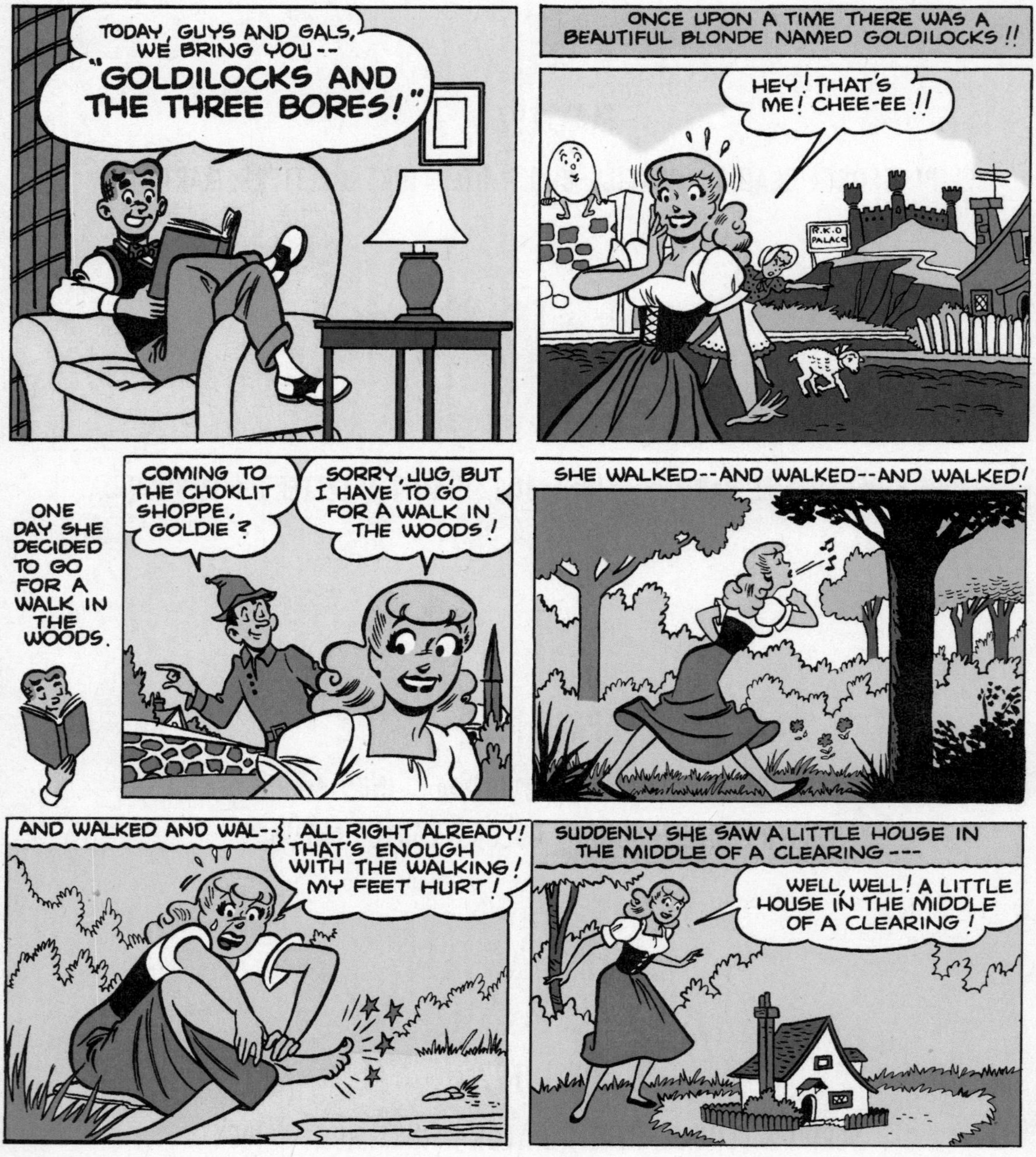
TODAY, GUYS AND GALS, WE BRING YOU-- "GOLDILOCKS AND THE THREE BORES!"
ONCE UPON A TIME THERE WAS A BEAUTIFUL BLONDE NAMED GOLDILOCKS!!
HEY! THAT'S ME! CHEE-EE!!
R.K.O PALACE
ONE DAY SHE DECIDED TO GO FOR A WALK IN THE WOODS.
COMING TO THE CHOKLIT SHOPPE, GOLDIE?
SORRY, JUG, BUT I HAVE TO GO FOR A WALK IN THE WOODS!
SHE WALKED--AND WALKED--AND WALKED!
AND WALKED AND WAL--
ALL RIGHT ALREADY! THAT'S ENOUGH WITH THE WALKING! MY FEET HURT!
SUDDENLY SHE SAW A LITTLE HOUSE IN THE MIDDLE OF A CLEARING---
WELL, WELL! A LITTLE HOUSE IN THE MIDDLE OF A CLEARING!

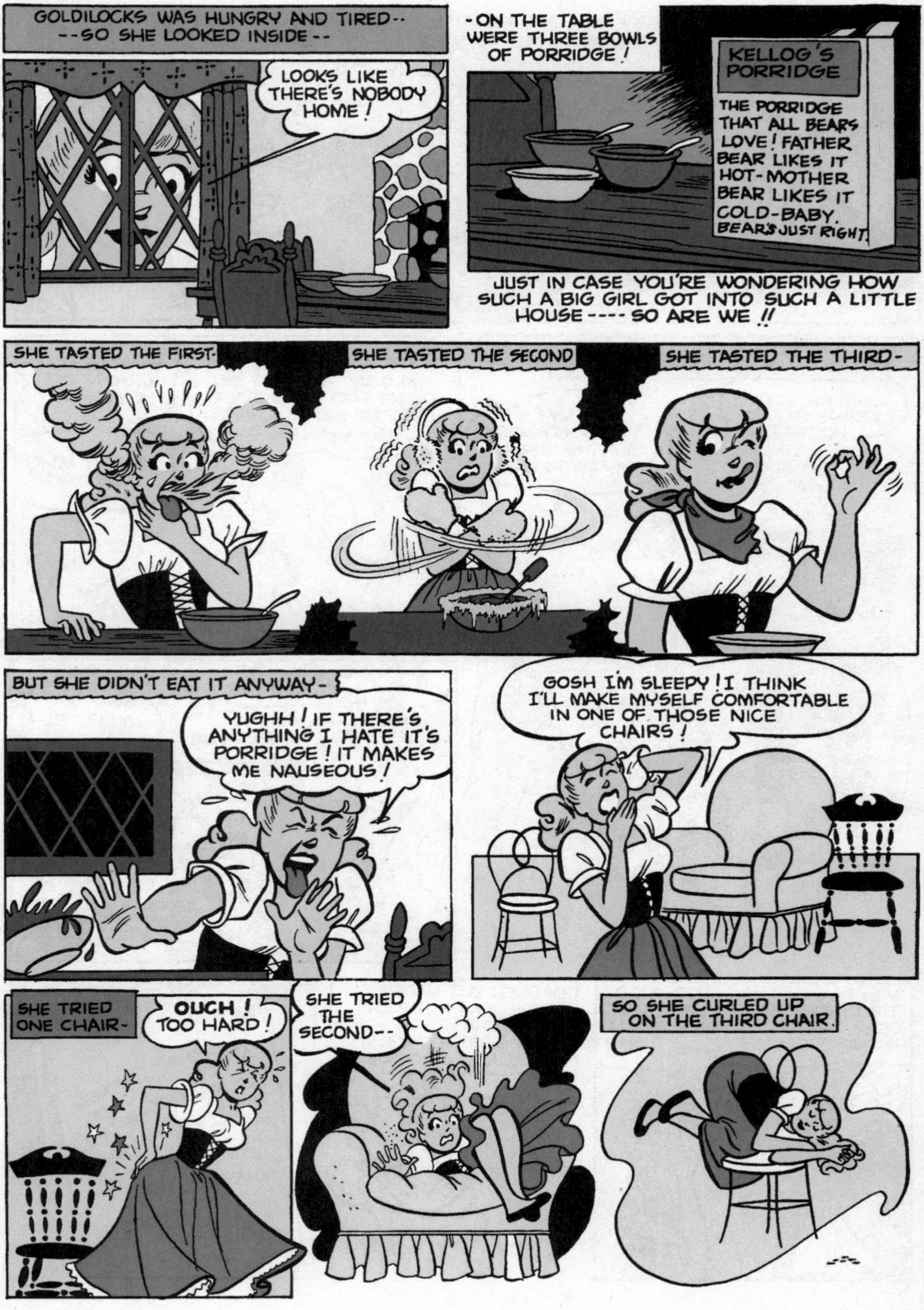
GOLDILOCKS WAS HUNGRY AND TIRED-- --SO SHE LOOKED INSIDE--
LOOKS LIKE THERE'S NOBODY HOME!
-ON THE TABLE WERE THREE BOWLS OF PORRIDGE!
KELLOG'S PORRIDGE
THE PORRIDGE THAT ALL BEARS LOVE! FATHER BEAR LIKES IT HOT-MOTHER BEAR LIKES IT COLD-BABY. BEAR'S JUST RIGHT.
JUST IN CASE YOU'RE WONDERING HOW SUCH A BIG GIRL GOT INTO SUCH A LITTLE HOUSE---- SO ARE WE!!
SHE TASTED THE FIRST-
SHE TASTED THE SECOND
SHE TASTED THE THIRD-
BUT SHE DIDN'T EAT IT ANYWAY-
YUGHH! IF THERE'S ANYTHING I HATE IT'S PORRIDGE! IT MAKES ME NAUSEOUS!
GOSH I'M SLEEPY! I THINK I'LL MAKE MYSELF COMFORTABLE IN ONE OF THOSE NICE CHAIRS!
SHE TRIED ONE CHAIR-
OUCH! TOO HARD!
SHE TRIED THE SECOND--
SO SHE CURLED UP ON THE THIRD CHAIR.

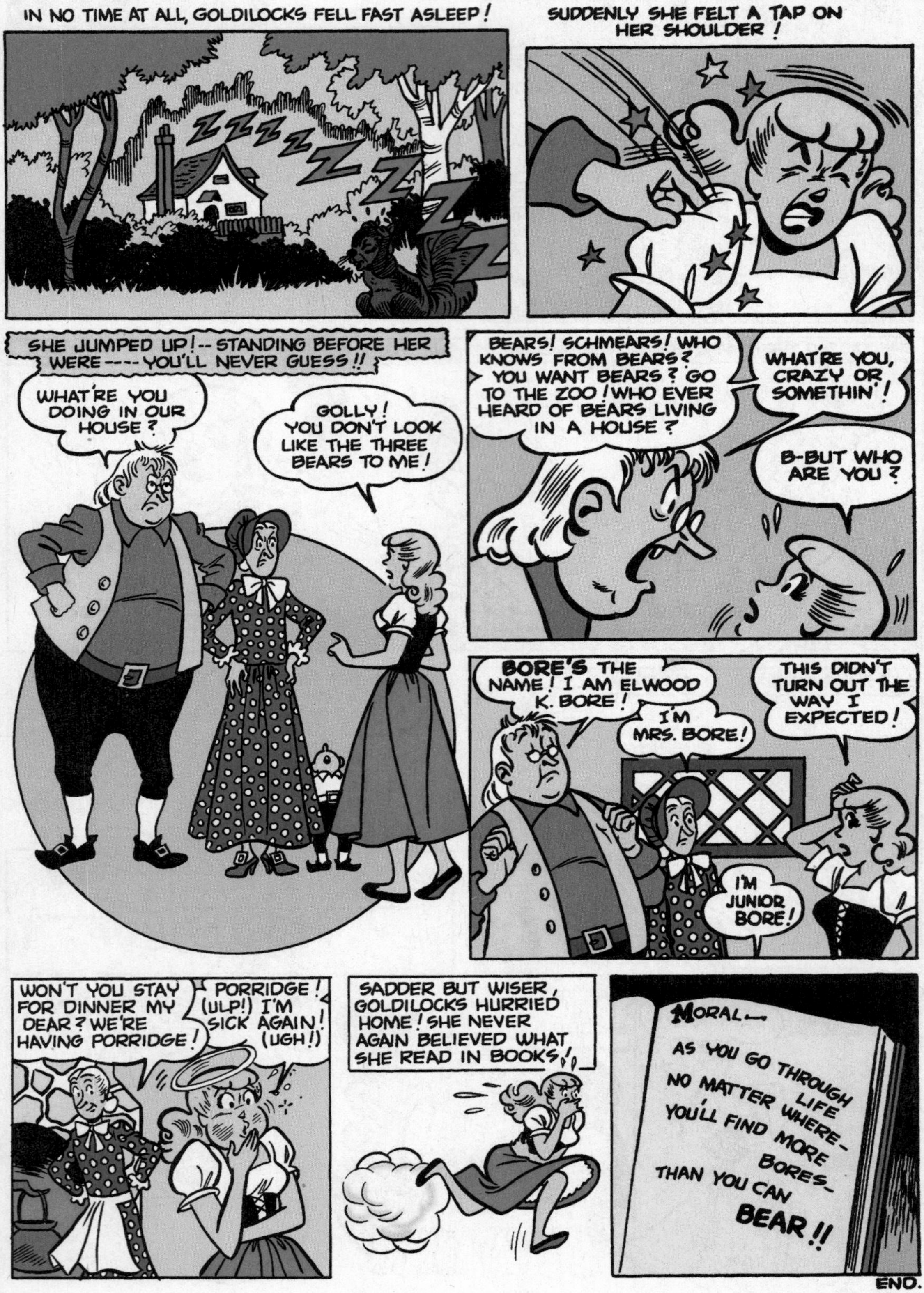
IN NO TIME AT ALL, GOLDILOCKS FELL FAST ASLEEP!
SUDDENLY SHE FELT A TAP ON HER SHOULDER!
SHE JUMPED UP! -- STANDING BEFORE HER WERE ---- YOU'LL NEVER GUESS!!
WHAT'RE YOU DOING IN OUR HOUSE?
GOLLY! YOU DON'T LOOK LIKE THE THREE BEARS TO ME!
BEARS! SCHMEARS! WHO KNOWS FROM BEARS? YOU WANT BEARS? GO TO THE ZOO! WHO EVER HEARD OF BEARS LIVING IN A HOUSE?
WHAT'RE YOU, CRAZY OR SOMETHIN'!
B-BUT WHO ARE YOU?
BORE'S THE NAME! I AM ELWOOD K. BORE!
I'M MRS. BORE!
THIS DIDN'T TURN OUT THE WAY I EXPECTED!
I'M JUNIOR BORE!
WON'T YOU STAY FOR DINNER MY DEAR? WE'RE HAVING PORRIDGE!
PORRIDGE! (ULP!) I'M SICK AGAIN! (UGH!)
SADDER BUT WISER, GOLDILOCKS HURRIED HOME! SHE NEVER AGAIN BELIEVED WHAT SHE READ IN BOOKS!
MORAL—
AS YOU GO THROUGH LIFE NO MATTER WHERE— YOU'LL FIND MORE BORES— THAN YOU CAN BEAR!!
END.

BETTY SAYS:

We recently ran an article called "ARCHIE IN SHAKESPEARE LAND." Our purpose was to combine LITERATURE and COMICS -- a sort of "laugh-while-you-learn" method..!

Well, if you think THAT was dopey -- wait until you read THIS one -- it's based on Lewis Carroll's famous classic, and we call it--

Archie in Wonderland!

I PROTEST! I OBJECT! I DON'T WANNA PLAY A DAME'S PART! NO, NO!

WHAT'RE YOU COMPLAINING ABOUT, ARCHIE--

--I'M THE WHITE RABBIT!

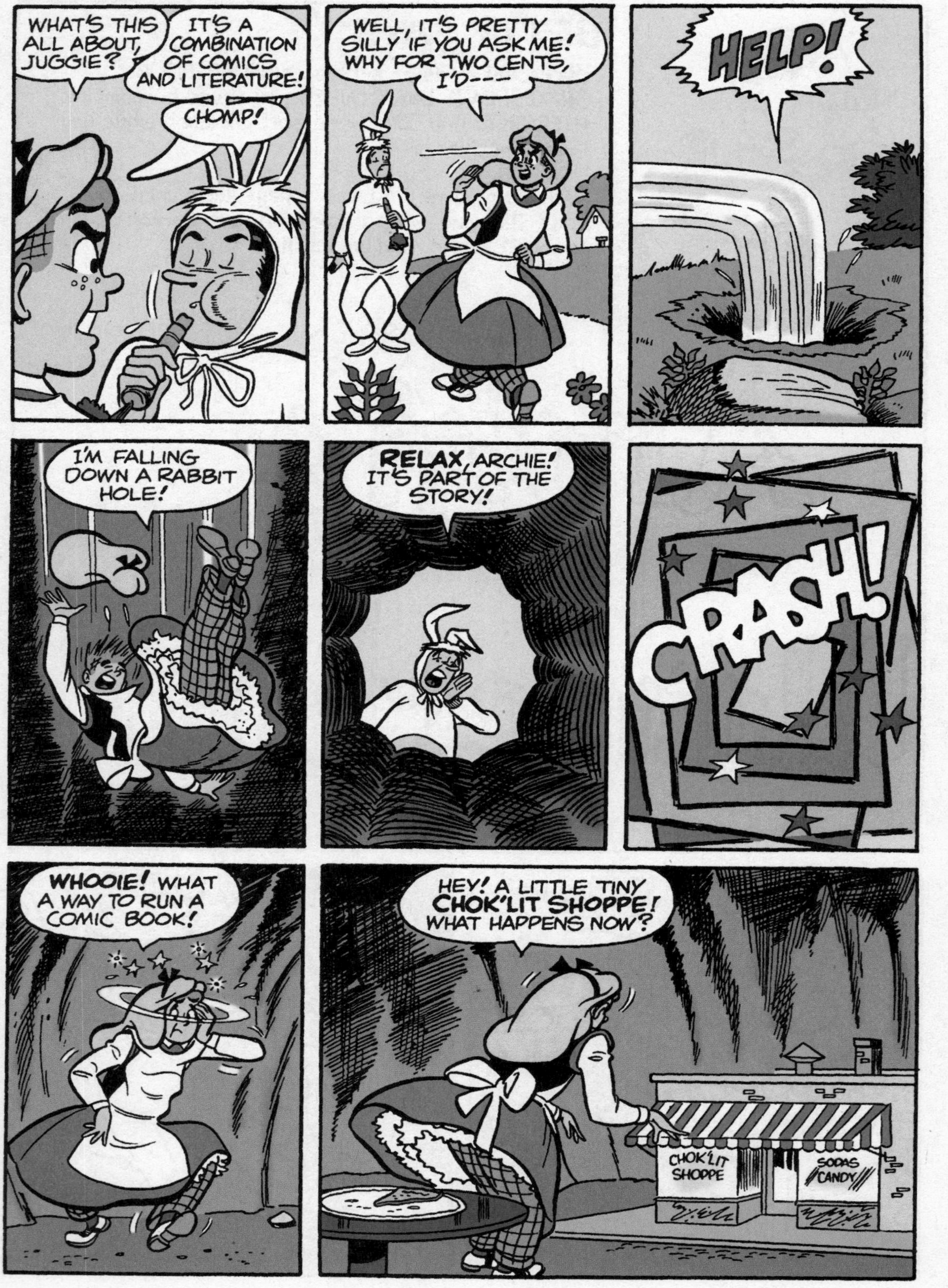
WHAT'S THIS ALL ABOUT, JUGGIE?
IT'S A COMBINATION OF COMICS AND LITERATURE!
CHOMP!
WELL, IT'S PRETTY SILLY IF YOU ASK ME! WHY FOR TWO CENTS, I'D---
HELP!
I'M FALLING DOWN A RABBIT HOLE!
RELAX, ARCHIE! IT'S PART OF THE STORY!
CRASH!
WHOOIE! WHAT A WAY TO RUN A COMIC BOOK!
HEY! A LITTLE TINY CHOK'LIT SHOPPE! WHAT HAPPENS NOW?
CHOK'LIT SHOPPE
SODAS CANDY

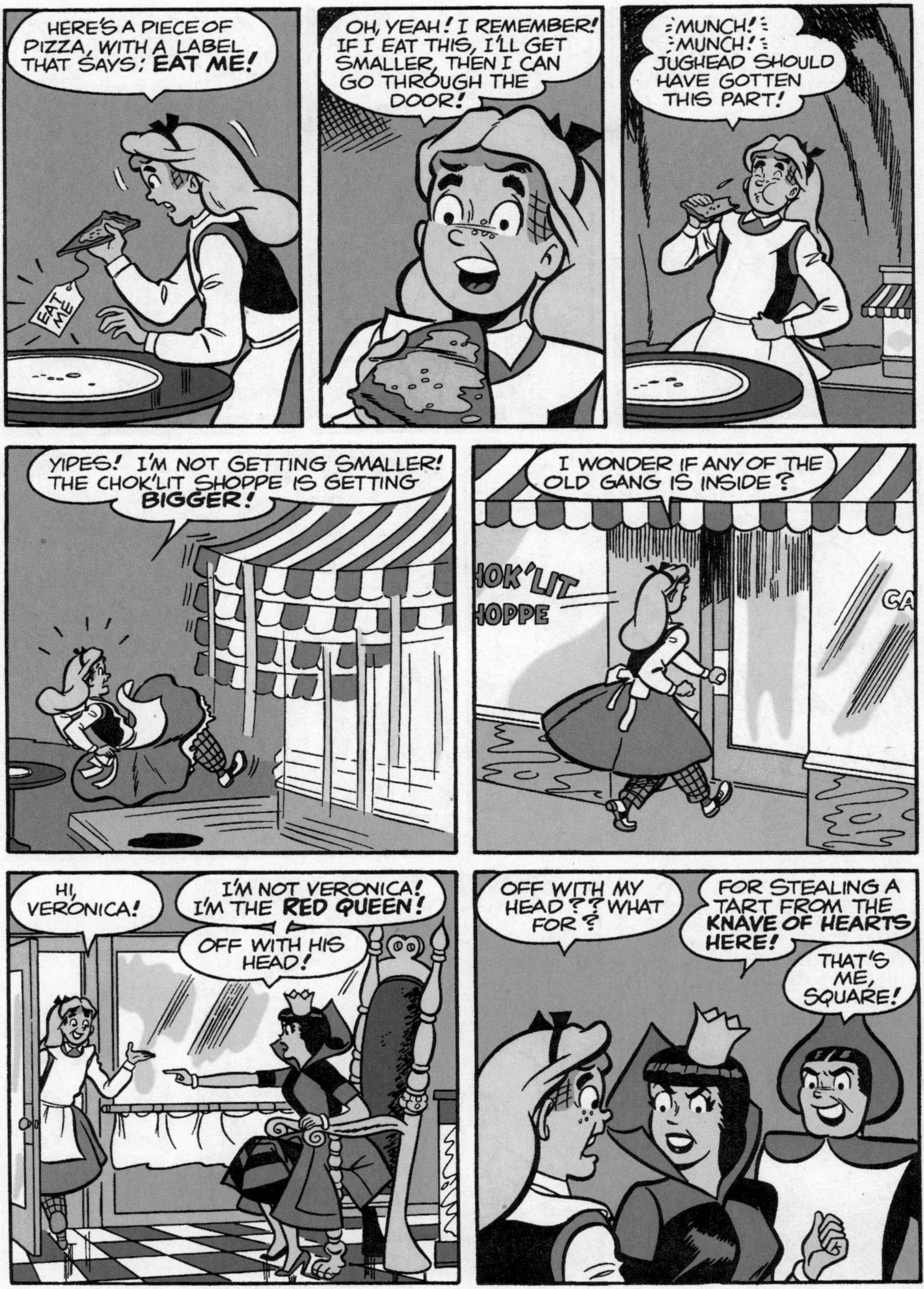
HERE'S A PIECE OF PIZZA, WITH A LABEL THAT SAYS: EAT ME!
EAT ME
OH, YEAH! I REMEMBER! IF I EAT THIS, I'LL GET SMALLER, THEN I CAN GO THROUGH THE DOOR!
MUNCH! MUNCH! JUGHEAD SHOULD HAVE GOTTEN THIS PART!
YIPES! I'M NOT GETTING SMALLER! THE CHOK'LIT SHOPPE IS GETTING BIGGER!
I WONDER IF ANY OF THE OLD GANG IS INSIDE?
HOK'LIT
HOPPE
HI, VERONICA!
I'M NOT VERONICA! I'M THE RED QUEEN!
OFF WITH HIS HEAD!
OFF WITH MY HEAD?? WHAT FOR?
FOR STEALING A TART FROM THE KNAVE OF HEARTS HERE!
THAT'S ME, SQUARE!

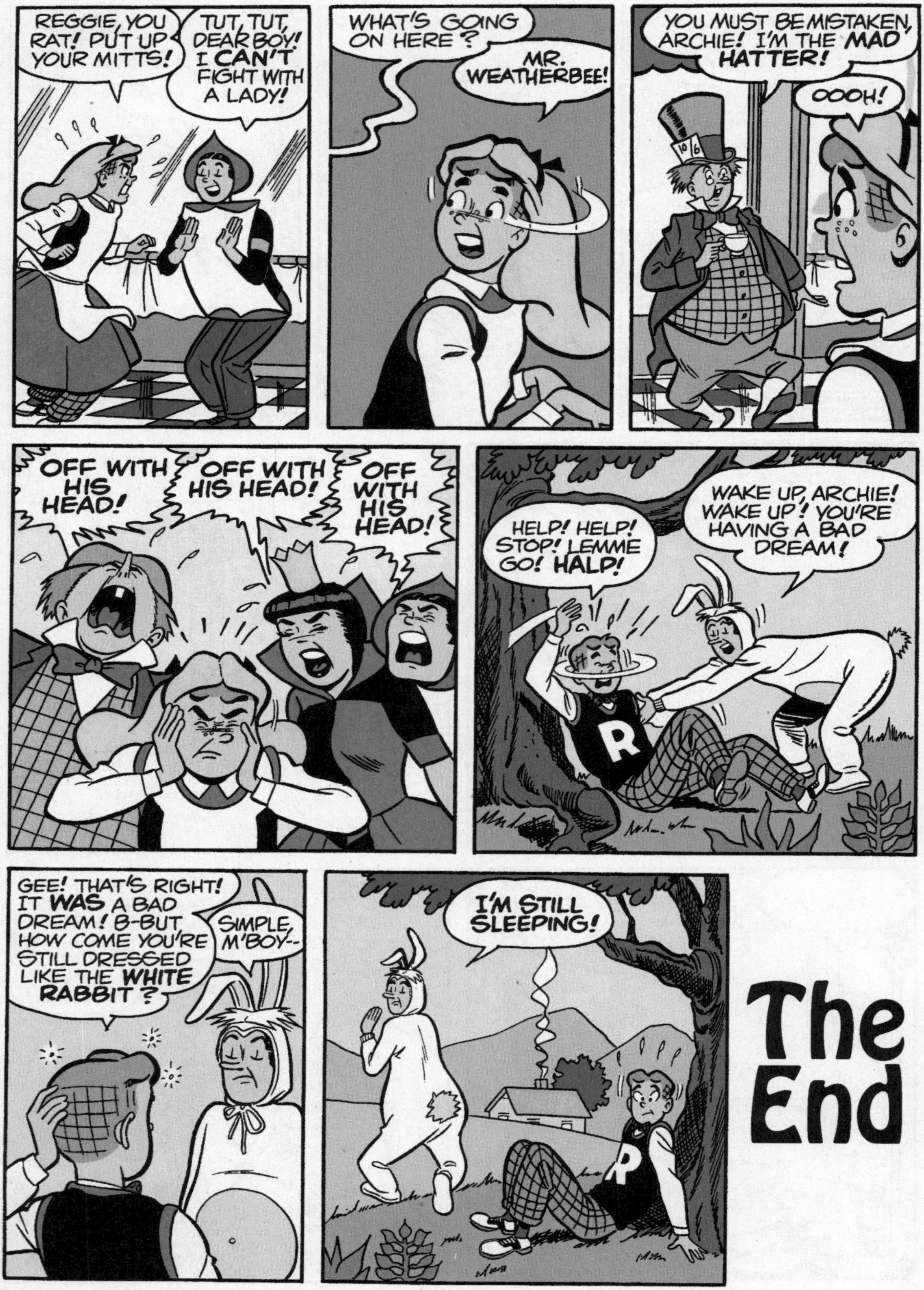
REGGIE, YOU RAT! PUT UP YOUR MITTS!
TUT, TUT, DEAR BOY! I CAN'T FIGHT WITH A LADY!
WHAT'S GOING ON HERE?
MR. WEATHERBEE!
YOU MUST BE MISTAKEN, ARCHIE! I'M THE MAD HATTER!
OOOH!
10/6
OFF WITH HIS HEAD!
OFF WITH HIS HEAD!
OFF WITH HIS HEAD!
HELP! HELP! STOP! LEMME GO! HALP!
WAKE UP, ARCHIE! WAKE UP! YOU'RE HAVING A BAD DREAM!
R
GEE! THAT'S RIGHT! IT WAS A BAD DREAM! B-BUT HOW COME YOU'RE STILL DRESSED LIKE THE WHITE RABBIT?
SIMPLE, M'BOY--
I'M STILL SLEEPING!
R

The End

Archie & Friends' Fables #1

"The Princess and the Party Pooper"

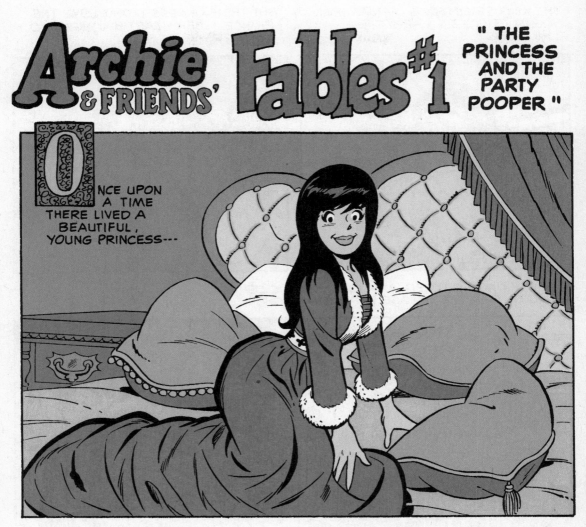

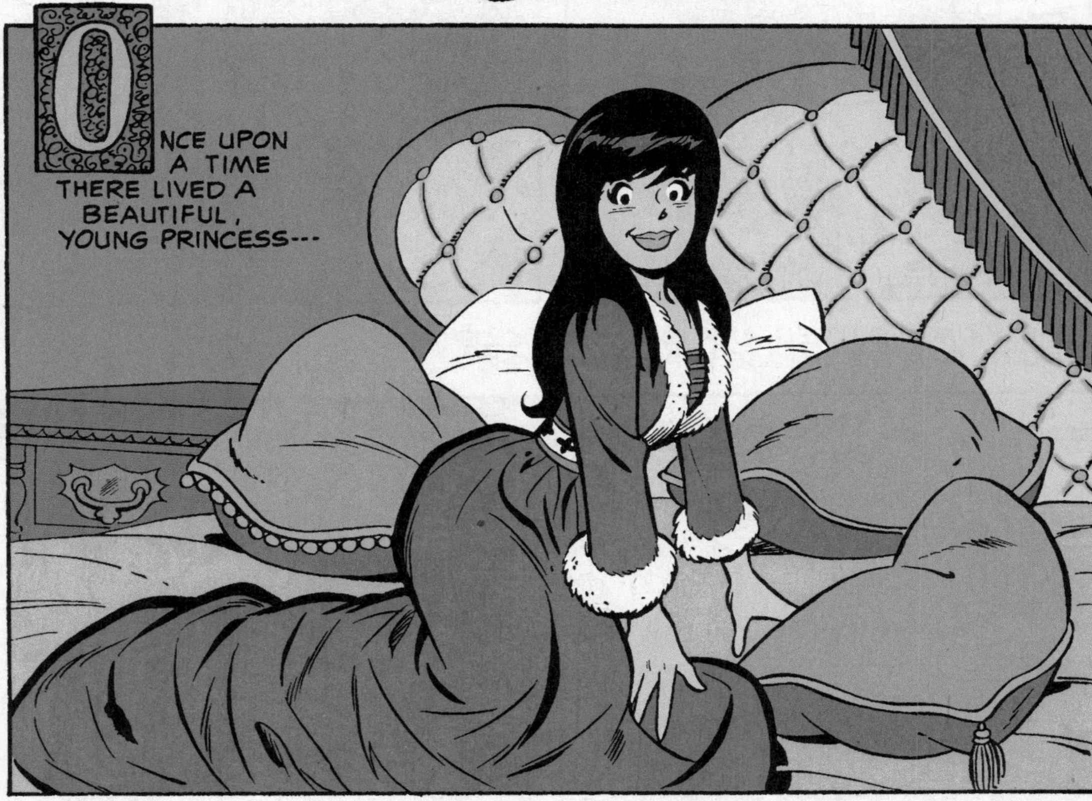
ONCE UPON A TIME THERE LIVED A BEAUTIFUL, YOUNG PRINCESS---

SHE LIVED IN A PALACE HIGH ON A HILL, AND THE SWIMMING POOL RAN ALL AROUND THE PALACE---

NOW THE PRINCESS' FATHER WAS KING OF ALL THE REALM AND HE LOVED HIS DAUGHTER VERY MUCH---

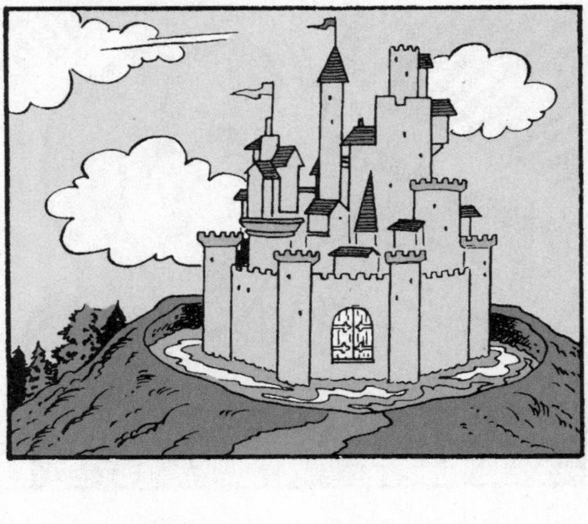

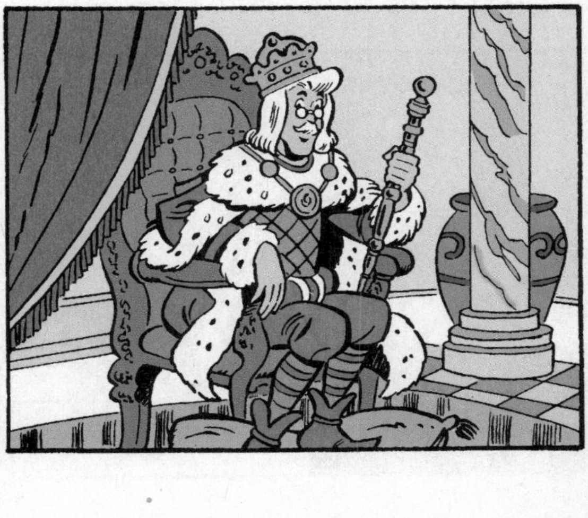

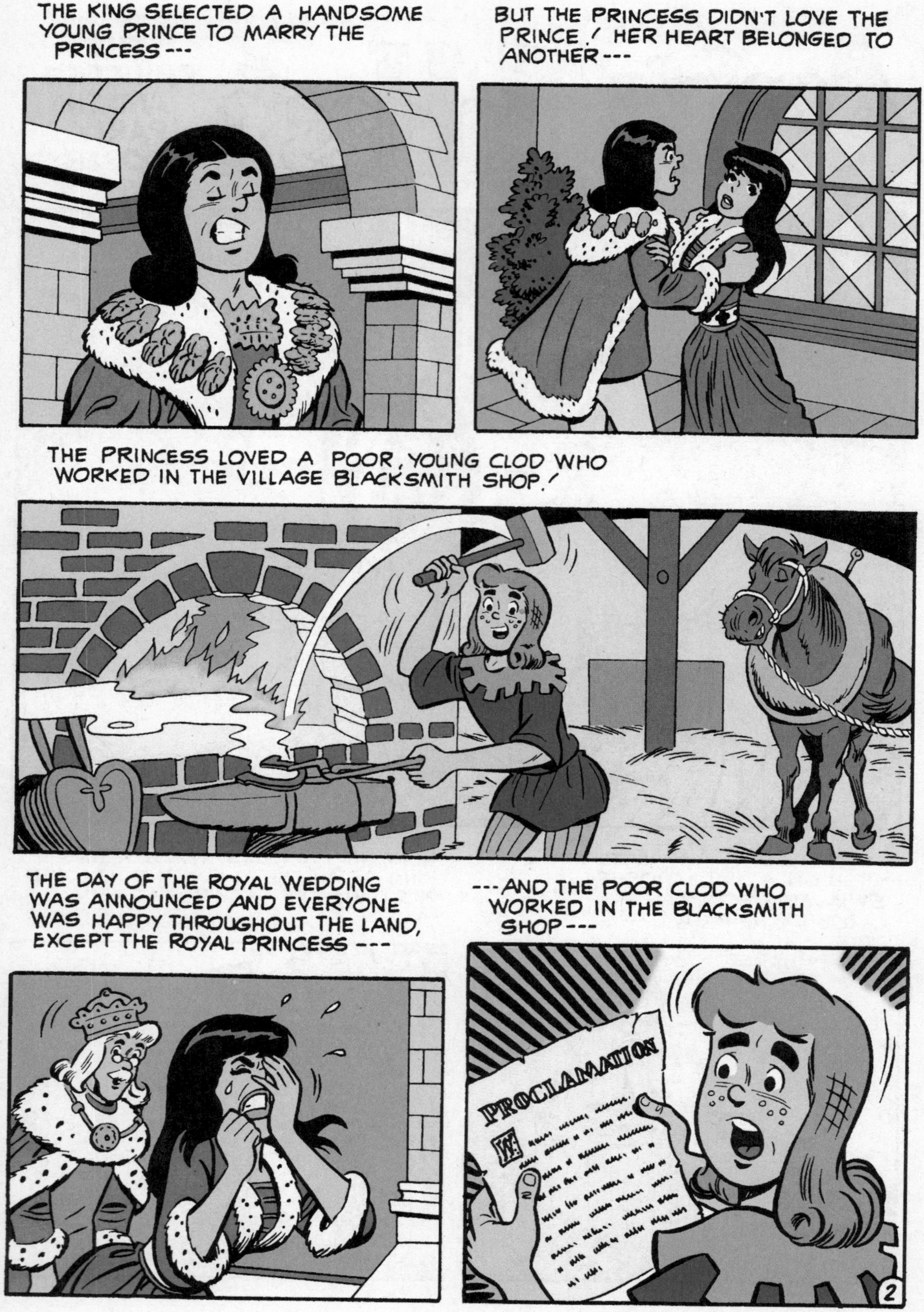
THE KING SELECTED A HANDSOME YOUNG PRINCE TO MARRY THE PRINCESS---
BUT THE PRINCESS DIDN'T LOVE THE PRINCE! HER HEART BELONGED TO ANOTHER---
THE PRINCESS LOVED A POOR, YOUNG CLOD WHO WORKED IN THE VILLAGE BLACKSMITH SHOP!
THE DAY OF THE ROYAL WEDDING WAS ANNOUNCED AND EVERYONE WAS HAPPY THROUGHOUT THE LAND, EXCEPT THE ROYAL PRINCESS---
---AND THE POOR CLOD WHO WORKED IN THE BLACKSMITH SHOP---
PROCLAMATION
2

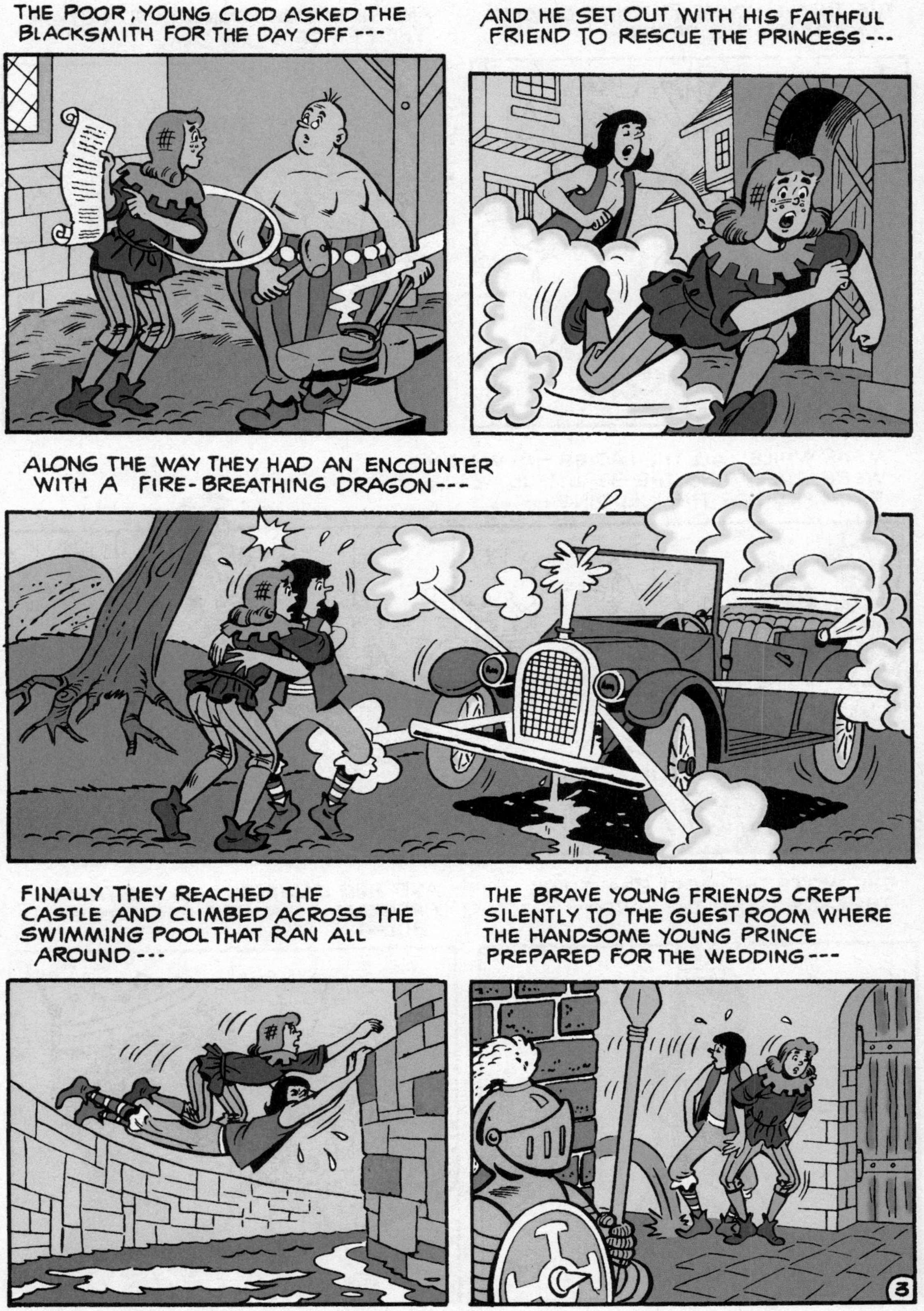
THE POOR, YOUNG CLOD ASKED THE BLACKSMITH FOR THE DAY OFF ---
AND HE SET OUT WITH HIS FAITHFUL FRIEND TO RESCUE THE PRINCESS ---
ALONG THE WAY THEY HAD AN ENCOUNTER WITH A FIRE-BREATHING DRAGON ---
FINALLY THEY REACHED THE CASTLE AND CLIMBED ACROSS THE SWIMMING POOL THAT RAN ALL AROUND ---
THE BRAVE YOUNG FRIENDS CREPT SILENTLY TO THE GUEST ROOM WHERE THE HANDSOME YOUNG PRINCE PREPARED FOR THE WEDDING ---
3

THE BRAVE YOUNG FRIENDS QUICKLY OVERCAME THE PRINCE---

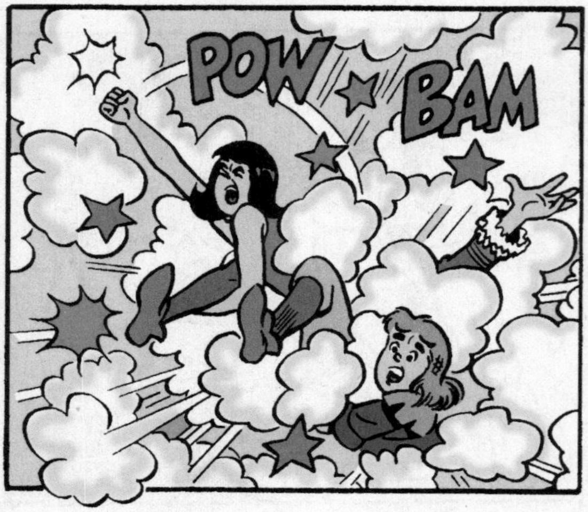
POW
BAM

AND THE POOR YOUNG CLOD PUT ON THE PRINCE'S UNIFORM---

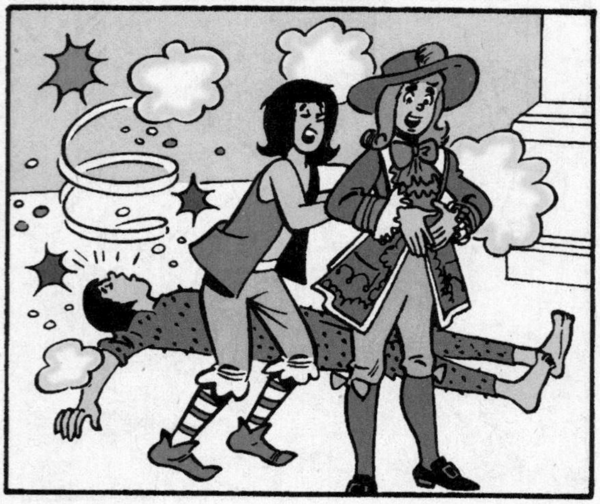

MEAN WHILE, ALL THE LADIES-IN-WAITING WERE PREPARING THE BEAUTIFUL, YOUNG PRINCESS FOR THE WEDDING---

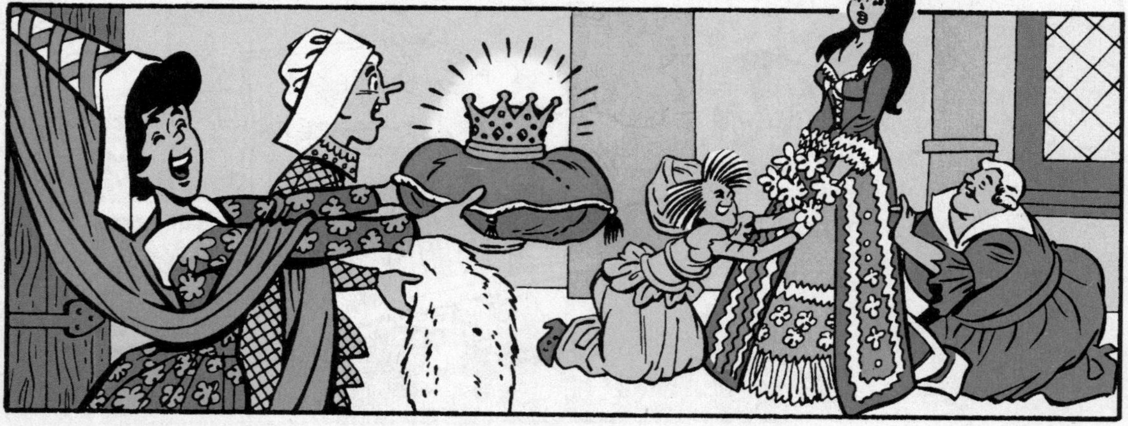

SHE WORE THE MOST BEAUTIFUL THREADS IN ALL THE LAND---

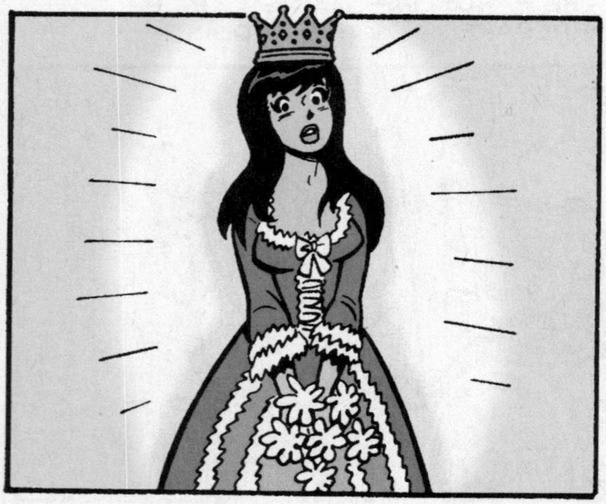

AND HER JEWELRY WAS THE MOST PRECIOUS IN ALL THE KINGDOM--- BUT---

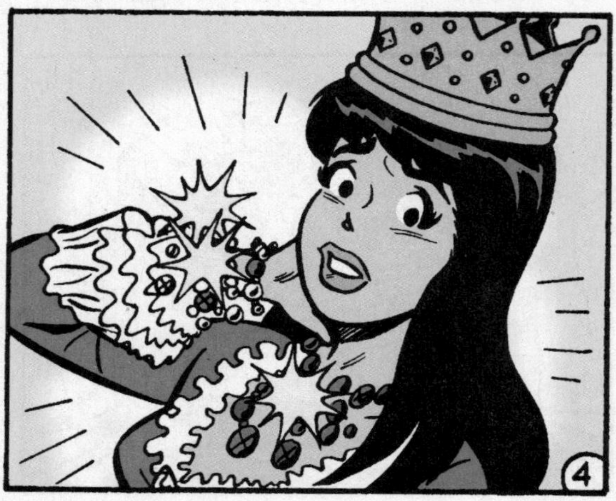

THE PRINCESS WAS VERY SAD AS SHE WALKED DOWN THE AISLE---

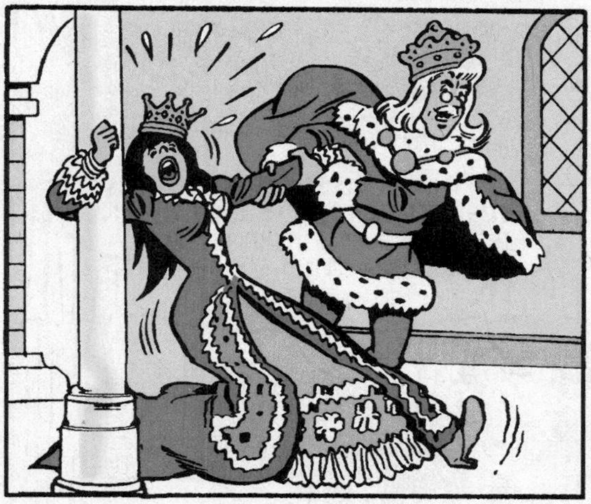

HOW WAS SHE TO KNOW THAT HER TRUE LOVER HAD SO CLEVERLY SAVED THE DAY---

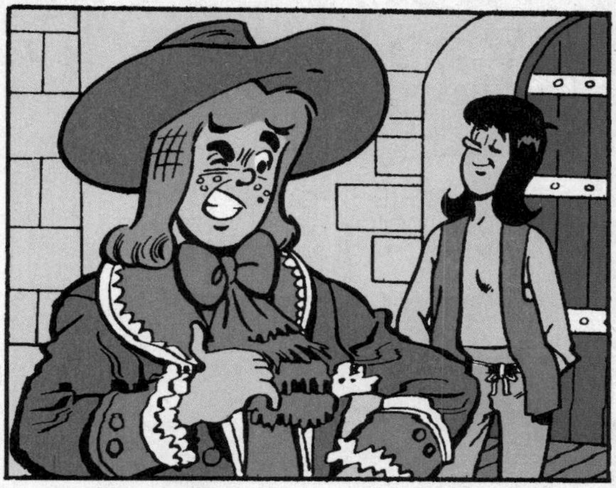

BUT AS THE POOR, YOUNG CLOD STEPPED FORWARD, HE TRIPPED ON THE ROYAL STAIRS AND FLIPPED HIS ROYAL MASQUERADE AND BLEW THE WHOLE BIT---

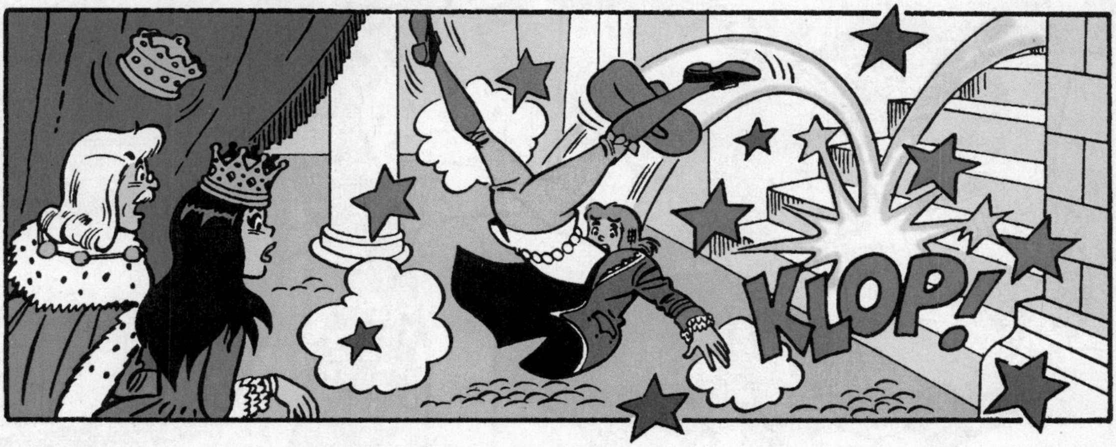
KLOP!

WHICH ONLY GOES TO PROVE THAT PEOPLE HAVE CHANGED ON THE OUTSIDE OVER THE YEARS, BUT THEY'RE STILL THE SAME ON THE INSIDE!

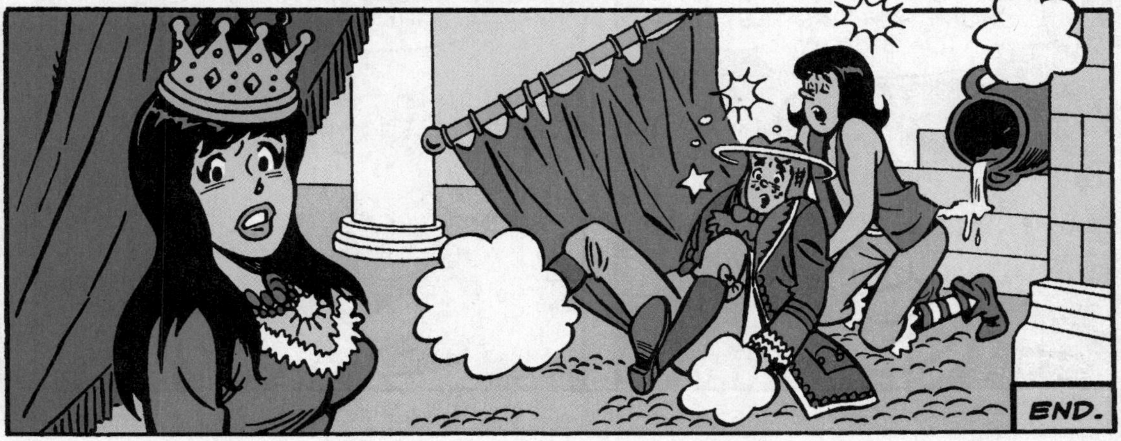
END.

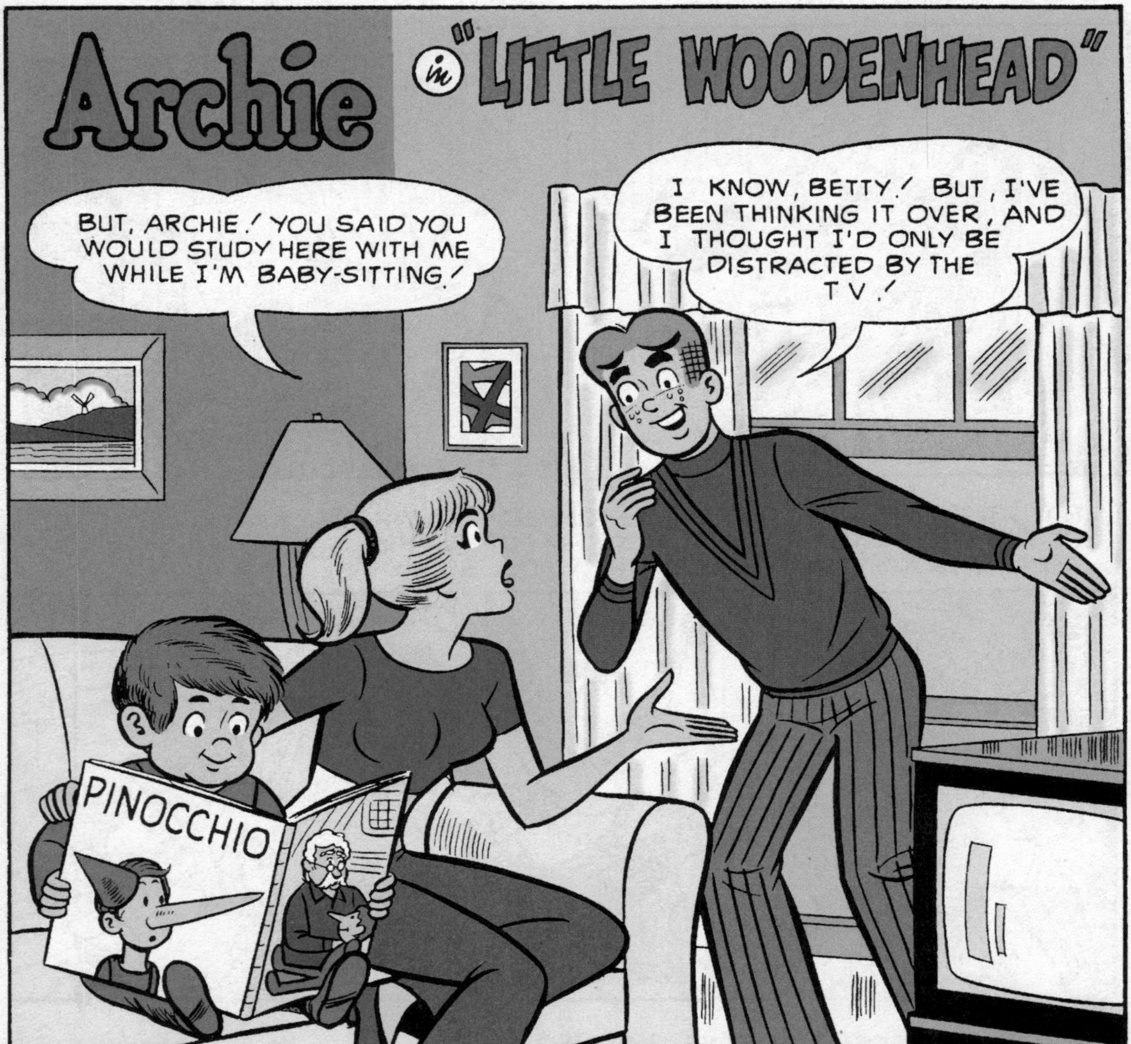
Archie in "LITTLE WOODENHEAD"
BUT, ARCHIE! YOU SAID YOU WOULD STUDY HERE WITH ME WHILE I'M BABY-SITTING!
I KNOW, BETTY! BUT, I'VE BEEN THINKING IT OVER, AND I THOUGHT I'D ONLY BE DISTRACTED BY THE T.V.!
PINOCCHIO

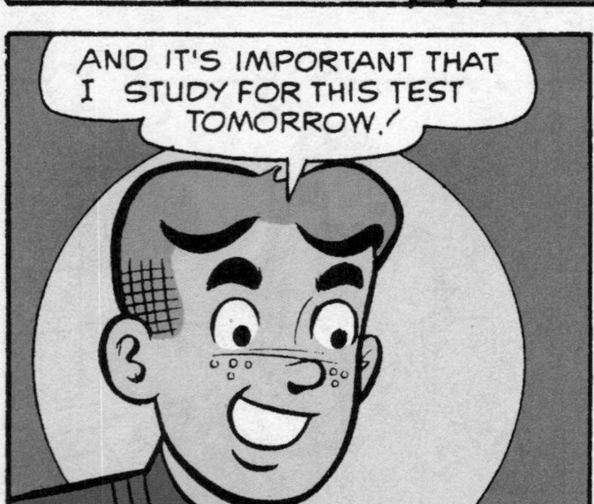
AND IT'S IMPORTANT THAT I STUDY FOR THIS TEST TOMORROW!

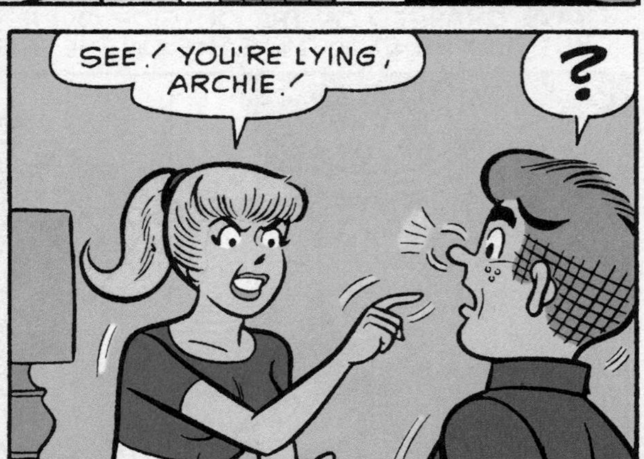
SEE! YOU'RE LYING, ARCHIE!
?

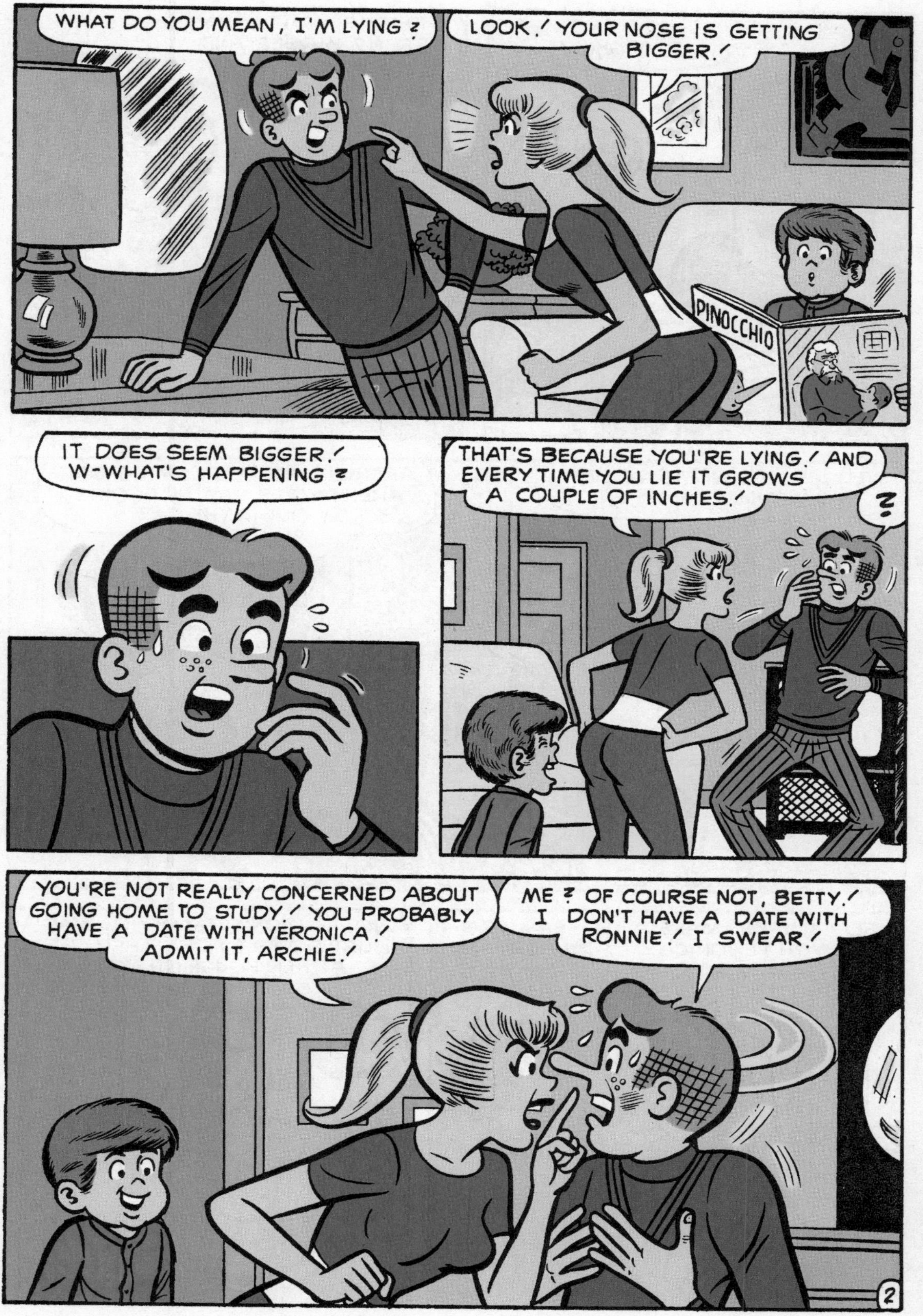
WHAT DO YOU MEAN, I'M LYING ?
LOOK! YOUR NOSE IS GETTING BIGGER!
PINOCCHIO
IT DOES SEEM BIGGER! W-WHAT'S HAPPENING ?
THAT'S BECAUSE YOU'RE LYING! AND EVERY TIME YOU LIE IT GROWS A COUPLE OF INCHES!
?
YOU'RE NOT REALLY CONCERNED ABOUT GOING HOME TO STUDY! YOU PROBABLY HAVE A DATE WITH VERONICA! ADMIT IT, ARCHIE!
ME ? OF COURSE NOT, BETTY! I DON'T HAVE A DATE WITH RONNIE! I SWEAR!
2

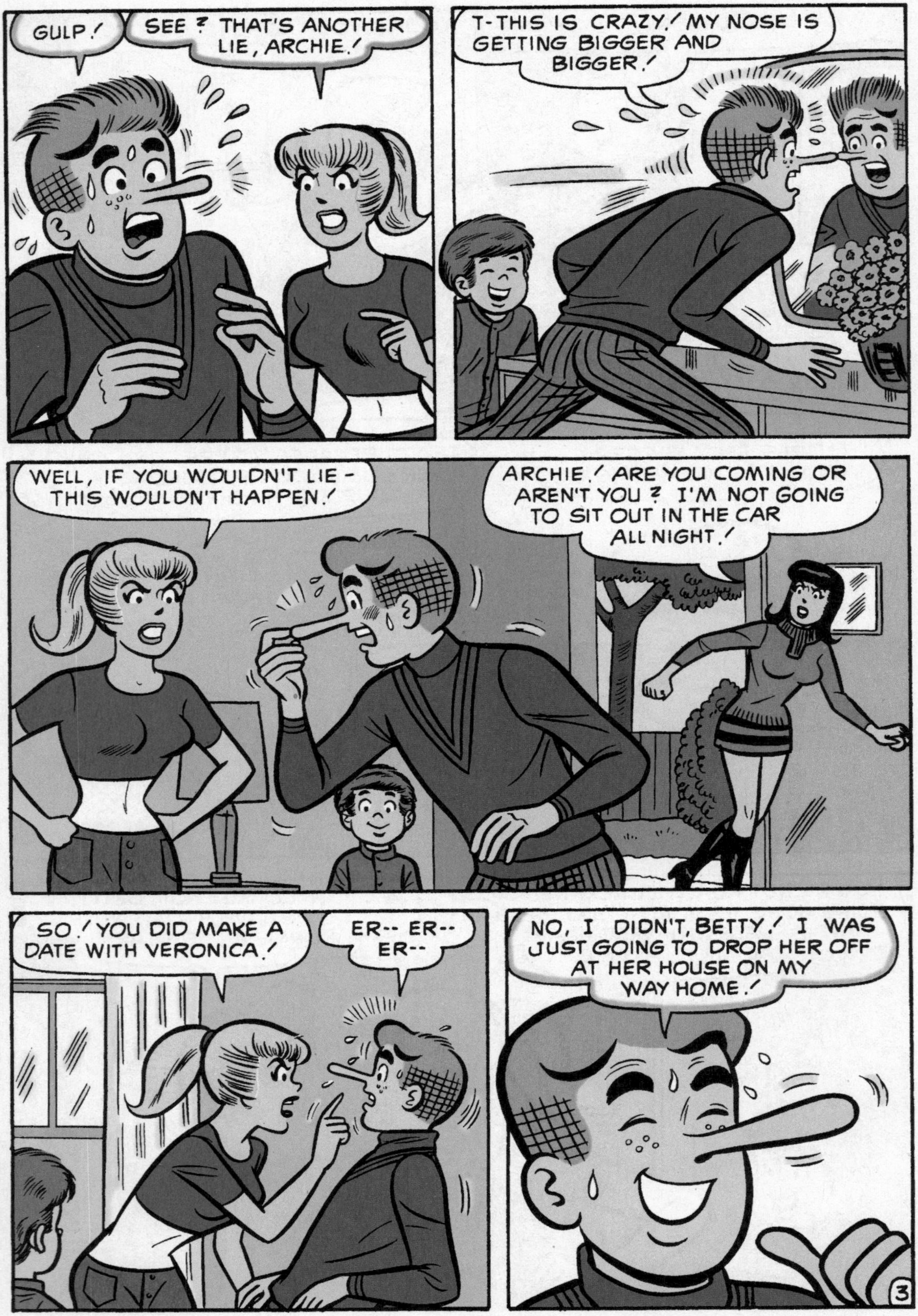
GULP!
SEE? THAT'S ANOTHER LIE, ARCHIE!
T-THIS IS CRAZY! MY NOSE IS GETTING BIGGER AND BIGGER!
WELL, IF YOU WOULDN'T LIE - THIS WOULDN'T HAPPEN!
ARCHIE! ARE YOU COMING OR AREN'T YOU? I'M NOT GOING TO SIT OUT IN THE CAR ALL NIGHT!
SO! YOU DID MAKE A DATE WITH VERONICA!
ER-- ER-- ER--
NO, I DIDN'T, BETTY! I WAS JUST GOING TO DROP HER OFF AT HER HOUSE ON MY WAY HOME!
3

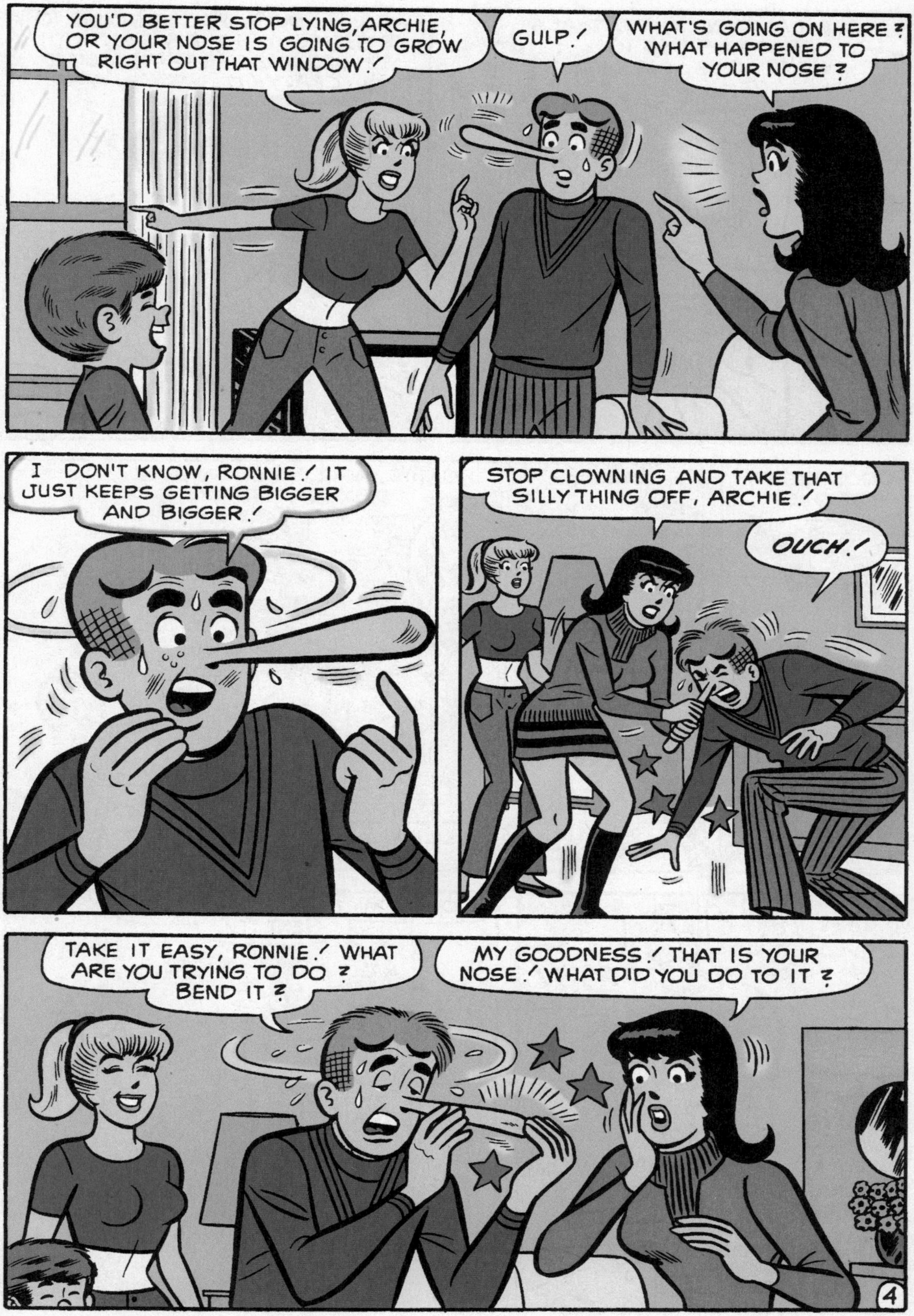
YOU'D BETTER STOP LYING, ARCHIE, OR YOUR NOSE IS GOING TO GROW RIGHT OUT THAT WINDOW!
GULP!
WHAT'S GOING ON HERE? WHAT HAPPENED TO YOUR NOSE?
I DON'T KNOW, RONNIE! IT JUST KEEPS GETTING BIGGER AND BIGGER!
STOP CLOWNING AND TAKE THAT SILLY THING OFF, ARCHIE!
OUCH!
TAKE IT EASY, RONNIE! WHAT ARE YOU TRYING TO DO? BEND IT?
MY GOODNESS! THAT IS YOUR NOSE! WHAT DID YOU DO TO IT?
4

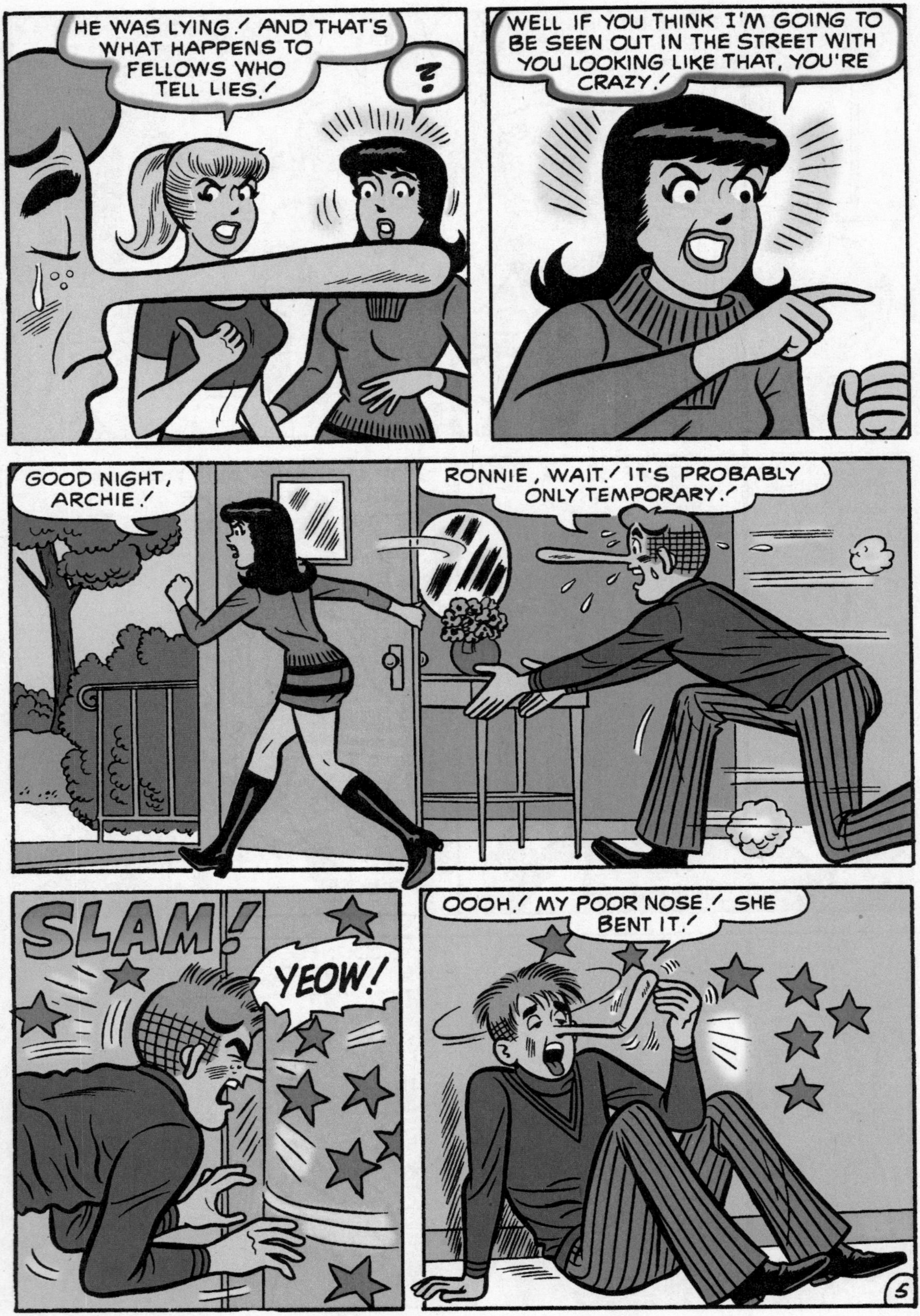
HE WAS LYING! AND THAT'S WHAT HAPPENS TO FELLOWS WHO TELL LIES!
?
WELL IF YOU THINK I'M GOING TO BE SEEN OUT IN THE STREET WITH YOU LOOKING LIKE THAT, YOU'RE CRAZY!
GOOD NIGHT, ARCHIE!
RONNIE, WAIT! IT'S PROBABLY ONLY TEMPORARY!
SLAM!
YEOW!
OOOH! MY POOR NOSE! SHE BENT IT!
5

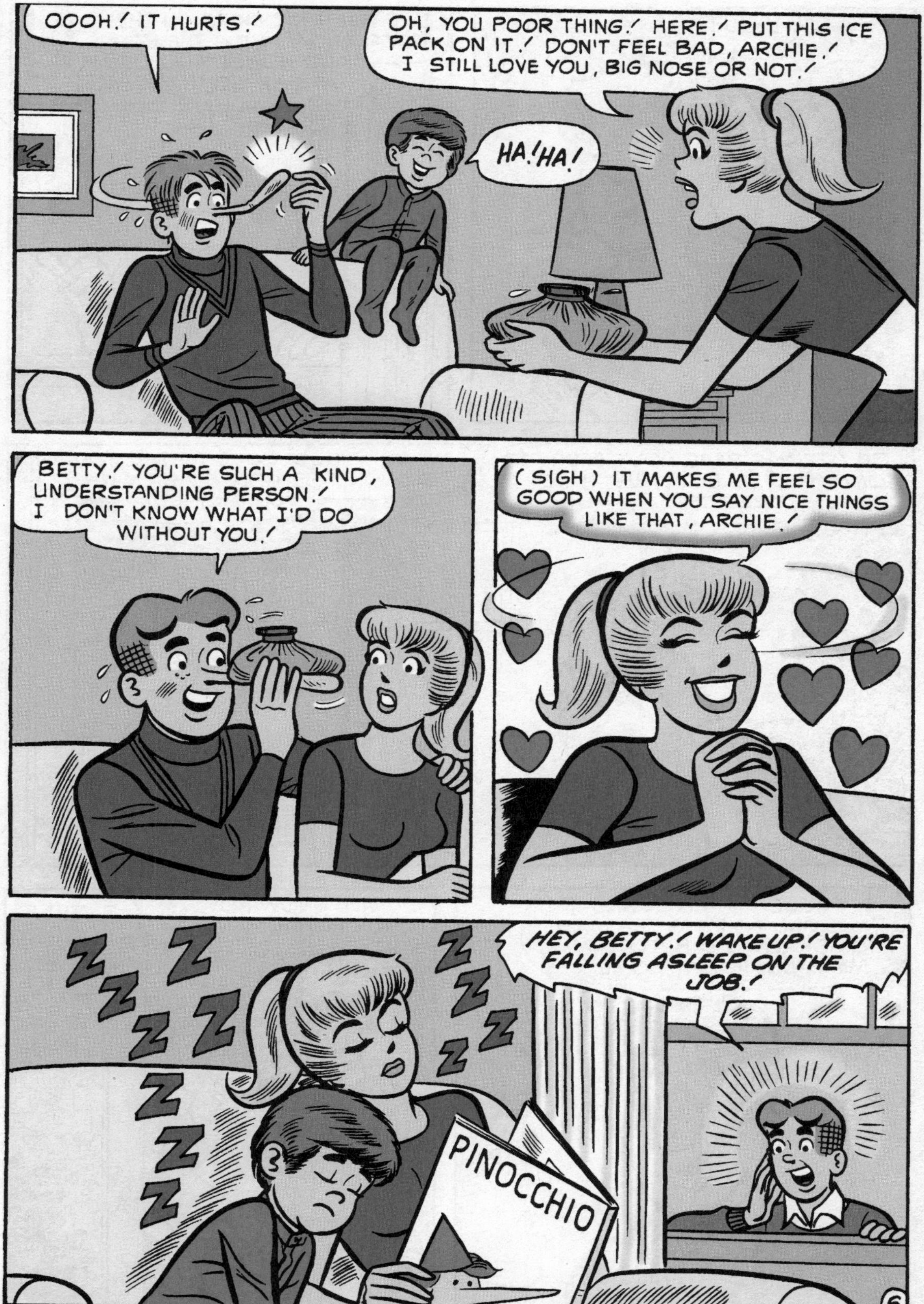

OOOH! IT HURTS!
HA! HA!
OH, YOU POOR THING! HERE! PUT THIS ICE PACK ON IT! DON'T FEEL BAD, ARCHIE! I STILL LOVE YOU, BIG NOSE OR NOT!
BETTY! YOU'RE SUCH A KIND, UNDERSTANDING PERSON! I DON'T KNOW WHAT I'D DO WITHOUT YOU!
(SIGH) IT MAKES ME FEEL SO GOOD WHEN YOU SAY NICE THINGS LIKE THAT, ARCHIE!
ZZZZZZZZZ
HEY, BETTY! WAKE UP! YOU'RE FALLING ASLEEP ON THE JOB!
PINOCCHIO
6

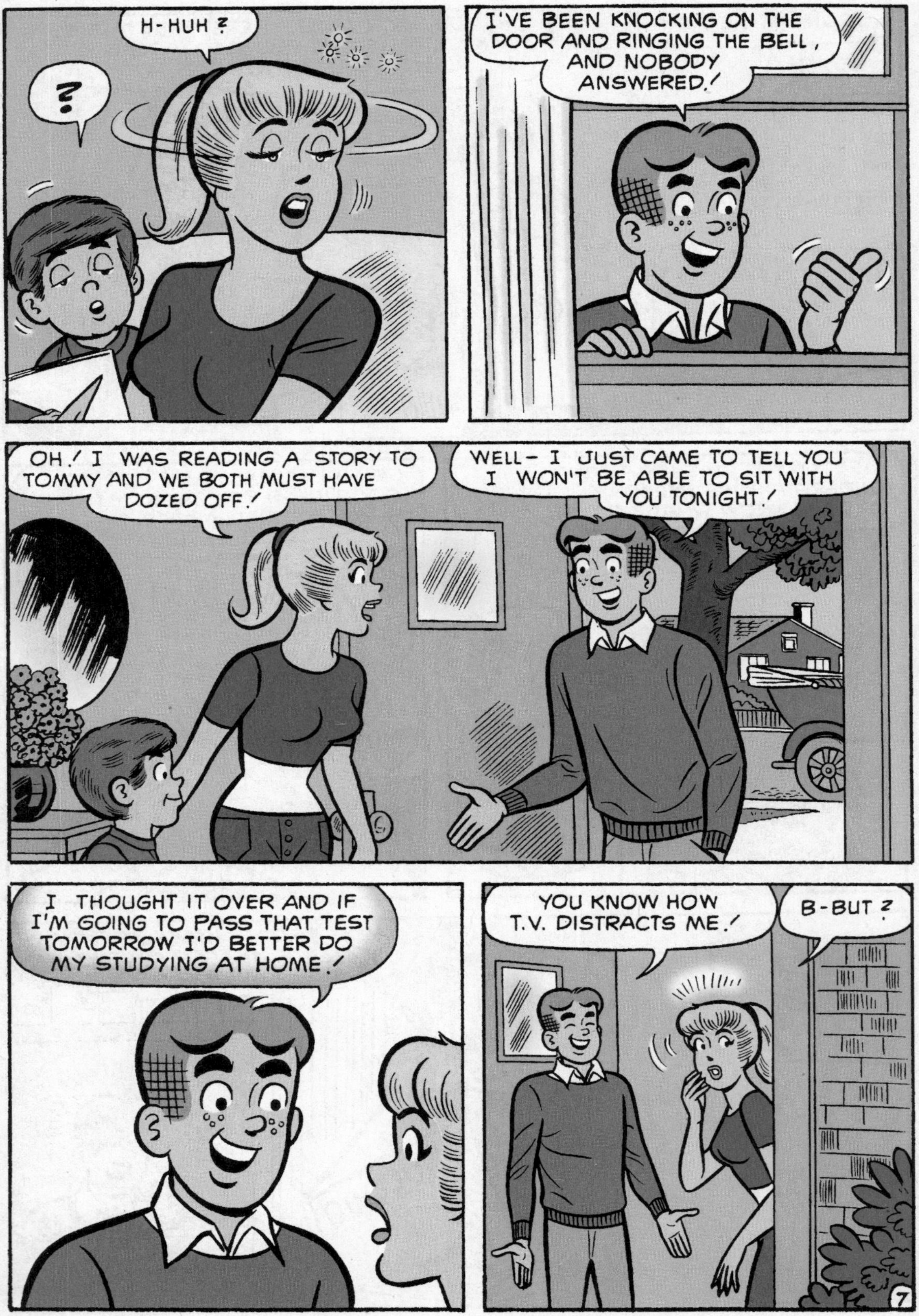
H-HUH ?
?
I'VE BEEN KNOCKING ON THE DOOR AND RINGING THE BELL, AND NOBODY ANSWERED!
OH! I WAS READING A STORY TO TOMMY AND WE BOTH MUST HAVE DOZED OFF!
WELL- I JUST CAME TO TELL YOU I WON'T BE ABLE TO SIT WITH YOU TONIGHT!
I THOUGHT IT OVER AND IF I'M GOING TO PASS THAT TEST TOMORROW I'D BETTER DO MY STUDYING AT HOME!
YOU KNOW HOW T.V. DISTRACTS ME!
B-BUT ?
7

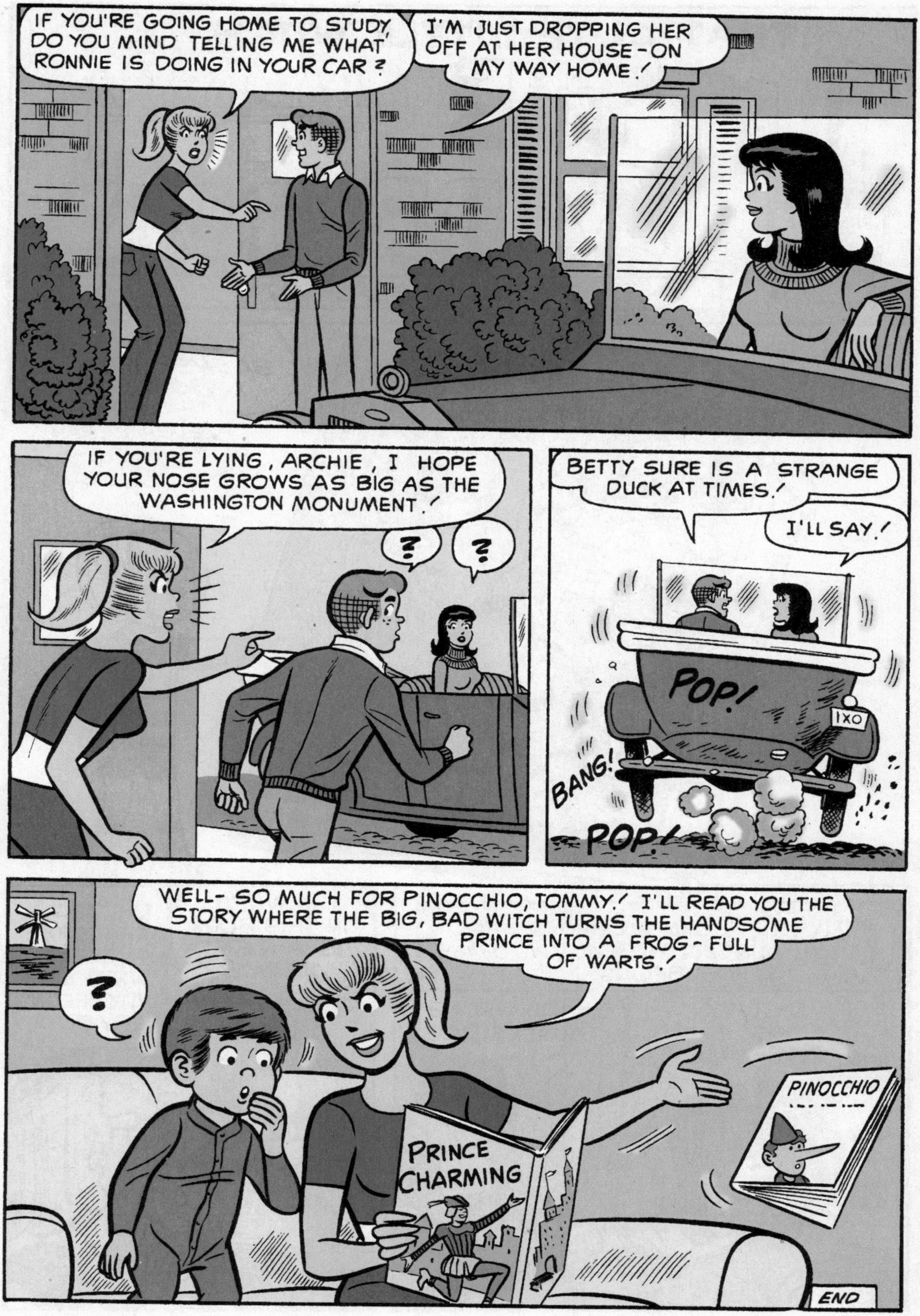
IF YOU'RE GOING HOME TO STUDY, DO YOU MIND TELLING ME WHAT RONNIE IS DOING IN YOUR CAR ?
I'M JUST DROPPING HER OFF AT HER HOUSE - ON MY WAY HOME !
IF YOU'RE LYING , ARCHIE , I HOPE YOUR NOSE GROWS AS BIG AS THE WASHINGTON MONUMENT !
?
?
BETTY SURE IS A STRANGE DUCK AT TIMES !
I'LL SAY !
POP!
1XO
BANG!
POP!
WELL- SO MUCH FOR PINOCCHIO, TOMMY ! I'LL READ YOU THE STORY WHERE THE BIG, BAD WITCH TURNS THE HANDSOME PRINCE INTO A FROG - FULL OF WARTS !
?
PRINCE CHARMING
PINOCCHIO
END

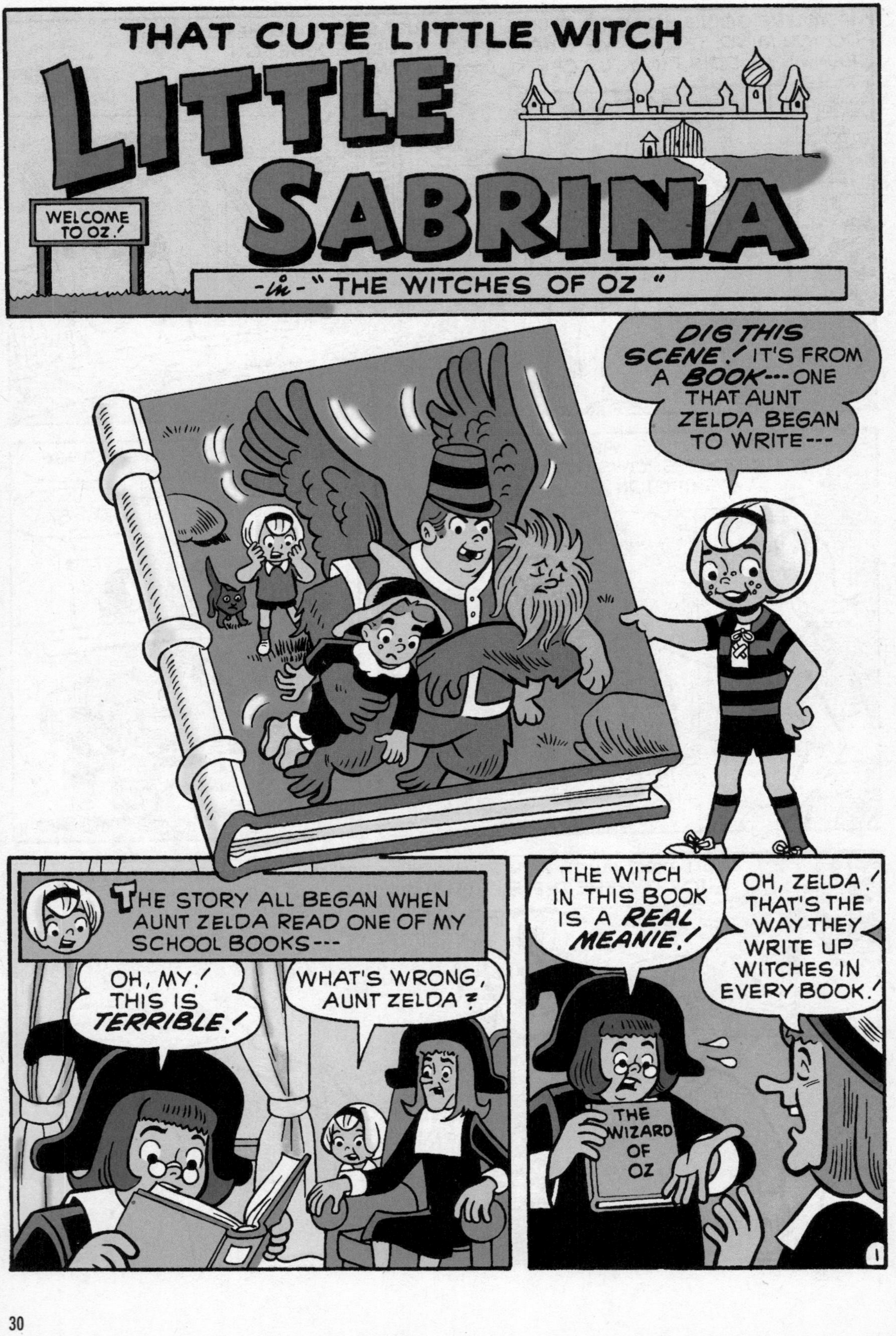
THAT CUTE LITTLE WITCH
LITTLE SABRINA
WELCOME TO OZ!
-in- "THE WITCHES OF OZ"
DIG THIS SCENE! IT'S FROM A BOOK--- ONE THAT AUNT ZELDA BEGAN TO WRITE---
THE STORY ALL BEGAN WHEN AUNT ZELDA READ ONE OF MY SCHOOL BOOKS---
OH, MY! THIS IS TERRIBLE!
WHAT'S WRONG, AUNT ZELDA?
THE WITCH IN THIS BOOK IS A REAL MEANIE!
OH, ZELDA! THAT'S THE WAY THEY WRITE UP WITCHES IN EVERY BOOK!
THE WIZARD OF OZ
1

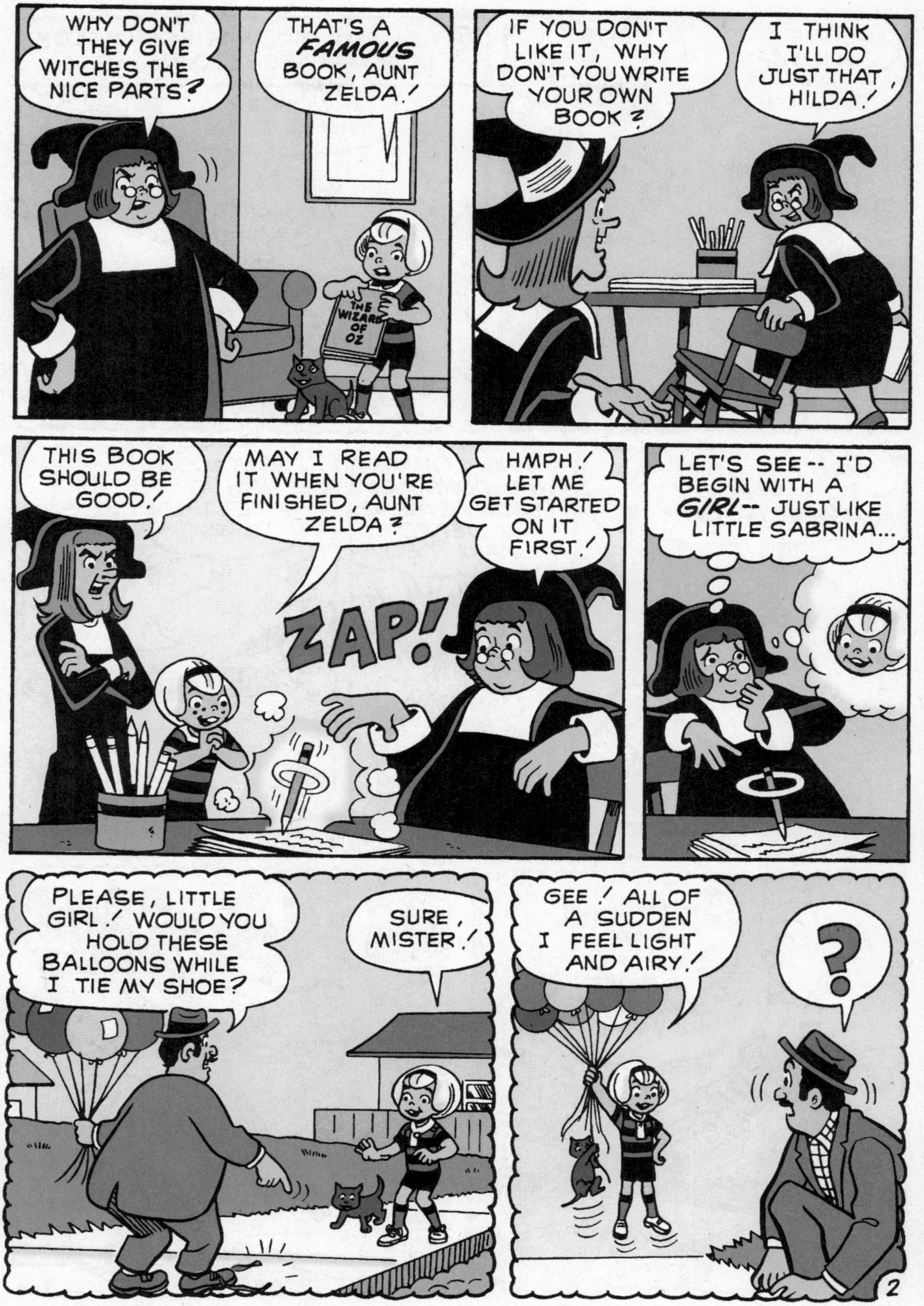

WHY DON'T THEY GIVE WITCHES THE NICE PARTS?
THAT'S A FAMOUS BOOK, AUNT ZELDA!
THE WIZARD OF OZ
IF YOU DON'T LIKE IT, WHY DON'T YOU WRITE YOUR OWN BOOK?
I THINK I'LL DO JUST THAT, HILDA!
THIS BOOK SHOULD BE GOOD!
MAY I READ IT WHEN YOU'RE FINISHED, AUNT ZELDA?
HMPH! LET ME GET STARTED ON IT FIRST!
ZAP!
LET'S SEE -- I'D BEGIN WITH A GIRL -- JUST LIKE LITTLE SABRINA...
PLEASE, LITTLE GIRL! WOULD YOU HOLD THESE BALLOONS WHILE I TIE MY SHOE?
SURE, MISTER!
GEE! ALL OF A SUDDEN I FEEL LIGHT AND AIRY!
?
2

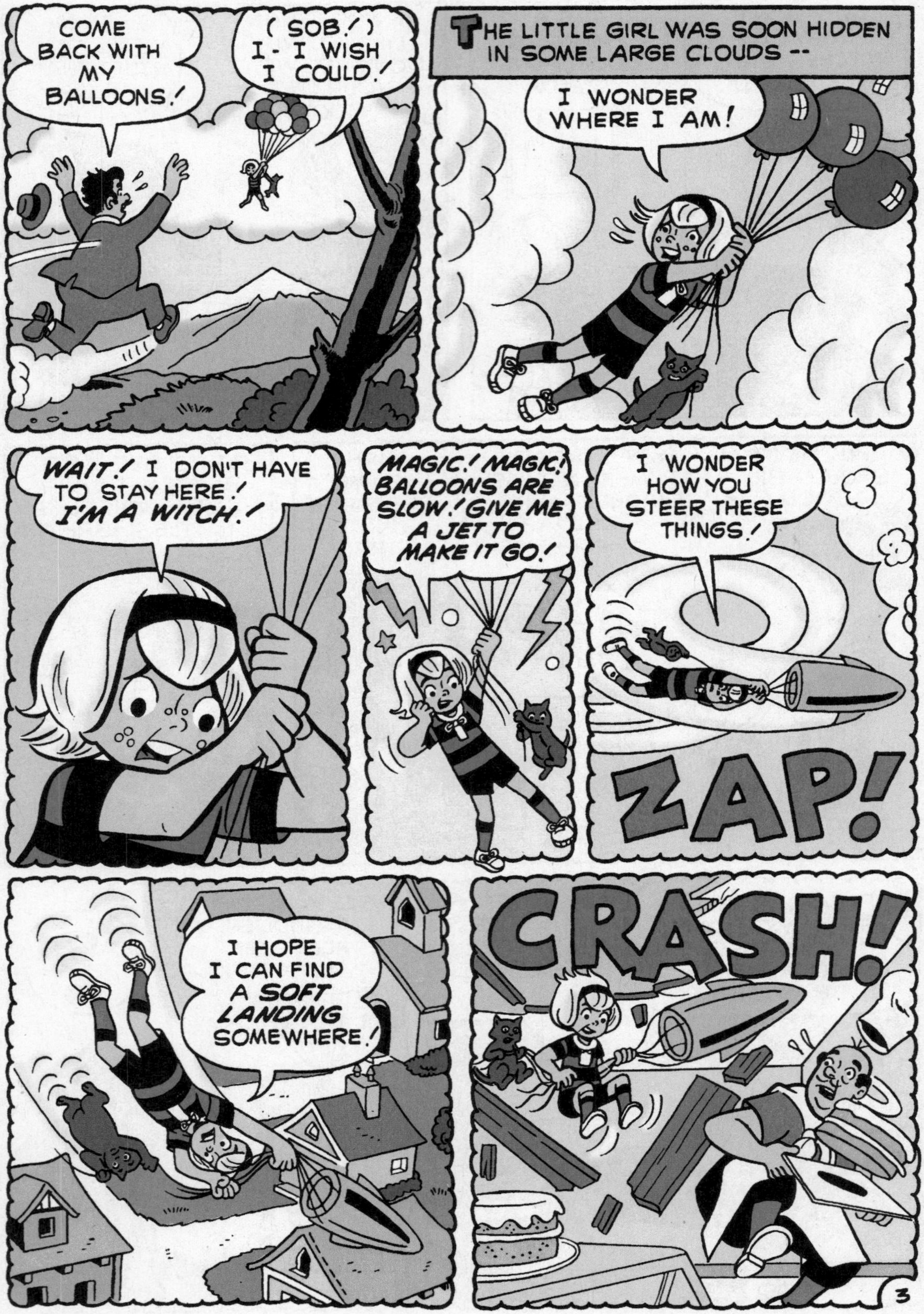
COME BACK WITH MY BALLOONS!
(SOB!) I - I WISH I COULD!
THE LITTLE GIRL WAS SOON HIDDEN IN SOME LARGE CLOUDS --
I WONDER WHERE I AM!
WAIT! I DON'T HAVE TO STAY HERE! I'M A WITCH!
MAGIC! MAGIC! BALLOONS ARE SLOW! GIVE ME A JET TO MAKE IT GO!
I WONDER HOW YOU STEER THESE THINGS!
ZAP!
I HOPE I CAN FIND A SOFT LANDING SOMEWHERE!
CRASH!
3

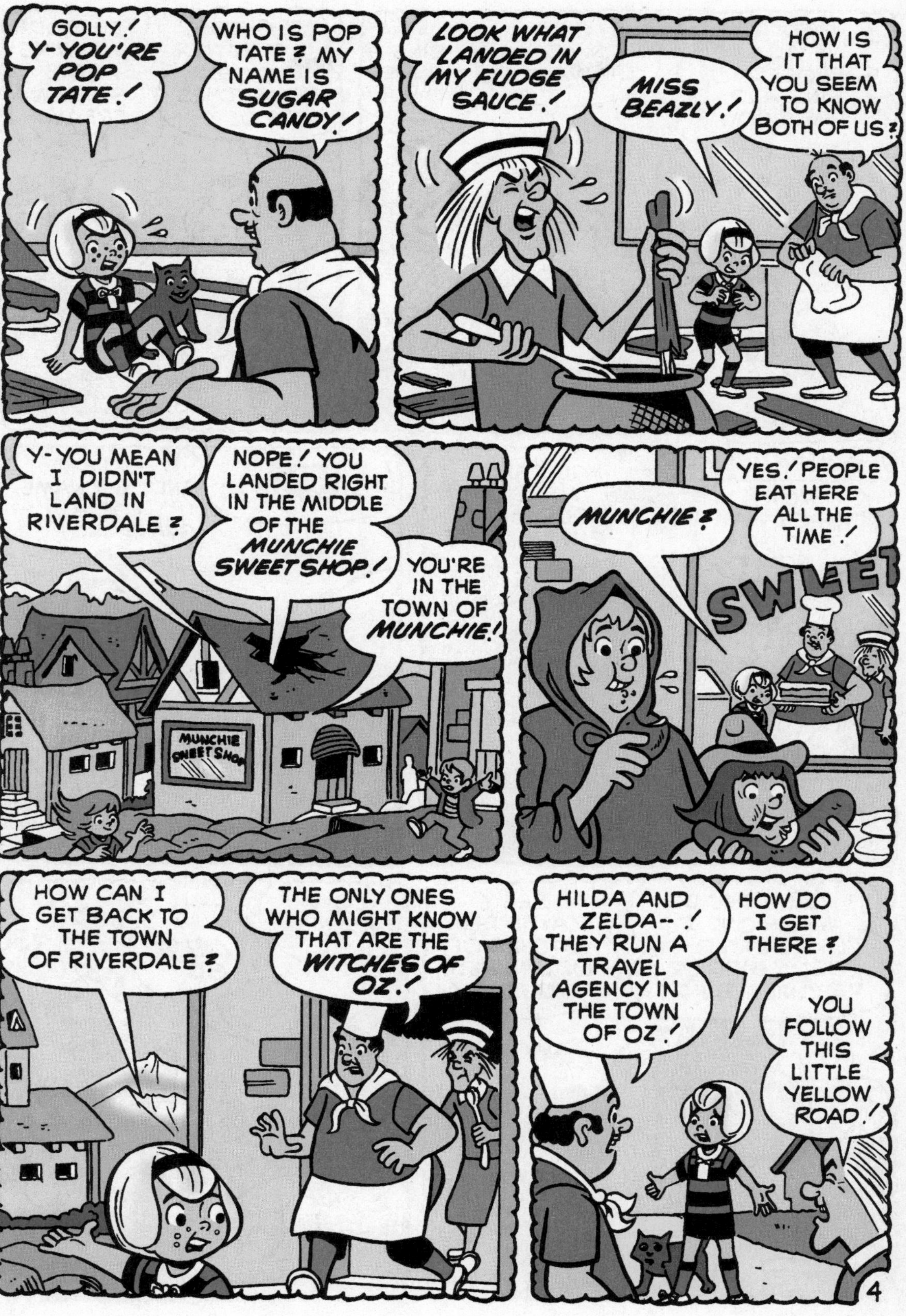
GOLLY! Y-YOU'RE POP TATE!
WHO IS POP TATE? MY NAME IS SUGAR CANDY!
LOOK WHAT LANDED IN MY FUDGE SAUCE!
MISS BEAZLY!
HOW IS IT THAT YOU SEEM TO KNOW BOTH OF US?
Y-YOU MEAN I DIDN'T LAND IN RIVERDALE?
NOPE! YOU LANDED RIGHT IN THE MIDDLE OF THE MUNCHIE SWEET SHOP!
YOU'RE IN THE TOWN OF MUNCHIE!
MUNCHIE SWEET SHOP
MUNCHIE?
YES! PEOPLE EAT HERE ALL THE TIME!
SWEET
HOW CAN I GET BACK TO THE TOWN OF RIVERDALE?
THE ONLY ONES WHO MIGHT KNOW THAT ARE THE WITCHES OF OZ!
HILDA AND ZELDA--! THEY RUN A TRAVEL AGENCY IN THE TOWN OF OZ!
HOW DO I GET THERE?
YOU FOLLOW THIS LITTLE YELLOW ROAD!
4

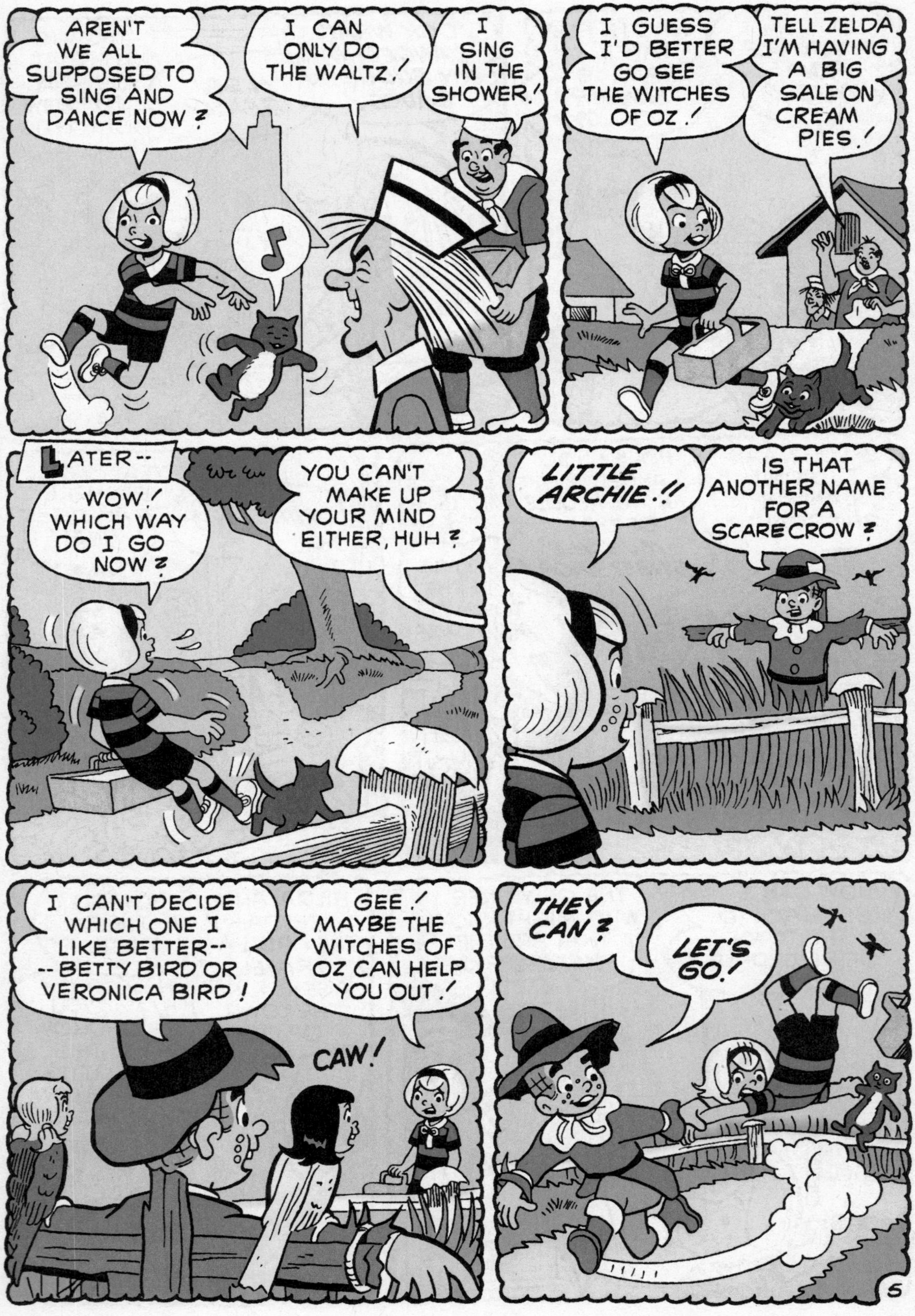
AREN'T WE ALL SUPPOSED TO SING AND DANCE NOW?
I CAN ONLY DO THE WALTZ!
I SING IN THE SHOWER!
I GUESS I'D BETTER GO SEE THE WITCHES OF OZ!
TELL ZELDA I'M HAVING A BIG SALE ON CREAM PIES!
LATER--
WOW! WHICH WAY DO I GO NOW?
YOU CAN'T MAKE UP YOUR MIND EITHER, HUH?
LITTLE ARCHIE!!
IS THAT ANOTHER NAME FOR A SCARECROW?
I CAN'T DECIDE WHICH ONE I LIKE BETTER-- --BETTY BIRD OR VERONICA BIRD!
GEE! MAYBE THE WITCHES OF OZ CAN HELP YOU OUT!
CAW!
THEY CAN?
LET'S GO!
5

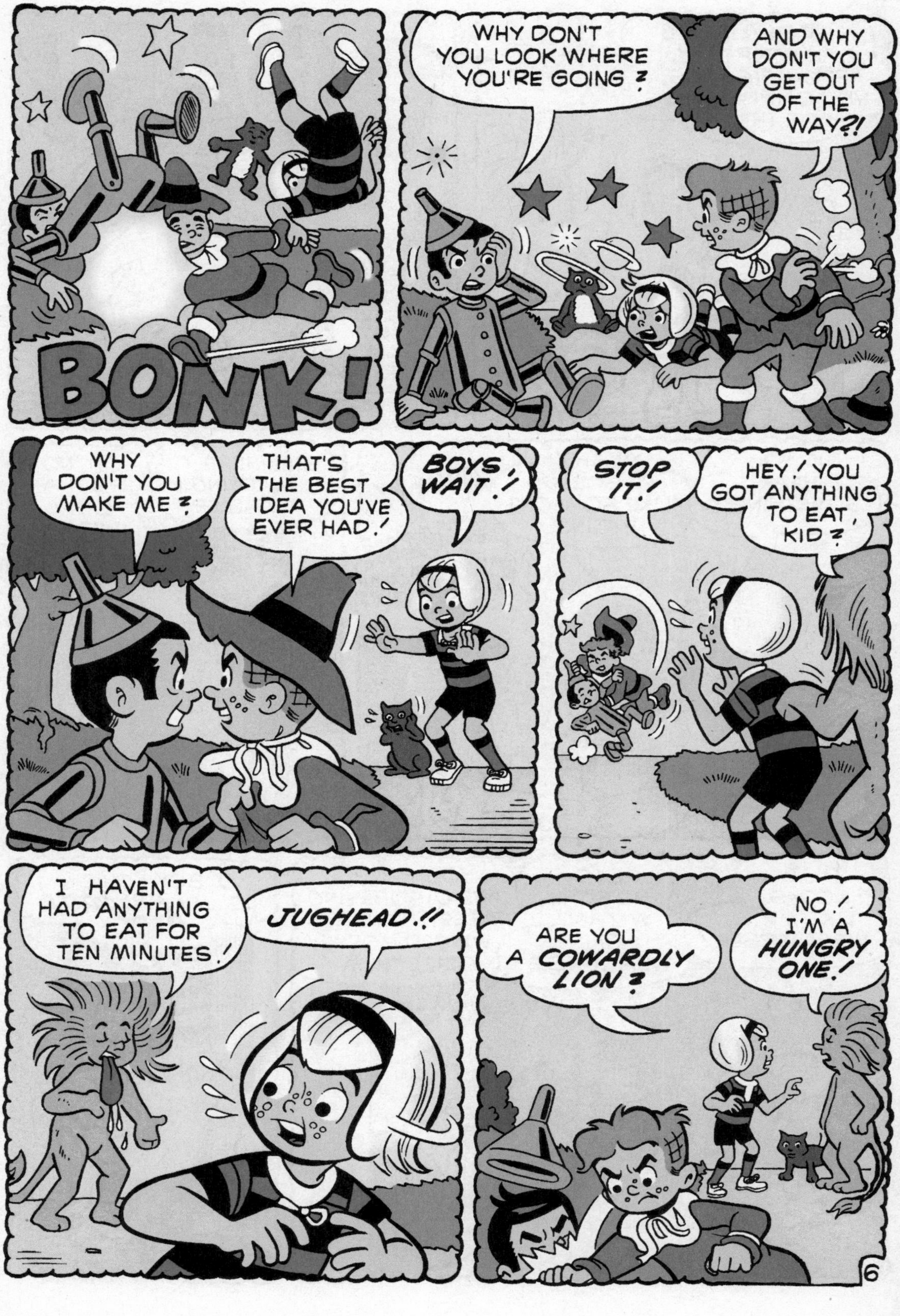
BONK!
WHY DON'T YOU LOOK WHERE YOU'RE GOING?
AND WHY DON'T YOU GET OUT OF THE WAY?!
WHY DON'T YOU MAKE ME?
THAT'S THE BEST IDEA YOU'VE EVER HAD!
BOYS, WAIT!
STOP IT!
HEY! YOU GOT ANYTHING TO EAT, KID?
I HAVEN'T HAD ANYTHING TO EAT FOR TEN MINUTES!
JUGHEAD!!!
ARE YOU A COWARDLY LION?
NO! I'M A HUNGRY ONE!
6

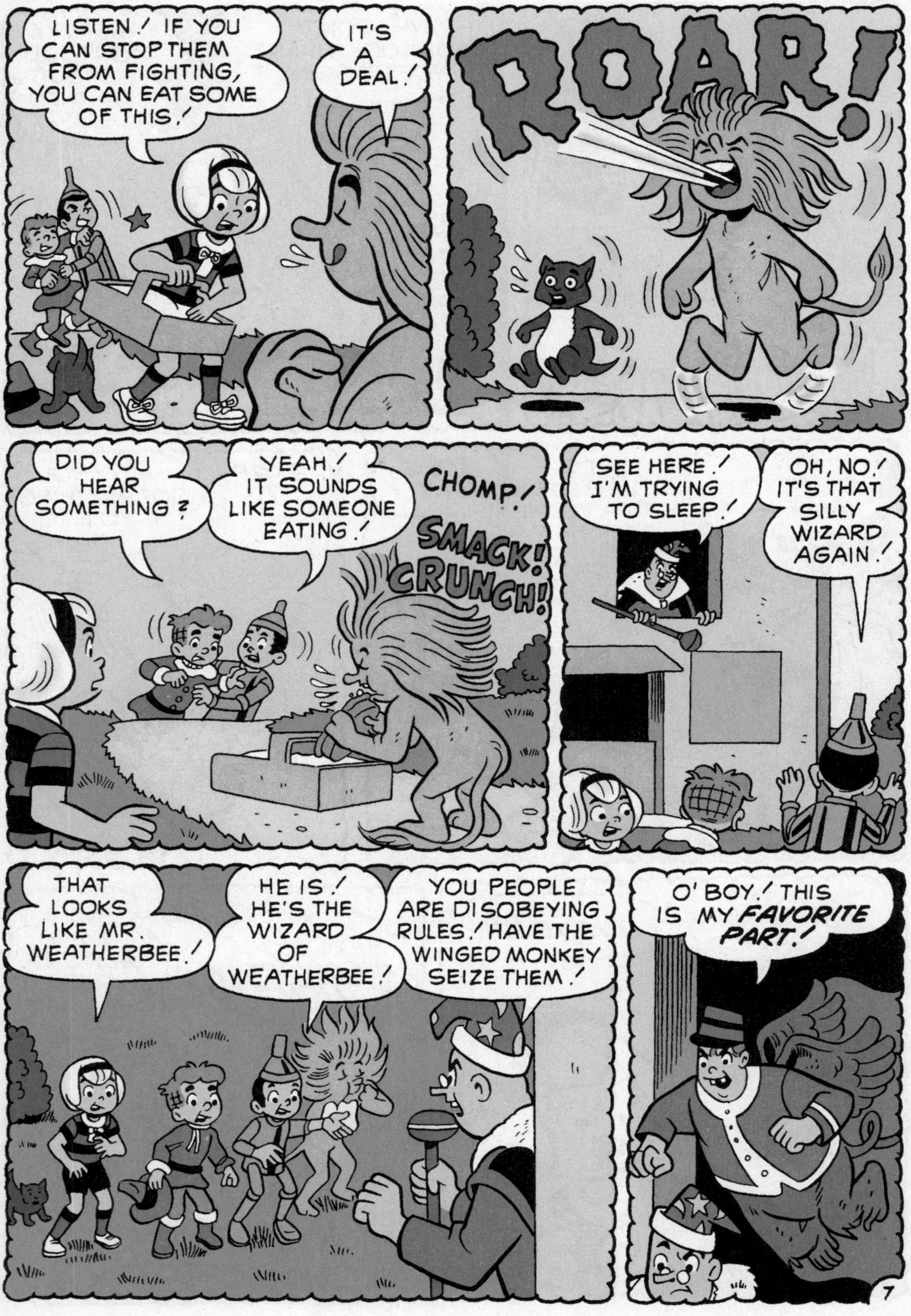
LISTEN! IF YOU CAN STOP THEM FROM FIGHTING, YOU CAN EAT SOME OF THIS!
IT'S A DEAL!
ROAR!
DID YOU HEAR SOMETHING?
YEAH! IT SOUNDS LIKE SOMEONE EATING!
CHOMP!
SMACK!
CRUNCH!
SEE HERE! I'M TRYING TO SLEEP!
OH, NO! IT'S THAT SILLY WIZARD AGAIN!
THAT LOOKS LIKE MR. WEATHERBEE!
HE IS! HE'S THE WIZARD OF WEATHERBEE!
YOU PEOPLE ARE DISOBEYING RULES! HAVE THE WINGED MONKEY SEIZE THEM!
O' BOY! THIS IS MY FAVORITE PART!
7

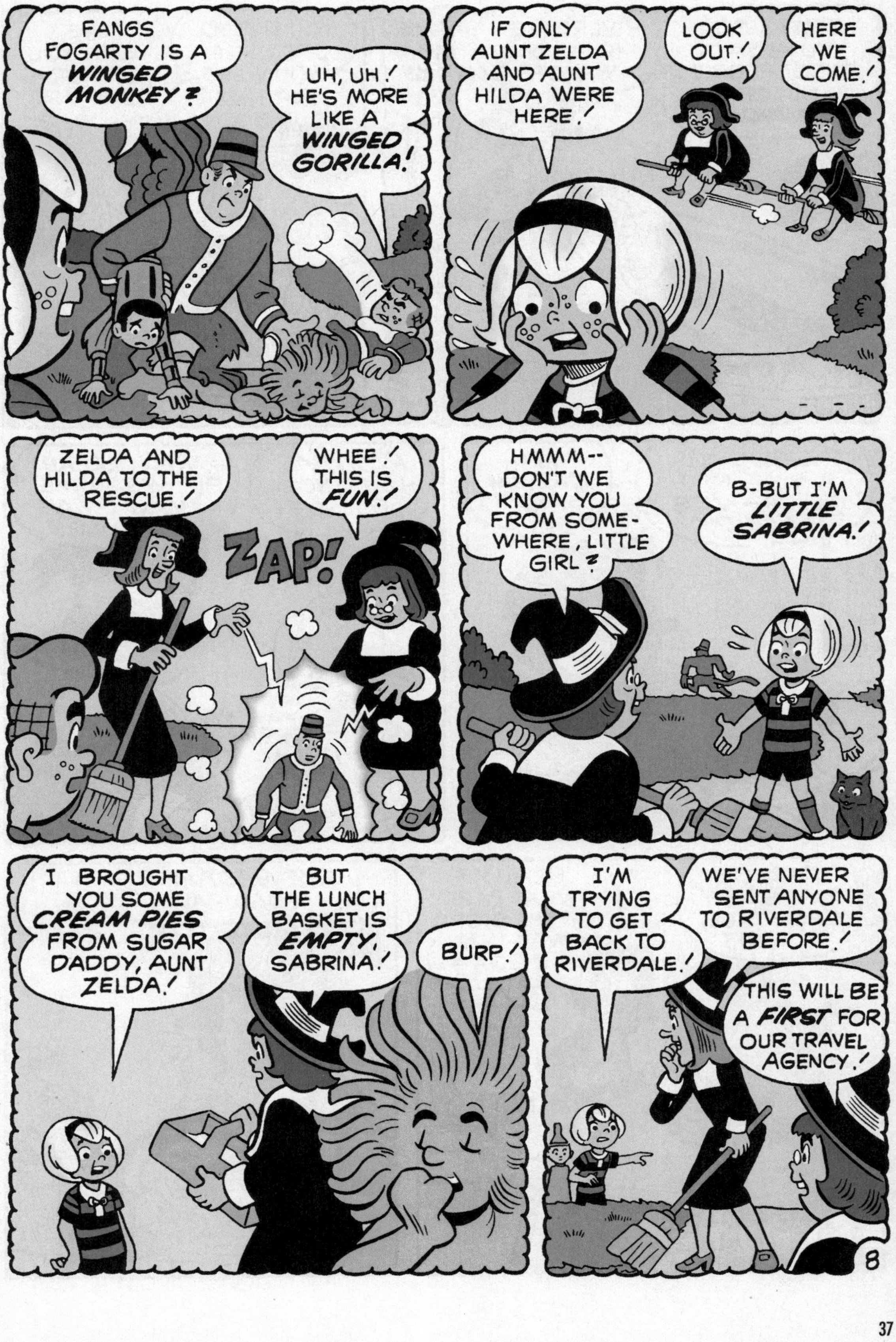
FANGS FOGARTY IS A WINGED MONKEY?
UH, UH! HE'S MORE LIKE A WINGED GORILLA!
IF ONLY AUNT ZELDA AND AUNT HILDA WERE HERE!
LOOK OUT!
HERE WE COME!
ZELDA AND HILDA TO THE RESCUE!
WHEE! THIS IS FUN!
ZAP!
HMMM-- DON'T WE KNOW YOU FROM SOME-WHERE, LITTLE GIRL?
B-BUT I'M LITTLE SABRINA!
I BROUGHT YOU SOME CREAM PIES FROM SUGAR DADDY, AUNT ZELDA!
BUT THE LUNCH BASKET IS EMPTY, SABRINA!
BURP!
I'M TRYING TO GET BACK TO RIVERDALE!
WE'VE NEVER SENT ANYONE TO RIVERDALE BEFORE!
THIS WILL BE A FIRST FOR OUR TRAVEL AGENCY!
8

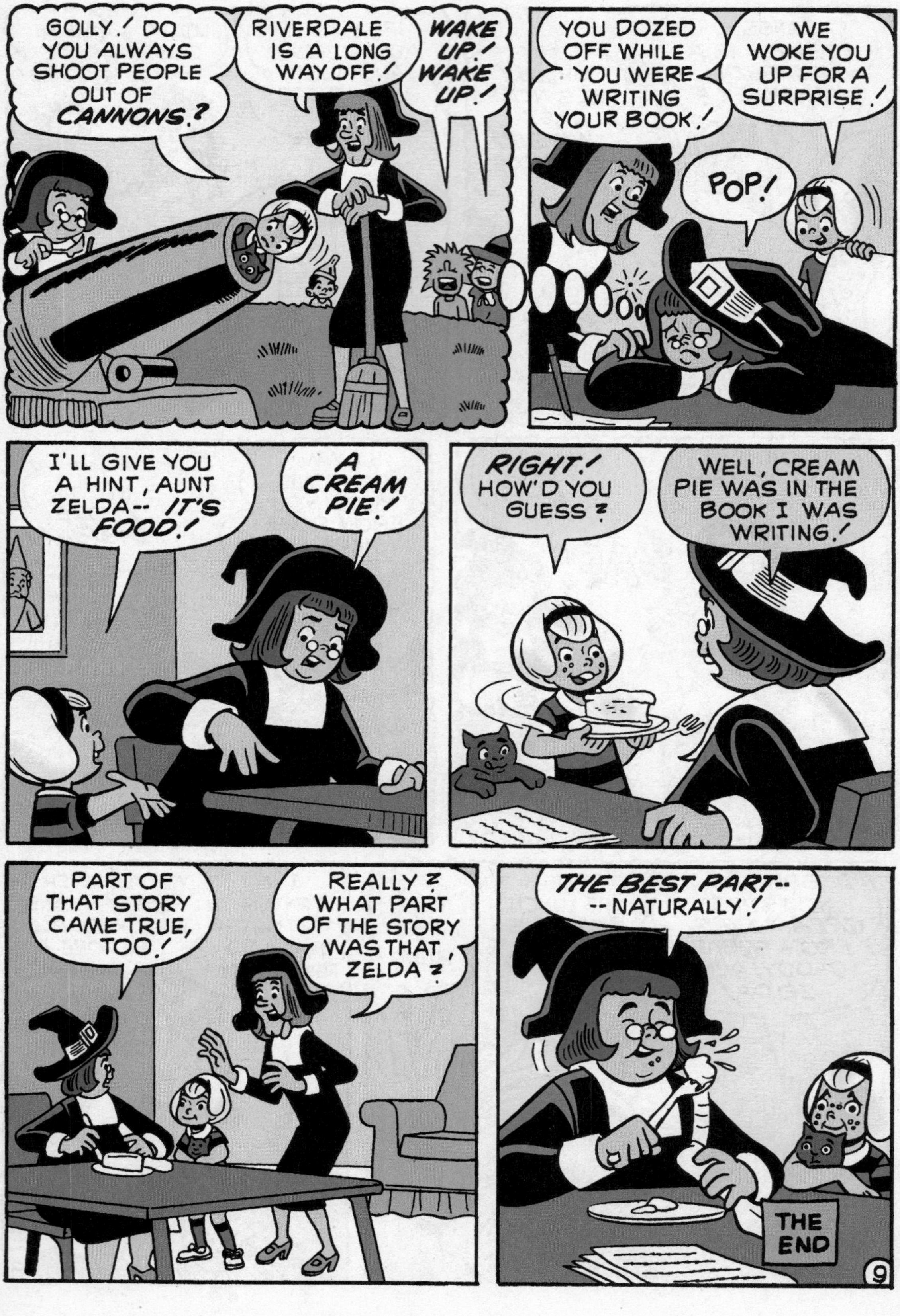
GOLLY! DO YOU ALWAYS SHOOT PEOPLE OUT OF CANNONS?
RIVERDALE IS A LONG WAY OFF!
WAKE UP! WAKE UP!
YOU DOZED OFF WHILE YOU WERE WRITING YOUR BOOK!
WE WOKE YOU UP FOR A SURPRISE!
POP!
I'LL GIVE YOU A HINT, AUNT ZELDA-- IT'S FOOD!
A CREAM PIE!
RIGHT! HOW'D YOU GUESS?
WELL, CREAM PIE WAS IN THE BOOK I WAS WRITING!
PART OF THAT STORY CAME TRUE, TOO!
REALLY? WHAT PART OF THE STORY WAS THAT, ZELDA?
THE BEST PART-- --NATURALLY!
THE END
9

CHAPTER TWO

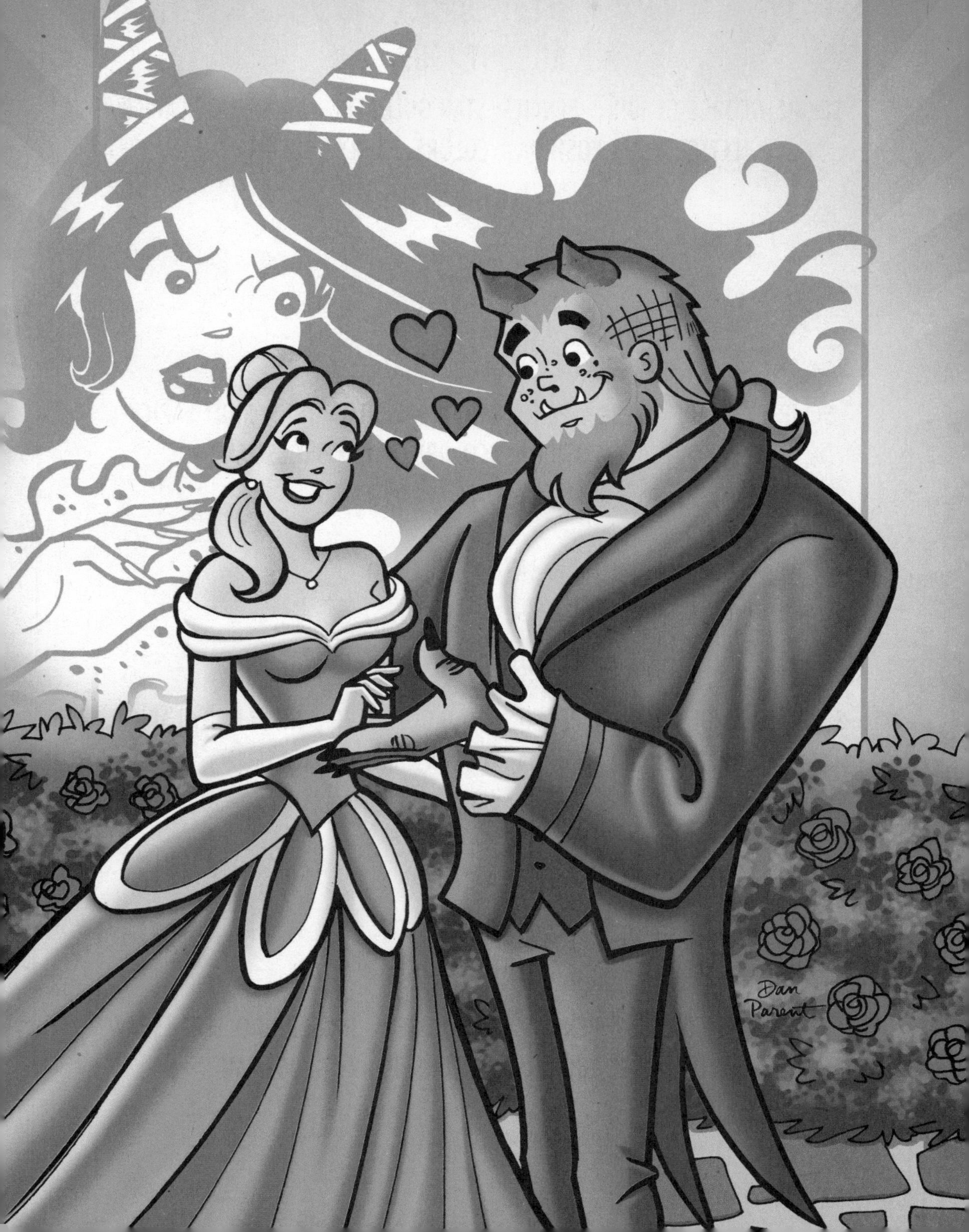
Dan Parent

THE MIGHTY ARCHIE ART PLAYERS IN
SNOW WHITE AND THE THREE GIANT DWARFS
AUGUST 1987

SCRIPT: GEORGE GLADIR   PENCILS: STAN GOLDBERG   INKS: RUDY LAPICK
LETTERS: BILL YOSHIDA   COLORS: BARRY GROSSMAN

BETTY & VERONICA IN
FAIRY TALE
DECEMBER 1987

SCRIPT: KATHLEEN WEBB   PENCILS: DAN DECARLO   INKS: RUDY LAPICK
LETTERS: BILL YOSHIDA   COLORS: BARRY GROSSMAN

THE MIGHTY ARCHIE ART PLAYERS IN
BEAUTY AND THE BEASTY
FEBRUARY 1989

SCRIPT: GEORGE GLADIR   PENCILS: STAN GOLDBERG   INKS: RUDY LAPICK
LETTERS: BILL YOSHIDA   COLORS: BARRY GROSSMAN

JUGHEAD IN
I WAS A TEENAGE JUGHEAD!
JUNE 1992

SCRIPT: TERRY COLLINS   PENCILS: REX LINDSEY   INKS: ROD OLLERENSHAW
LETTERS: BILL YOSHIDA   COLORS: BARRY GROSSMAN

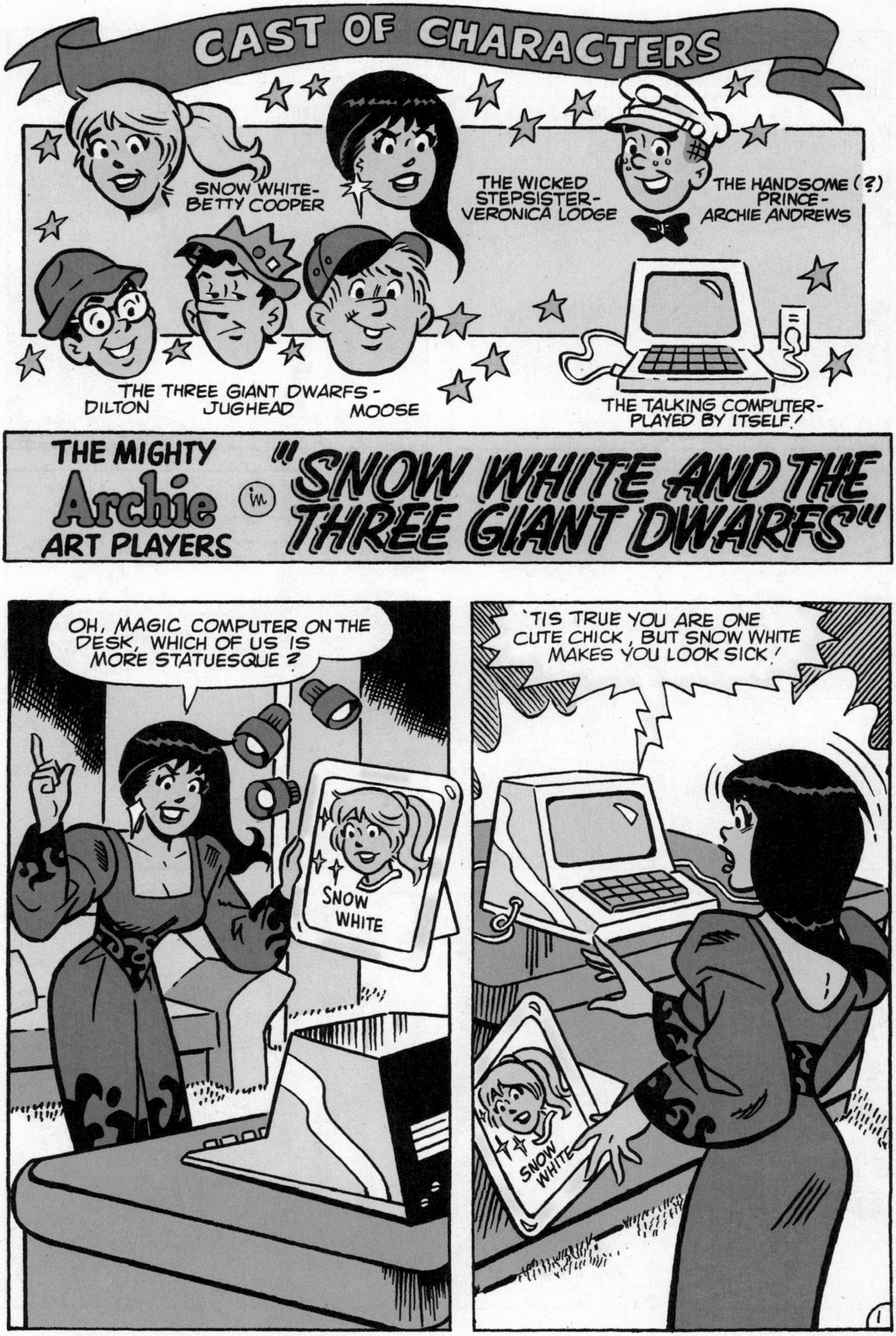

CAST OF CHARACTERS
SNOW WHITE- BETTY COOPER
THE WICKED STEPSISTER- VERONICA LODGE
THE HANDSOME (?) PRINCE- ARCHIE ANDREWS
THE THREE GIANT DWARFS -
DILTON
JUGHEAD
MOOSE
THE TALKING COMPUTER- PLAYED BY ITSELF!
THE MIGHTY Archie ART PLAYERS in "SNOW WHITE AND THE THREE GIANT DWARFS"
OH, MAGIC COMPUTER ON THE DESK, WHICH OF US IS MORE STATUESQUE?
SNOW WHITE
'TIS TRUE YOU ARE ONE CUTE CHICK, BUT SNOW WHITE MAKES YOU LOOK SICK!
SNOW WHITE
1

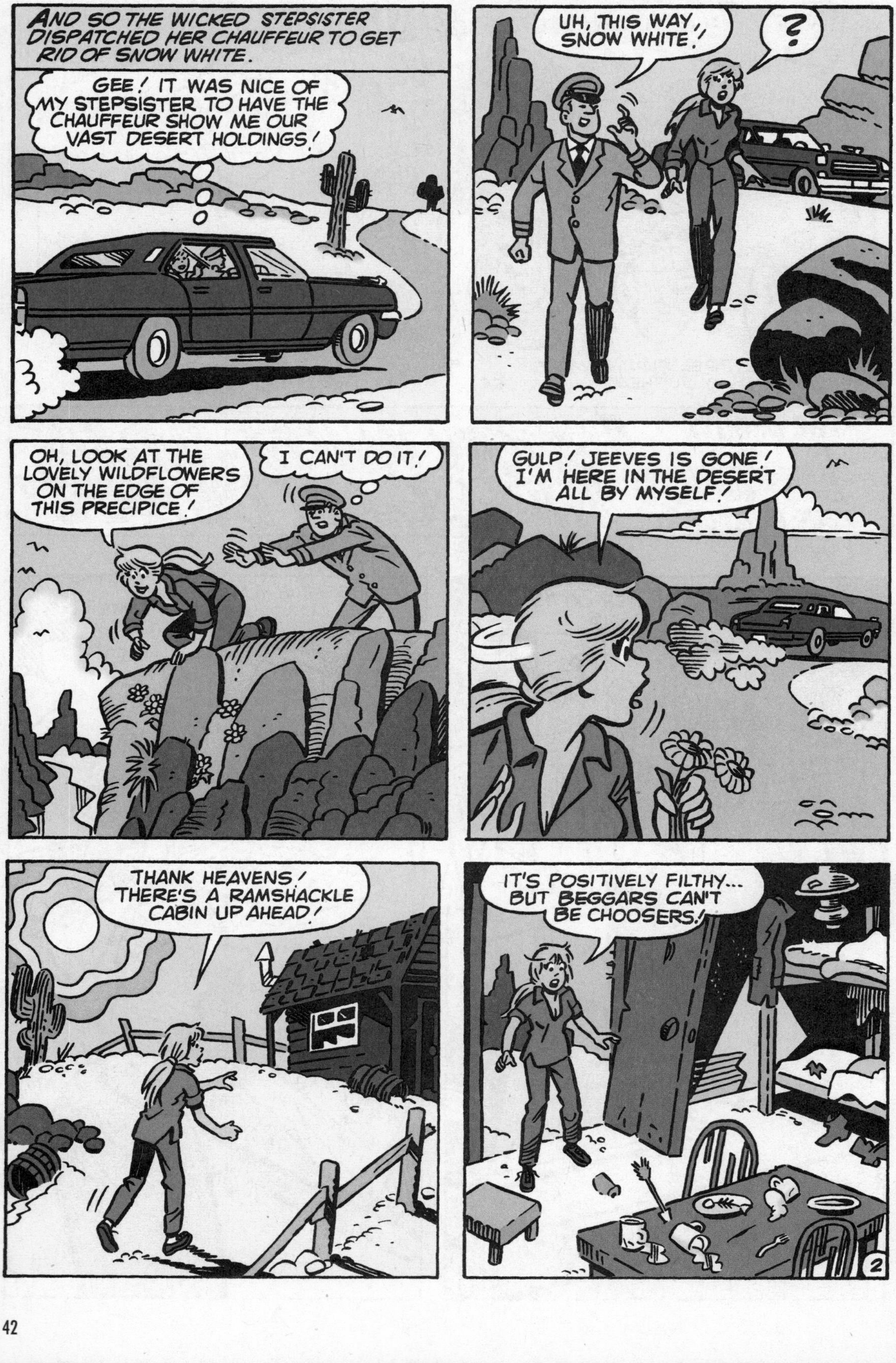
AND SO THE WICKED STEPSISTER DISPATCHED HER CHAUFFEUR TO GET RID OF SNOW WHITE.
GEE! IT WAS NICE OF MY STEPSISTER TO HAVE THE CHAUFFEUR SHOW ME OUR VAST DESERT HOLDINGS!
UH, THIS WAY, SNOW WHITE!
?
OH, LOOK AT THE LOVELY WILDFLOWERS ON THE EDGE OF THIS PRECIPICE!
I CAN'T DO IT!
GULP! JEEVES IS GONE! I'M HERE IN THE DESERT ALL BY MYSELF!
THANK HEAVENS! THERE'S A RAMSHACKLE CABIN UP AHEAD!
IT'S POSITIVELY FILTHY... BUT BEGGARS CAN'T BE CHOOSERS!
2

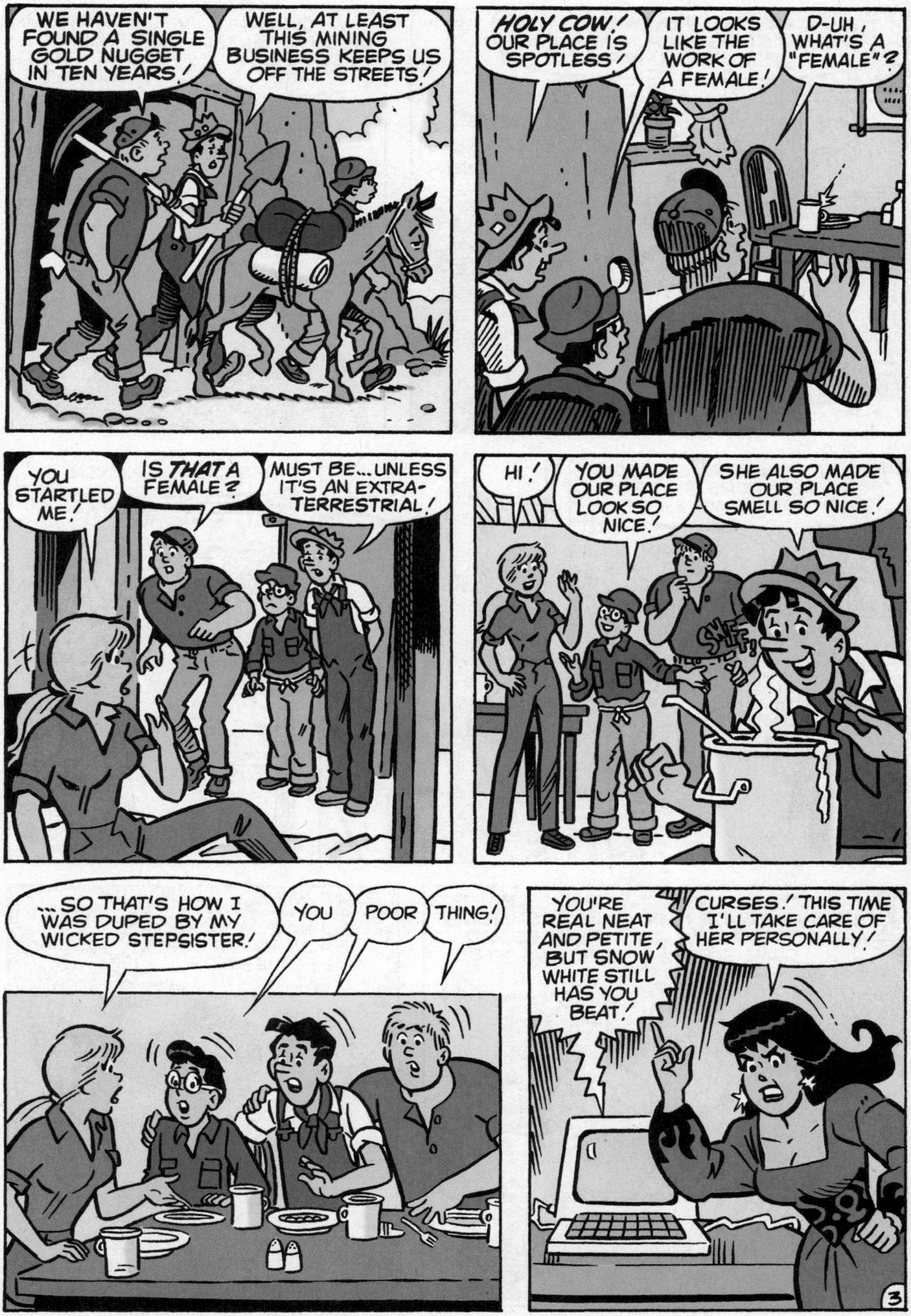
WE HAVEN'T FOUND A SINGLE GOLD NUGGET IN TEN YEARS!
WELL, AT LEAST THIS MINING BUSINESS KEEPS US OFF THE STREETS!
HOLY COW! OUR PLACE IS SPOTLESS!
IT LOOKS LIKE THE WORK OF A FEMALE!
D-UH, WHAT'S A "FEMALE"?
YOU STARTLED ME!
IS THAT A FEMALE?
MUST BE...UNLESS IT'S AN EXTRA-TERRESTRIAL!
HI!
YOU MADE OUR PLACE LOOK SO NICE!
SHE ALSO MADE OUR PLACE SMELL SO NICE!
SNIFF
...SO THAT'S HOW I WAS DUPED BY MY WICKED STEPSISTER!
YOU
POOR
THING!
YOU'RE REAL NEAT AND PETITE, BUT SNOW WHITE STILL HAS YOU BEAT!
CURSES! THIS TIME I'LL TAKE CARE OF HER PERSONALLY!
3

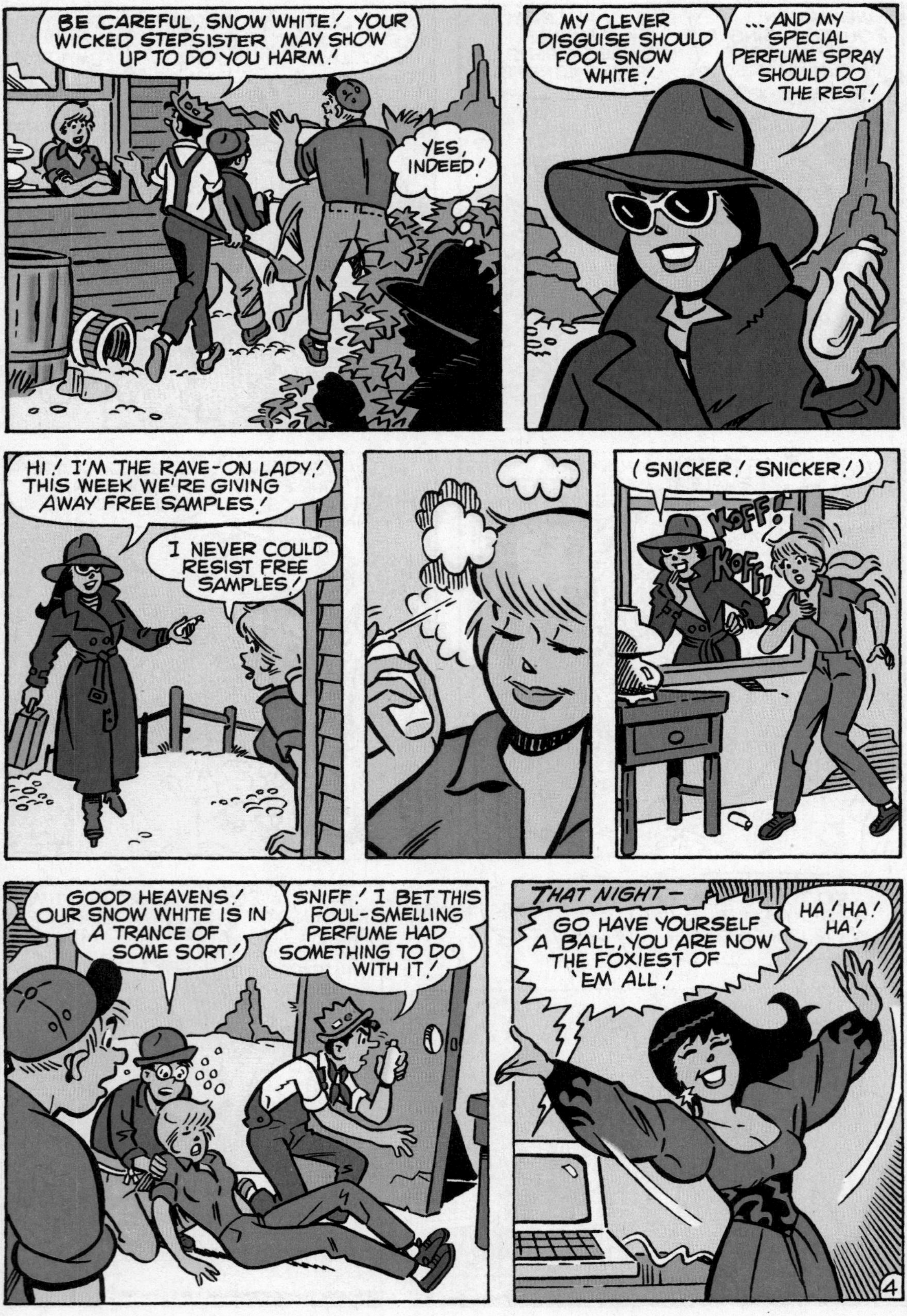
BE CAREFUL, SNOW WHITE! YOUR WICKED STEPSISTER MAY SHOW UP TO DO YOU HARM!
YES, INDEED!
MY CLEVER DISGUISE SHOULD FOOL SNOW WHITE!
... AND MY SPECIAL PERFUME SPRAY SHOULD DO THE REST!
HI! I'M THE RAVE-ON LADY! THIS WEEK WE'RE GIVING AWAY FREE SAMPLES!
I NEVER COULD RESIST FREE SAMPLES!
(SNICKER! SNICKER!)
KOFF!
KOFF!
GOOD HEAVENS! OUR SNOW WHITE IS IN A TRANCE OF SOME SORT!
SNIFF! I BET THIS FOUL-SMELLING PERFUME HAD SOMETHING TO DO WITH IT!
THAT NIGHT—
GO HAVE YOURSELF A BALL, YOU ARE NOW THE FOXIEST OF 'EM ALL!
HA! HA! HA!
4

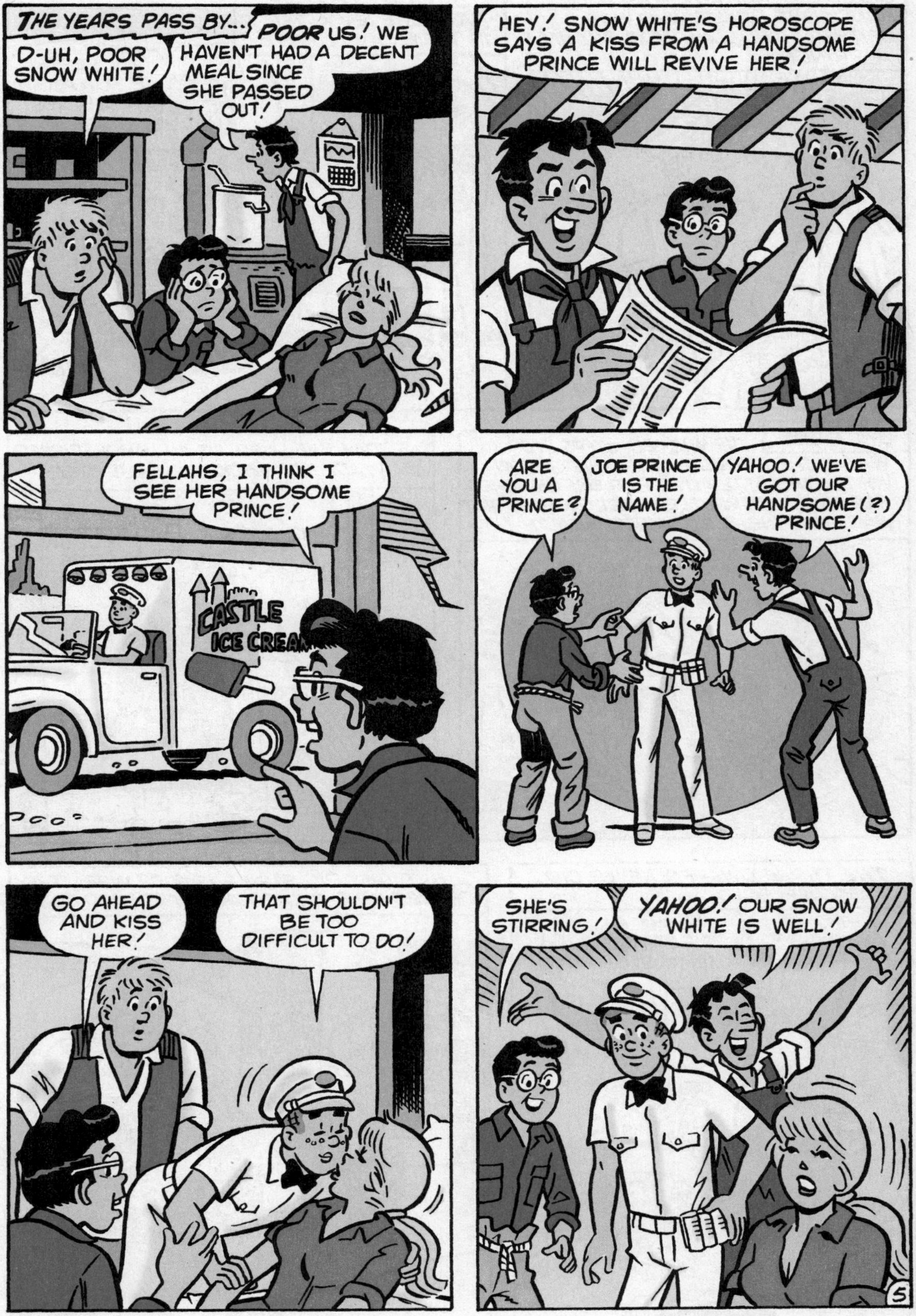
THE YEARS PASS BY...
D-UH, POOR SNOW WHITE!
POOR US! WE HAVEN'T HAD A DECENT MEAL SINCE SHE PASSED OUT!
HEY! SNOW WHITE'S HOROSCOPE SAYS A KISS FROM A HANDSOME PRINCE WILL REVIVE HER!
FELLAHS, I THINK I SEE HER HANDSOME PRINCE!
CASTLE ICE CREAM
ARE YOU A PRINCE?
JOE PRINCE IS THE NAME!
YAHOO! WE'VE GOT OUR HANDSOME (?) PRINCE!
GO AHEAD AND KISS HER!
THAT SHOULDN'T BE TOO DIFFICULT TO DO!
SHE'S STIRRING!
YAHOO! OUR SNOW WHITE IS WELL!
5

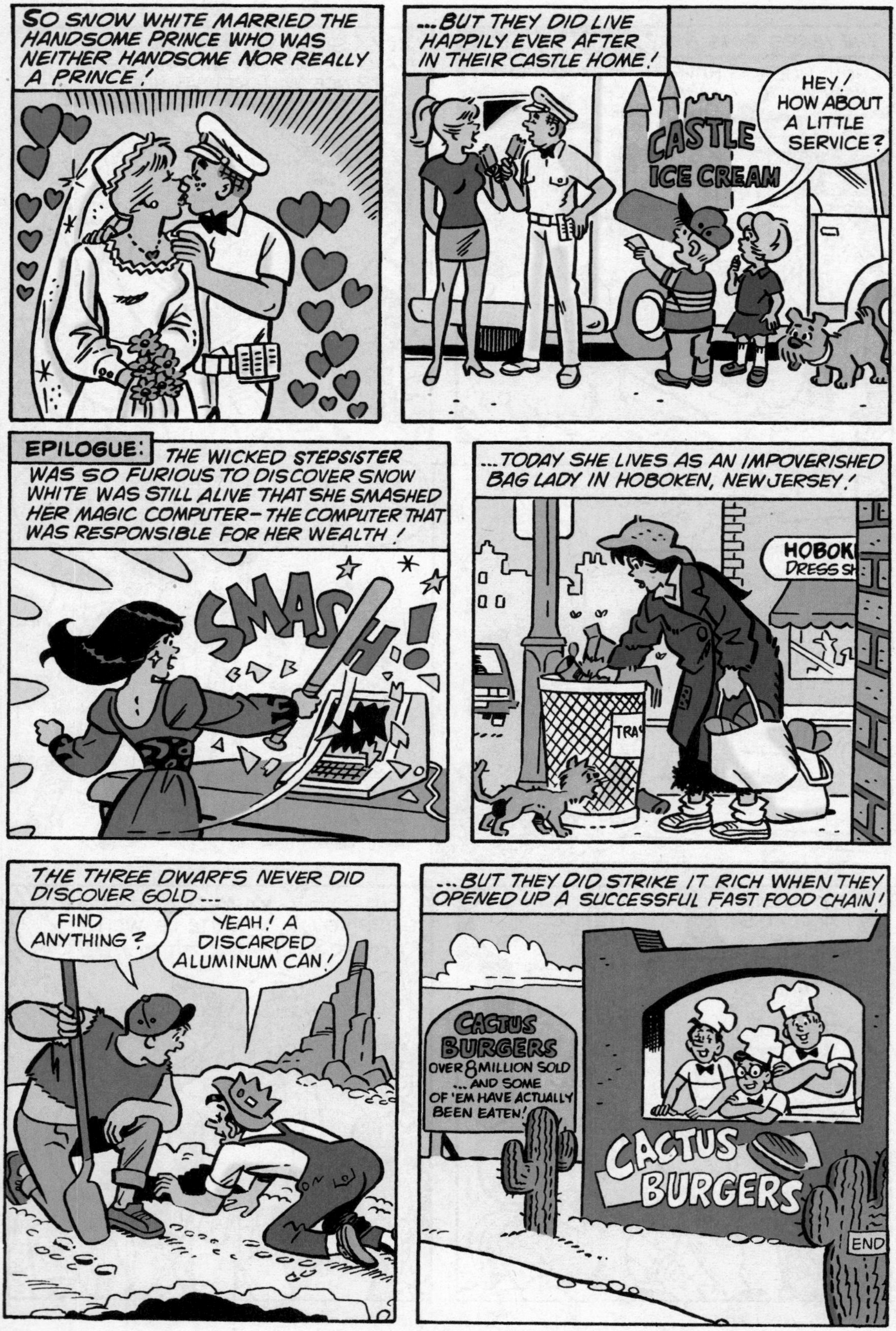
SO SNOW WHITE MARRIED THE HANDSOME PRINCE WHO WAS NEITHER HANDSOME NOR REALLY A PRINCE!
...BUT THEY DID LIVE HAPPILY EVER AFTER IN THEIR CASTLE HOME!
CASTLE ICE CREAM
HEY! HOW ABOUT A LITTLE SERVICE?
EPILOGUE: THE WICKED STEPSISTER WAS SO FURIOUS TO DISCOVER SNOW WHITE WAS STILL ALIVE THAT SHE SMASHED HER MAGIC COMPUTER—THE COMPUTER THAT WAS RESPONSIBLE FOR HER WEALTH!
SMASH!
...TODAY SHE LIVES AS AN IMPOVERISHED BAG LADY IN HOBOKEN, NEW JERSEY!
HOBOK
DRESS SH
TRA
THE THREE DWARFS NEVER DID DISCOVER GOLD...
FIND ANYTHING?
YEAH! A DISCARDED ALUMINUM CAN!
...BUT THEY DID STRIKE IT RICH WHEN THEY OPENED UP A SUCCESSFUL FAST FOOD CHAIN!
CACTUS BURGERS
OVER 8 MILLION SOLD ...AND SOME OF 'EM HAVE ACTUALLY BEEN EATEN!
CACTUS BURGERS
END

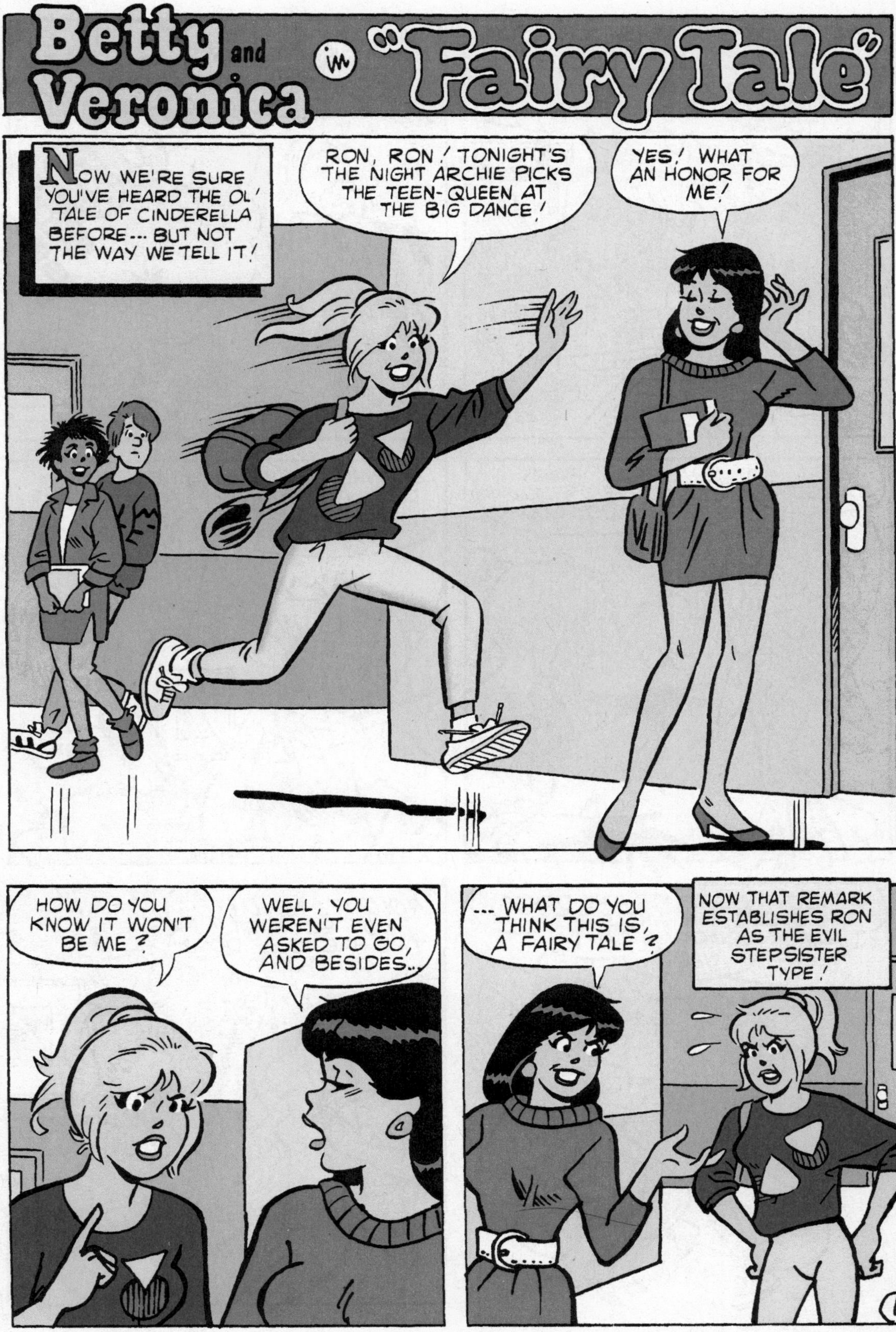
Betty and Veronica in "Fairy Tale"
NOW WE'RE SURE YOU'VE HEARD THE OL' TALE OF CINDERELLA BEFORE... BUT NOT THE WAY WE TELL IT!
RON, RON! TONIGHT'S THE NIGHT ARCHIE PICKS THE TEEN-QUEEN AT THE BIG DANCE!
YES! WHAT AN HONOR FOR ME!
HOW DO YOU KNOW IT WON'T BE ME?
WELL, YOU WEREN'T EVEN ASKED TO GO, AND BESIDES...
...WHAT DO YOU THINK THIS IS, A FAIRY TALE?
NOW THAT REMARK ESTABLISHES RON AS THE EVIL STEPSISTER TYPE!
1

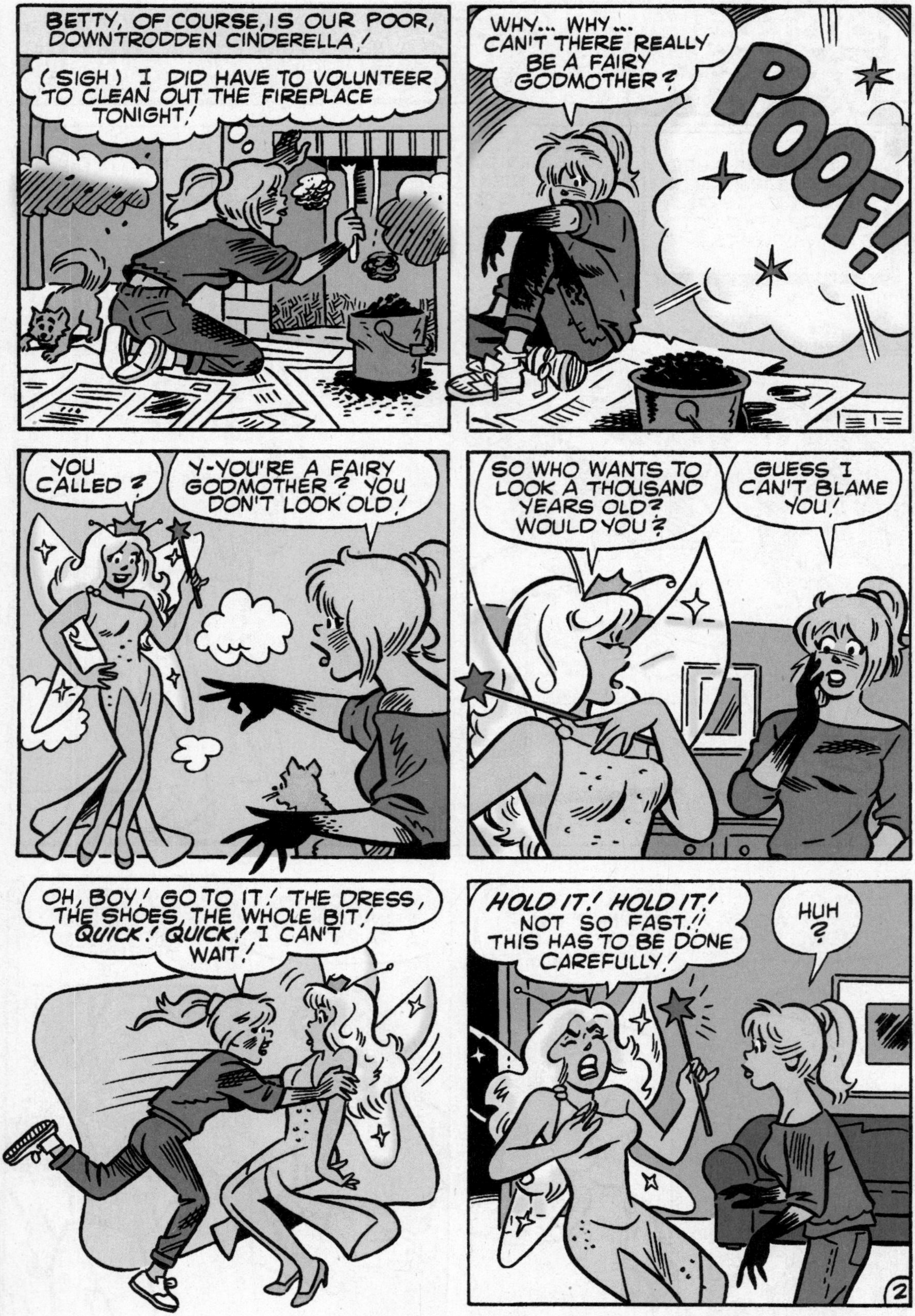

BETTY, OF COURSE, IS OUR POOR, DOWNTRODDEN CINDERELLA!
(SIGH) I DID HAVE TO VOLUNTEER TO CLEAN OUT THE FIREPLACE TONIGHT!
WHY... WHY... CAN'T THERE REALLY BE A FAIRY GODMOTHER?
POOF!
YOU CALLED?
Y-YOU'RE A FAIRY GODMOTHER? YOU DON'T LOOK OLD!
SO WHO WANTS TO LOOK A THOUSAND YEARS OLD? WOULD YOU?
GUESS I CAN'T BLAME YOU!
OH, BOY! GO TO IT! THE DRESS, THE SHOES, THE WHOLE BIT! QUICK! QUICK! I CAN'T WAIT!
HOLD IT! HOLD IT! NOT SO FAST!! THIS HAS TO BE DONE CAREFULLY!
HUH?
2

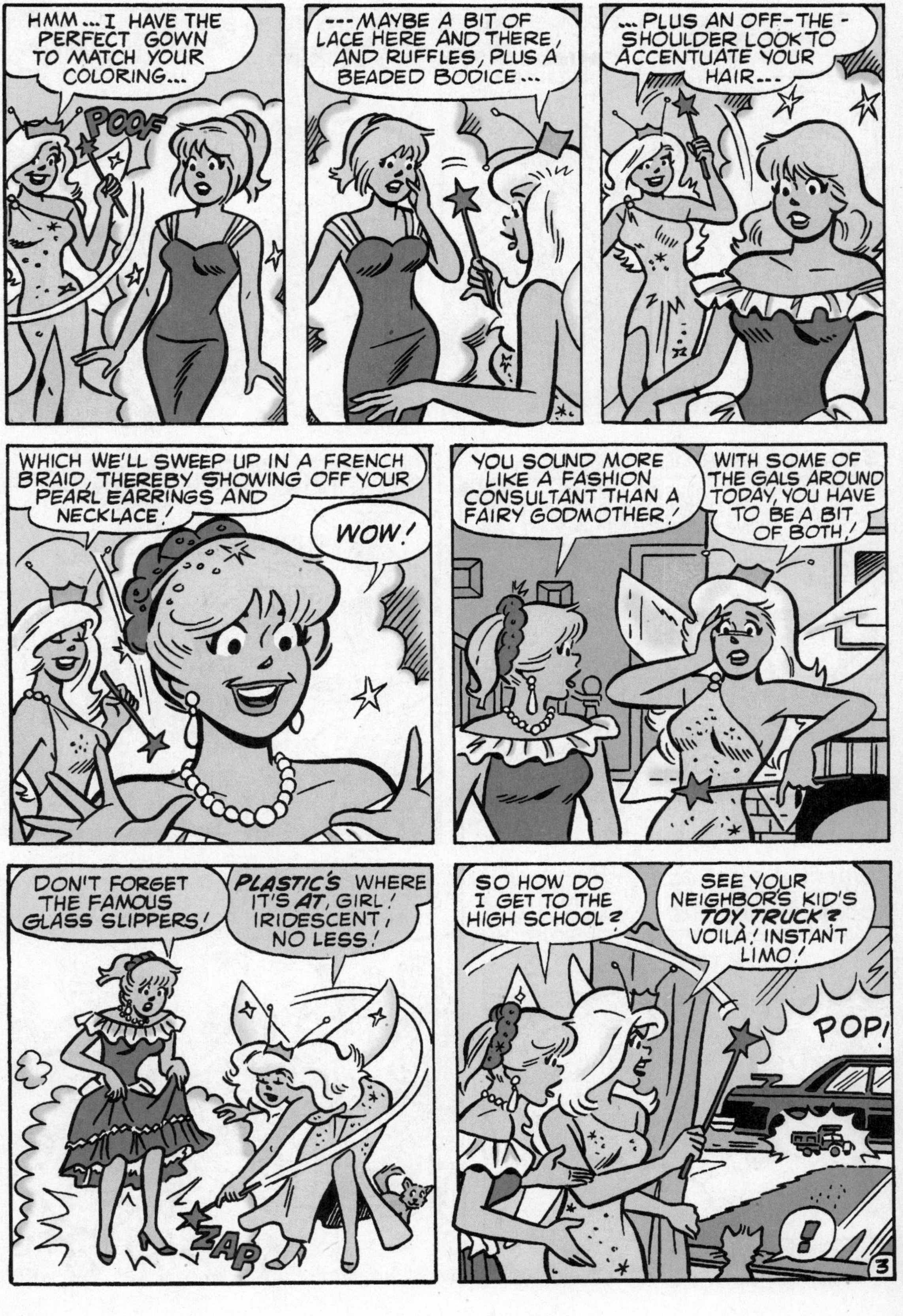
HMM... I HAVE THE PERFECT GOWN TO MATCH YOUR COLORING...
POOF
---MAYBE A BIT OF LACE HERE AND THERE, AND RUFFLES, PLUS A BEADED BODICE...
...PLUS AN OFF-THE-SHOULDER LOOK TO ACCENTUATE YOUR HAIR---
WHICH WE'LL SWEEP UP IN A FRENCH BRAID, THEREBY SHOWING OFF YOUR PEARL EARRINGS AND NECKLACE!
WOW!
YOU SOUND MORE LIKE A FASHION CONSULTANT THAN A FAIRY GODMOTHER!
WITH SOME OF THE GALS AROUND TODAY, YOU HAVE TO BE A BIT OF BOTH!
DON'T FORGET THE FAMOUS GLASS SLIPPERS!
PLASTIC'S WHERE IT'S AT, GIRL! IRIDESCENT, NO LESS!
ZAP
SO HOW DO I GET TO THE HIGH SCHOOL?
SEE YOUR NEIGHBOR'S KID'S TOY TRUCK? VOILÀ! INSTANT LIMO!
POP!
!
3

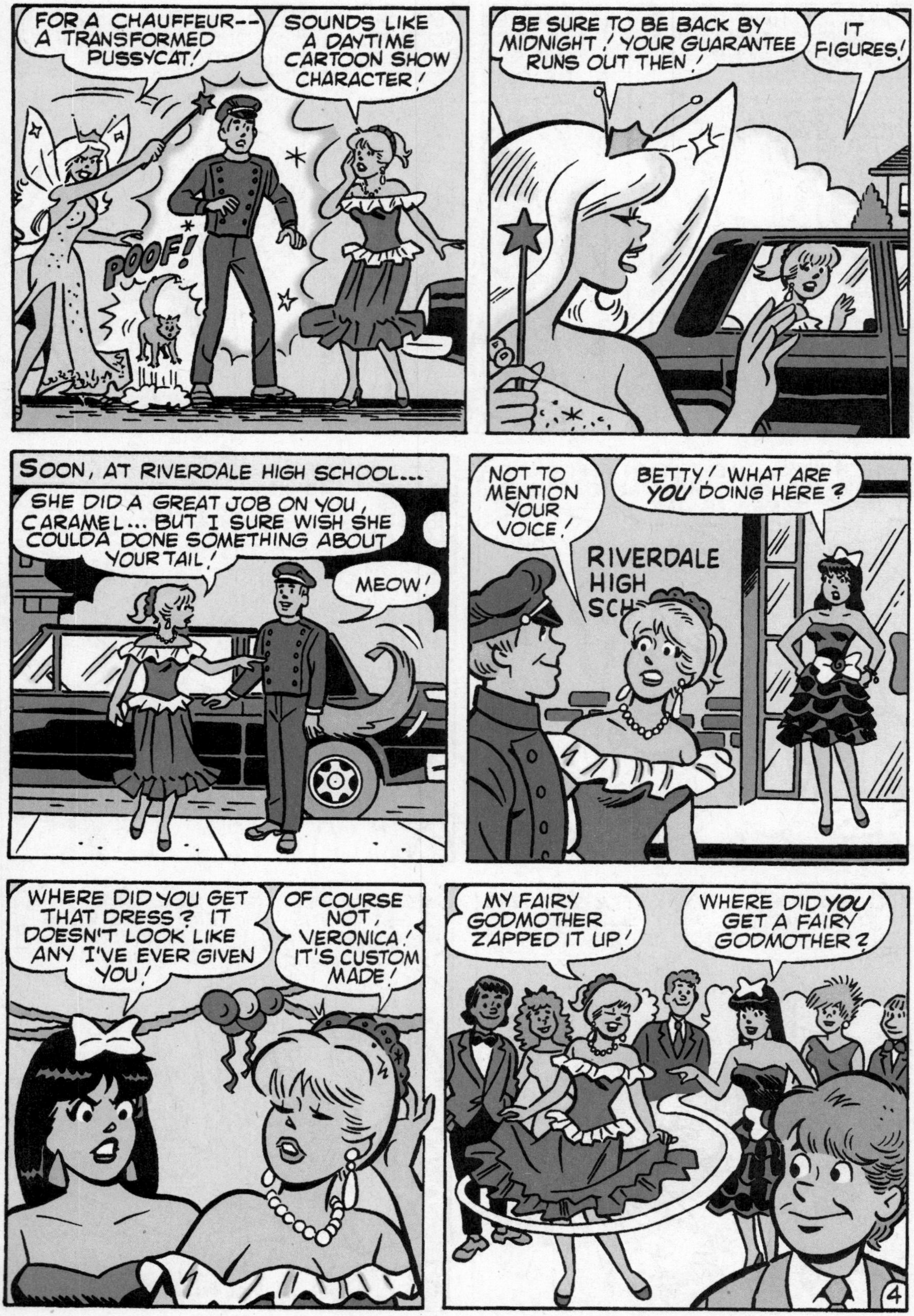
FOR A CHAUFFEUR-- A TRANSFORMED PUSSYCAT!
SOUNDS LIKE A DAYTIME CARTOON SHOW CHARACTER!
POOF!
BE SURE TO BE BACK BY MIDNIGHT! YOUR GUARANTEE RUNS OUT THEN!
IT FIGURES!
SOON, AT RIVERDALE HIGH SCHOOL...
SHE DID A GREAT JOB ON YOU, CARAMEL... BUT I SURE WISH SHE COULDA DONE SOMETHING ABOUT YOUR TAIL!
MEOW!
NOT TO MENTION YOUR VOICE!
BETTY! WHAT ARE YOU DOING HERE?
RIVERDALE HIGH SCH
WHERE DID YOU GET THAT DRESS? IT DOESN'T LOOK LIKE ANY I'VE EVER GIVEN YOU!
OF COURSE NOT, VERONICA! IT'S CUSTOM MADE!
MY FAIRY GODMOTHER ZAPPED IT UP!
WHERE DID YOU GET A FAIRY GODMOTHER?
4

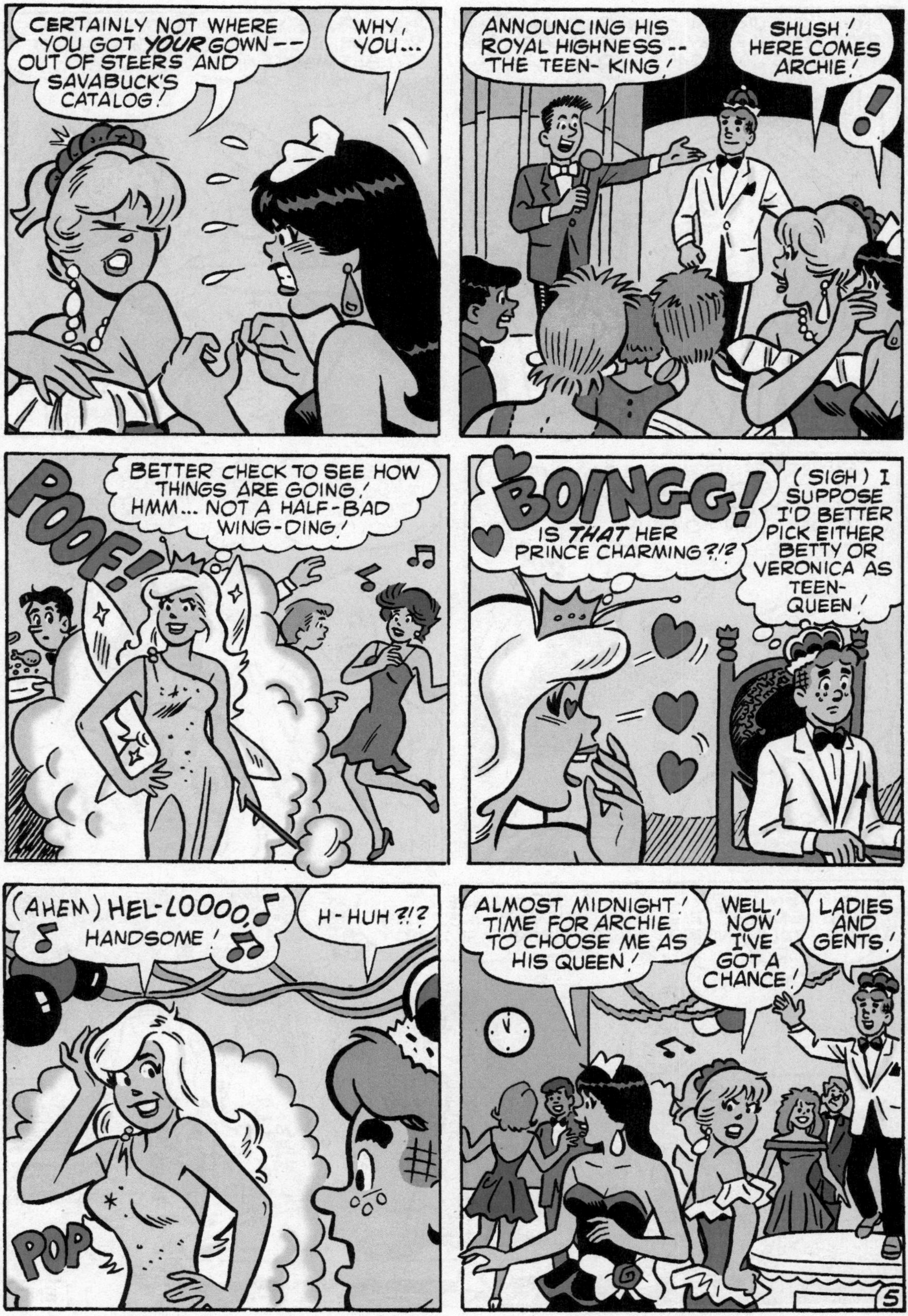
CERTAINLY NOT WHERE YOU GOT YOUR GOWN -- OUT OF STEERS AND SAVABUCK'S CATALOG!
WHY, YOU...
ANNOUNCING HIS ROYAL HIGHNESS -- THE TEEN-KING!
SHUSH! HERE COMES ARCHIE!
!
POOF!!
BETTER CHECK TO SEE HOW THINGS ARE GOING! HMM... NOT A HALF-BAD WING-DING!
BOINGG!
IS THAT HER PRINCE CHARMING?!?
(SIGH) I SUPPOSE I'D BETTER PICK EITHER BETTY OR VERONICA AS TEEN-QUEEN!
(AHEM) HEL-LOOOO, HANDSOME!
H-HUH ?!?
POP
ALMOST MIDNIGHT! TIME FOR ARCHIE TO CHOOSE ME AS HIS QUEEN!
WELL, NOW I'VE GOT A CHANCE!
LADIES AND GENTS!
5

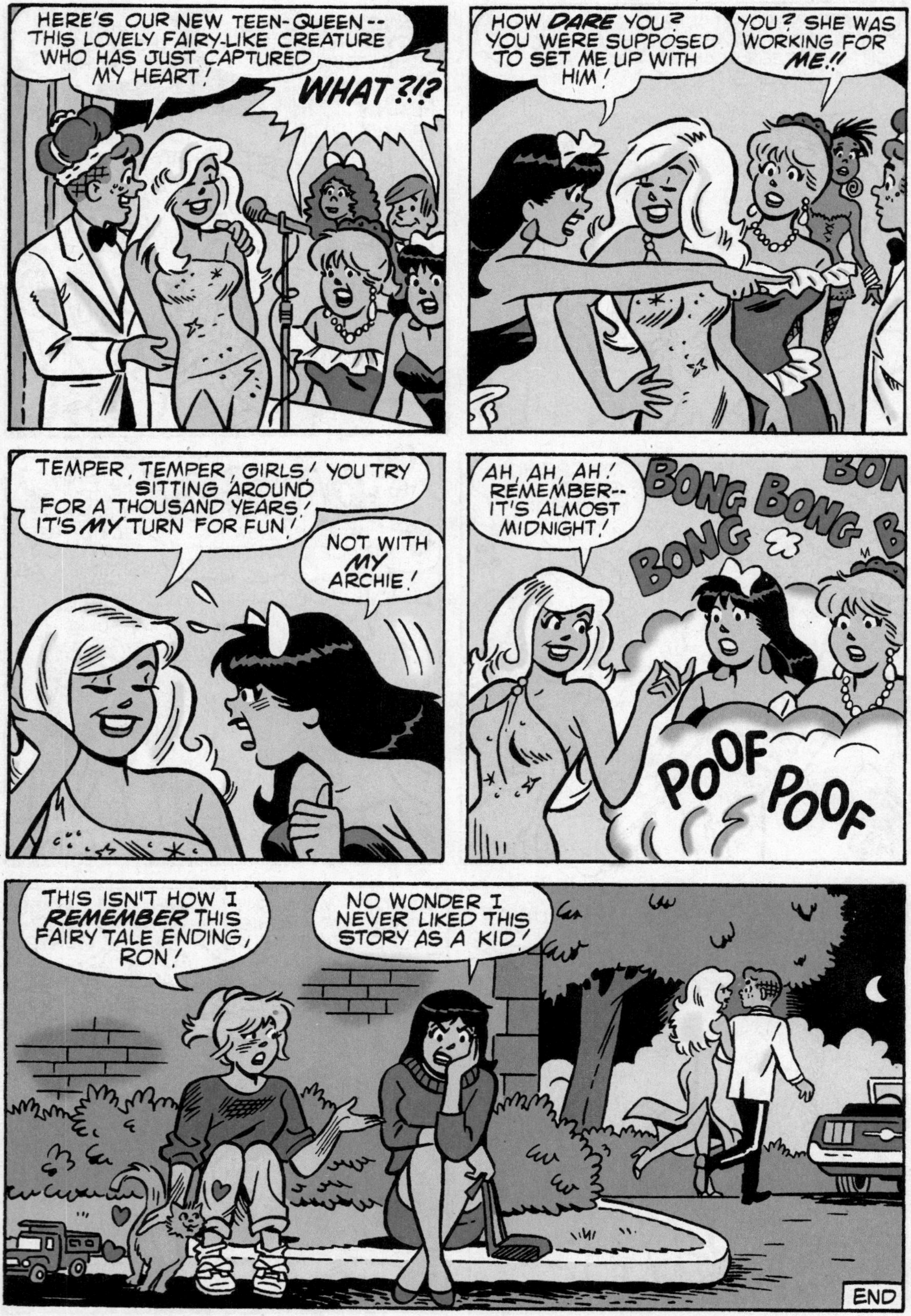
HERE'S OUR NEW TEEN-QUEEN -- THIS LOVELY FAIRY-LIKE CREATURE WHO HAS JUST CAPTURED MY HEART!
WHAT?!?
HOW DARE YOU? YOU WERE SUPPOSED TO SET ME UP WITH HIM!
YOU? SHE WAS WORKING FOR ME!!
TEMPER, TEMPER, GIRLS! YOU TRY SITTING AROUND FOR A THOUSAND YEARS! IT'S MY TURN FOR FUN!
NOT WITH MY ARCHIE!
AH, AH, AH! REMEMBER-- IT'S ALMOST MIDNIGHT!
BONG BONG BONG BONG
POOF POOF
THIS ISN'T HOW I REMEMBER THIS FAIRY TALE ENDING, RON!
NO WONDER I NEVER LIKED THIS STORY AS A KID!
END

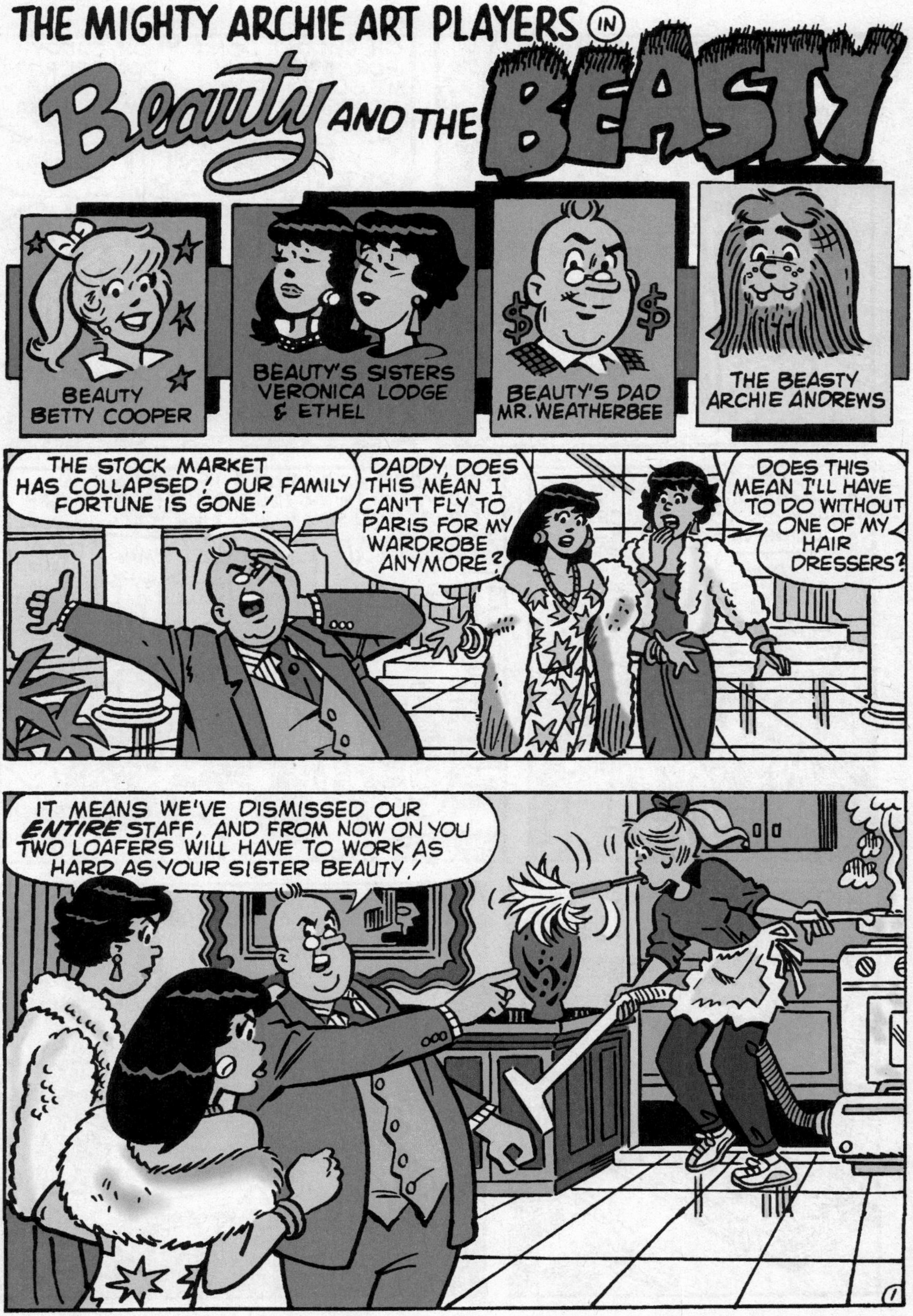
THE MIGHTY ARCHIE ART PLAYERS IN
Beauty AND THE BEASTY
BEAUTY
BETTY COOPER
BEAUTY'S SISTERS
VERONICA LODGE
& ETHEL
BEAUTY'S DAD
MR. WEATHERBEE
THE BEASTY
ARCHIE ANDREWS
THE STOCK MARKET HAS COLLAPSED! OUR FAMILY FORTUNE IS GONE!
DADDY, DOES THIS MEAN I CAN'T FLY TO PARIS FOR MY WARDROBE ANYMORE?
DOES THIS MEAN I'LL HAVE TO DO WITHOUT ONE OF MY HAIR DRESSERS?
IT MEANS WE'VE DISMISSED OUR ENTIRE STAFF, AND FROM NOW ON YOU TWO LOAFERS WILL HAVE TO WORK AS HARD AS YOUR SISTER BEAUTY!
1

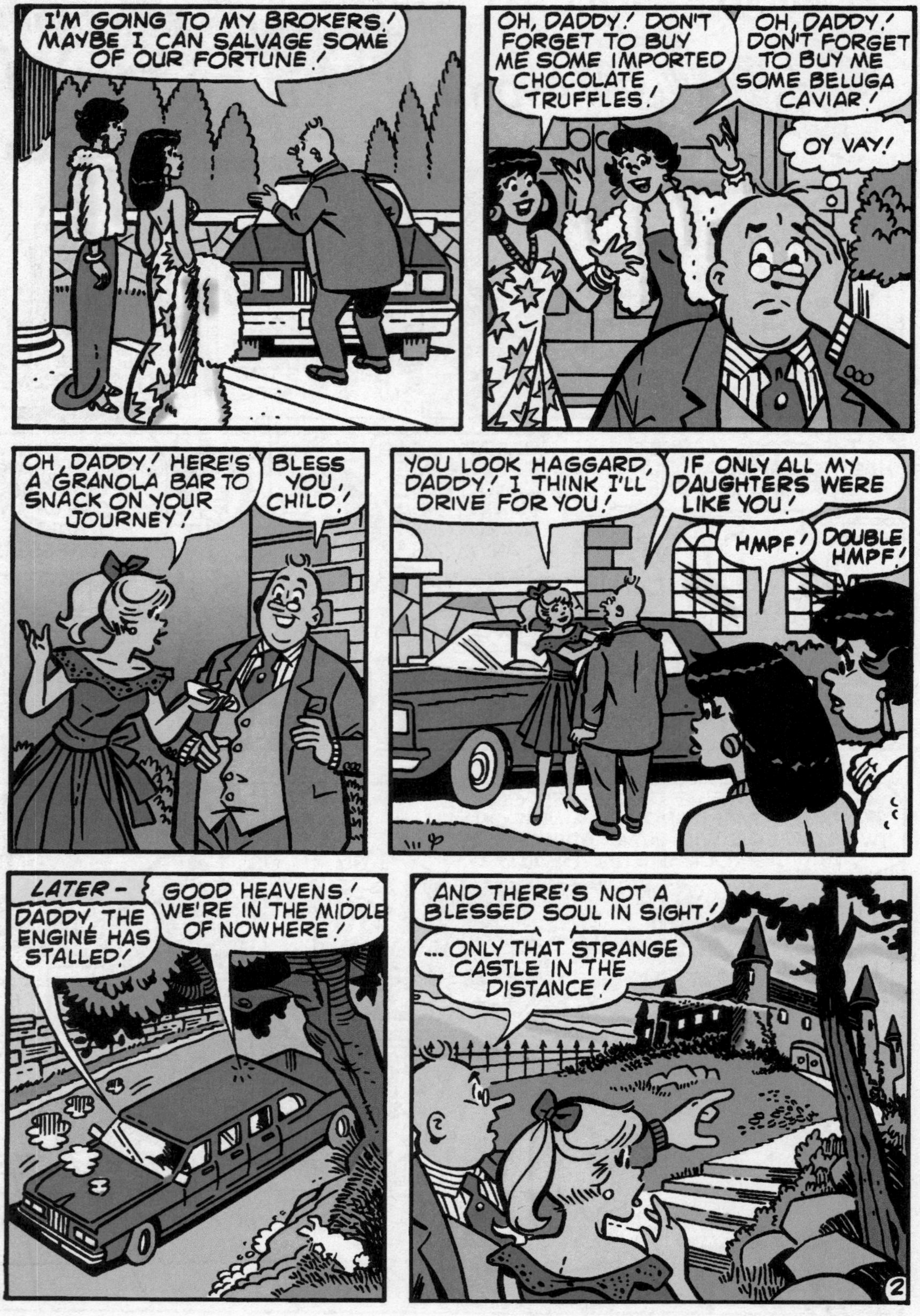
I'M GOING TO MY BROKERS! MAYBE I CAN SALVAGE SOME OF OUR FORTUNE!
OH, DADDY! DON'T FORGET TO BUY ME SOME IMPORTED CHOCOLATE TRUFFLES!
OH, DADDY! DON'T FORGET TO BUY ME SOME BELUGA CAVIAR!
OY VAY!
OH, DADDY! HERE'S A GRANOLA BAR TO SNACK ON YOUR JOURNEY!
BLESS YOU, CHILD!
YOU LOOK HAGGARD, DADDY! I THINK I'LL DRIVE FOR YOU!
IF ONLY ALL MY DAUGHTERS WERE LIKE YOU!
HMPF!
DOUBLE HMPF!
LATER -
DADDY, THE ENGINE HAS STALLED!
GOOD HEAVENS! WE'RE IN THE MIDDLE OF NOWHERE!
AND THERE'S NOT A BLESSED SOUL IN SIGHT!
...ONLY THAT STRANGE CASTLE IN THE DISTANCE!
2

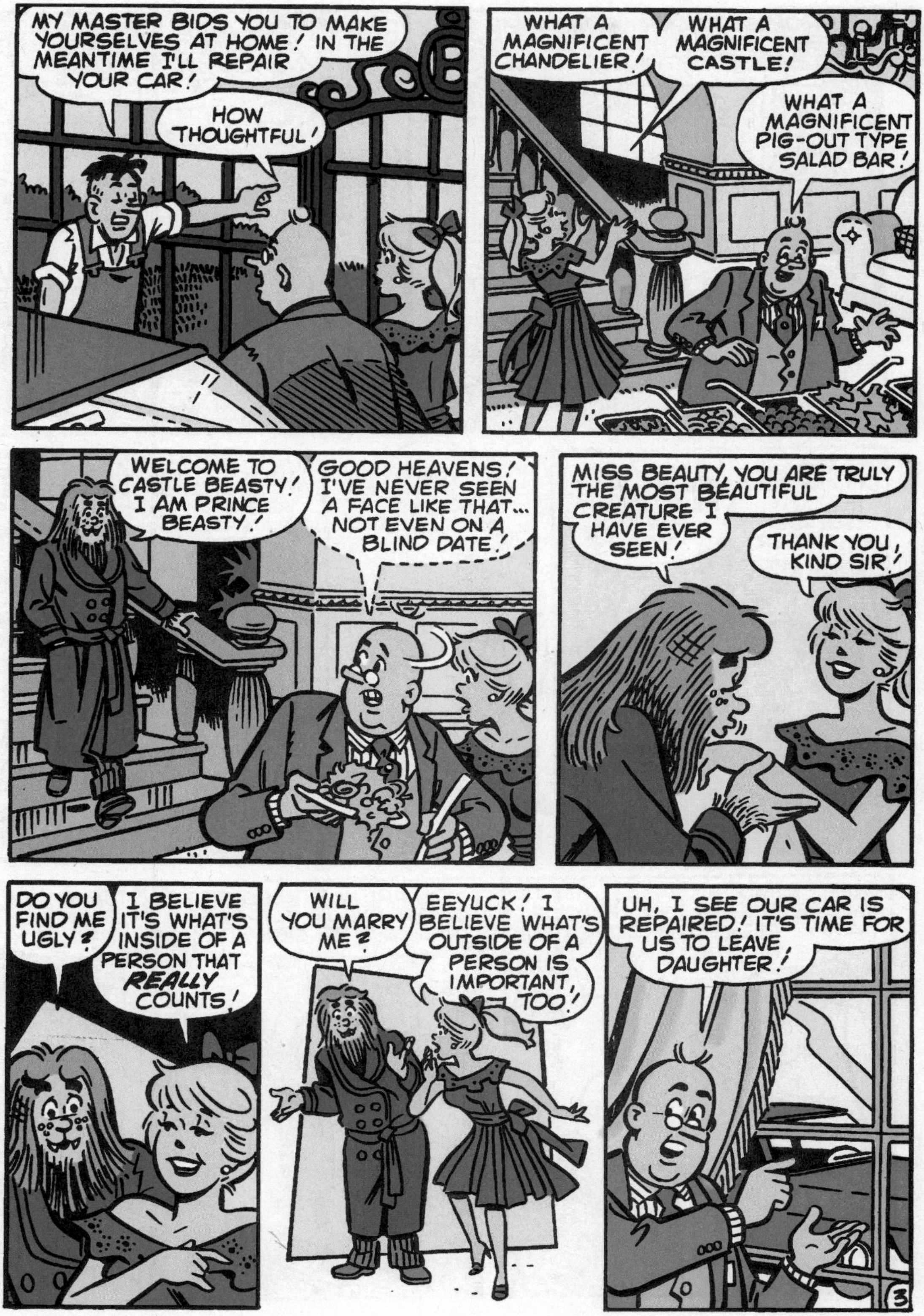
MY MASTER BIDS YOU TO MAKE YOURSELVES AT HOME! IN THE MEANTIME I'LL REPAIR YOUR CAR!
HOW THOUGHTFUL!
WHAT A MAGNIFICENT CHANDELIER!
WHAT A MAGNIFICENT CASTLE!
WHAT A MAGNIFICENT PIG-OUT TYPE SALAD BAR!
WELCOME TO CASTLE BEASTY! I AM PRINCE BEASTY!
GOOD HEAVENS! I'VE NEVER SEEN A FACE LIKE THAT... NOT EVEN ON A BLIND DATE!
MISS BEAUTY, YOU ARE TRULY THE MOST BEAUTIFUL CREATURE I HAVE EVER SEEN!
THANK YOU, KIND SIR!
DO YOU FIND ME UGLY?
I BELIEVE IT'S WHAT'S INSIDE OF A PERSON THAT REALLY COUNTS!
WILL YOU MARRY ME?
EEYUCK! I BELIEVE WHAT'S OUTSIDE OF A PERSON IS IMPORTANT, TOO!
UH, I SEE OUR CAR IS REPAIRED! IT'S TIME FOR US TO LEAVE, DAUGHTER!
3

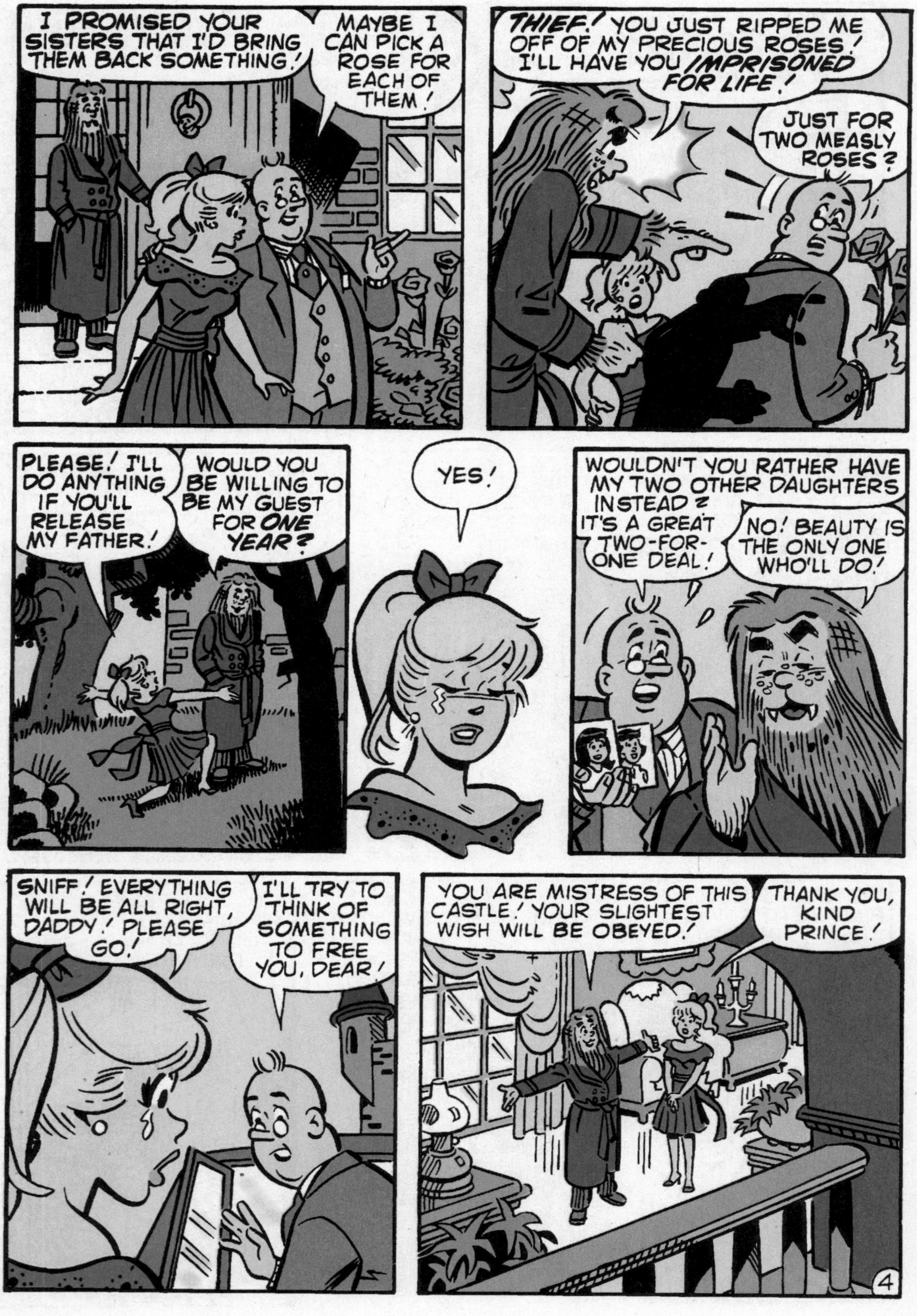
I PROMISED YOUR SISTERS THAT I'D BRING THEM BACK SOMETHING!
MAYBE I CAN PICK A ROSE FOR EACH OF THEM!
THIEF! YOU JUST RIPPED ME OFF OF MY PRECIOUS ROSES! I'LL HAVE YOU IMPRISONED FOR LIFE!
JUST FOR TWO MEASLY ROSES?
PLEASE! I'LL DO ANYTHING IF YOU'LL RELEASE MY FATHER!
WOULD YOU BE WILLING TO BE MY GUEST FOR ONE YEAR?
YES!
WOULDN'T YOU RATHER HAVE MY TWO OTHER DAUGHTERS INSTEAD?
IT'S A GREAT TWO-FOR-ONE DEAL!
NO! BEAUTY IS THE ONLY ONE WHO'LL DO!
SNIFF! EVERYTHING WILL BE ALL RIGHT, DADDY! PLEASE GO!
I'LL TRY TO THINK OF SOMETHING TO FREE YOU, DEAR!
YOU ARE MISTRESS OF THIS CASTLE! YOUR SLIGHTEST WISH WILL BE OBEYED!
THANK YOU, KIND PRINCE!
4

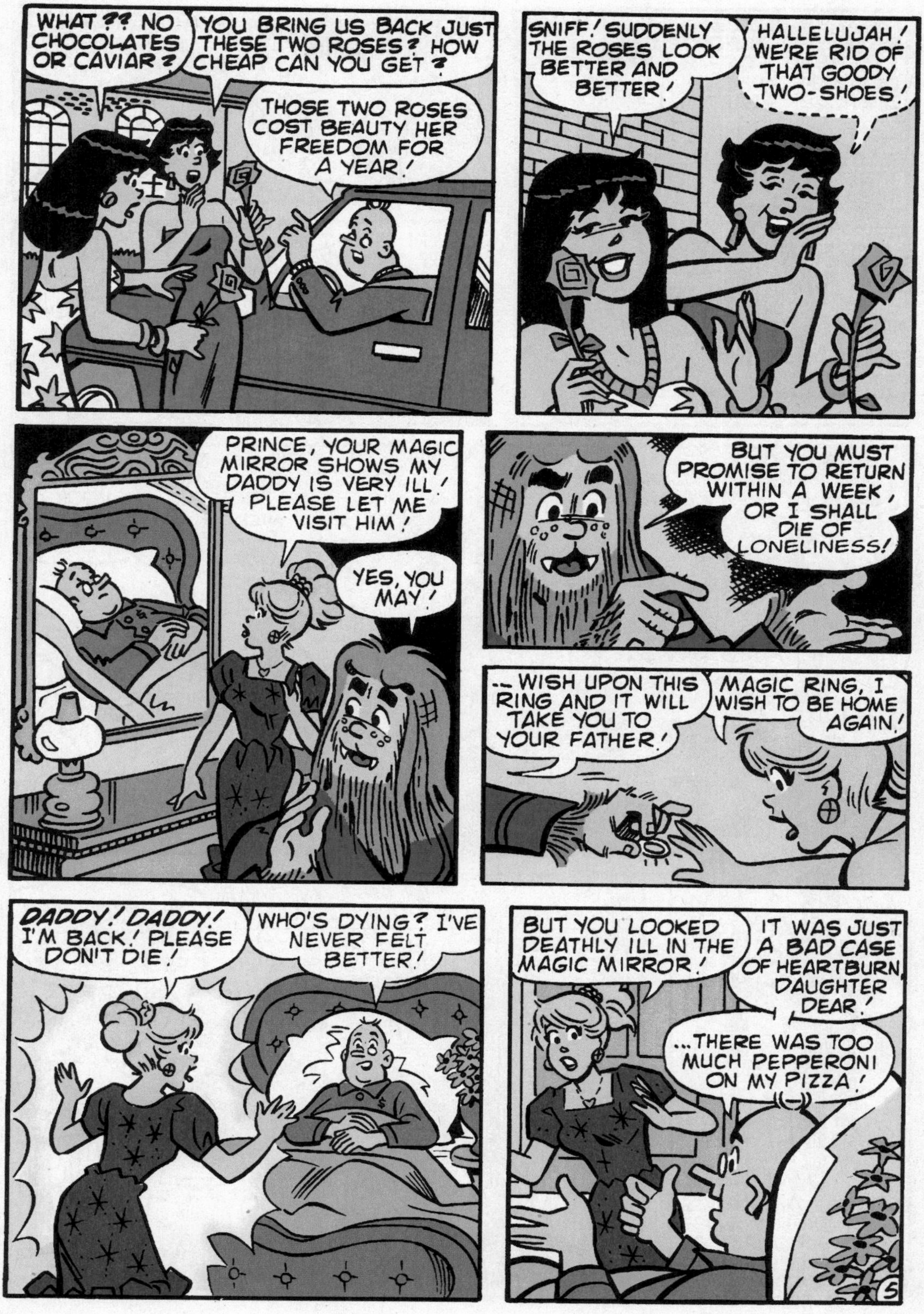
WHAT ?? NO CHOCOLATES OR CAVIAR ?
YOU BRING US BACK JUST THESE TWO ROSES ? HOW CHEAP CAN YOU GET ?
THOSE TWO ROSES COST BEAUTY HER FREEDOM FOR A YEAR!
SNIFF! SUDDENLY THE ROSES LOOK BETTER AND BETTER!
HALLELUJAH! WE'RE RID OF THAT GOODY TWO-SHOES!
PRINCE, YOUR MAGIC MIRROR SHOWS MY DADDY IS VERY ILL! PLEASE LET ME VISIT HIM!
YES, YOU MAY!
BUT YOU MUST PROMISE TO RETURN WITHIN A WEEK, OR I SHALL DIE OF LONELINESS!
-- WISH UPON THIS RING AND IT WILL TAKE YOU TO YOUR FATHER!
MAGIC RING, I WISH TO BE HOME AGAIN!
DADDY! DADDY! I'M BACK! PLEASE DON'T DIE!
WHO'S DYING? I'VE NEVER FELT BETTER!
BUT YOU LOOKED DEATHLY ILL IN THE MAGIC MIRROR!
IT WAS JUST A BAD CASE OF HEARTBURN, DAUGHTER DEAR!
...THERE WAS TOO MUCH PEPPERONI ON MY PIZZA!
5

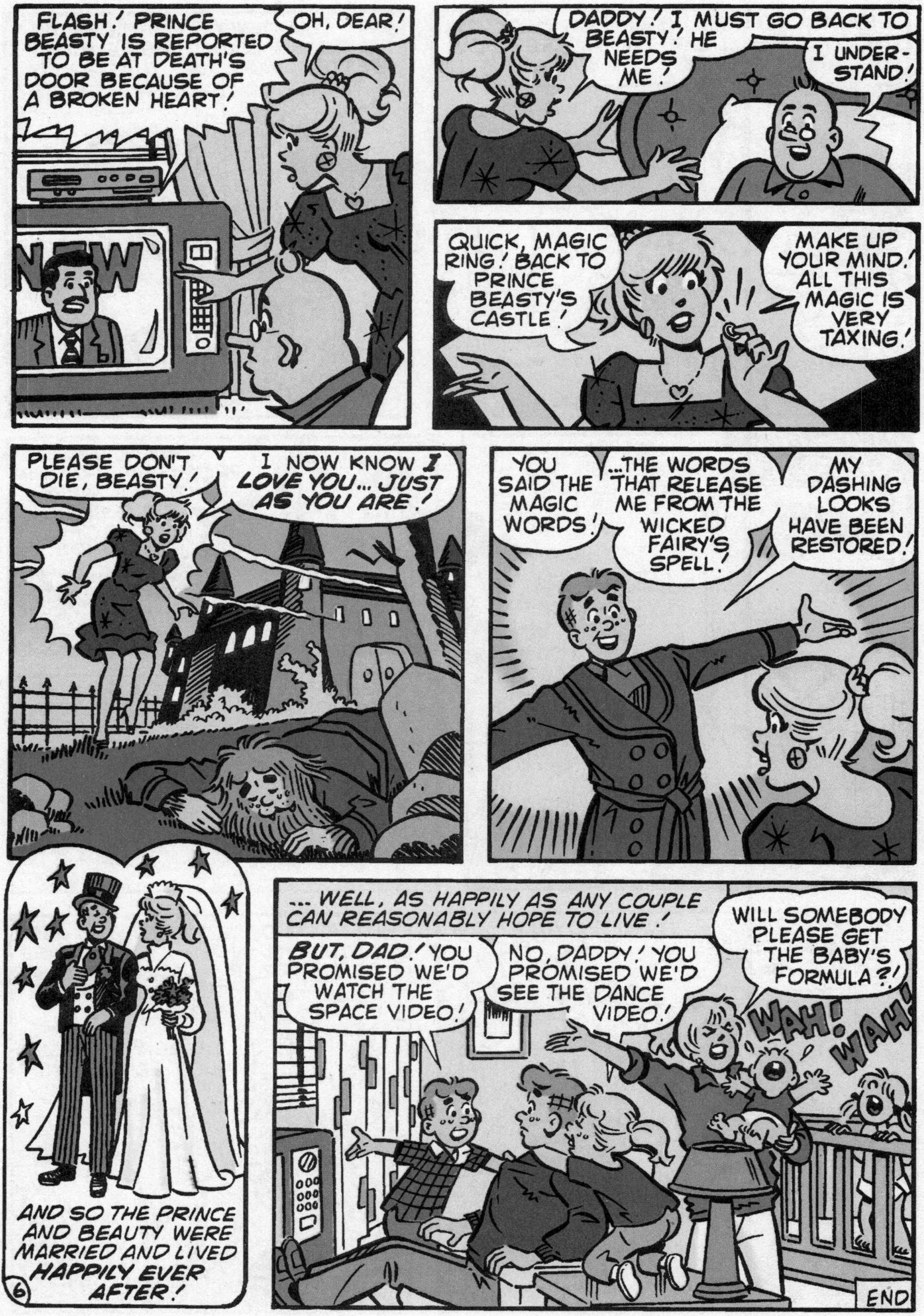
FLASH! PRINCE BEASTY IS REPORTED TO BE AT DEATH'S DOOR BECAUSE OF A BROKEN HEART!
OH, DEAR!
DADDY! I MUST GO BACK TO BEASTY! HE NEEDS ME!
I UNDERSTAND!
QUICK, MAGIC RING! BACK TO PRINCE BEASTY'S CASTLE!
MAKE UP YOUR MIND! ALL THIS MAGIC IS VERY TAXING!
PLEASE DON'T DIE, BEASTY!
I NOW KNOW I LOVE YOU... JUST AS YOU ARE!
YOU SAID THE MAGIC WORDS!
...THE WORDS THAT RELEASE ME FROM THE WICKED FAIRY'S SPELL!
MY DASHING LOOKS HAVE BEEN RESTORED!
AND SO THE PRINCE AND BEAUTY WERE MARRIED AND LIVED HAPPILY EVER AFTER!
6
... WELL, AS HAPPILY AS ANY COUPLE CAN REASONABLY HOPE TO LIVE!
BUT, DAD! YOU PROMISED WE'D WATCH THE SPACE VIDEO!
NO, DADDY! YOU PROMISED WE'D SEE THE DANCE VIDEO!
WILL SOMEBODY PLEASE GET THE BABY'S FORMULA?!
WAH! WAH!
END

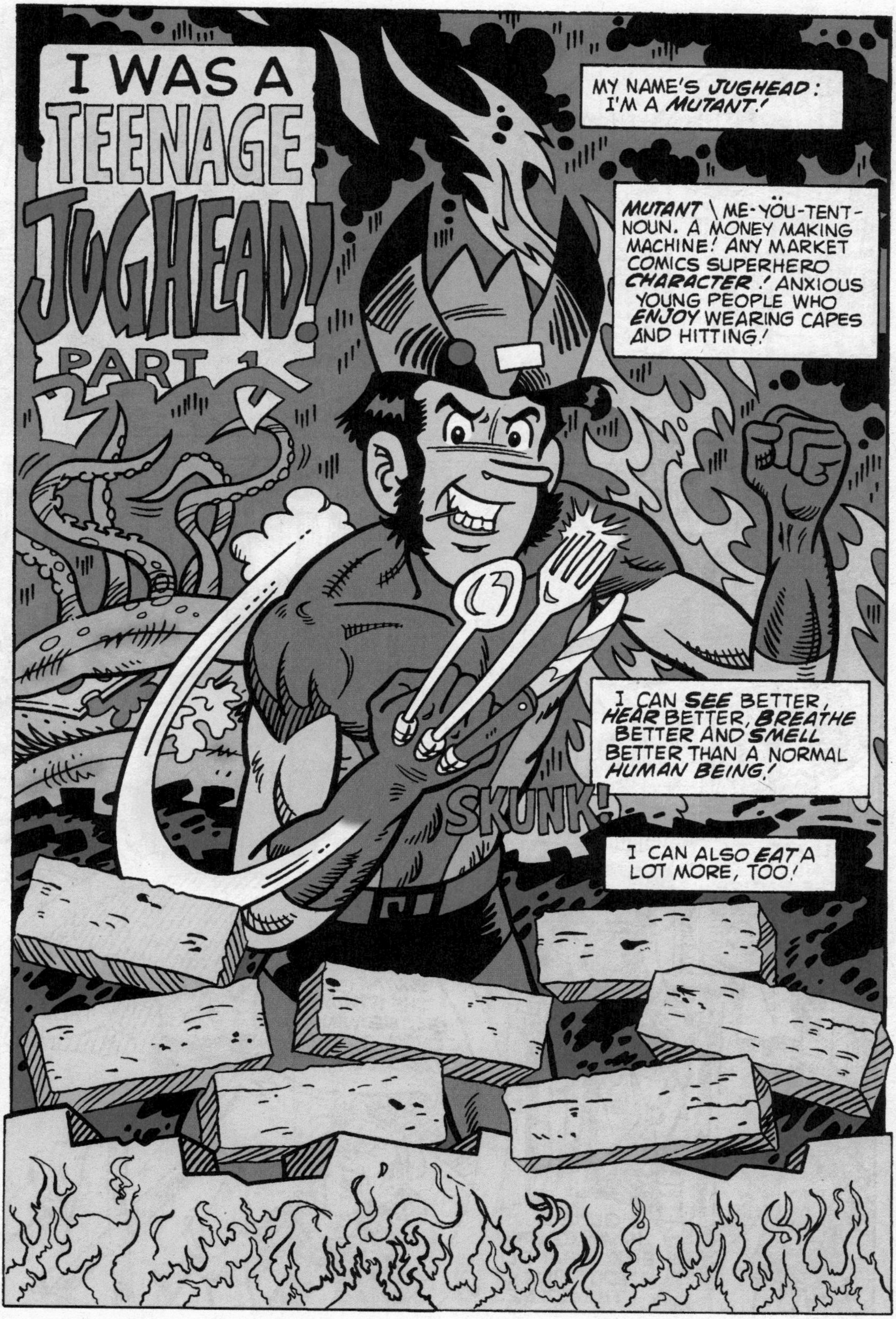

I WAS A TEENAGE JUGHEAD! PART 1
MY NAME'S JUGHEAD: I'M A MUTANT!
MUTANT \ ME-YÖU-TENT-NOUN. A MONEY MAKING MACHINE! ANY MARKET COMICS SUPERHERO CHARACTER! ANXIOUS YOUNG PEOPLE WHO ENJOY WEARING CAPES AND HITTING!
I CAN SEE BETTER, HEAR BETTER, BREATHE BETTER AND SMELL BETTER THAN A NORMAL HUMAN BEING!
SKUNK!
I CAN ALSO EAT A LOT MORE, TOO!

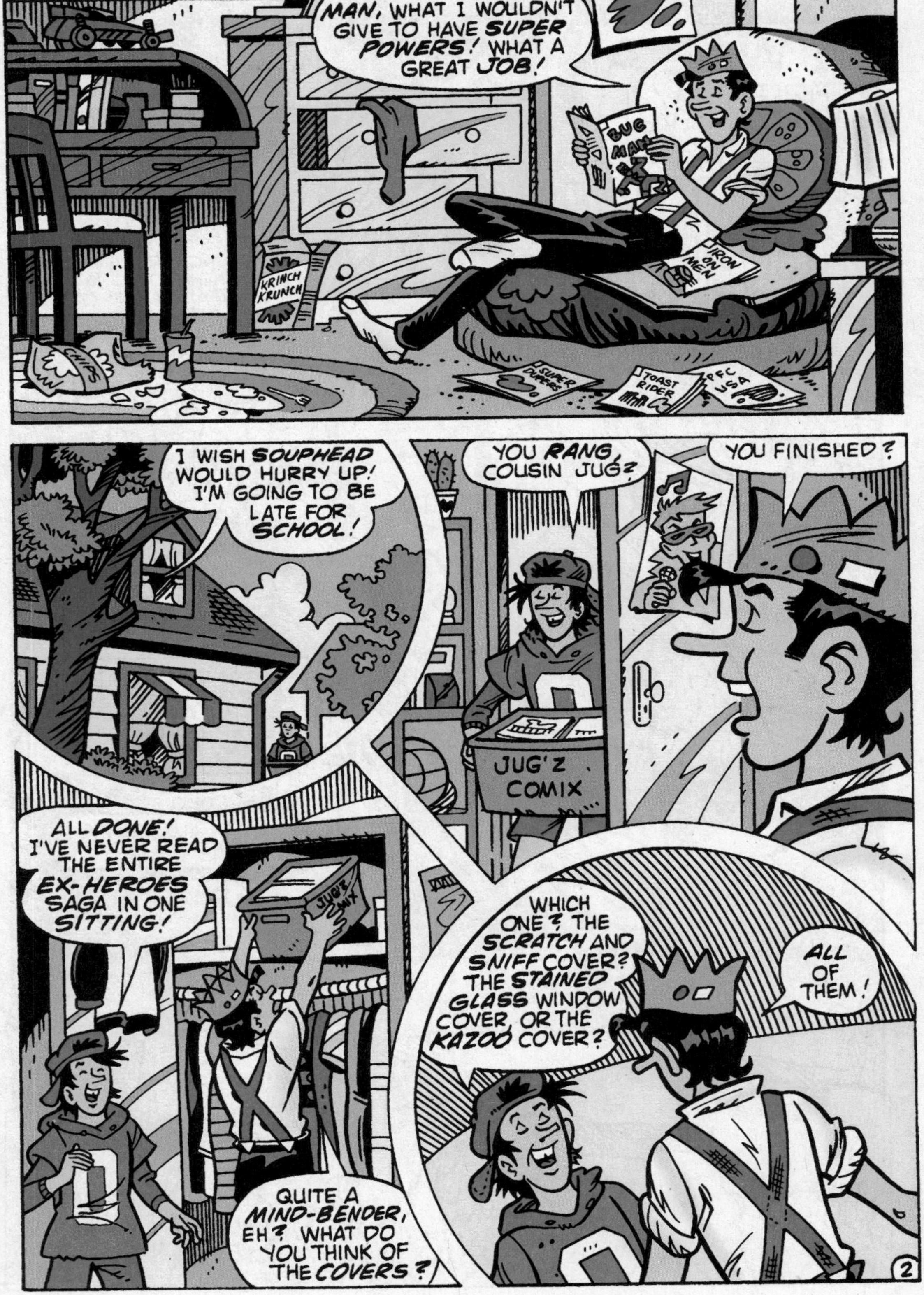
MAN, WHAT I WOULDN'T GIVE TO HAVE SUPER POWERS! WHAT A GREAT JOB!
BUG MAN
IRON ON MEN
KRINCH KRUNCH
CHIPS
SUPER DUPERS
TOAST RIDER
PFC USA
I WISH SOUPHEAD WOULD HURRY UP! I'M GOING TO BE LATE FOR SCHOOL!
YOU RANG, COUSIN JUG?
YOU FINISHED?
JUG'Z COMIX
ALL DONE! I'VE NEVER READ THE ENTIRE EX-HEROES SAGA IN ONE SITTING!
QUITE A MIND-BENDER, EH? WHAT DO YOU THINK OF THE COVERS?
WHICH ONE? THE SCRATCH AND SNIFF COVER? THE STAINED GLASS WINDOW COVER, OR THE KAZOO COVER?
ALL OF THEM!
2

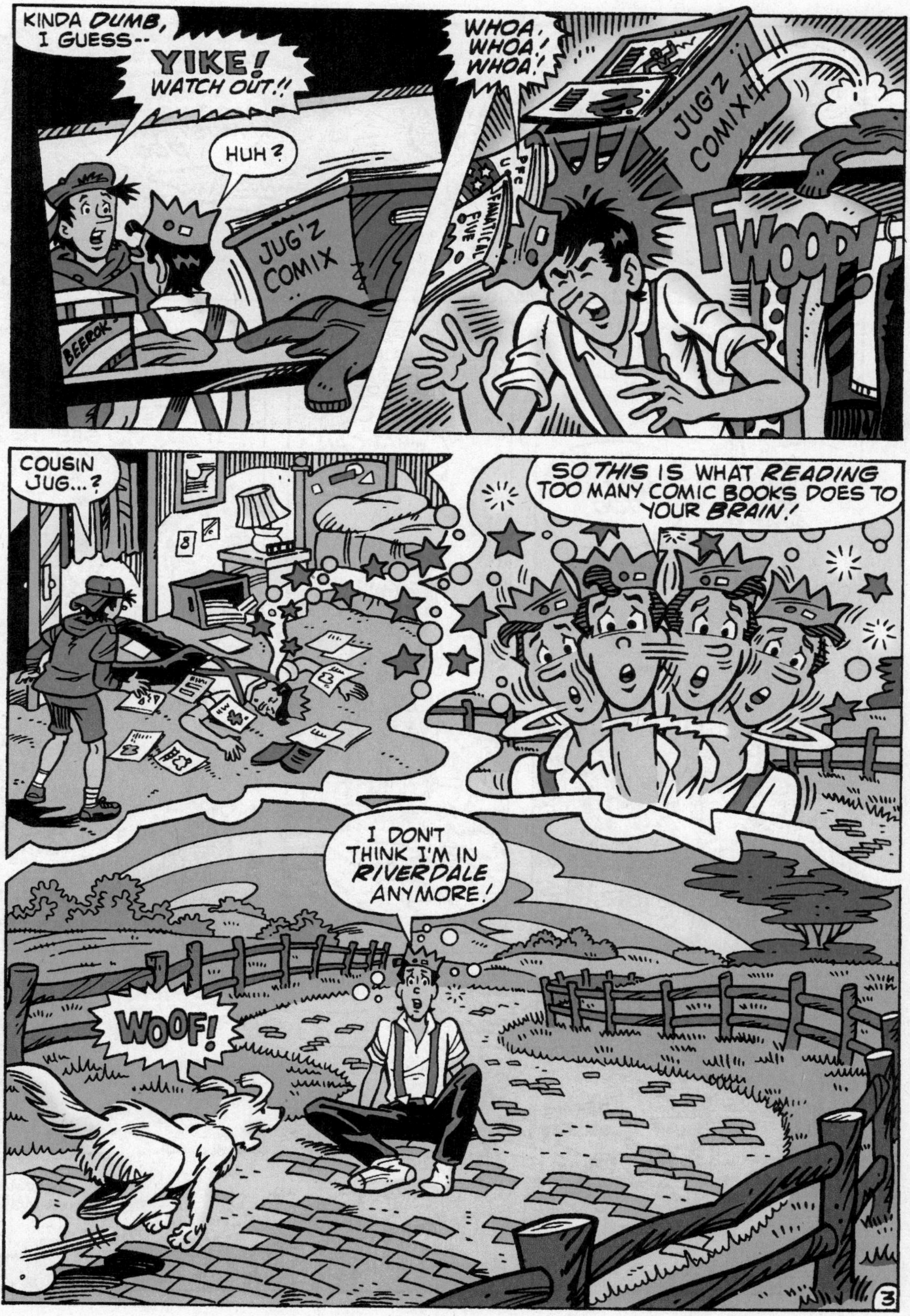
KINDA DUMB, I GUESS--
YIKE! WATCH OUT!!
HUH?
JUG'Z COMIX
BEEROK
WHOA, WHOA! WHOA!
JUG'Z COMIX!!
FANTASTICAL FIVE
FWOOP!
COUSIN JUG...?
SO THIS IS WHAT READING TOO MANY COMIC BOOKS DOES TO YOUR BRAIN!
I DON'T THINK I'M IN RIVERDALE ANYMORE!
WOOF!
3

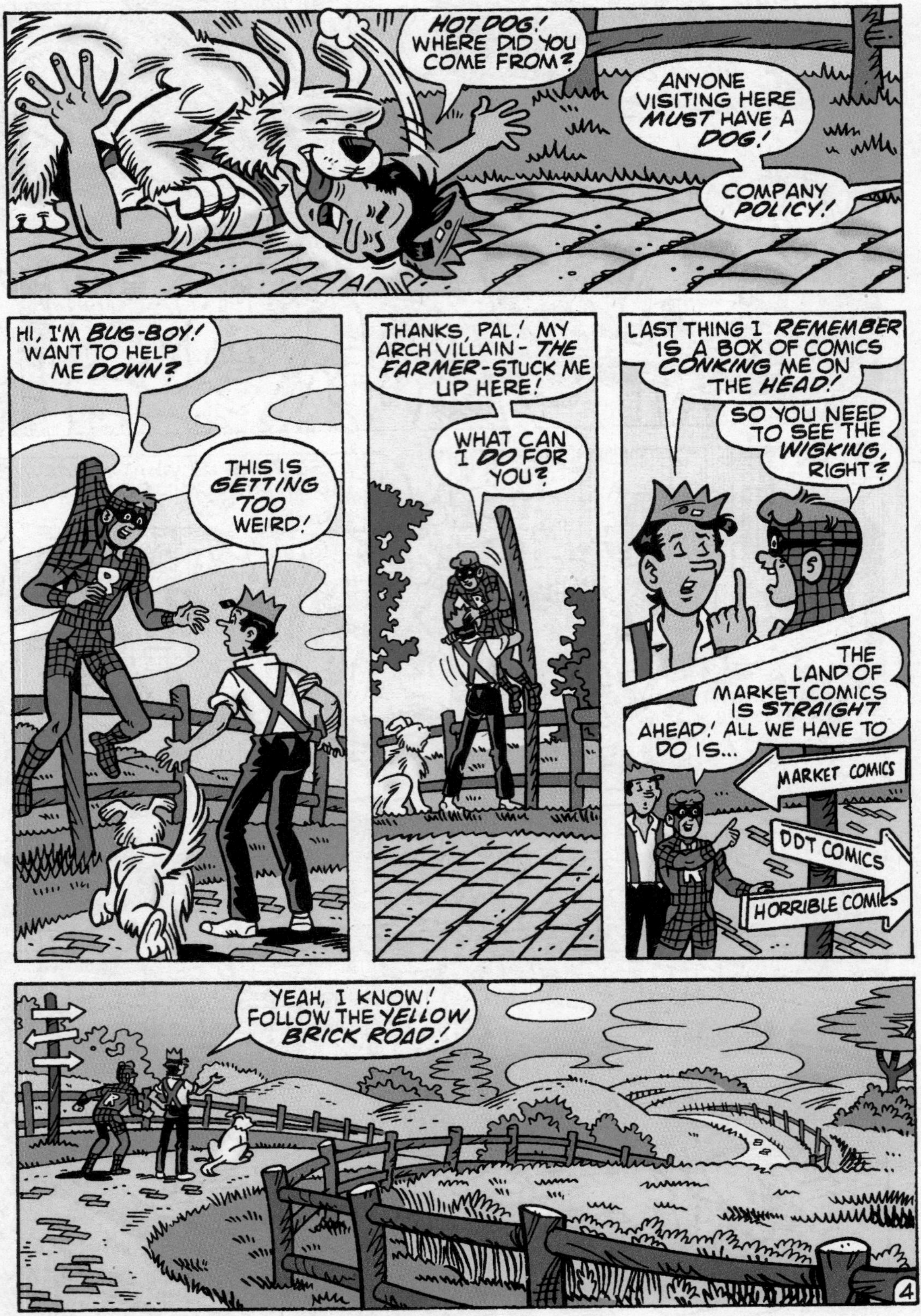
HOT DOG! WHERE DID YOU COME FROM?
ANYONE VISITING HERE MUST HAVE A DOG!
COMPANY POLICY!
AAAAA
HI, I'M BUG-BOY! WANT TO HELP ME DOWN?
THIS IS GETTING TOO WEIRD!
THANKS, PAL! MY ARCH VILLAIN - THE FARMER - STUCK ME UP HERE!
WHAT CAN I DO FOR YOU?
LAST THING I REMEMBER IS A BOX OF COMICS CONKING ME ON THE HEAD!
SO YOU NEED TO SEE THE WIGKING, RIGHT?
THE LAND OF MARKET COMICS IS STRAIGHT AHEAD! ALL WE HAVE TO DO IS...
MARKET COMICS
DDT COMICS
HORRIBLE COMICS
YEAH, I KNOW! FOLLOW THE YELLOW BRICK ROAD!
4

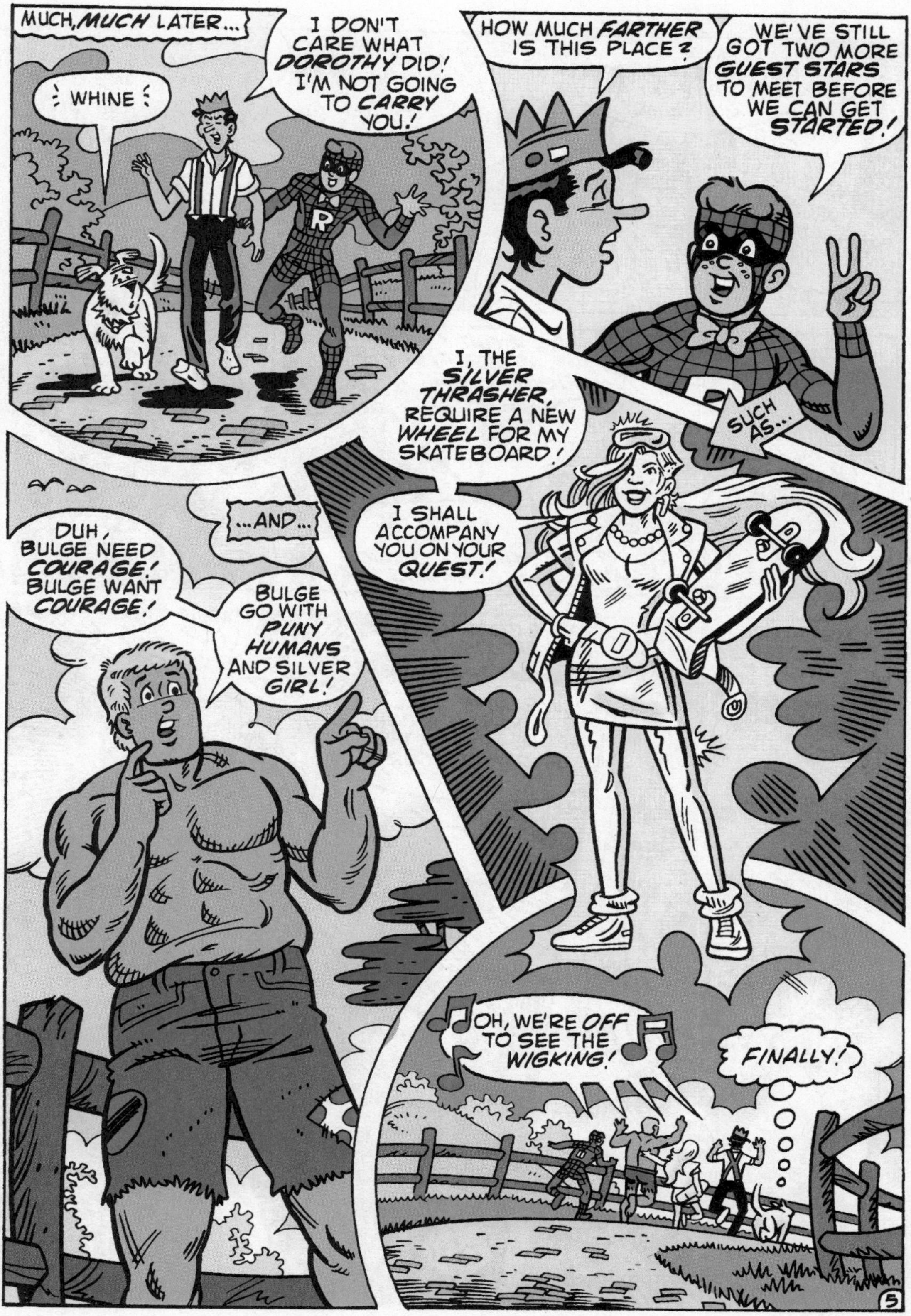
MUCH, MUCH LATER...
I DON'T CARE WHAT DOROTHY DID! I'M NOT GOING TO CARRY YOU!
WHINE
HOW MUCH FARTHER IS THIS PLACE?
WE'VE STILL GOT TWO MORE GUEST STARS TO MEET BEFORE WE CAN GET STARTED!
SUCH AS...
I, THE SILVER THRASHER, REQUIRE A NEW WHEEL FOR MY SKATEBOARD!
I SHALL ACCOMPANY YOU ON YOUR QUEST!
...AND...
DUH, BULGE NEED COURAGE! BULGE WANT COURAGE!
BULGE GO WITH PUNY HUMANS AND SILVER GIRL!
OH, WE'RE OFF TO SEE THE WIGKING!
FINALLY!
5

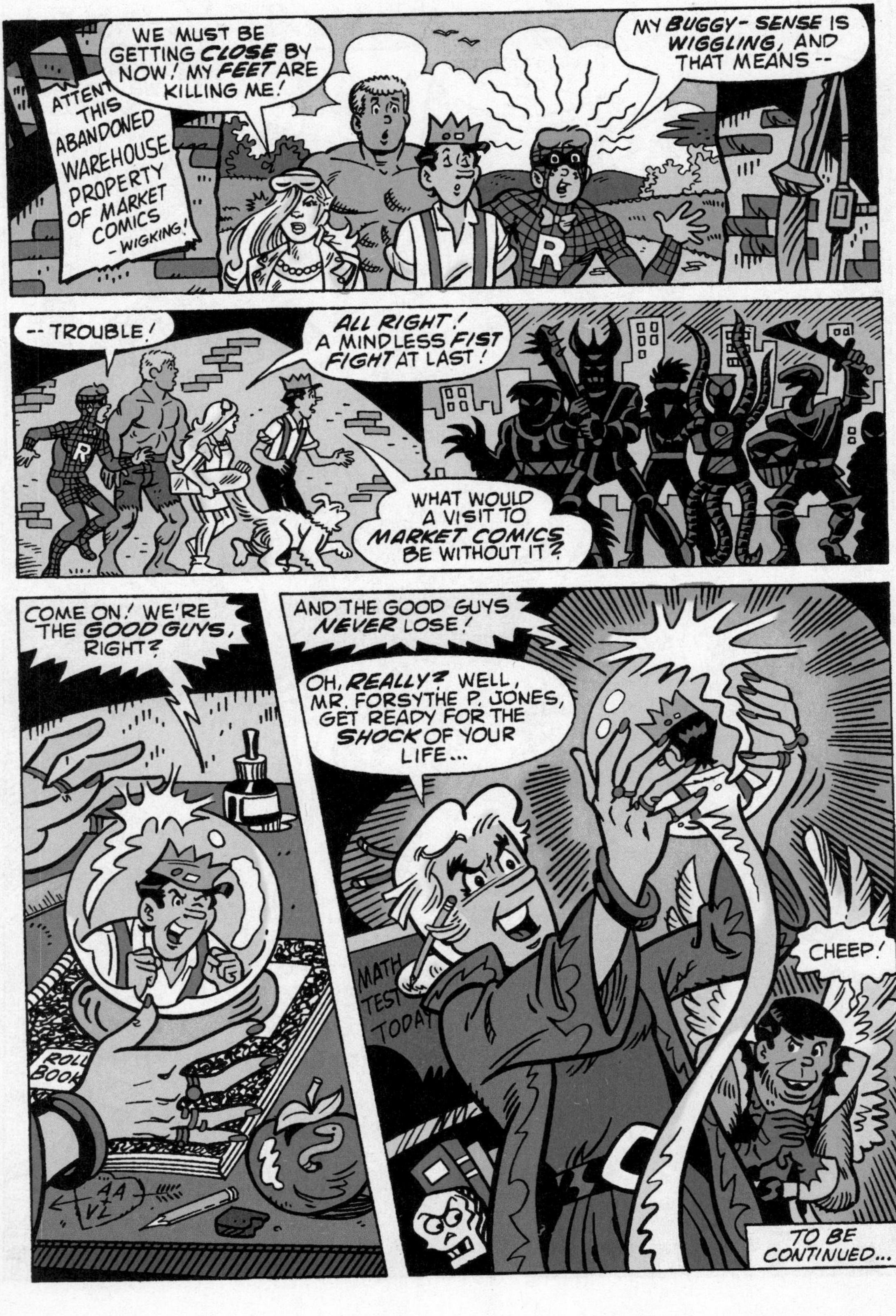
ATTENT
THIS
ABANDONED
WAREHOUSE
PROPERTY
OF MARKET
COMICS
-WIGKING!
WE MUST BE GETTING CLOSE BY NOW! MY FEET ARE KILLING ME!
MY BUGGY-SENSE IS WIGGLING, AND THAT MEANS --
-- TROUBLE!
ALL RIGHT! A MINDLESS FIST FIGHT AT LAST!
WHAT WOULD A VISIT TO MARKET COMICS BE WITHOUT IT?
COME ON! WE'RE THE GOOD GUYS, RIGHT?
ROLL BOOK
AND THE GOOD GUYS NEVER LOSE!
OH, REALLY? WELL, MR. FORSYTHE P. JONES, GET READY FOR THE SHOCK OF YOUR LIFE...
MATH TEST TODAY
CHEEP!
TO BE CONTINUED...

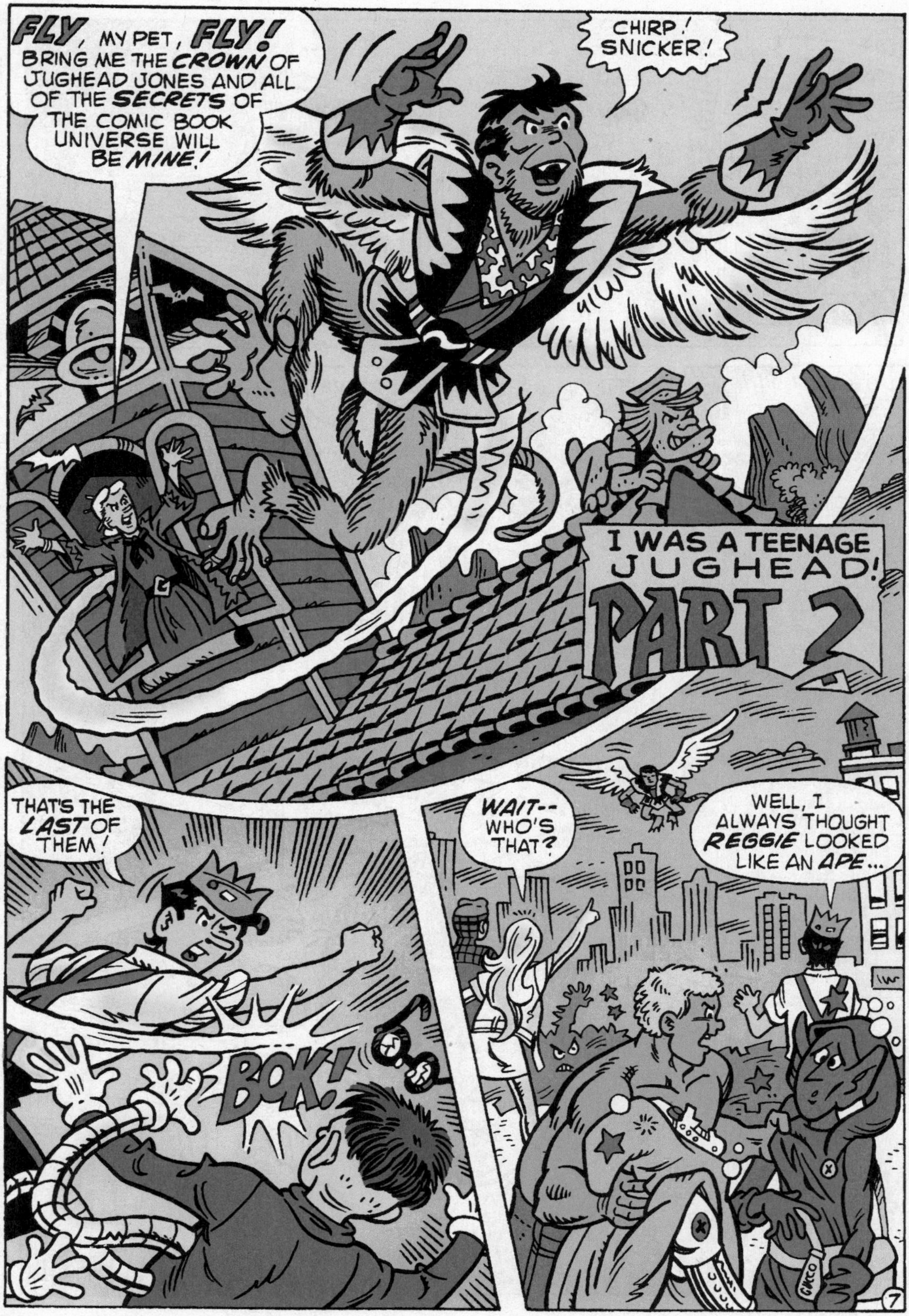
FLY, MY PET, FLY! BRING ME THE CROWN OF JUGHEAD JONES AND ALL OF THE SECRETS OF THE COMIC BOOK UNIVERSE WILL BE MINE!
CHIRP! SNICKER!
I WAS A TEENAGE JUGHEAD!
PART 2
THAT'S THE LAST OF THEM!
BOK!
WAIT-- WHO'S THAT?
WELL, I ALWAYS THOUGHT REGGIE LOOKED LIKE AN APE...
7

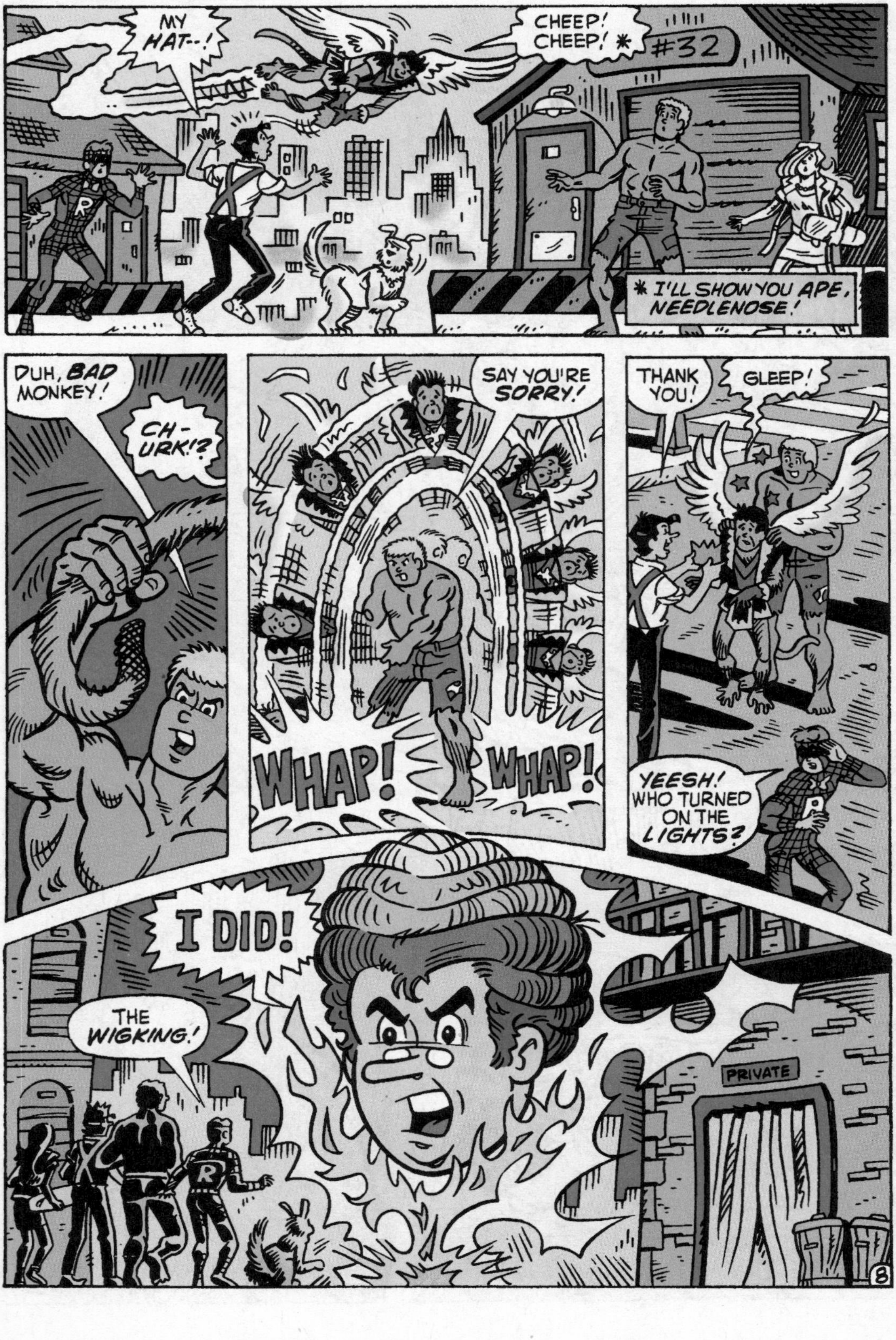

MY HAT--!
CHEEP! CHEEP! *
#32
* I'LL SHOW YOU APE, NEEDLENOSE!
DUH, BAD MONKEY!
CH-URK!?
SAY YOU'RE SORRY!
WHAP! WHAP!
THANK YOU!
GLEEP!
YEESH! WHO TURNED ON THE LIGHTS?
I DID!
THE WIGKING!
PRIVATE
8

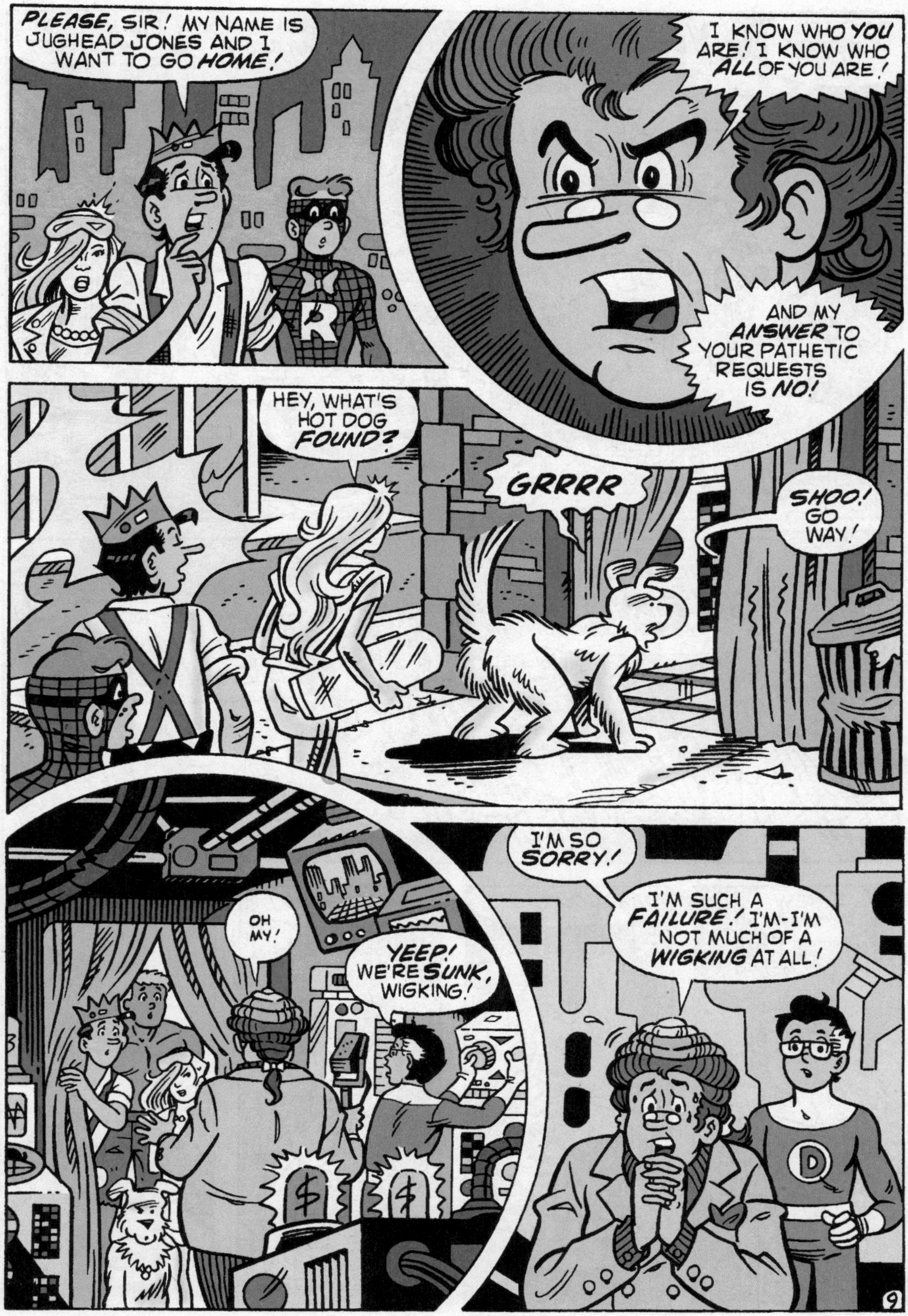
PLEASE, SIR! MY NAME IS JUGHEAD JONES AND I WANT TO GO HOME!
I KNOW WHO YOU ARE! I KNOW WHO ALL OF YOU ARE!
AND MY ANSWER TO YOUR PATHETIC REQUESTS IS NO!
HEY, WHAT'S HOT DOG FOUND?
GRRRR
SHOO! GO WAY!
OH MY!
YEEP! WE'RE SUNK, WIGKING!
I'M SO SORRY!
I'M SUCH A FAILURE! I'M-I'M NOT MUCH OF A WIGKING AT ALL!
9

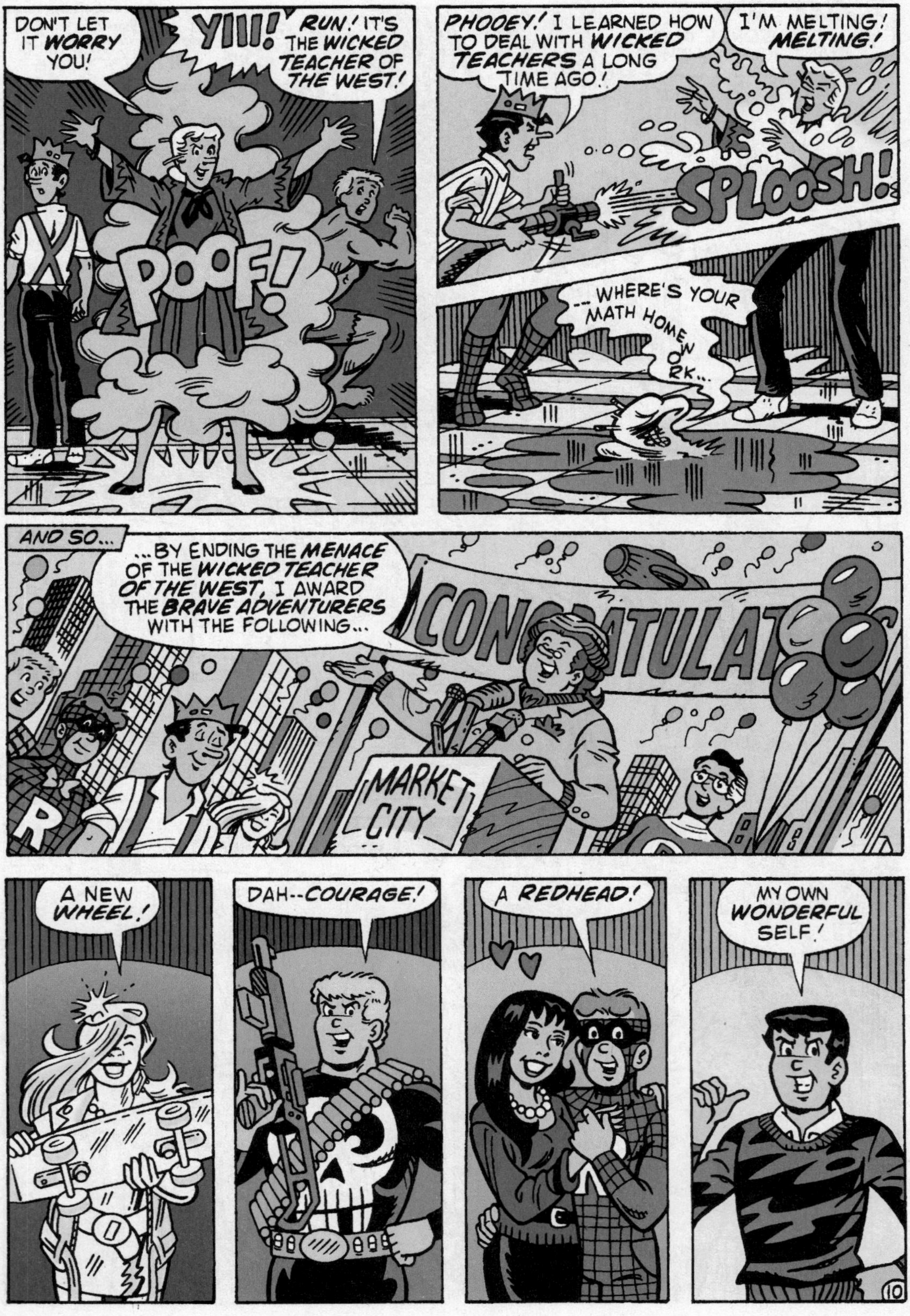
DON'T LET IT WORRY YOU!
YIII!
RUN! IT'S THE WICKED TEACHER OF THE WEST!
POOF!
PHOOEY! I LEARNED HOW TO DEAL WITH WICKED TEACHERS A LONG TIME AGO!
I'M MELTING! MELTING!
SPLOOSH!
... WHERE'S YOUR MATH HOMEWORK...
AND SO...
...BY ENDING THE MENACE OF THE WICKED TEACHER OF THE WEST, I AWARD THE BRAVE ADVENTURERS WITH THE FOLLOWING...
CONGRATULAT
MARKET CITY
A NEW WHEEL!
DAH--COURAGE!
A REDHEAD!
MY OWN WONDERFUL SELF!
10

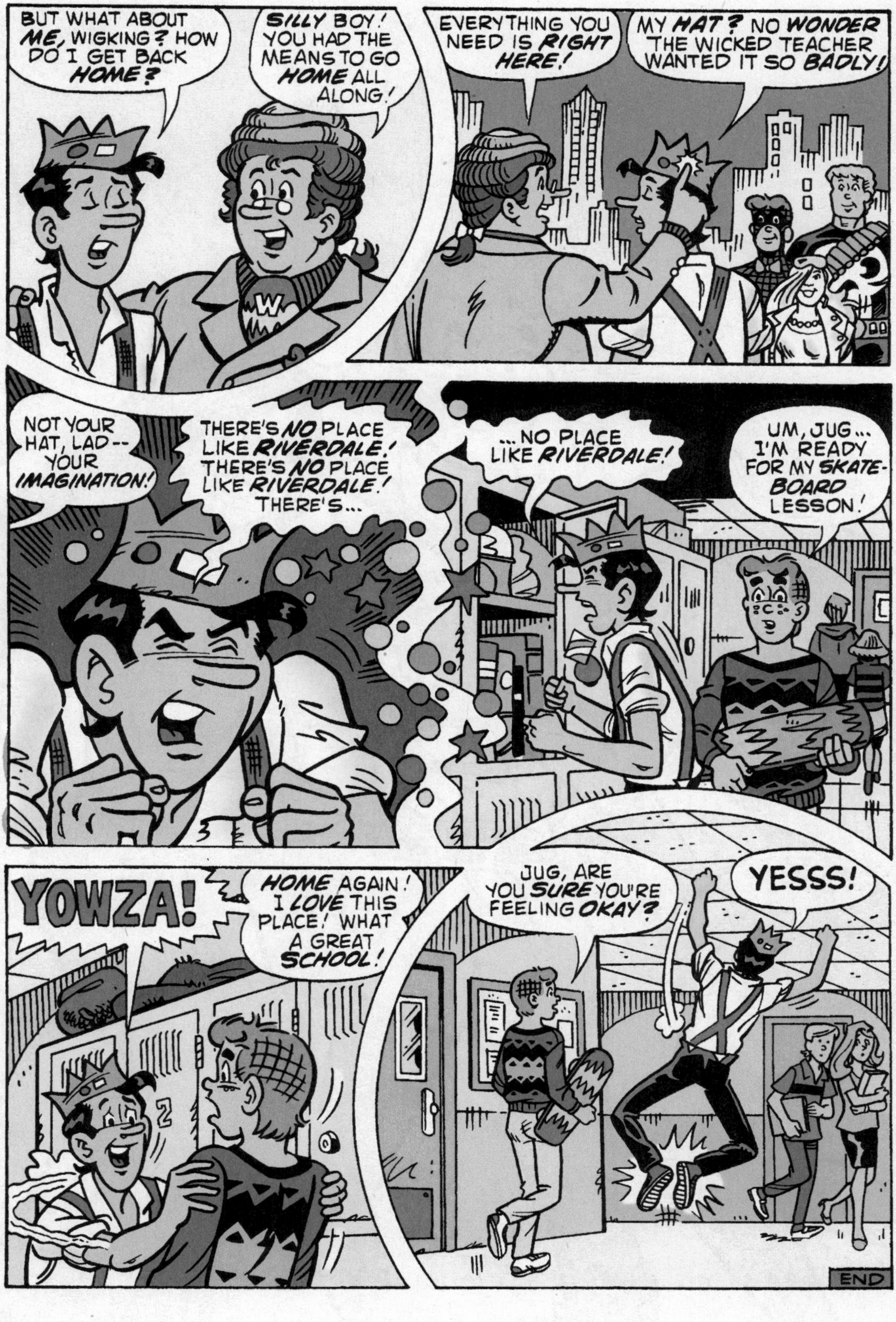
BUT WHAT ABOUT ME, WIGKING? HOW DO I GET BACK HOME?
SILLY BOY! YOU HAD THE MEANS TO GO HOME ALL ALONG!
EVERYTHING YOU NEED IS RIGHT HERE!
MY HAT? NO WONDER THE WICKED TEACHER WANTED IT SO BADLY!
NOT YOUR HAT, LAD-- YOUR IMAGINATION!
THERE'S NO PLACE LIKE RIVERDALE! THERE'S NO PLACE LIKE RIVERDALE! THERE'S...
...NO PLACE LIKE RIVERDALE!
UM, JUG... I'M READY FOR MY SKATE-BOARD LESSON!
YOWZA!
HOME AGAIN! I LOVE THIS PLACE! WHAT A GREAT SCHOOL!
JUG, ARE YOU SURE YOU'RE FEELING OKAY?
YESSS!
END

CHAPTER THREE

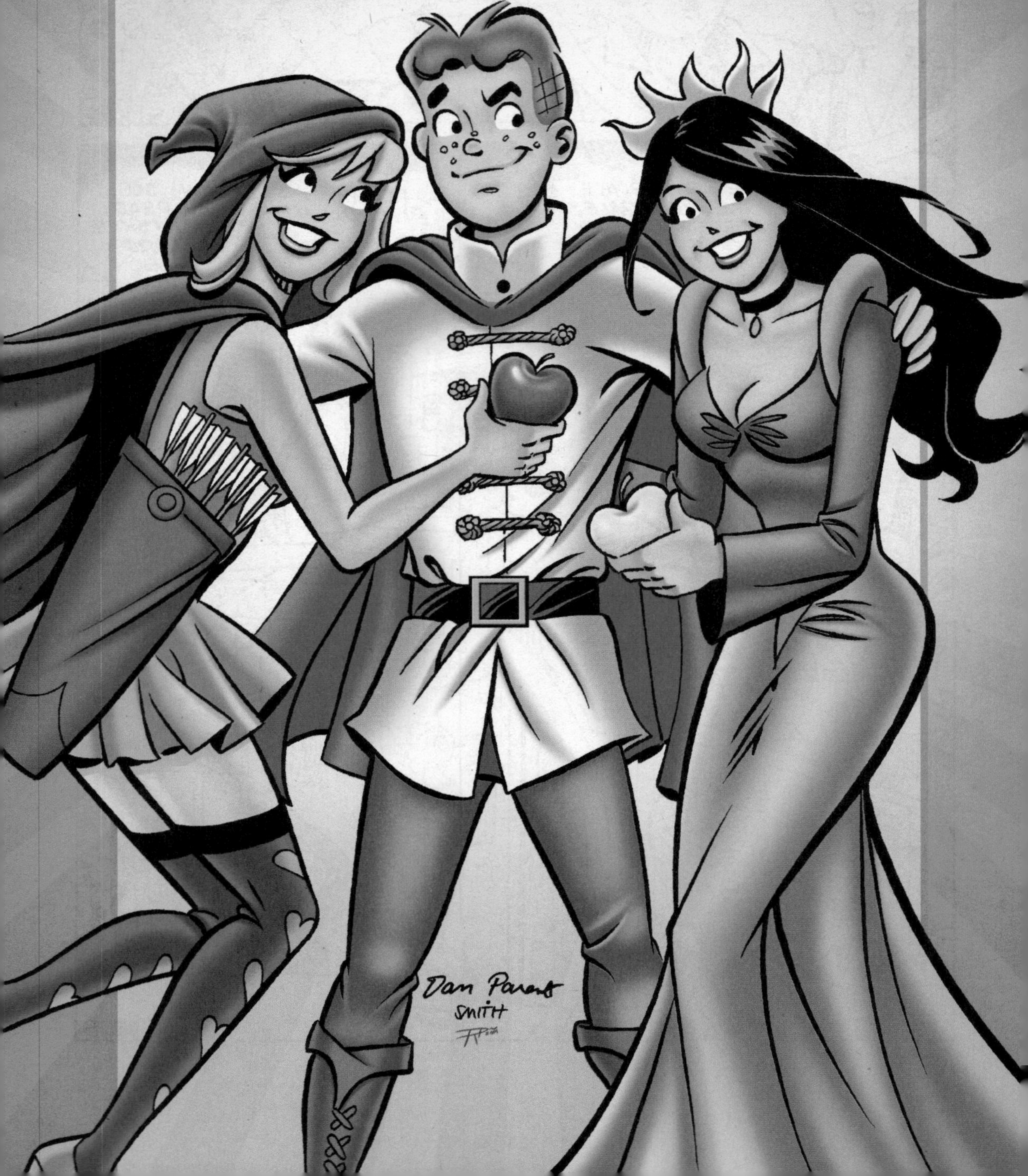
Dan Parent
SMITH

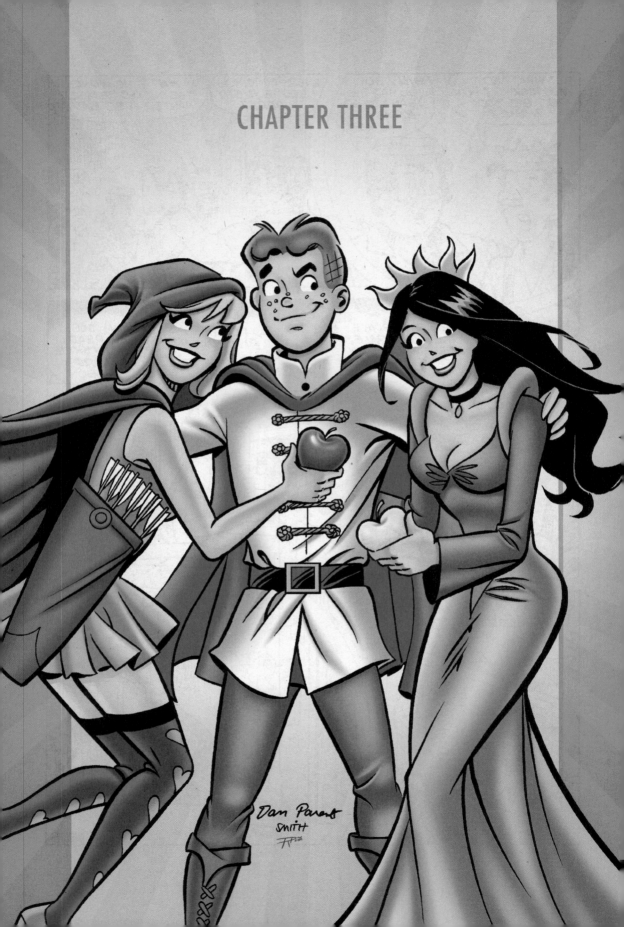

BETTY AND VERONICA IN
PRINCE FROG
AUGUST 2000

SCRIPT: KATHLEEN WEBB   PENCILS: DAN DECARLO   INKS: HENRY SCARPELLI
LETTERS: BILL YOSHIDA   COLORS: BARRY GROSSMAN

BETTY & VERONICA IN
ROBIN HOOD WINKED
JULY 2002

SCRIPT: MIKE PELLOWSKI   PENCILS: JEFF SHULTZ   INKS: HENRY SCARPELLI
LETTERS: BILL YOSHIDA   COLORS: BARRY GROSSMAN

BETTY & VERONICA IN
SLEEPING BETTY
NOVEMBER 2007

SCRIPT & PENCILS: DAN PARENT   INKS: JIM AMASH
LETTERS: JANICE CHIANG   COLORS: BARRY GROSSMAN

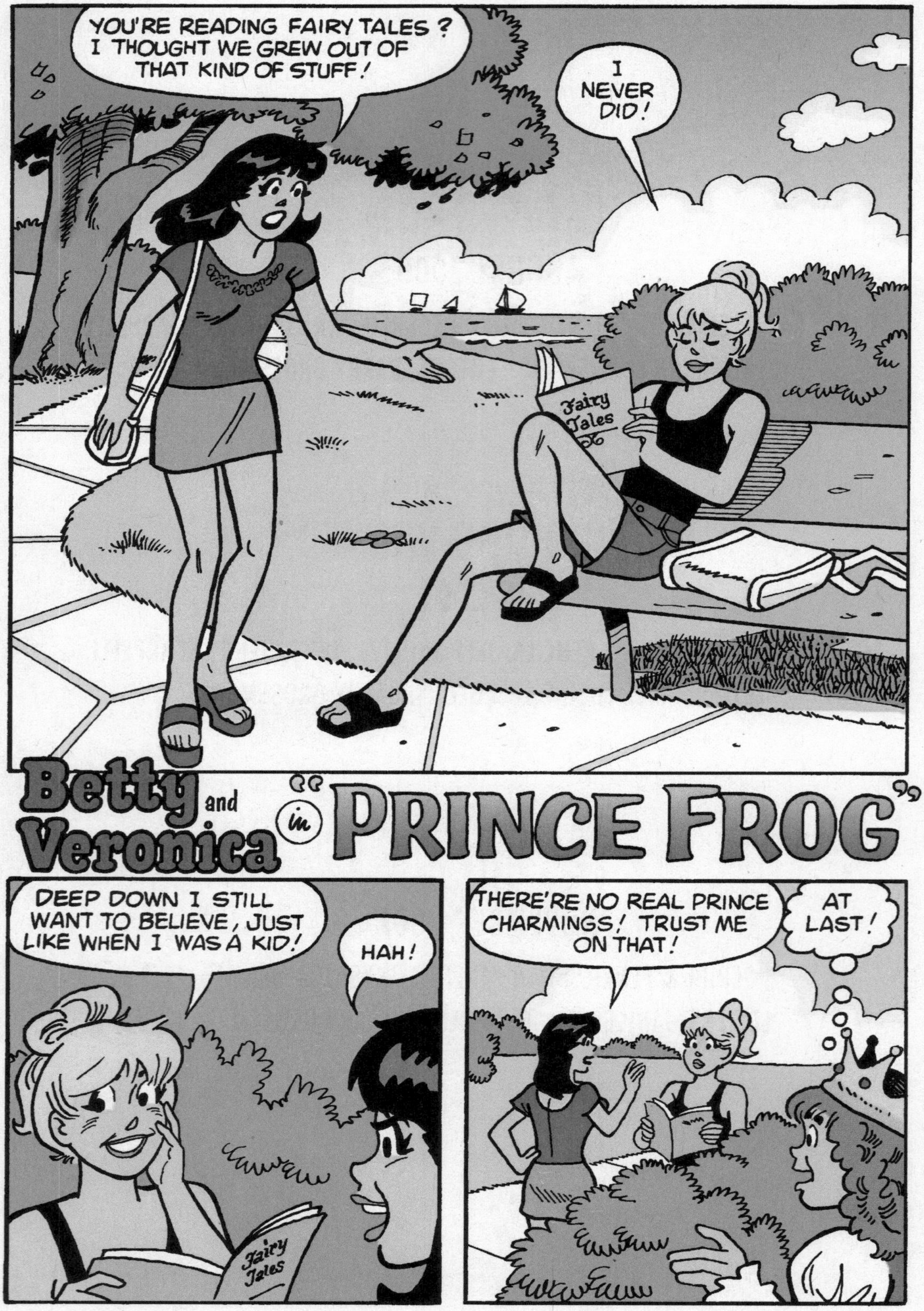
YOU'RE READING FAIRY TALES? I THOUGHT WE GREW OUT OF THAT KIND OF STUFF!
I NEVER DID!
Fairy Tales
Betty and Veronica in "PRINCE FROG"
DEEP DOWN I STILL WANT TO BELIEVE, JUST LIKE WHEN I WAS A KID!
HAH!
Fairy Tales
THERE'RE NO REAL PRINCE CHARMINGS! TRUST ME ON THAT!
AT LAST!

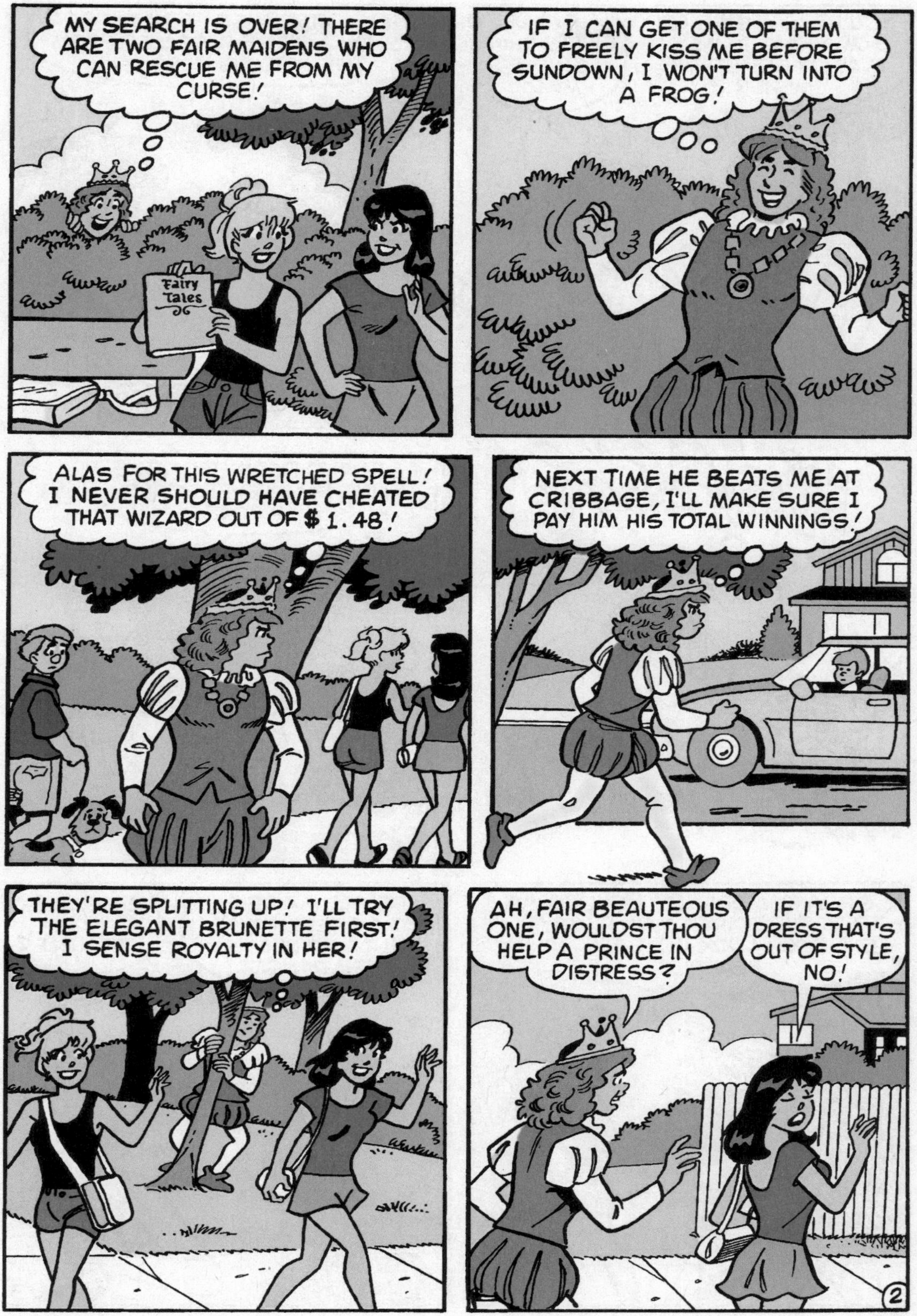
MY SEARCH IS OVER! THERE ARE TWO FAIR MAIDENS WHO CAN RESCUE ME FROM MY CURSE!
Fairy Tales
IF I CAN GET ONE OF THEM TO FREELY KISS ME BEFORE SUNDOWN, I WON'T TURN INTO A FROG!
ALAS FOR THIS WRETCHED SPELL! I NEVER SHOULD HAVE CHEATED THAT WIZARD OUT OF $ 1.48!
NEXT TIME HE BEATS ME AT CRIBBAGE, I'LL MAKE SURE I PAY HIM HIS TOTAL WINNINGS!
THEY'RE SPLITTING UP! I'LL TRY THE ELEGANT BRUNETTE FIRST! I SENSE ROYALTY IN HER!
AH, FAIR BEAUTEOUS ONE, WOULDST THOU HELP A PRINCE IN DISTRESS?
IF IT'S A DRESS THAT'S OUT OF STYLE, NO!
2

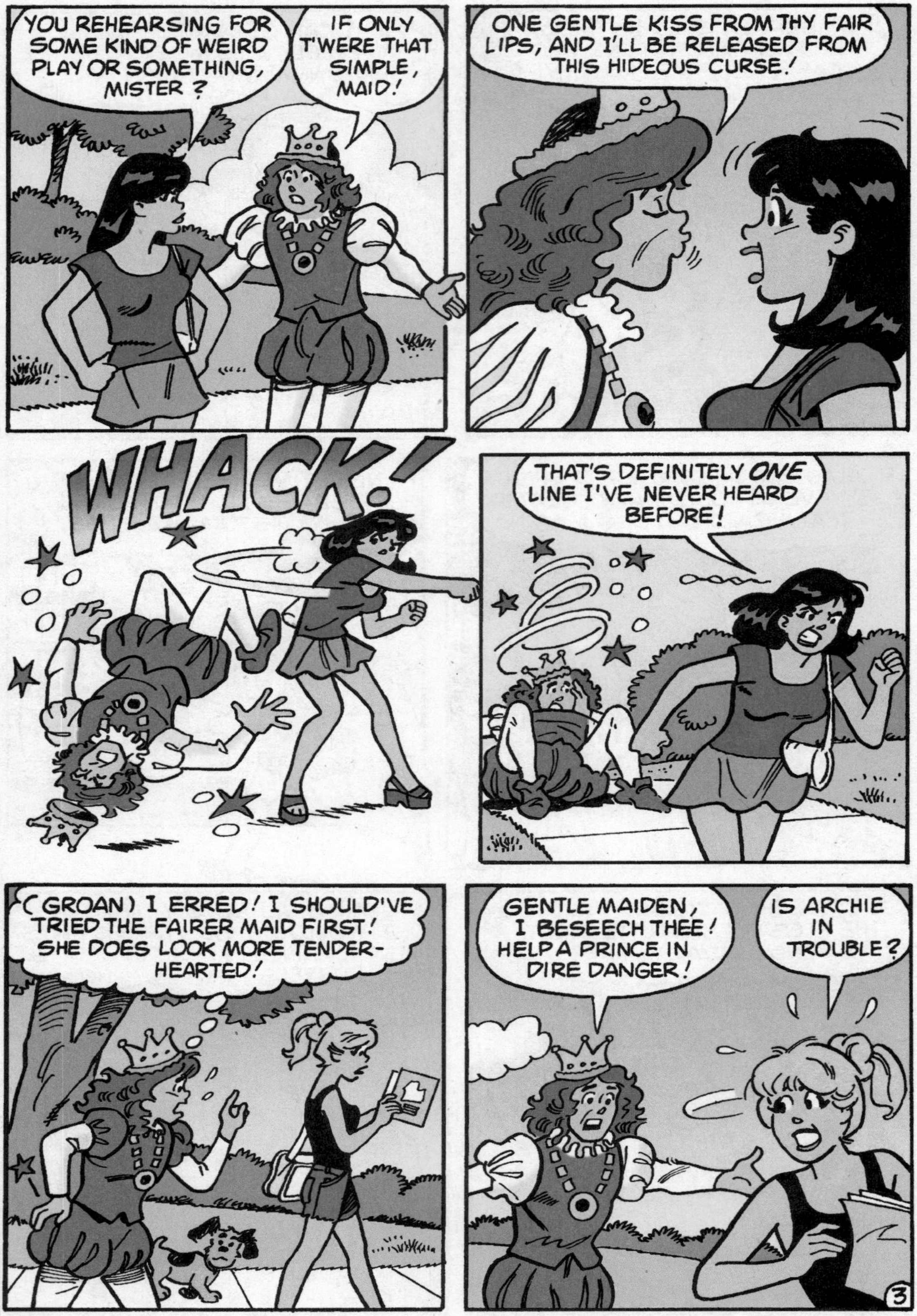
YOU REHEARSING FOR SOME KIND OF WEIRD PLAY OR SOMETHING, MISTER ?
IF ONLY T'WERE THAT SIMPLE, MAID!
ONE GENTLE KISS FROM THY FAIR LIPS, AND I'LL BE RELEASED FROM THIS HIDEOUS CURSE!
WHACK!
THAT'S DEFINITELY ONE LINE I'VE NEVER HEARD BEFORE!
(GROAN) I ERRED! I SHOULD'VE TRIED THE FAIRER MAID FIRST! SHE DOES LOOK MORE TENDER-HEARTED!
GENTLE MAIDEN, I BESEECH THEE! HELP A PRINCE IN DIRE DANGER!
IS ARCHIE IN TROUBLE?
3

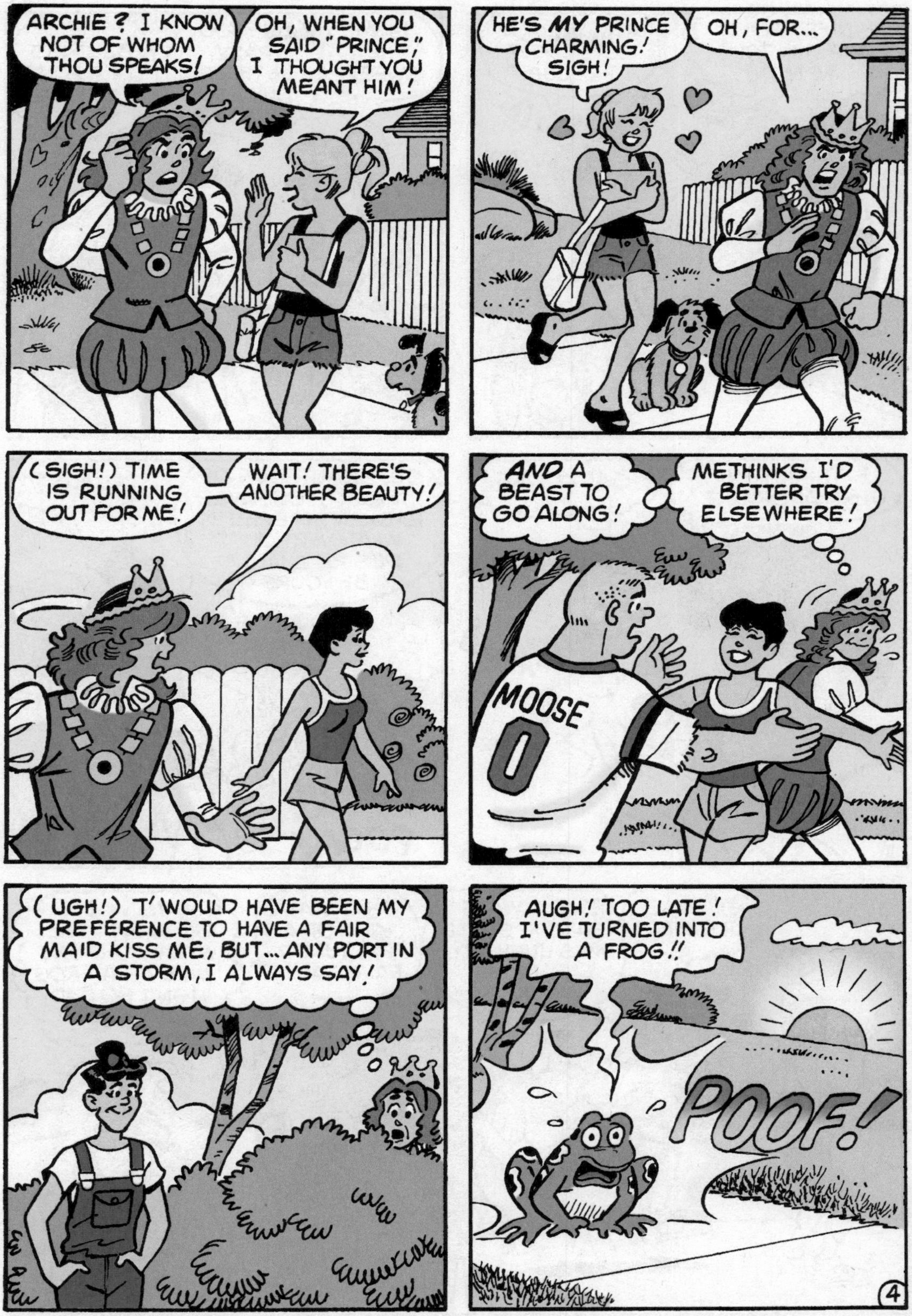
ARCHIE ? I KNOW NOT OF WHOM THOU SPEAKS!
OH, WHEN YOU SAID "PRINCE," I THOUGHT YOU MEANT HIM!
HE'S *MY* PRINCE CHARMING! SIGH!
OH, FOR...
(SIGH!) TIME IS RUNNING OUT FOR ME!
WAIT! THERE'S ANOTHER BEAUTY!
AND A BEAST TO GO ALONG!
METHINKS I'D BETTER TRY ELSEWHERE!
MOOSE
0
(UGH!) T' WOULD HAVE BEEN MY PREFERENCE TO HAVE A FAIR MAID KISS ME, BUT... ANY PORT IN A STORM, I ALWAYS SAY!
AUGH! TOO LATE! I'VE TURNED INTO A FROG!!
POOF!
4

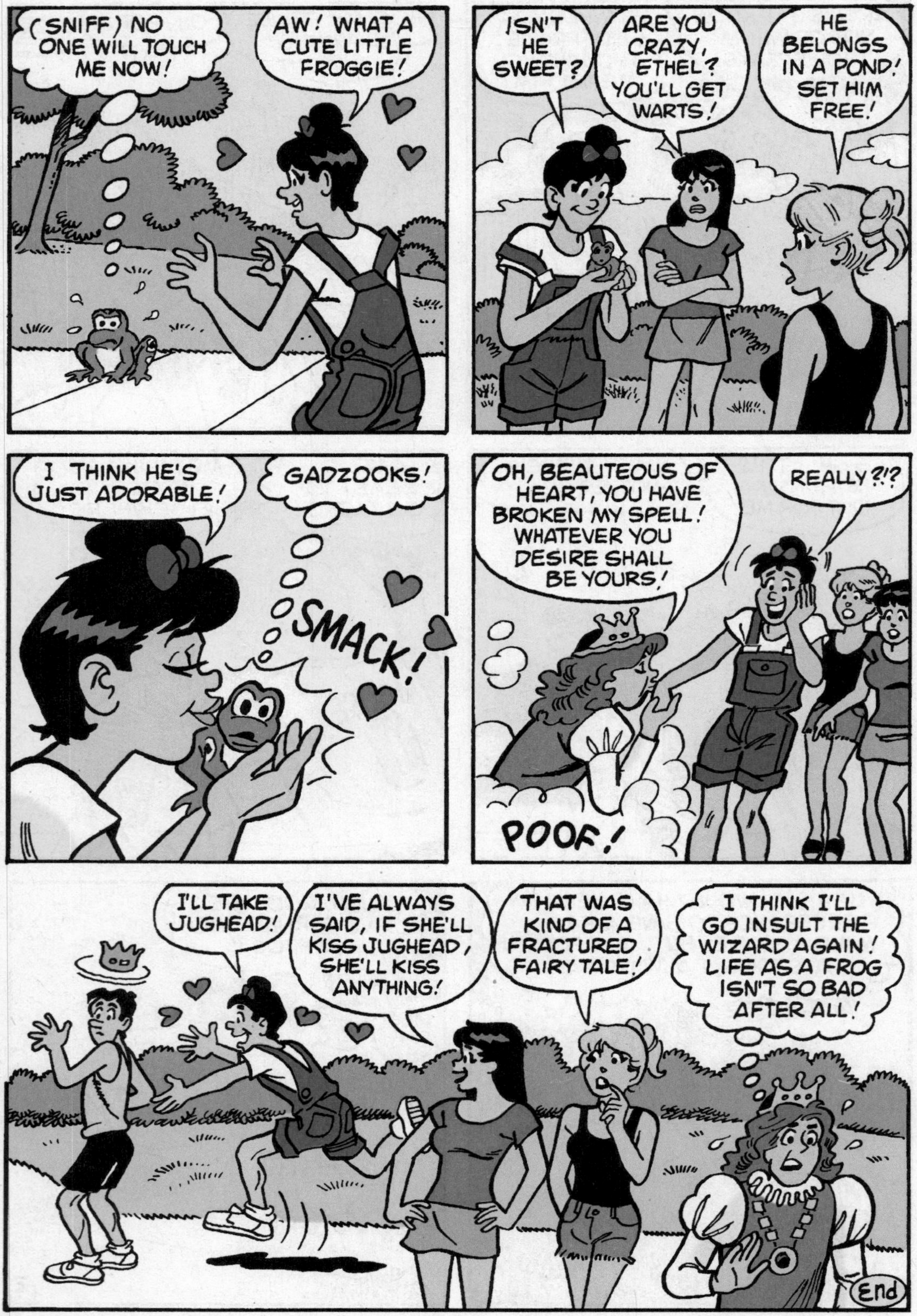
(SNIFF) NO ONE WILL TOUCH ME NOW!
AW! WHAT A CUTE LITTLE FROGGIE!
ISN'T HE SWEET?
ARE YOU CRAZY, ETHEL? YOU'LL GET WARTS!
HE BELONGS IN A POND! SET HIM FREE!
I THINK HE'S JUST ADORABLE!
GADZOOKS!
SMACK!
OH, BEAUTEOUS OF HEART, YOU HAVE BROKEN MY SPELL! WHATEVER YOU DESIRE SHALL BE YOURS!
REALLY?!?
POOF!
I'LL TAKE JUGHEAD!
I'VE ALWAYS SAID, IF SHE'LL KISS JUGHEAD, SHE'LL KISS ANYTHING!
THAT WAS KIND OF A FRACTURED FAIRY TALE!
I THINK I'LL GO INSULT THE WIZARD AGAIN! LIFE AS A FROG ISN'T SO BAD AFTER ALL!
End

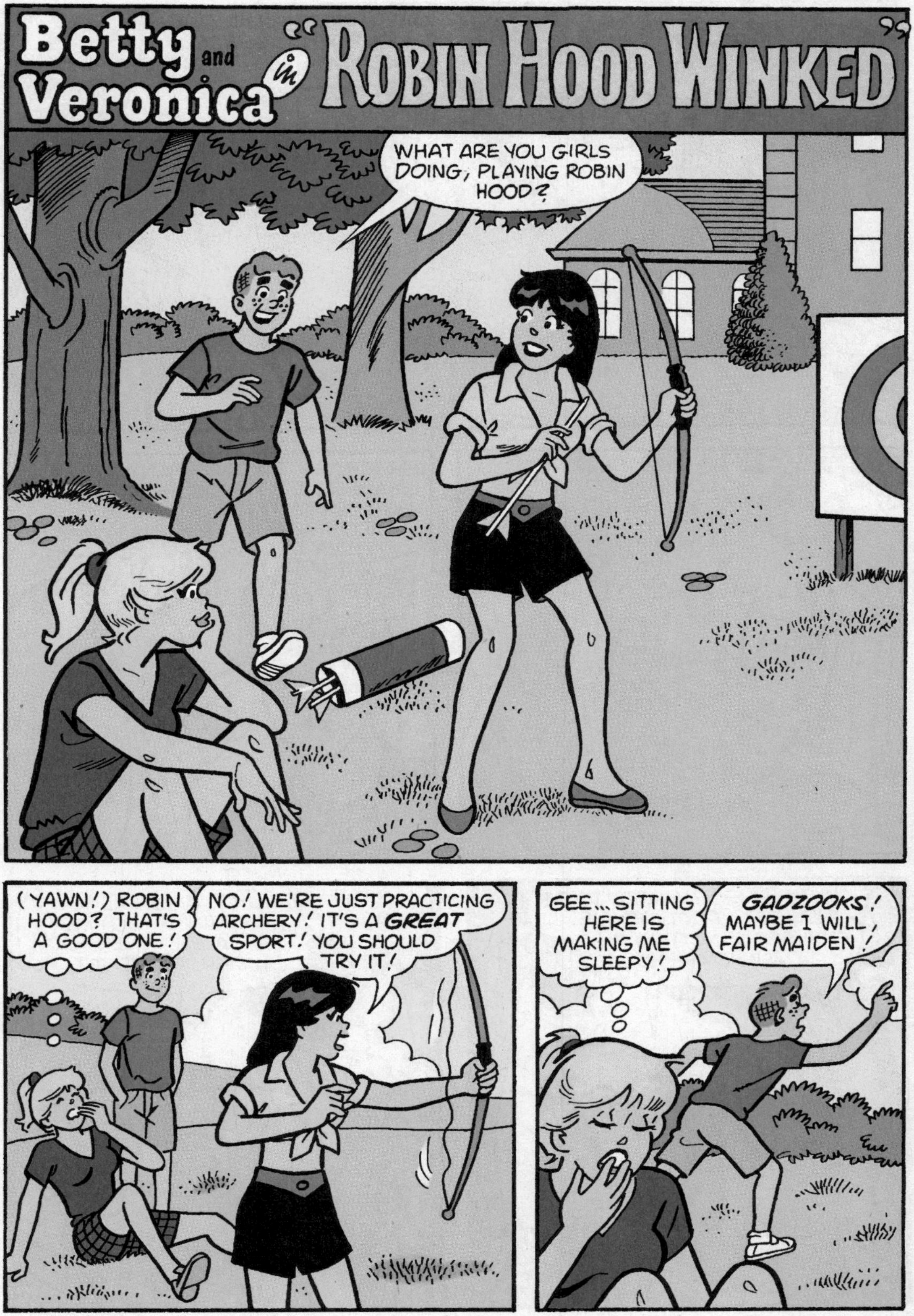
Betty and Veronica in "ROBIN HOOD WINKED"
WHAT ARE YOU GIRLS DOING, PLAYING ROBIN HOOD?
(YAWN!) ROBIN HOOD? THAT'S A GOOD ONE!
NO! WE'RE JUST PRACTICING ARCHERY! IT'S A GREAT SPORT! YOU SHOULD TRY IT!
GEE... SITTING HERE IS MAKING ME SLEEPY!
GADZOOKS! MAYBE I WILL, FAIR MAIDEN!

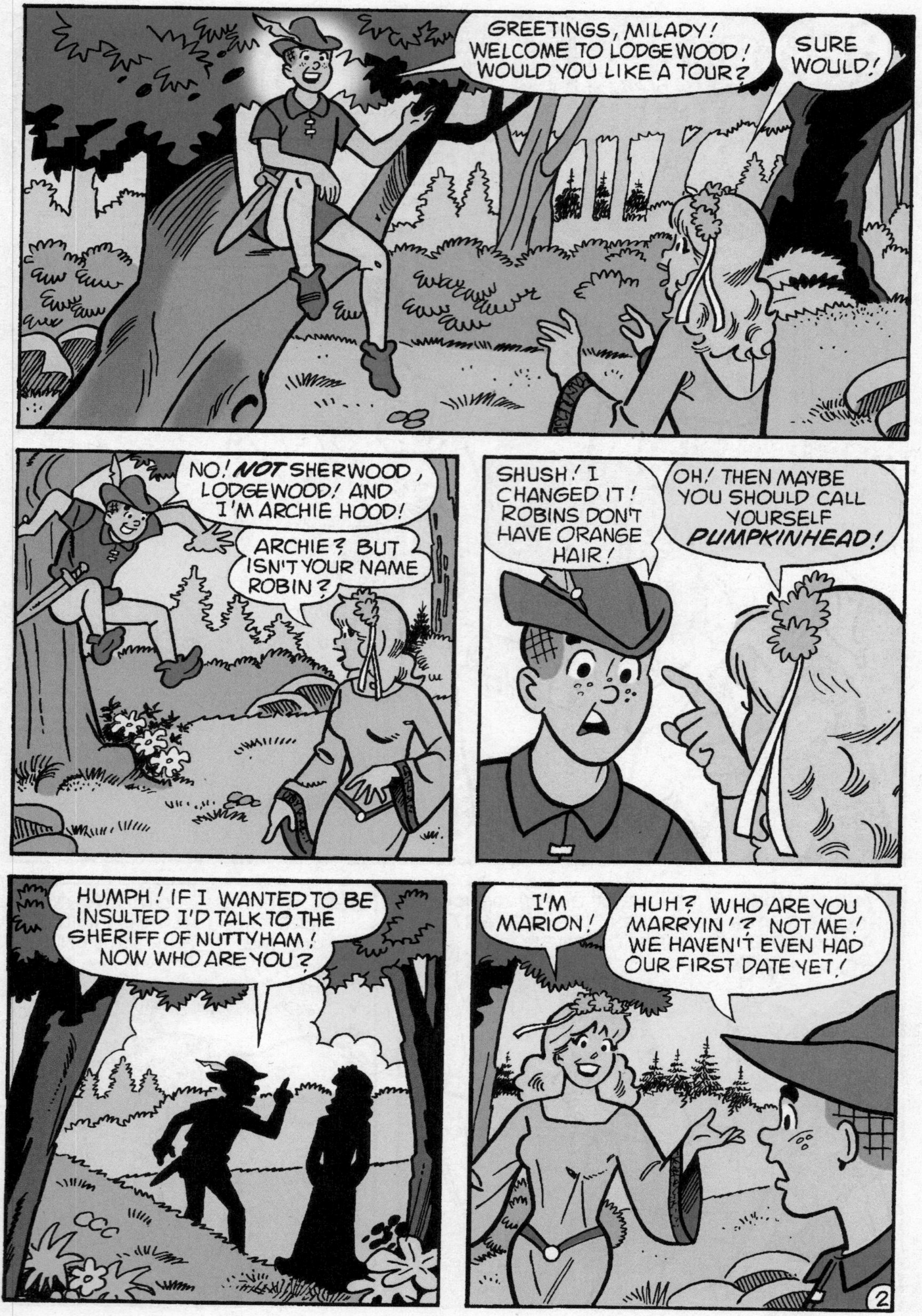
GREETINGS, MILADY! WELCOME TO LODGEWOOD! WOULD YOU LIKE A TOUR?
SURE WOULD!
NO! NOT SHERWOOD, LODGEWOOD! AND I'M ARCHIE HOOD!
ARCHIE? BUT ISN'T YOUR NAME ROBIN?
SHUSH! I CHANGED IT! ROBINS DON'T HAVE ORANGE HAIR!
OH! THEN MAYBE YOU SHOULD CALL YOURSELF PUMPKINHEAD!
HUMPH! IF I WANTED TO BE INSULTED I'D TALK TO THE SHERIFF OF NUTTYHAM! NOW WHO ARE YOU?
I'M MARION!
HUH? WHO ARE YOU MARRYIN'? NOT ME! WE HAVEN'T EVEN HAD OUR FIRST DATE YET!
2

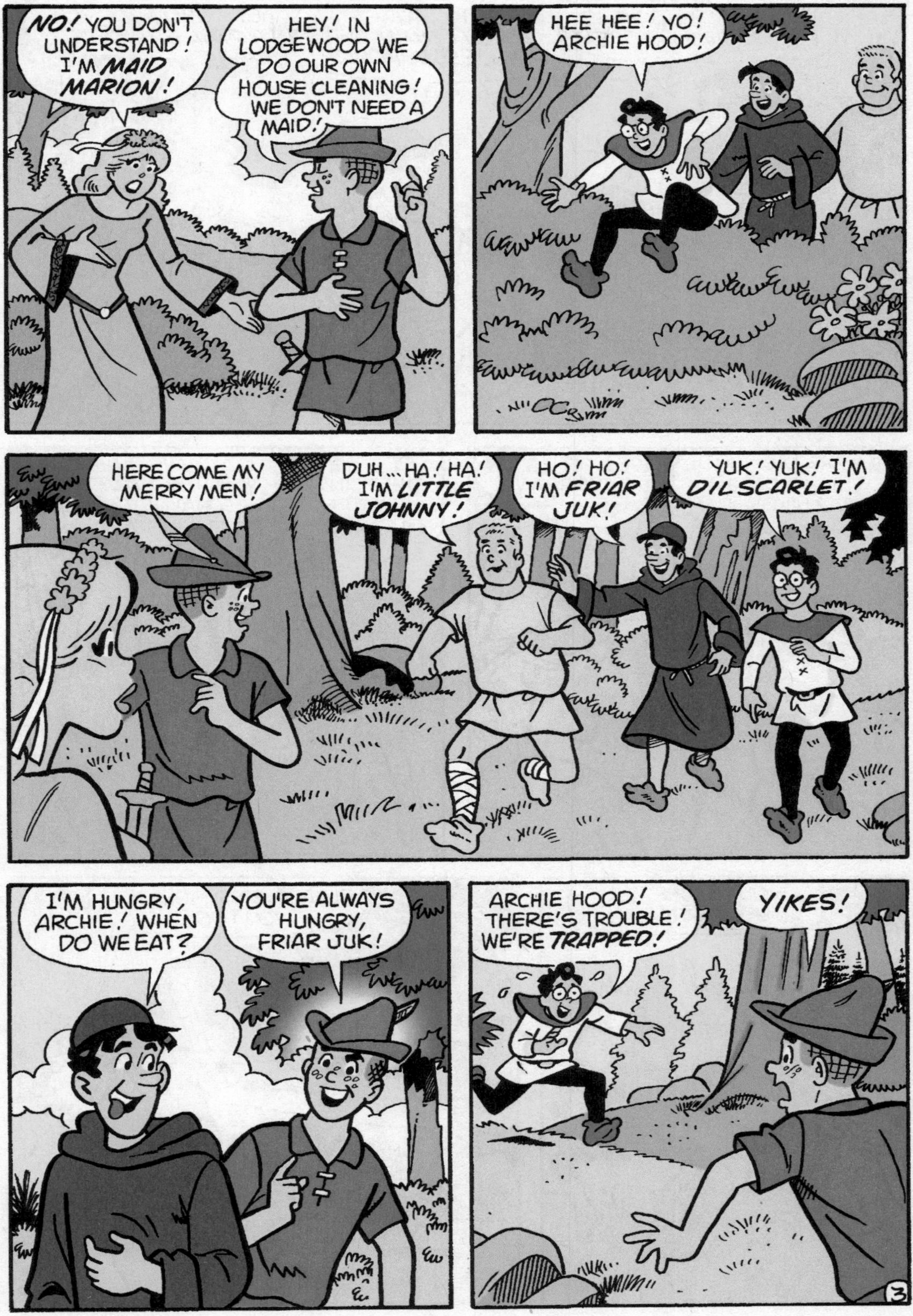
NO! YOU DON'T UNDERSTAND! I'M MAID MARION!
HEY! IN LODGEWOOD WE DO OUR OWN HOUSE CLEANING! WE DON'T NEED A MAID!
HEE HEE! YO! ARCHIE HOOD!
HERE COME MY MERRY MEN!
DUH... HA! HA! I'M LITTLE JOHNNY!
HO! HO! I'M FRIAR JUK!
YUK! YUK! I'M DIL SCARLET!
I'M HUNGRY, ARCHIE! WHEN DO WE EAT?
YOU'RE ALWAYS HUNGRY, FRIAR JUK!
ARCHIE HOOD! THERE'S TROUBLE! WE'RE TRAPPED!
YIKES!
3

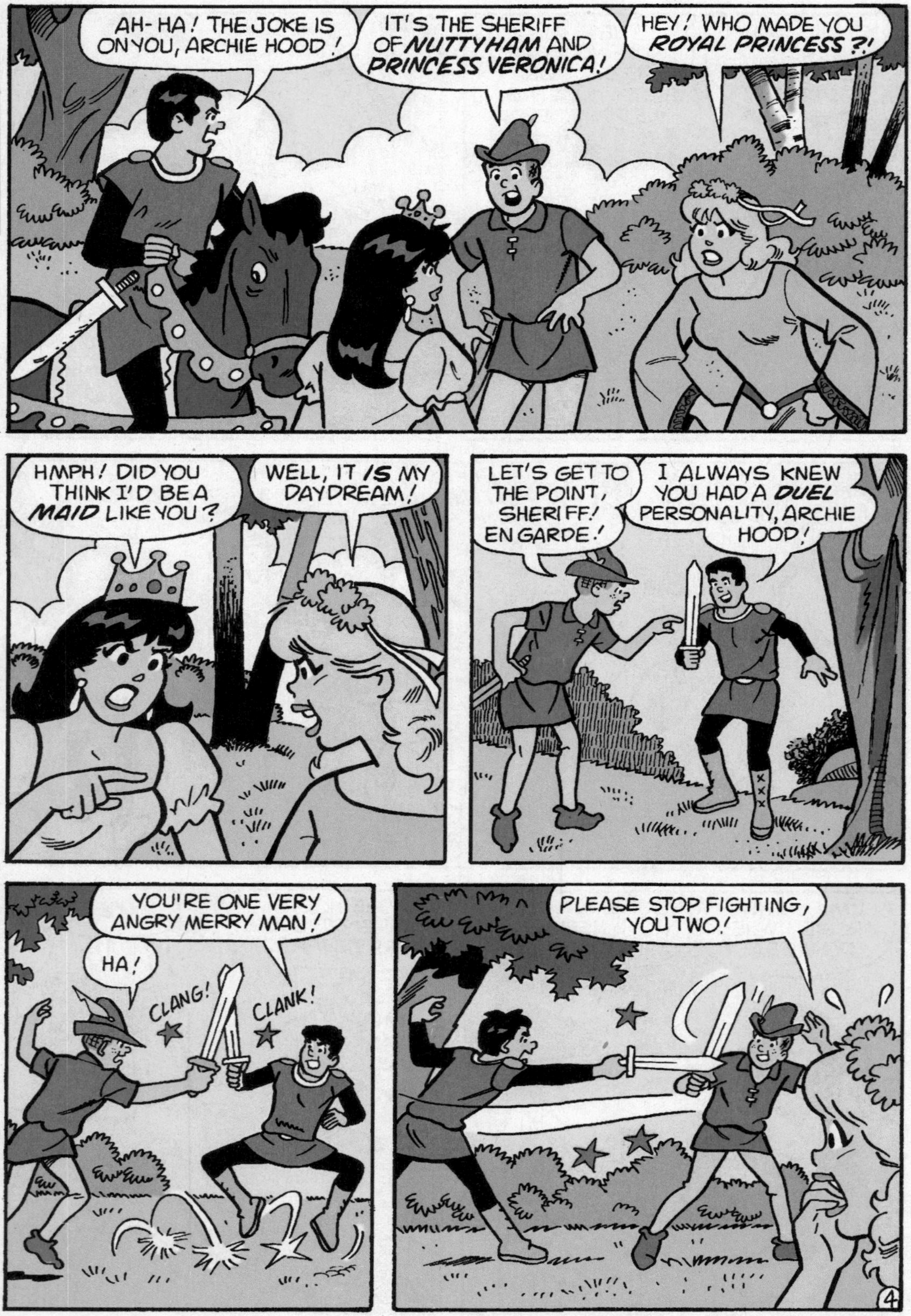
AH-HA! THE JOKE IS ON YOU, ARCHIE HOOD!
IT'S THE SHERIFF OF NUTTYHAM AND PRINCESS VERONICA!
HEY! WHO MADE YOU ROYAL PRINCESS ?!
HMPH! DID YOU THINK I'D BE A MAID LIKE YOU?
WELL, IT IS MY DAYDREAM!
LET'S GET TO THE POINT, SHERIFF! EN GARDE!
I ALWAYS KNEW YOU HAD A DUEL PERSONALITY, ARCHIE HOOD!
YOU'RE ONE VERY ANGRY MERRY MAN!
HA!
CLANG!
CLANK!
PLEASE STOP FIGHTING, YOU TWO!
4

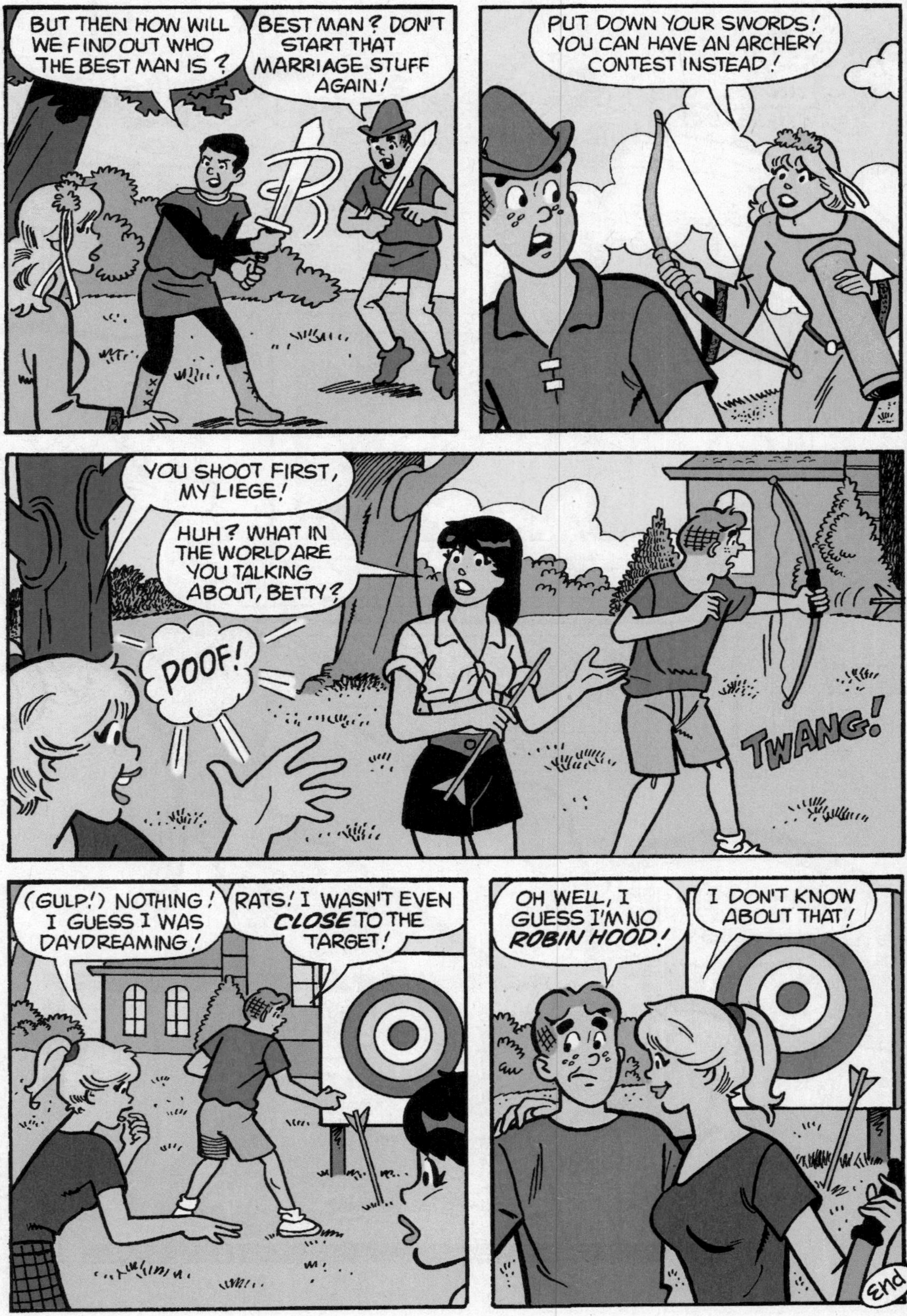
BUT THEN HOW WILL WE FIND OUT WHO THE BEST MAN IS?
BEST MAN? DON'T START THAT MARRIAGE STUFF AGAIN!
PUT DOWN YOUR SWORDS! YOU CAN HAVE AN ARCHERY CONTEST INSTEAD!
YOU SHOOT FIRST, MY LIEGE!
HUH? WHAT IN THE WORLD ARE YOU TALKING ABOUT, BETTY?
POOF!
TWANG!
(GULP!) NOTHING! I GUESS I WAS DAYDREAMING!
RATS! I WASN'T EVEN CLOSE TO THE TARGET!
OH WELL, I GUESS I'M NO ROBIN HOOD!
I DON'T KNOW ABOUT THAT!
End

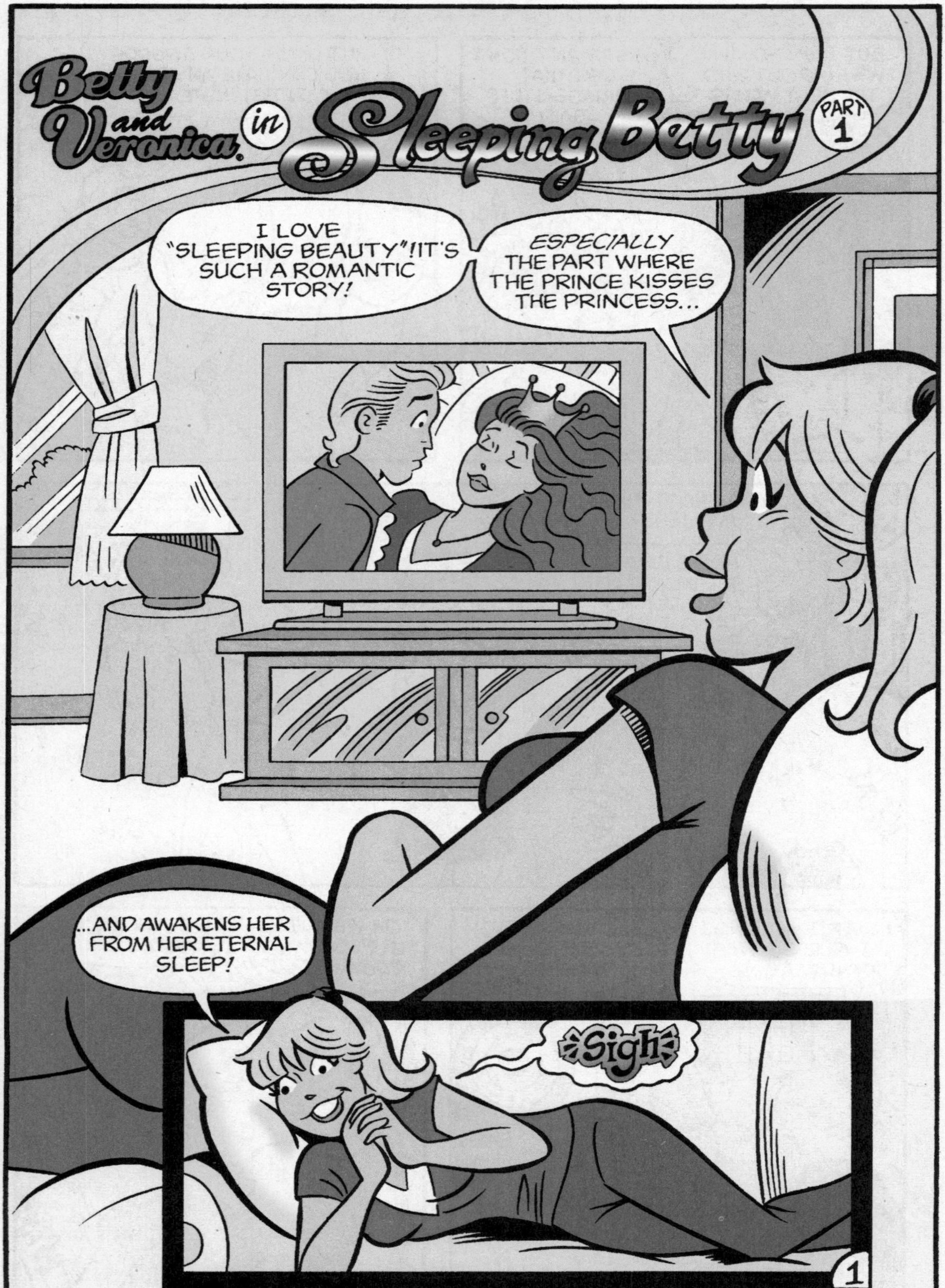
Betty and Veronica in Sleeping Betty PART 1
I LOVE "SLEEPING BEAUTY"!IT'S SUCH A ROMANTIC STORY!
ESPECIALLY THE PART WHERE THE PRINCE KISSES THE PRINCESS...
...AND AWAKENS HER FROM HER ETERNAL SLEEP!
Sigh
1

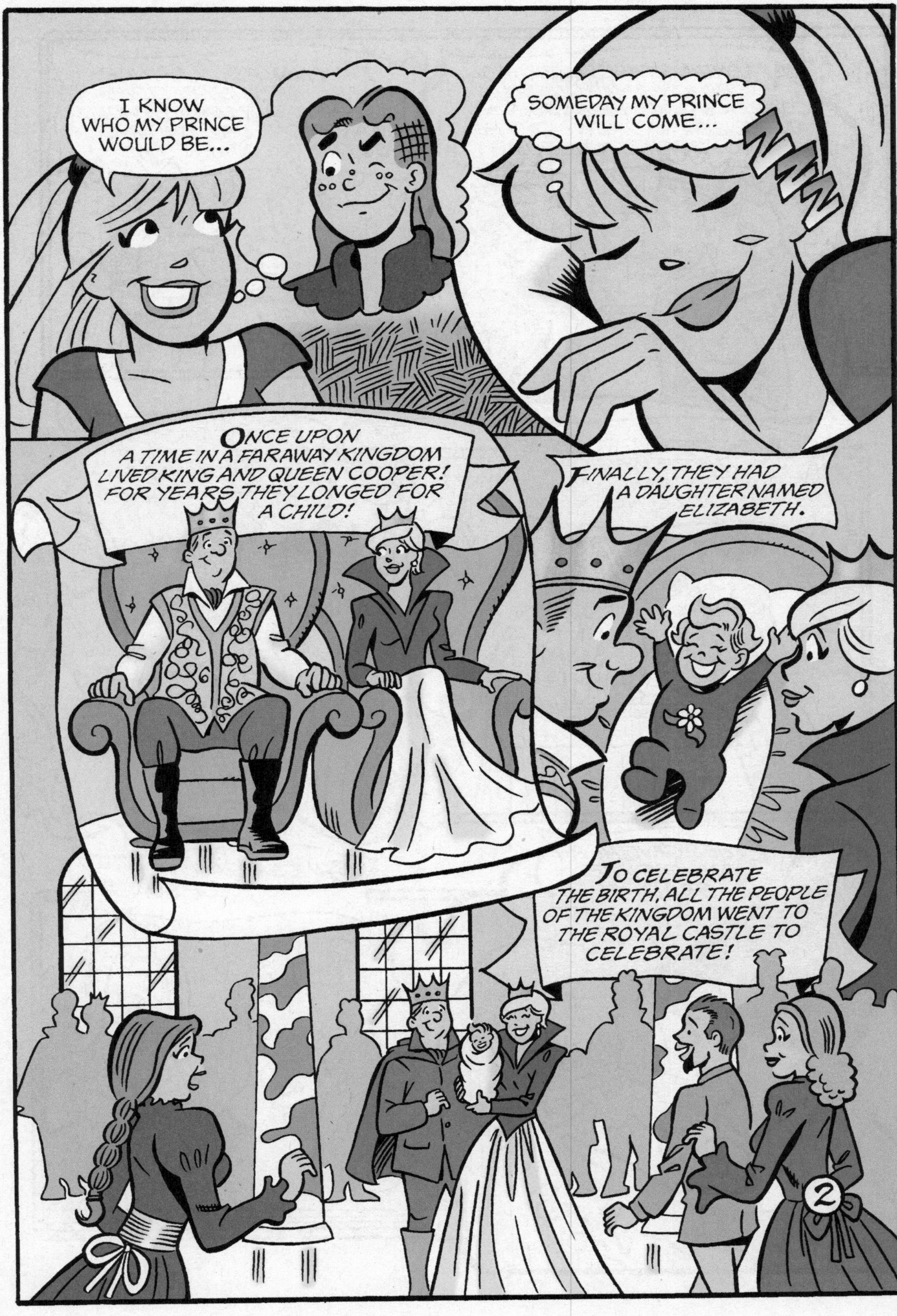
I KNOW WHO MY PRINCE WOULD BE...
SOMEDAY MY PRINCE WILL COME...
ZZZ
ONCE UPON A TIME IN A FARAWAY KINGDOM LIVED KING AND QUEEN COOPER! FOR YEARS, THEY LONGED FOR A CHILD!
FINALLY, THEY HAD A DAUGHTER NAMED ELIZABETH.
TO CELEBRATE THE BIRTH, ALL THE PEOPLE OF THE KINGDOM WENT TO THE ROYAL CASTLE TO CELEBRATE!
2

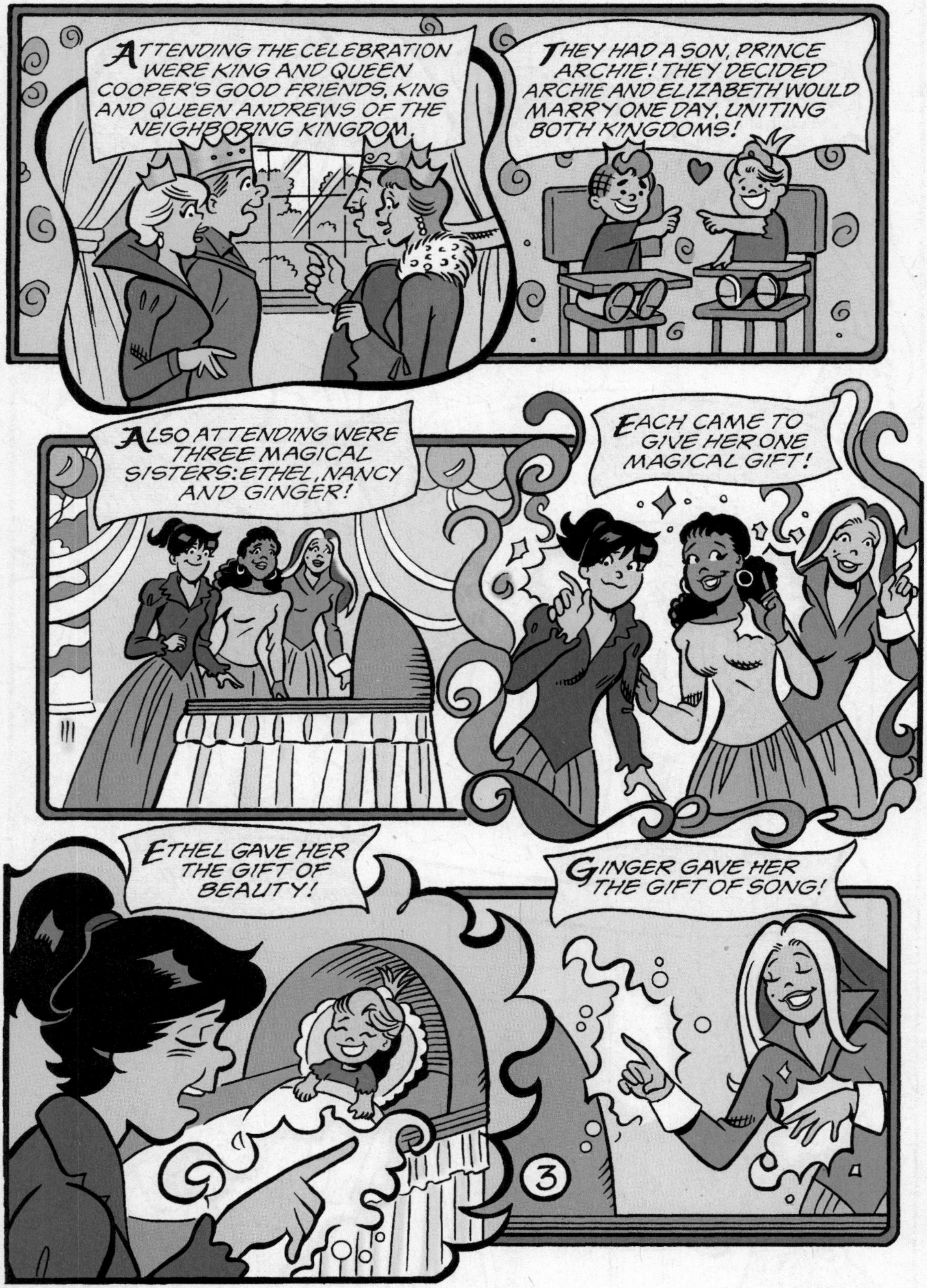
ATTENDING THE CELEBRATION WERE KING AND QUEEN COOPER'S GOOD FRIENDS, KING AND QUEEN ANDREWS OF THE NEIGHBORING KINGDOM.
THEY HAD A SON, PRINCE ARCHIE! THEY DECIDED ARCHIE AND ELIZABETH WOULD MARRY ONE DAY, UNITING BOTH KINGDOMS!
ALSO ATTENDING WERE THREE MAGICAL SISTERS: ETHEL, NANCY AND GINGER!
EACH CAME TO GIVE HER ONE MAGICAL GIFT!
ETHEL GAVE HER THE GIFT OF BEAUTY!
GINGER GAVE HER THE GIFT OF SONG!
3

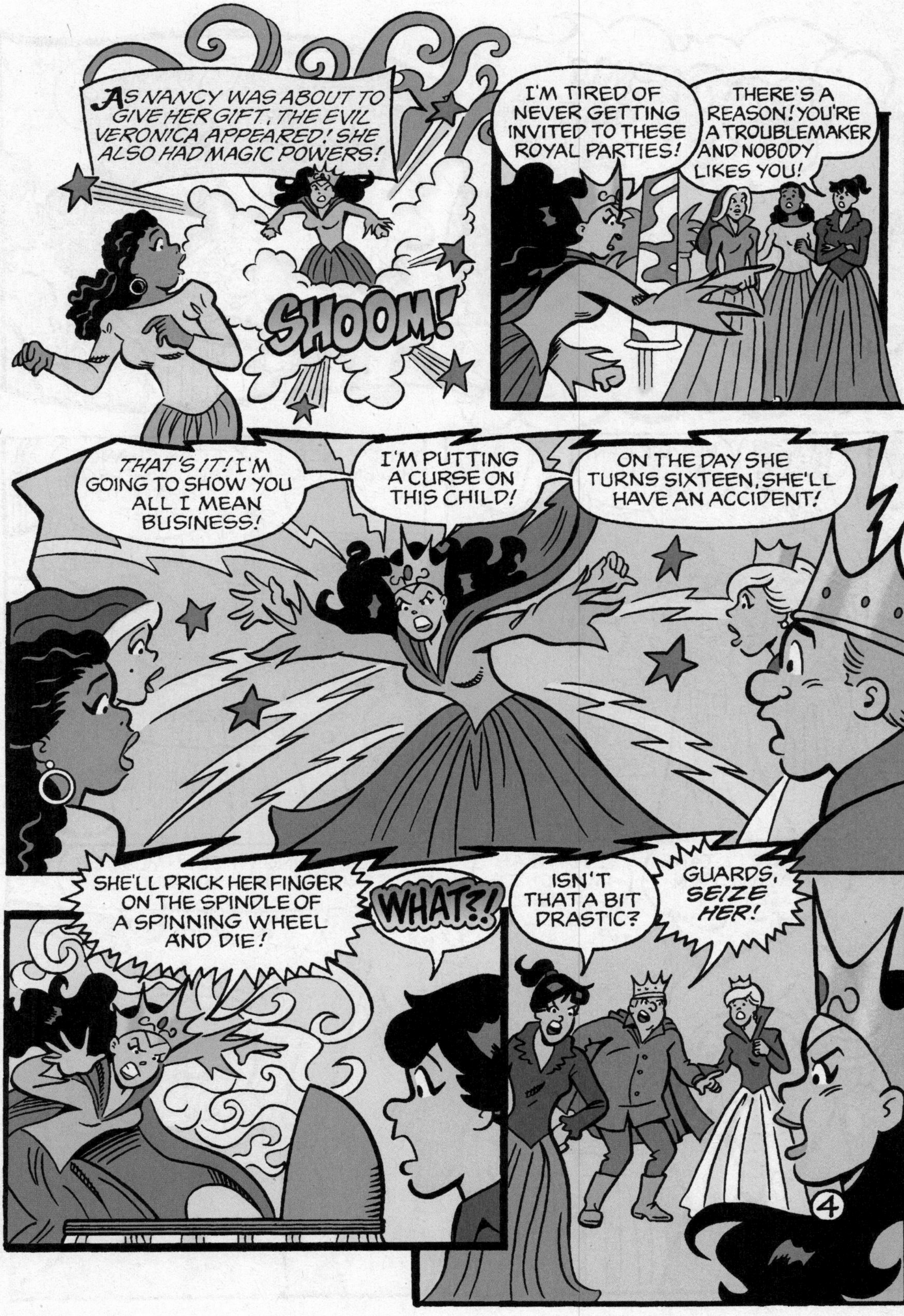

AS NANCY WAS ABOUT TO GIVE HER GIFT, THE EVIL VERONICA APPEARED! SHE ALSO HAD MAGIC POWERS!
SHOOM!
I'M TIRED OF NEVER GETTING INVITED TO THESE ROYAL PARTIES!
THERE'S A REASON! YOU'RE A TROUBLEMAKER AND NOBODY LIKES YOU!
THAT'S IT! I'M GOING TO SHOW YOU ALL I MEAN BUSINESS!
I'M PUTTING A CURSE ON THIS CHILD!
ON THE DAY SHE TURNS SIXTEEN, SHE'LL HAVE AN ACCIDENT!
SHE'LL PRICK HER FINGER ON THE SPINDLE OF A SPINNING WHEEL AND DIE!
WHAT?!
ISN'T THAT A BIT DRASTIC?
GUARDS, SEIZE HER!
4

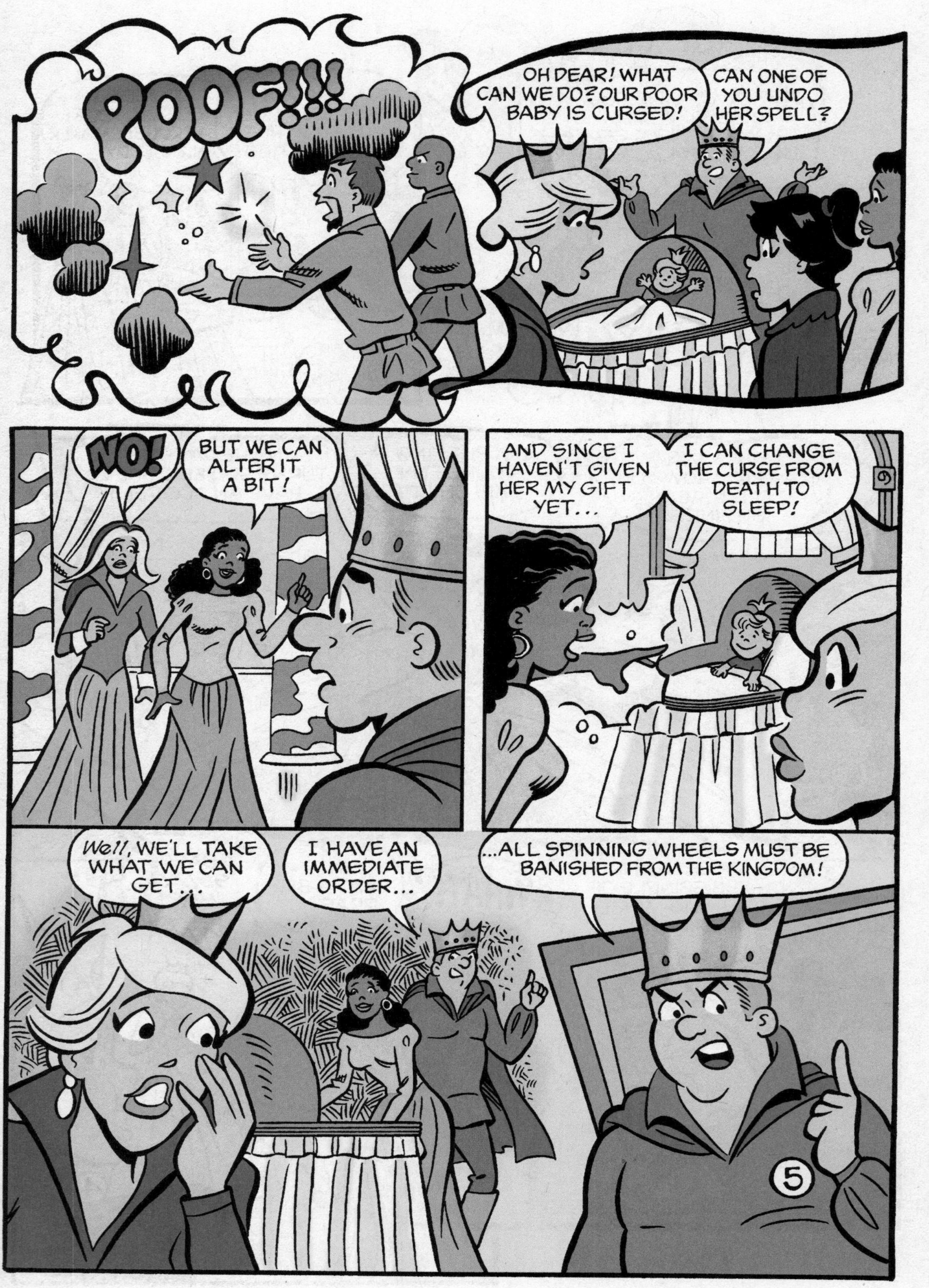
POOF!!!
OH DEAR! WHAT CAN WE DO? OUR POOR BABY IS CURSED!
CAN ONE OF YOU UNDO HER SPELL?
NO!
BUT WE CAN ALTER IT A BIT!
AND SINCE I HAVEN'T GIVEN HER MY GIFT YET...
I CAN CHANGE THE CURSE FROM DEATH TO SLEEP!
Well, WE'LL TAKE WHAT WE CAN GET...
I HAVE AN IMMEDIATE ORDER...
...ALL SPINNING WHEELS MUST BE BANISHED FROM THE KINGDOM!
5

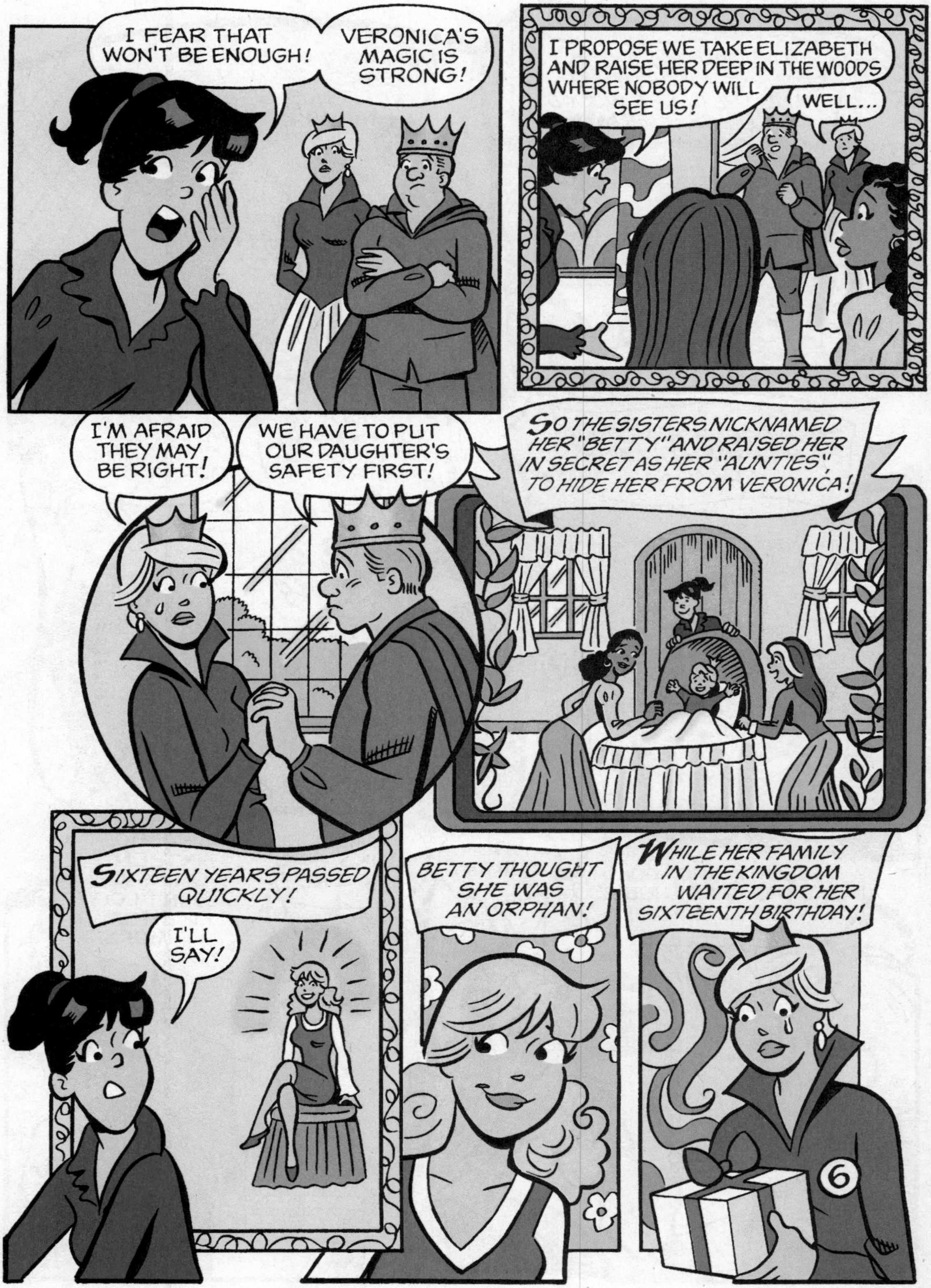
I FEAR THAT WON'T BE ENOUGH!
VERONICA'S MAGIC IS STRONG!
I PROPOSE WE TAKE ELIZABETH AND RAISE HER DEEP IN THE WOODS WHERE NOBODY WILL SEE US!
WELL...
I'M AFRAID THEY MAY BE RIGHT!
WE HAVE TO PUT OUR DAUGHTER'S SAFETY FIRST!
SO THE SISTERS NICKNAMED HER "BETTY" AND RAISED HER IN SECRET AS HER "AUNTIES", TO HIDE HER FROM VERONICA!
SIXTEEN YEARS PASSED QUICKLY!
I'LL SAY!
BETTY THOUGHT SHE WAS AN ORPHAN!
WHILE HER FAMILY IN THE KINGDOM WAITED FOR HER SIXTEENTH BIRTHDAY!
6

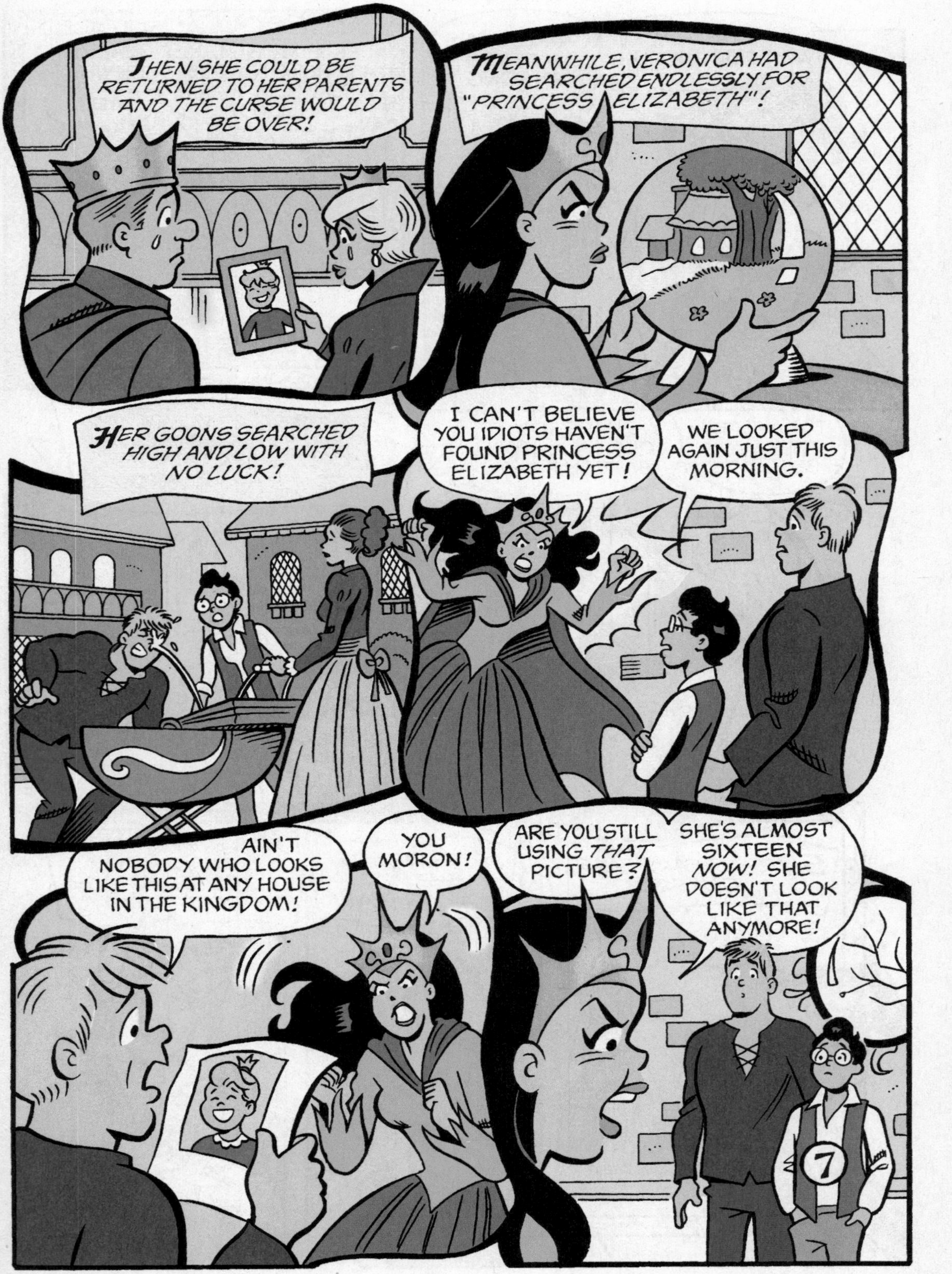
THEN SHE COULD BE RETURNED TO HER PARENTS AND THE CURSE WOULD BE OVER!
MEANWHILE, VERONICA HAD SEARCHED ENDLESSLY FOR "PRINCESS ELIZABETH"!
HER GOONS SEARCHED HIGH AND LOW WITH NO LUCK!
I CAN'T BELIEVE YOU IDIOTS HAVEN'T FOUND PRINCESS ELIZABETH YET!
WE LOOKED AGAIN JUST THIS MORNING.
AIN'T NOBODY WHO LOOKS LIKE THIS AT ANY HOUSE IN THE KINGDOM!
YOU MORON!
ARE YOU STILL USING THAT PICTURE?
SHE'S ALMOST SIXTEEN NOW! SHE DOESN'T LOOK LIKE THAT ANYMORE!

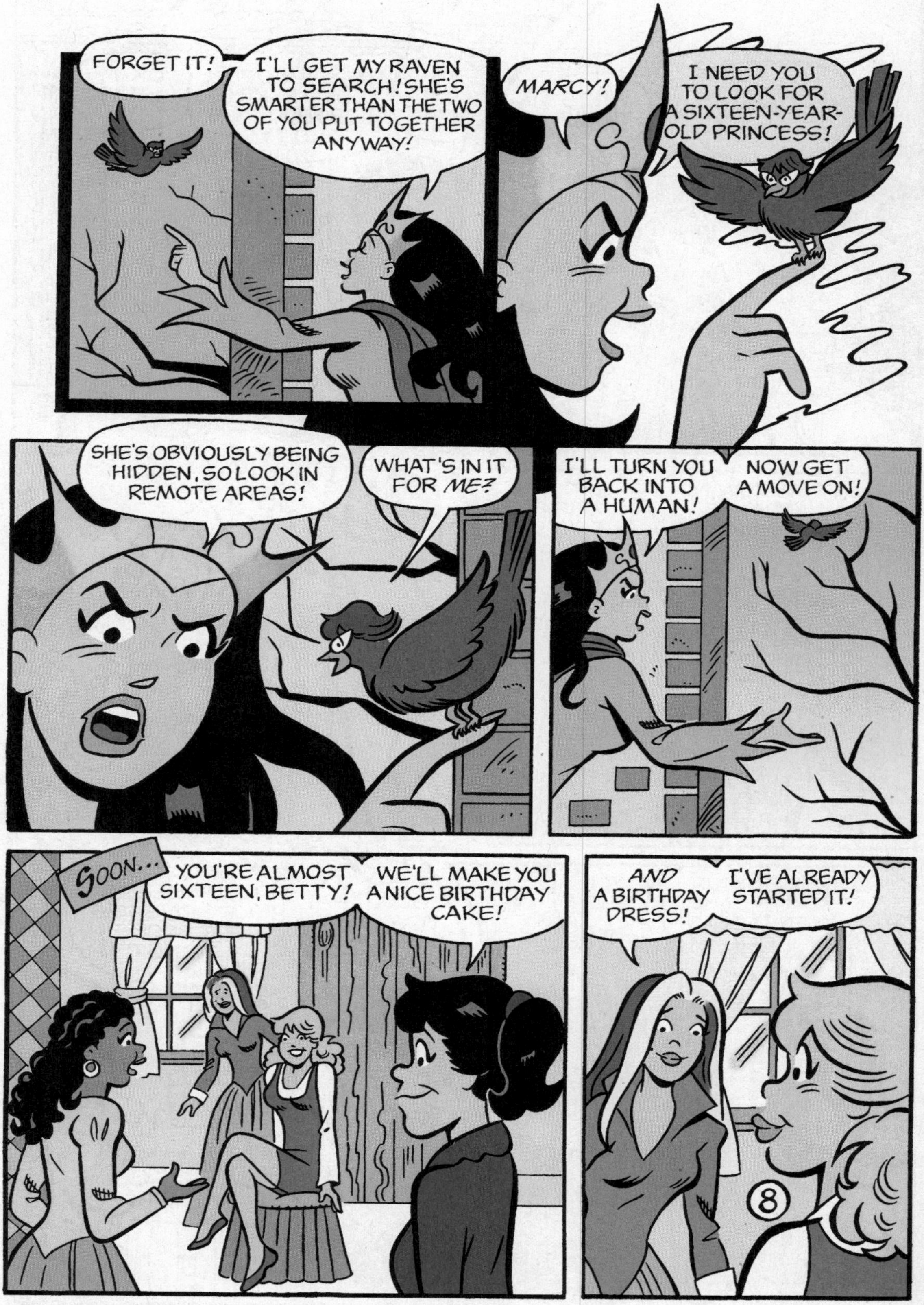
FORGET IT!
I'LL GET MY RAVEN TO SEARCH! SHE'S SMARTER THAN THE TWO OF YOU PUT TOGETHER ANYWAY!
MARCY!
I NEED YOU TO LOOK FOR A SIXTEEN-YEAR-OLD PRINCESS!
SHE'S OBVIOUSLY BEING HIDDEN, SO LOOK IN REMOTE AREAS!
WHAT'S IN IT FOR *ME?*
I'LL TURN YOU BACK INTO A HUMAN!
NOW GET A MOVE ON!
SOON...
YOU'RE ALMOST SIXTEEN, BETTY!
WE'LL MAKE YOU A NICE BIRTHDAY CAKE!
AND A BIRTHDAY DRESS!
I'VE ALREADY STARTED IT!
8

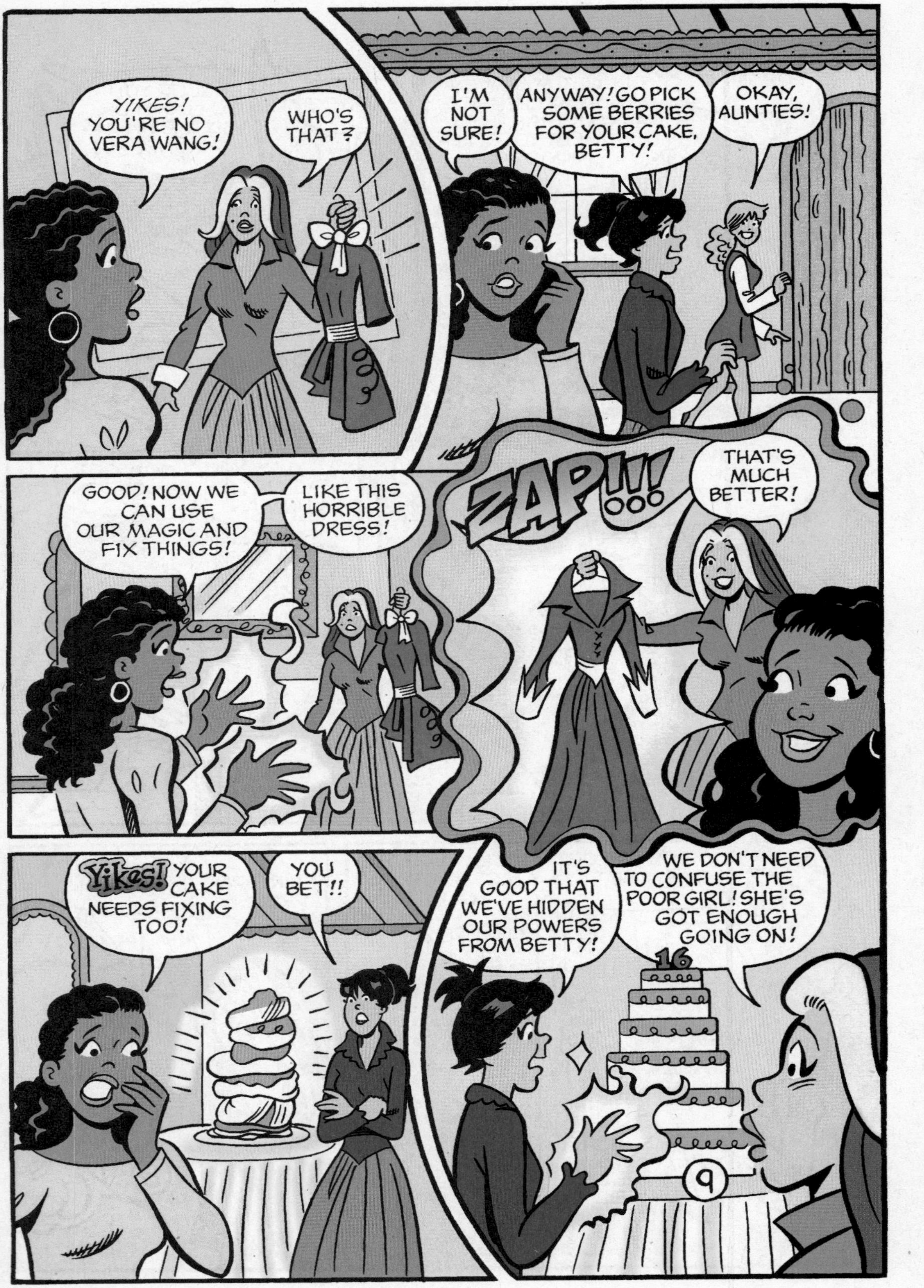
YIKES! YOU'RE NO VERA WANG!
WHO'S THAT?
I'M NOT SURE!
ANYWAY! GO PICK SOME BERRIES FOR YOUR CAKE, BETTY!
OKAY, AUNTIES!
GOOD! NOW WE CAN USE OUR MAGIC AND FIX THINGS!
LIKE THIS HORRIBLE DRESS!
ZAP!!!
THAT'S MUCH BETTER!
YIKES! YOUR CAKE NEEDS FIXING TOO!
YOU BET!!
IT'S GOOD THAT WE'VE HIDDEN OUR POWERS FROM BETTY!
WE DON'T NEED TO CONFUSE THE POOR GIRL! SHE'S GOT ENOUGH GOING ON!
16
9

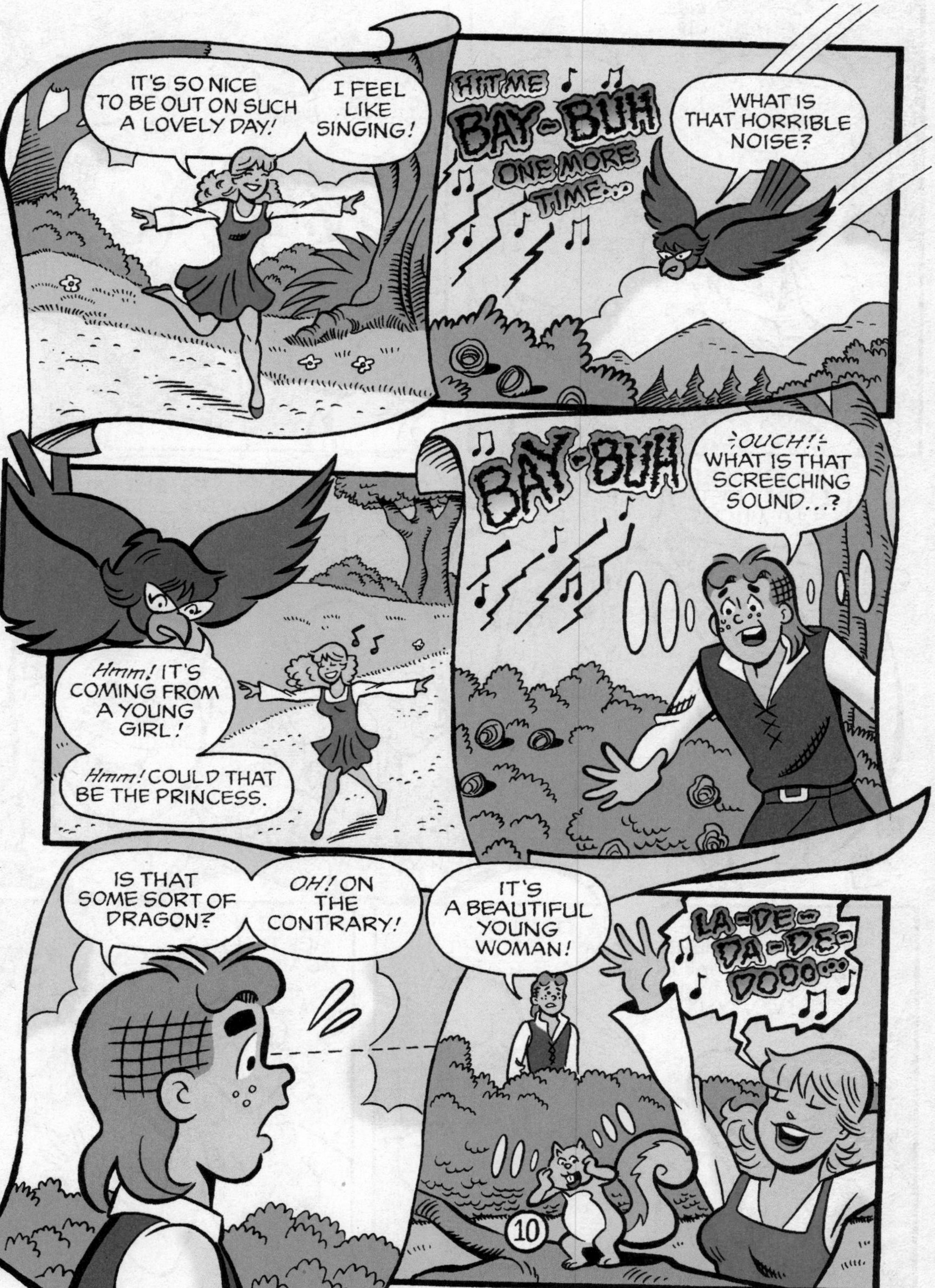
IT'S SO NICE TO BE OUT ON SUCH A LOVELY DAY!
I FEEL LIKE SINGING!
HIT ME BAY-BUH ONE MORE TIME...
WHAT IS THAT HORRIBLE NOISE?
Hmm! IT'S COMING FROM A YOUNG GIRL!
Hmm! COULD THAT BE THE PRINCESS.
BAY-BUH
OUCH! WHAT IS THAT SCREECHING SOUND...?
IS THAT SOME SORT OF DRAGON?
OH! ON THE CONTRARY!
IT'S A BEAUTIFUL YOUNG WOMAN!
LA-DE-DA-DE-DOOO...
10

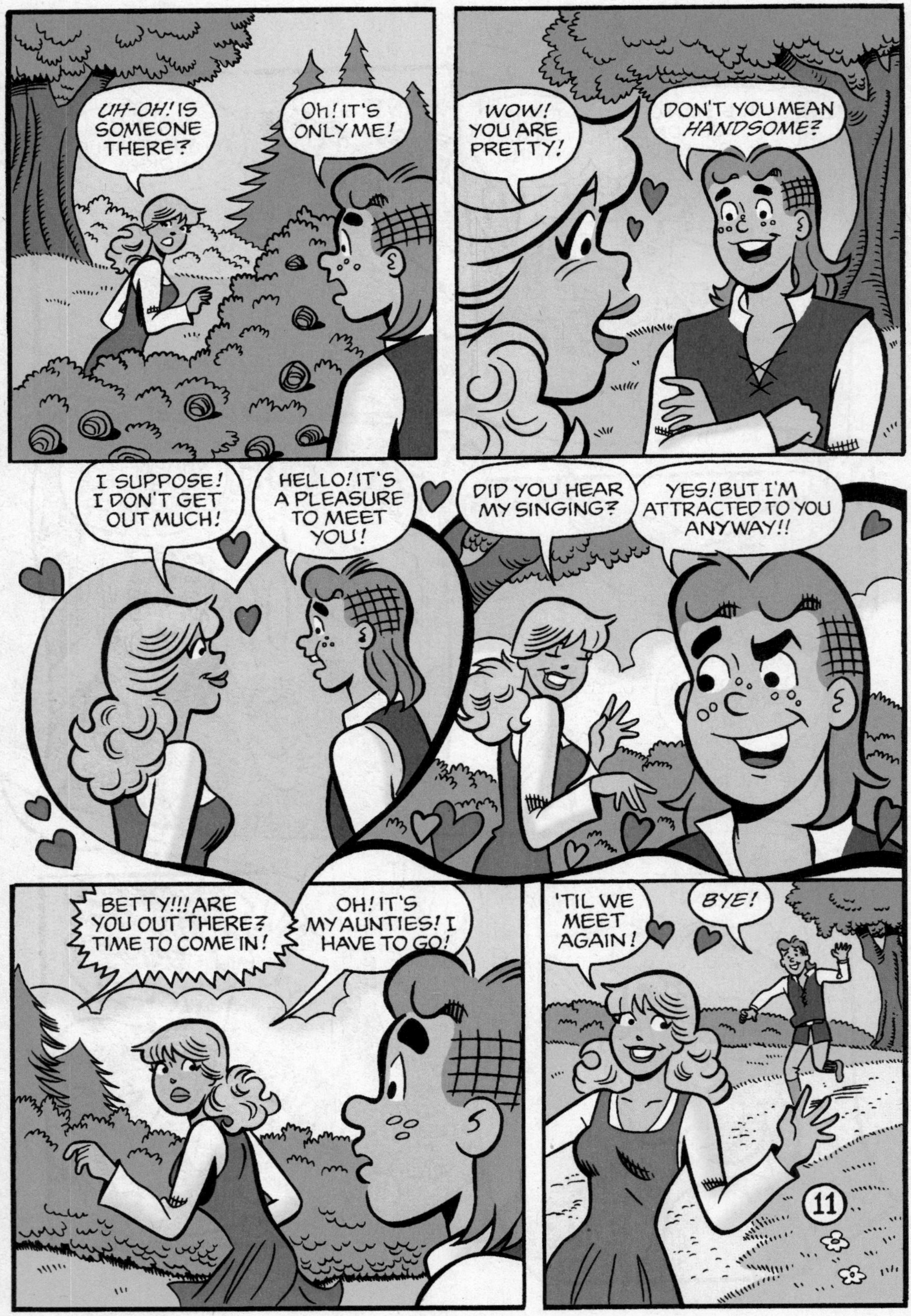
UH-OH! IS SOMEONE THERE?
OH! IT'S ONLY ME!
WOW! YOU ARE PRETTY!
DON'T YOU MEAN HANDSOME?
I SUPPOSE! I DON'T GET OUT MUCH!
HELLO! IT'S A PLEASURE TO MEET YOU!
DID YOU HEAR MY SINGING?
YES! BUT I'M ATTRACTED TO YOU ANYWAY!!
BETTY!!! ARE YOU OUT THERE? TIME TO COME IN!
OH! IT'S MY AUNTIES! I HAVE TO GO!
'TIL WE MEET AGAIN!
BYE!
11

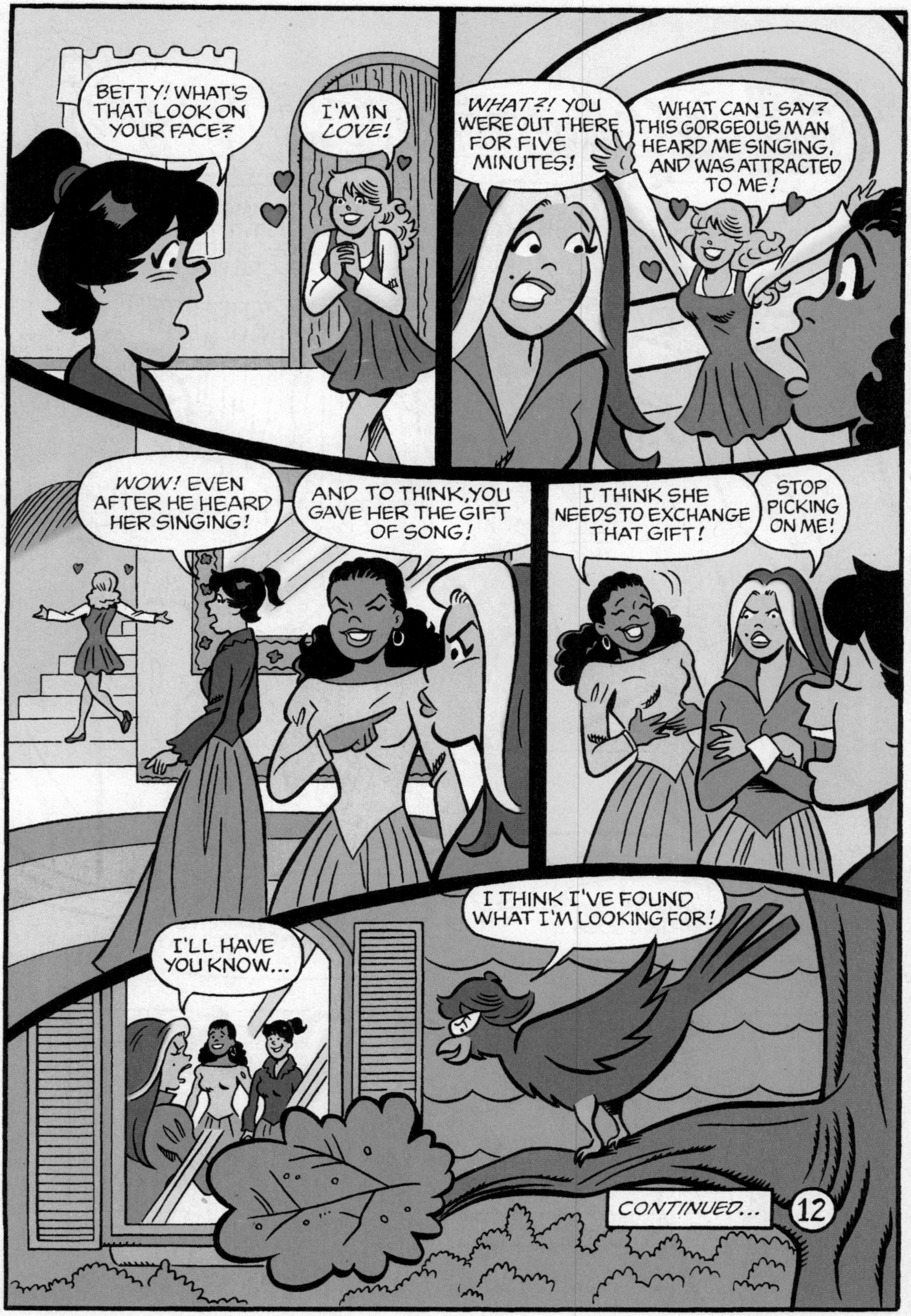
BETTY! WHAT'S THAT LOOK ON YOUR FACE?
I'M IN LOVE!
WHAT?! YOU WERE OUT THERE FOR FIVE MINUTES!
WHAT CAN I SAY? THIS GORGEOUS MAN HEARD ME SINGING, AND WAS ATTRACTED TO ME!
WOW! EVEN AFTER HE HEARD HER SINGING!
AND TO THINK, YOU GAVE HER THE GIFT OF SONG!
I THINK SHE NEEDS TO EXCHANGE THAT GIFT!
STOP PICKING ON ME!
I'LL HAVE YOU KNOW...
I THINK I'VE FOUND WHAT I'M LOOKING FOR!
CONTINUED...
12

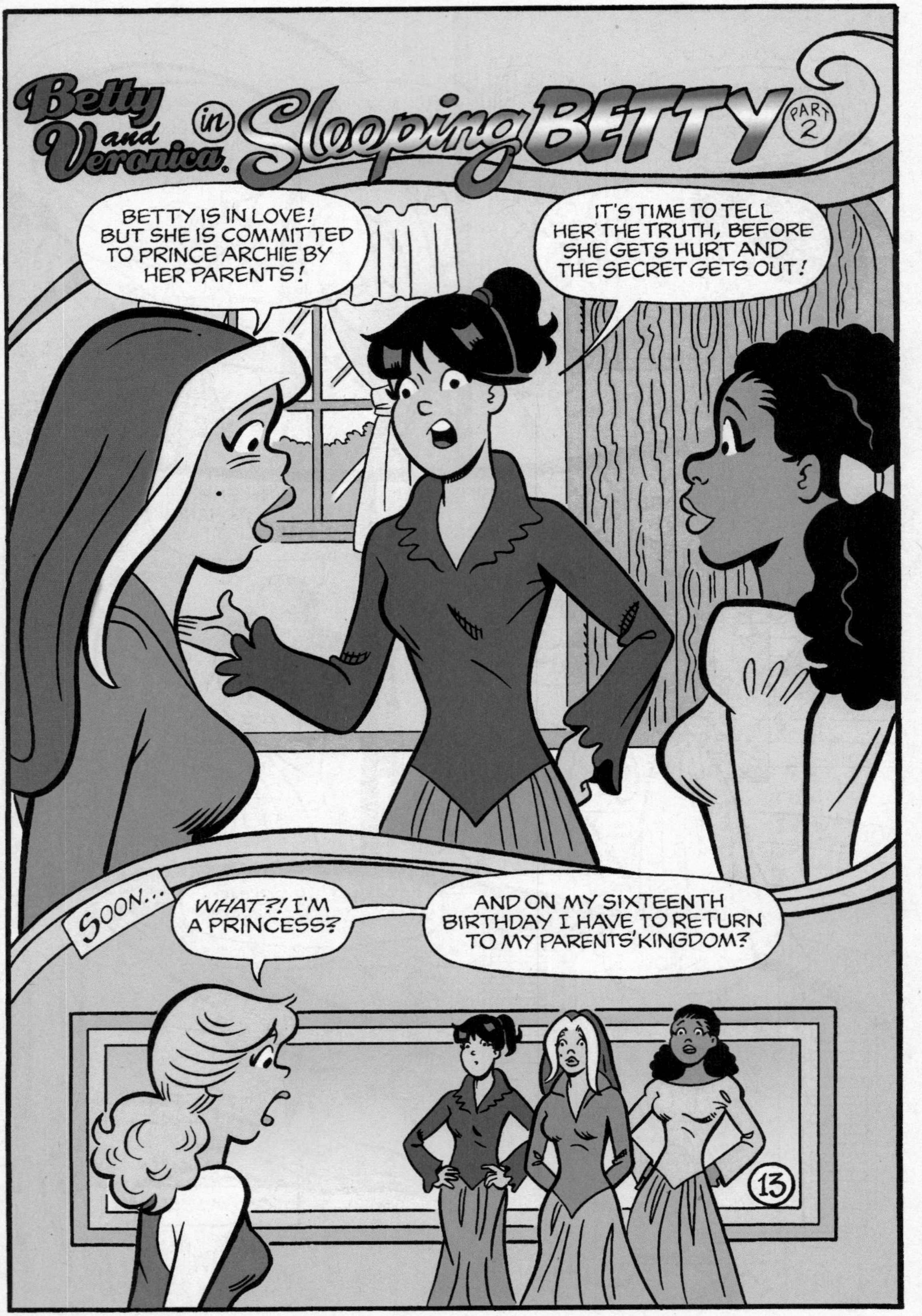
Betty and Veronica in Sleeping BETTY PART 2
BETTY IS IN LOVE! BUT SHE IS COMMITTED TO PRINCE ARCHIE BY HER PARENTS!
IT'S TIME TO TELL HER THE TRUTH, BEFORE SHE GETS HURT AND THE SECRET GETS OUT!
SOON...
WHAT?! I'M A PRINCESS?
AND ON MY SIXTEENTH BIRTHDAY I HAVE TO RETURN TO MY PARENTS' KINGDOM?
13

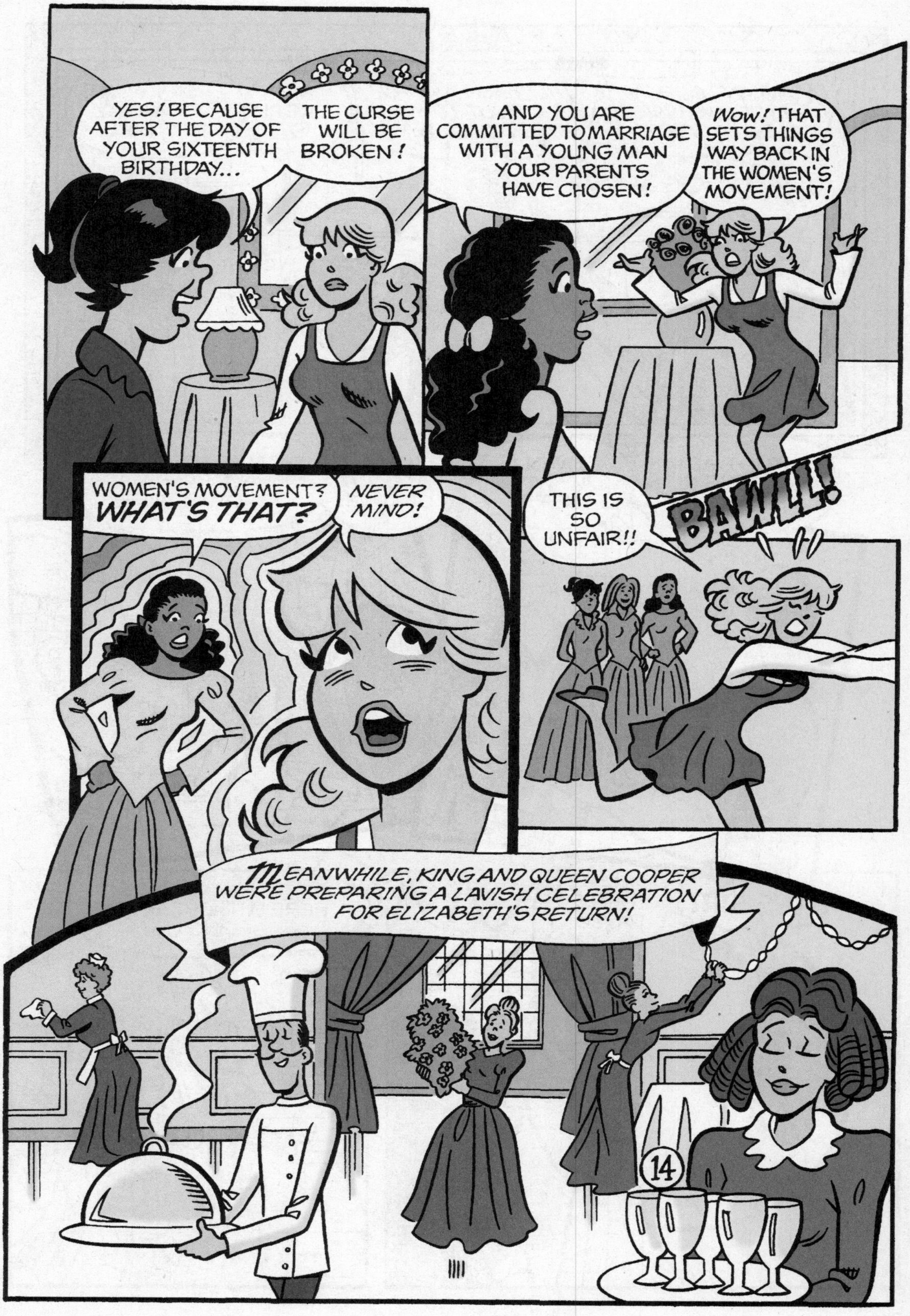
YES! BECAUSE AFTER THE DAY OF YOUR SIXTEENTH BIRTHDAY...
THE CURSE WILL BE BROKEN!
AND YOU ARE COMMITTED TO MARRIAGE WITH A YOUNG MAN YOUR PARENTS HAVE CHOSEN!
Wow! THAT SETS THINGS WAY BACK IN THE WOMEN'S MOVEMENT!
WOMEN'S MOVEMENT? WHAT'S THAT?
NEVER MIND!
THIS IS SO UNFAIR!!
BAWLL!
MEANWHILE, KING AND QUEEN COOPER WERE PREPARING A LAVISH CELEBRATION FOR ELIZABETH'S RETURN!
14

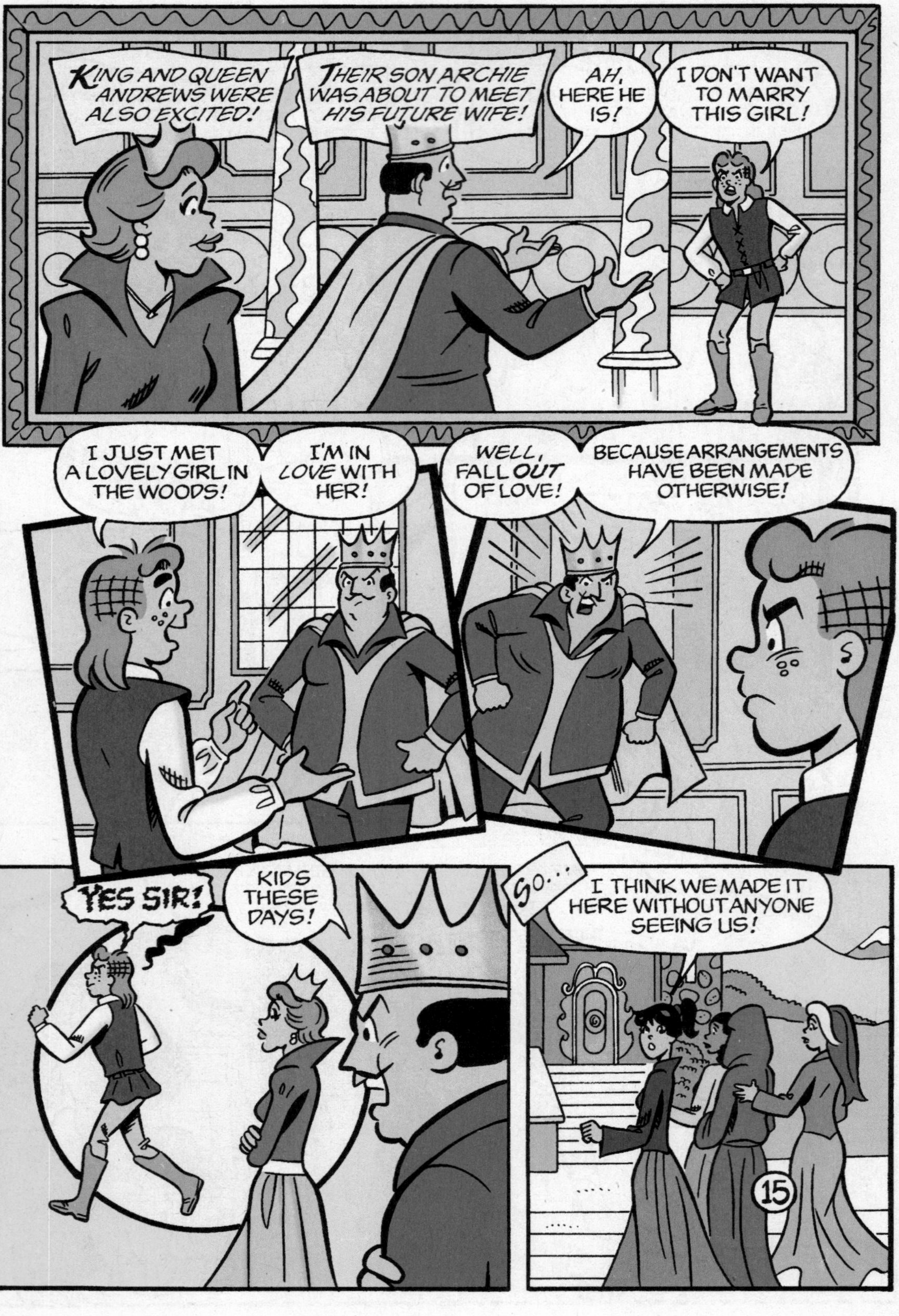
KING AND QUEEN ANDREWS WERE ALSO EXCITED!
THEIR SON ARCHIE WAS ABOUT TO MEET HIS FUTURE WIFE!
AH, HERE HE IS!
I DON'T WANT TO MARRY THIS GIRL!
I JUST MET A LOVELY GIRL IN THE WOODS!
I'M IN LOVE WITH HER!
WELL, FALL OUT OF LOVE!
BECAUSE ARRANGEMENTS HAVE BEEN MADE OTHERWISE!
YES SIR!
KIDS THESE DAYS!
SO...
I THINK WE MADE IT HERE WITHOUT ANYONE SEEING US!
.....
.....
15

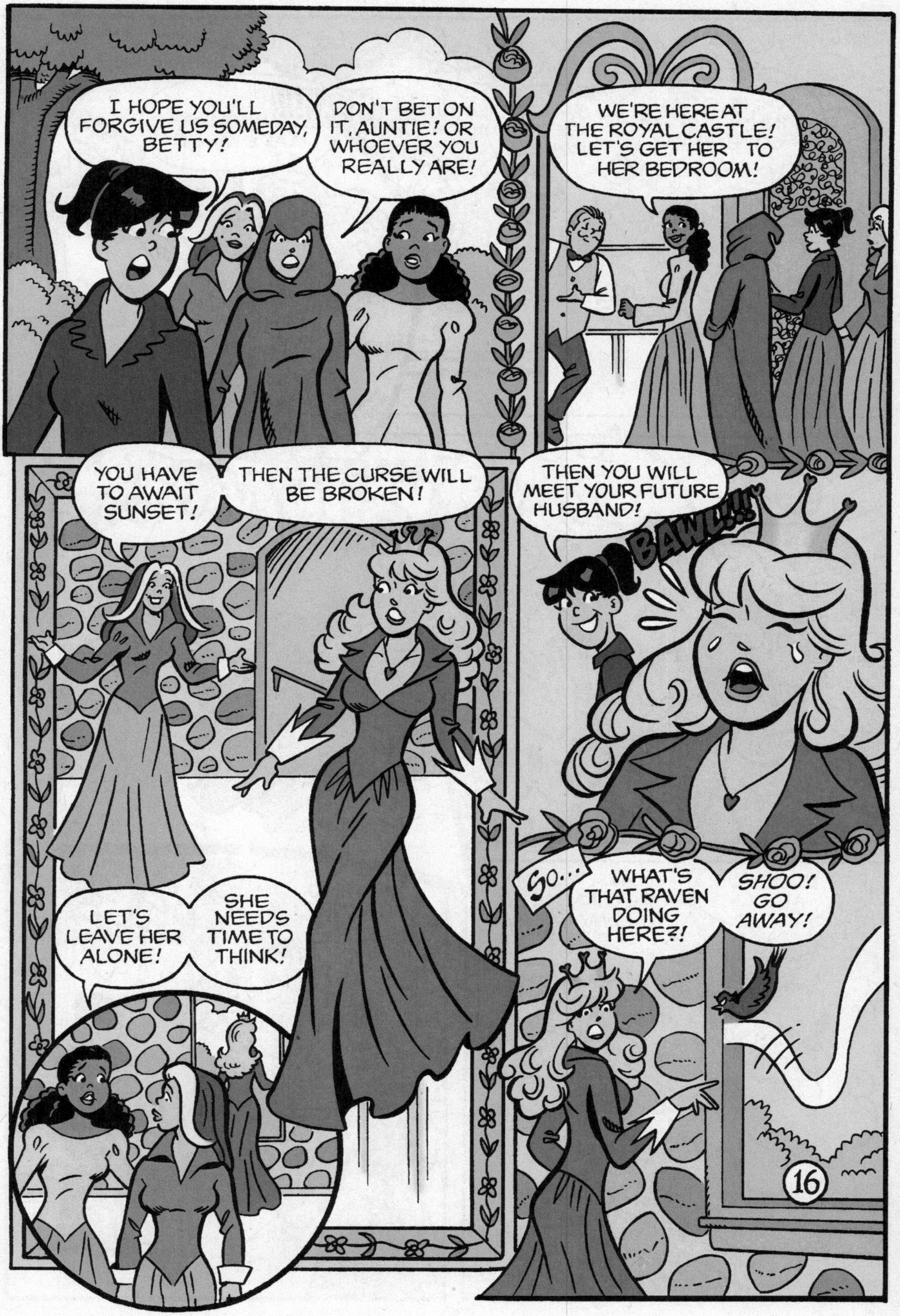

I HOPE YOU'LL FORGIVE US SOMEDAY, BETTY!
DON'T BET ON IT, AUNTIE! OR WHOEVER YOU REALLY ARE!
WE'RE HERE AT THE ROYAL CASTLE! LET'S GET HER TO HER BEDROOM!
YOU HAVE TO AWAIT SUNSET!
THEN THE CURSE WILL BE BROKEN!
THEN YOU WILL MEET YOUR FUTURE HUSBAND!
BAWL!!!
LET'S LEAVE HER ALONE!
SHE NEEDS TIME TO THINK!
SO...
WHAT'S THAT RAVEN DOING HERE?!
SHOO! GO AWAY!
16

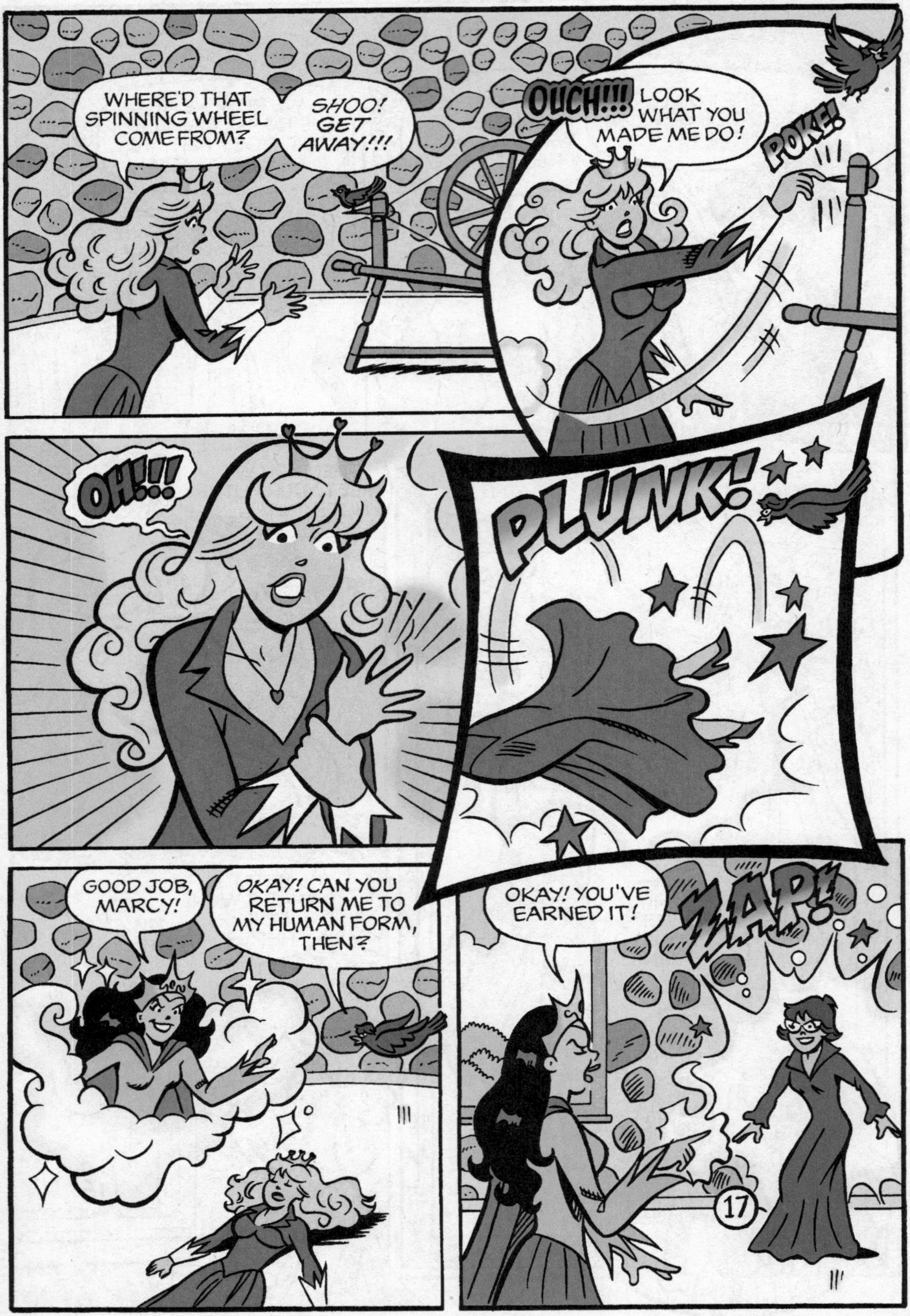
WHERE'D THAT SPINNING WHEEL COME FROM?
SHOO! GET AWAY!!!
OUCH!!!
LOOK WHAT YOU MADE ME DO!
POKE!
OH!!!
PLUNK!
GOOD JOB, MARCY!
OKAY! CAN YOU RETURN ME TO MY HUMAN FORM, THEN?
OKAY! YOU'VE EARNED IT!
ZAP!
17

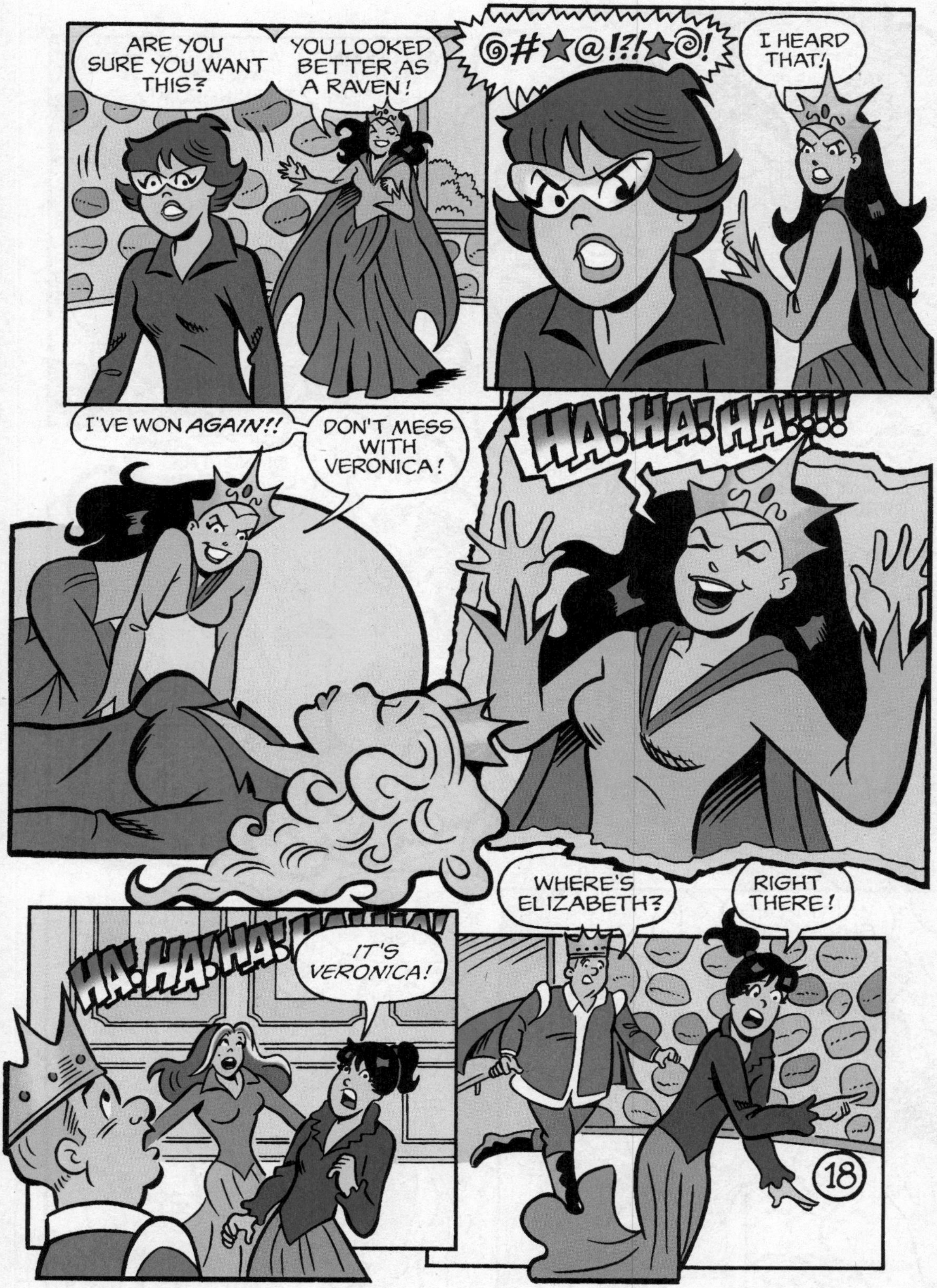
ARE YOU SURE YOU WANT THIS?
YOU LOOKED BETTER AS A RAVEN!
I HEARD THAT!
I'VE WON AGAIN!!
DON'T MESS WITH VERONICA!
HA! HA! HA!!!!
HA! HA! HA!
IT'S VERONICA!
WHERE'S ELIZABETH?
RIGHT THERE!
18

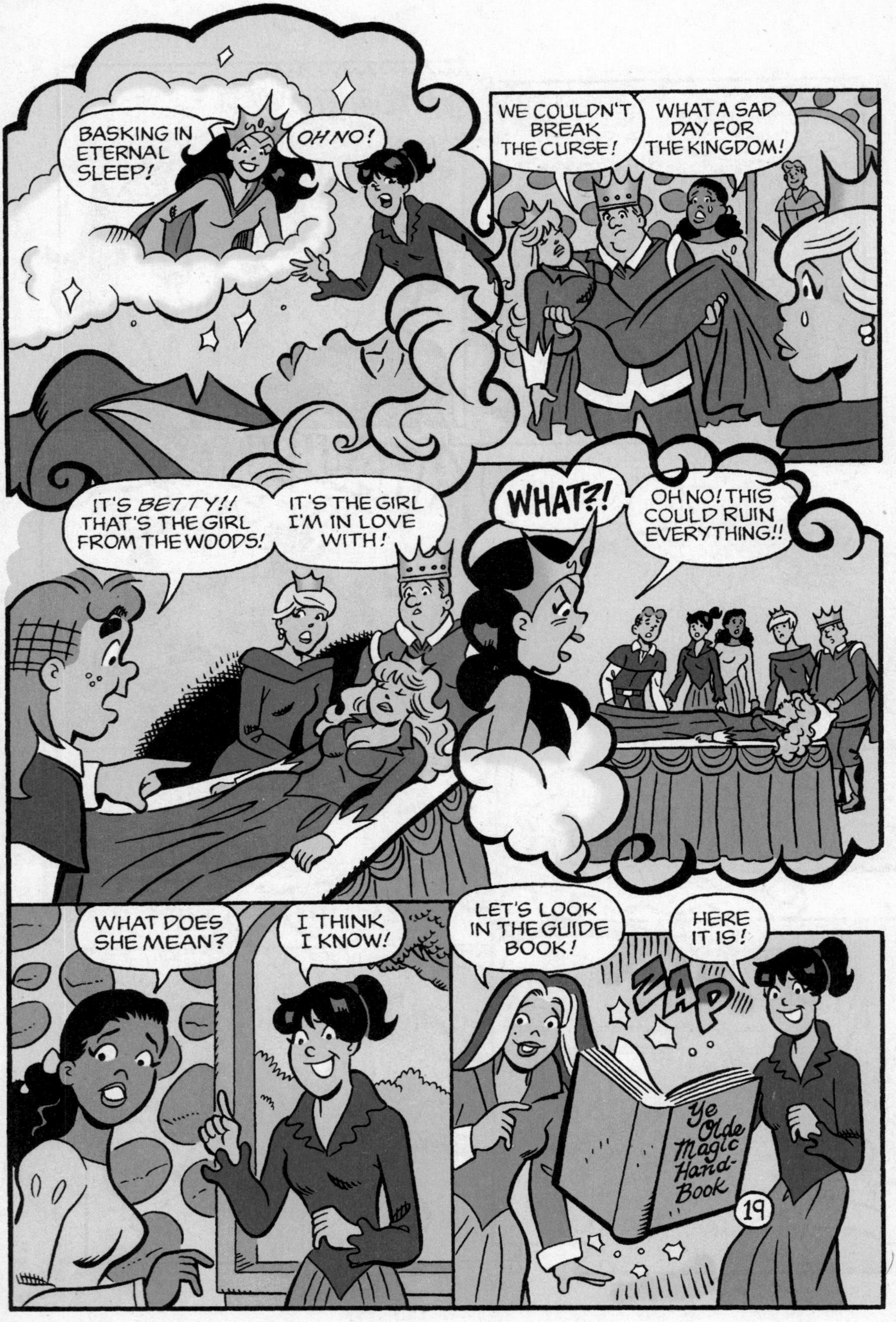
BASKING IN ETERNAL SLEEP!
OH NO!
WE COULDN'T BREAK THE CURSE!
WHAT A SAD DAY FOR THE KINGDOM!
IT'S BETTY!! THAT'S THE GIRL FROM THE WOODS!
IT'S THE GIRL I'M IN LOVE WITH!
WHAT?!
OH NO! THIS COULD RUIN EVERYTHING!!
WHAT DOES SHE MEAN?
I THINK I KNOW!
LET'S LOOK IN THE GUIDE BOOK!
HERE IT IS!
ZAP
Ye Olde Magic Hand-Book
19

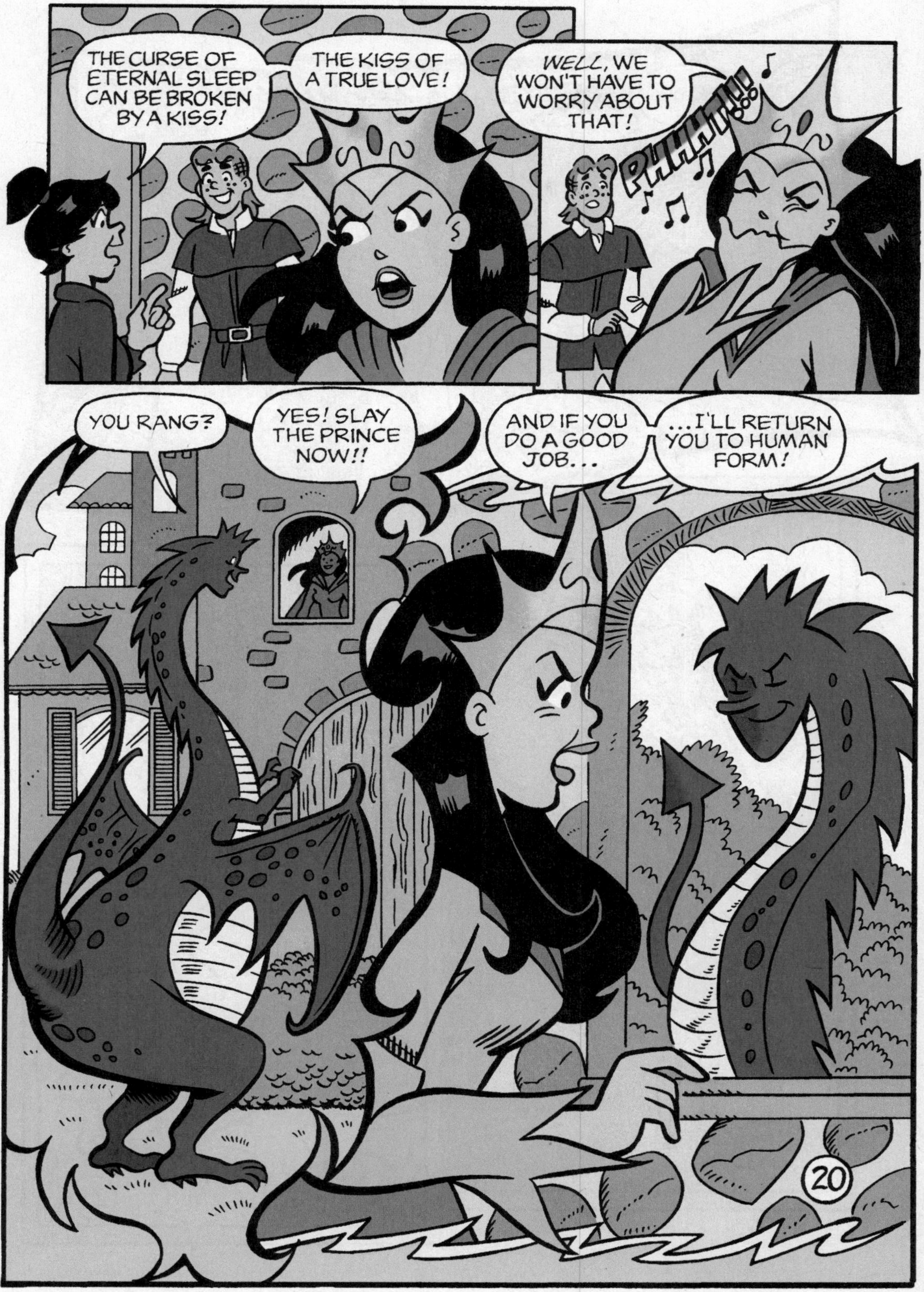
THE CURSE OF ETERNAL SLEEP CAN BE BROKEN BY A KISS!
THE KISS OF A TRUE LOVE!
WELL, WE WON'T HAVE TO WORRY ABOUT THAT!
PHHHT!!!
YOU RANG?
YES! SLAY THE PRINCE NOW!!
AND IF YOU DO A GOOD JOB...
...I'LL RETURN YOU TO HUMAN FORM!
20

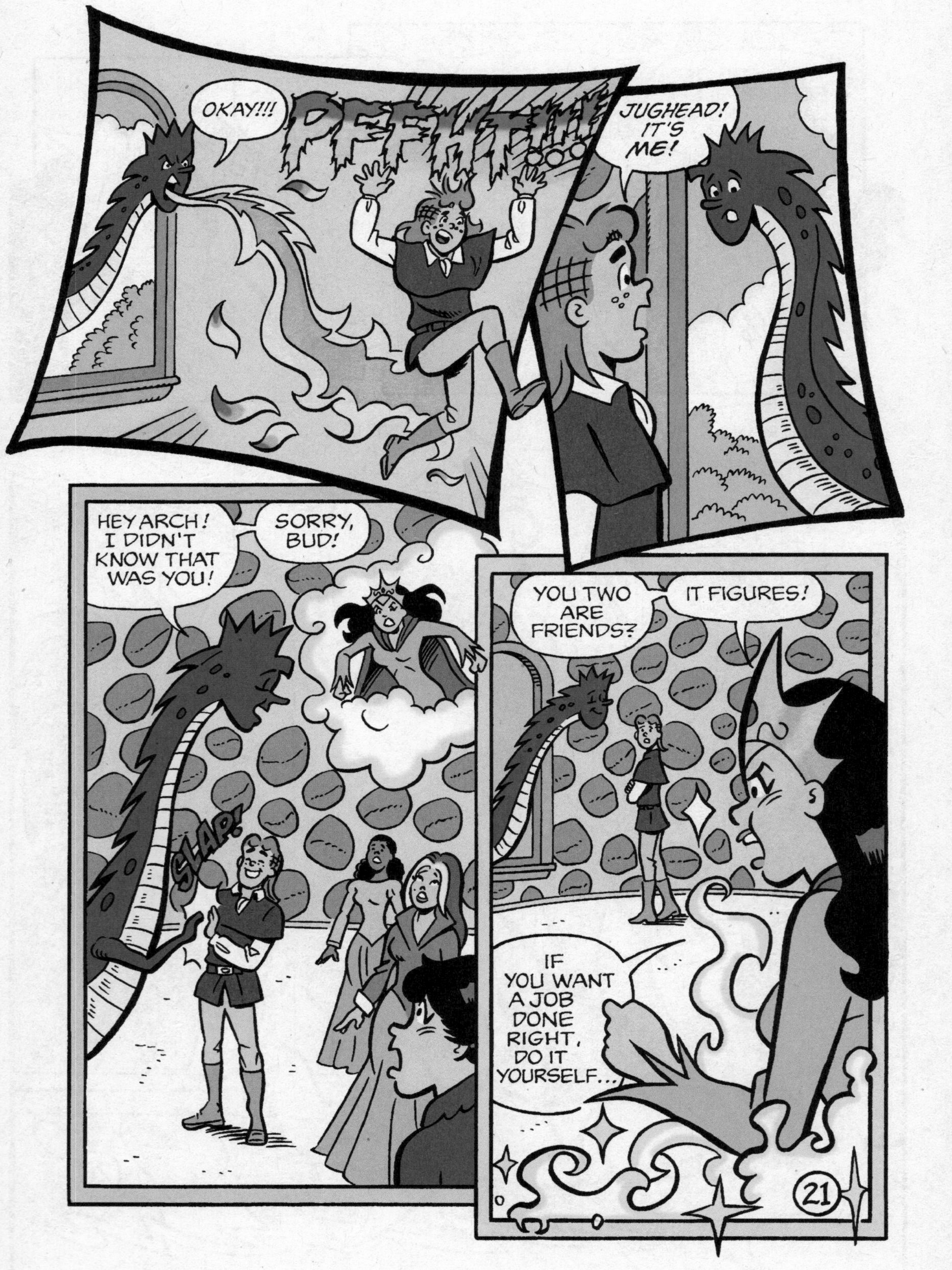
OKAY!!!
PFFUTTT!
JUGHEAD! IT'S ME!
HEY ARCH! I DIDN'T KNOW THAT WAS YOU!
SORRY, BUD!
SLAP!
YOU TWO ARE FRIENDS?
IT FIGURES!
IF YOU WANT A JOB DONE RIGHT, DO IT YOURSELF...
21

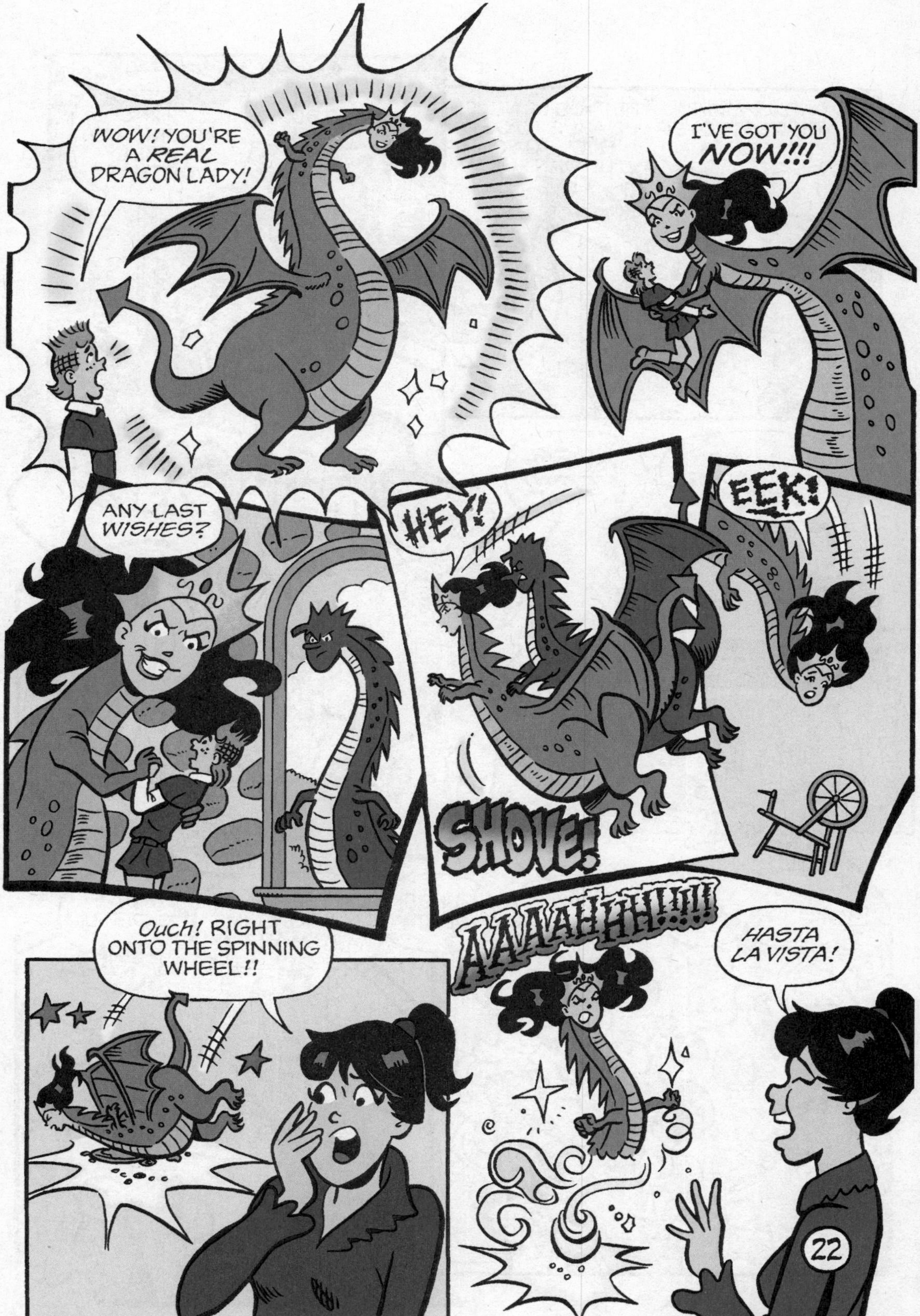
WOW! YOU'RE A REAL DRAGON LADY!
I'VE GOT YOU NOW!!!
ANY LAST WISHES?
HEY!
SHOVE!
EEK!
AAAAHHH!!!!!
Ouch! RIGHT ONTO THE SPINNING WHEEL!!
HASTA LA VISTA!
22

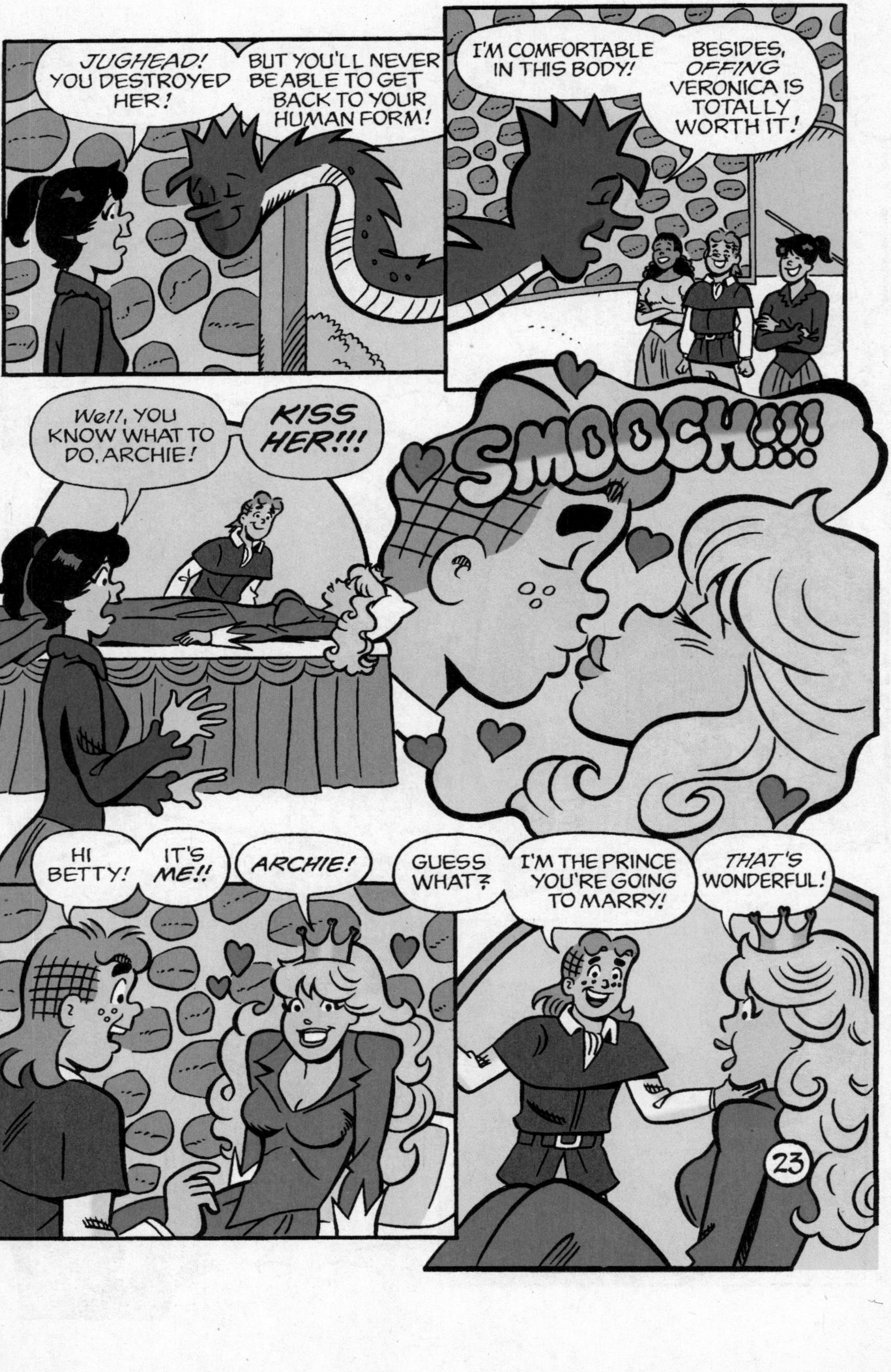
JUGHEAD! YOU DESTROYED HER!
BUT YOU'LL NEVER BE ABLE TO GET BACK TO YOUR HUMAN FORM!
I'M COMFORTABLE IN THIS BODY!
BESIDES, OFFING VERONICA IS TOTALLY WORTH IT!
Well, YOU KNOW WHAT TO DO, ARCHIE!
KISS HER!!!
SMOOCH!!!
HI BETTY!
IT'S ME!!
ARCHIE!
GUESS WHAT?
I'M THE PRINCE YOU'RE GOING TO MARRY!
THAT'S WONDERFUL!
23

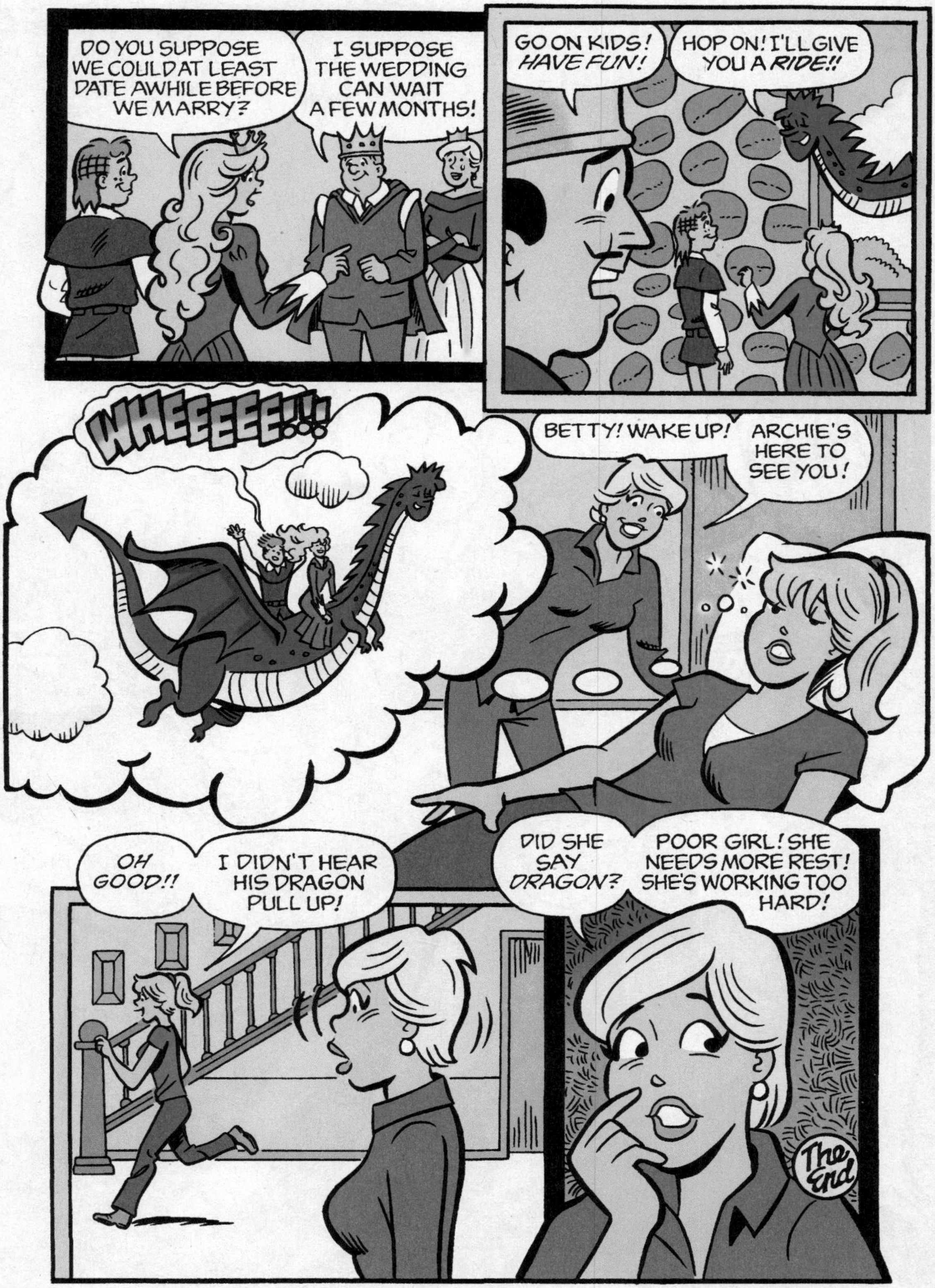
DO YOU SUPPOSE WE COULD AT LEAST DATE AWHILE BEFORE WE MARRY?
I SUPPOSE THE WEDDING CAN WAIT A FEW MONTHS!
GO ON KIDS! *HAVE FUN!*
HOP ON! I'LL GIVE YOU A *RIDE!!*
WHEEEEEE!!!
BETTY! WAKE UP!
ARCHIE'S HERE TO SEE YOU!
OH GOOD!!
I DIDN'T HEAR HIS DRAGON PULL UP!
DID SHE SAY *DRAGON?*
POOR GIRL! SHE NEEDS MORE REST! SHE'S WORKING TOO HARD!
The End

CHAPTER FOUR

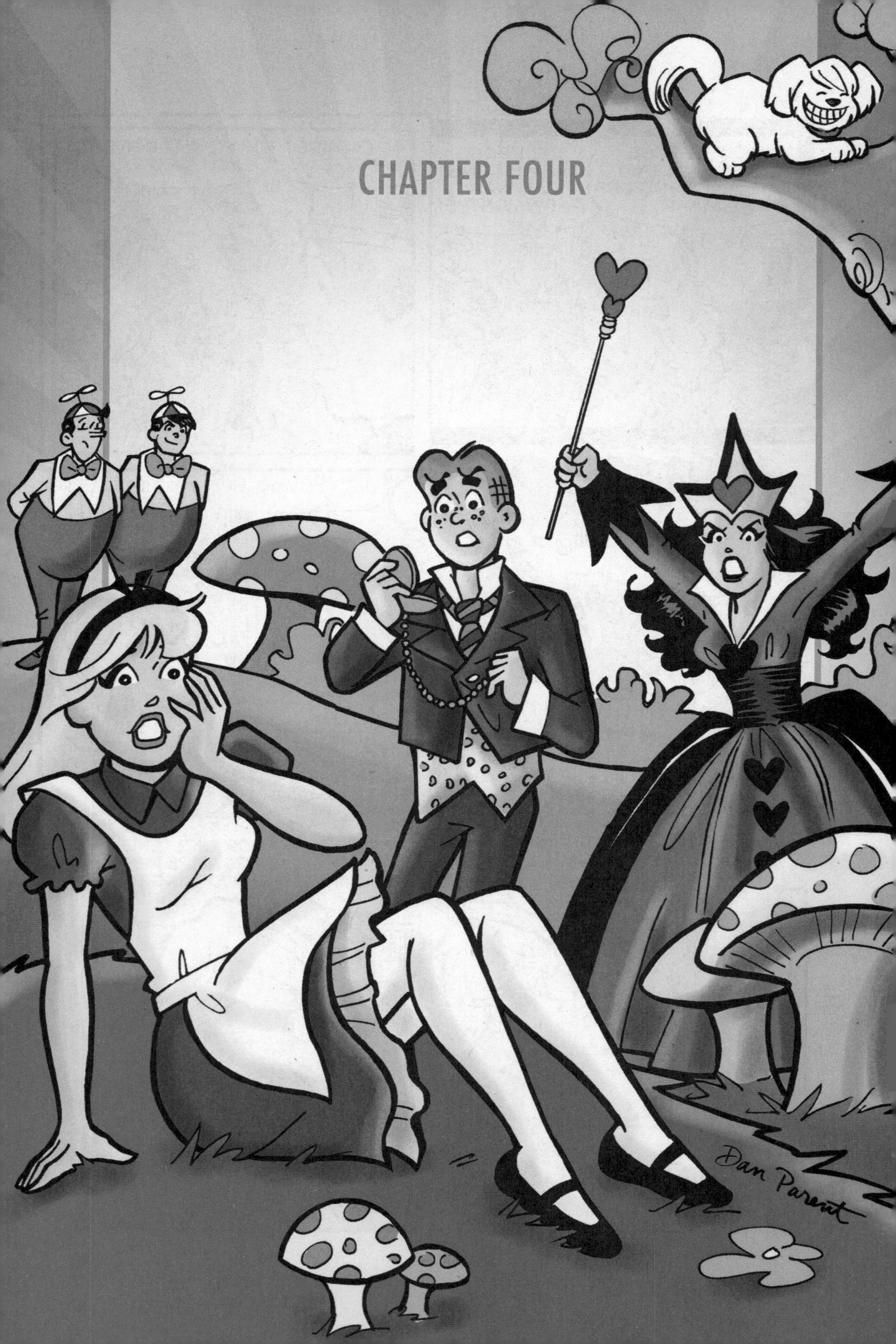
Dan Parent

BETTY & VERONICA IN

THERE'S NO PLACE LIKE... RIVERDALE

DECEMBER 2008

SCRIPT & PENCILS: DAN PARENT   INKS: RICH KOSLOWSKI
LETTERS: JACK MORELLI   COLORS: BARRY GROSSMAN

BETTY IN

WONDERLAND!

AUGUST 2009

SCRIPT & PENCILS: DAN PARENT   INKS: JIM AMASH
LETTERS: TERESA DAVIDSON   COLORS: BARRY GROSSMAN

BETTY & VERONICA IN

A TALE OF TWO CINDERELLAS

NOVEMBER 2010

SCRIPT & PENCILS: DAN PARENT   INKS: JIM AMASH
LETTERS: TERESA DAVIDSON   COLORS: BARRY GROSSMAN

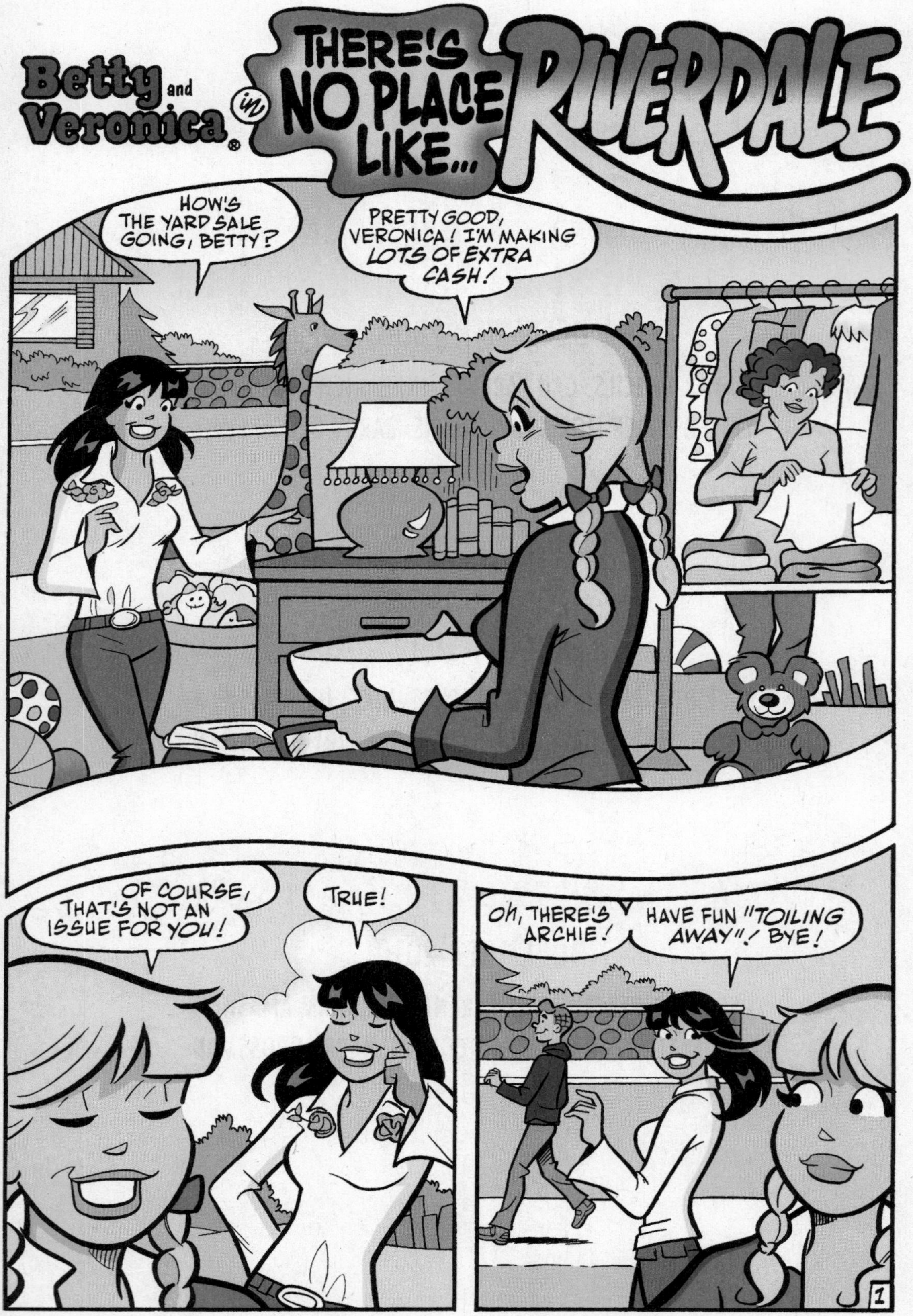
Betty and Veronica in
THERE'S NO PLACE LIKE... RIVERDALE
HOW'S THE YARD SALE GOING, BETTY?
PRETTY GOOD, VERONICA! I'M MAKING LOTS OF EXTRA CASH!
OF COURSE, THAT'S NOT AN ISSUE FOR YOU!
TRUE!
OH, THERE'S ARCHIE!
HAVE FUN "TOILING AWAY"! BYE!
1

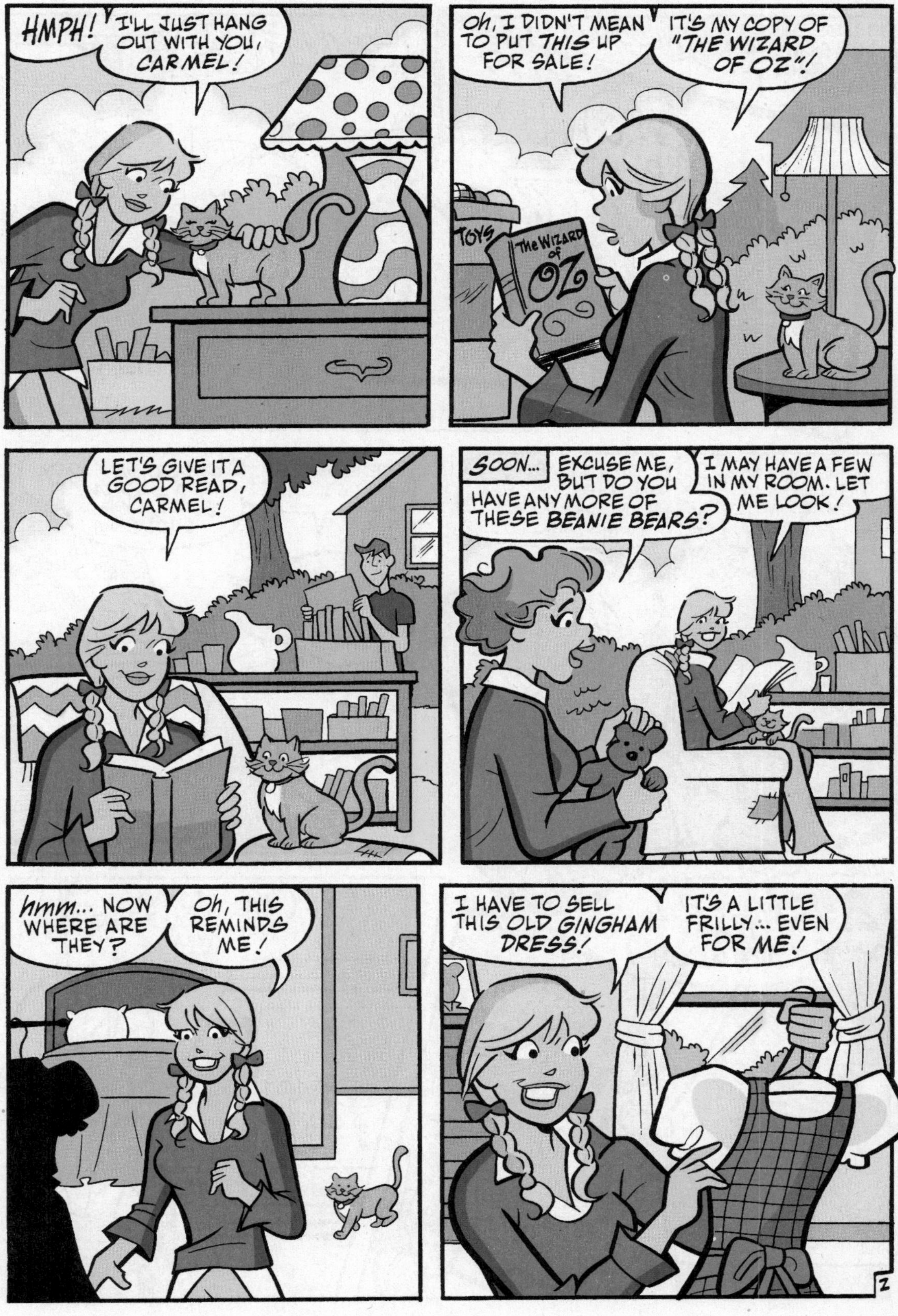
HMPH!
I'LL JUST HANG OUT WITH YOU, CARMEL!
Oh, I DIDN'T MEAN TO PUT THIS UP FOR SALE!
IT'S MY COPY OF "THE WIZARD OF OZ"!
TOYS
The WIZARD of OZ
LET'S GIVE IT A GOOD READ, CARMEL!
SOON...
EXCUSE ME, BUT DO YOU HAVE ANY MORE OF THESE BEANIE BEARS?
I MAY HAVE A FEW IN MY ROOM. LET ME LOOK!
hmm... NOW WHERE ARE THEY?
Oh, THIS REMINDS ME!
I HAVE TO SELL THIS OLD GINGHAM DRESS!
IT'S A LITTLE FRILLY... EVEN FOR ME!

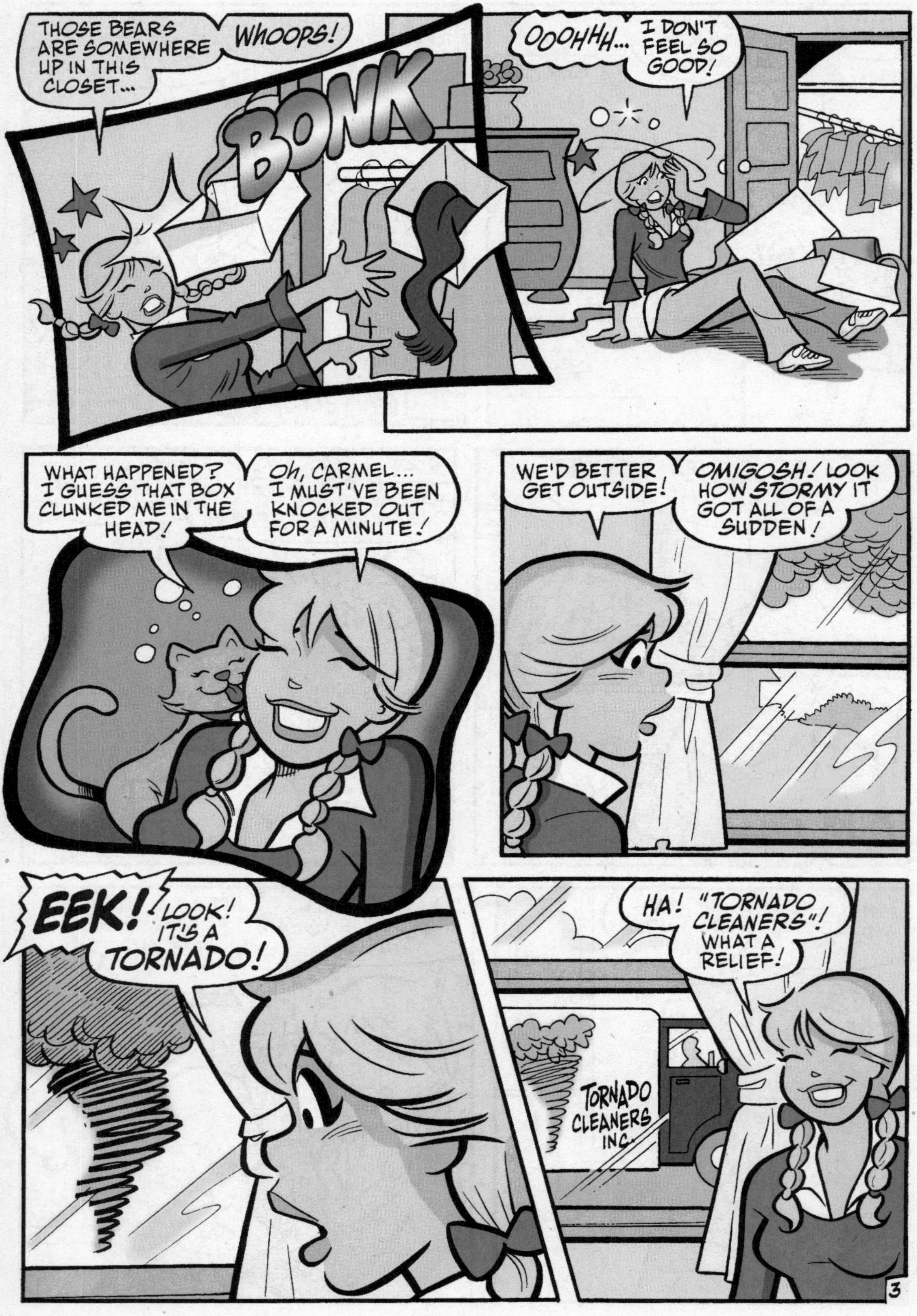
THOSE BEARS ARE SOMEWHERE UP IN THIS CLOSET...
WHOOPS!
BONK
OOOHHH... I DON'T FEEL SO GOOD!
WHAT HAPPENED? I GUESS THAT BOX CLUNKED ME IN THE HEAD!
OH, CARMEL... I MUST'VE BEEN KNOCKED OUT FOR A MINUTE!
WE'D BETTER GET OUTSIDE!
OMIGOSH! LOOK HOW STORMY IT GOT ALL OF A SUDDEN!
EEK! LOOK! IT'S A TORNADO!
HA! "TORNADO CLEANERS"! WHAT A RELIEF!
TORNADO CLEANERS INC.
3

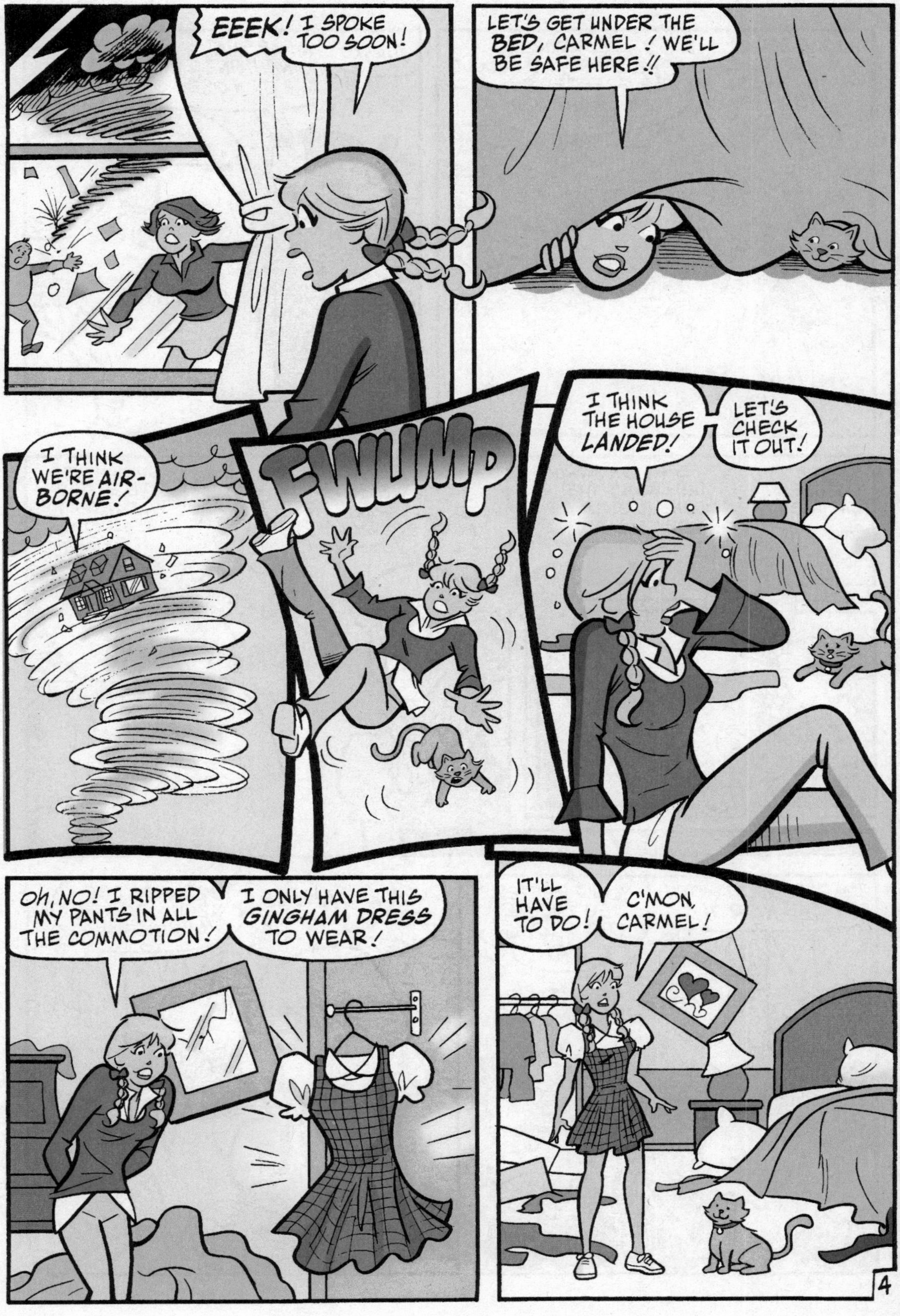
EEEK! I SPOKE TOO SOON!
LET'S GET UNDER THE BED, CARMEL! WE'LL BE SAFE HERE!!
I THINK WE'RE AIR-BORNE!
FWUMP
I THINK THE HOUSE LANDED!
LET'S CHECK IT OUT!
Oh, NO! I RIPPED MY PANTS IN ALL THE COMMOTION!
I ONLY HAVE THIS GINGHAM DRESS TO WEAR!
IT'LL HAVE TO DO!
C'MON, CARMEL!
4

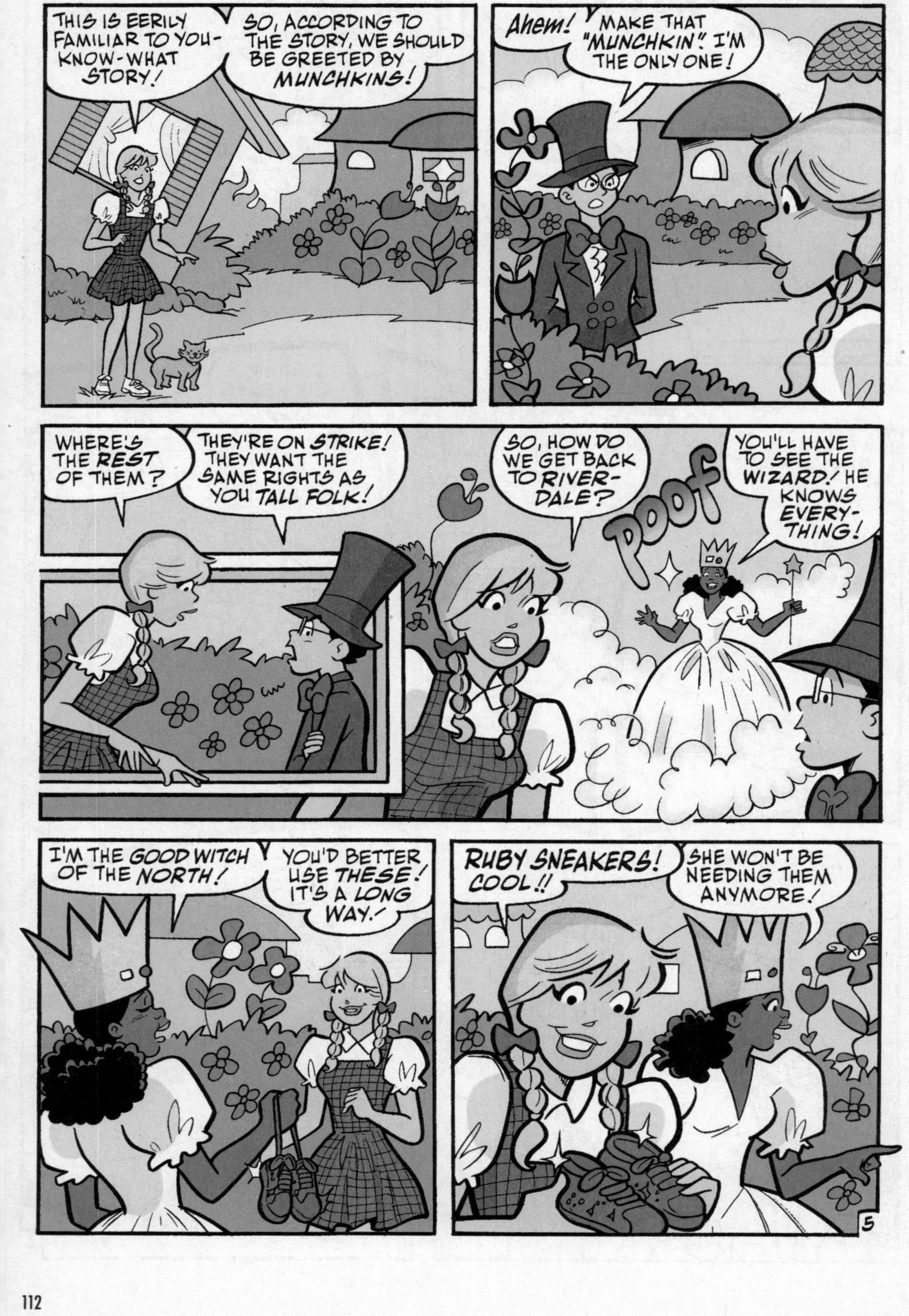
THIS IS EERILY FAMILIAR TO YOU-KNOW-WHAT STORY!
SO, ACCORDING TO THE STORY, WE SHOULD BE GREETED BY MUNCHKINS!
Ahem!
MAKE THAT "MUNCHKIN". I'M THE ONLY ONE!
WHERE'S THE REST OF THEM?
THEY'RE ON STRIKE! THEY WANT THE SAME RIGHTS AS YOU TALL FOLK!
SO, HOW DO WE GET BACK TO RIVER-DALE?
POOF
YOU'LL HAVE TO SEE THE WIZARD! HE KNOWS EVERY-THING!
I'M THE GOOD WITCH OF THE NORTH!
YOU'D BETTER USE THESE! IT'S A LONG WAY.
RUBY SNEAKERS! COOL!!
SHE WON'T BE NEEDING THEM ANYMORE!
5

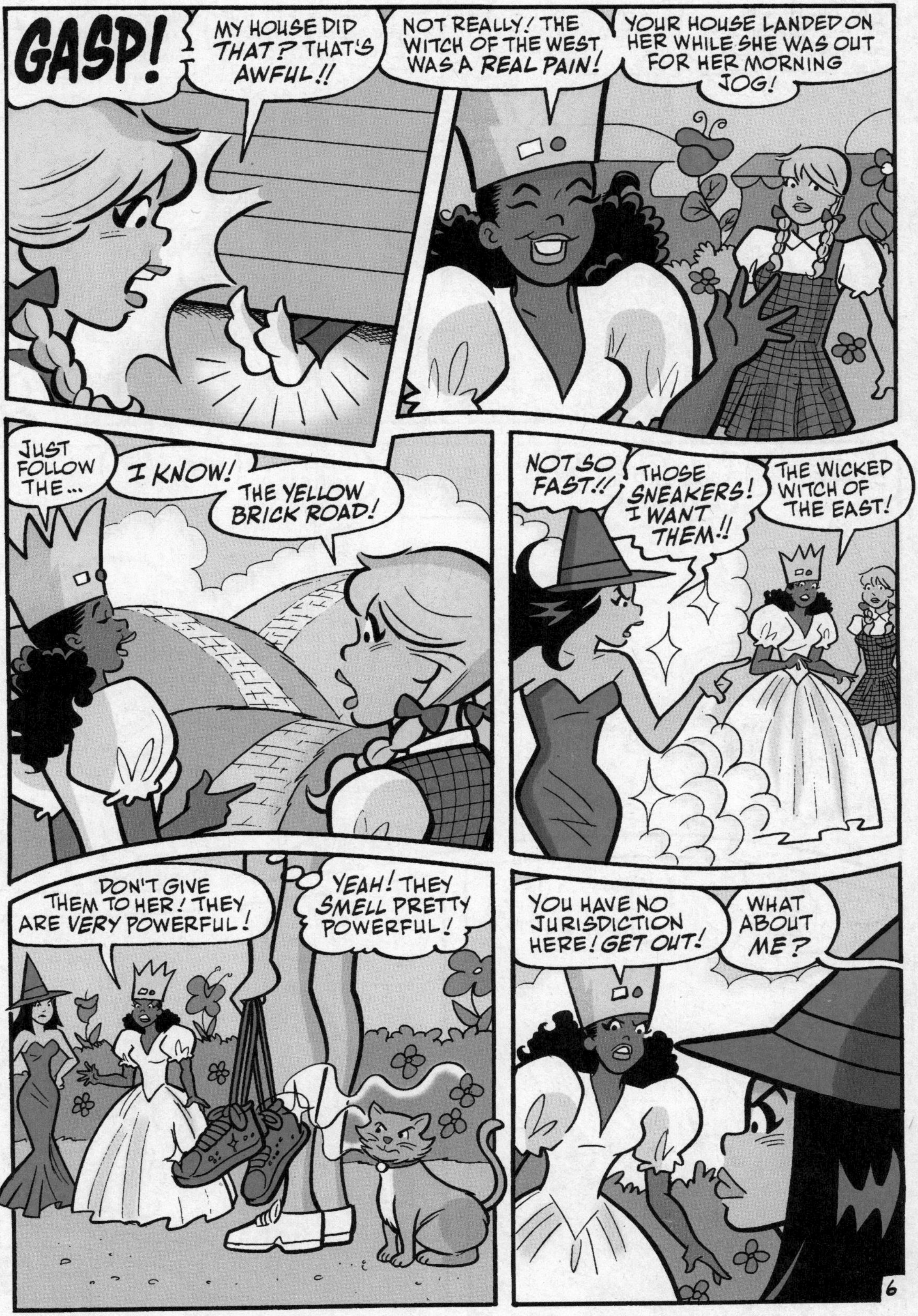
GASP!
MY HOUSE DID THAT? THAT'S AWFUL!!
NOT REALLY! THE WITCH OF THE WEST WAS A REAL PAIN!
YOUR HOUSE LANDED ON HER WHILE SHE WAS OUT FOR HER MORNING JOG!
JUST FOLLOW THE...
I KNOW!
THE YELLOW BRICK ROAD!
NOT SO FAST!!
THOSE SNEAKERS! I WANT THEM!!
THE WICKED WITCH OF THE EAST!
DON'T GIVE THEM TO HER! THEY ARE VERY POWERFUL!
YEAH! THEY SMELL PRETTY POWERFUL!
YOU HAVE NO JURISDICTION HERE! GET OUT!
WHAT ABOUT ME?
6

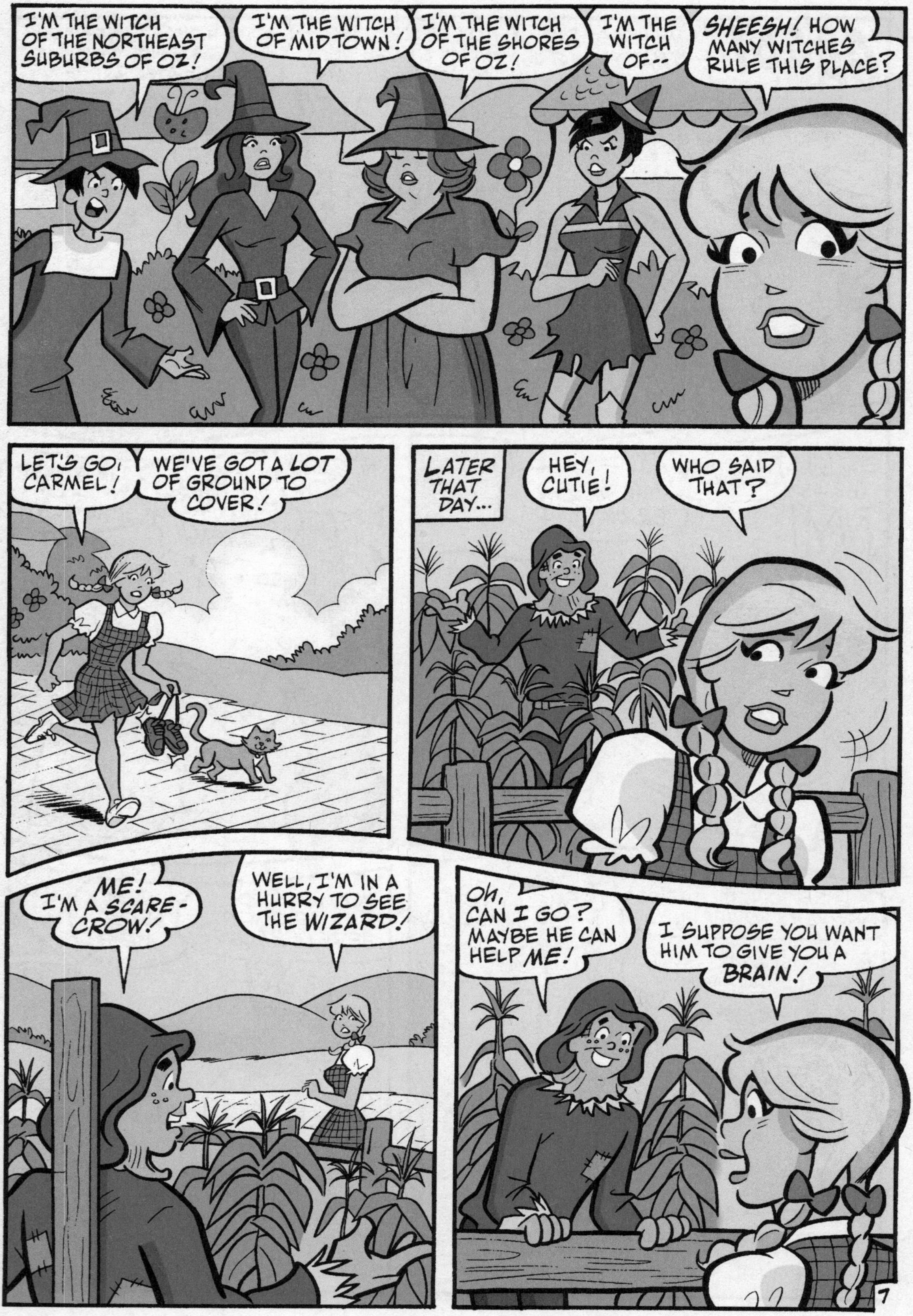
I'M THE WITCH OF THE NORTHEAST SUBURBS OF OZ!
I'M THE WITCH OF MIDTOWN!
I'M THE WITCH OF THE SHORES OF OZ!
I'M THE WITCH OF--
SHEESH! HOW MANY WITCHES RULE THIS PLACE?
LET'S GO, CARMEL!
WE'VE GOT A LOT OF GROUND TO COVER!
LATER THAT DAY...
HEY, CUTIE!
WHO SAID THAT?
ME! I'M A SCARE-CROW!
WELL, I'M IN A HURRY TO SEE THE WIZARD!
OH, CAN I GO? MAYBE HE CAN HELP ME!
I SUPPOSE YOU WANT HIM TO GIVE YOU A BRAIN!
7

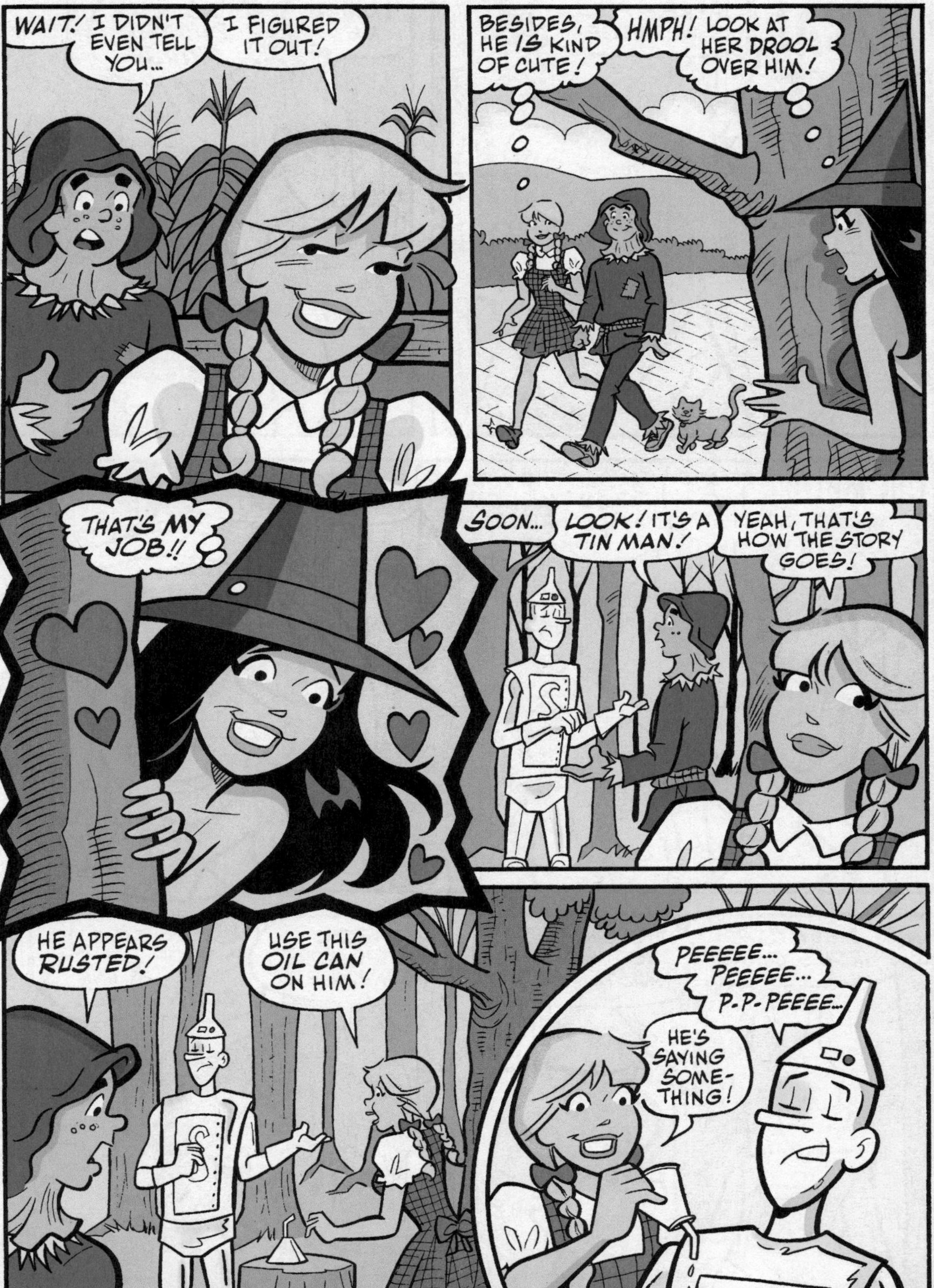

WAIT! I DIDN'T EVEN TELL YOU...
I FIGURED IT OUT!
BESIDES, HE IS KIND OF CUTE!
HMPH! LOOK AT HER DROOL OVER HIM!
THAT'S MY JOB!!
SOON...
LOOK! IT'S A TIN MAN!
YEAH, THAT'S HOW THE STORY GOES!
HE APPEARS RUSTED!
USE THIS OIL CAN ON HIM!
PEEEEE... PEEEEE... P-P-PEEEE...
HE'S SAYING SOME-THING!
8

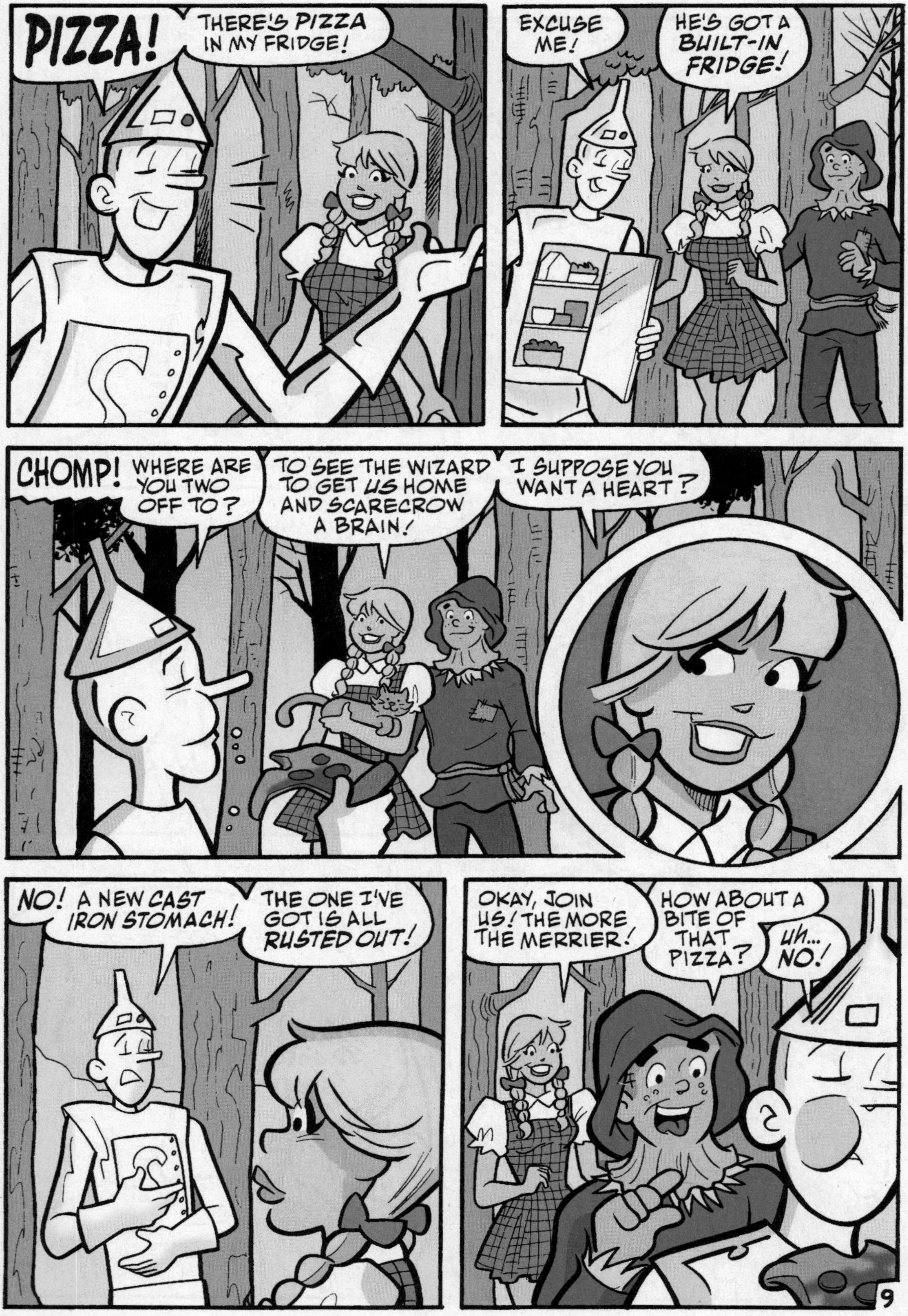
PIZZA!
THERE'S PIZZA IN MY FRIDGE!
EXCUSE ME!
HE'S GOT A BUILT-IN FRIDGE!
CHOMP!
WHERE ARE YOU TWO OFF TO?
TO SEE THE WIZARD TO GET US HOME AND SCARECROW A BRAIN!
I SUPPOSE YOU WANT A HEART?
NO! A NEW CAST IRON STOMACH!
THE ONE I'VE GOT IS ALL RUSTED OUT!
OKAY, JOIN US! THE MORE THE MERRIER!
HOW ABOUT A BITE OF THAT PIZZA?
uh... NO!
9

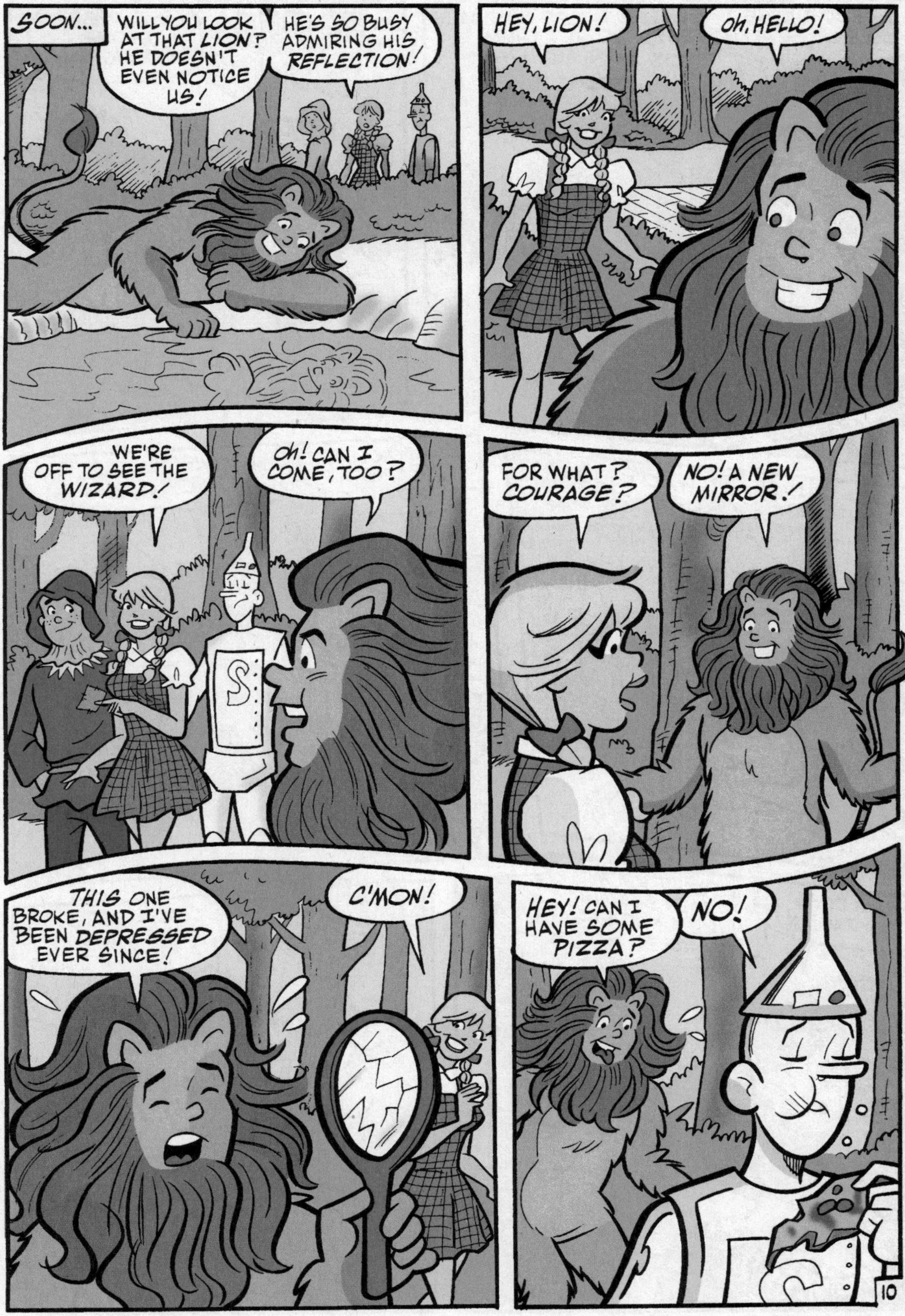
SOON...
WILL YOU LOOK AT THAT LION? HE DOESN'T EVEN NOTICE US!
HE'S SO BUSY ADMIRING HIS REFLECTION!
HEY, LION!
Oh, HELLO!
WE'RE OFF TO SEE THE WIZARD!
Oh! CAN I COME, TOO?
FOR WHAT? COURAGE?
NO! A NEW MIRROR!
THIS ONE BROKE, AND I'VE BEEN DEPRESSED EVER SINCE!
C'MON!
HEY! CAN I HAVE SOME PIZZA?
NO!
10

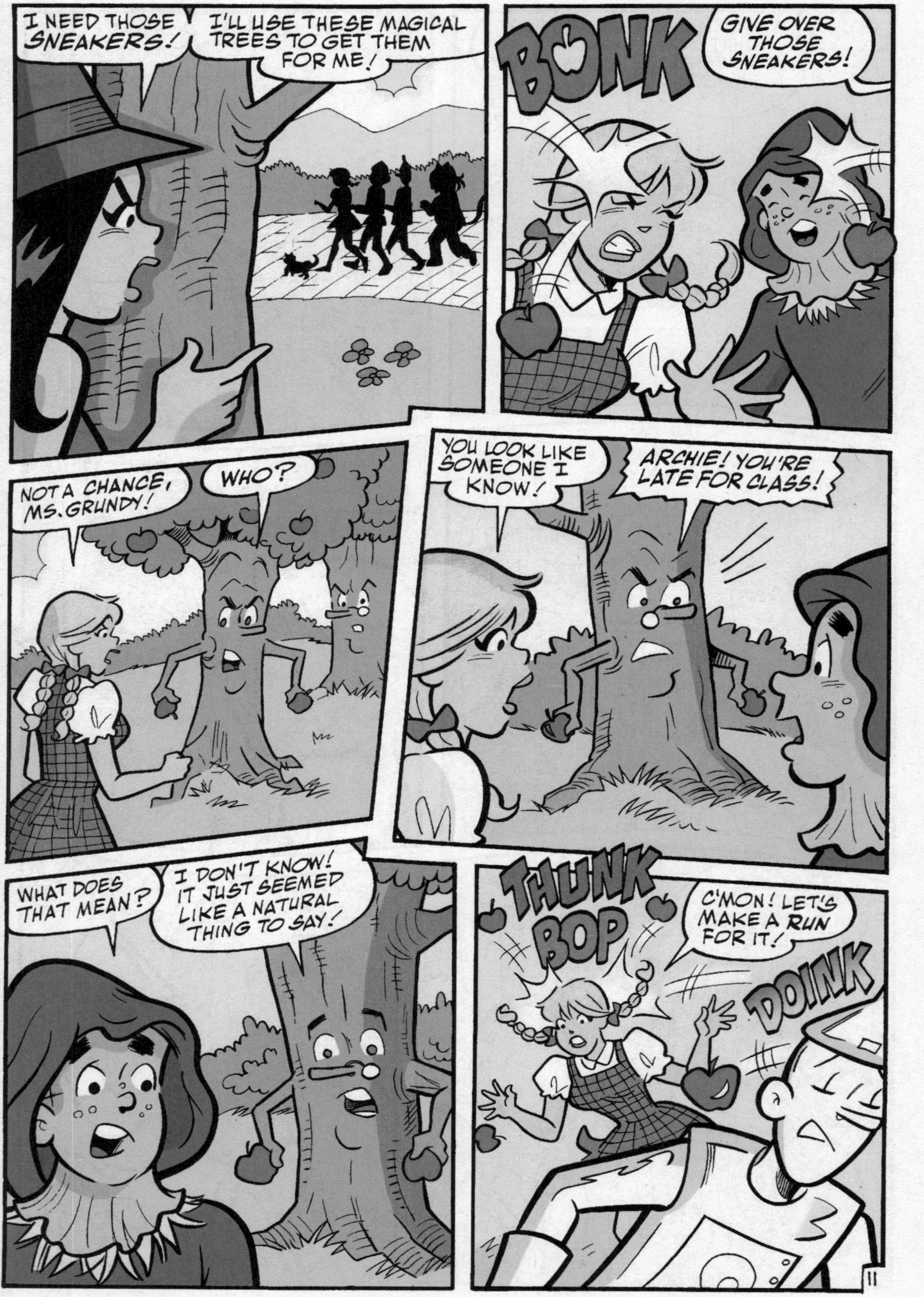
I NEED THOSE SNEAKERS!
I'LL USE THESE MAGICAL TREES TO GET THEM FOR ME!
BONK
GIVE OVER THOSE SNEAKERS!
NOT A CHANCE, MS. GRUNDY!
WHO?
YOU LOOK LIKE SOMEONE I KNOW!
ARCHIE! YOU'RE LATE FOR CLASS!
WHAT DOES THAT MEAN?
I DON'T KNOW! IT JUST SEEMED LIKE A NATURAL THING TO SAY!
THUNK
BOP
C'MON! LET'S MAKE A RUN FOR IT!
DOINK
11

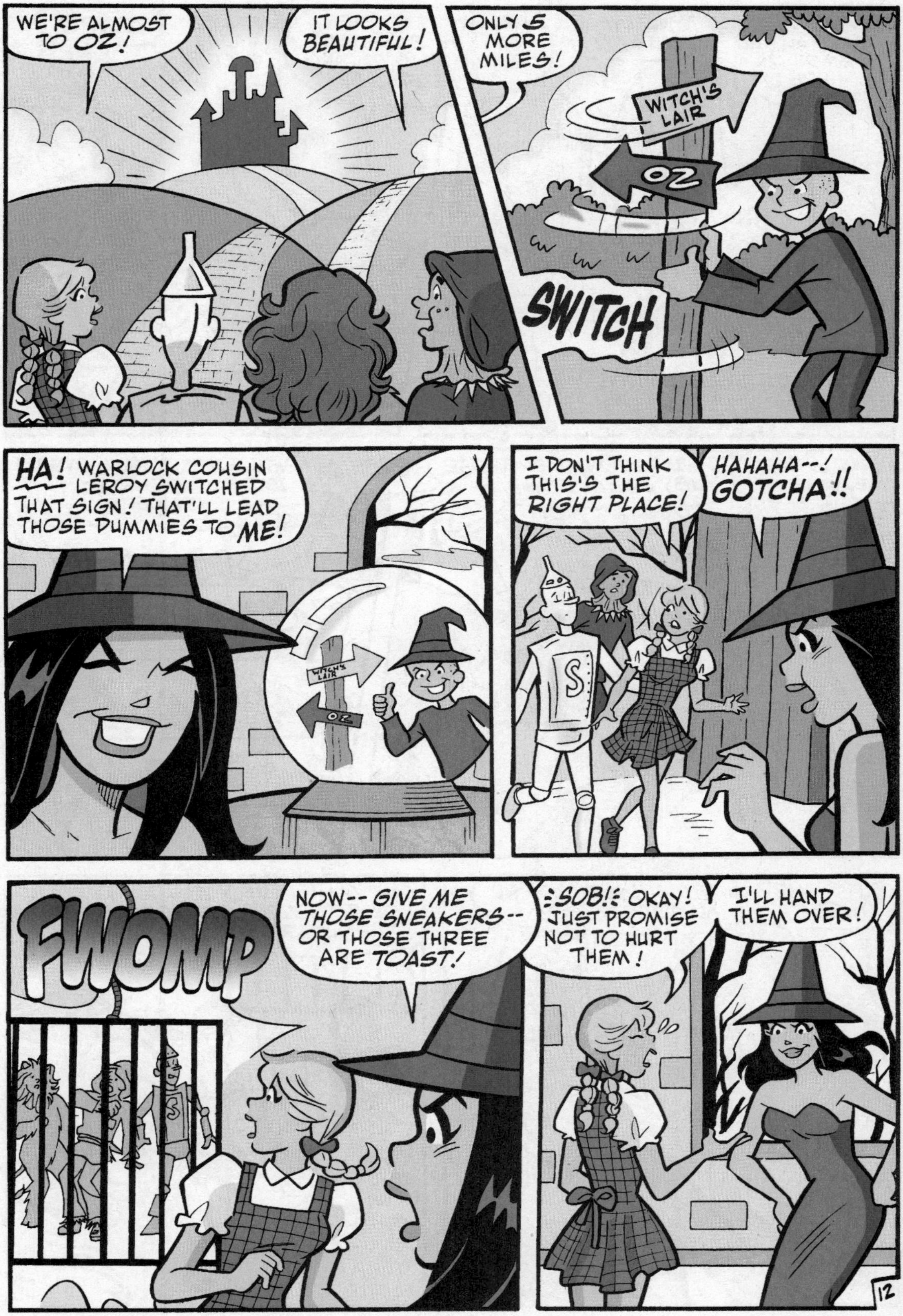
WE'RE ALMOST TO OZ!
IT LOOKS BEAUTIFUL!
ONLY 5 MORE MILES!
WITCH'S LAIR
OZ
SWITCH
HA! WARLOCK COUSIN LEROY SWITCHED THAT SIGN! THAT'LL LEAD THOSE DUMMIES TO ME!
I DON'T THINK THIS'S THE RIGHT PLACE!
HAHAHA--! GOTCHA!!
FWOMP
NOW-- GIVE ME THOSE SNEAKERS-- OR THOSE THREE ARE TOAST!
:SOB!: OKAY! JUST PROMISE NOT TO HURT THEM!
I'LL HAND THEM OVER!
12

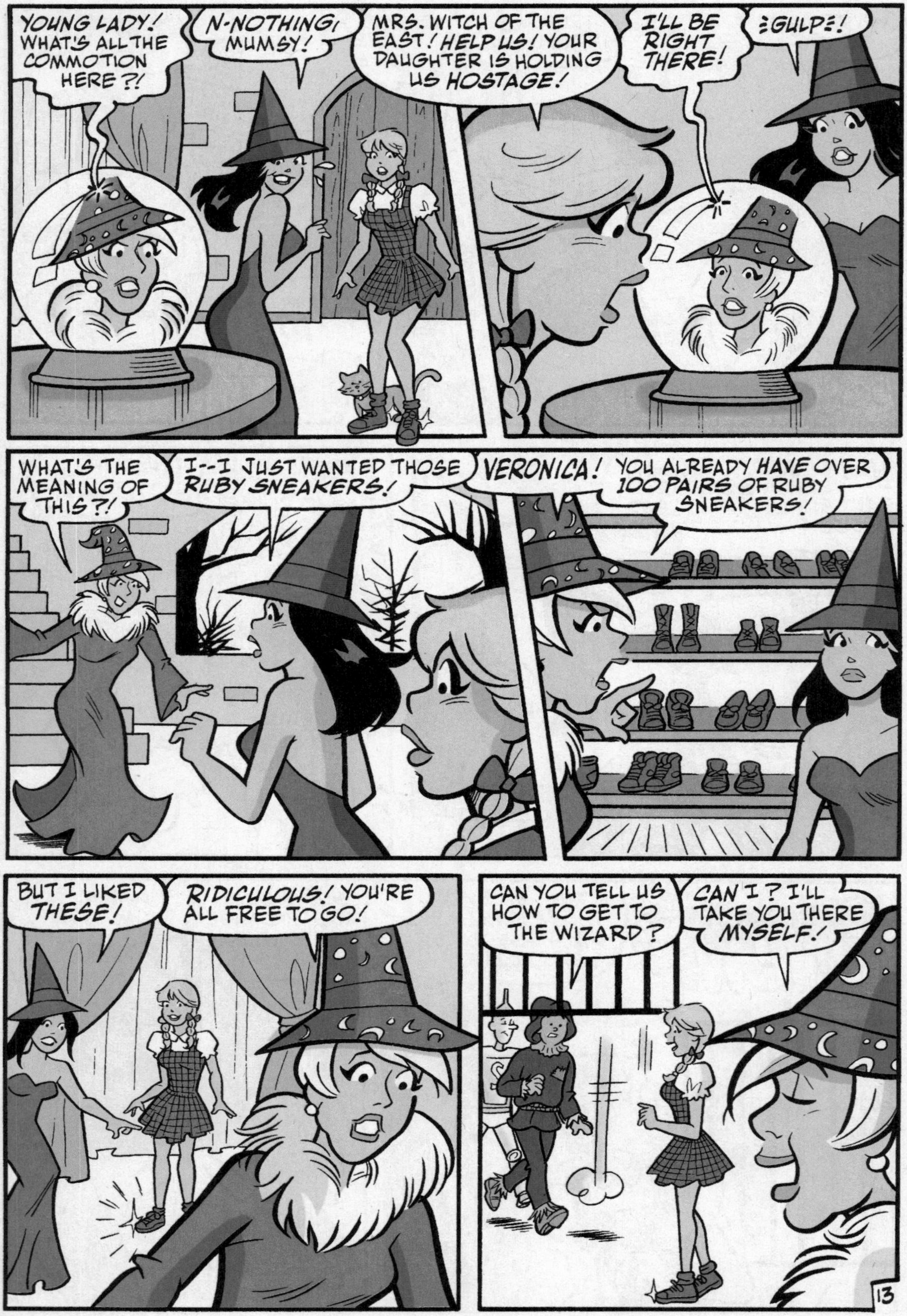
YOUNG LADY! WHAT'S ALL THE COMMOTION HERE?!
N-NOTHING, MUMSY!
MRS. WITCH OF THE EAST! HELP US! YOUR DAUGHTER IS HOLDING US HOSTAGE!
I'LL BE RIGHT THERE!
GULP!
WHAT'S THE MEANING OF THIS?!
I--I JUST WANTED THOSE RUBY SNEAKERS!
VERONICA!
YOU ALREADY HAVE OVER 100 PAIRS OF RUBY SNEAKERS!
BUT I LIKED THESE!
RIDICULOUS! YOU'RE ALL FREE TO GO!
CAN YOU TELL US HOW TO GET TO THE WIZARD?
CAN I? I'LL TAKE YOU THERE MYSELF!
13

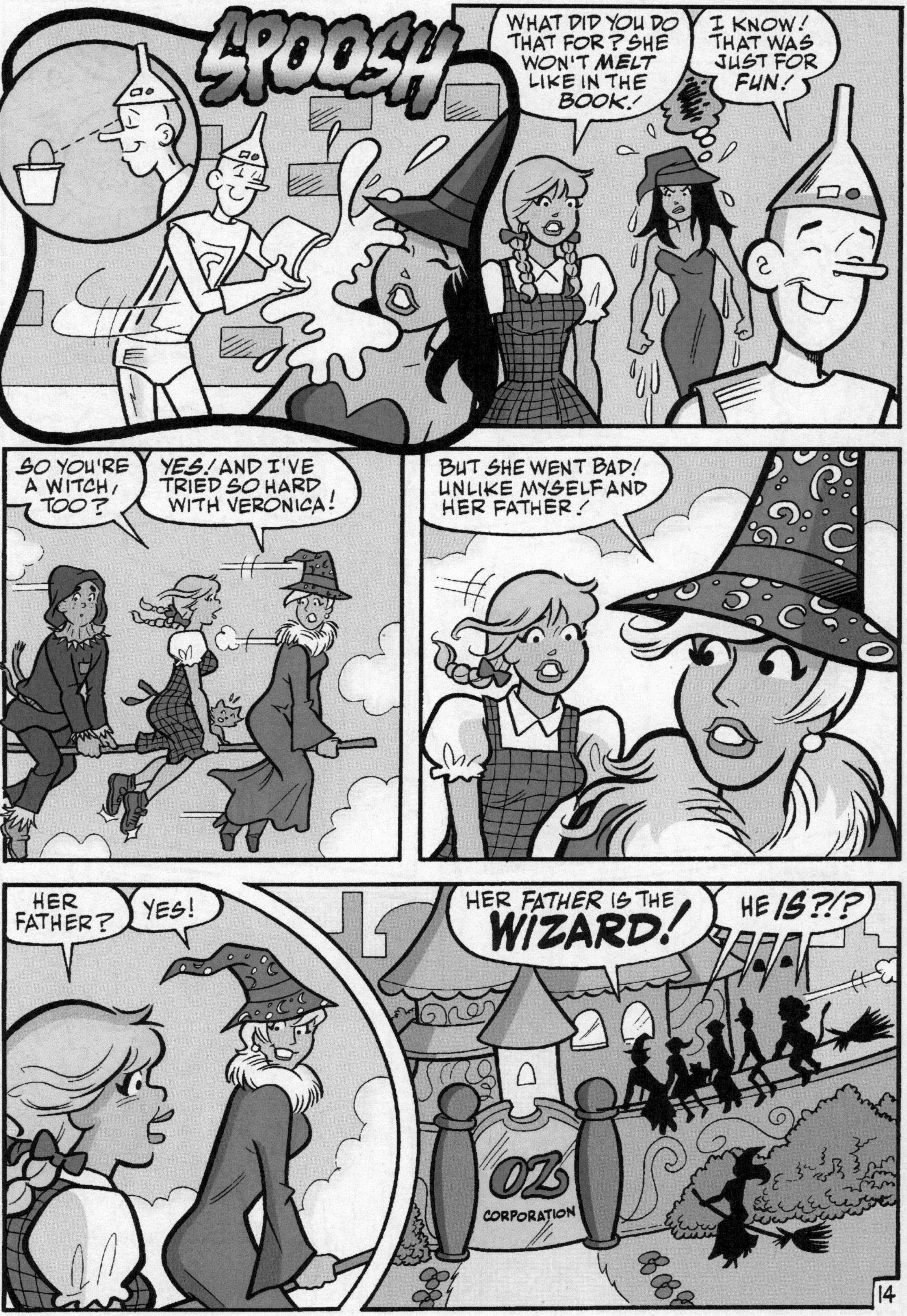
SPOOSH
WHAT DID YOU DO THAT FOR? SHE WON'T MELT LIKE IN THE BOOK!
I KNOW! THAT WAS JUST FOR FUN!
SO YOU'RE A WITCH, TOO?
YES! AND I'VE TRIED SO HARD WITH VERONICA!
BUT SHE WENT BAD! UNLIKE MYSELF AND HER FATHER!
HER FATHER?
YES!
HER FATHER IS THE WIZARD!
HE IS?!?
OZ
CORPORATION
14

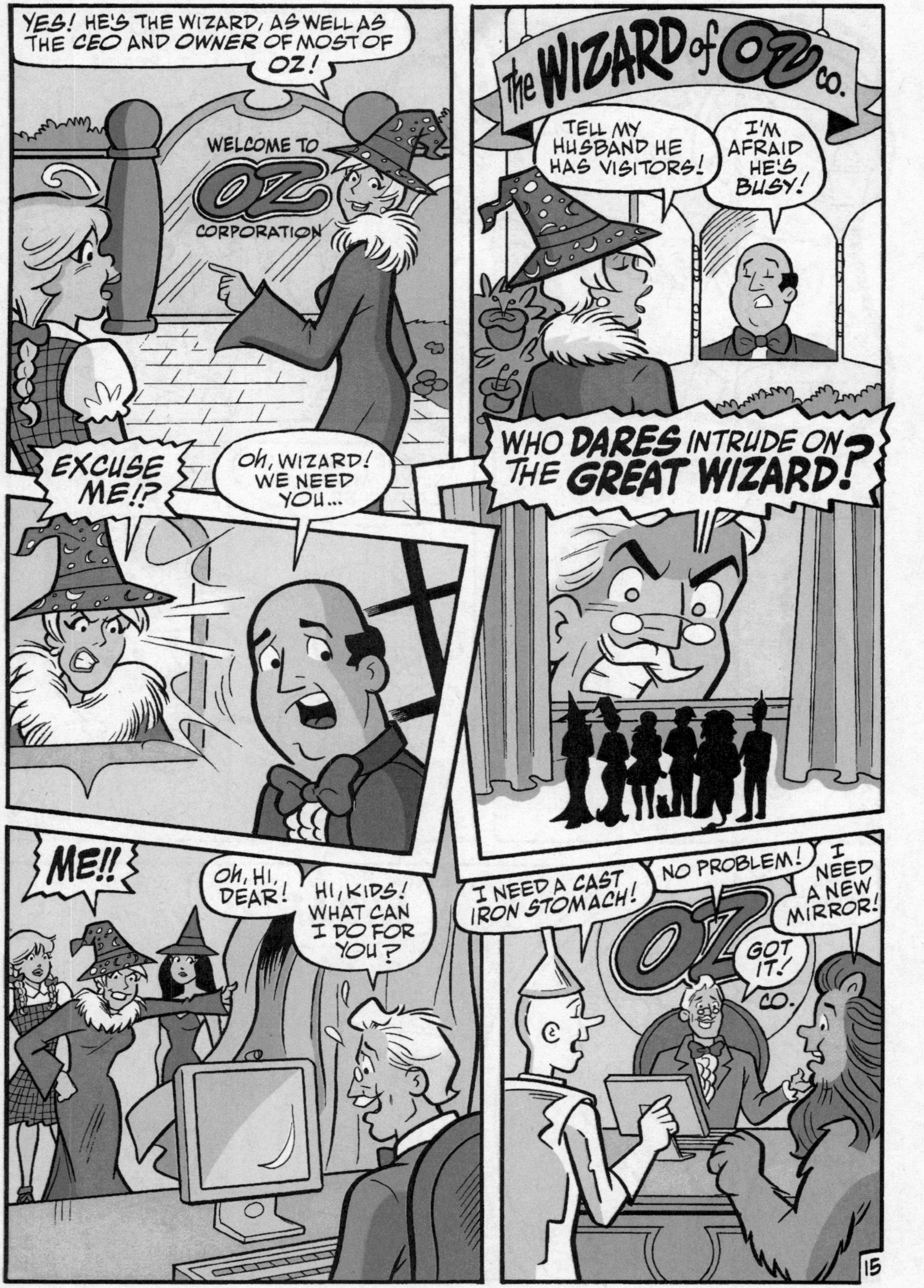
YES! HE'S THE WIZARD, AS WELL AS THE CEO AND OWNER OF MOST OF OZ!
WELCOME TO OZ CORPORATION
the WIZARD of OZ co.
TELL MY HUSBAND HE HAS VISITORS!
I'M AFRAID HE'S BUSY!
EXCUSE ME!?
Oh, WIZARD! WE NEED YOU...
WHO DARES INTRUDE ON THE GREAT WIZARD?
ME!!
Oh, HI, DEAR!
HI, KIDS! WHAT CAN I DO FOR YOU?
I NEED A CAST IRON STOMACH!
NO PROBLEM!
I NEED A NEW MIRROR!
GOT IT!
OZ CO.
15

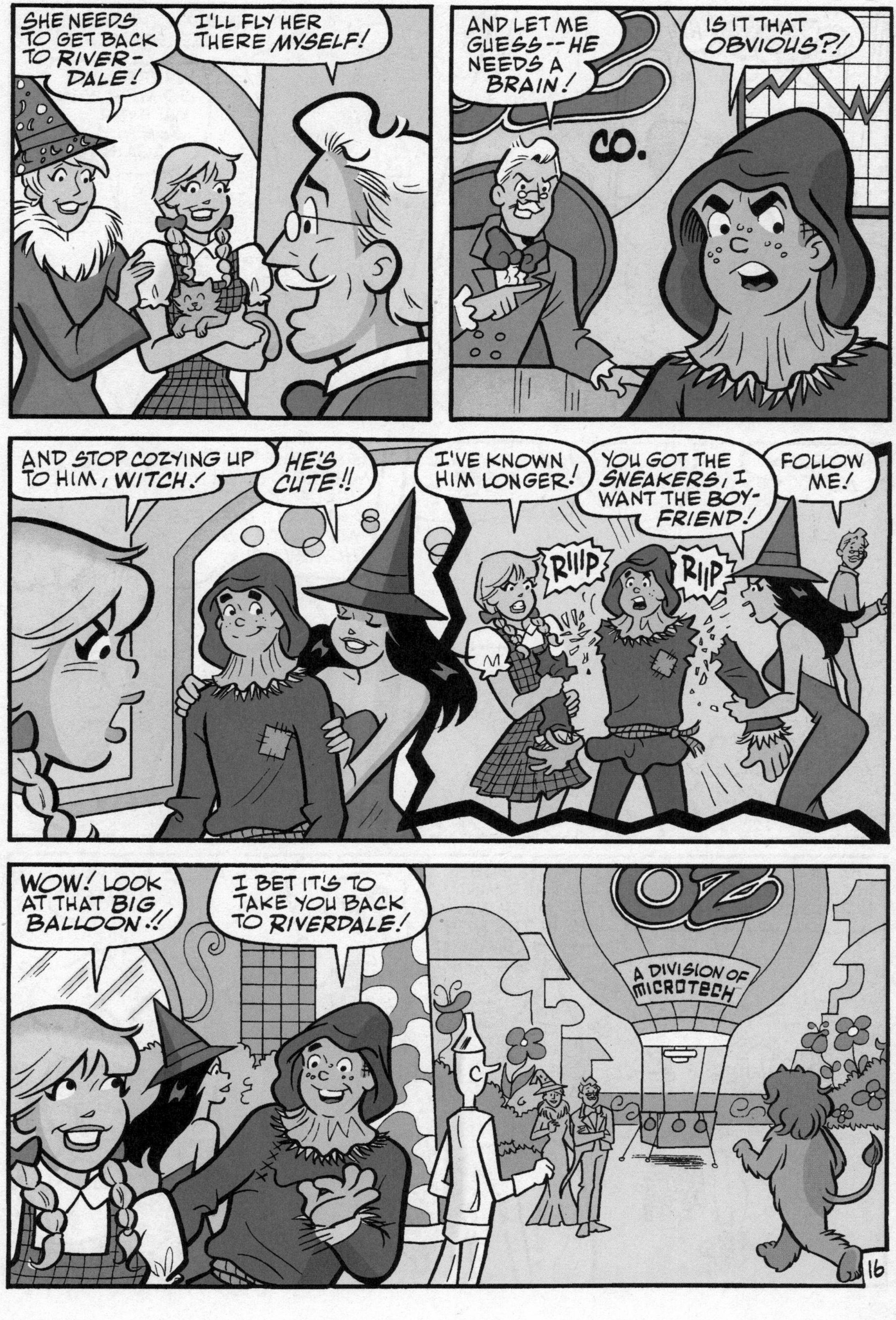
SHE NEEDS TO GET BACK TO RIVER-DALE!
I'LL FLY HER THERE MYSELF!
AND LET ME GUESS-- HE NEEDS A BRAIN!
CO.
IS IT THAT OBVIOUS?!
AND STOP COZYING UP TO HIM, WITCH!
HE'S CUTE!!
I'VE KNOWN HIM LONGER!
YOU GOT THE SNEAKERS, I WANT THE BOY-FRIEND!
FOLLOW ME!
RIIIP
RIIP
WOW! LOOK AT THAT BIG BALLOON!!
I BET IT'S TO TAKE YOU BACK TO RIVERDALE!
OZ
A DIVISION OF MICROTECH
16

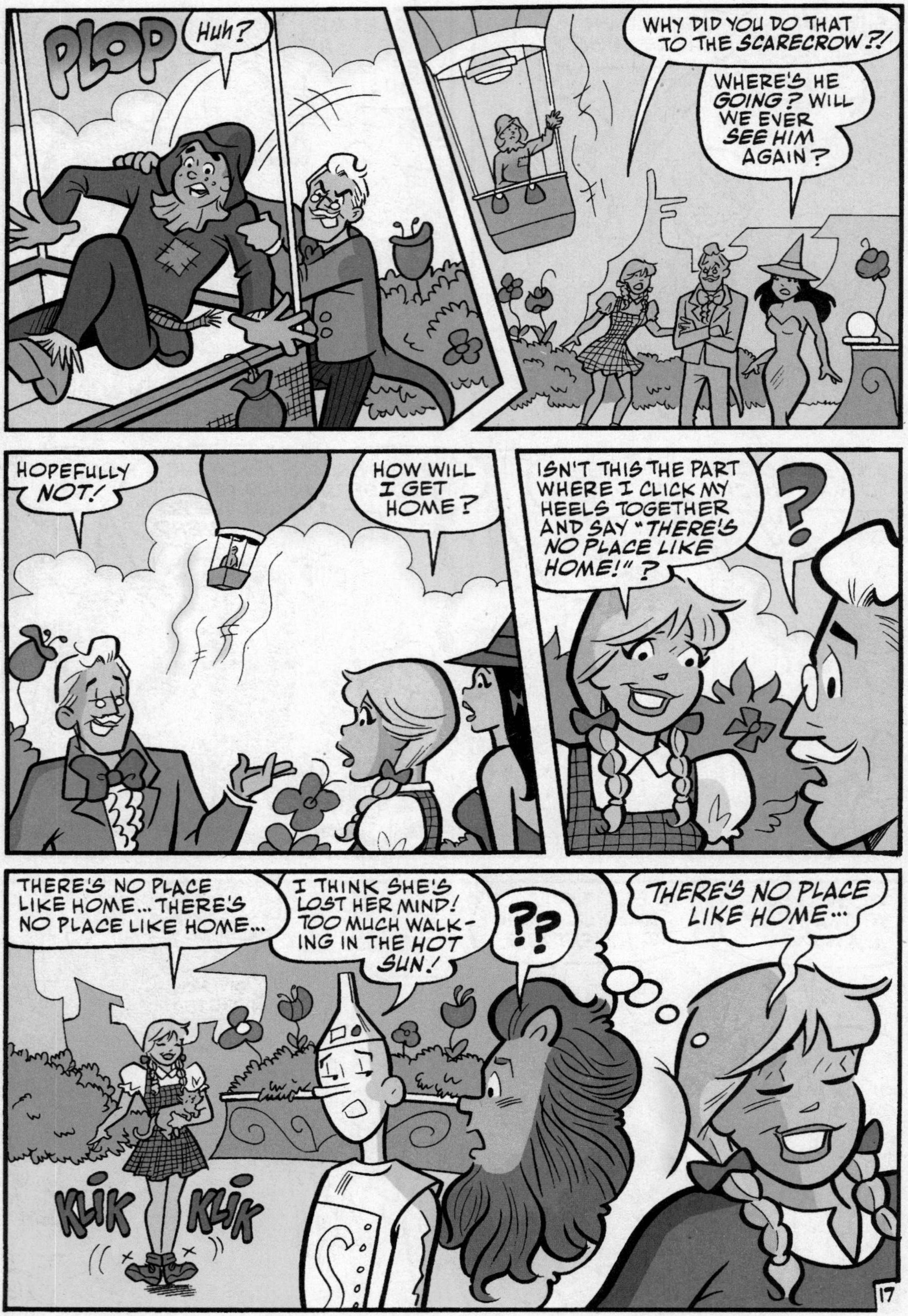
PLOP
Huh?
WHY DID YOU DO THAT TO THE SCARECROW?!
WHERE'S HE GOING? WILL WE EVER SEE HIM AGAIN?
HOPEFULLY NOT!
HOW WILL I GET HOME?
ISN'T THIS THE PART WHERE I CLICK MY HEELS TOGETHER AND SAY "THERE'S NO PLACE LIKE HOME!"?
?
THERE'S NO PLACE LIKE HOME... THERE'S NO PLACE LIKE HOME...
I THINK SHE'S LOST HER MIND! TOO MUCH WALKING IN THE HOT SUN!
??
THERE'S NO PLACE LIKE HOME...
KLIK KLIK
17

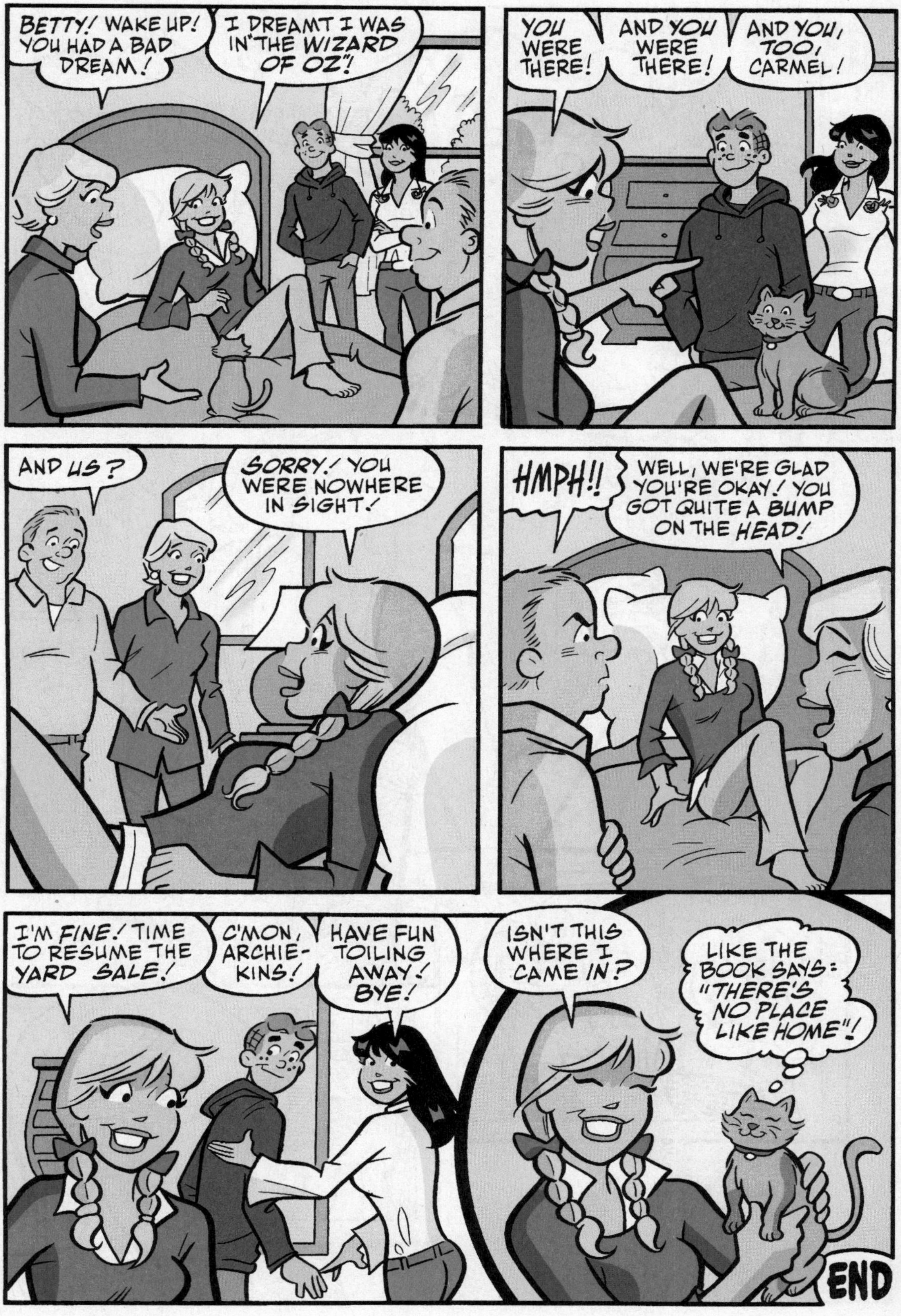
BETTY! WAKE UP! YOU HAD A BAD DREAM!
I DREAMT I WAS IN "THE WIZARD OF OZ"!
YOU WERE THERE!
AND YOU WERE THERE!
AND YOU, TOO, CARMEL!
AND US?
SORRY! YOU WERE NOWHERE IN SIGHT!
HMPH!!
WELL, WE'RE GLAD YOU'RE OKAY! YOU GOT QUITE A BUMP ON THE HEAD!
I'M FINE! TIME TO RESUME THE YARD SALE!
C'MON, ARCHIE-KINS!
HAVE FUN TOILING AWAY! BYE!
ISN'T THIS WHERE I CAME IN?
LIKE THE BOOK SAYS: "THERE'S NO PLACE LIKE HOME"!
END

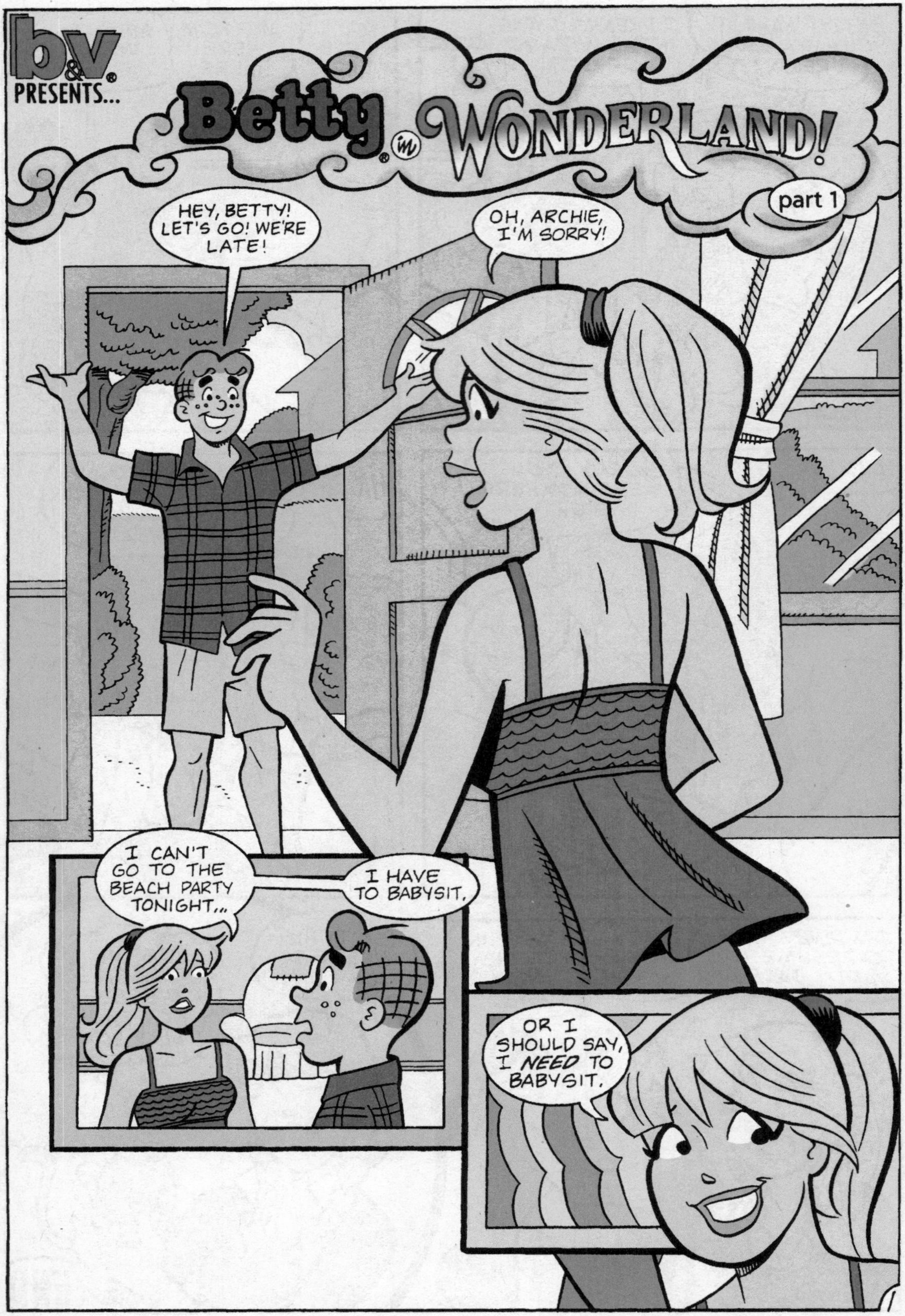
b&v PRESENTS...
Betty in WONDERLAND!
part 1
HEY, BETTY! LET'S GO! WE'RE LATE!
OH, ARCHIE, I'M SORRY!
I CAN'T GO TO THE BEACH PARTY TONIGHT...
I HAVE TO BABYSIT.
OR I SHOULD SAY, I *NEED* TO BABYSIT.
1

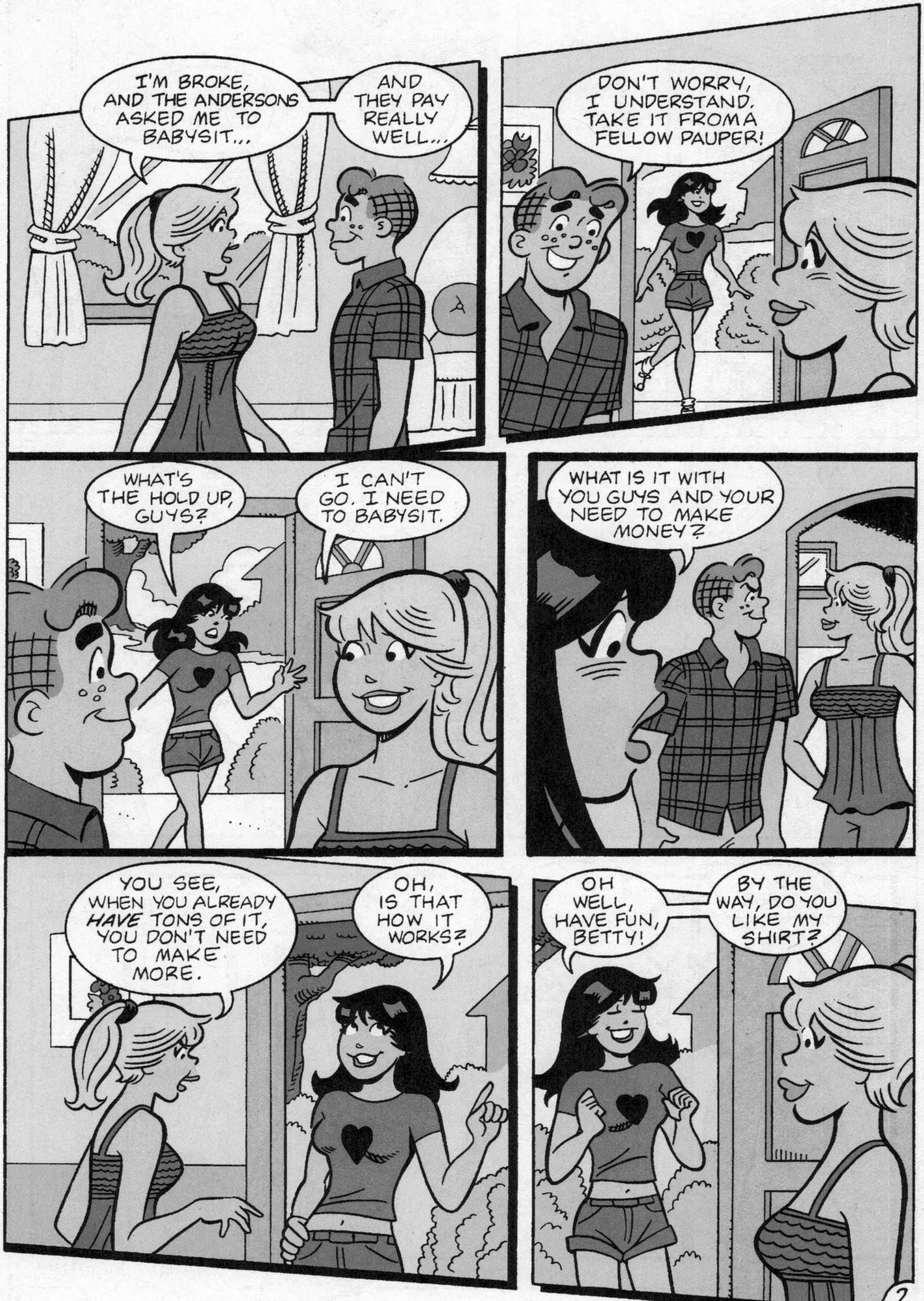
I'M BROKE, AND THE ANDERSONS ASKED ME TO BABYSIT...
AND THEY PAY REALLY WELL...
DON'T WORRY, I UNDERSTAND. TAKE IT FROM A FELLOW PAUPER!
WHAT'S THE HOLD UP, GUYS?
I CAN'T GO. I NEED TO BABYSIT.
WHAT IS IT WITH YOU GUYS AND YOUR NEED TO MAKE MONEY?
YOU SEE, WHEN YOU ALREADY *HAVE* TONS OF IT, YOU DON'T NEED TO MAKE MORE.
OH, IS THAT HOW IT WORKS?
OH WELL, HAVE FUN, BETTY!
BY THE WAY, DO YOU LIKE MY SHIRT?
2

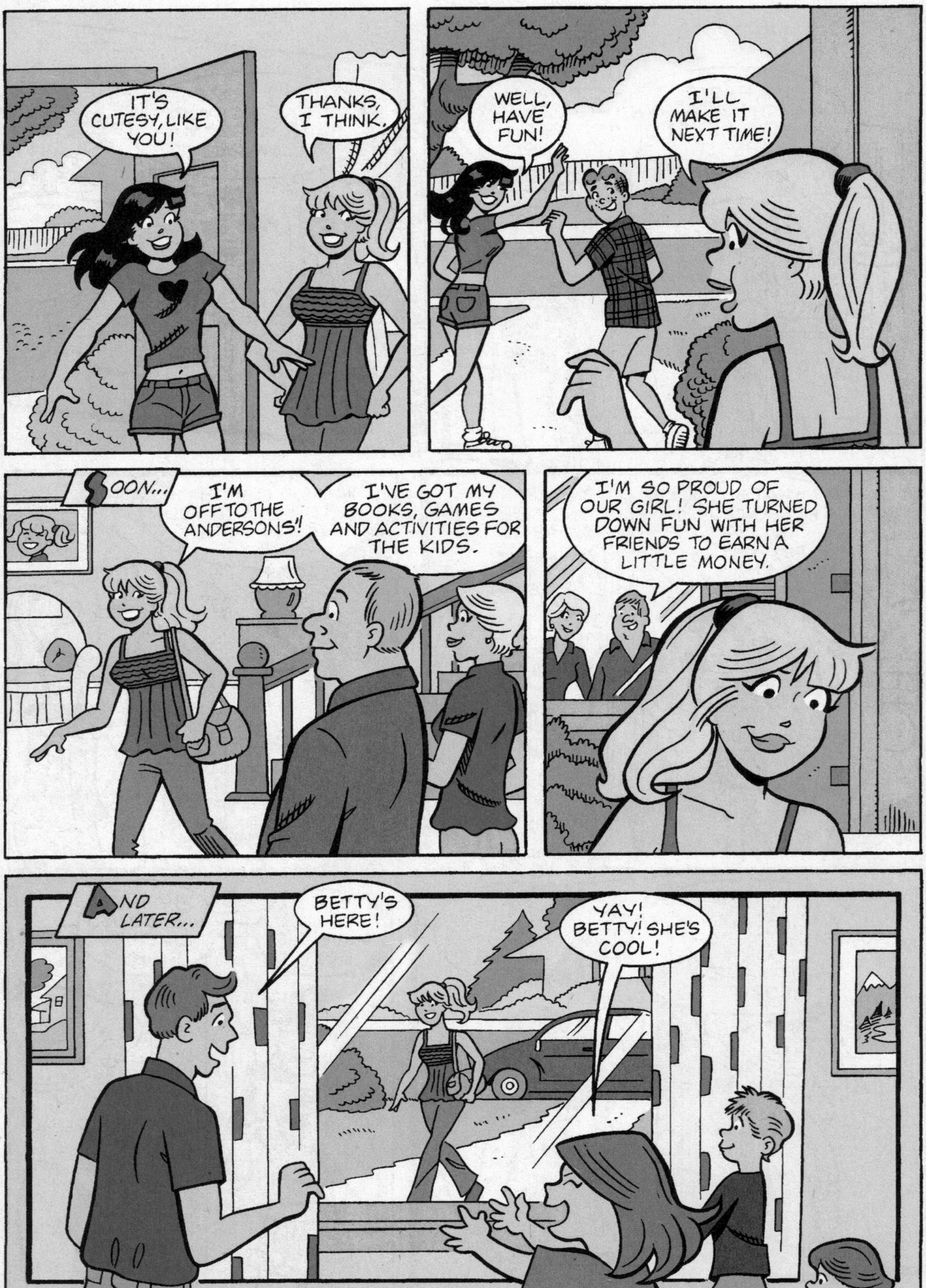
IT'S CUTESY, LIKE YOU!
THANKS, I THINK.
WELL, HAVE FUN!
I'LL MAKE IT NEXT TIME!
SOON...
I'M OFF TO THE ANDERSONS'!
I'VE GOT MY BOOKS, GAMES AND ACTIVITIES FOR THE KIDS.
I'M SO PROUD OF OUR GIRL! SHE TURNED DOWN FUN WITH HER FRIENDS TO EARN A LITTLE MONEY.
AND LATER...
BETTY'S HERE!
YAY! BETTY! SHE'S COOL!
3

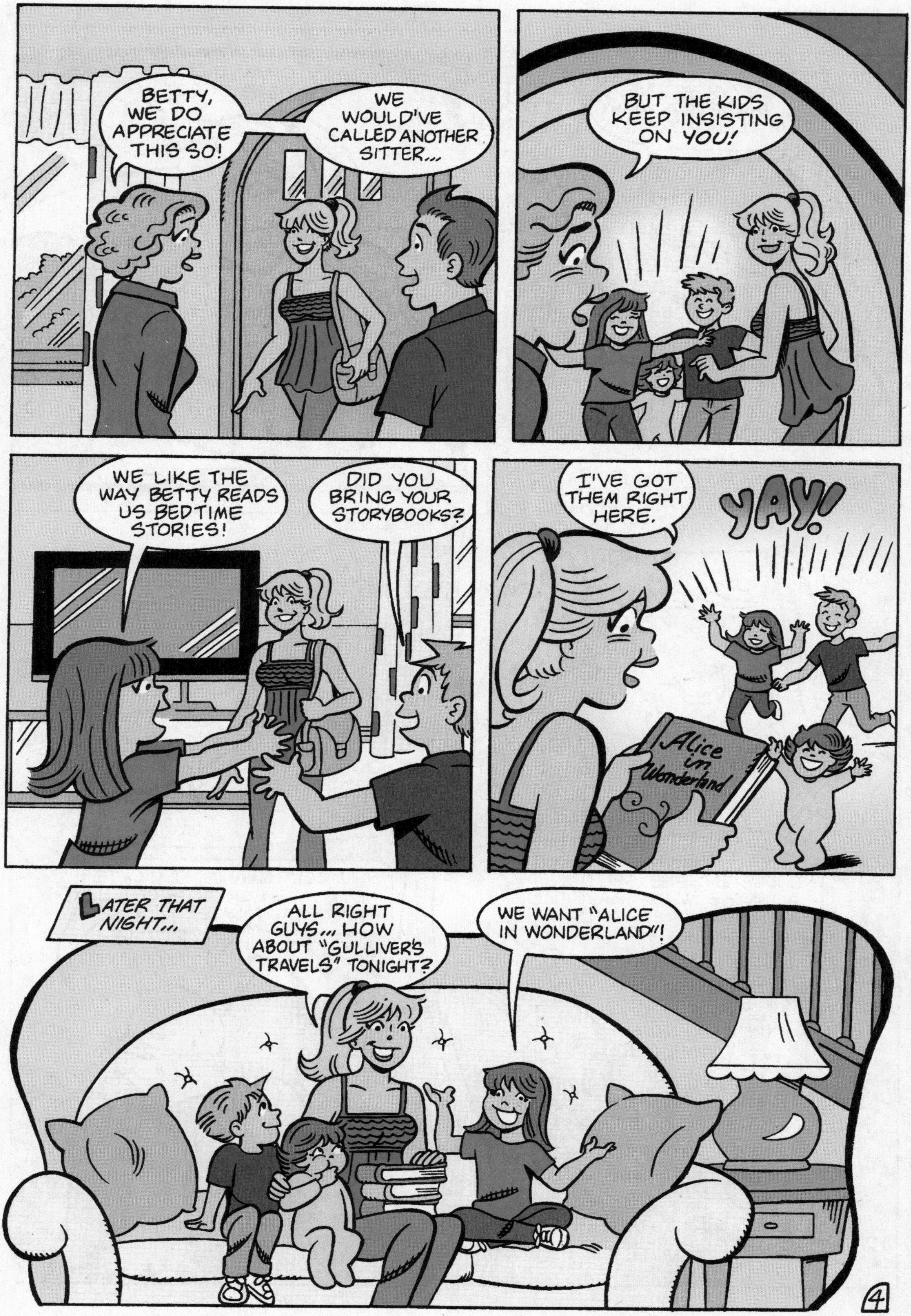
BETTY, WE DO APPRECIATE THIS SO!
WE WOULD'VE CALLED ANOTHER SITTER...
BUT THE KIDS KEEP INSISTING ON YOU!
WE LIKE THE WAY BETTY READS US BEDTIME STORIES!
DID YOU BRING YOUR STORYBOOKS?
I'VE GOT THEM RIGHT HERE.
YAY!
Alice in Wonderland
LATER THAT NIGHT...
ALL RIGHT GUYS... HOW ABOUT "GULLIVER'S TRAVELS" TONIGHT?
WE WANT "ALICE IN WONDERLAND"!
4

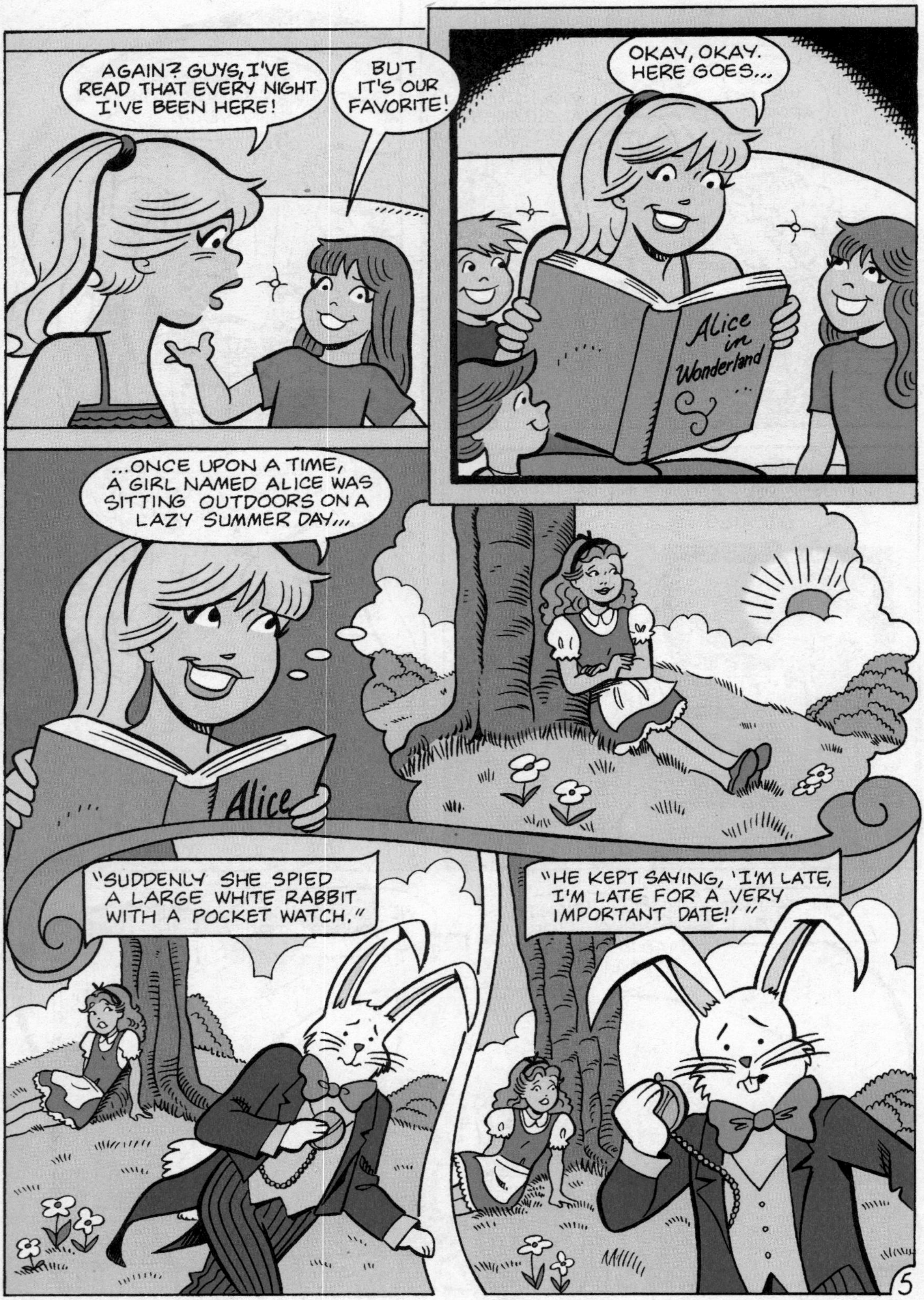
AGAIN? GUYS, I'VE READ THAT EVERY NIGHT I'VE BEEN HERE!
BUT IT'S OUR FAVORITE!
OKAY, OKAY. HERE GOES...
Alice in Wonderland
...ONCE UPON A TIME, A GIRL NAMED ALICE WAS SITTING OUTDOORS ON A LAZY SUMMER DAY...
Alice
"SUDDENLY SHE SPIED A LARGE WHITE RABBIT WITH A POCKET WATCH."
"HE KEPT SAYING, 'I'M LATE, I'M LATE FOR A VERY IMPORTANT DATE!'"
5

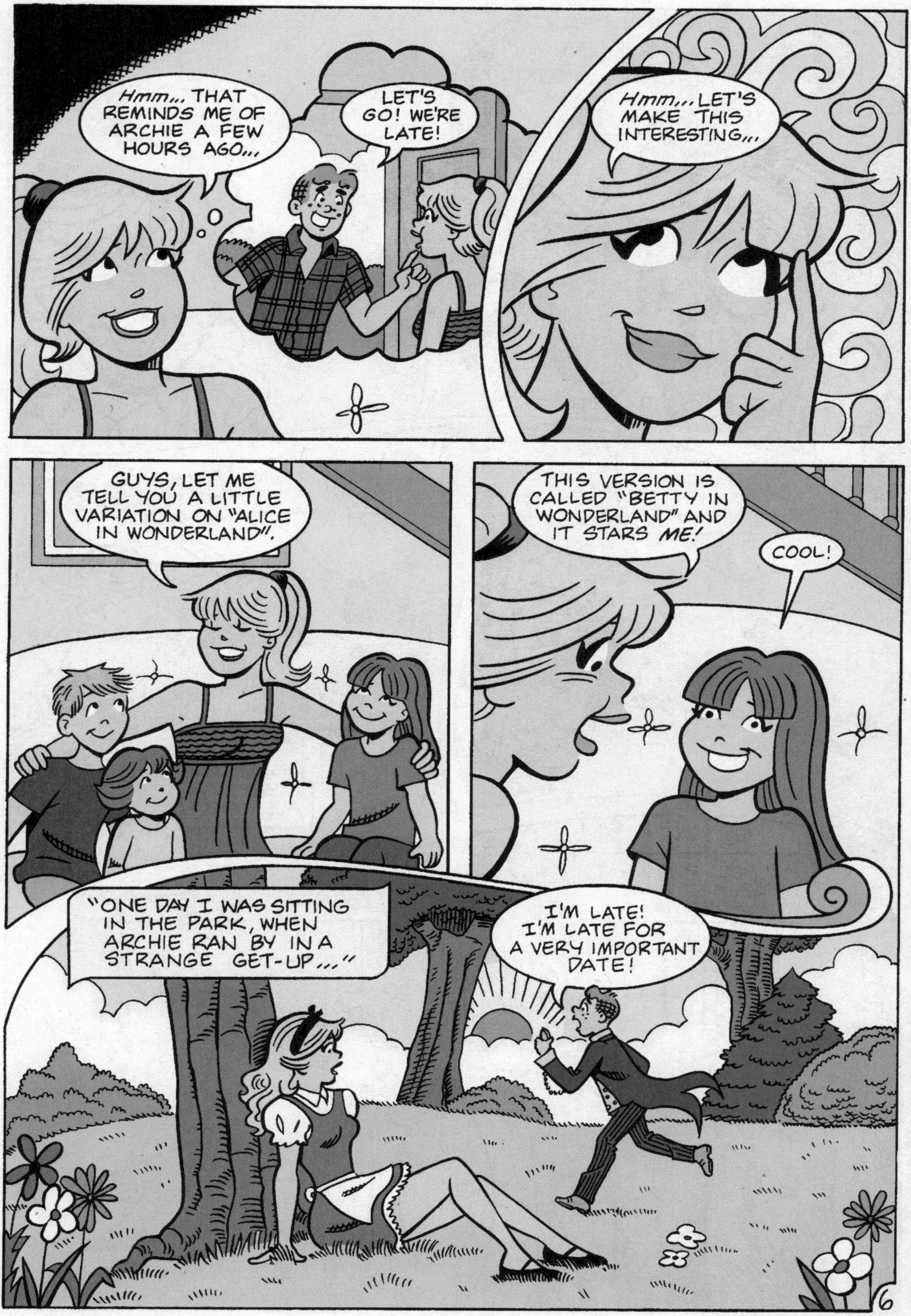
Hmm... THAT REMINDS ME OF ARCHIE A FEW HOURS AGO...
LET'S GO! WE'RE LATE!
Hmm... LET'S MAKE THIS INTERESTING...
GUYS, LET ME TELL YOU A LITTLE VARIATION ON "ALICE IN WONDERLAND".
THIS VERSION IS CALLED "BETTY IN WONDERLAND" AND IT STARS ME!
COOL!
"ONE DAY I WAS SITTING IN THE PARK, WHEN ARCHIE RAN BY IN A STRANGE GET-UP..."
I'M LATE! I'M LATE FOR A VERY IMPORTANT DATE!
6

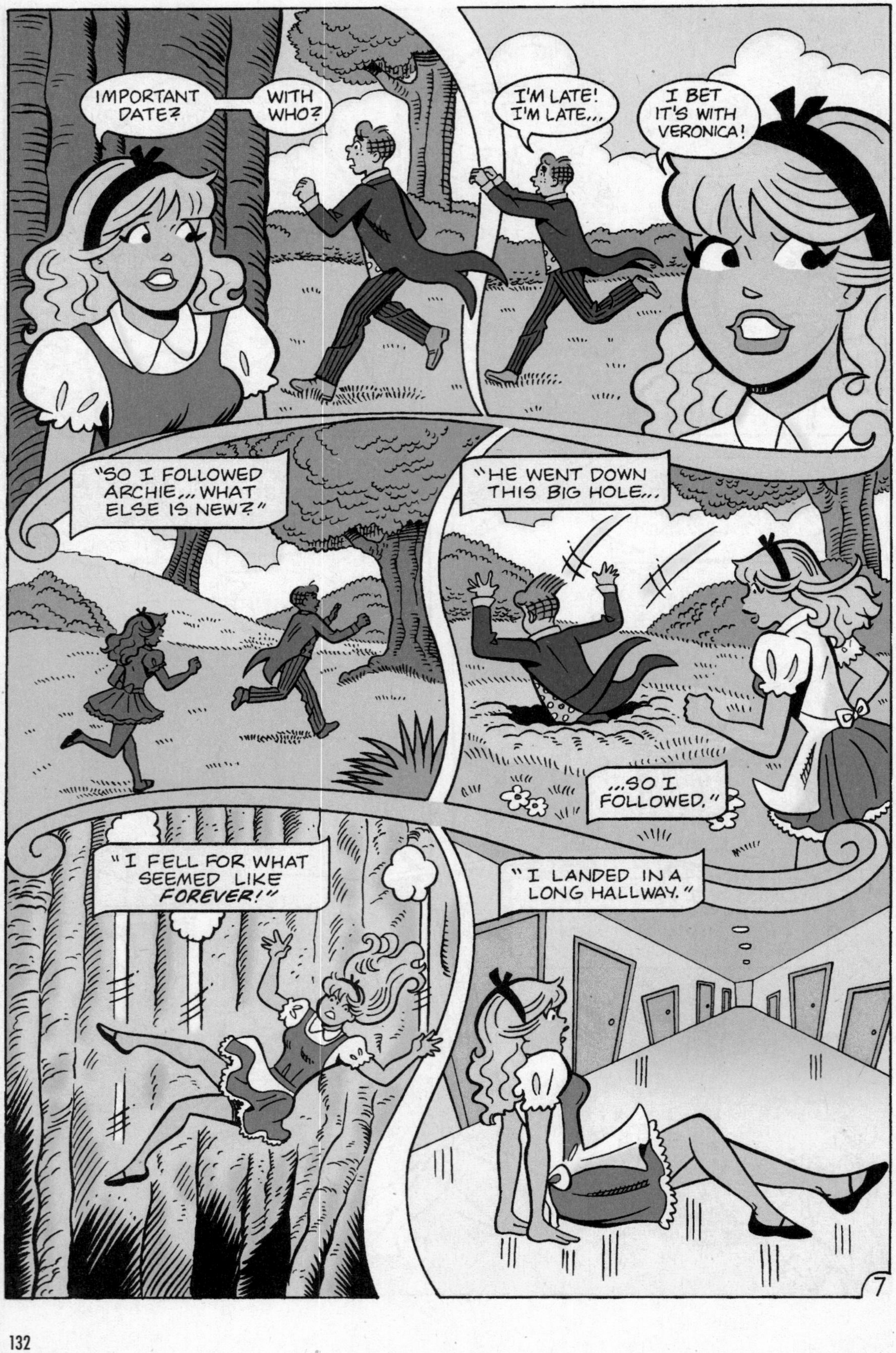
IMPORTANT DATE?
WITH WHO?
I'M LATE! I'M LATE...
I BET IT'S WITH VERONICA!
"SO I FOLLOWED ARCHIE... WHAT ELSE IS NEW?"
"HE WENT DOWN THIS BIG HOLE...
...SO I FOLLOWED."
"I FELL FOR WHAT SEEMED LIKE *FOREVER!*"
"I LANDED IN A LONG HALLWAY."
7

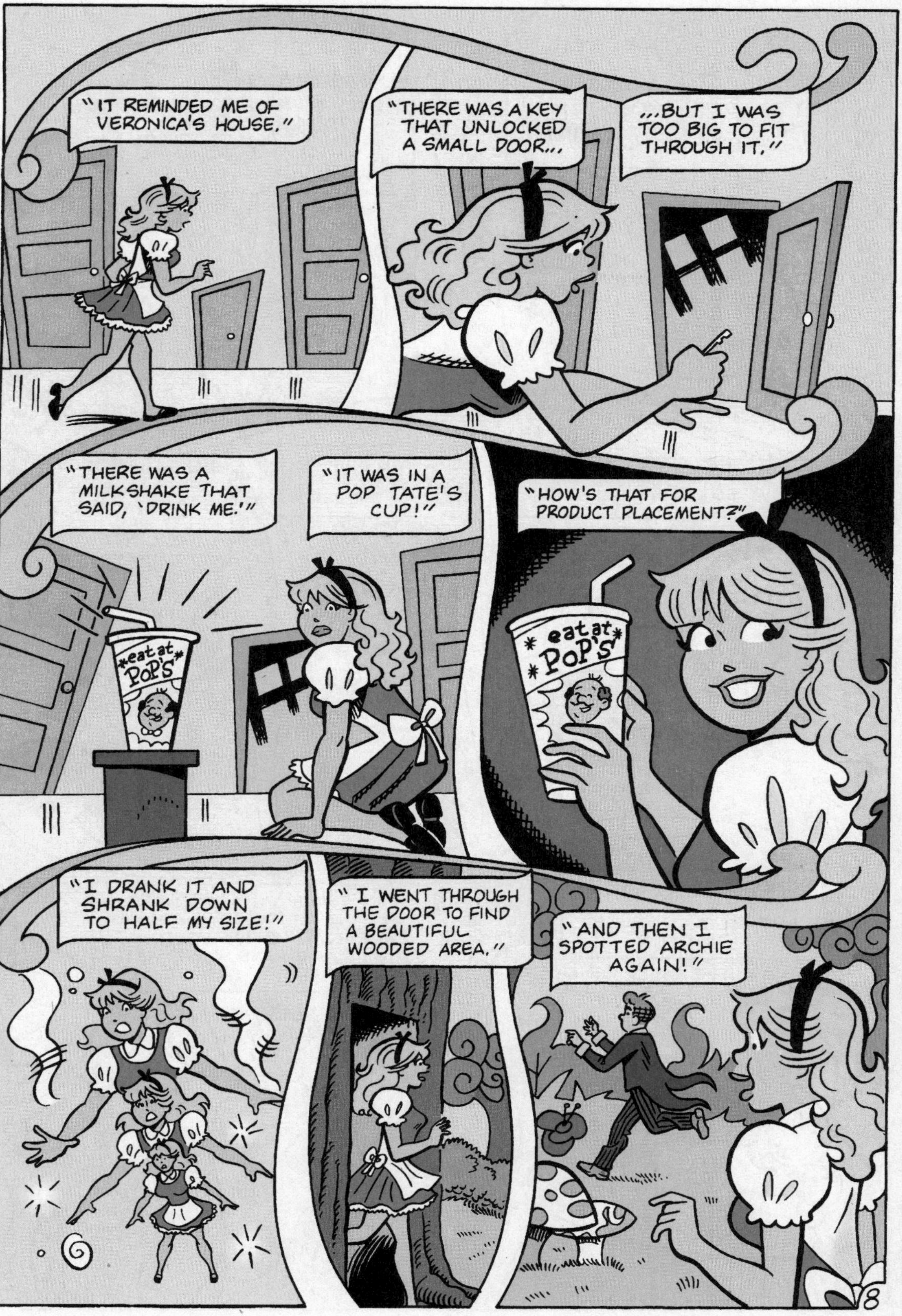
"IT REMINDED ME OF VERONICA'S HOUSE."
"THERE WAS A KEY THAT UNLOCKED A SMALL DOOR...
...BUT I WAS TOO BIG TO FIT THROUGH IT."
"THERE WAS A MILKSHAKE THAT SAID, 'DRINK ME.'"
"IT WAS IN A POP TATE'S CUP!"
eat at POP'S
"HOW'S THAT FOR PRODUCT PLACEMENT?"
eat at POP'S
"I DRANK IT AND SHRANK DOWN TO HALF MY SIZE!"
" I WENT THROUGH THE DOOR TO FIND A BEAUTIFUL WOODED AREA."
"AND THEN I SPOTTED ARCHIE AGAIN!"
8

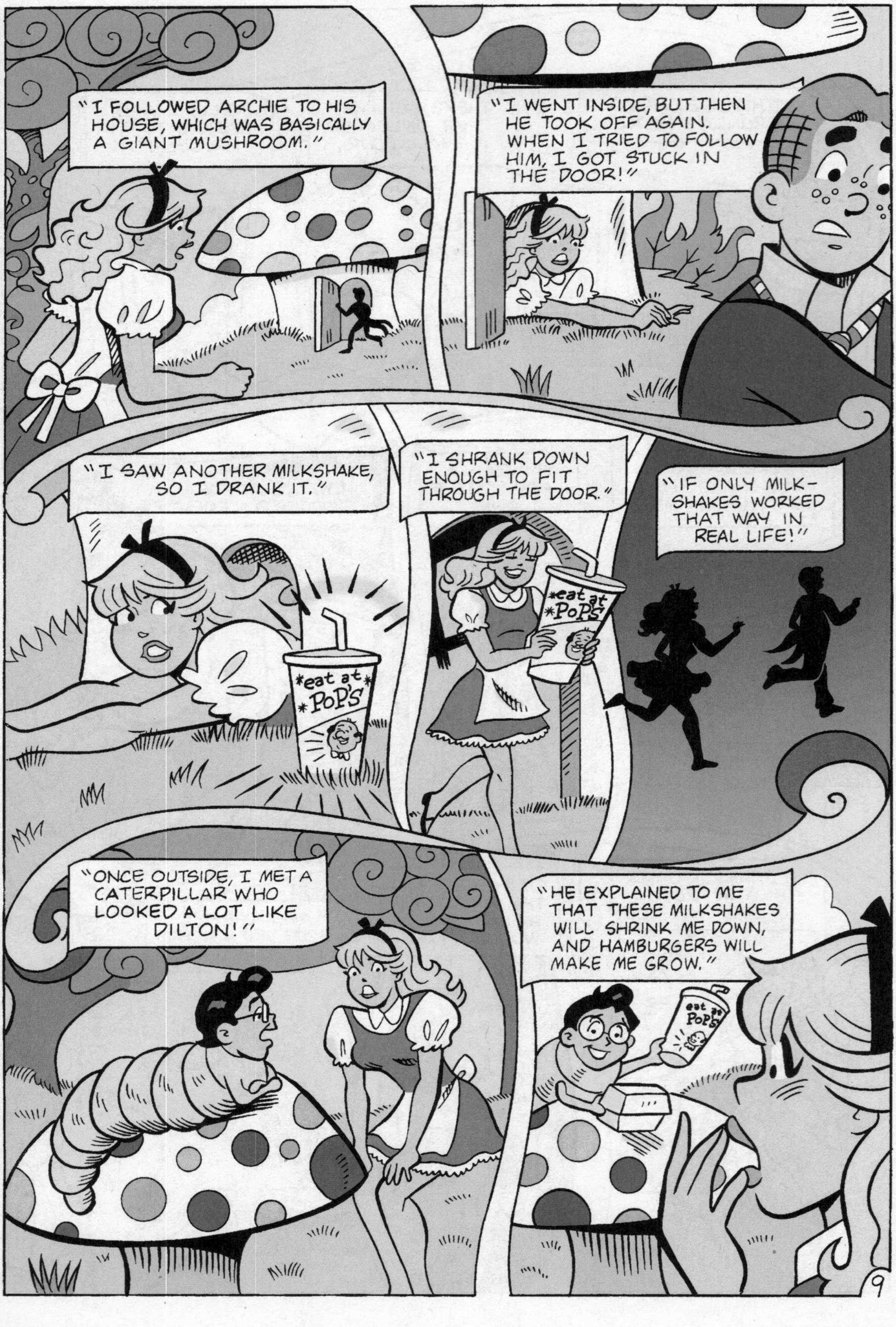
"I FOLLOWED ARCHIE TO HIS HOUSE, WHICH WAS BASICALLY A GIANT MUSHROOM."
"I WENT INSIDE, BUT THEN HE TOOK OFF AGAIN. WHEN I TRIED TO FOLLOW HIM, I GOT STUCK IN THE DOOR!"
"I SAW ANOTHER MILKSHAKE, SO I DRANK IT."
eat at POP'S
"I SHRANK DOWN ENOUGH TO FIT THROUGH THE DOOR."
eat at POP'S
"IF ONLY MILK-SHAKES WORKED THAT WAY IN REAL LIFE!"
"ONCE OUTSIDE, I MET A CATERPILLAR WHO LOOKED A LOT LIKE DILTON!"
"HE EXPLAINED TO ME THAT THESE MILKSHAKES WILL SHRINK ME DOWN, AND HAMBURGERS WILL MAKE ME GROW."
eat at POP'S
9

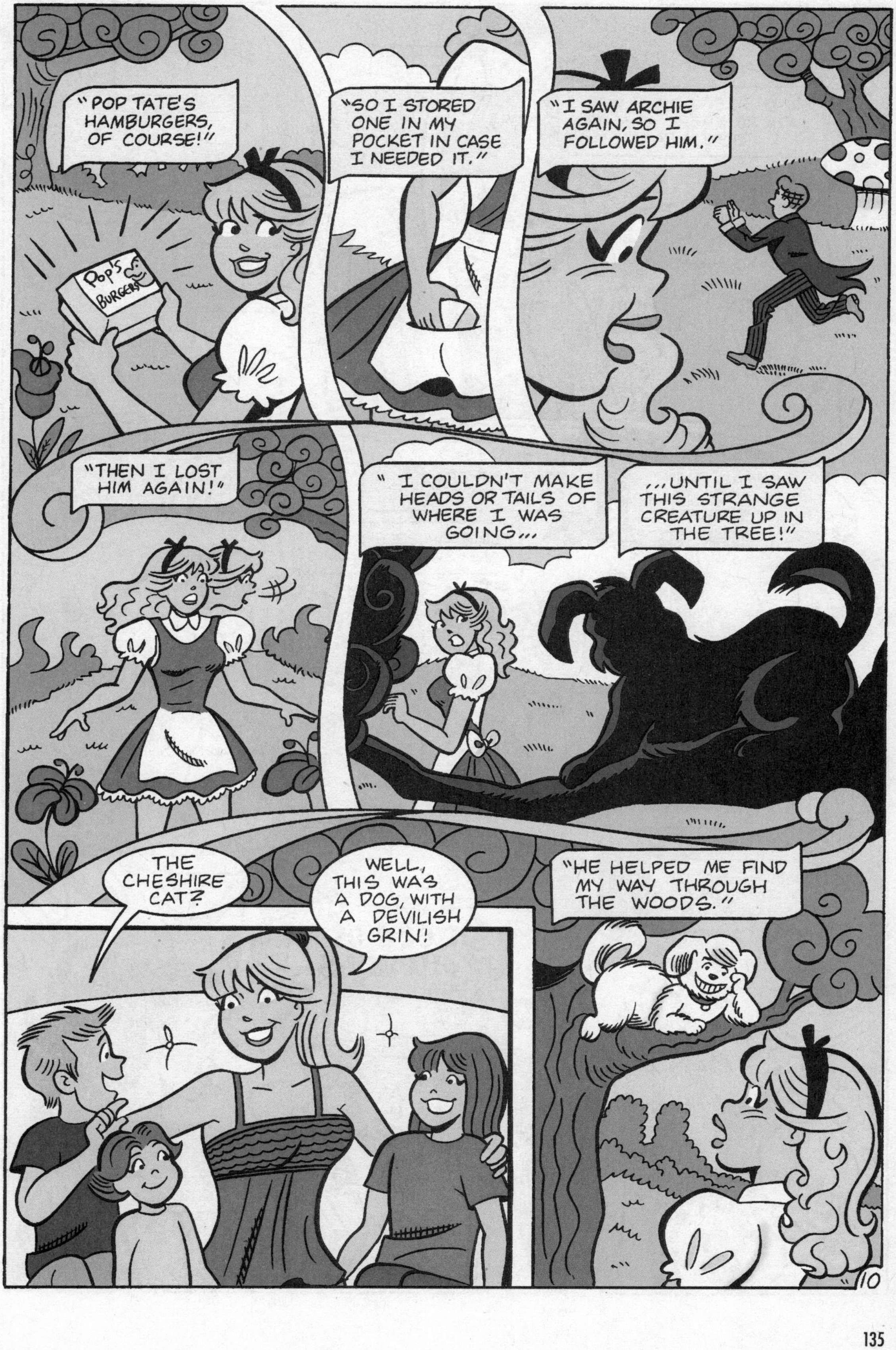
"POP TATE'S HAMBURGERS, OF COURSE!"
POP'S BURGERS
"SO I STORED ONE IN MY POCKET IN CASE I NEEDED IT."
"I SAW ARCHIE AGAIN, SO I FOLLOWED HIM."
"THEN I LOST HIM AGAIN!"
" I COULDN'T MAKE HEADS OR TAILS OF WHERE I WAS GOING...
...UNTIL I SAW THIS STRANGE CREATURE UP IN THE TREE!"
THE CHESHIRE CAT?
WELL, THIS WAS A DOG, WITH A DEVILISH GRIN!
"HE HELPED ME FIND MY WAY THROUGH THE WOODS."
10

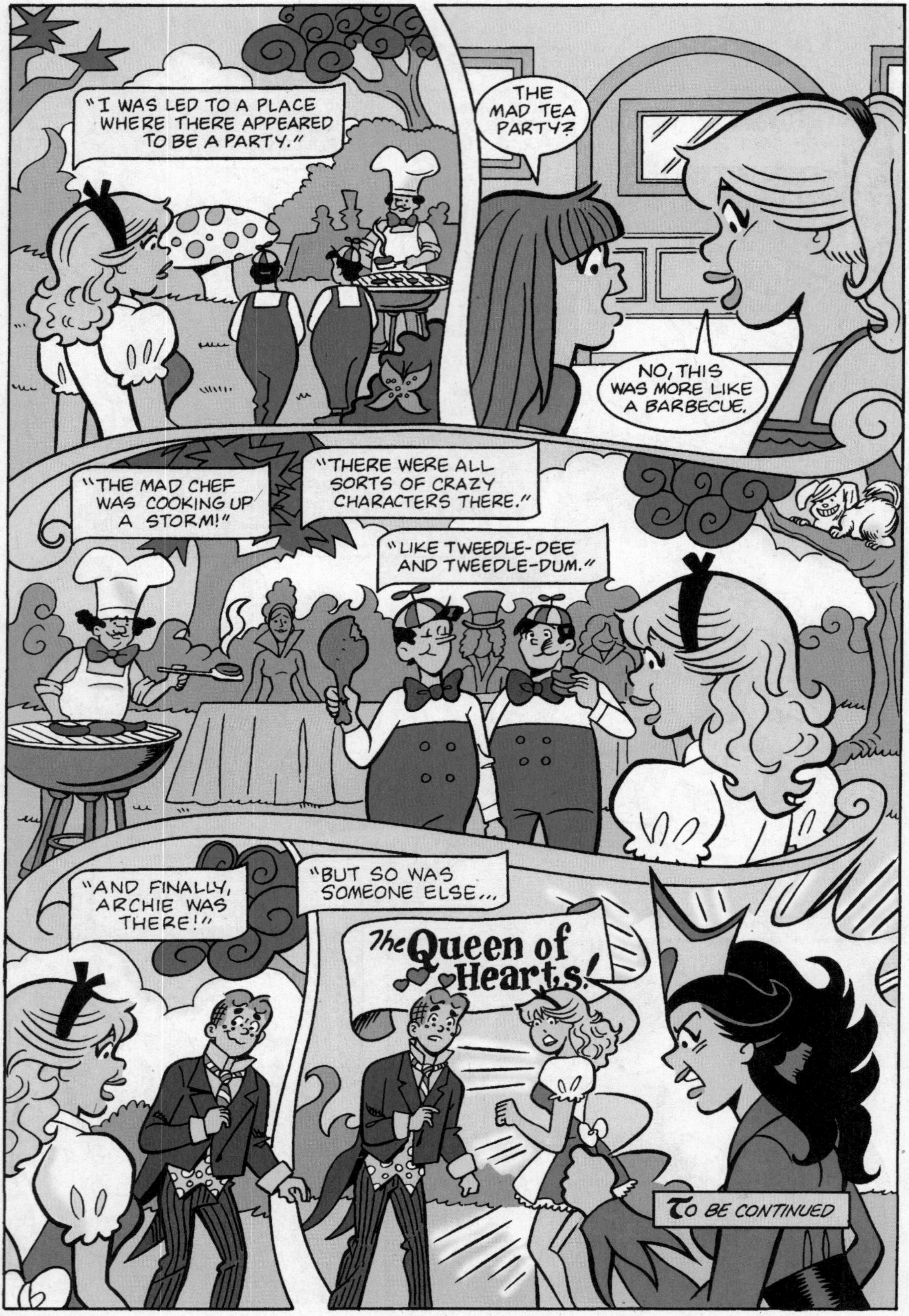
"I WAS LED TO A PLACE WHERE THERE APPEARED TO BE A PARTY."
THE MAD TEA PARTY?
NO, THIS WAS MORE LIKE A BARBECUE.
"THE MAD CHEF WAS COOKING UP A STORM!"
"THERE WERE ALL SORTS OF CRAZY CHARACTERS THERE."
"LIKE TWEEDLE-DEE AND TWEEDLE-DUM."
"AND FINALLY, ARCHIE WAS THERE!"
"BUT SO WAS SOMEONE ELSE...
The Queen of Hearts!
TO BE CONTINUED

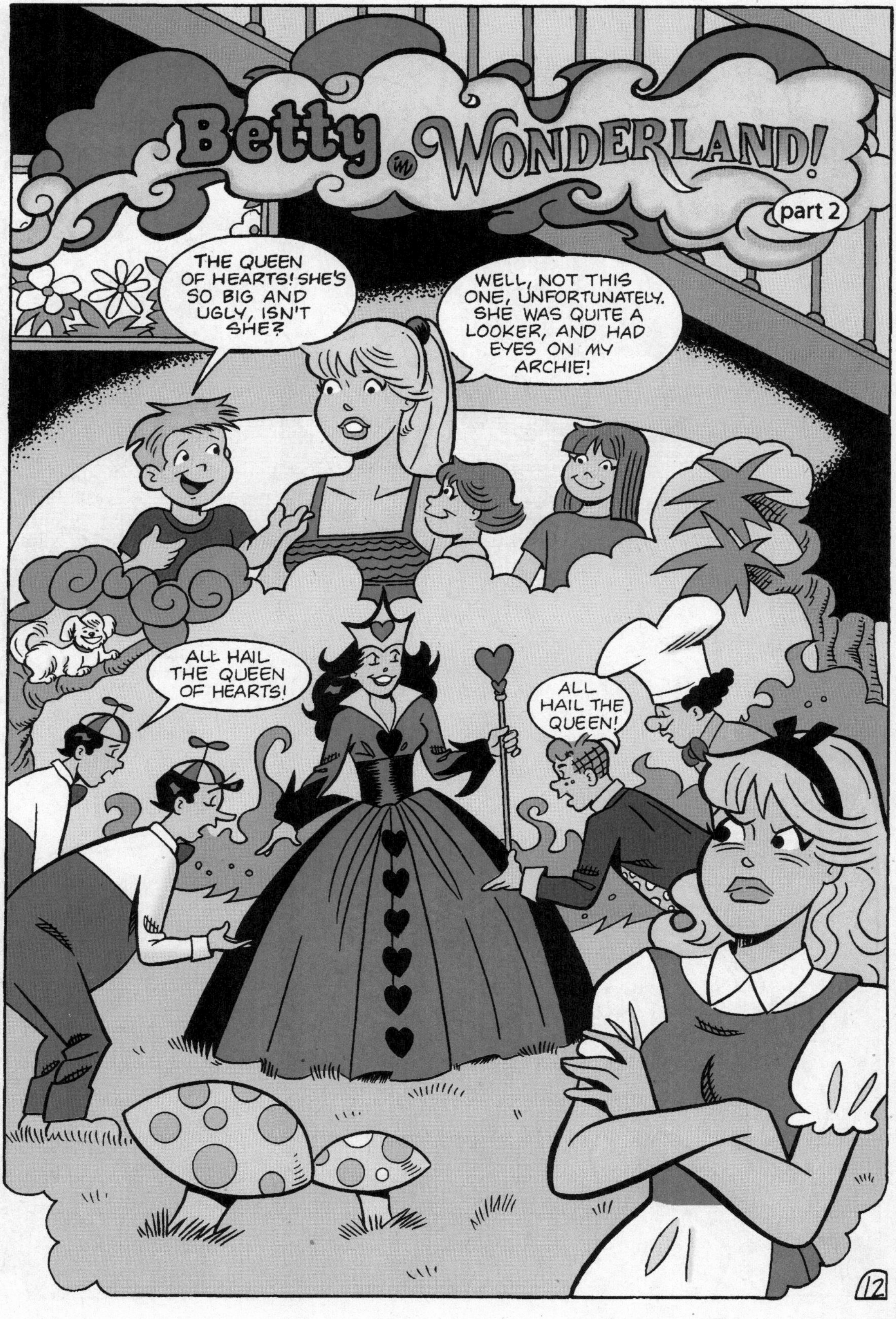
Betty in WONDERLAND!
part 2
THE QUEEN OF HEARTS! SHE'S SO BIG AND UGLY, ISN'T SHE?
WELL, NOT THIS ONE, UNFORTUNATELY. SHE WAS QUITE A LOOKER, AND HAD EYES ON MY ARCHIE!
ALL HAIL THE QUEEN OF HEARTS!
ALL HAIL THE QUEEN!
12

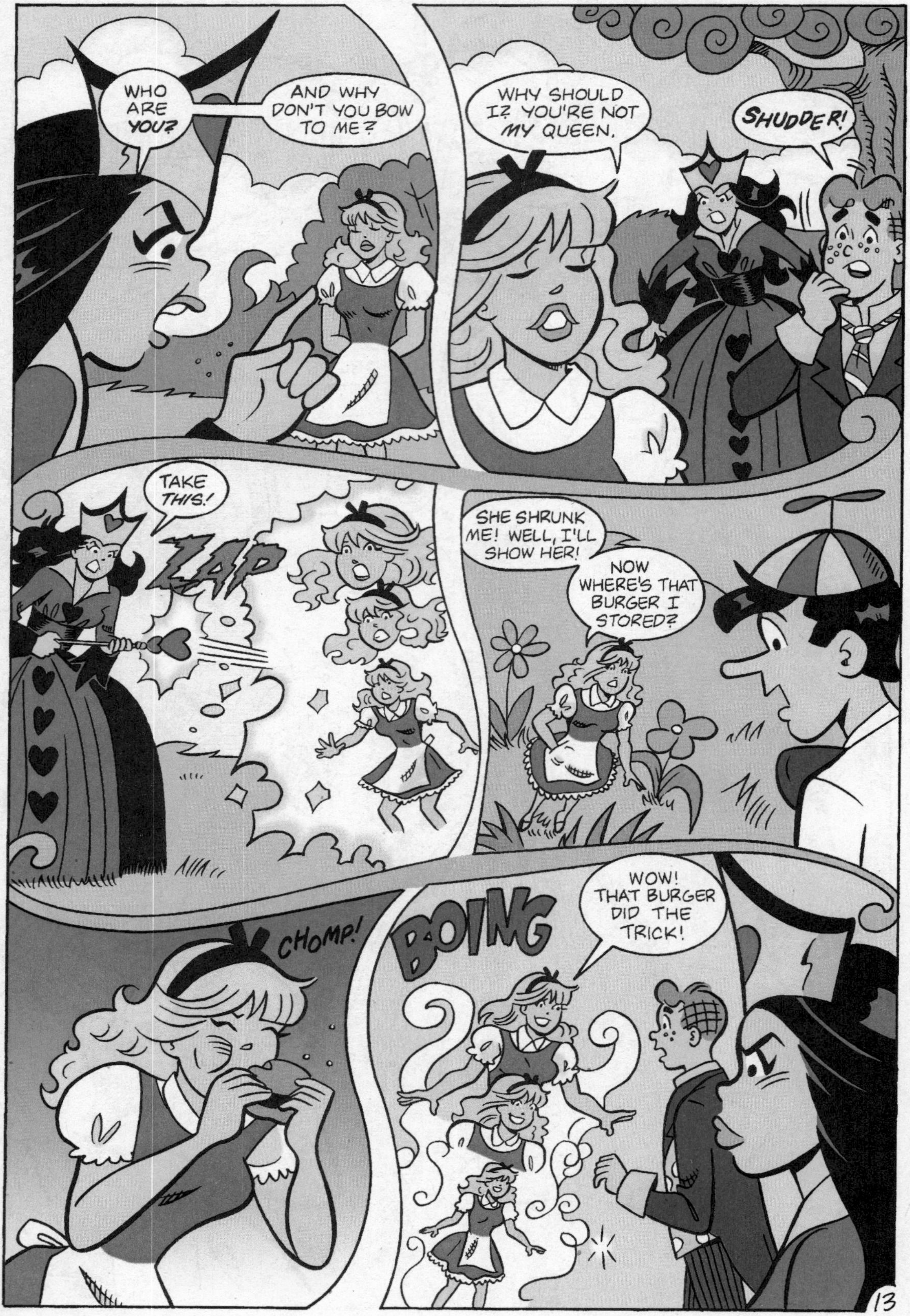
WHO ARE YOU?
AND WHY DON'T YOU BOW TO ME?
WHY SHOULD I? YOU'RE NOT MY QUEEN.
SHUDDER!
TAKE THIS!
ZAP
SHE SHRUNK ME! WELL, I'LL SHOW HER!
NOW WHERE'S THAT BURGER I STORED?
CHOMP!
BOING
WOW! THAT BURGER DID THE TRICK!
13

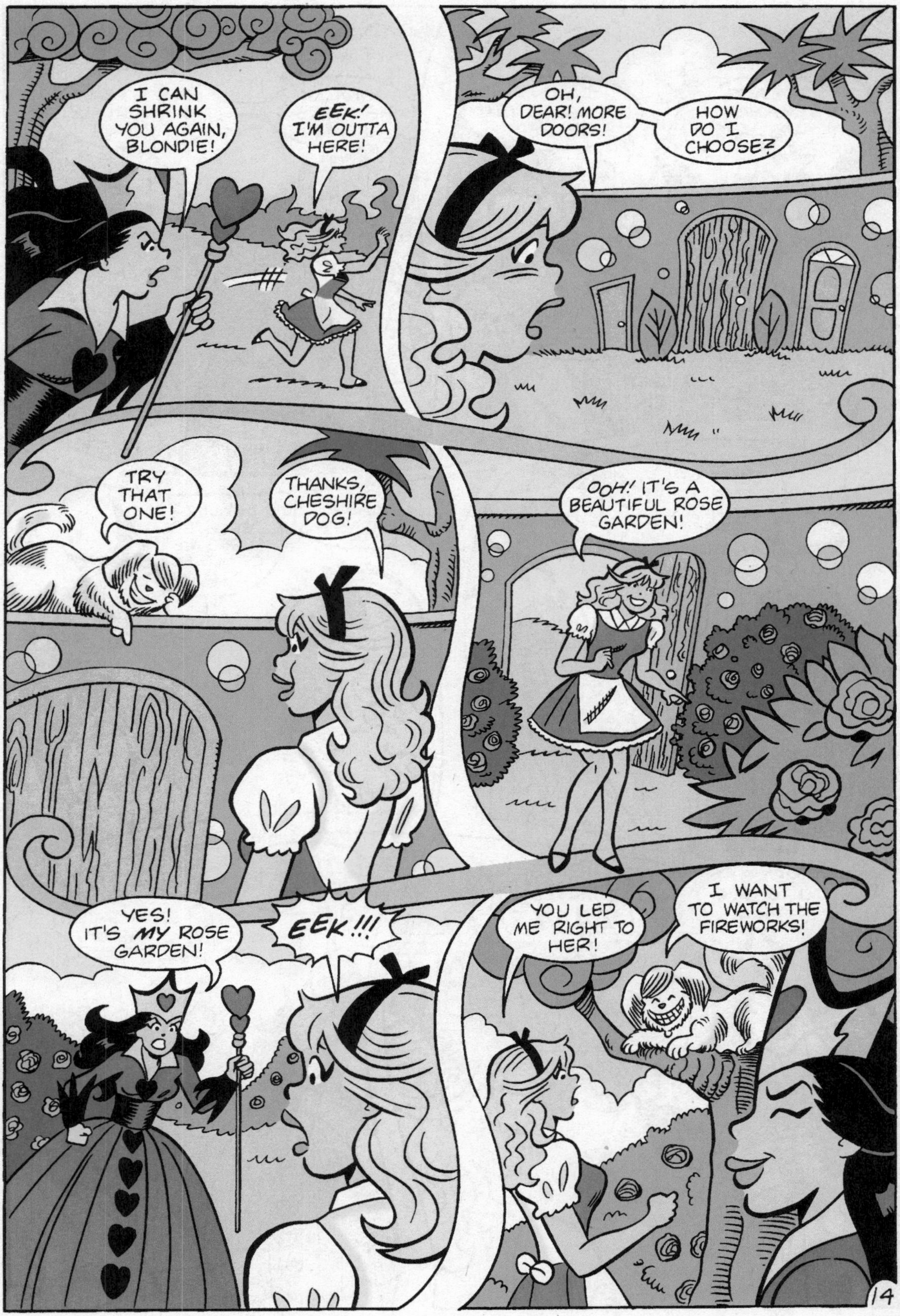
I CAN SHRINK YOU AGAIN, BLONDIE!
EEK! I'M OUTTA HERE!
OH, DEAR! MORE DOORS!
HOW DO I CHOOSE?
TRY THAT ONE!
THANKS, CHESHIRE DOG!
OOH! IT'S A BEAUTIFUL ROSE GARDEN!
YES! IT'S MY ROSE GARDEN!
EEK!!!
YOU LED ME RIGHT TO HER!
I WANT TO WATCH THE FIREWORKS!
14

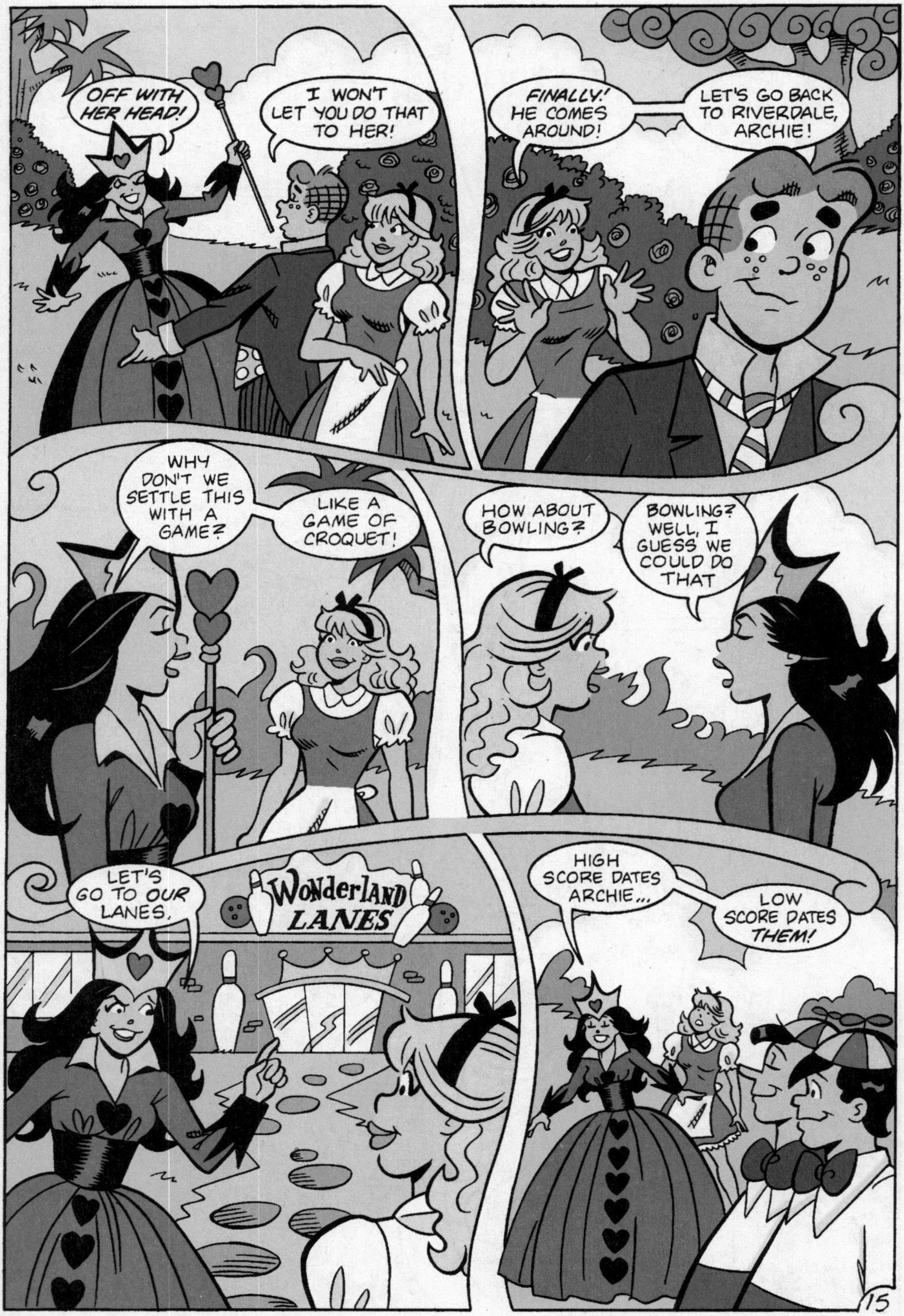
OFF WITH HER HEAD!
I WON'T LET YOU DO THAT TO HER!
FINALLY! HE COMES AROUND!
LET'S GO BACK TO RIVERDALE, ARCHIE!
WHY DON'T WE SETTLE THIS WITH A GAME?
LIKE A GAME OF CROQUET!
HOW ABOUT BOWLING?
BOWLING? WELL, I GUESS WE COULD DO THAT
LET'S GO TO OUR LANES.
WONDERLAND LANES
HIGH SCORE DATES ARCHIE...
LOW SCORE DATES THEM!
15

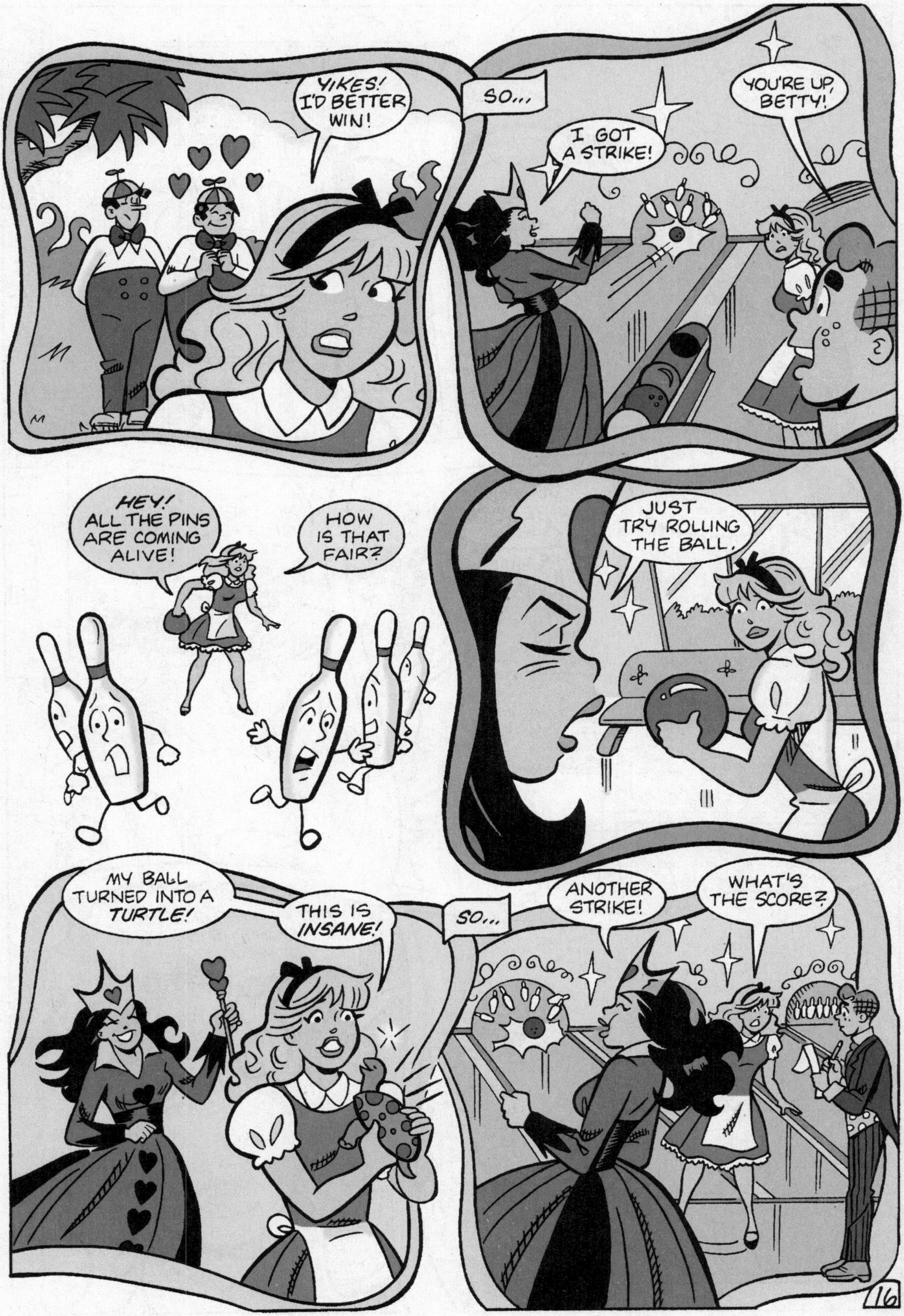
YIKES! I'D BETTER WIN!
SO...
I GOT A STRIKE!
YOU'RE UP, BETTY!
HEY! ALL THE PINS ARE COMING ALIVE!
HOW IS THAT FAIR?
JUST TRY ROLLING THE BALL.
MY BALL TURNED INTO A TURTLE!
THIS IS INSANE!
SO...
ANOTHER STRIKE!
WHAT'S THE SCORE?
16

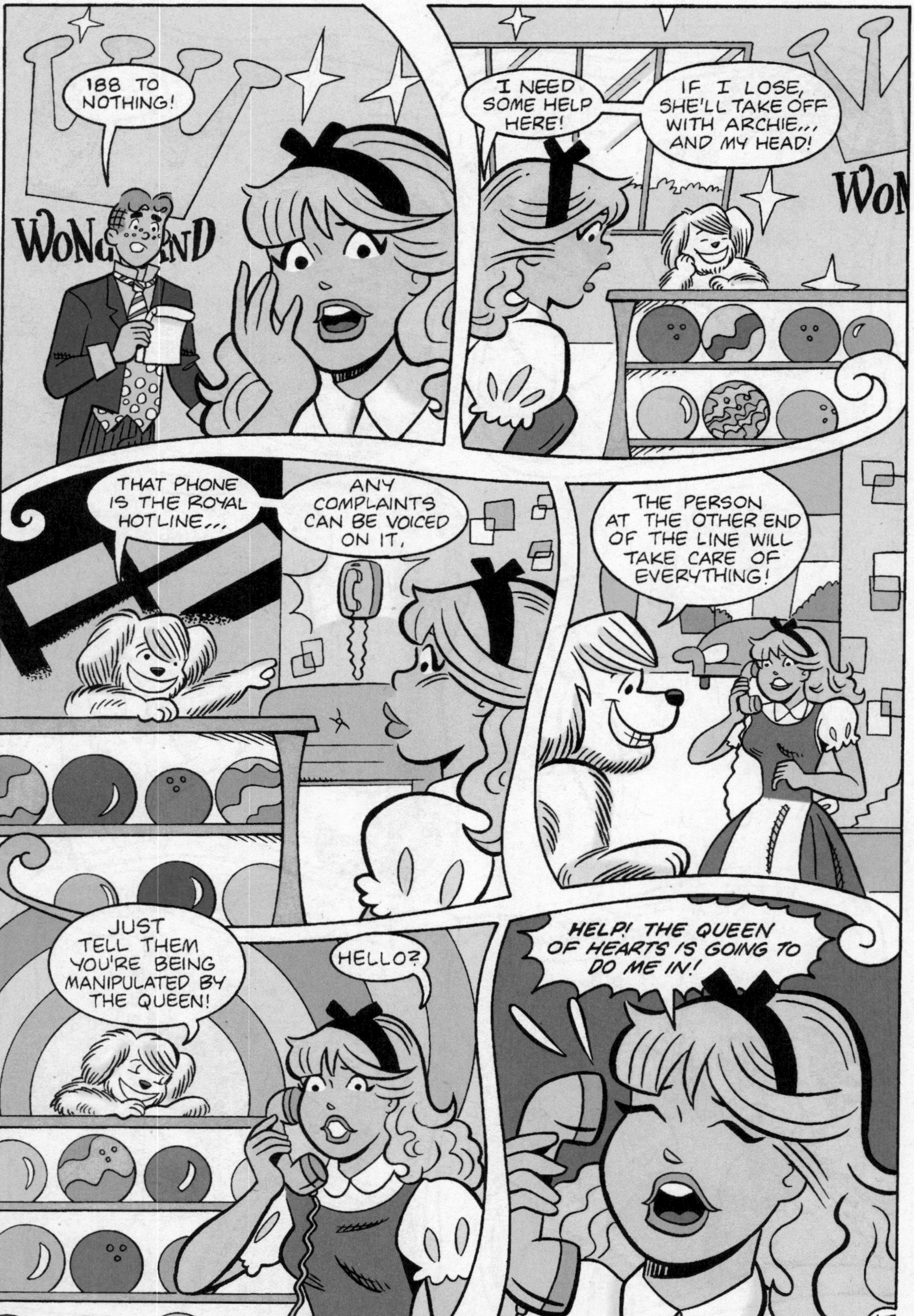
188 TO NOTHING!
WONDERLAND
I NEED SOME HELP HERE!
IF I LOSE, SHE'LL TAKE OFF WITH ARCHIE... AND MY HEAD!
THAT PHONE IS THE ROYAL HOTLINE...
ANY COMPLAINTS CAN BE VOICED ON IT.
THE PERSON AT THE OTHER END OF THE LINE WILL TAKE CARE OF EVERYTHING!
JUST TELL THEM YOU'RE BEING MANIPULATED BY THE QUEEN!
HELLO?
HELP! THE QUEEN OF HEARTS IS GOING TO DO ME IN!
17

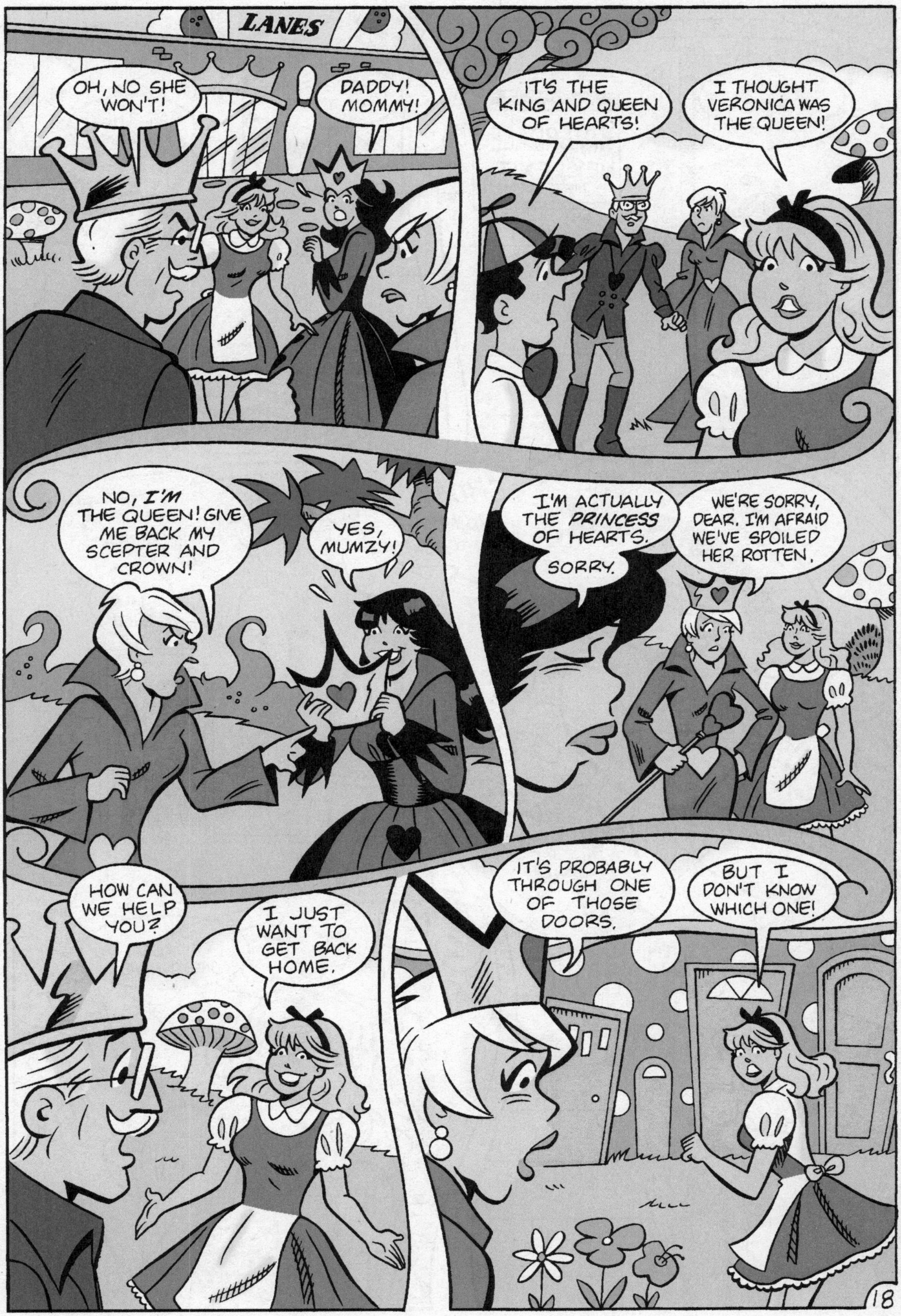
LANES
OH, NO SHE WON'T!
DADDY! MOMMY!
IT'S THE KING AND QUEEN OF HEARTS!
I THOUGHT VERONICA WAS THE QUEEN!
NO, I'M THE QUEEN! GIVE ME BACK MY SCEPTER AND CROWN!
YES, MUMZY!
I'M ACTUALLY THE PRINCESS OF HEARTS.
SORRY.
WE'RE SORRY, DEAR. I'M AFRAID WE'VE SPOILED HER ROTTEN.
HOW CAN WE HELP YOU?
I JUST WANT TO GET BACK HOME.
IT'S PROBABLY THROUGH ONE OF THOSE DOORS.
BUT I DON'T KNOW WHICH ONE!
18

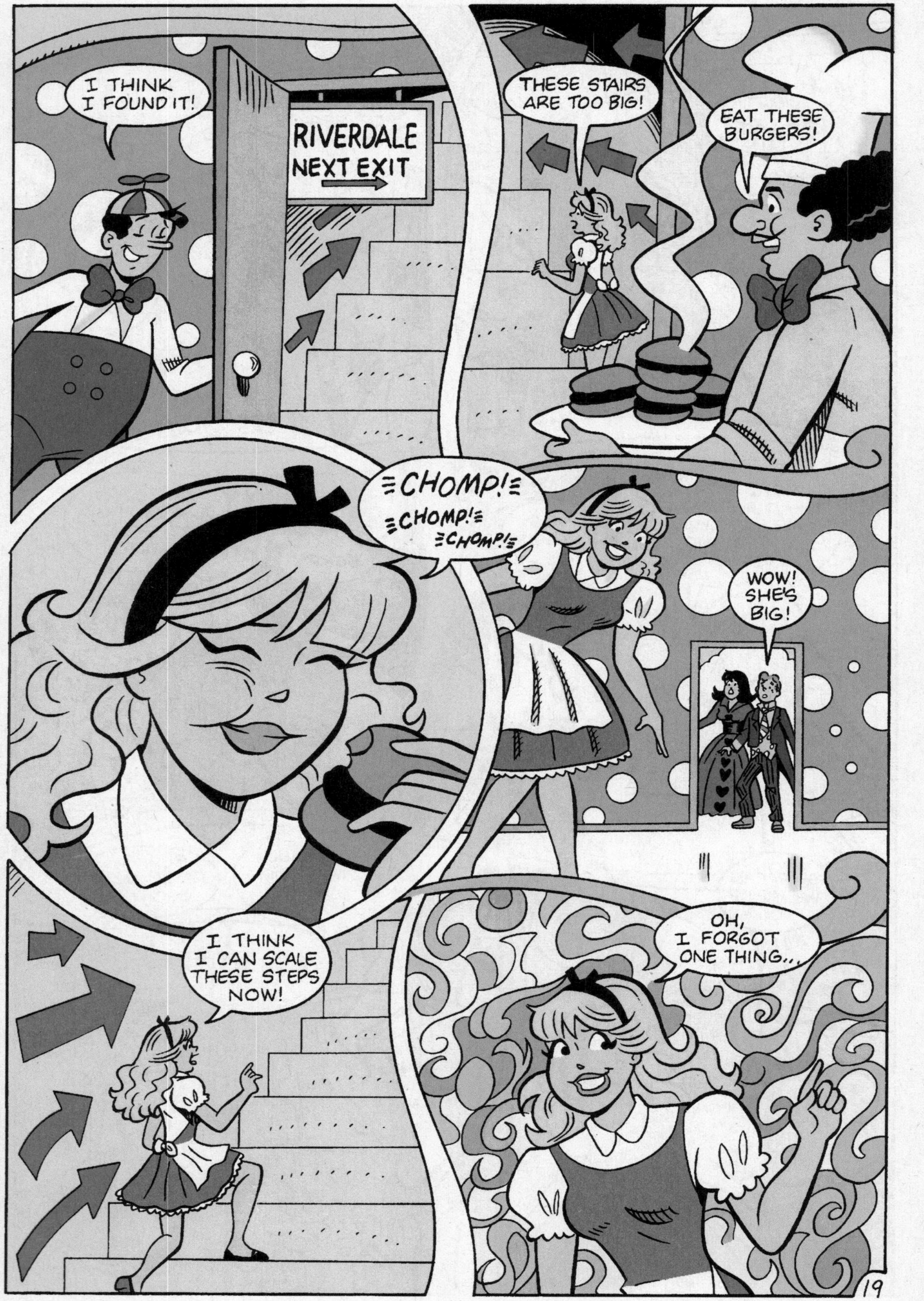
I THINK I FOUND IT!
RIVERDALE NEXT EXIT
THESE STAIRS ARE TOO BIG!
EAT THESE BURGERS!
CHOMP! CHOMP! CHOMP!
WOW! SHE'S BIG!
I THINK I CAN SCALE THESE STEPS NOW!
OH, I FORGOT ONE THING...
19

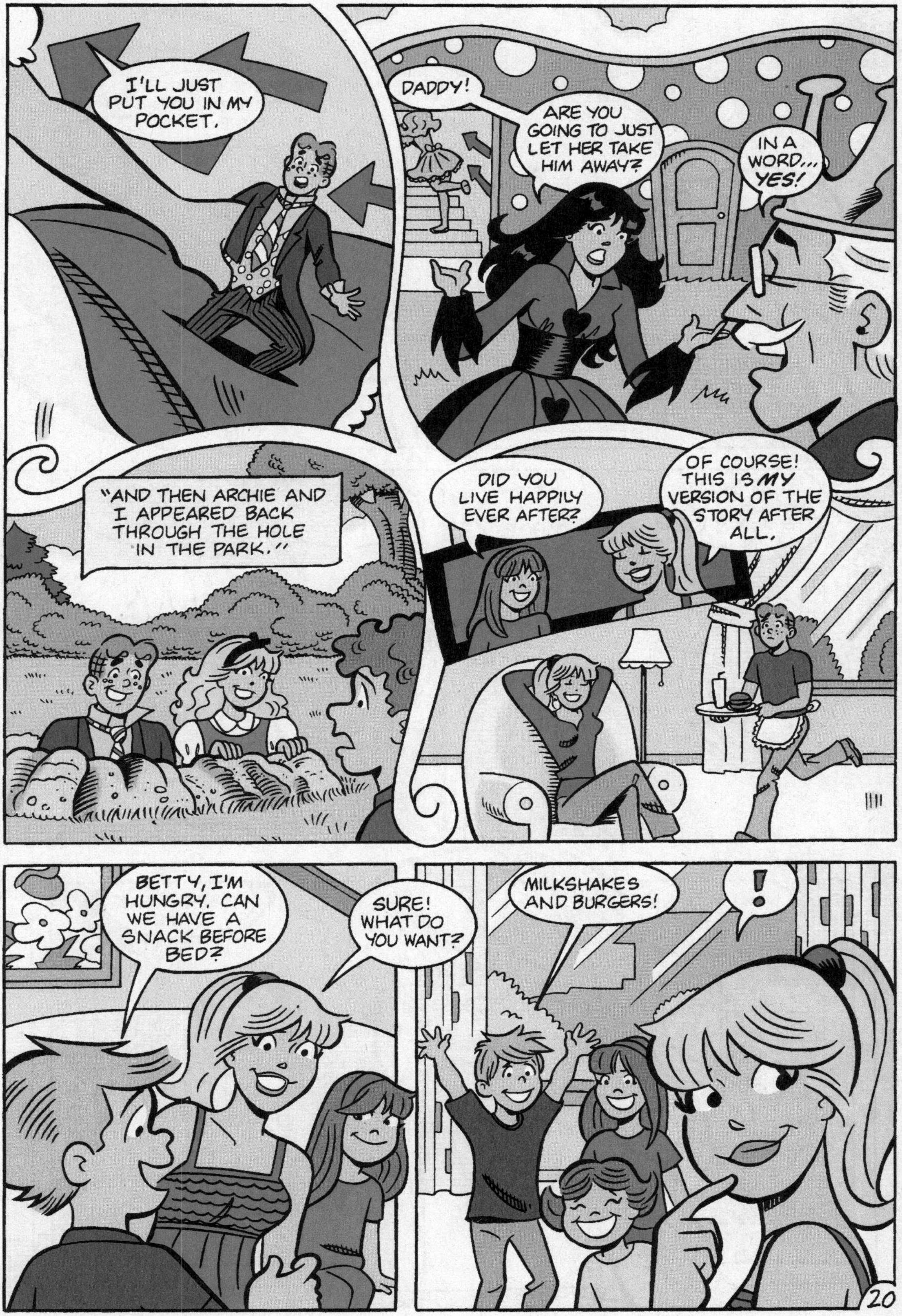
I'LL JUST PUT YOU IN MY POCKET.
DADDY!
ARE YOU GOING TO JUST LET HER TAKE HIM AWAY?
IN A WORD... YES!
"AND THEN ARCHIE AND I APPEARED BACK THROUGH THE HOLE IN THE PARK."
DID YOU LIVE HAPPILY EVER AFTER?
OF COURSE! THIS IS MY VERSION OF THE STORY AFTER ALL.
BETTY, I'M HUNGRY. CAN WE HAVE A SNACK BEFORE BED?
SURE! WHAT DO YOU WANT?
MILKSHAKES AND BURGERS!
!
20

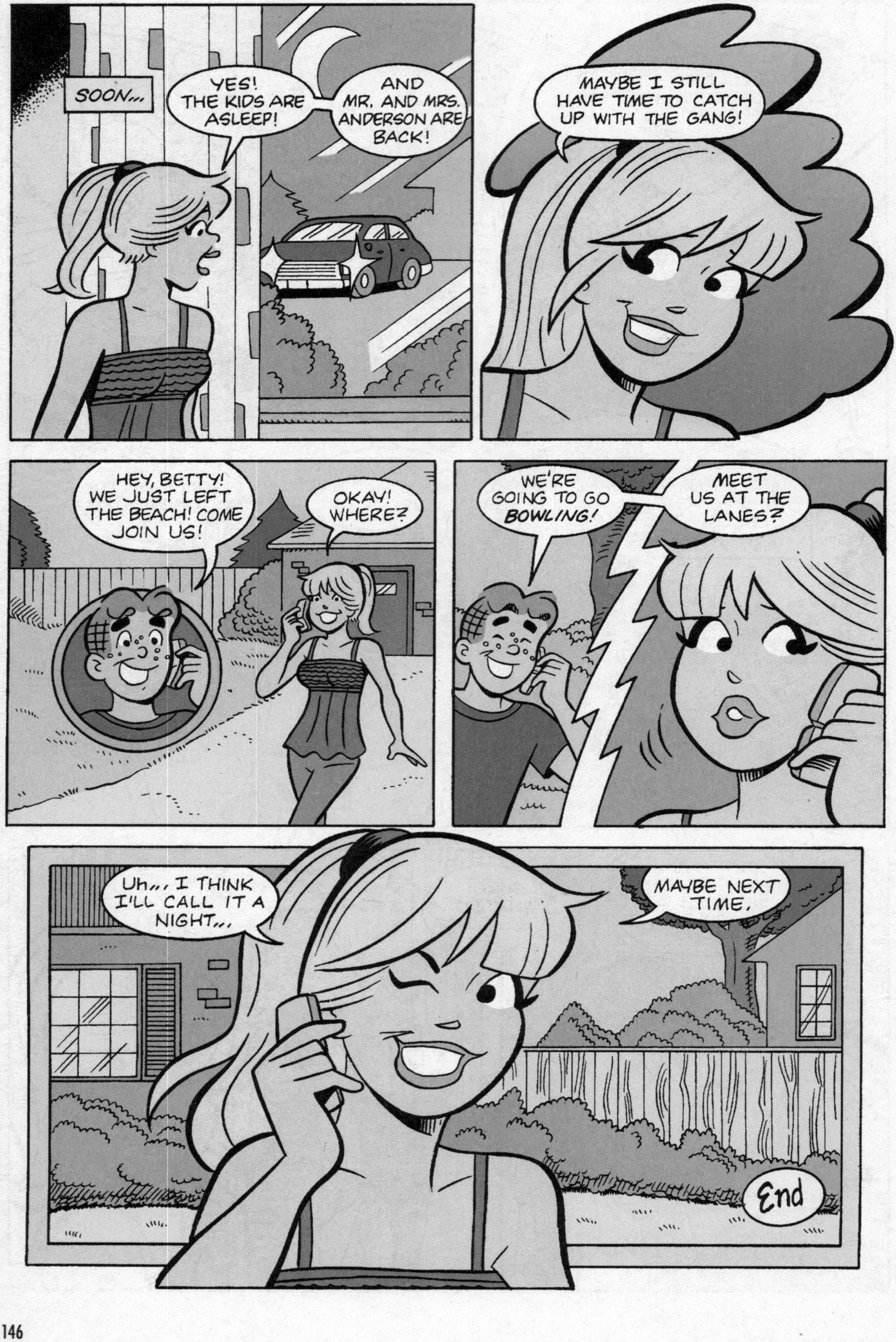
SOON...
YES! THE KIDS ARE ASLEEP!
AND MR. AND MRS. ANDERSON ARE BACK!
MAYBE I STILL HAVE TIME TO CATCH UP WITH THE GANG!
HEY, BETTY! WE JUST LEFT THE BEACH! COME JOIN US!
OKAY! WHERE?
WE'RE GOING TO GO BOWLING!
MEET US AT THE LANES?
Uh... I THINK I'LL CALL IT A NIGHT...
MAYBE NEXT TIME.
End

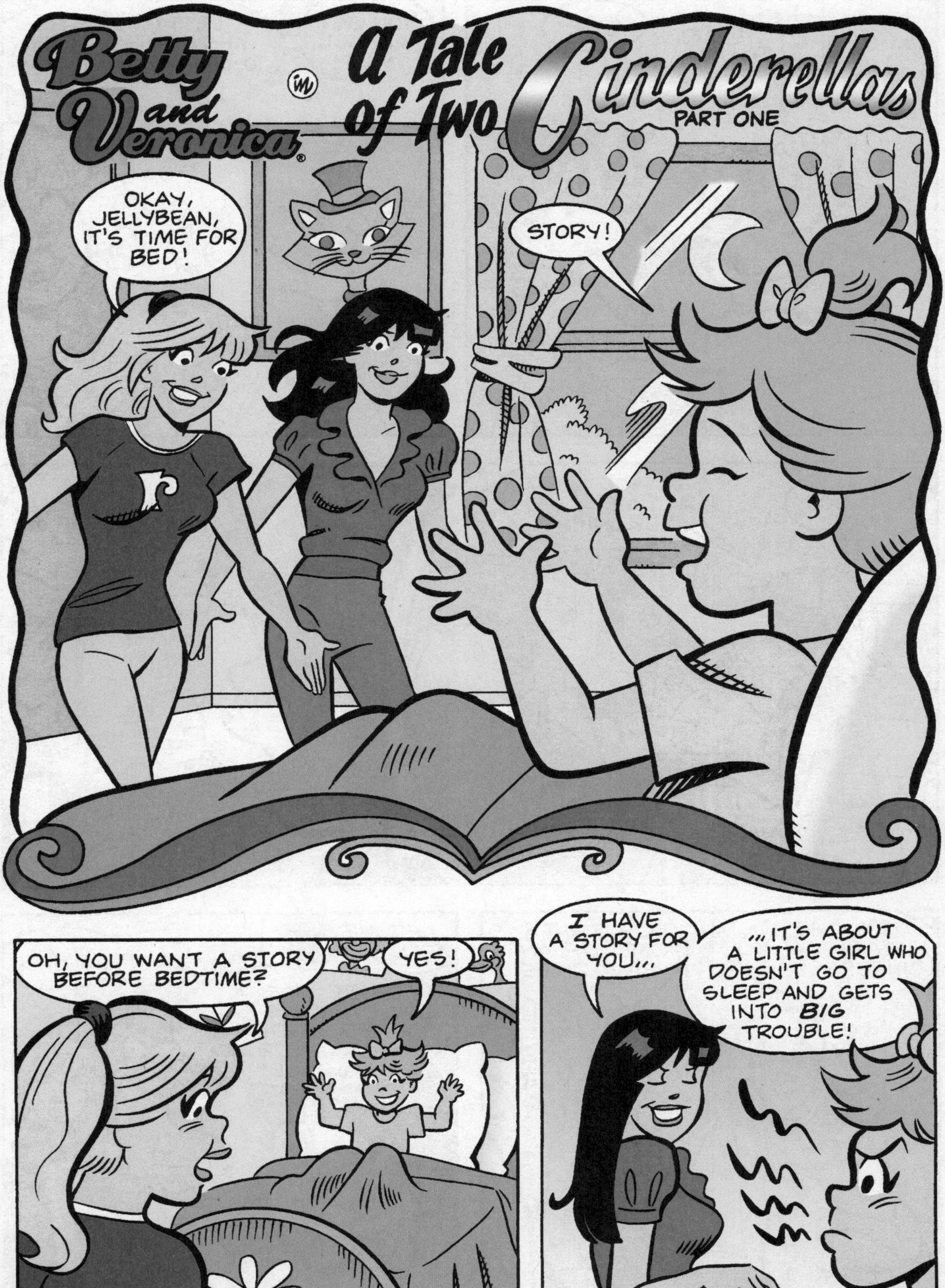
Betty and Veronica
in
A Tale of Two Cinderellas
PART ONE
OKAY, JELLYBEAN, IT'S TIME FOR BED!
STORY!
OH, YOU WANT A STORY BEFORE BEDTIME?
YES!
I HAVE A STORY FOR YOU...
...IT'S ABOUT A LITTLE GIRL WHO DOESN'T GO TO SLEEP AND GETS INTO BIG TROUBLE!

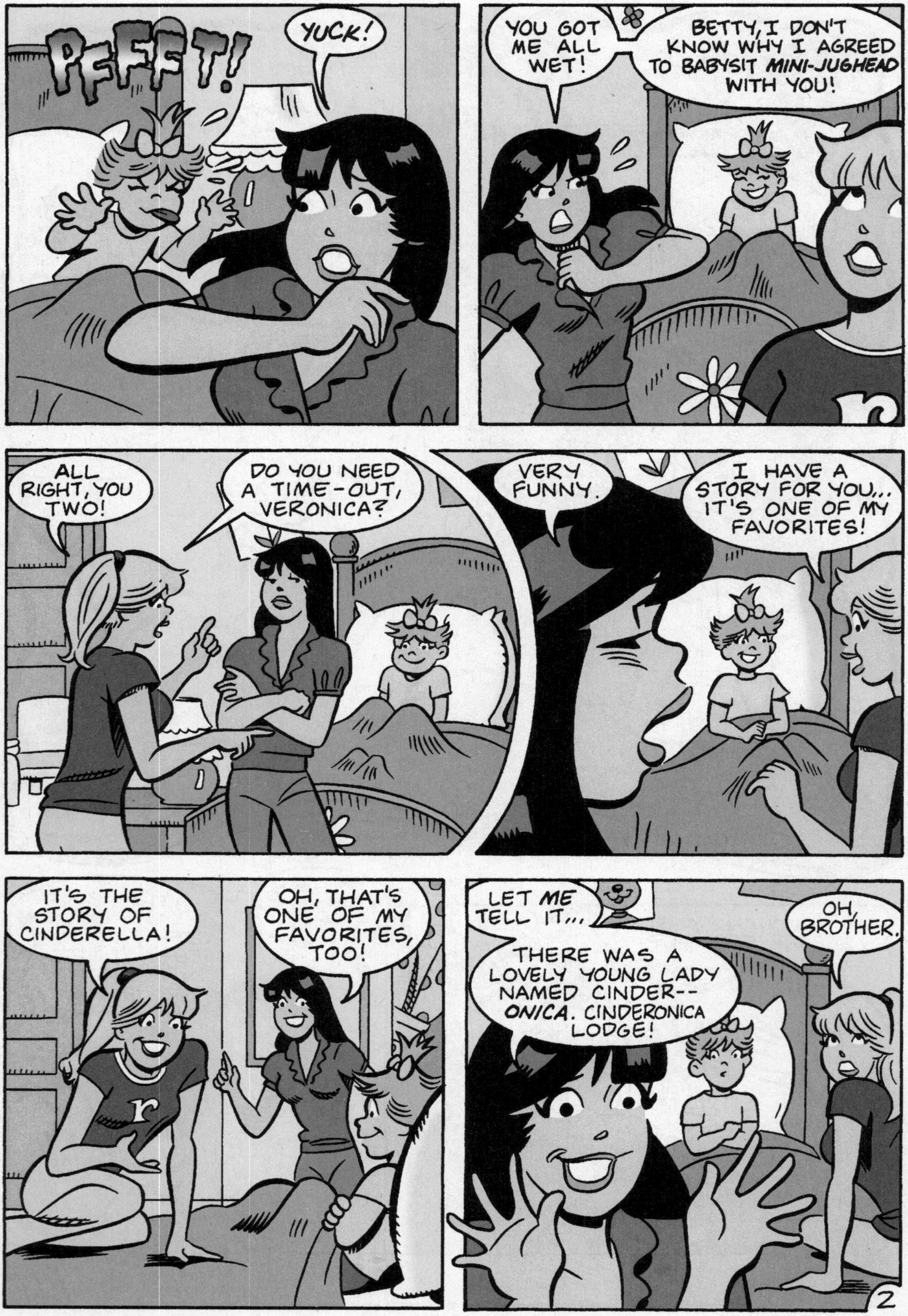
PFFFT!
YUCK!
YOU GOT ME ALL WET!
BETTY, I DON'T KNOW WHY I AGREED TO BABYSIT MINI-JUGHEAD WITH YOU!
ALL RIGHT, YOU TWO!
DO YOU NEED A TIME-OUT, VERONICA?
VERY FUNNY.
I HAVE A STORY FOR YOU... IT'S ONE OF MY FAVORITES!
IT'S THE STORY OF CINDERELLA!
OH, THAT'S ONE OF MY FAVORITES, TOO!
LET ME TELL IT...
THERE WAS A LOVELY YOUNG LADY NAMED CINDER--ONICA. CINDERONICA LODGE!
OH, BROTHER.
2

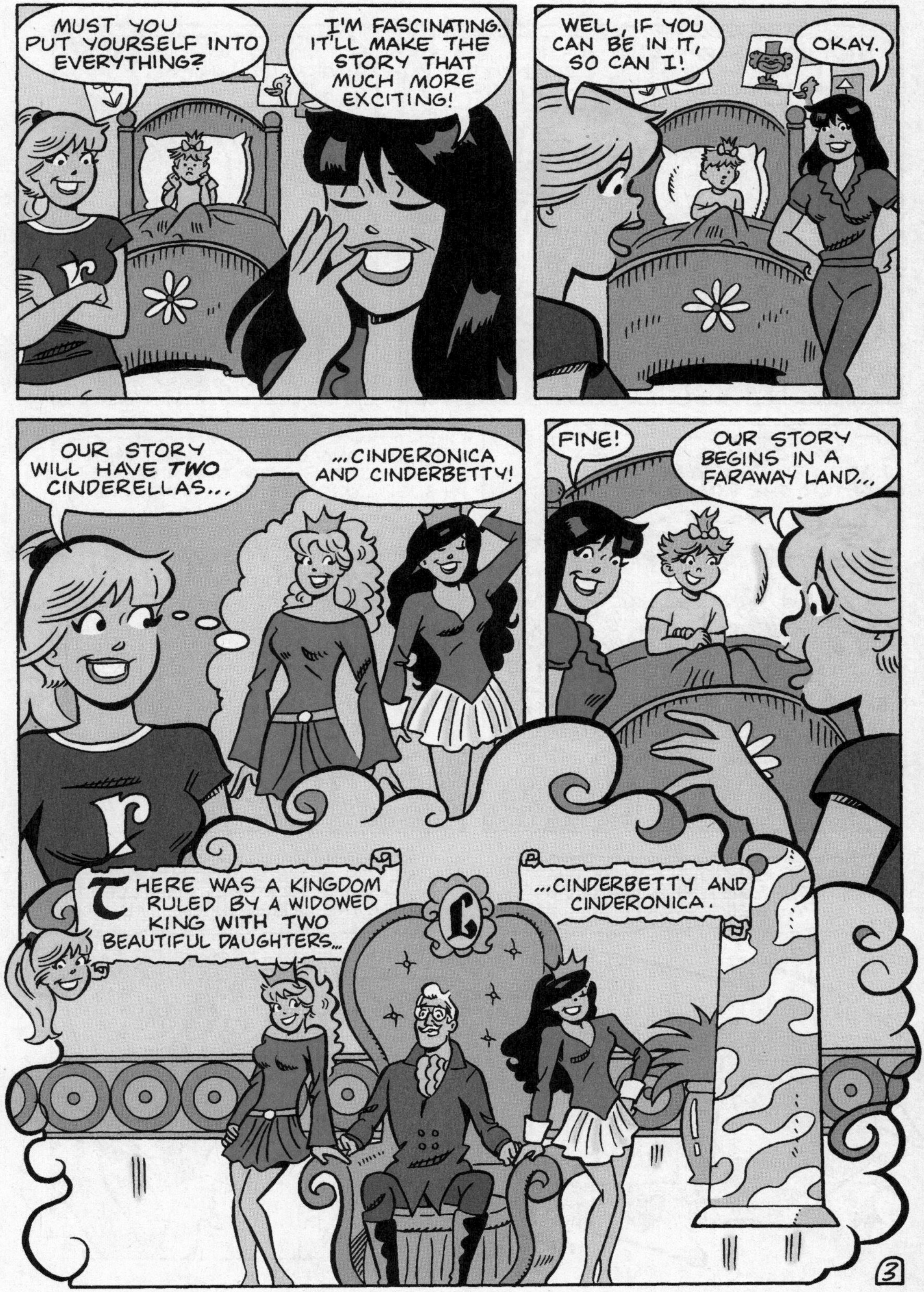

MUST YOU PUT YOURSELF INTO EVERYTHING?
I'M FASCINATING. IT'LL MAKE THE STORY THAT MUCH MORE EXCITING!
WELL, IF YOU CAN BE IN IT, SO CAN I!
OKAY.
OUR STORY WILL HAVE TWO CINDERELLAS...
...CINDERONICA AND CINDERBETTY!
FINE!
OUR STORY BEGINS IN A FARAWAY LAND...
THERE WAS A KINGDOM RULED BY A WIDOWED KING WITH TWO BEAUTIFUL DAUGHTERS...
...CINDERBETTY AND CINDERONICA.
3

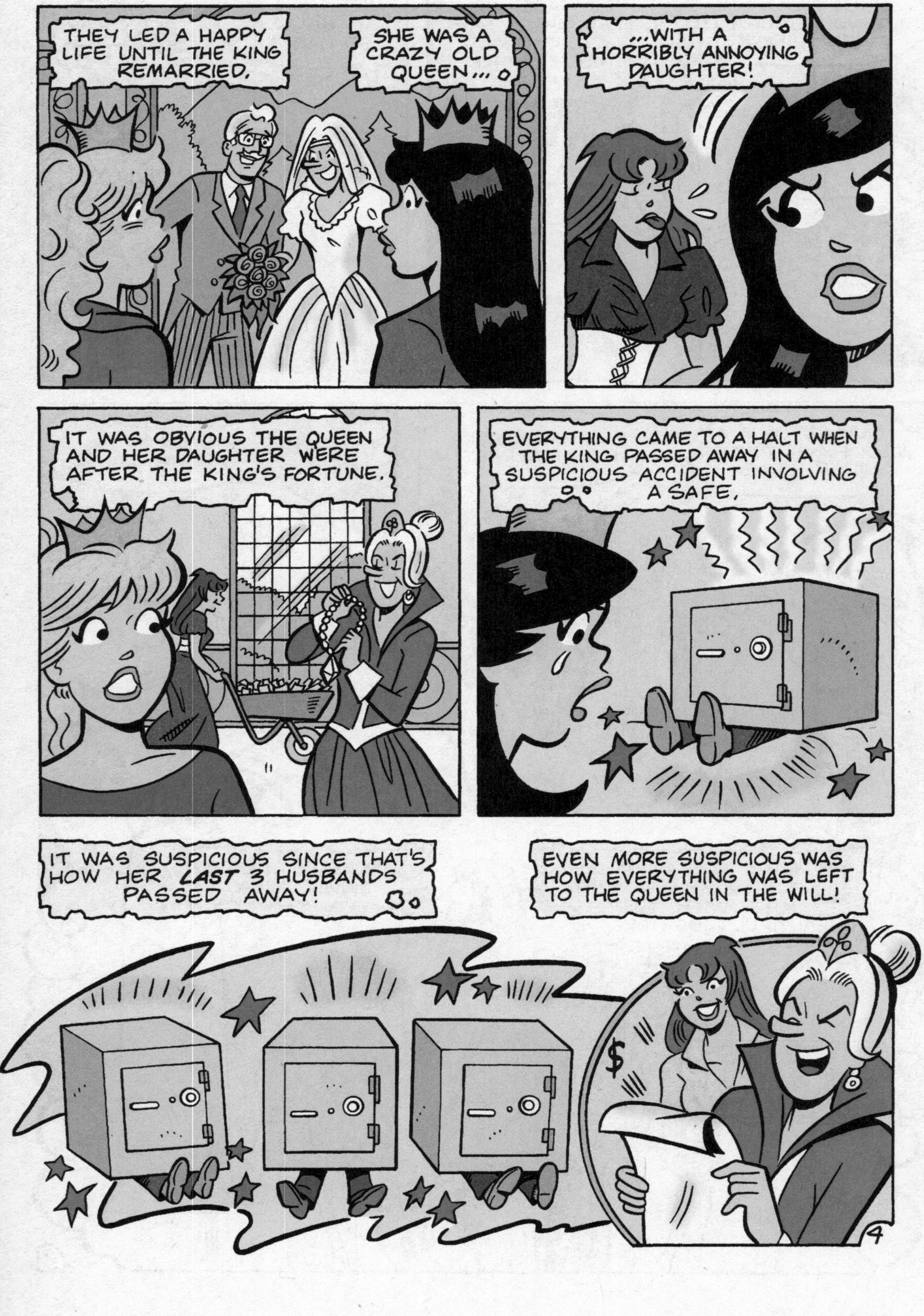
THEY LED A HAPPY LIFE UNTIL THE KING REMARRIED.
SHE WAS A CRAZY OLD QUEEN...
...WITH A HORRIBLY ANNOYING DAUGHTER!
IT WAS OBVIOUS THE QUEEN AND HER DAUGHTER WERE AFTER THE KING'S FORTUNE.
EVERYTHING CAME TO A HALT WHEN THE KING PASSED AWAY IN A SUSPICIOUS ACCIDENT INVOLVING A SAFE.
IT WAS SUSPICIOUS SINCE THAT'S HOW HER *LAST* 3 HUSBANDS PASSED AWAY!
EVEN MORE SUSPICIOUS WAS HOW EVERYTHING WAS LEFT TO THE QUEEN IN THE WILL!
$
4

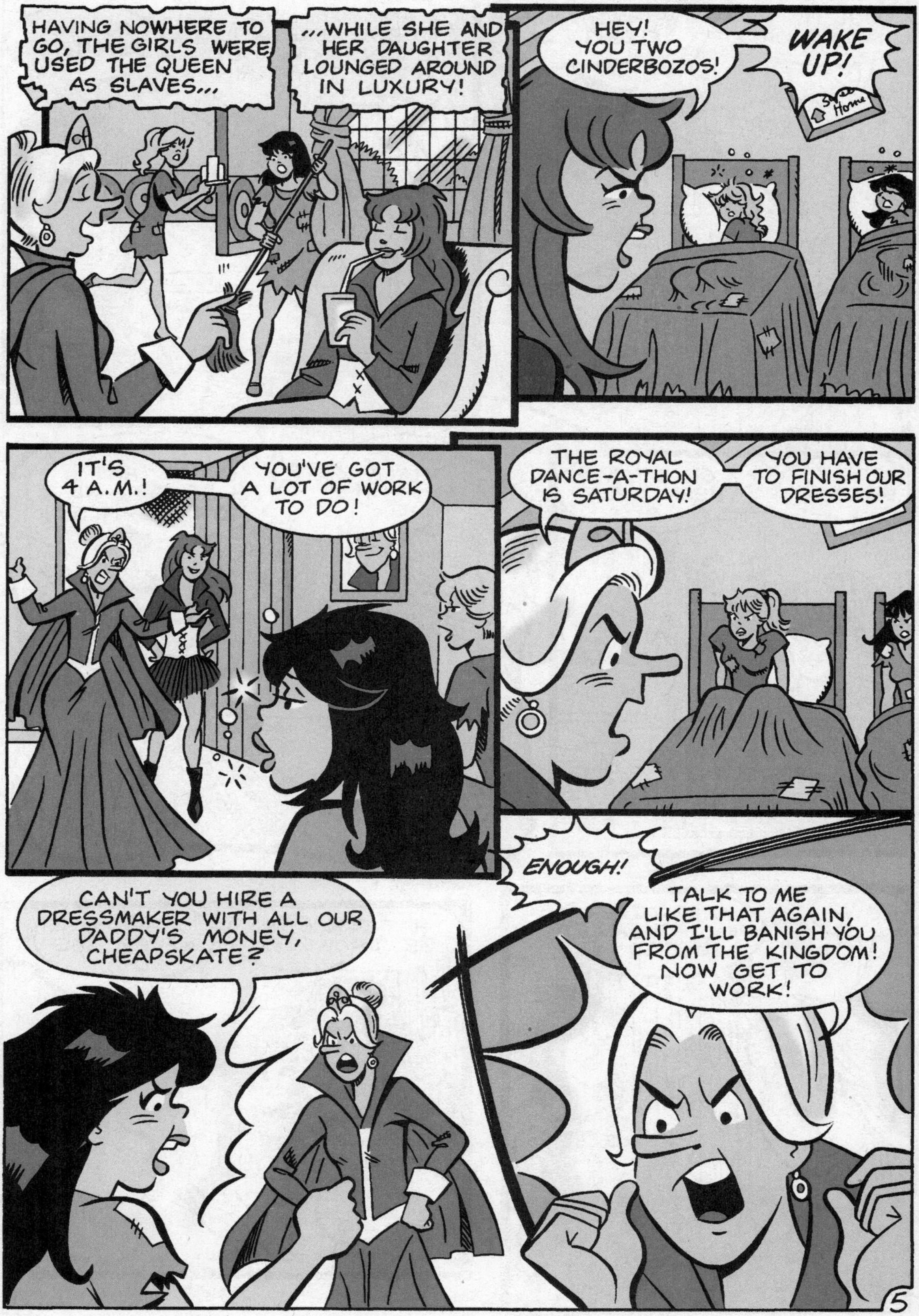
HAVING NOWHERE TO GO, THE GIRLS WERE USED THE QUEEN AS SLAVES...
...WHILE SHE AND HER DAUGHTER LOUNGED AROUND IN LUXURY!
HEY! YOU TWO CINDERBOZOS!
WAKE UP!
IT'S 4 A.M.!
YOU'VE GOT A LOT OF WORK TO DO!
THE ROYAL DANCE-A-THON IS SATURDAY!
YOU HAVE TO FINISH OUR DRESSES!
CAN'T YOU HIRE A DRESSMAKER WITH ALL OUR DADDY'S MONEY, CHEAPSKATE?
ENOUGH!
TALK TO ME LIKE THAT AGAIN, AND I'LL BANISH YOU FROM THE KINGDOM! NOW GET TO WORK!
5

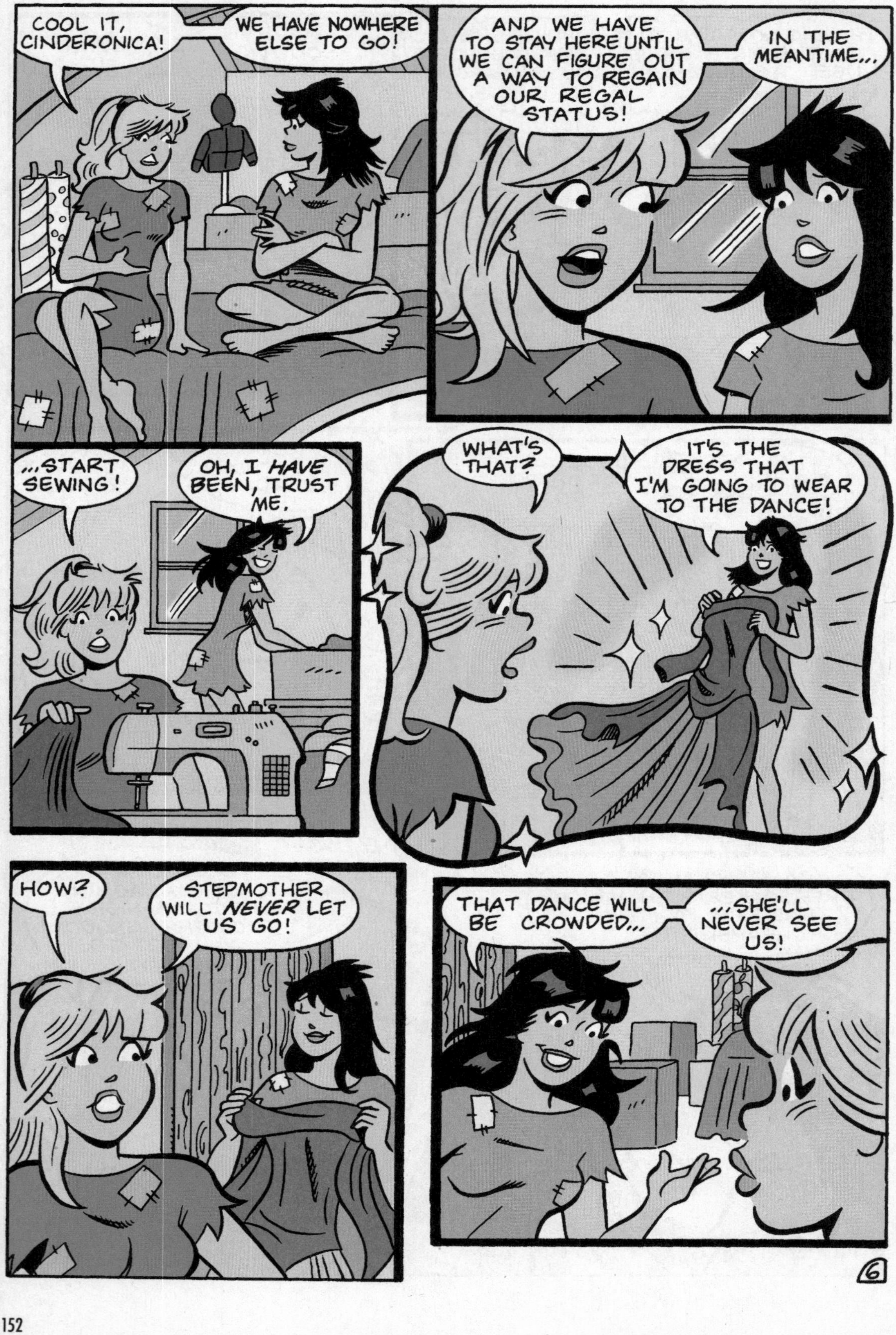
COOL IT, CINDERONICA!
WE HAVE NOWHERE ELSE TO GO!
AND WE HAVE TO STAY HERE UNTIL WE CAN FIGURE OUT A WAY TO REGAIN OUR REGAL STATUS!
IN THE MEANTIME...
...START SEWING!
OH, I *HAVE* BEEN, TRUST ME.
WHAT'S THAT?
IT'S THE DRESS THAT I'M GOING TO WEAR TO THE DANCE!
HOW?
STEPMOTHER WILL *NEVER* LET US GO!
THAT DANCE WILL BE CROWDED...
...SHE'LL NEVER SEE US!
6

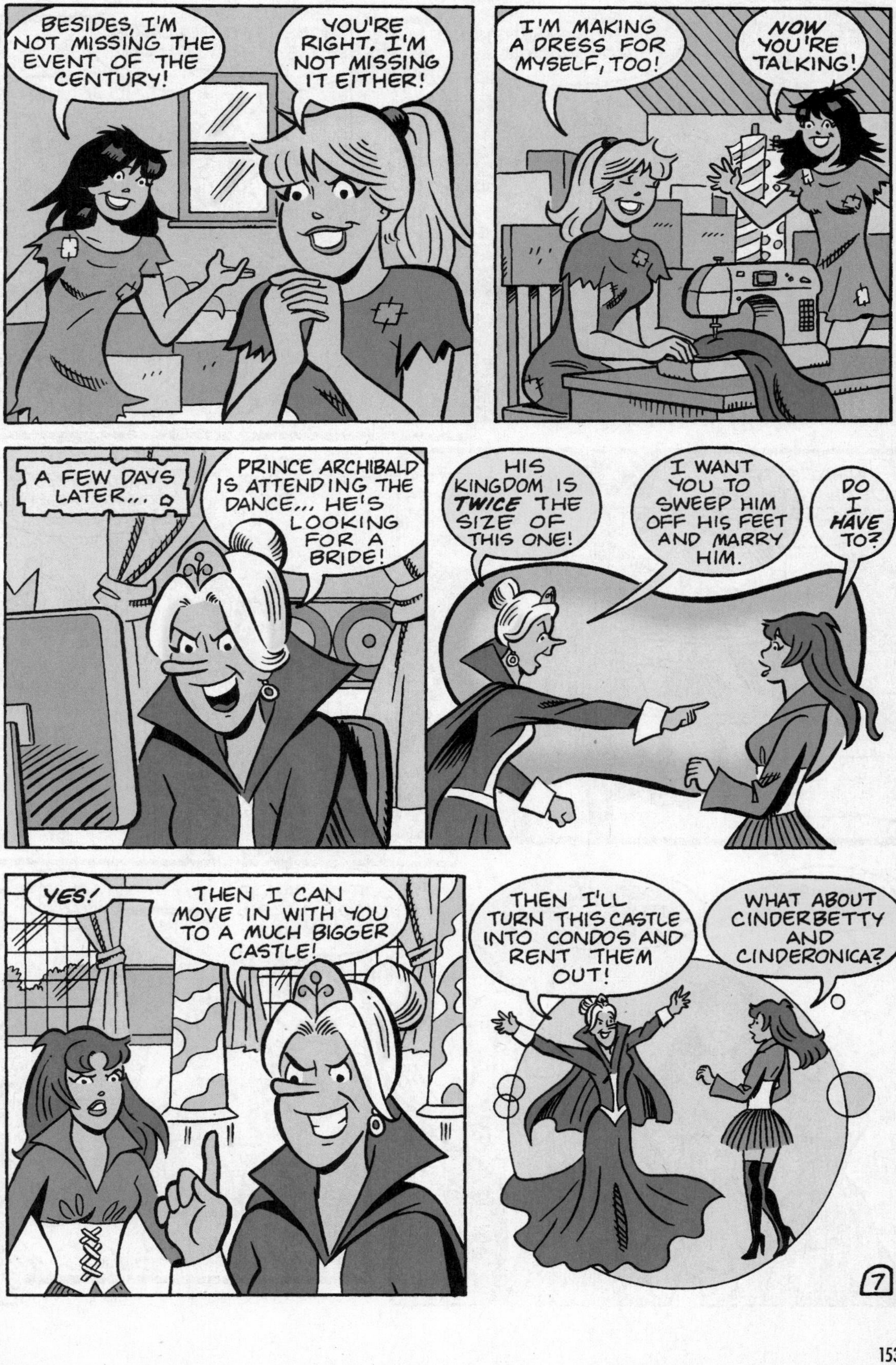

BESIDES, I'M NOT MISSING THE EVENT OF THE CENTURY!
YOU'RE RIGHT. I'M NOT MISSING IT EITHER!
I'M MAKING A DRESS FOR MYSELF, TOO!
NOW YOU'RE TALKING!
A FEW DAYS LATER...
PRINCE ARCHIBALD IS ATTENDING THE DANCE... HE'S LOOKING FOR A BRIDE!
HIS KINGDOM IS TWICE THE SIZE OF THIS ONE!
I WANT YOU TO SWEEP HIM OFF HIS FEET AND MARRY HIM.
DO I HAVE TO?
YES!
THEN I CAN MOVE IN WITH YOU TO A MUCH BIGGER CASTLE!
THEN I'LL TURN THIS CASTLE INTO CONDOS AND RENT THEM OUT!
WHAT ABOUT CINDERBETTY AND CINDERONICA?
7

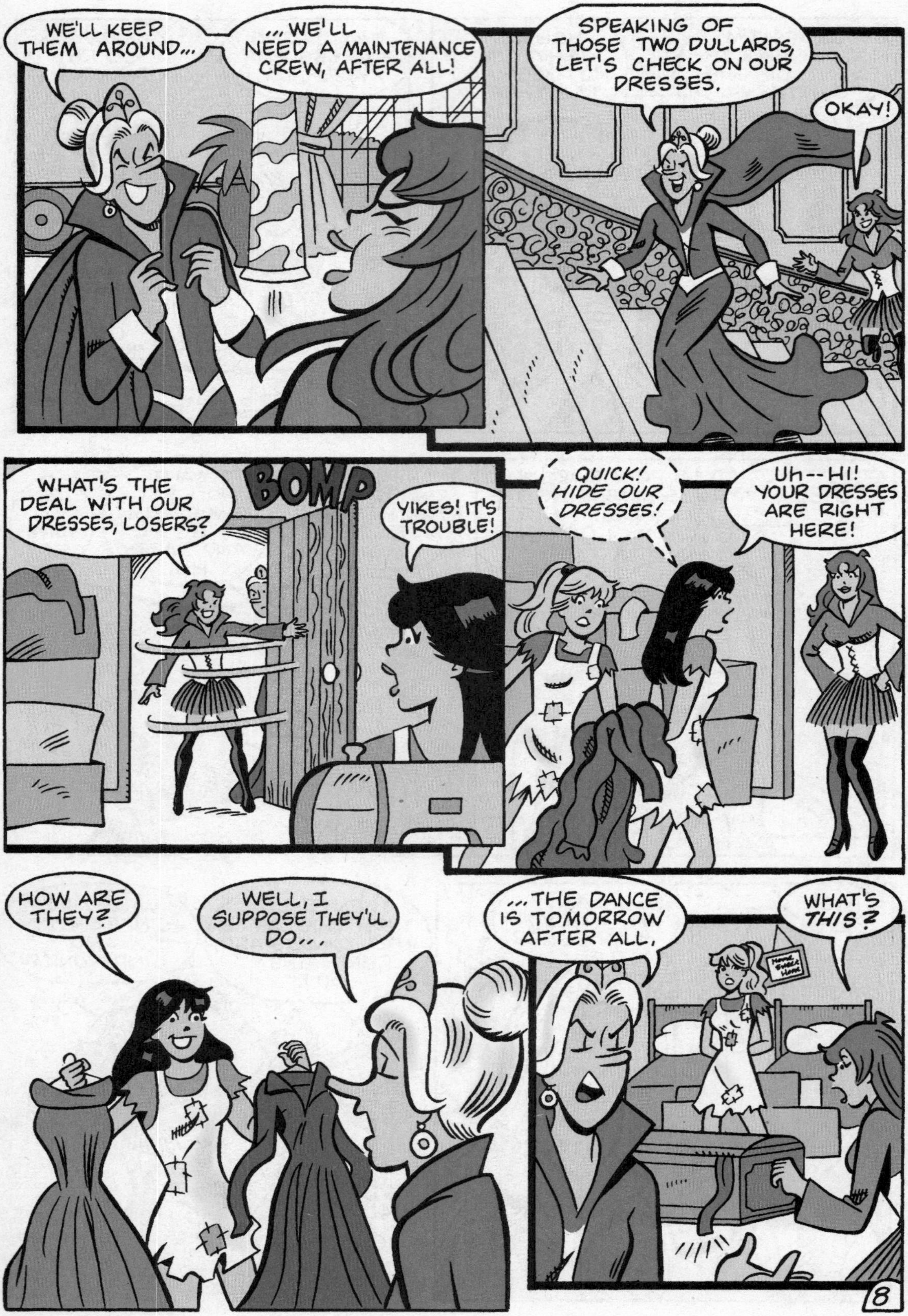
WE'LL KEEP THEM AROUND...
...WE'LL NEED A MAINTENANCE CREW, AFTER ALL!
SPEAKING OF THOSE TWO DULLARDS, LET'S CHECK ON OUR DRESSES.
OKAY!
BOMP
WHAT'S THE DEAL WITH OUR DRESSES, LOSERS?
YIKES! IT'S TROUBLE!
QUICK! HIDE OUR DRESSES!
Uh--HI! YOUR DRESSES ARE RIGHT HERE!
HOW ARE THEY?
WELL, I SUPPOSE THEY'LL DO...
...THE DANCE IS TOMORROW AFTER ALL.
WHAT'S THIS?
8

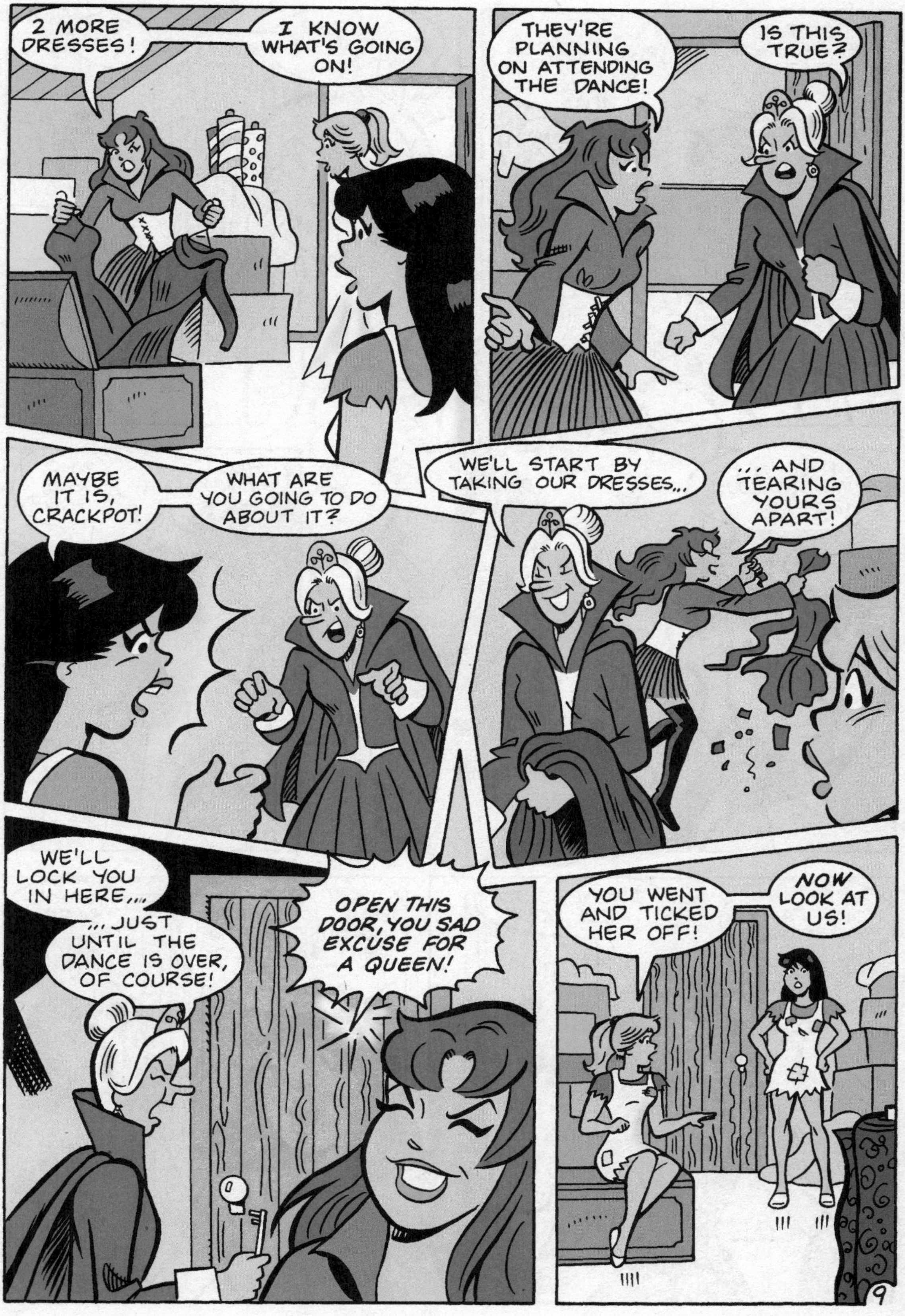
2 MORE DRESSES!
I KNOW WHAT'S GOING ON!
THEY'RE PLANNING ON ATTENDING THE DANCE!
IS THIS TRUE?
MAYBE IT IS, CRACKPOT!
WHAT ARE YOU GOING TO DO ABOUT IT?
WE'LL START BY TAKING OUR DRESSES...
... AND TEARING YOURS APART!
WE'LL LOCK YOU IN HERE,...
... JUST UNTIL THE DANCE IS OVER, OF COURSE!
OPEN THIS DOOR, YOU SAD EXCUSE FOR A QUEEN!
YOU WENT AND TICKED HER OFF!
NOW LOOK AT US!
9

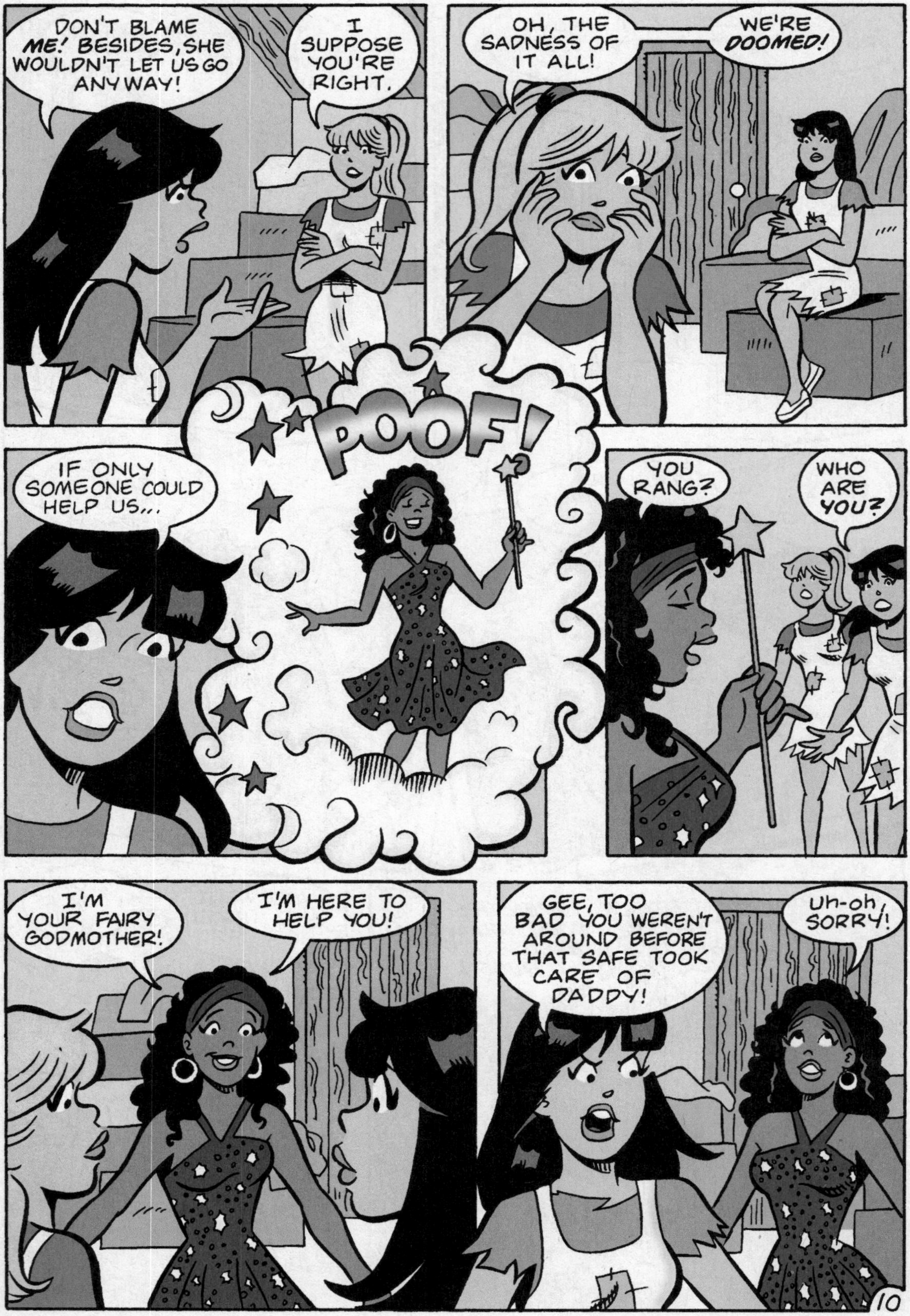
DON'T BLAME ME! BESIDES, SHE WOULDN'T LET US GO ANYWAY!
I SUPPOSE YOU'RE RIGHT.
OH, THE SADNESS OF IT ALL!
WE'RE DOOMED!
POOF!
IF ONLY SOMEONE COULD HELP US...
YOU RANG?
WHO ARE YOU?
I'M YOUR FAIRY GODMOTHER!
I'M HERE TO HELP YOU!
GEE, TOO BAD YOU WEREN'T AROUND BEFORE THAT SAFE TOOK CARE OF DADDY!
Uh-oh, SORRY!
10

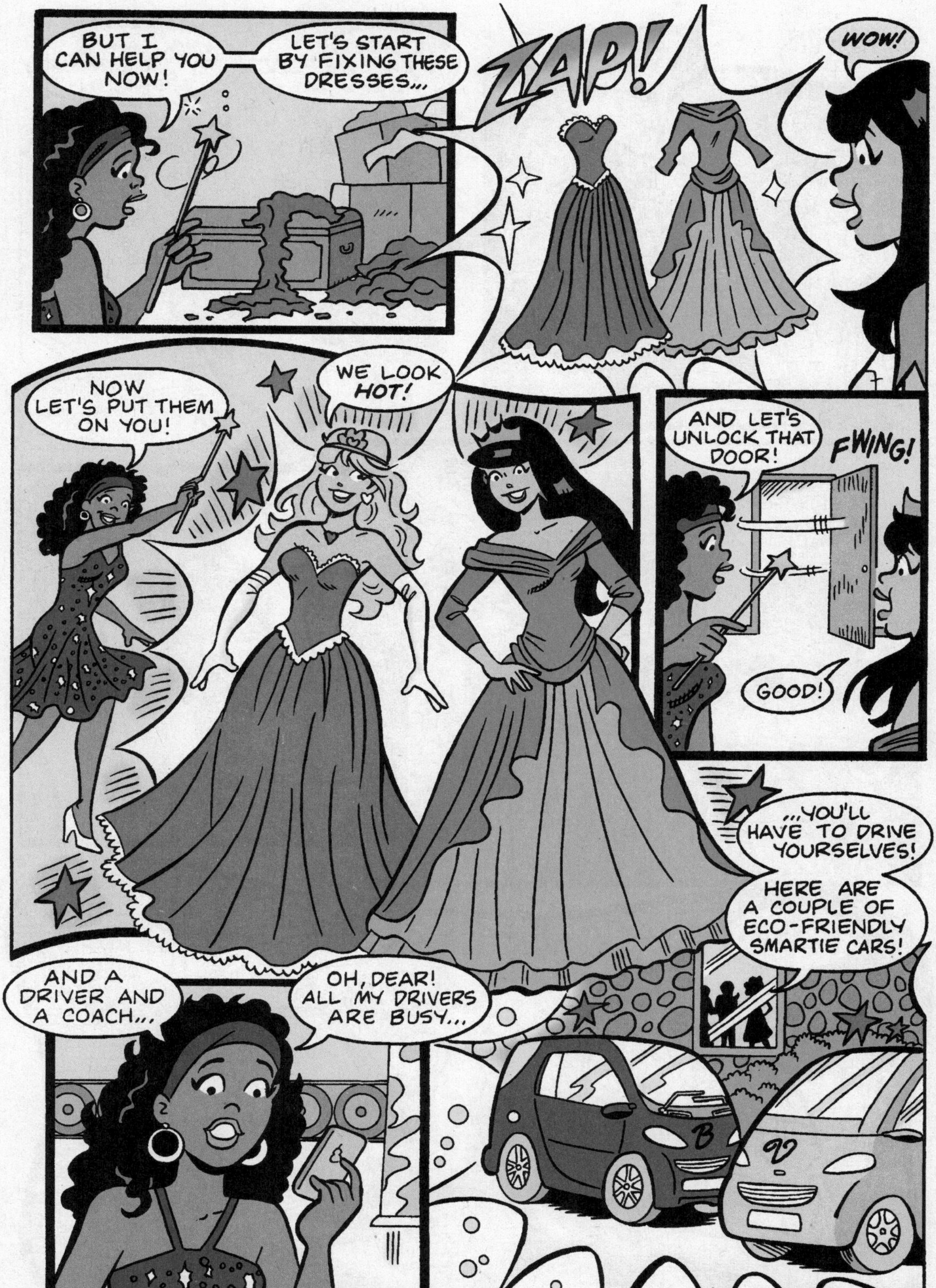
BUT I CAN HELP YOU NOW!
LET'S START BY FIXING THESE DRESSES...
ZAP!
WOW!
NOW LET'S PUT THEM ON YOU!
WE LOOK HOT!
AND LET'S UNLOCK THAT DOOR!
FWING!
GOOD!
AND A DRIVER AND A COACH...
OH, DEAR! ALL MY DRIVERS ARE BUSY...
...YOU'LL HAVE TO DRIVE YOURSELVES!
HERE ARE A COUPLE OF ECO-FRIENDLY SMARTIE CARS!
11

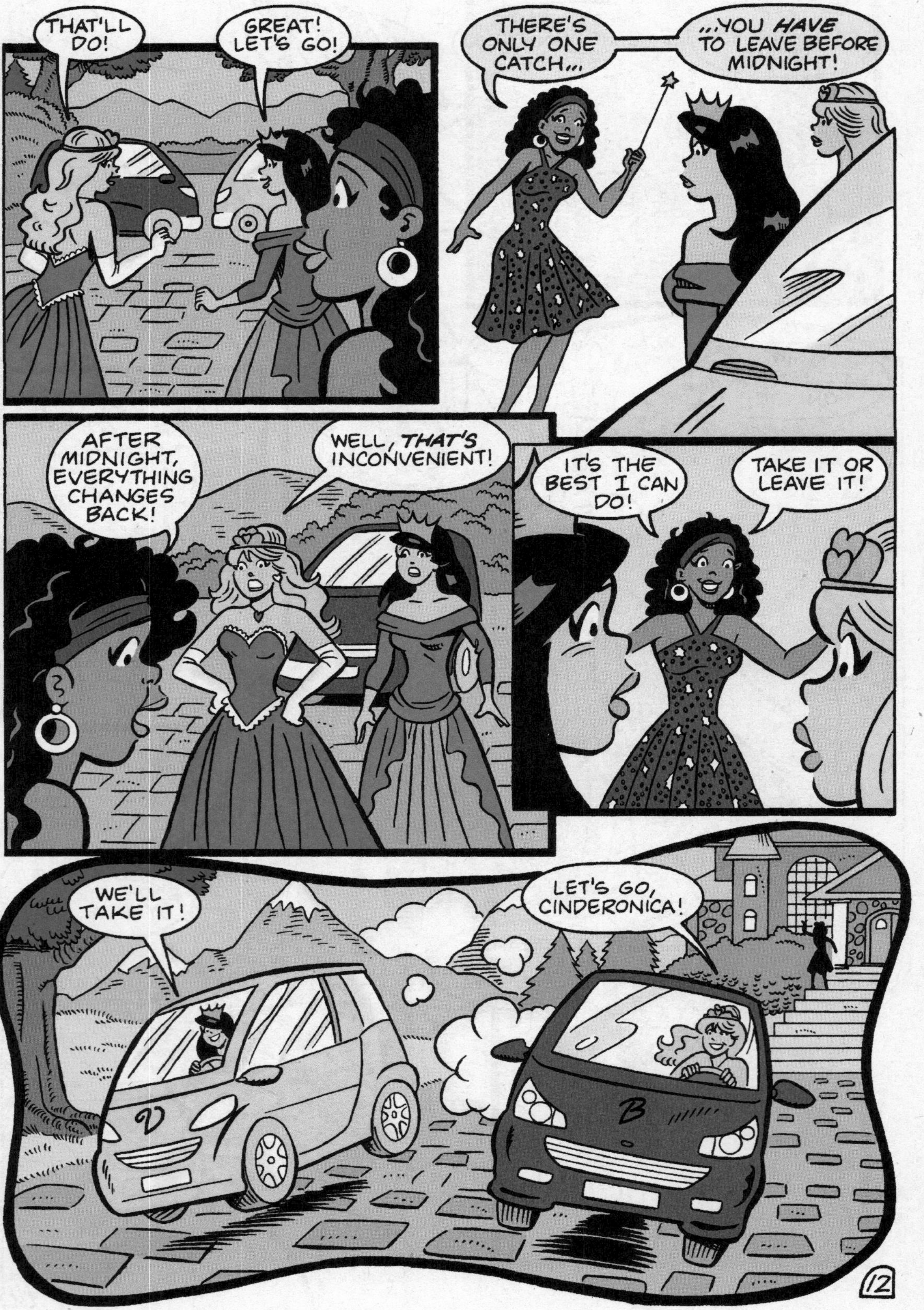
THAT'LL DO!
GREAT! LET'S GO!
THERE'S ONLY ONE CATCH...
...YOU *HAVE* TO LEAVE BEFORE MIDNIGHT!
AFTER MIDNIGHT, EVERYTHING CHANGES BACK!
WELL, *THAT'S* INCONVENIENT!
IT'S THE BEST I CAN DO!
TAKE IT OR LEAVE IT!
WE'LL TAKE IT!
LET'S GO, CINDERONICA!
12

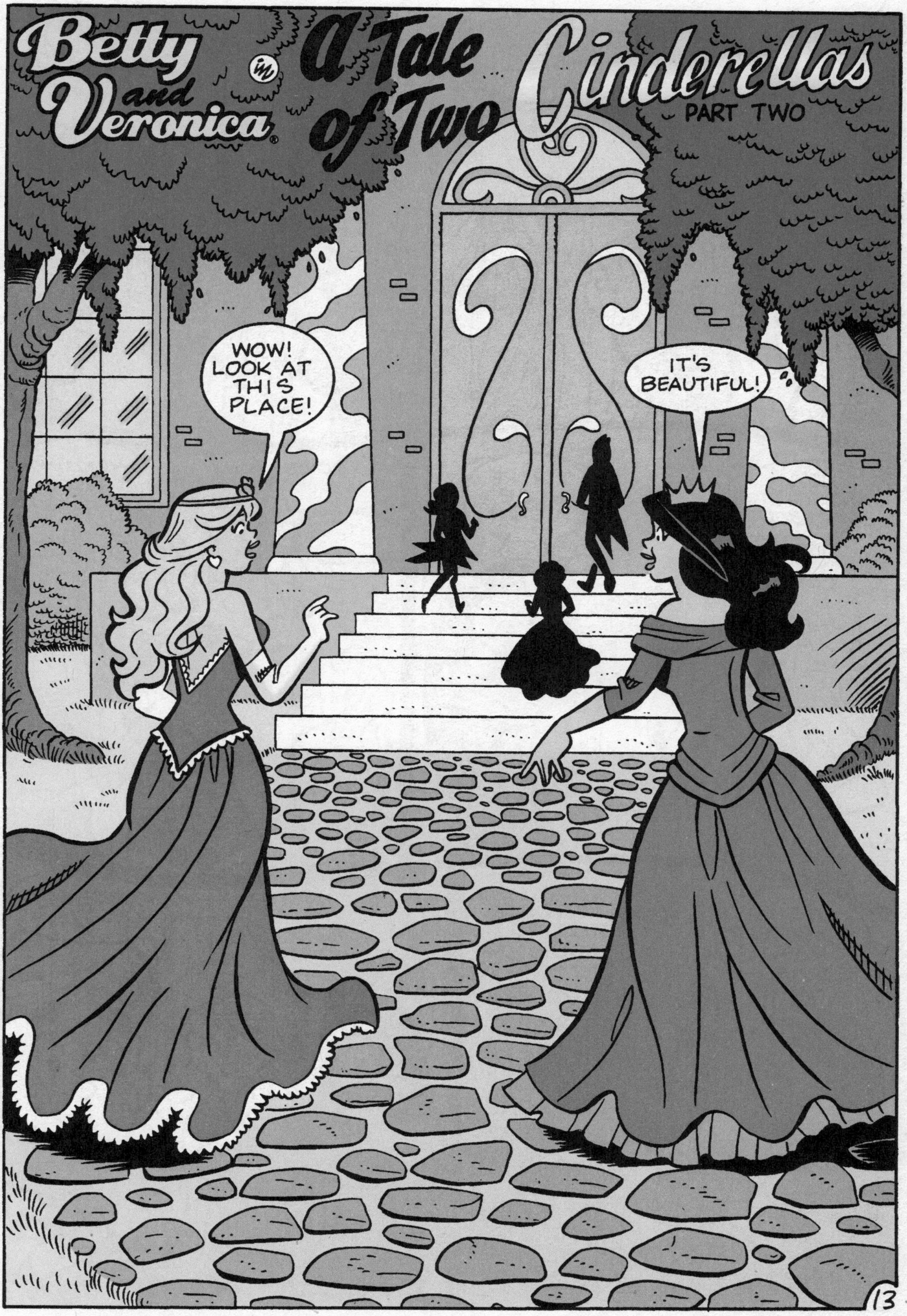
Betty and Veronica in A Tale of Two Cinderellas
PART TWO
WOW! LOOK AT THIS PLACE!
IT'S BEAUTIFUL!
13

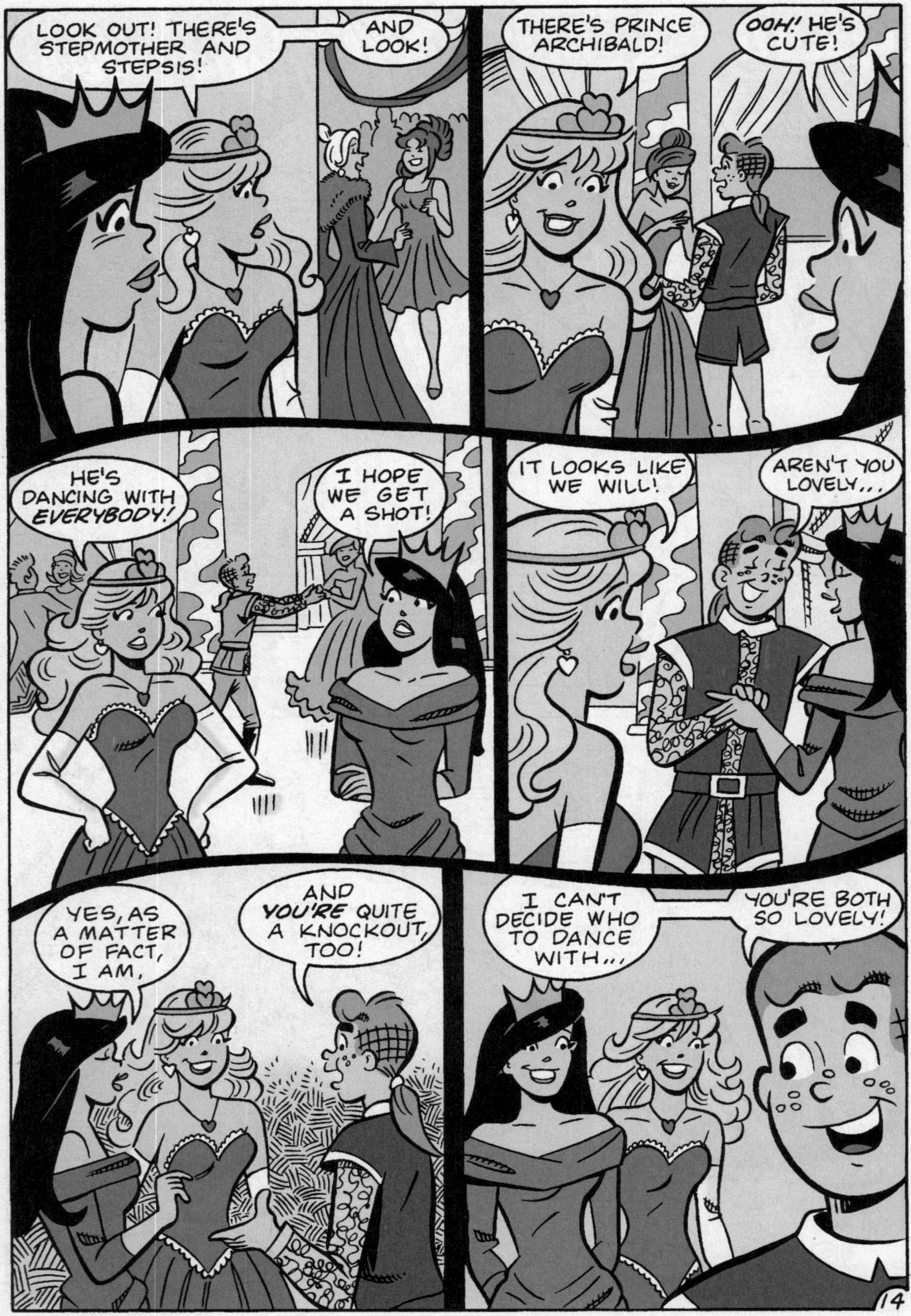
LOOK OUT! THERE'S STEPMOTHER AND STEPSIS!
AND LOOK!
THERE'S PRINCE ARCHIBALD!
OOH! HE'S CUTE!
HE'S DANCING WITH EVERYBODY!
I HOPE WE GET A SHOT!
IT LOOKS LIKE WE WILL!
AREN'T YOU LOVELY...
YES, AS A MATTER OF FACT, I AM.
AND YOU'RE QUITE A KNOCKOUT, TOO!
I CAN'T DECIDE WHO TO DANCE WITH...
YOU'RE BOTH SO LOVELY!
14

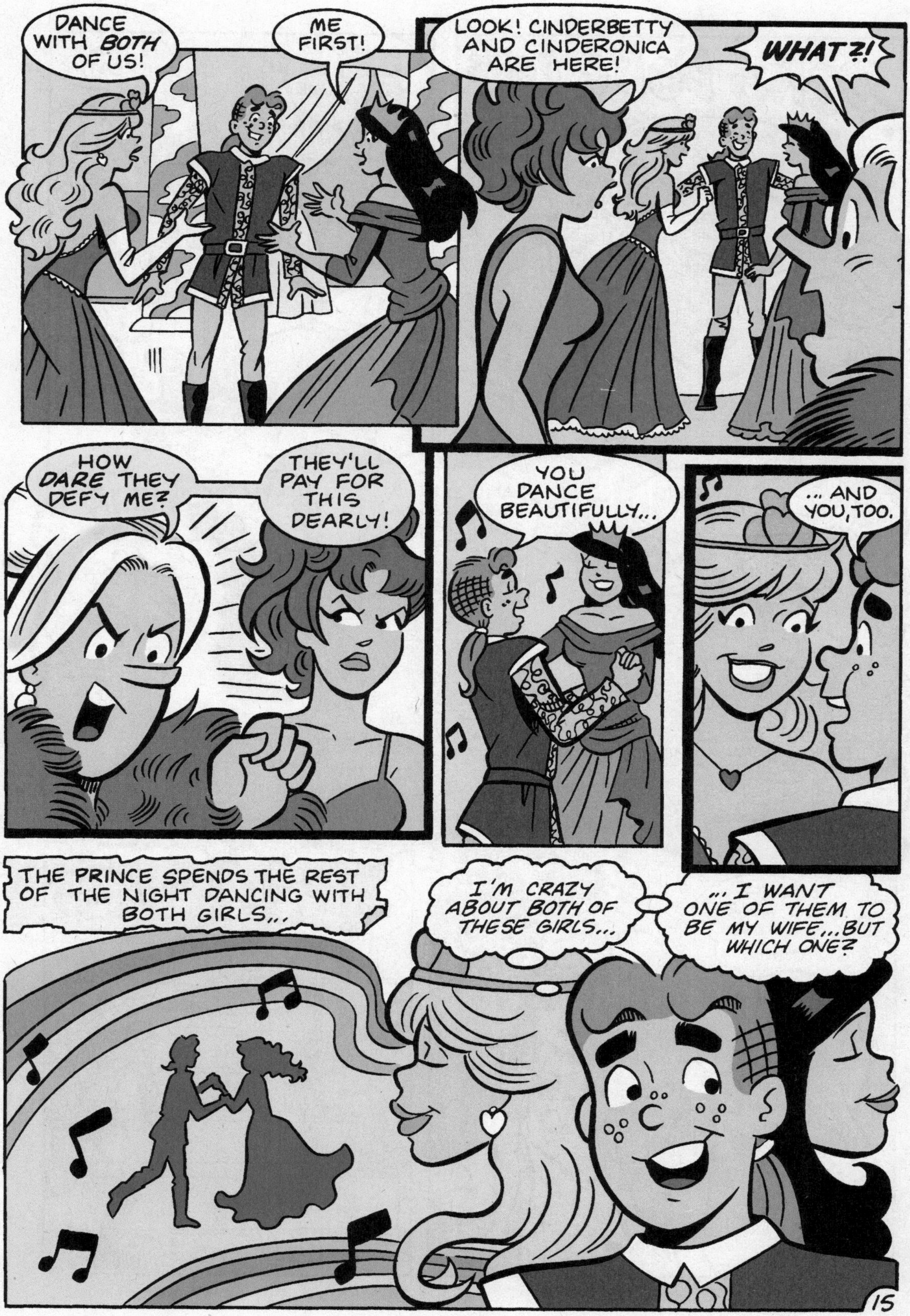
DANCE WITH *BOTH* OF US!
ME FIRST!
LOOK! CINDERBETTY AND CINDERONICA ARE HERE!
WHAT?!
HOW *DARE* THEY DEFY ME?
THEY'LL PAY FOR THIS DEARLY!
YOU DANCE BEAUTIFULLY...
... AND YOU, TOO.
THE PRINCE SPENDS THE REST OF THE NIGHT DANCING WITH BOTH GIRLS...
I'M CRAZY ABOUT BOTH OF THESE GIRLS...
... I WANT ONE OF THEM TO BE MY WIFE... BUT WHICH ONE?
15

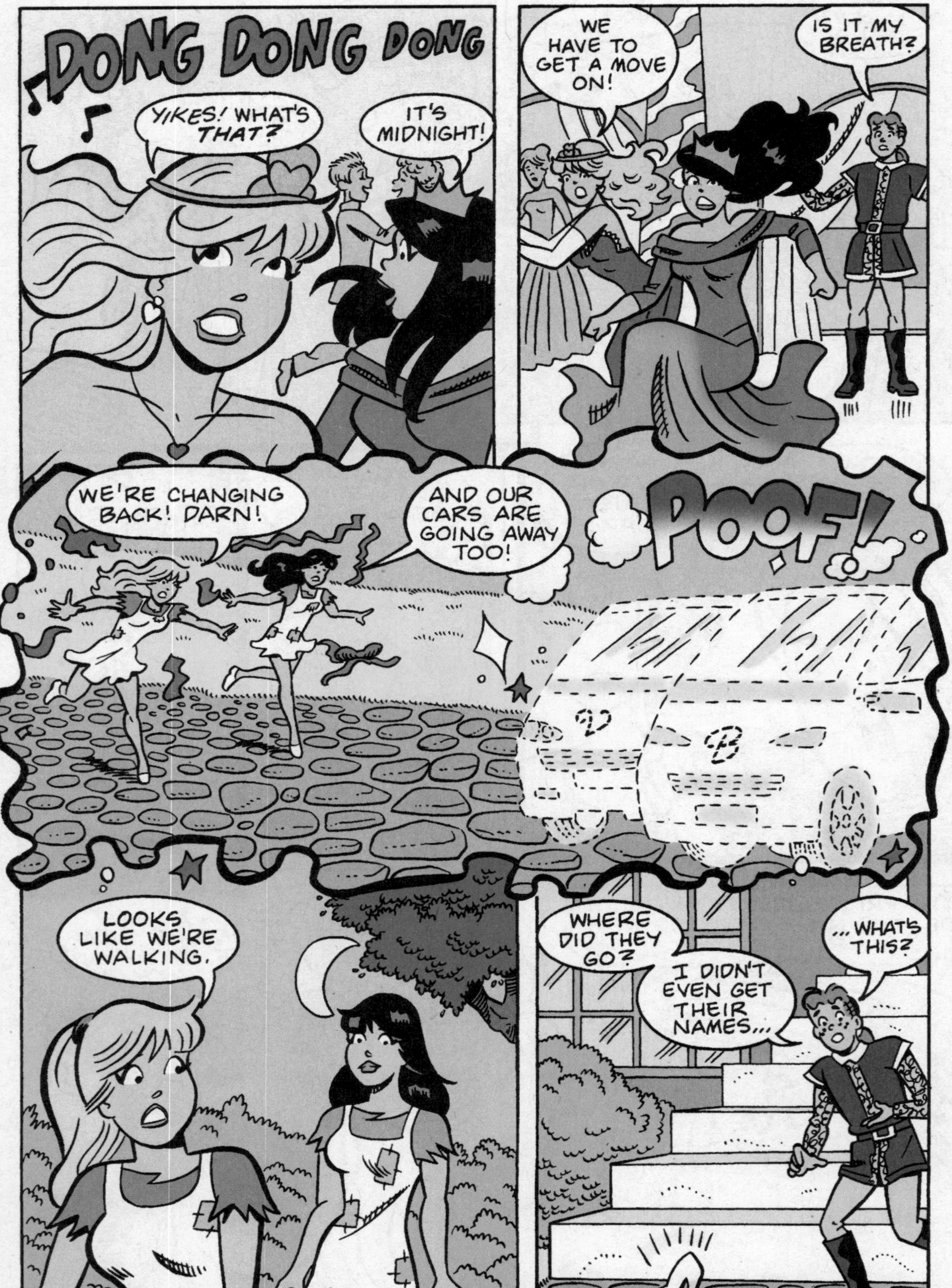
DONG DONG DONG
YIKES! WHAT'S THAT?
IT'S MIDNIGHT!
WE HAVE TO GET A MOVE ON!
IS IT MY BREATH?
WE'RE CHANGING BACK! DARN!
AND OUR CARS ARE GOING AWAY TOO!
POOF!
LOOKS LIKE WE'RE WALKING.
WHERE DID THEY GO?
I DIDN'T EVEN GET THEIR NAMES...
...WHAT'S THIS?
16

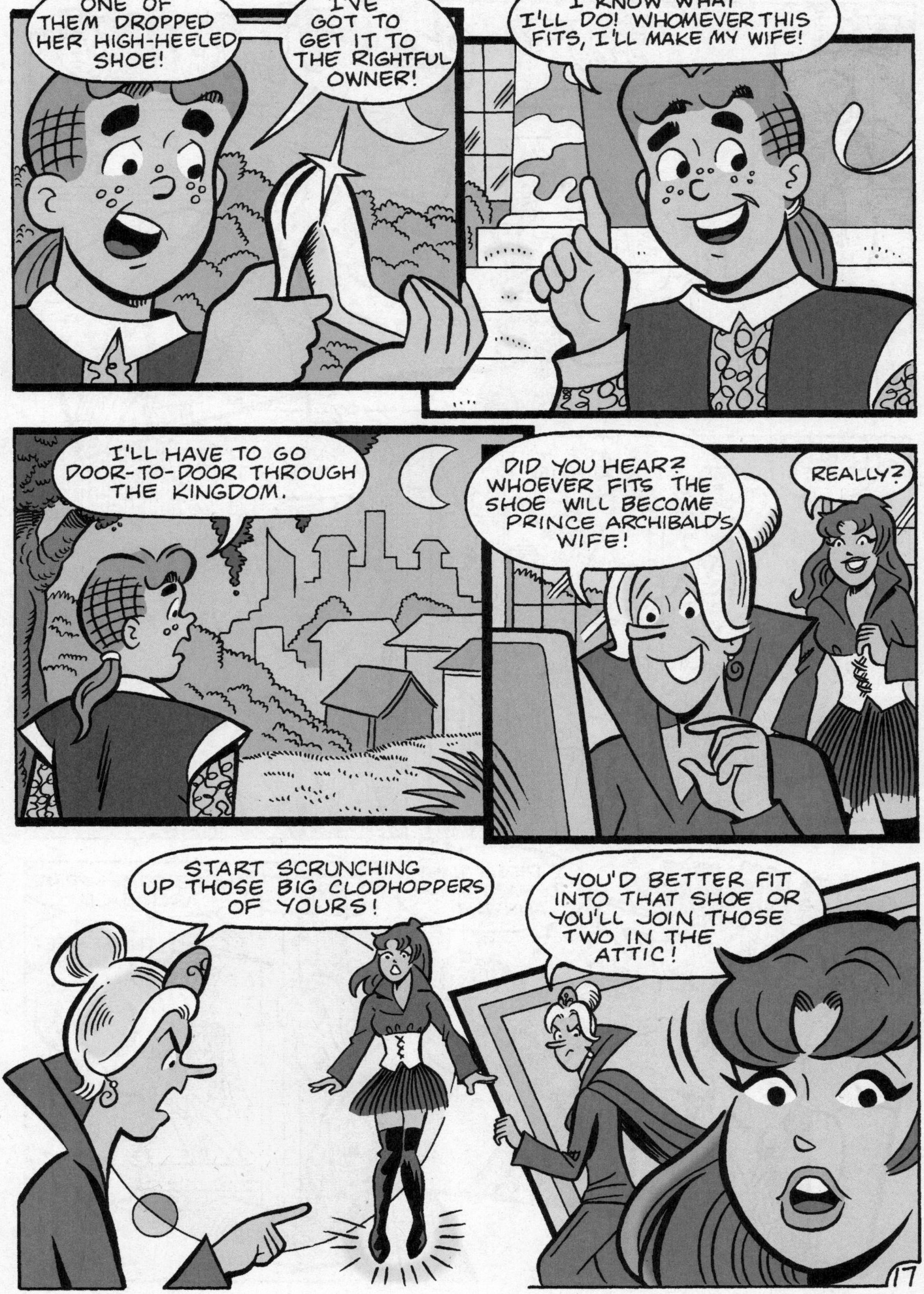
ONE OF THEM DROPPED HER HIGH-HEELED SHOE!
I'VE GOT TO GET IT TO THE RIGHTFUL OWNER!
I KNOW WHAT I'LL DO! WHOMEVER THIS FITS, I'LL MAKE MY WIFE!
I'LL HAVE TO GO DOOR-TO-DOOR THROUGH THE KINGDOM.
DID YOU HEAR? WHOEVER FITS THE SHOE WILL BECOME PRINCE ARCHIBALD'S WIFE!
REALLY?
START SCRUNCHING UP THOSE BIG CLODHOPPERS OF YOURS!
YOU'D BETTER FIT INTO THAT SHOE OR YOU'LL JOIN THOSE TWO IN THE ATTIC!
17

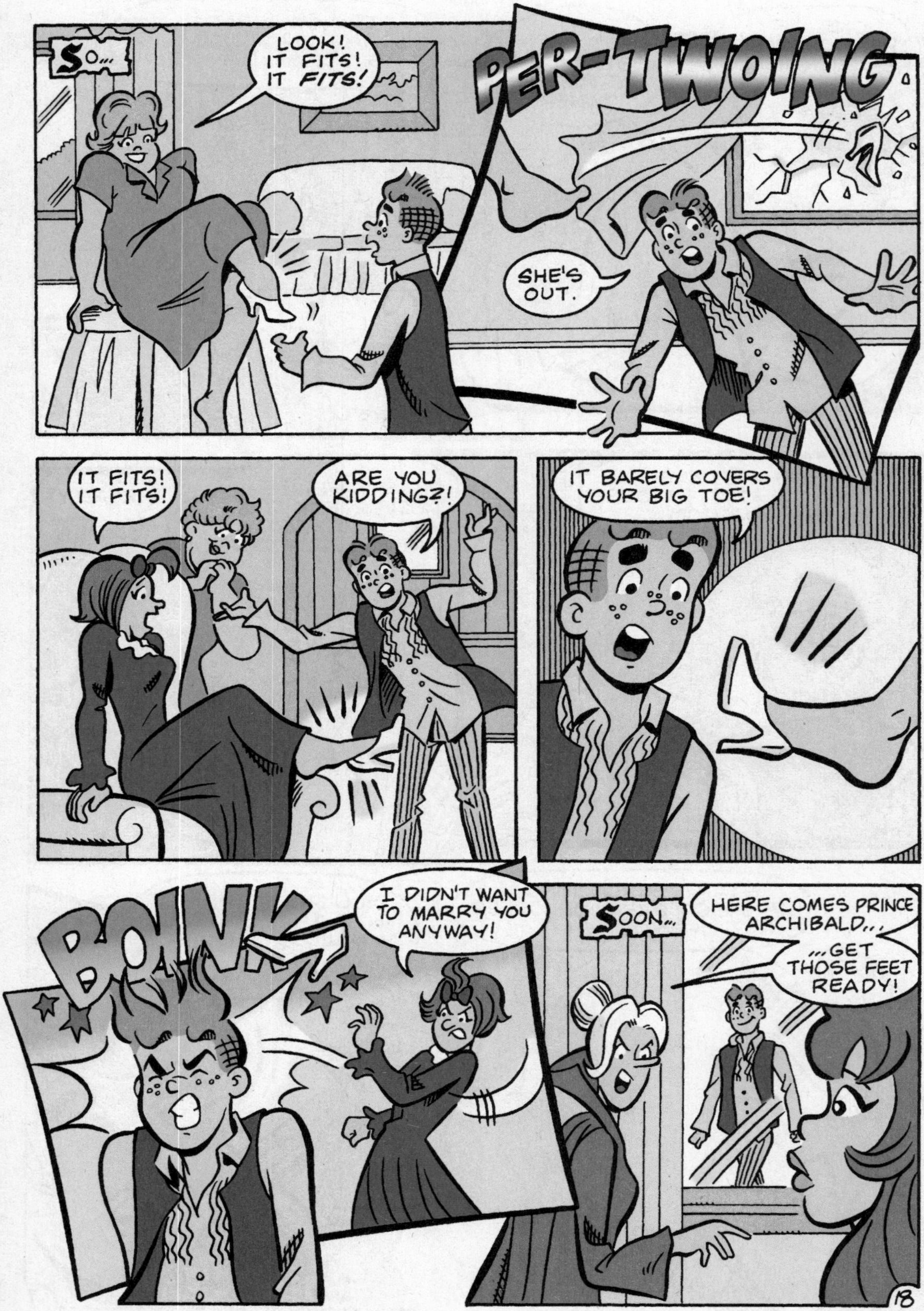
SO...
LOOK! IT FITS! IT FITS!
PER-TWOING
SHE'S OUT.
IT FITS! IT FITS!
ARE YOU KIDDING?!
IT BARELY COVERS YOUR BIG TOE!
BOINK
I DIDN'T WANT TO MARRY YOU ANYWAY!
SOON...
HERE COMES PRINCE ARCHIBALD...
...GET THOSE FEET READY!
18

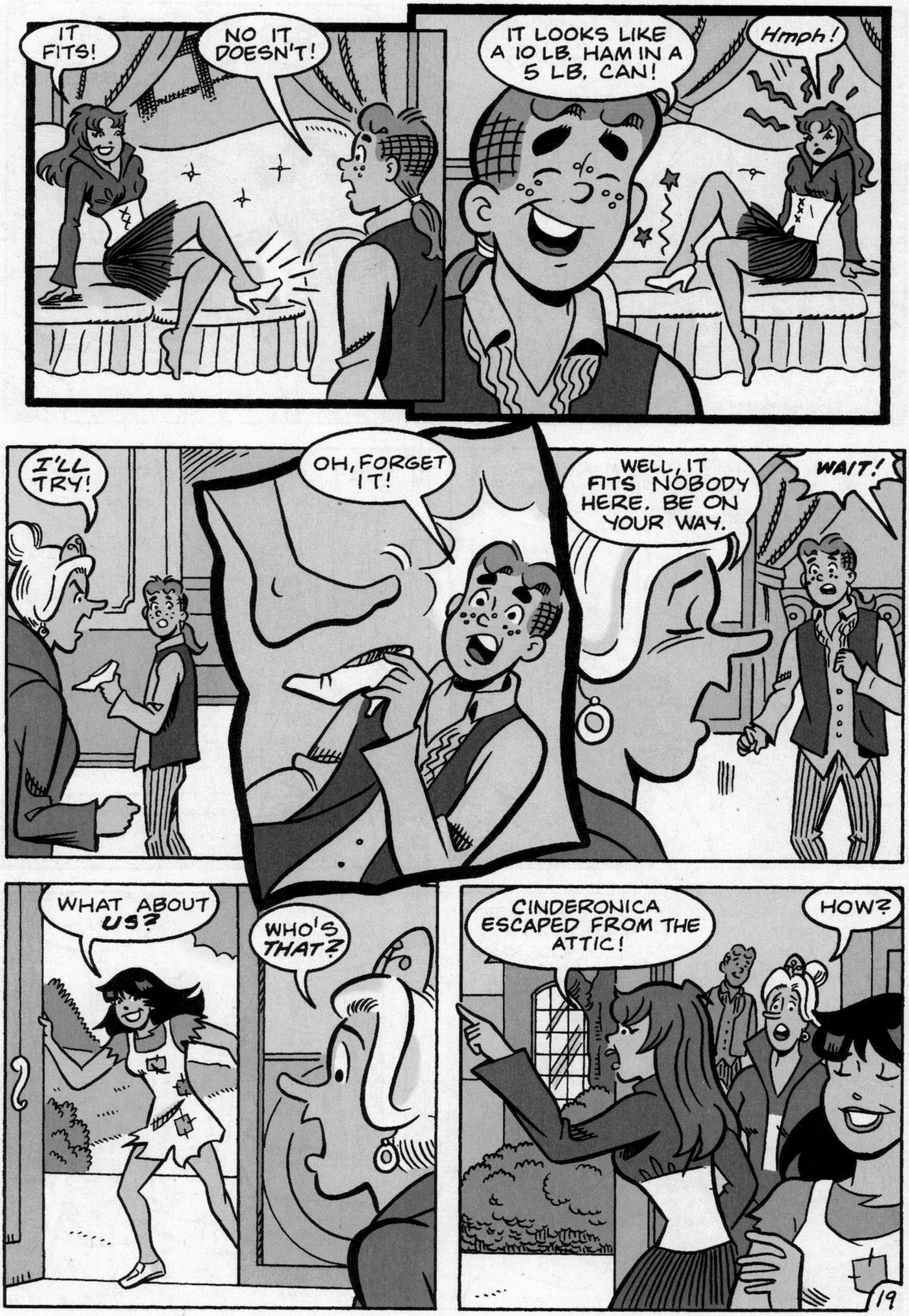
IT FITS!
NO IT DOESN'T!
IT LOOKS LIKE A 10 LB. HAM IN A 5 LB. CAN!
Hmph!
I'LL TRY!
OH, FORGET IT!
WELL, IT FITS NOBODY HERE. BE ON YOUR WAY.
WAIT!
WHAT ABOUT US?
WHO'S THAT?
CINDERONICA ESCAPED FROM THE ATTIC!
HOW?
19

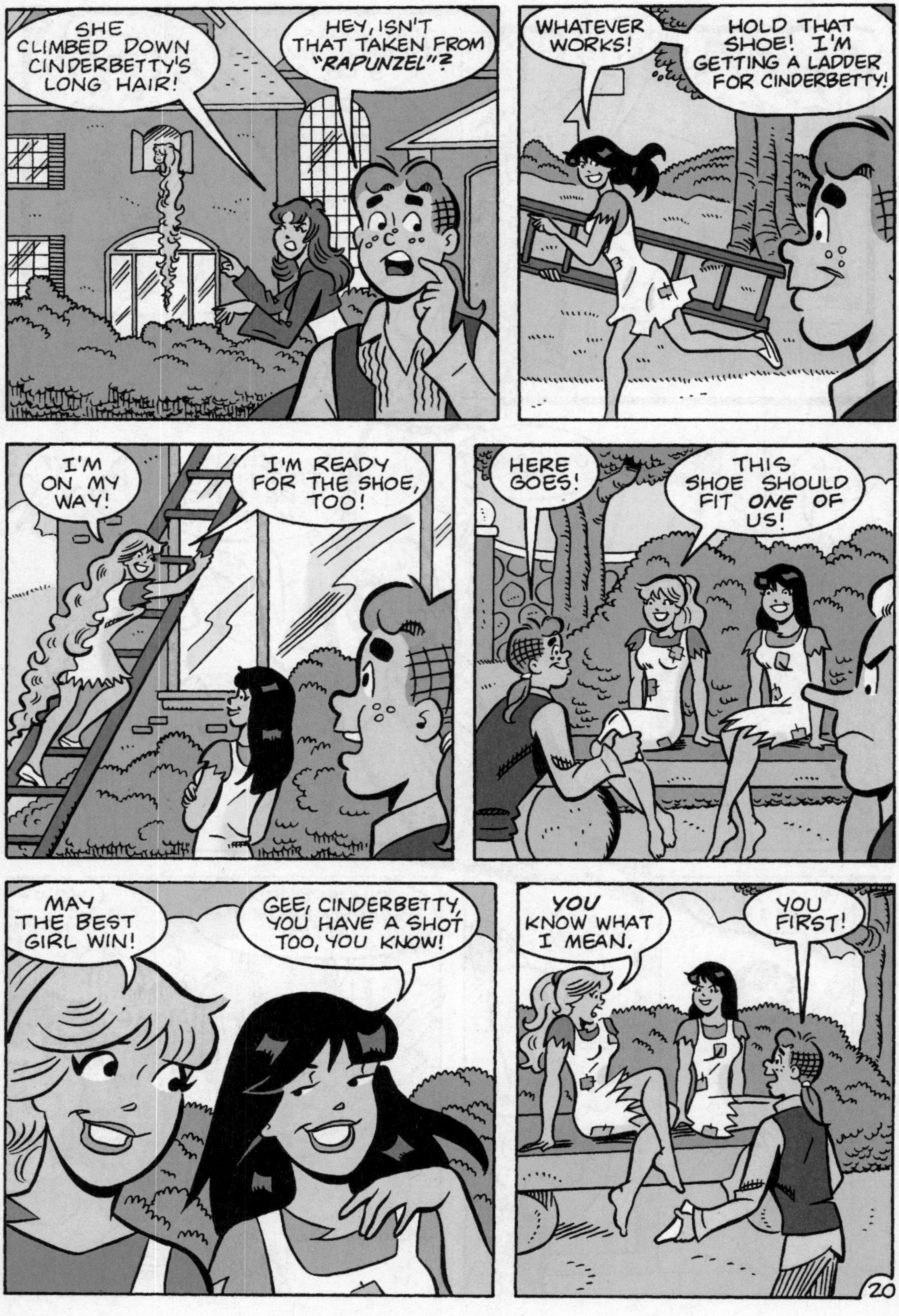
SHE CLIMBED DOWN CINDERBETTY'S LONG HAIR!
HEY, ISN'T THAT TAKEN FROM "RAPUNZEL"?
WHATEVER WORKS!
HOLD THAT SHOE! I'M GETTING A LADDER FOR CINDERBETTY!
I'M ON MY WAY!
I'M READY FOR THE SHOE, TOO!
HERE GOES!
THIS SHOE SHOULD FIT ONE OF US!
MAY THE BEST GIRL WIN!
GEE, CINDERBETTY, YOU HAVE A SHOT TOO, YOU KNOW!
YOU KNOW WHAT I MEAN.
YOU FIRST!
20

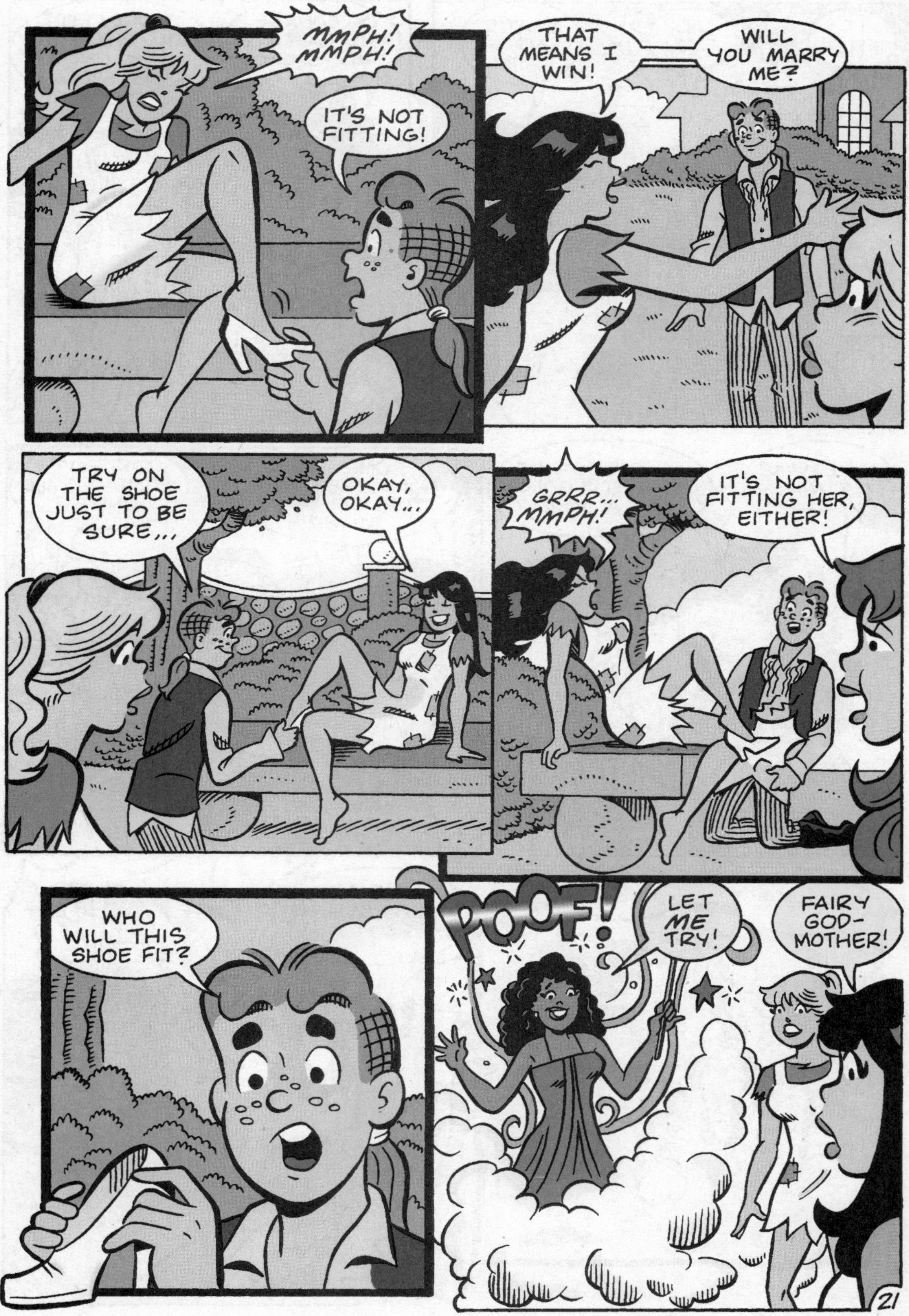

MMPH! MMPH!
IT'S NOT FITTING!
THAT MEANS I WIN!
WILL YOU MARRY ME?
TRY ON THE SHOE JUST TO BE SURE...
OKAY, OKAY...
GRRR... MMPH!
IT'S NOT FITTING HER, EITHER!
WHO WILL THIS SHOE FIT?
POOF!
LET ME TRY!
FAIRY GOD-MOTHER!
21

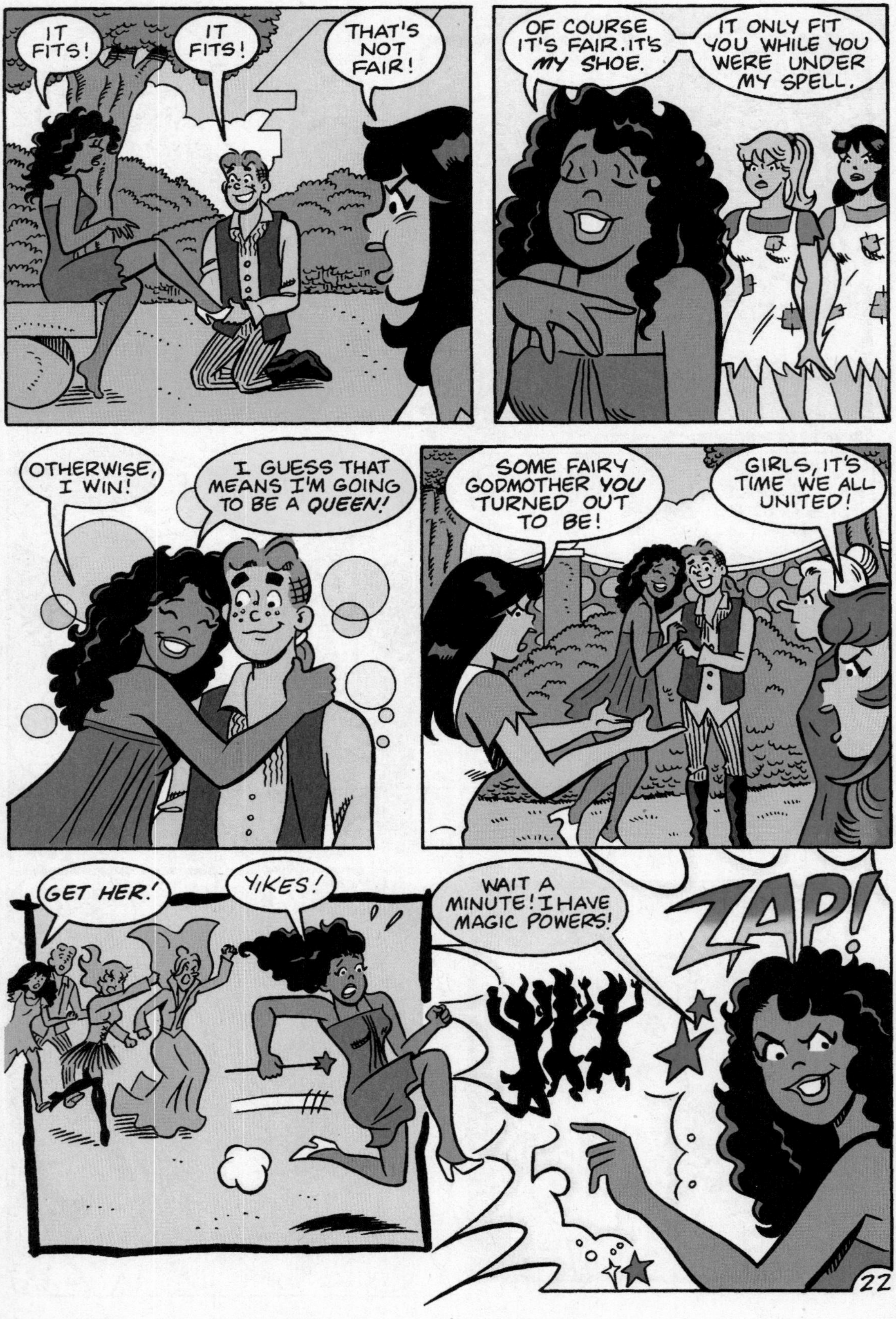
IT FITS!
IT FITS!
THAT'S NOT FAIR!
OF COURSE IT'S FAIR. IT'S MY SHOE.
IT ONLY FIT YOU WHILE YOU WERE UNDER MY SPELL.
OTHERWISE, I WIN!
I GUESS THAT MEANS I'M GOING TO BE A QUEEN!
SOME FAIRY GODMOTHER YOU TURNED OUT TO BE!
GIRLS, IT'S TIME WE ALL UNITED!
GET HER!
YIKES!
WAIT A MINUTE! I HAVE MAGIC POWERS!
ZAP!
22

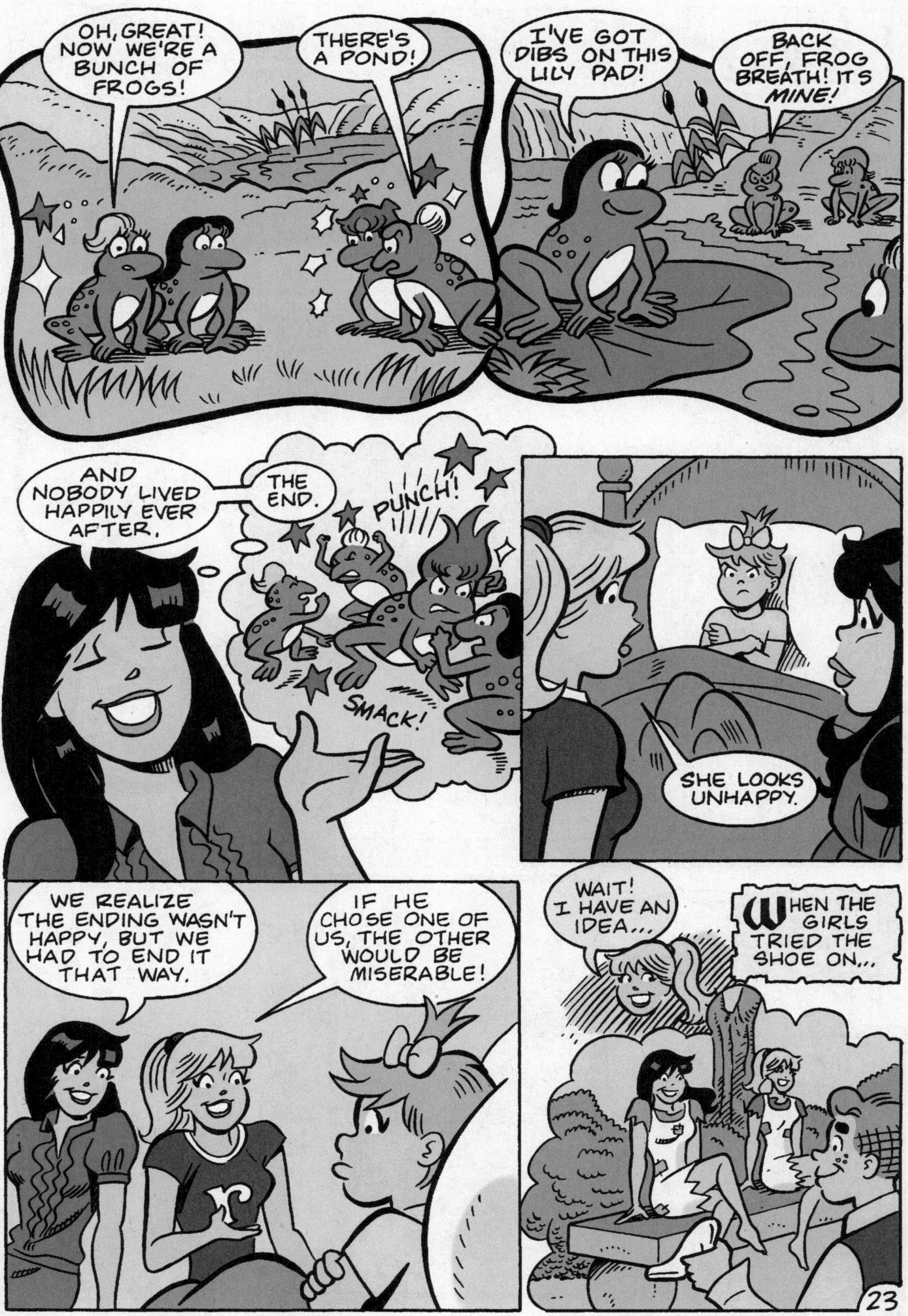
OH, GREAT! NOW WE'RE A BUNCH OF FROGS!
THERE'S A POND!
I'VE GOT DIBS ON THIS LILY PAD!
BACK OFF, FROG BREATH! IT'S MINE!
AND NOBODY LIVED HAPPILY EVER AFTER.
THE END.
PUNCH!
SMACK!
SHE LOOKS UNHAPPY.
WE REALIZE THE ENDING WASN'T HAPPY, BUT WE HAD TO END IT THAT WAY.
IF HE CHOSE ONE OF US, THE OTHER WOULD BE MISERABLE!
WAIT! I HAVE AN IDEA...
WHEN THE GIRLS TRIED THE SHOE ON...
23

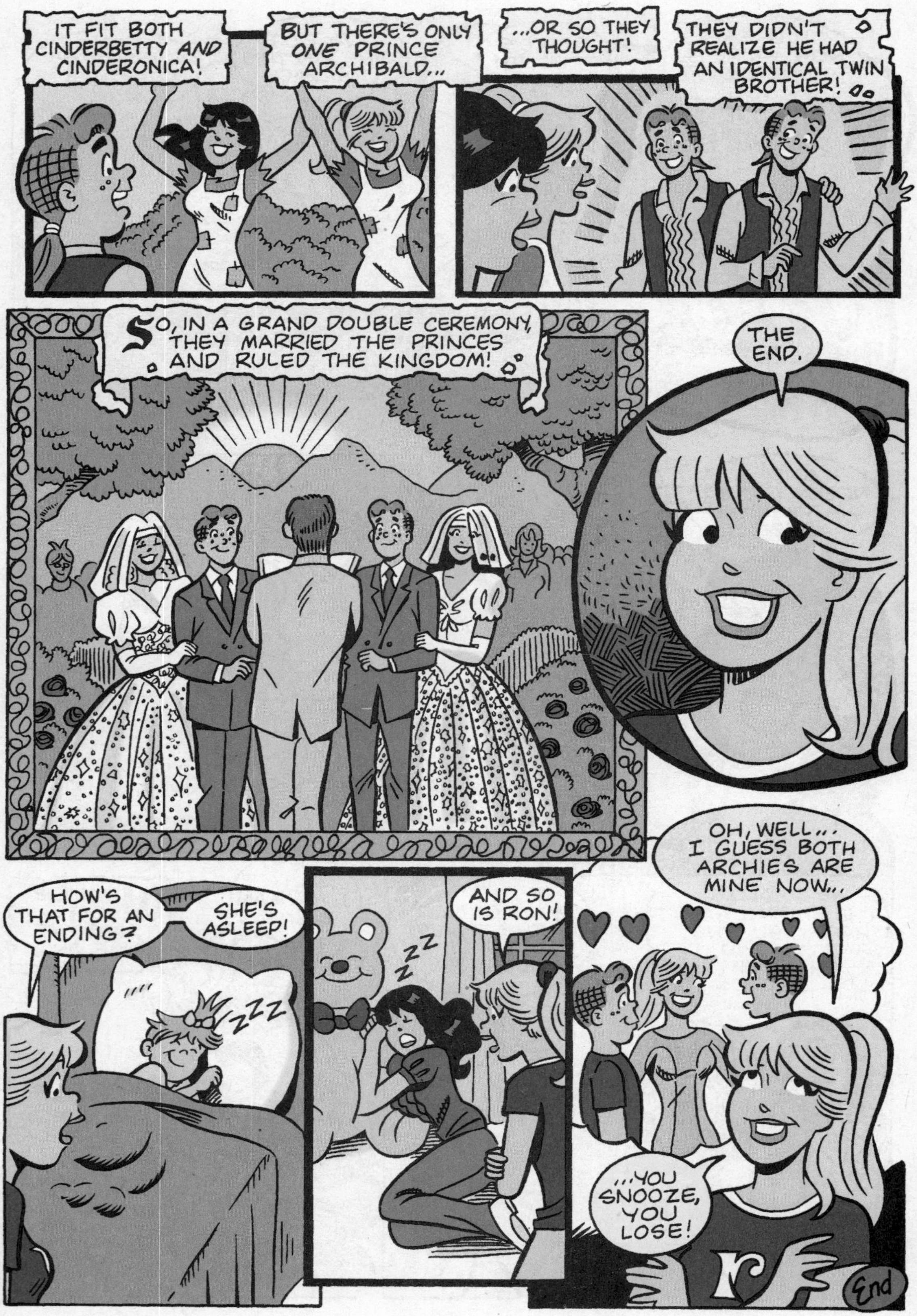
IT FIT BOTH CINDERBETTY *AND* CINDERONICA!
BUT THERE'S ONLY *ONE* PRINCE ARCHIBALD...
...OR SO THEY THOUGHT!
THEY DIDN'T REALIZE HE HAD AN IDENTICAL TWIN BROTHER!
SO, IN A GRAND DOUBLE CEREMONY, THEY MARRIED THE PRINCES AND RULED THE KINGDOM!
THE END.
HOW'S THAT FOR AN ENDING?
SHE'S ASLEEP!
ZZZ
AND SO IS RON!
ZZZ
OH, WELL... I GUESS BOTH ARCHIES ARE MINE NOW...
...YOU SNOOZE, YOU LOSE!
End

CHAPTER FIVE

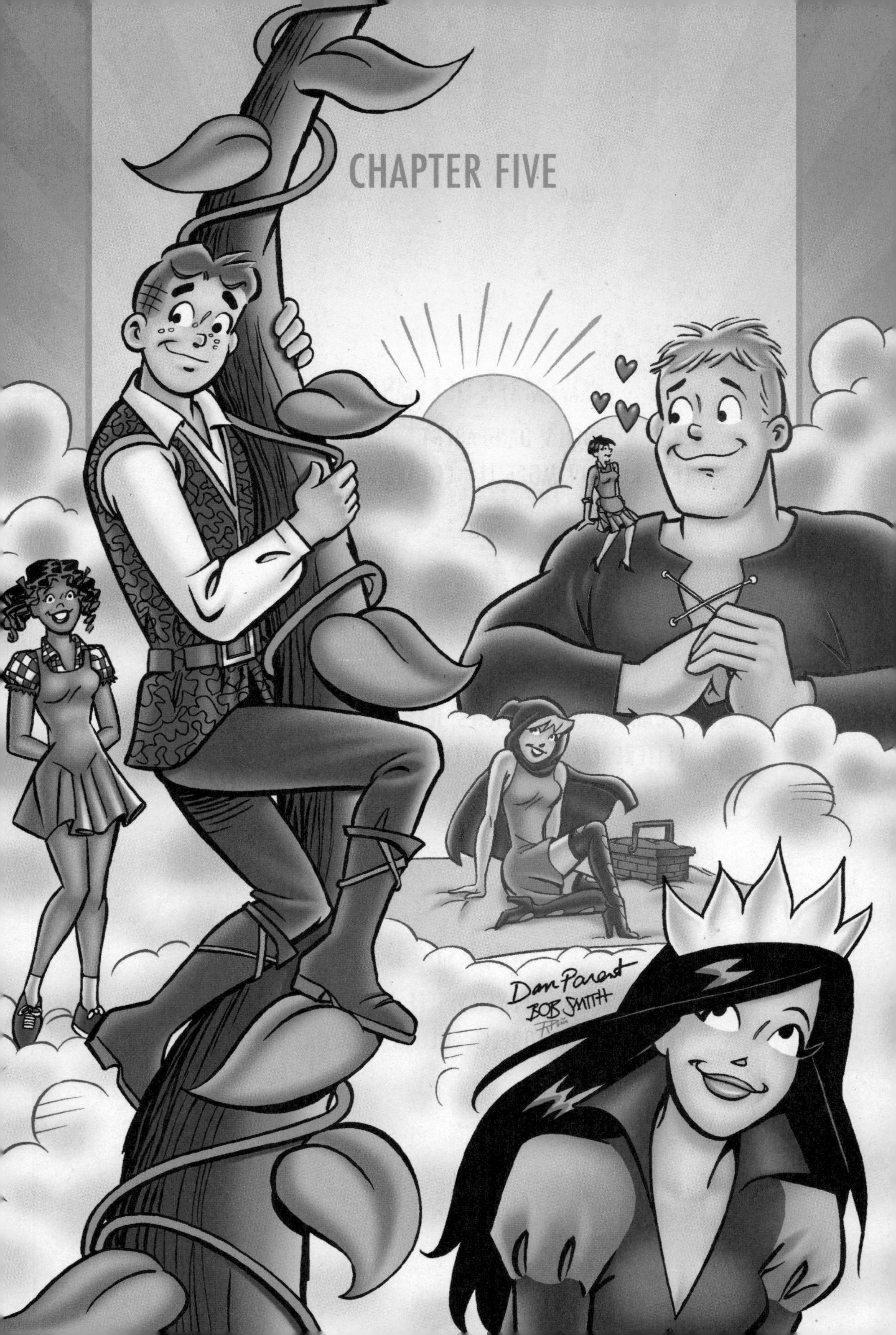
Dan Parent
BOB SMITH

ARCHIE IN
WHAT'S THE STORY? PTS 1 & 2
NOVEMBER-DECEMBER 2012
SCRIPT & PENCILS: DAN PARENT   INKS: RICH KOSLOWSKI
LETTERS: JACK MORELLI   COLORS: DIGIKORE STUDIOS

BETTY & VERONICA IN
BETTY AND THE BEAST
JUNE 2013
SCRIPT: DAN PARENT   PENCILS: JEFF SHULTZ   INKS: BOB SMITH
LETTERS: JACK MORELLI COLORS: DIGIKORE STUDIOS

BETTY & VERONICA IN
SNOW WHITE AND THE RIVERDALE DWARVES
AUGUST 2013
SCRIPT: DAN PARENT   PENCILS: JEFF SHULTZ   INKS: BOB SMITH
LETTERS: JACK MORELLI COLORS: DIGIKORE STUDIOS

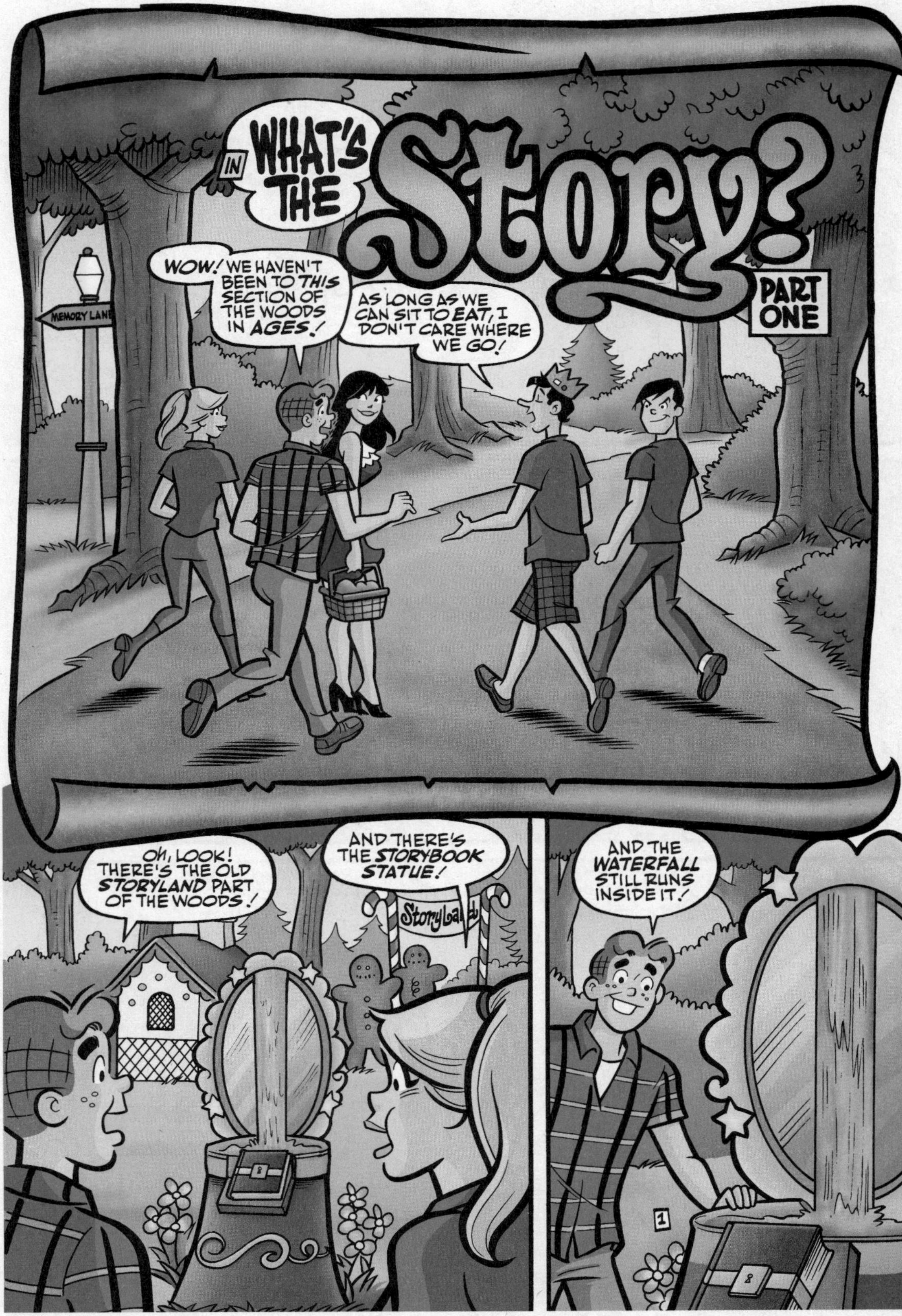

IN WHAT'S THE Story? PART ONE
MEMORY LANE
WOW! WE HAVEN'T BEEN TO THIS SECTION OF THE WOODS IN AGES!
AS LONG AS WE CAN SIT TO EAT, I DON'T CARE WHERE WE GO!
OH, LOOK! THERE'S THE OLD STORYLAND PART OF THE WOODS!
AND THERE'S THE STORYBOOK STATUE!
StoryLand
AND THE WATERFALL STILL RUNS INSIDE IT!
1

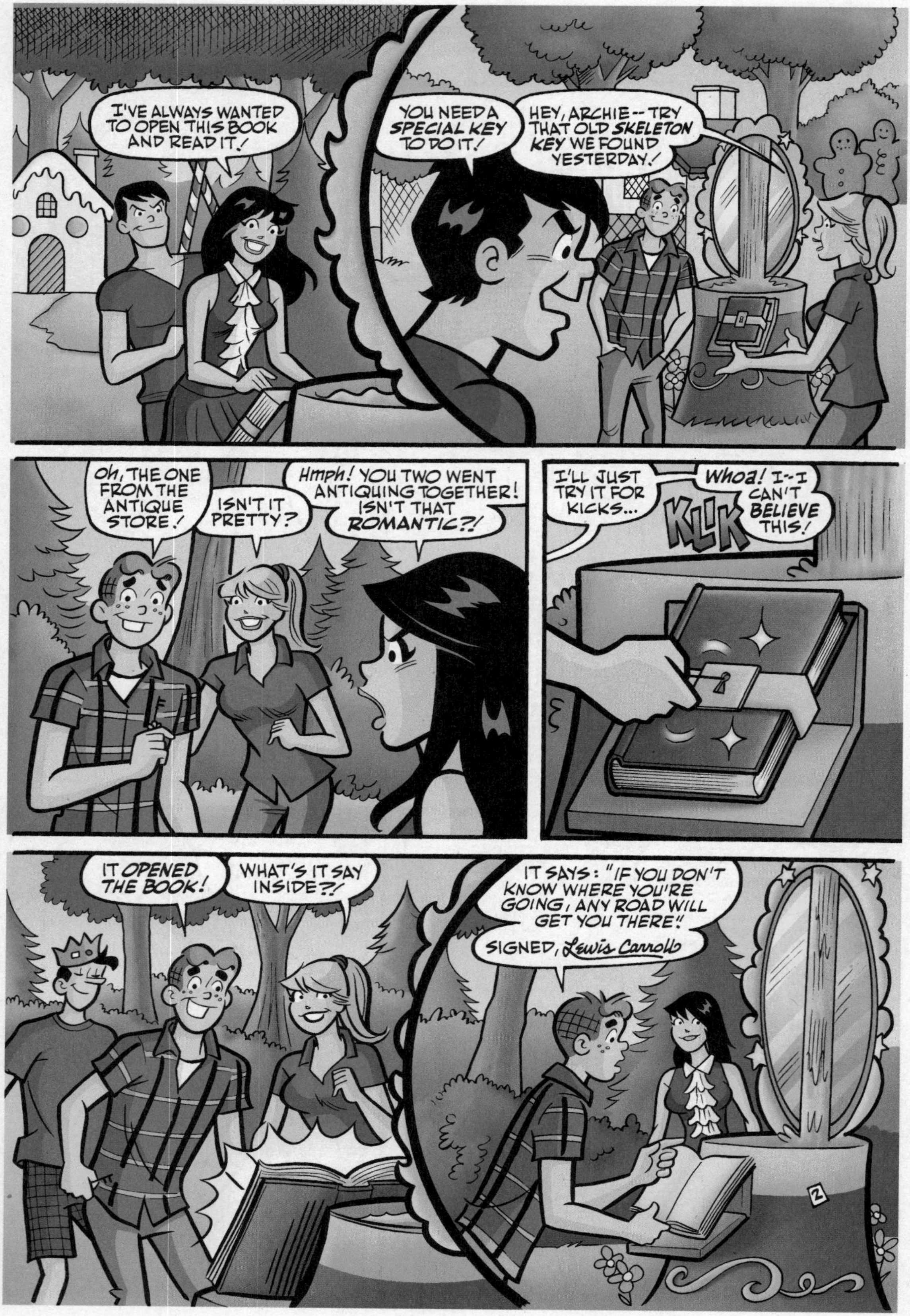
I'VE ALWAYS WANTED TO OPEN THIS BOOK AND READ IT!
YOU NEED A SPECIAL KEY TO DO IT!
HEY, ARCHIE-- TRY THAT OLD SKELETON KEY WE FOUND YESTERDAY!
Oh, THE ONE FROM THE ANTIQUE STORE!
ISN'T IT PRETTY?
Hmph! YOU TWO WENT ANTIQUING TOGETHER! ISN'T THAT ROMANTIC?!
I'LL JUST TRY IT FOR KICKS...
KLIK
Whoa! I--I CAN'T BELIEVE THIS!
IT OPENED THE BOOK!
WHAT'S IT SAY INSIDE?!
IT SAYS: "IF YOU DON'T KNOW WHERE YOU'RE GOING, ANY ROAD WILL GET YOU THERE!"
SIGNED, Lewis Carroll
2

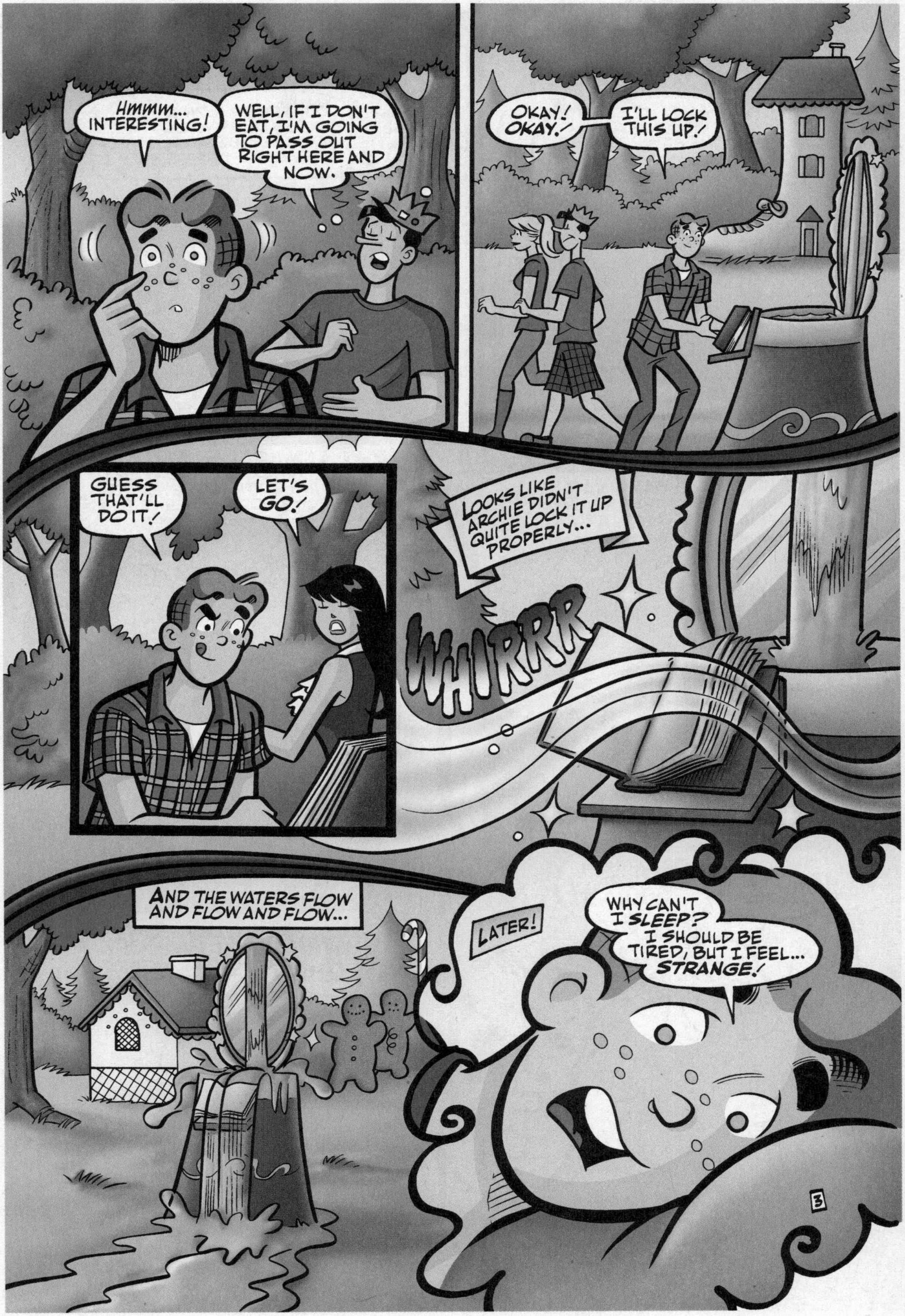
HMMM... INTERESTING!
WELL, IF I DON'T EAT, I'M GOING TO PASS OUT RIGHT HERE AND NOW.
OKAY! OKAY.!
I'LL LOCK THIS UP.!
GUESS THAT'LL DO IT.!
LET'S GO!
LOOKS LIKE ARCHIE DIDN'T QUITE LOCK IT UP PROPERLY...
WHIRRR
AND THE WATERS FLOW AND FLOW AND FLOW...
LATER!
WHY CAN'T I SLEEP? I SHOULD BE TIRED, BUT I FEEL... STRANGE!
3

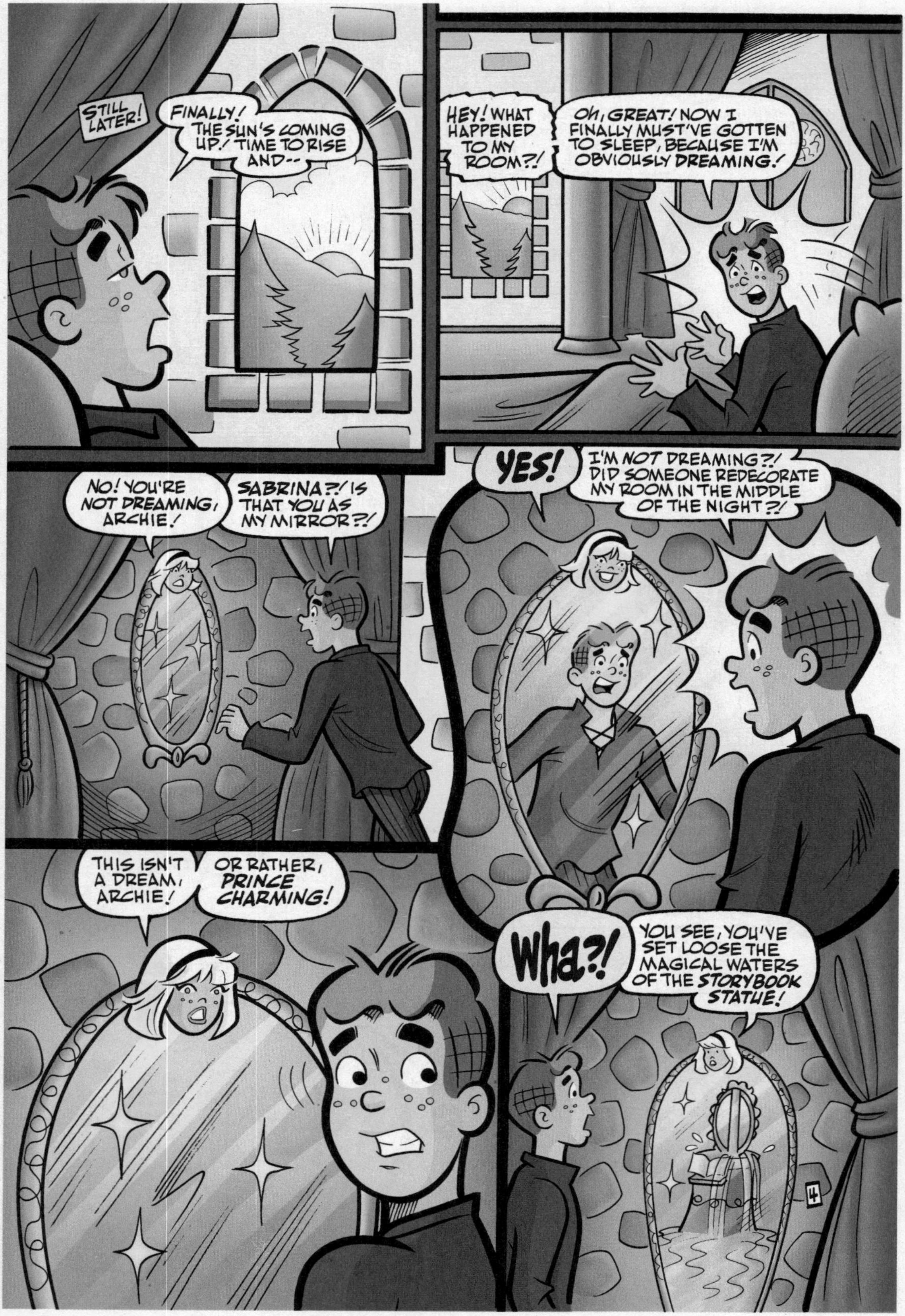
STILL LATER!
FINALLY! THE SUN'S COMING UP! TIME TO RISE AND--
HEY! WHAT HAPPENED TO MY ROOM?!
OH, GREAT! NOW I FINALLY MUST'VE GOTTEN TO SLEEP, BECAUSE I'M OBVIOUSLY DREAMING!
NO! YOU'RE NOT DREAMING, ARCHIE!
SABRINA?! IS THAT YOU AS MY MIRROR?!
YES!
I'M NOT DREAMING?! DID SOMEONE REDECORATE MY ROOM IN THE MIDDLE OF THE NIGHT?!
THIS ISN'T A DREAM, ARCHIE!
OR RATHER, PRINCE CHARMING!
WHA?!
YOU SEE, YOU'VE SET LOOSE THE MAGICAL WATERS OF THE STORYBOOK STATUE!
4

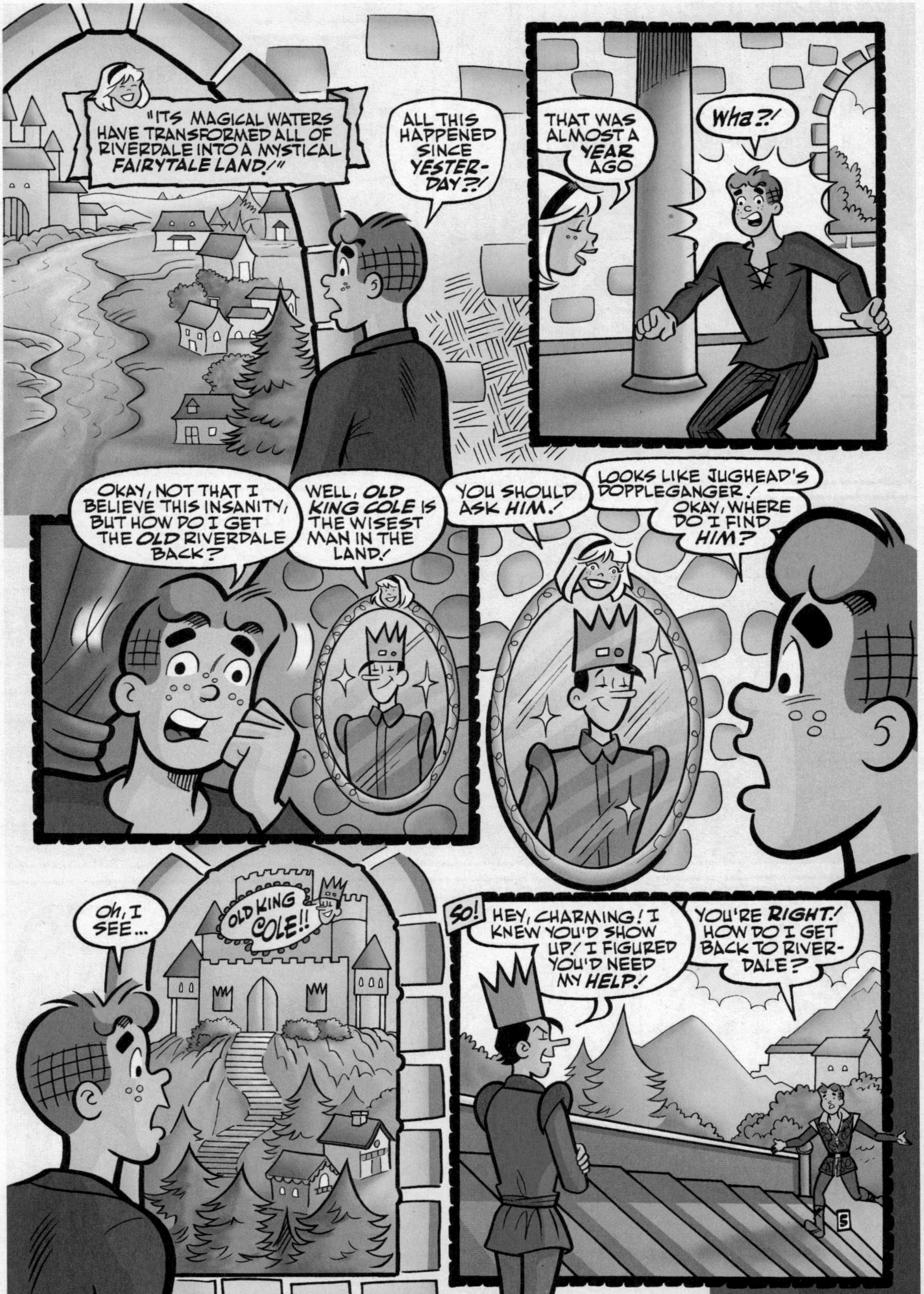

"ITS MAGICAL WATERS HAVE TRANSFORMED ALL OF RIVERDALE INTO A MYSTICAL FAIRYTALE LAND!"
ALL THIS HAPPENED SINCE YESTER-DAY?!
THAT WAS ALMOST A YEAR AGO
Wha?!
OKAY, NOT THAT I BELIEVE THIS INSANITY, BUT HOW DO I GET THE OLD RIVERDALE BACK?
WELL, OLD KING COLE IS THE WISEST MAN IN THE LAND!
YOU SHOULD ASK HIM!
LOOKS LIKE JUGHEAD'S DOPPLEGANGER!
OKAY, WHERE DO I FIND HIM?
Oh, I SEE...
OLD KING COLE!!
SO!
HEY, CHARMING! I KNEW YOU'D SHOW UP! I FIGURED YOU'D NEED MY HELP!
YOU'RE RIGHT! HOW DO I GET BACK TO RIVER-DALE?
5

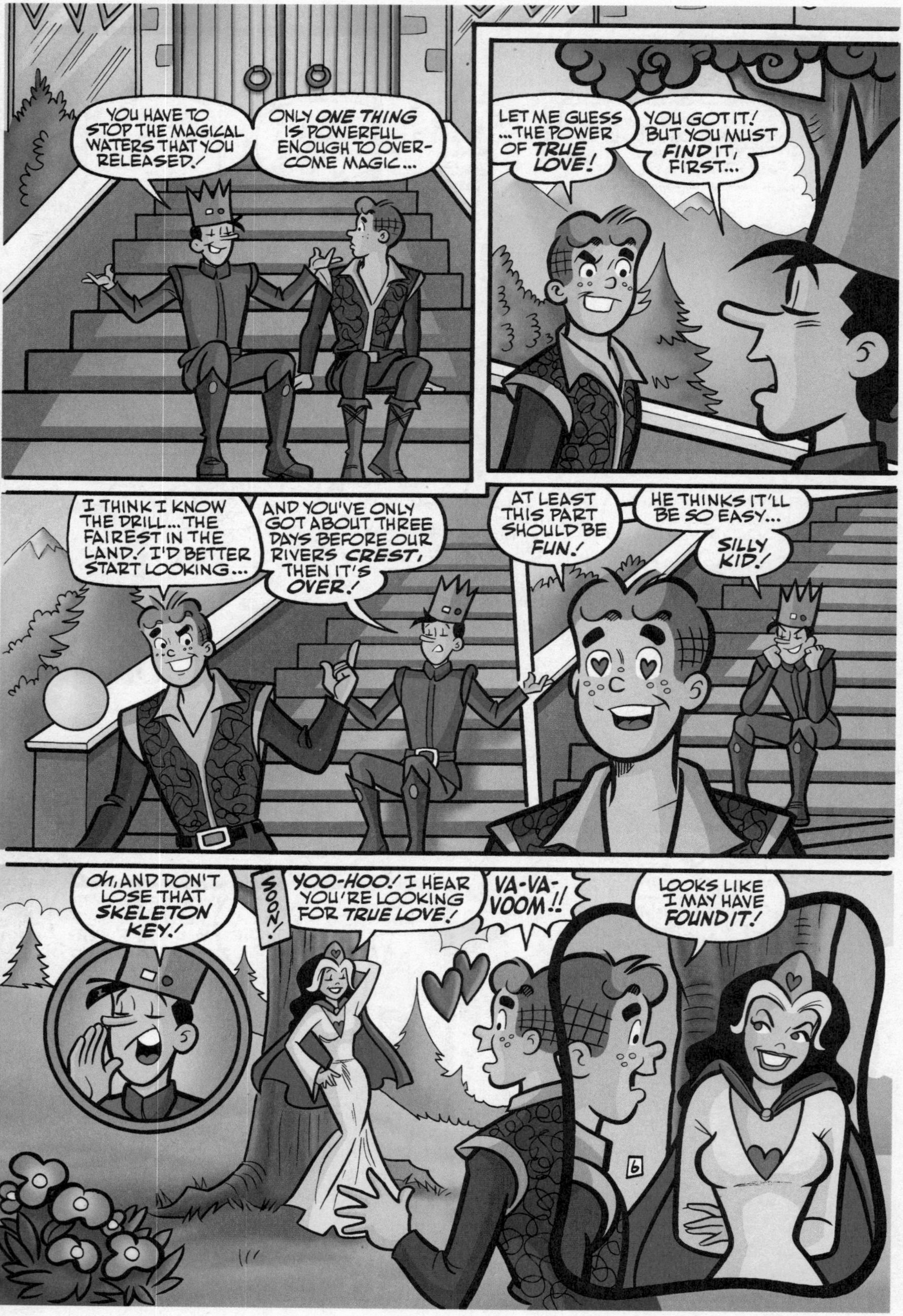
YOU HAVE TO STOP THE MAGICAL WATERS THAT YOU RELEASED!
ONLY ONE THING IS POWERFUL ENOUGH TO OVER-COME MAGIC...
LET ME GUESS ...THE POWER OF TRUE LOVE!
YOU GOT IT! BUT YOU MUST FIND IT, FIRST...
I THINK I KNOW THE DRILL... THE FAIREST IN THE LAND! I'D BETTER START LOOKING...
AND YOU'VE ONLY GOT ABOUT THREE DAYS BEFORE OUR RIVERS CREST, THEN IT'S OVER!
AT LEAST THIS PART SHOULD BE FUN!
HE THINKS IT'LL BE SO EASY...
SILLY KID!
OH, AND DON'T LOSE THAT SKELETON KEY!
SOON!
YOO-HOO! I HEAR YOU'RE LOOKING FOR TRUE LOVE!
VA-VA-VOOM!!
LOOKS LIKE I MAY HAVE FOUND IT!
6

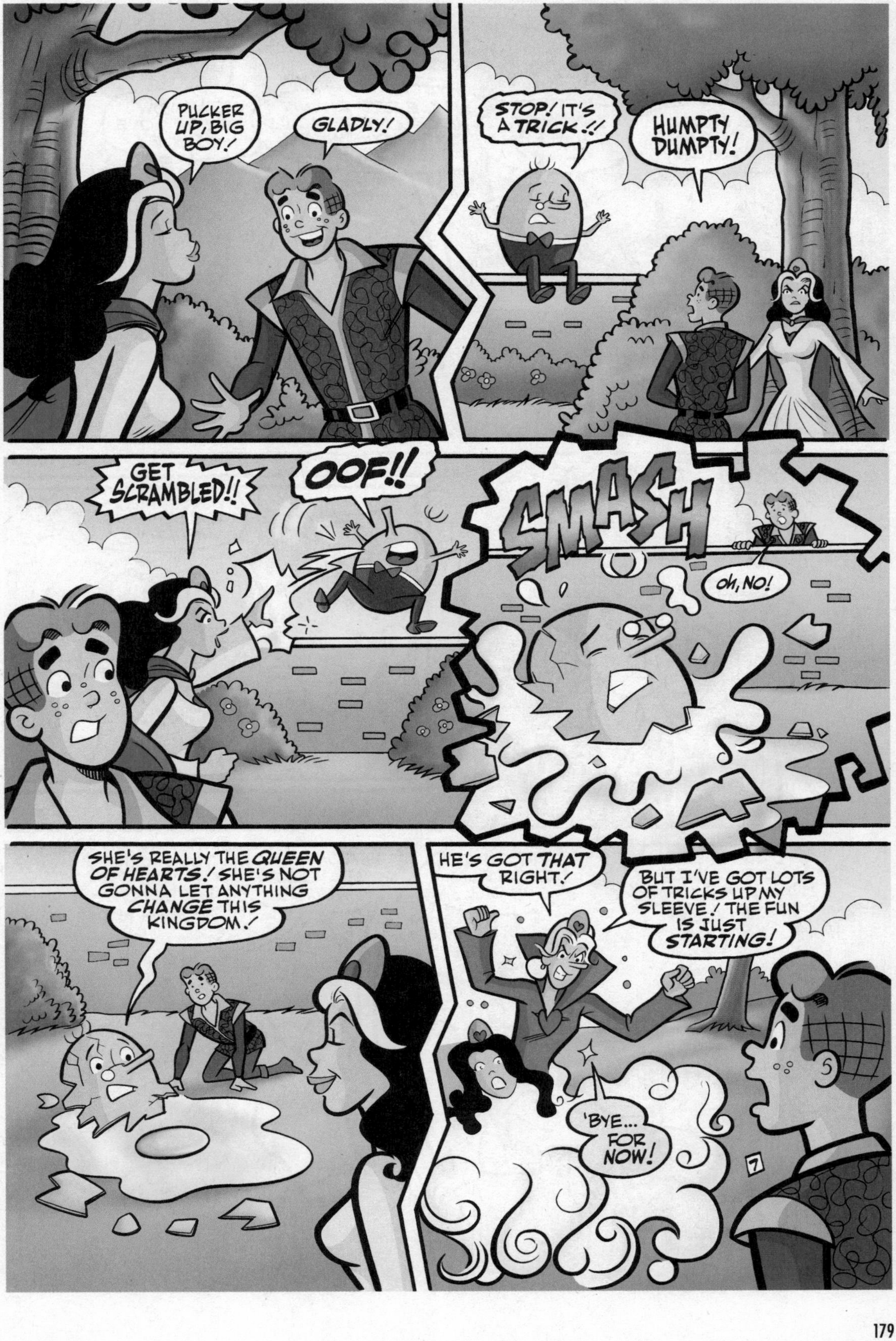
PUCKER UP, BIG BOY!
GLADLY!
STOP! IT'S A TRICK!!
HUMPTY DUMPTY!
GET SCRAMBLED!!
OOF!!
SMASH
oh, NO!
SHE'S REALLY THE QUEEN OF HEARTS! SHE'S NOT GONNA LET ANYTHING CHANGE THIS KINGDOM!
HE'S GOT THAT RIGHT!
BUT I'VE GOT LOTS OF TRICKS UP MY SLEEVE! THE FUN IS JUST STARTING!
'BYE... FOR NOW!
7

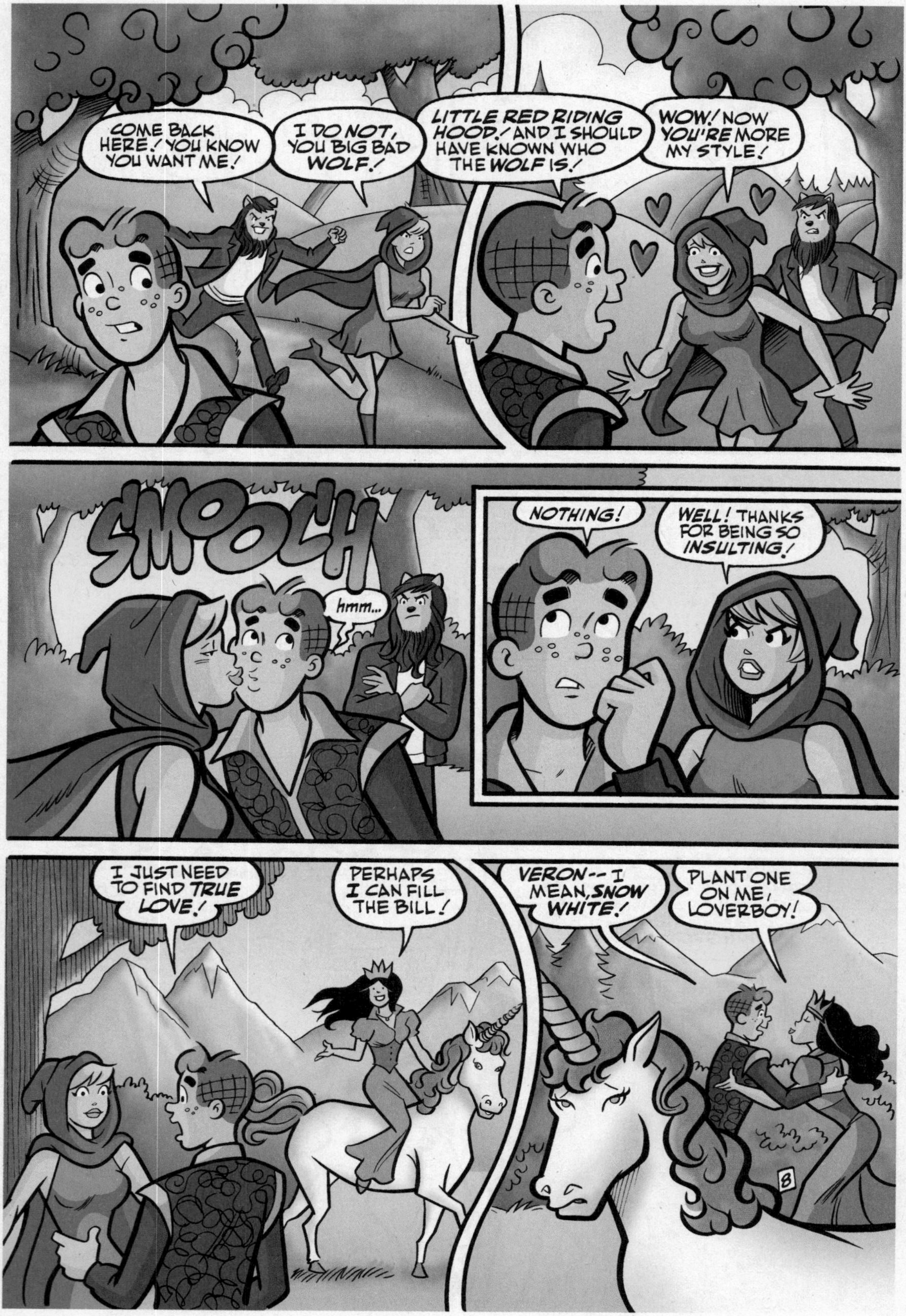
COME BACK HERE! YOU KNOW YOU WANT ME!
I DO NOT, YOU BIG BAD WOLF!
LITTLE RED RIDING HOOD! AND I SHOULD HAVE KNOWN WHO THE WOLF IS!
WOW! NOW YOU'RE MORE MY STYLE!
SMOOCH
hmm...
NOTHING!
WELL! THANKS FOR BEING SO INSULTING!
I JUST NEED TO FIND TRUE LOVE!
PERHAPS I CAN FILL THE BILL!
VERON-- I MEAN, SNOW WHITE!
PLANT ONE ON ME, LOVERBOY!

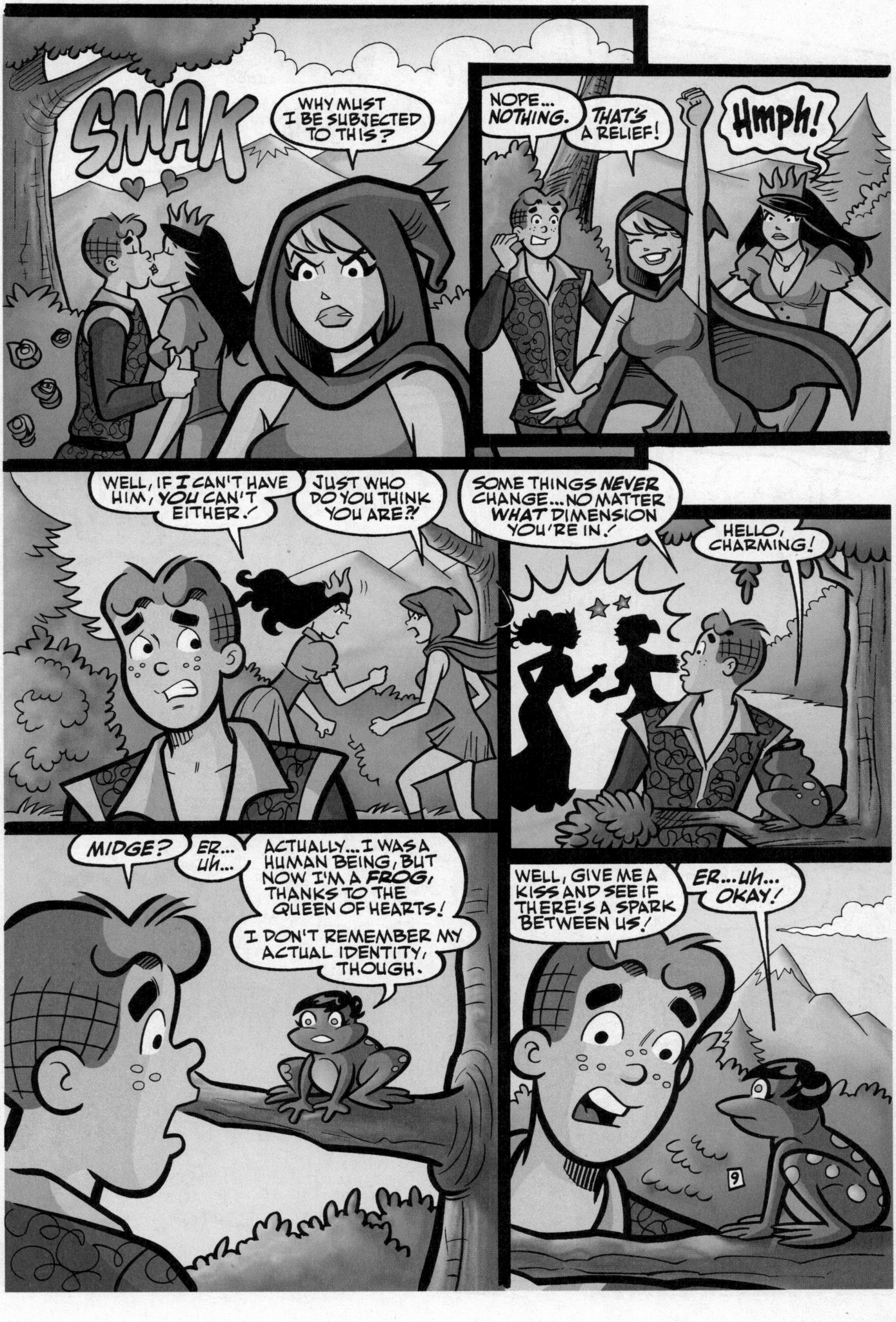

SMAK
WHY MUST I BE SUBJECTED TO THIS?
NOPE... NOTHING.
THAT'S A RELIEF!
Hmph!
WELL, IF I CAN'T HAVE HIM, YOU CAN'T EITHER!
JUST WHO DO YOU THINK YOU ARE?!
SOME THINGS NEVER CHANGE... NO MATTER WHAT DIMENSION YOU'RE IN!
HELLO, CHARMING!
MIDGE?
ER... UH...
ACTUALLY... I WAS A HUMAN BEING, BUT NOW I'M A FROG, THANKS TO THE QUEEN OF HEARTS!
I DON'T REMEMBER MY ACTUAL IDENTITY, THOUGH.
WELL, GIVE ME A KISS AND SEE IF THERE'S A SPARK BETWEEN US!
ER... UH... OKAY!
9

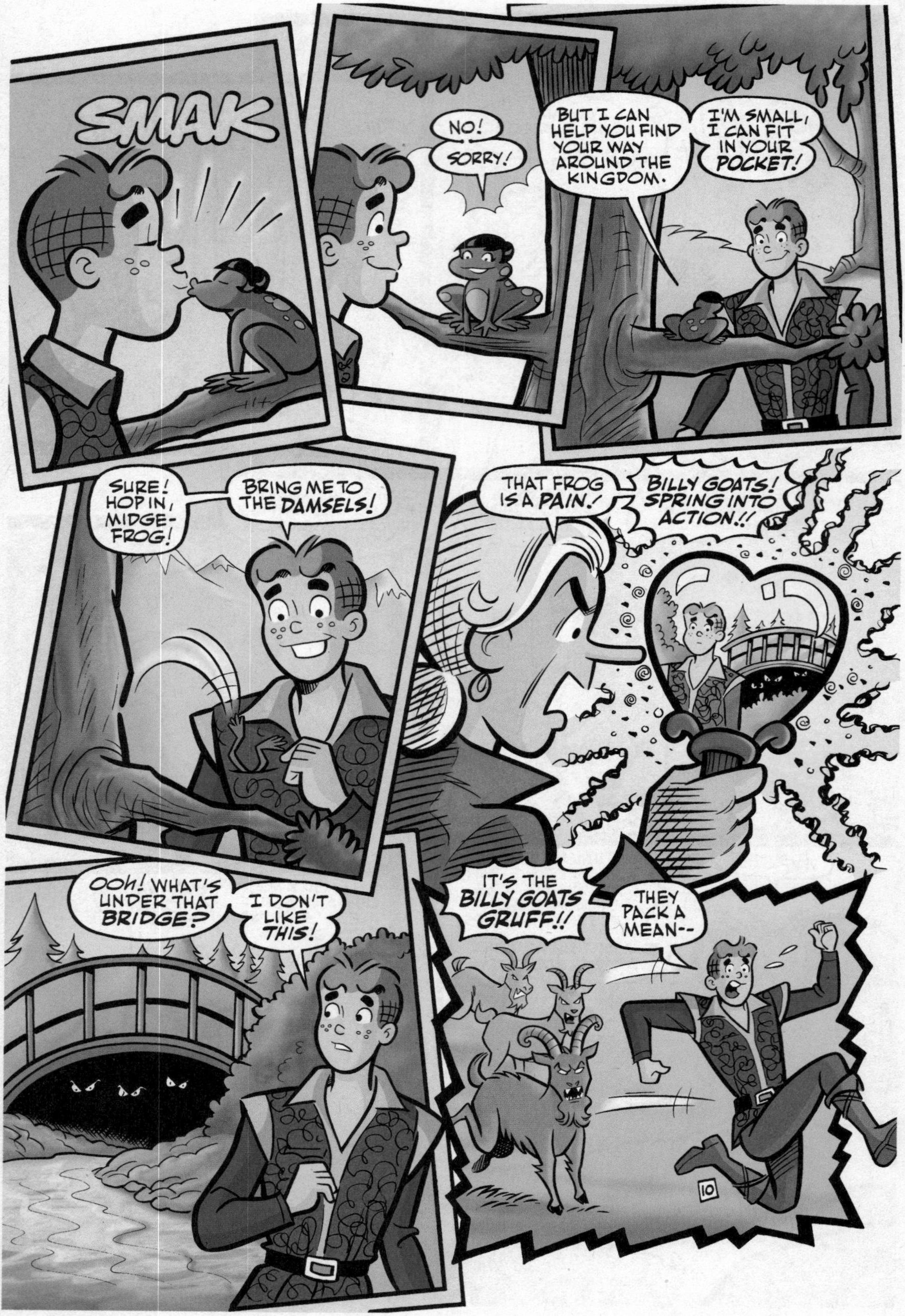
SMAK
NO!
SORRY!
BUT I CAN HELP YOU FIND YOUR WAY AROUND THE KINGDOM.
I'M SMALL, I CAN FIT IN YOUR POCKET!
SURE! HOP IN, MIDGE-FROG!
BRING ME TO THE DAMSELS!
THAT FROG IS A PAIN!
BILLY GOATS! SPRING INTO ACTION!!
OOH! WHAT'S UNDER THAT BRIDGE?
I DON'T LIKE THIS!
IT'S THE BILLY GOATS GRUFF!!
THEY PACK A MEAN--
10

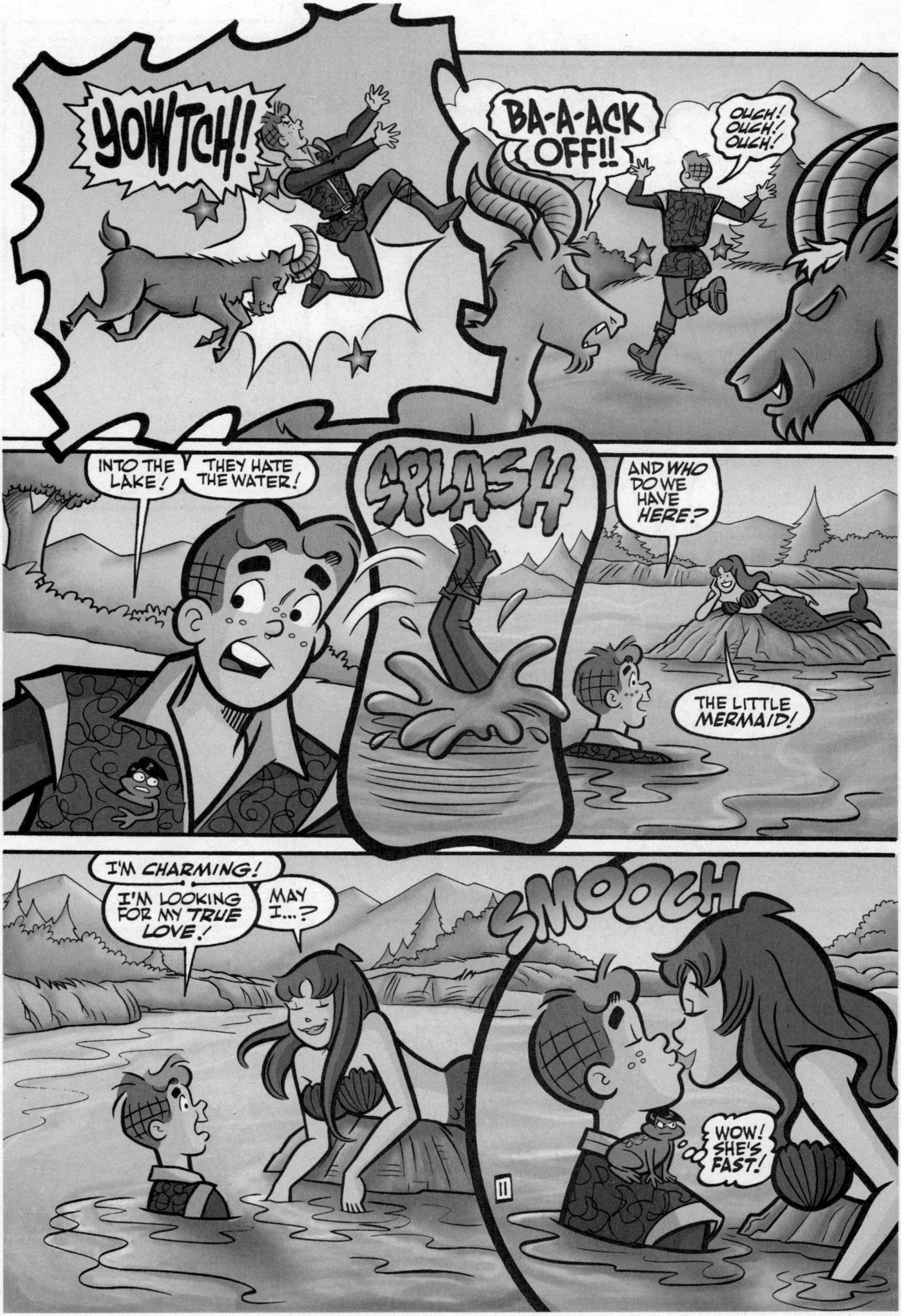
YOWTCH!
BA-A-ACK OFF!!
OUCH! OUCH! OUCH!
INTO THE LAKE!
THEY HATE THE WATER!
SPLASH
AND WHO DO WE HAVE HERE?
THE LITTLE MERMAID!
I'M CHARMING!
I'M LOOKING FOR MY TRUE LOVE!
MAY I...?
SMOOCH
WOW! SHE'S FAST!

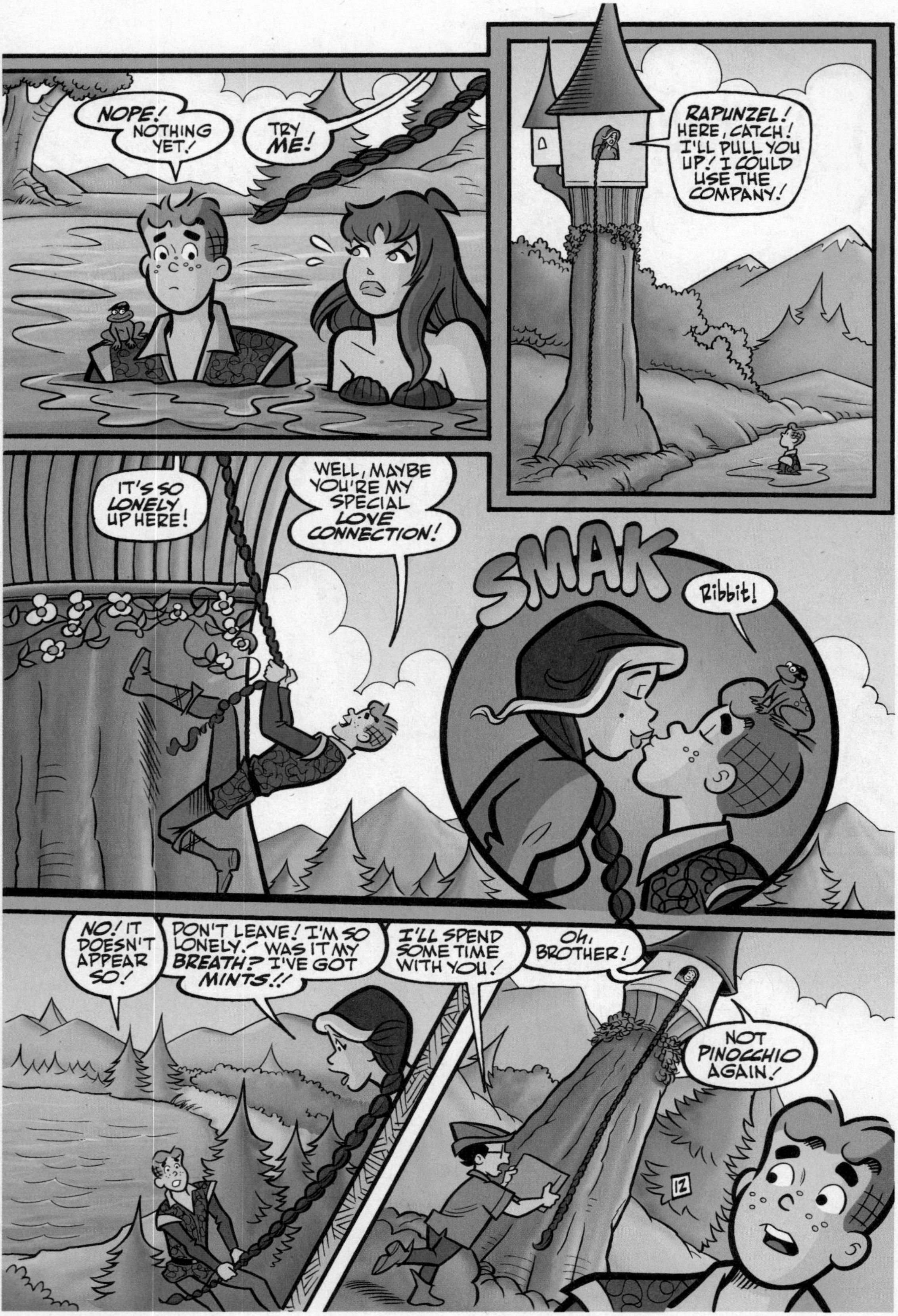
NOPE! NOTHING YET!
TRY ME!
RAPUNZEL! HERE, CATCH! I'LL PULL YOU UP! I COULD USE THE COMPANY!
IT'S SO LONELY UP HERE!
WELL, MAYBE YOU'RE MY SPECIAL LOVE CONNECTION!
SMAK
Ribbit!
NO! IT DOESN'T APPEAR SO!
DON'T LEAVE! I'M SO LONELY! WAS IT MY BREATH? I'VE GOT MINTS!!
I'LL SPEND SOME TIME WITH YOU!
Oh, BROTHER!
NOT PINOCCHIO AGAIN!
12

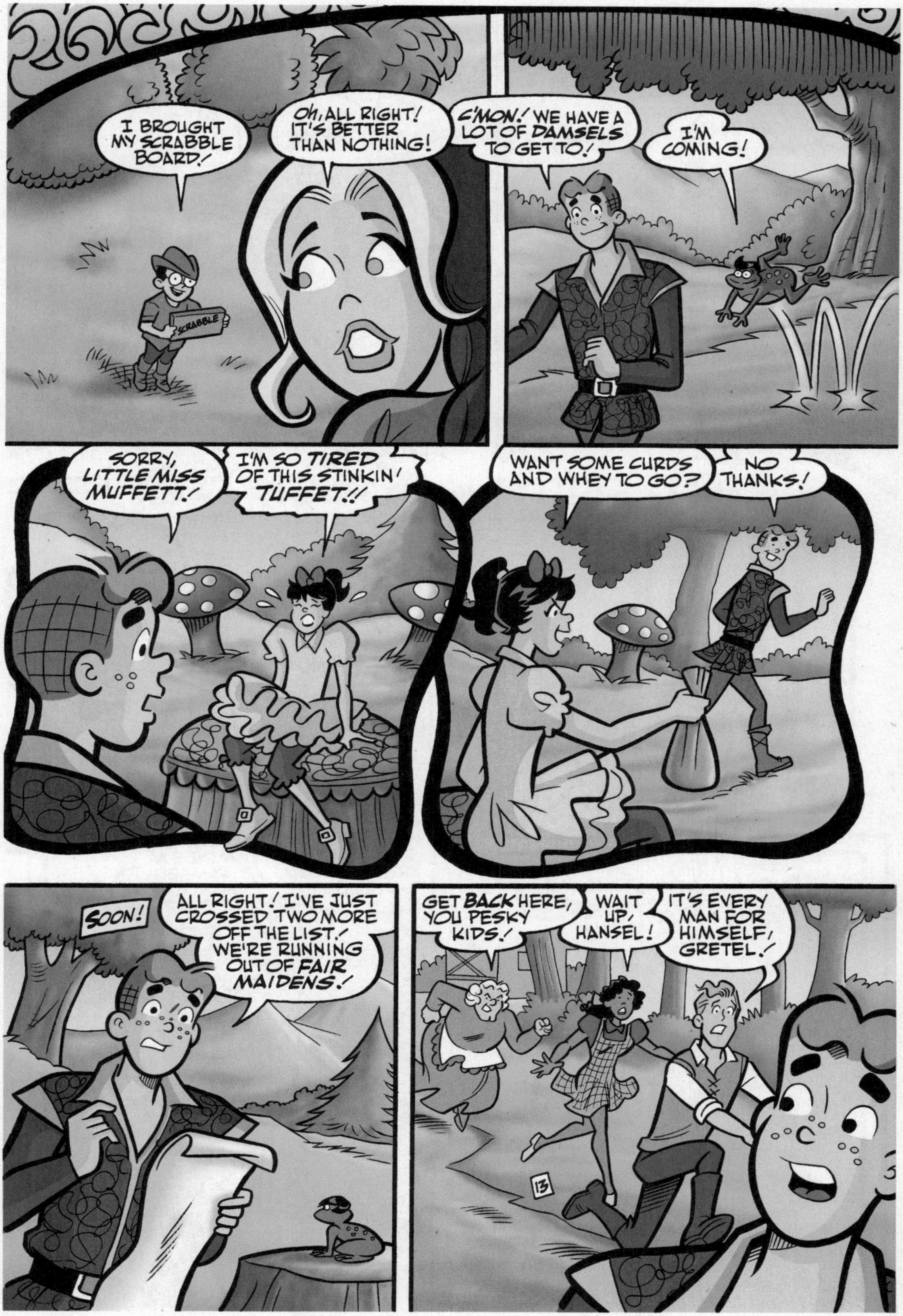
I BROUGHT MY SCRABBLE BOARD!
SCRABBLE
OH, ALL RIGHT! IT'S BETTER THAN NOTHING!
C'MON! WE HAVE A LOT OF DAMSELS TO GET TO!
I'M COMING!
SORRY, LITTLE MISS MUFFETT!
I'M SO TIRED OF THIS STINKIN' TUFFET!!
WANT SOME CURDS AND WHEY TO GO?
NO THANKS!
SOON!
ALL RIGHT! I'VE JUST CROSSED TWO MORE OFF THE LIST! WE'RE RUNNING OUT OF FAIR MAIDENS!
GET BACK HERE, YOU PESKY KIDS!
WAIT UP, HANSEL!
IT'S EVERY MAN FOR HIMSELF, GRETEL!
13

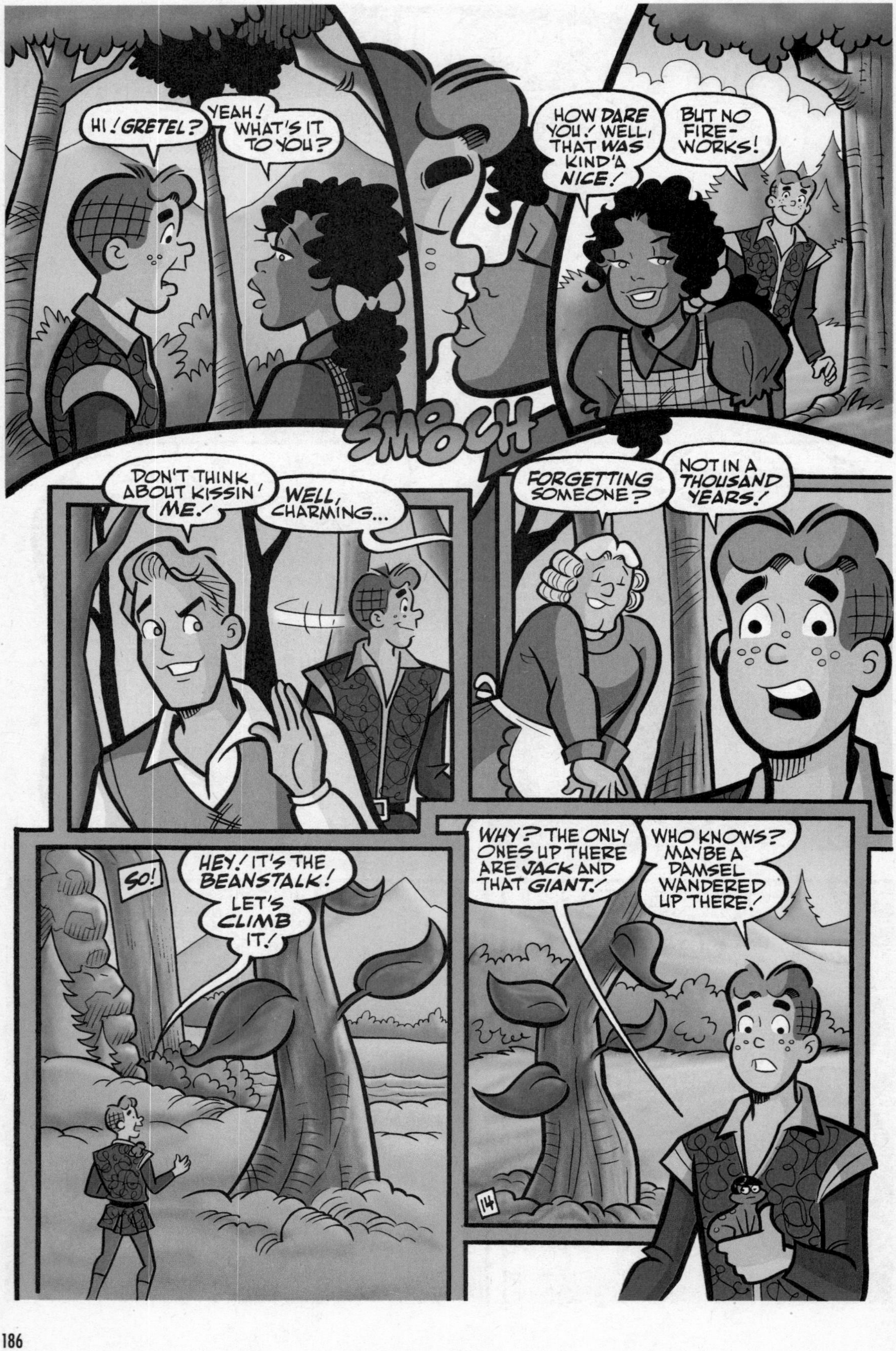
HI! GRETEL?
YEAH! WHAT'S IT TO YOU?
SMOOCH
HOW DARE YOU! WELL, THAT WAS KIND'A NICE!
BUT NO FIRE-WORKS!
DON'T THINK ABOUT KISSIN' ME!
WELL, CHARMING...
FORGETTING SOMEONE?
NOT IN A THOUSAND YEARS!
SO!
HEY! IT'S THE BEANSTALK! LET'S CLIMB IT!
WHY? THE ONLY ONES UP THERE ARE JACK AND THAT GIANT!
WHO KNOWS? MAYBE A DAMSEL WANDERED UP THERE!
14

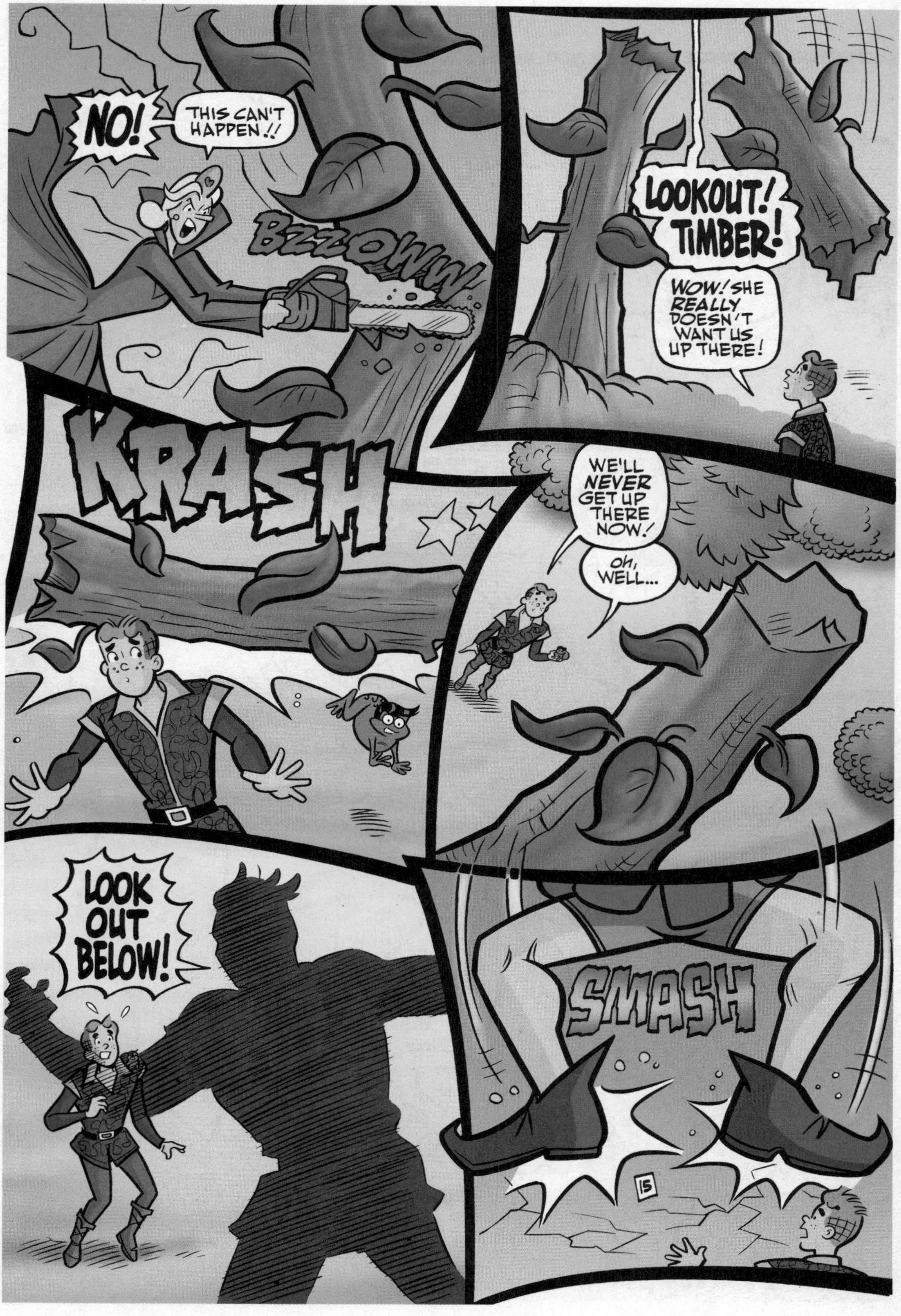
NO!
THIS CAN'T HAPPEN !!
BZZOWW
LOOKOUT! TIMBER!
WOW! SHE REALLY DOESN'T WANT US UP THERE!
KRASH
WE'LL NEVER GET UP THERE NOW!
oh, WELL...
LOOK OUT BELOW!
SMASH
15

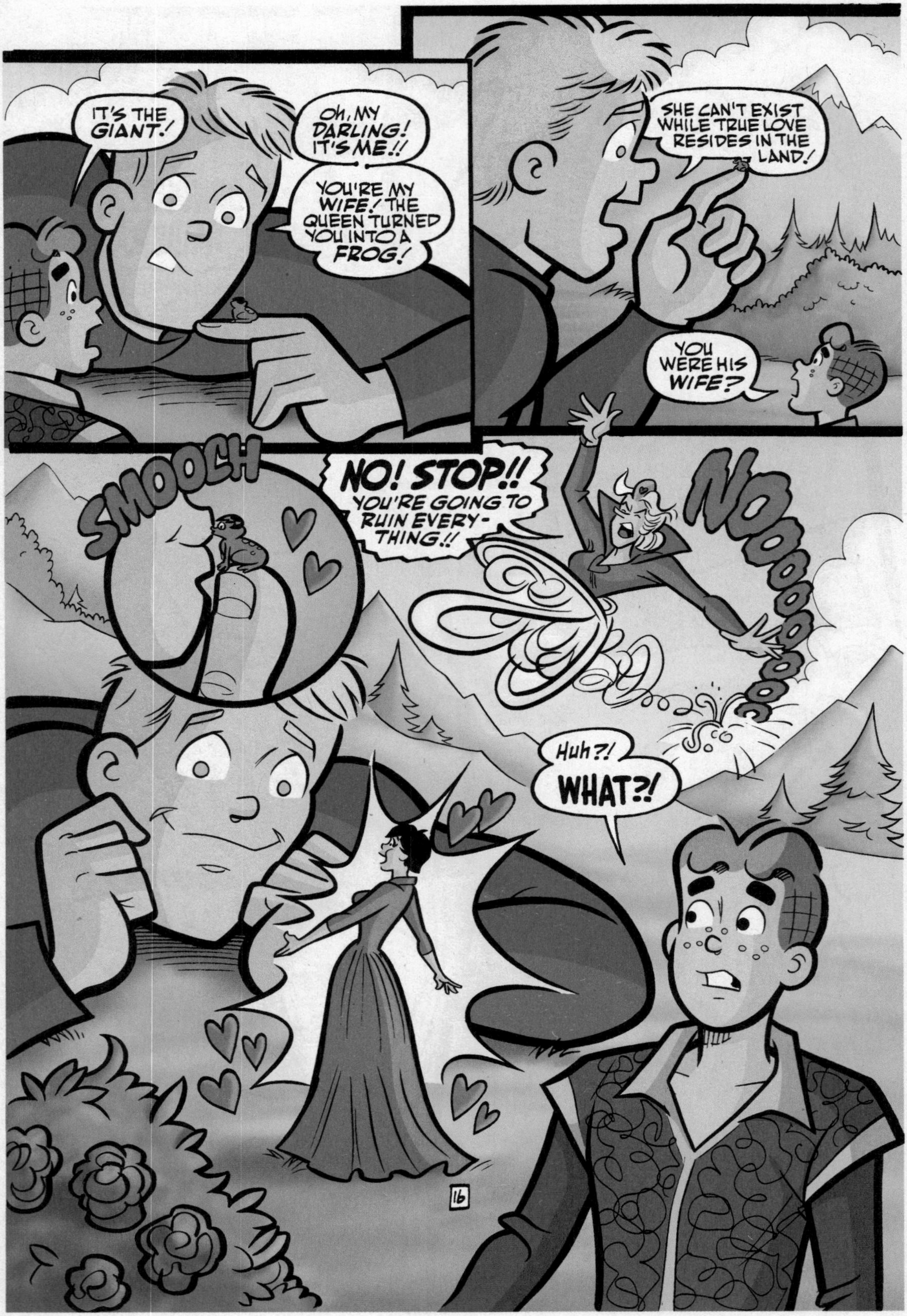
IT'S THE GIANT!
Oh, MY DARLING! IT'S ME!!
YOU'RE MY WIFE! THE QUEEN TURNED YOU INTO A FROG!
SHE CAN'T EXIST WHILE TRUE LOVE RESIDES IN THE LAND!
YOU WERE HIS WIFE?
SMOOCH
NO! STOP!! YOU'RE GOING TO RUIN EVERY-THING!!
NOOOOOOOOOO
Huh?! WHAT?!
16

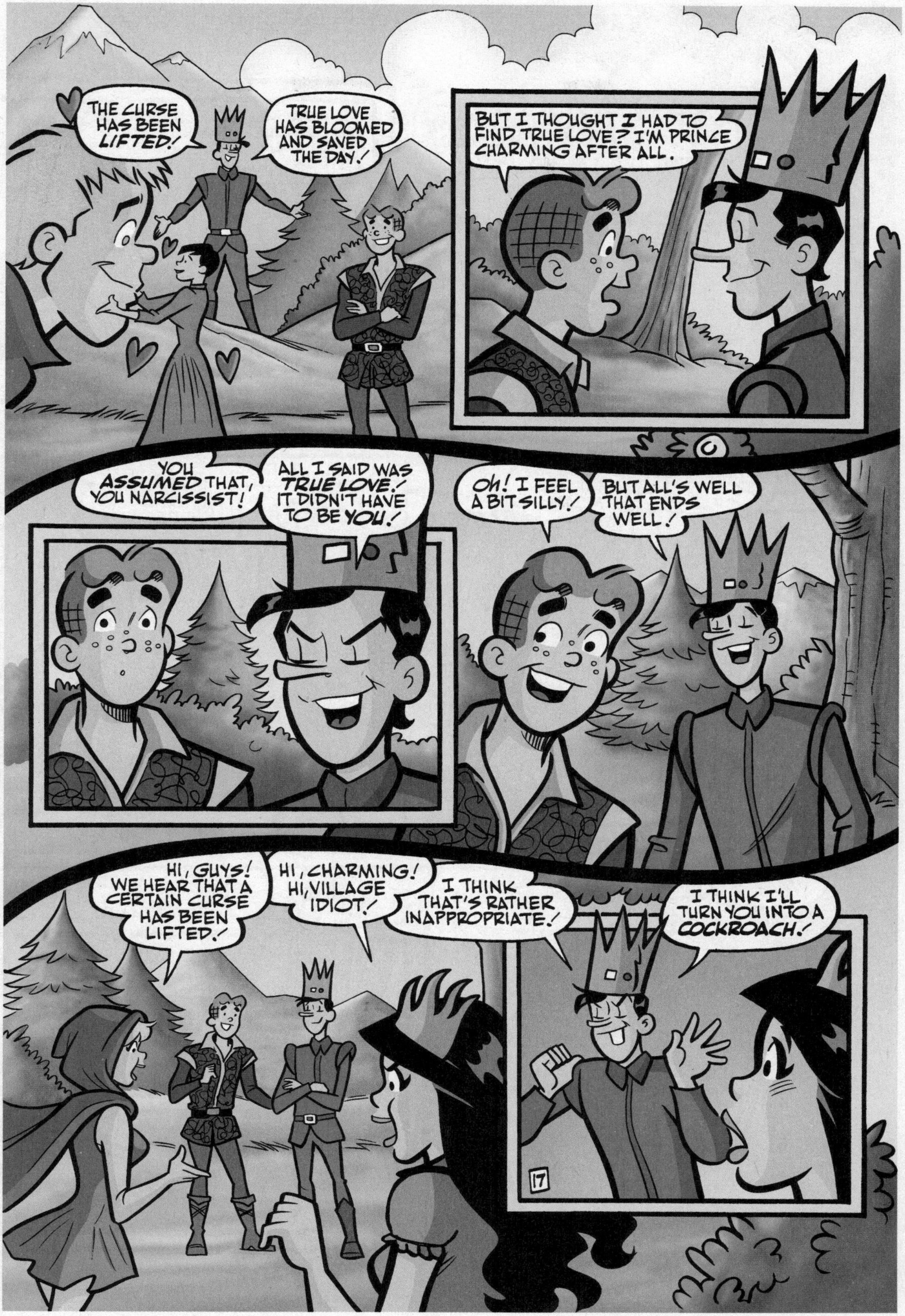
THE CURSE HAS BEEN LIFTED!
TRUE LOVE HAS BLOOMED AND SAVED THE DAY!
BUT I THOUGHT I HAD TO FIND TRUE LOVE? I'M PRINCE CHARMING AFTER ALL.
YOU ASSUMED THAT, YOU NARCISSIST!
ALL I SAID WAS TRUE LOVE! IT DIDN'T HAVE TO BE YOU!
Oh! I FEEL A BIT SILLY!
BUT ALL'S WELL THAT ENDS WELL!
HI, GUYS! WE HEAR THAT A CERTAIN CURSE HAS BEEN LIFTED!
HI, CHARMING! HI, VILLAGE IDIOT!
I THINK THAT'S RATHER INAPPROPRIATE!
I THINK I'LL TURN YOU INTO A COCKROACH!
17

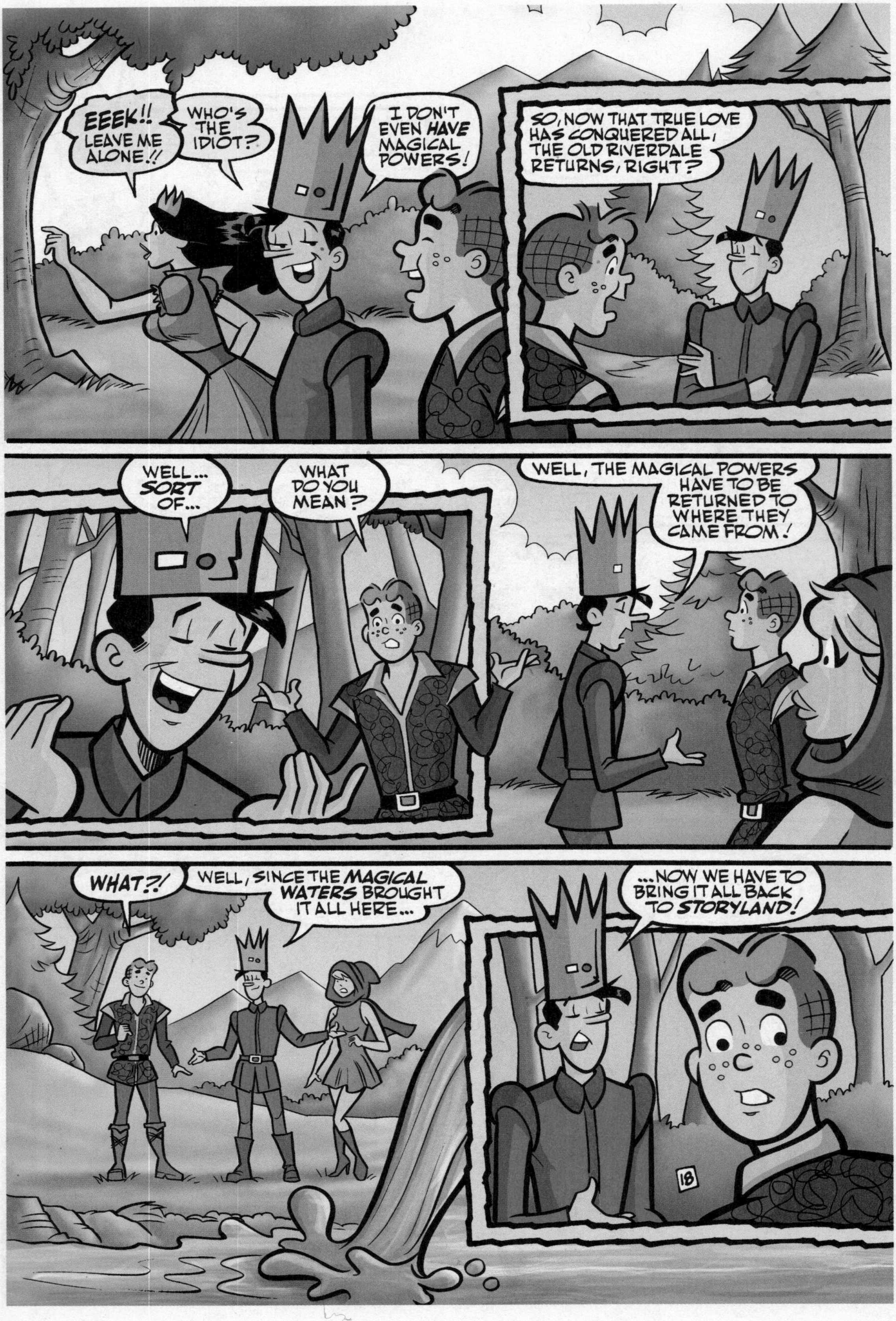
EEEK!! LEAVE ME ALONE!!
WHO'S THE IDIOT?
I DON'T EVEN HAVE MAGICAL POWERS!
SO, NOW THAT TRUE LOVE HAS CONQUERED ALL, THE OLD RIVERDALE RETURNS, RIGHT?
WELL... SORT OF...
WHAT DO YOU MEAN?
WELL, THE MAGICAL POWERS HAVE TO BE RETURNED TO WHERE THEY CAME FROM!
WHAT?!
WELL, SINCE THE MAGICAL WATERS BROUGHT IT ALL HERE...
...NOW WE HAVE TO BRING IT ALL BACK TO STORYLAND!
18

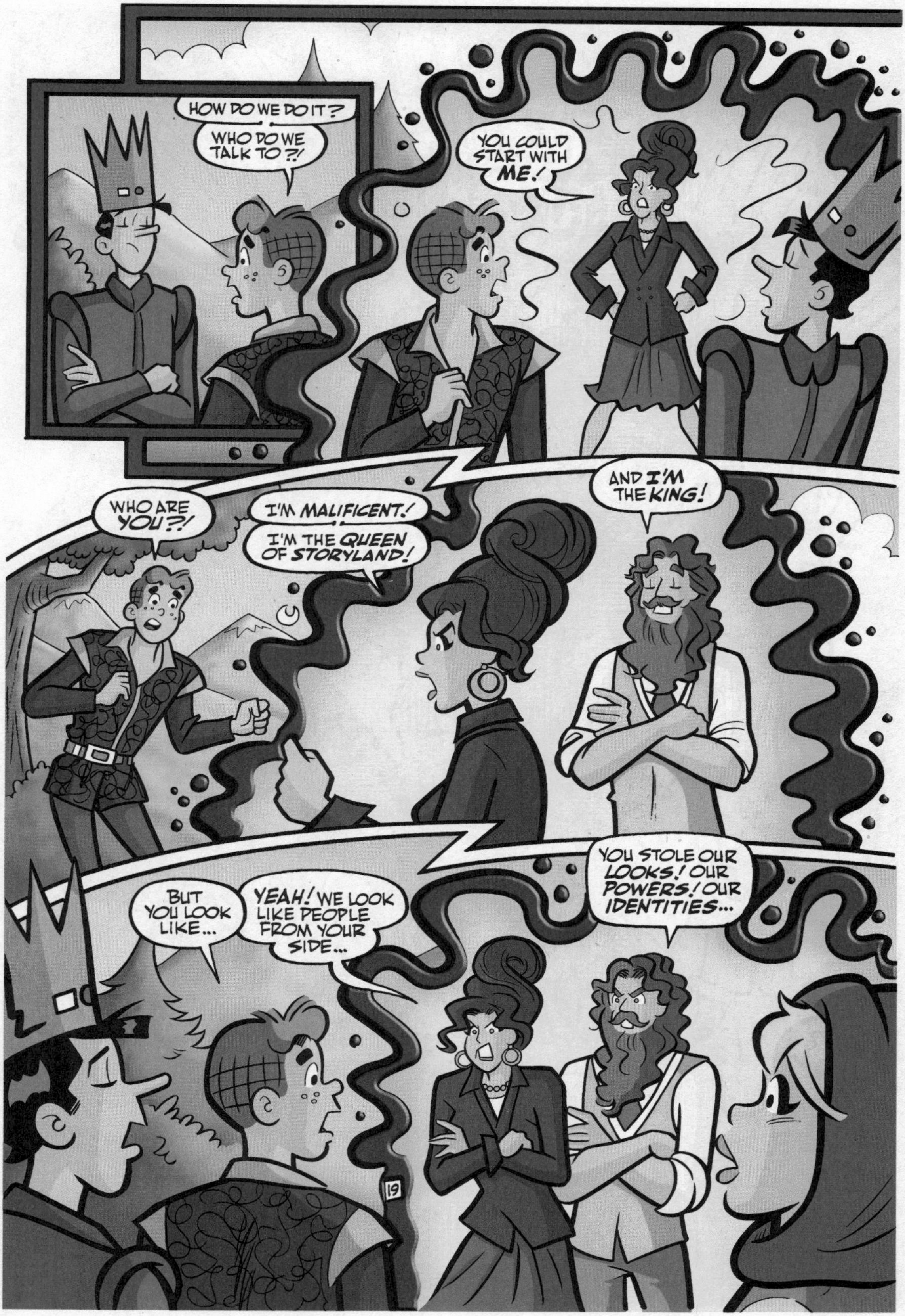
HOW DO WE DO IT?
WHO DO WE TALK TO?!
YOU COULD START WITH ME!
WHO ARE YOU?!
I'M MALIFICENT!
I'M THE QUEEN OF STORYLAND!
AND I'M THE KING!
BUT YOU LOOK LIKE...
YEAH! WE LOOK LIKE PEOPLE FROM YOUR SIDE...
YOU STOLE OUR LOOKS! OUR POWERS! OUR IDENTITIES...
19

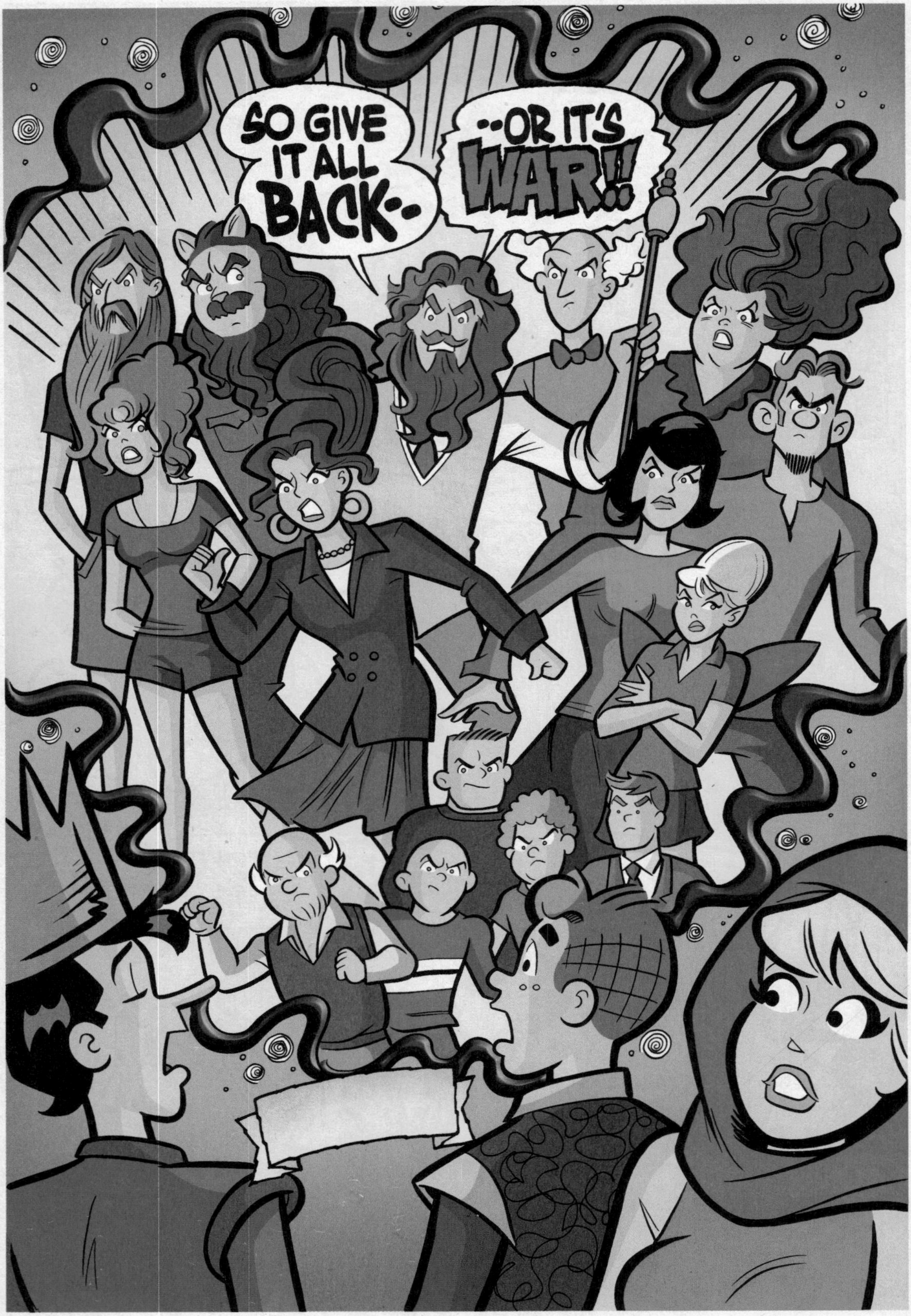
SO GIVE IT ALL BACK--
--OR IT'S WAR!!

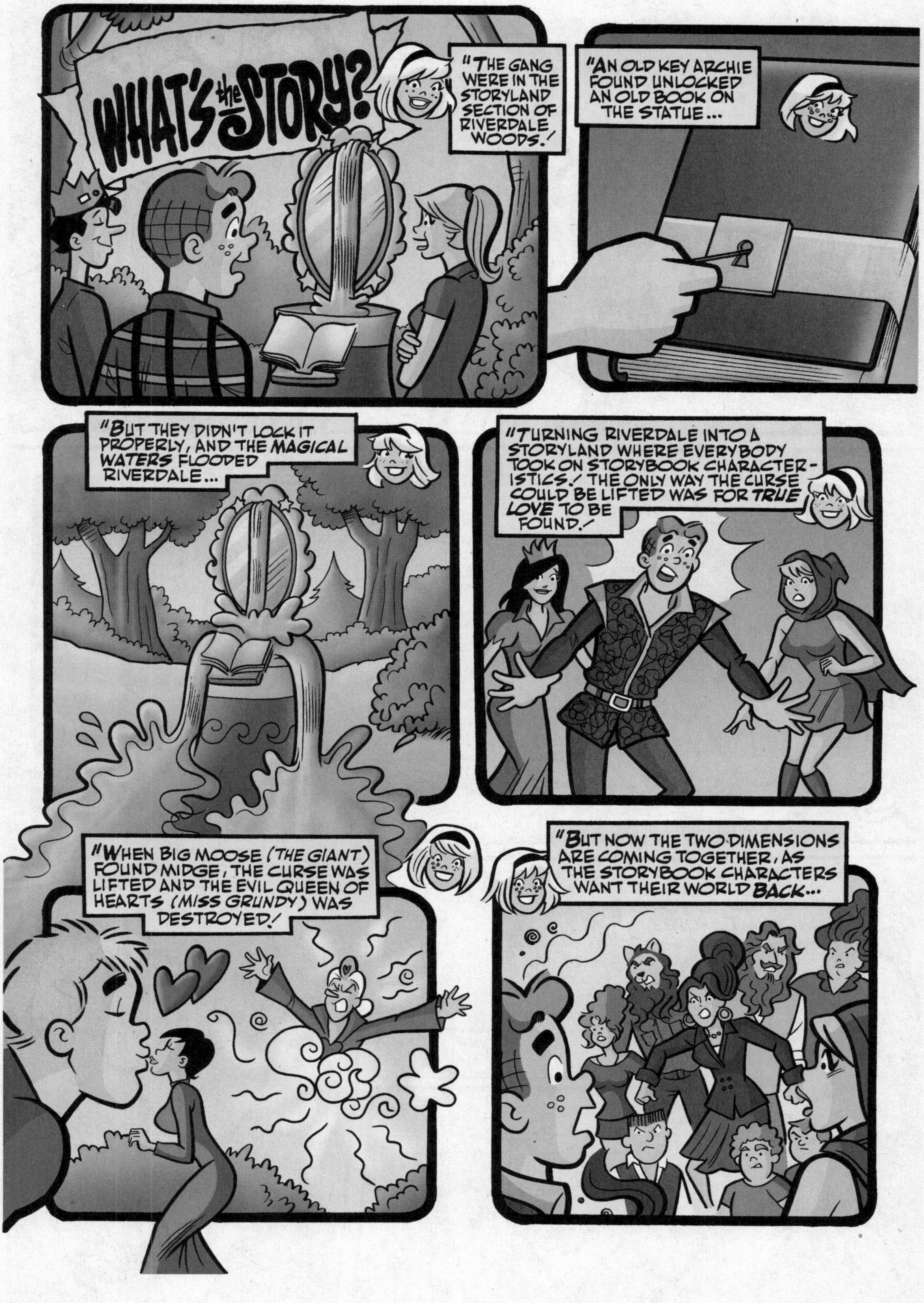
WHAT'S the STORY?
"THE GANG WERE IN THE STORYLAND SECTION OF RIVERDALE WOODS!
"AN OLD KEY ARCHIE FOUND UNLOCKED AN OLD BOOK ON THE STATUE...
"BUT THEY DIDN'T LOCK IT PROPERLY, AND THE MAGICAL WATERS FLOODED RIVERDALE...
"TURNING RIVERDALE INTO A STORYLAND WHERE EVERYBODY TOOK ON STORYBOOK CHARACTER-ISTICS! THE ONLY WAY THE CURSE COULD BE LIFTED WAS FOR TRUE LOVE TO BE FOUND!
"WHEN BIG MOOSE (THE GIANT) FOUND MIDGE, THE CURSE WAS LIFTED AND THE EVIL QUEEN OF HEARTS (MISS GRUNDY) WAS DESTROYED!
"BUT NOW THE TWO DIMENSIONS ARE COMING TOGETHER, AS THE STORYBOOK CHARACTERS WANT THEIR WORLD BACK...

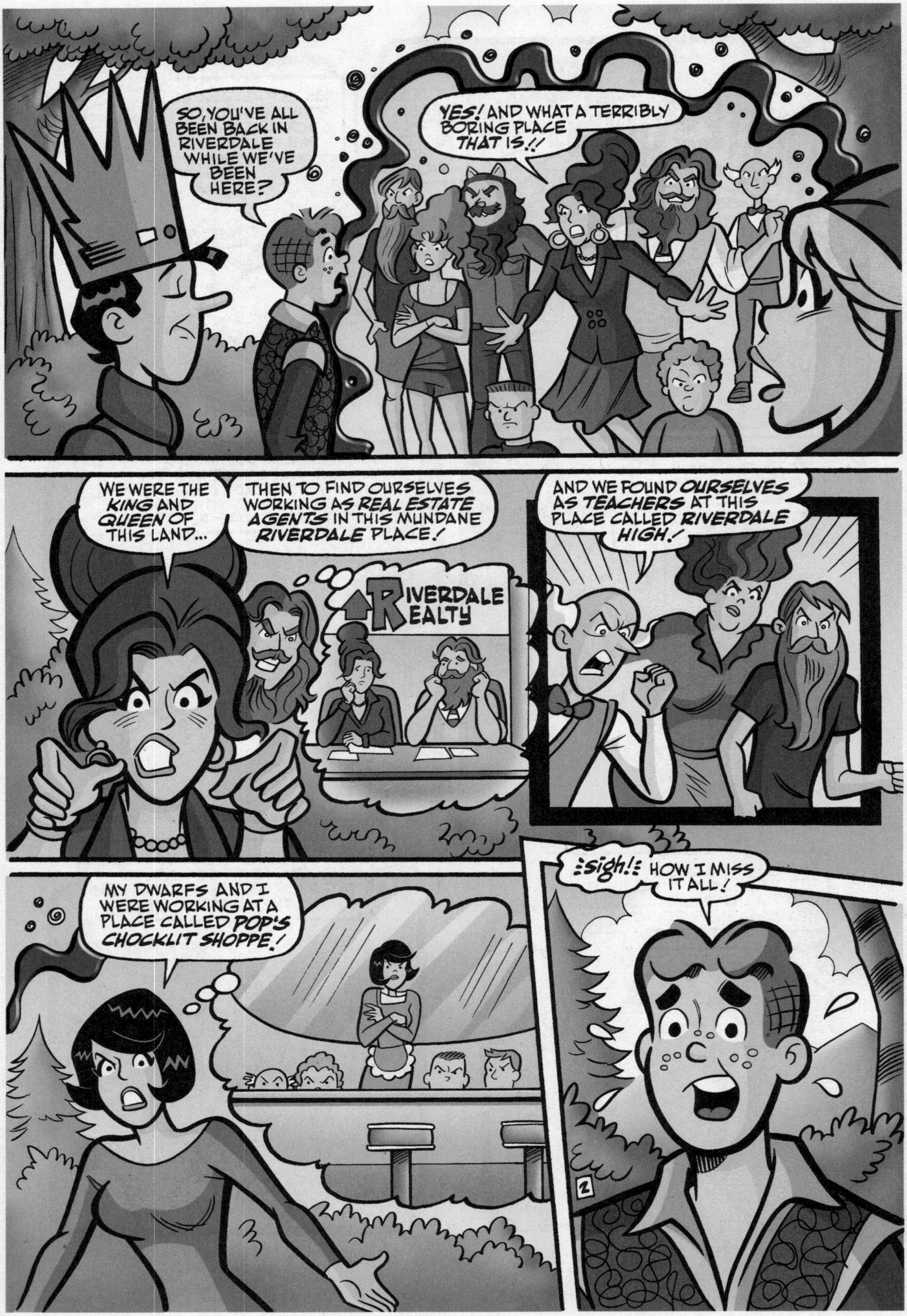
SO, YOU'VE ALL BEEN BACK IN RIVERDALE WHILE WE'VE BEEN HERE?
YES! AND WHAT A TERRIBLY BORING PLACE THAT IS!!
WE WERE THE KING AND QUEEN OF THIS LAND...
THEN TO FIND OURSELVES WORKING AS REAL ESTATE AGENTS IN THIS MUNDANE RIVERDALE PLACE!
RIVERDALE REALTY
AND WE FOUND OURSELVES AS TEACHERS AT THIS PLACE CALLED RIVERDALE HIGH!
MY DWARFS AND I WERE WORKING AT A PLACE CALLED POP'S CHOCKLIT SHOPPE!
sigh! HOW I MISS IT ALL!
2

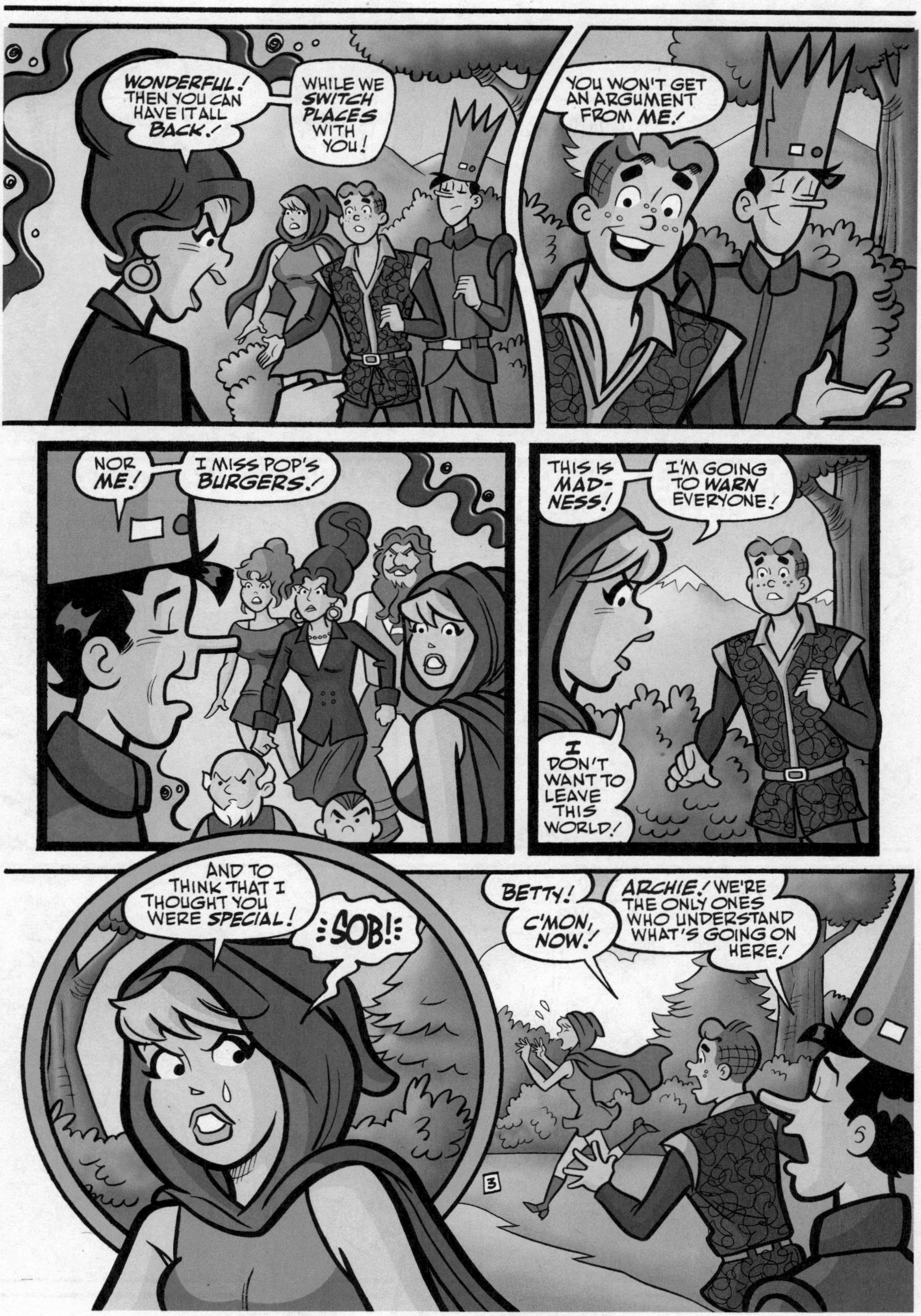
WONDERFUL! THEN YOU CAN HAVE IT ALL BACK!
WHILE WE SWITCH PLACES WITH YOU!
YOU WON'T GET AN ARGUMENT FROM ME!
NOR ME!
I MISS POP'S BURGERS!
THIS IS MADNESS!
I'M GOING TO WARN EVERYONE!
I DON'T WANT TO LEAVE THIS WORLD!
AND TO THINK THAT I THOUGHT YOU WERE SPECIAL!
SOB!
BETTY!
C'MON, NOW!
ARCHIE! WE'RE THE ONLY ONES WHO UNDERSTAND WHAT'S GOING ON HERE!
3

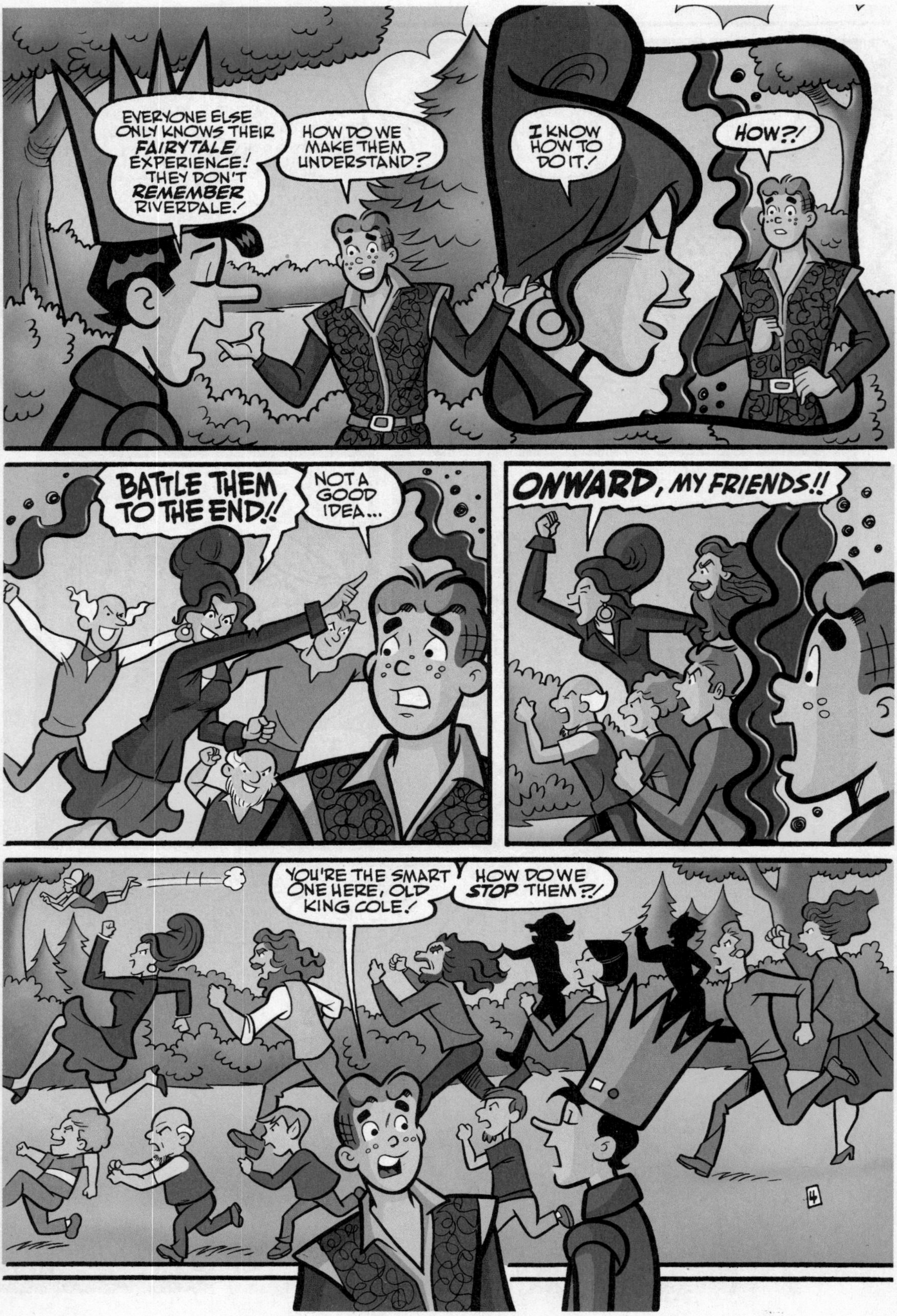
EVERYONE ELSE ONLY KNOWS THEIR FAIRYTALE EXPERIENCE! THEY DON'T REMEMBER RIVERDALE!
HOW DO WE MAKE THEM UNDERSTAND?
I KNOW HOW TO DO IT!
HOW?!
BATTLE THEM TO THE END!!
NOT A GOOD IDEA...
ONWARD, MY FRIENDS!!
YOU'RE THE SMART ONE HERE, OLD KING COLE!
HOW DO WE STOP THEM?!

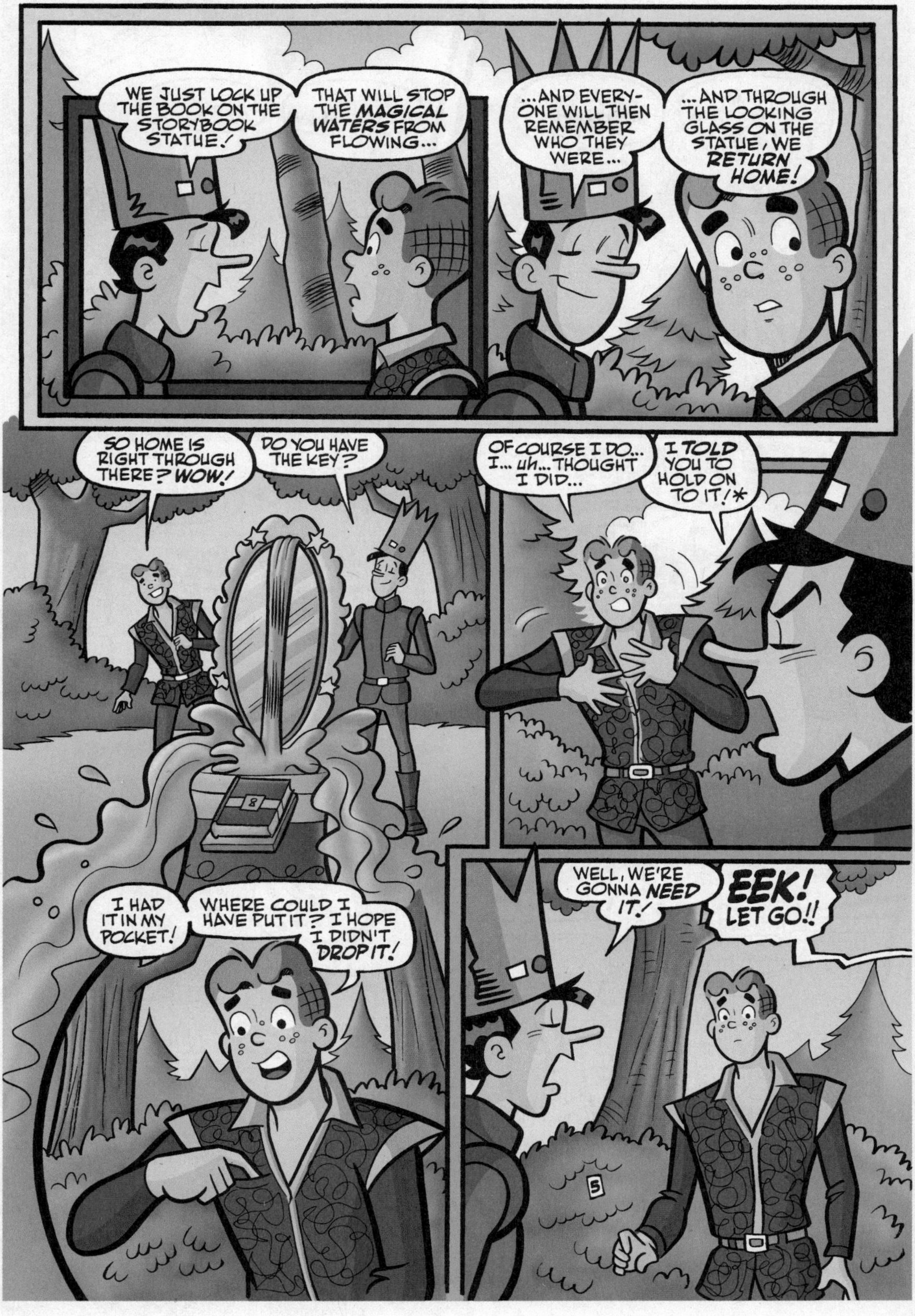
WE JUST LOCK UP THE BOOK ON THE STORYBOOK STATUE!
THAT WILL STOP THE MAGICAL WATERS FROM FLOWING...
...AND EVERY-ONE WILL THEN REMEMBER WHO THEY WERE...
...AND THROUGH THE LOOKING GLASS ON THE STATUE, WE RETURN HOME!
SO HOME IS RIGHT THROUGH THERE? WOW!
DO YOU HAVE THE KEY?
OF COURSE I DO... I... uh... THOUGHT I DID...
I TOLD YOU TO HOLD ON TO IT!*
I HAD IT IN MY POCKET!
WHERE COULD I HAVE PUT IT? I HOPE I DIDN'T DROP IT!
WELL, WE'RE GONNA NEED IT!
EEK! LET GO!!

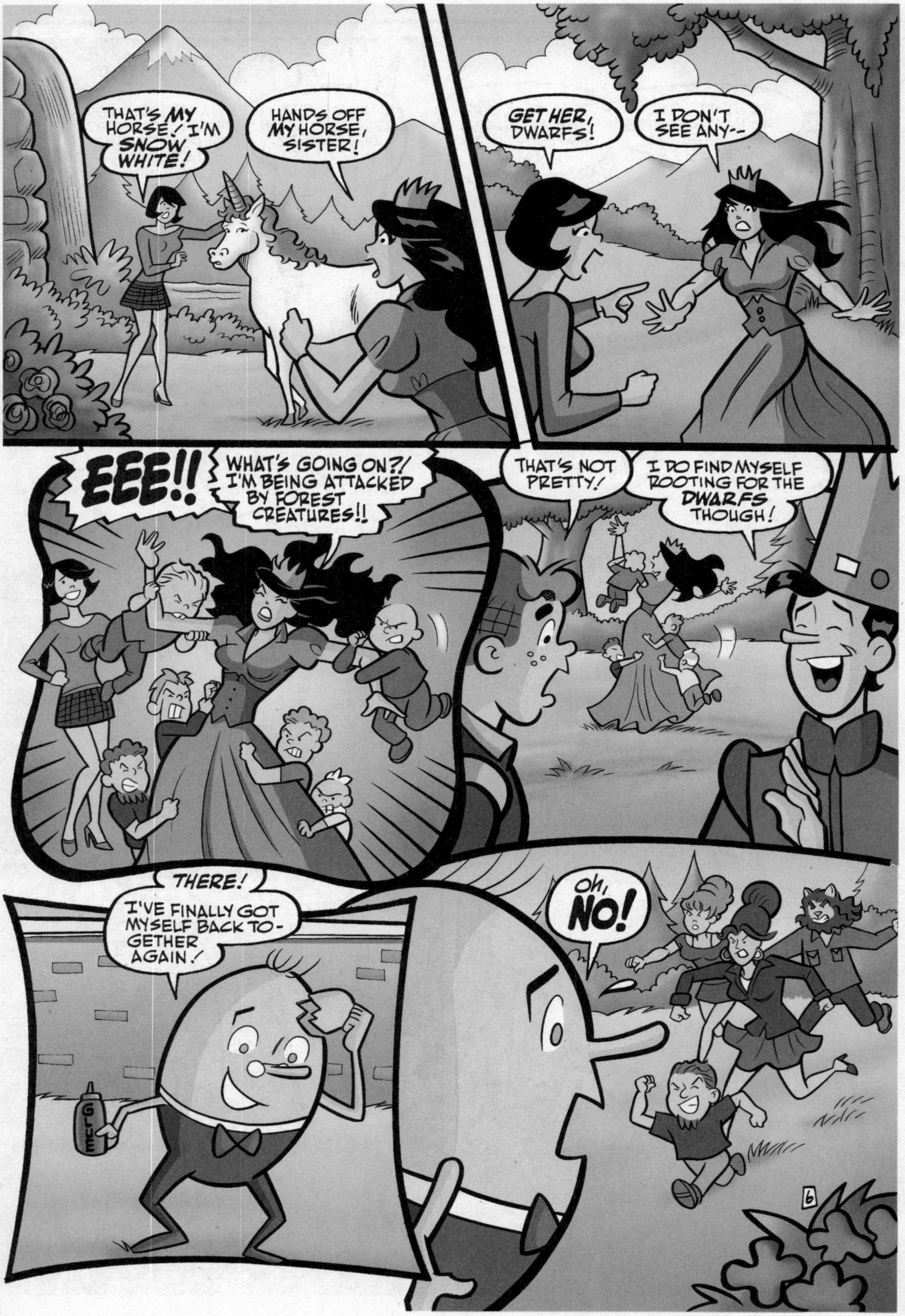
THAT'S MY HORSE! I'M SNOW WHITE!
HANDS OFF MY HORSE, SISTER!
GET HER, DWARFS!
I DON'T SEE ANY--
EEE!!
WHAT'S GOING ON?! I'M BEING ATTACKED BY FOREST CREATURES!!
THAT'S NOT PRETTY!
I DO FIND MYSELF ROOTING FOR THE DWARFS THOUGH!
THERE! I'VE FINALLY GOT MYSELF BACK TOGETHER AGAIN!
GLUE
OH, NO!
6

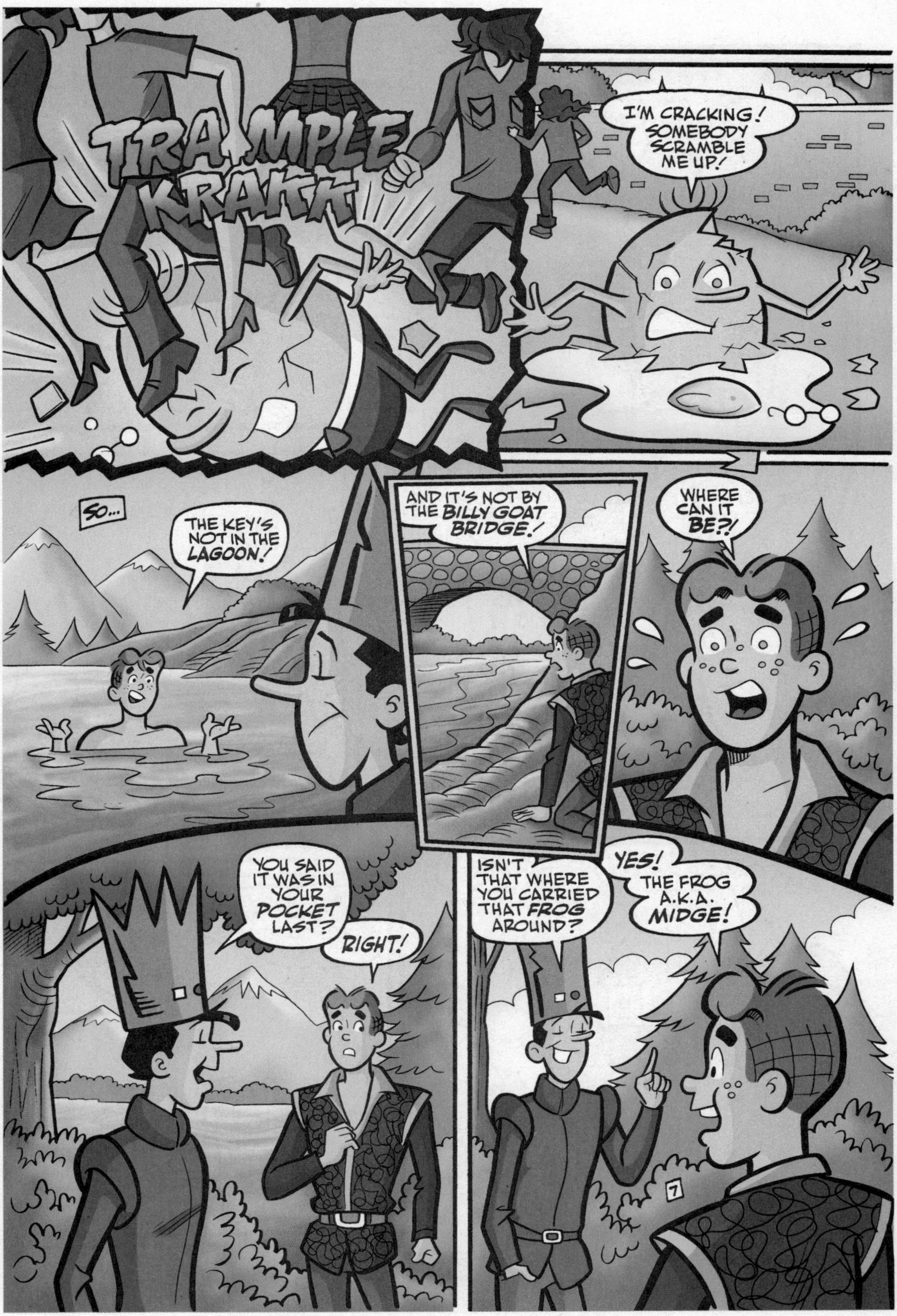
TRAMPLE
KRAKK
I'M CRACKING! SOMEBODY SCRAMBLE ME UP!
SO...
THE KEY'S NOT IN THE LAGOON!
AND IT'S NOT BY THE BILLY GOAT BRIDGE!
WHERE CAN IT BE?!
YOU SAID IT WAS IN YOUR POCKET LAST?
RIGHT!
ISN'T THAT WHERE YOU CARRIED THAT FROG AROUND?
YES!
THE FROG A.K.A. MIDGE!
7

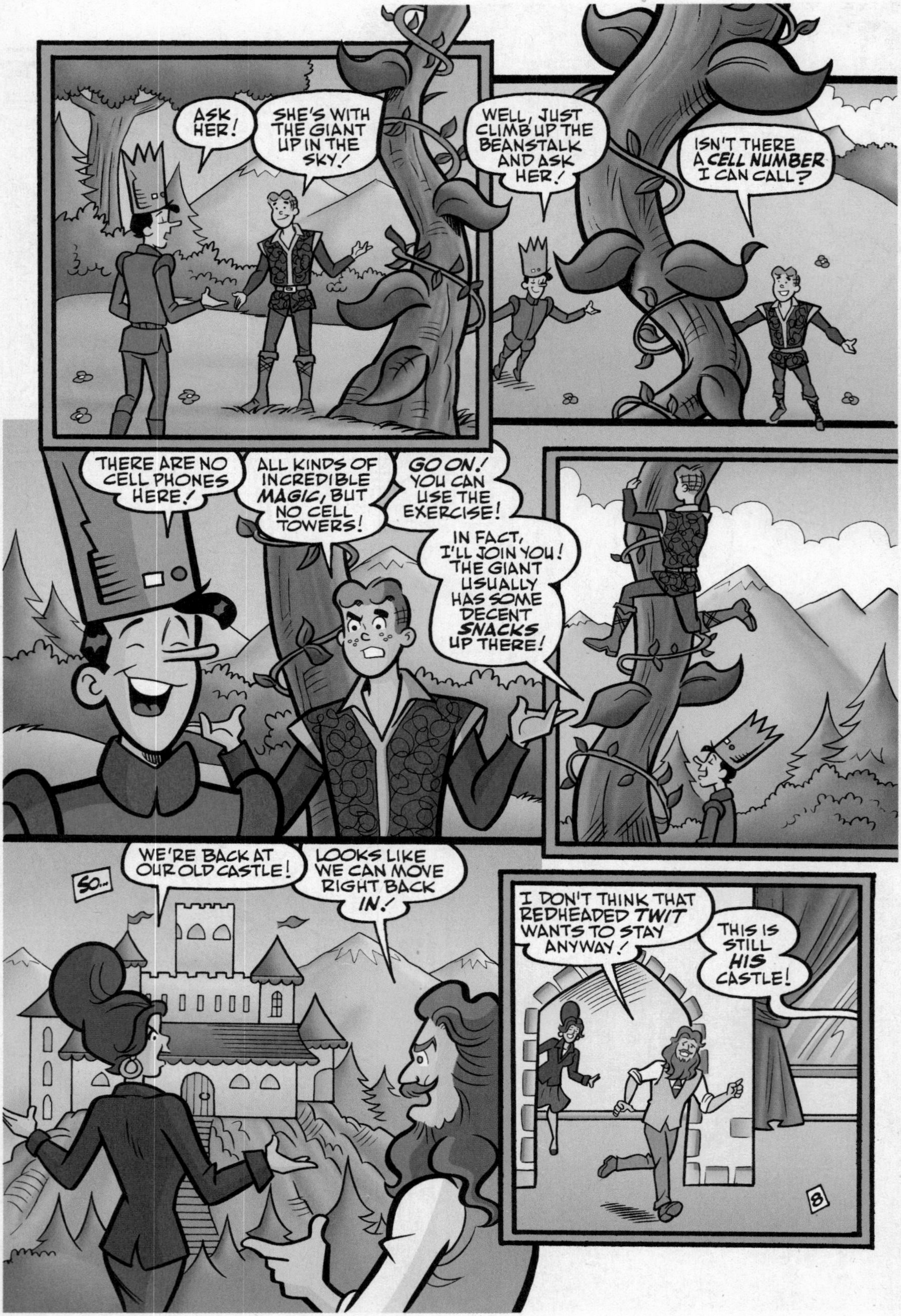
ASK HER!
SHE'S WITH THE GIANT UP IN THE SKY!
WELL, JUST CLIMB UP THE BEANSTALK AND ASK HER!
ISN'T THERE A CELL NUMBER I CAN CALL?
THERE ARE NO CELL PHONES HERE!
ALL KINDS OF INCREDIBLE MAGIC, BUT NO CELL TOWERS!
GO ON! YOU CAN USE THE EXERCISE!
IN FACT, I'LL JOIN YOU! THE GIANT USUALLY HAS SOME DECENT SNACKS UP THERE!
SO...
WE'RE BACK AT OUR OLD CASTLE!
LOOKS LIKE WE CAN MOVE RIGHT BACK IN!
I DON'T THINK THAT REDHEADED TWIT WANTS TO STAY ANYWAY!
THIS IS STILL HIS CASTLE!
8

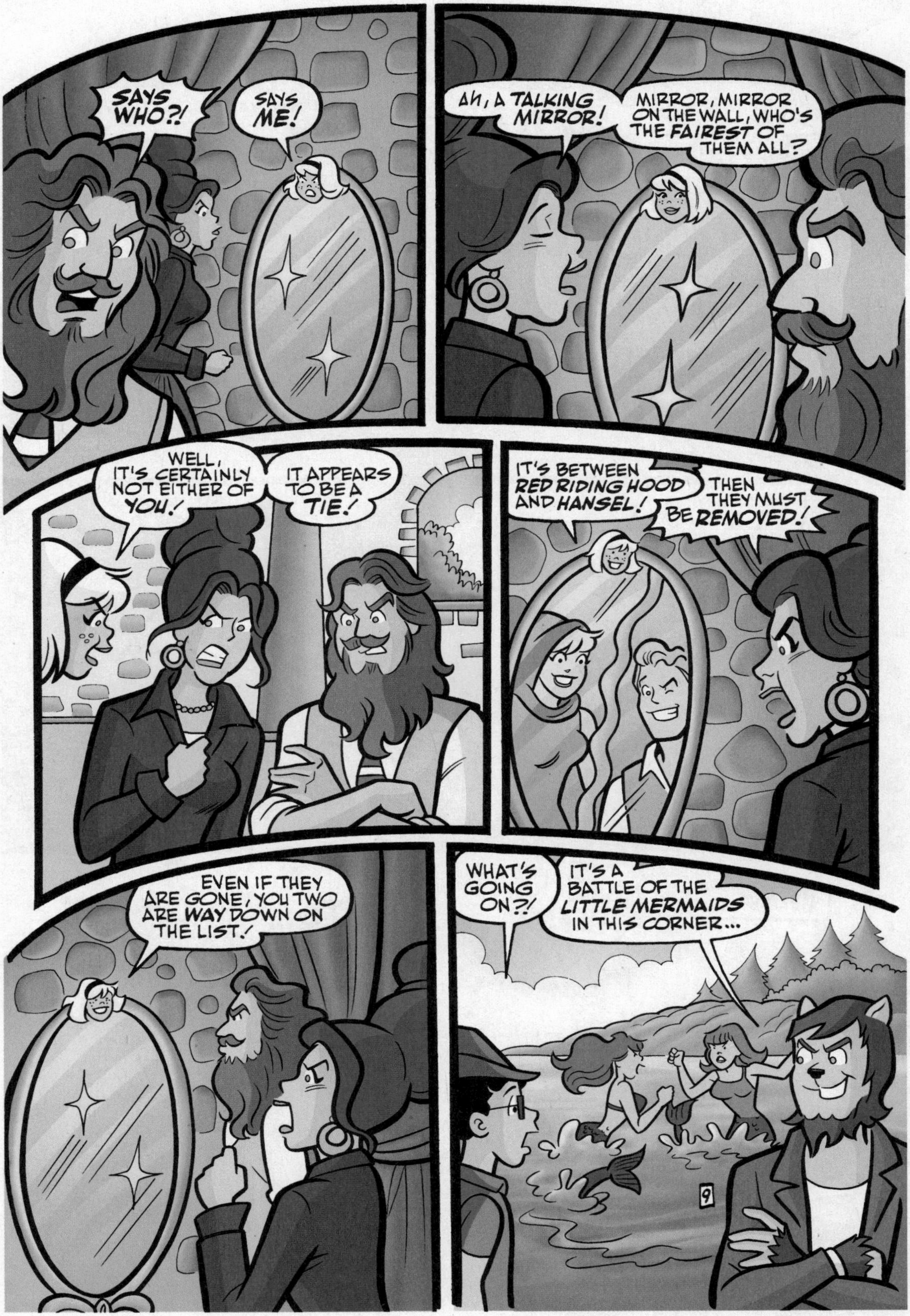
SAYS WHO?!
SAYS ME!
AH, A TALKING MIRROR!
MIRROR, MIRROR ON THE WALL, WHO'S THE FAIREST OF THEM ALL?
WELL, IT'S CERTAINLY NOT EITHER OF YOU!
IT APPEARS TO BE A TIE!
IT'S BETWEEN RED RIDING HOOD AND HANSEL!
THEN THEY MUST BE REMOVED!
EVEN IF THEY ARE GONE, YOU TWO ARE WAY DOWN ON THE LIST!
WHAT'S GOING ON?!
IT'S A BATTLE OF THE LITTLE MERMAIDS IN THIS CORNER...
9

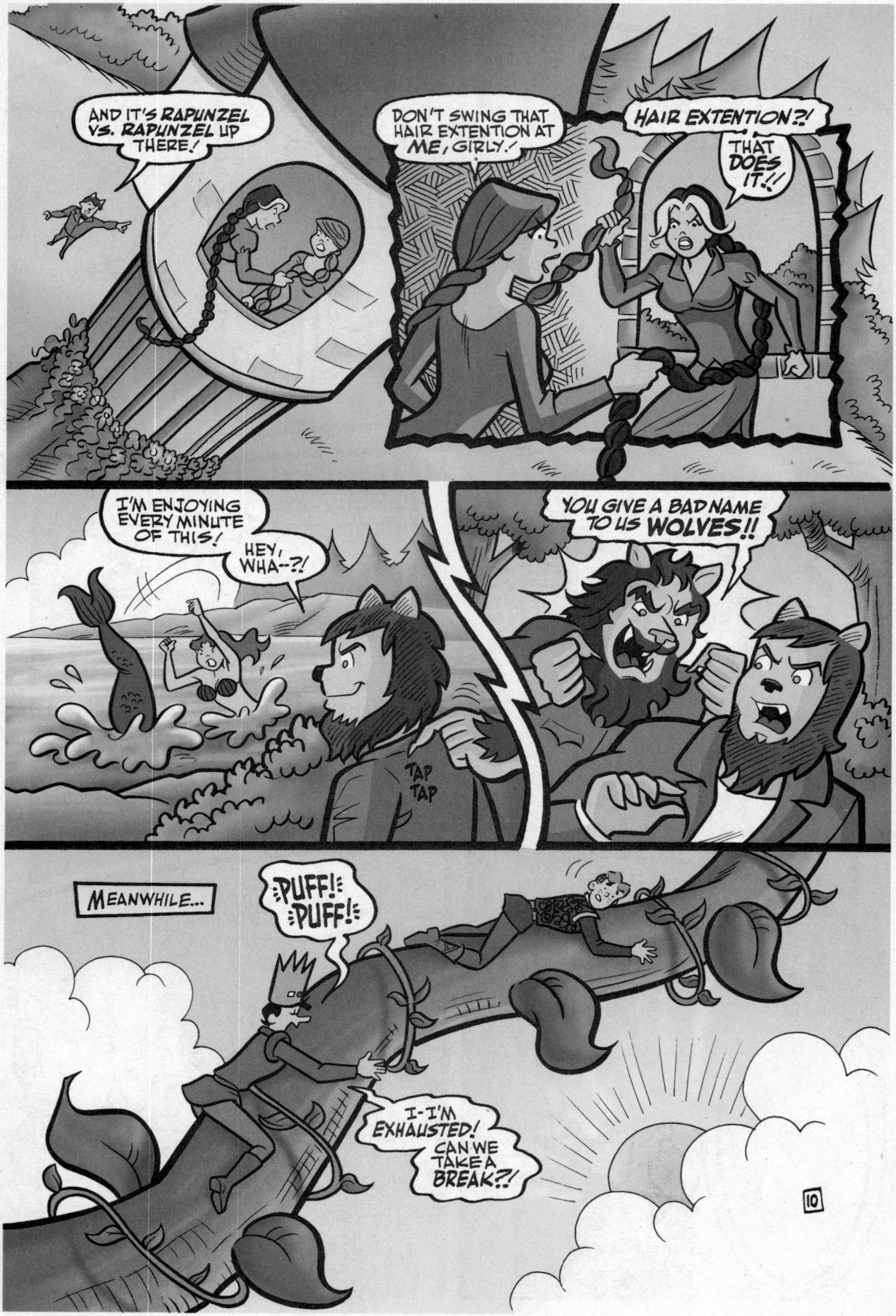
AND IT'S RAPUNZEL VS. RAPUNZEL UP THERE!
DON'T SWING THAT HAIR EXTENTION AT ME, GIRLY!
HAIR EXTENTION?!
THAT DOES IT!!
I'M ENJOYING EVERY MINUTE OF THIS!
HEY, WHA--?!
TAP TAP
YOU GIVE A BAD NAME TO US WOLVES!!
MEANWHILE...
PUFF! PUFF!
I-I'M EXHAUSTED! CAN WE TAKE A BREAK?!
10

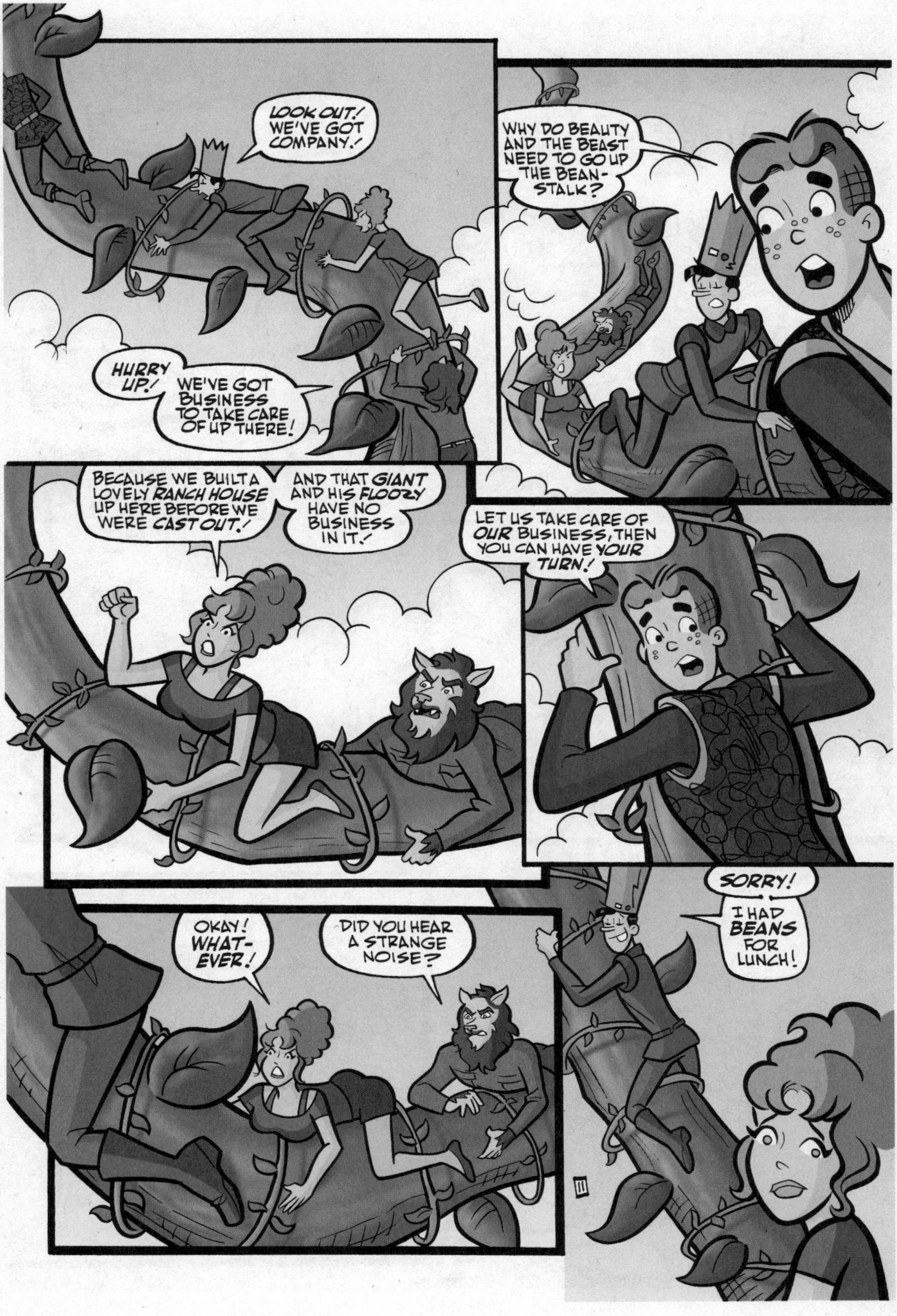
LOOK OUT! WE'VE GOT COMPANY.!
HURRY UP!
WE'VE GOT BUSINESS TO TAKE CARE OF UP THERE!
WHY DO BEAUTY AND THE BEAST NEED TO GO UP THE BEAN-STALK?
BECAUSE WE BUILT A LOVELY RANCH HOUSE UP HERE BEFORE WE WERE CAST OUT.!
AND THAT GIANT AND HIS FLOOZY HAVE NO BUSINESS IN IT.!
LET US TAKE CARE OF OUR BUSINESS, THEN YOU CAN HAVE YOUR TURN!
OKAY! WHAT-EVER!
DID YOU HEAR A STRANGE NOISE?
SORRY!
I HAD BEANS FOR LUNCH!

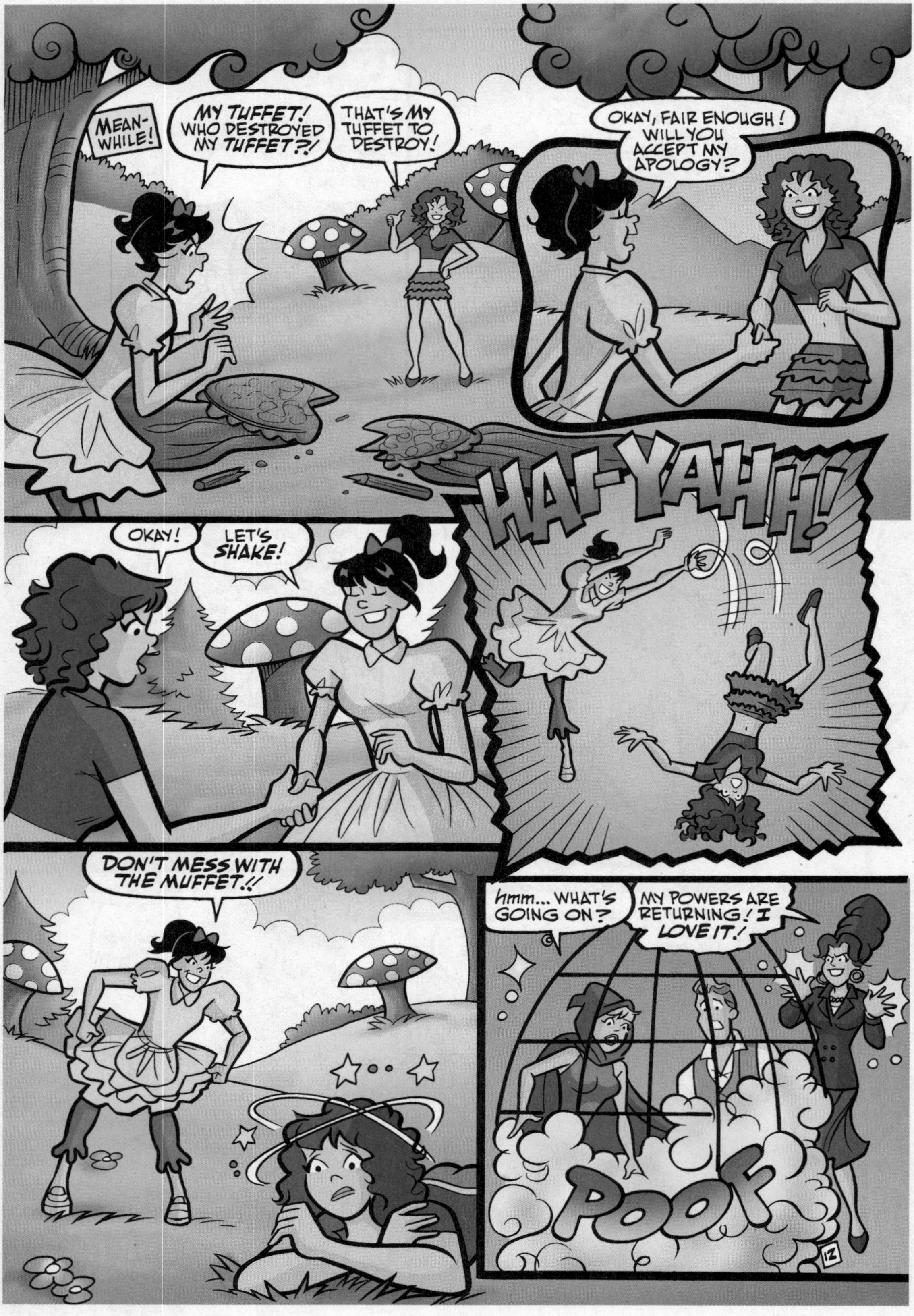
MEAN-WHILE!
MY TUFFET! WHO DESTROYED MY TUFFET?!
THAT'S MY TUFFET TO DESTROY!
OKAY, FAIR ENOUGH! WILL YOU ACCEPT MY APOLOGY?
OKAY!
LET'S SHAKE!
HAI-YAHH!
DON'T MESS WITH THE MUFFET!!
hmm... WHAT'S GOING ON?
MY POWERS ARE RETURNING! I LOVE IT!
POOF
12

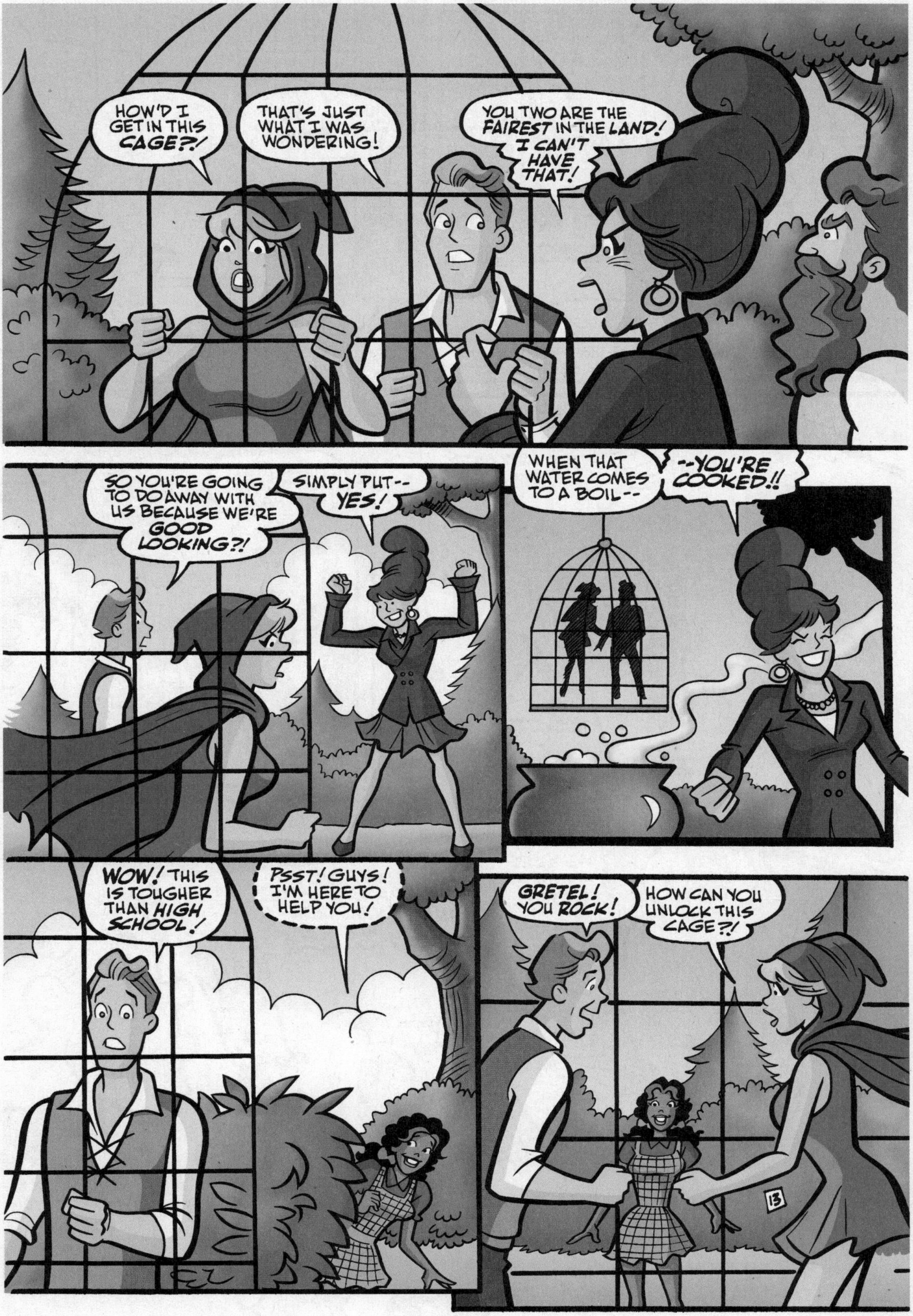
HOW'D I GET IN THIS CAGE?!
THAT'S JUST WHAT I WAS WONDERING!
YOU TWO ARE THE FAIREST IN THE LAND! I CAN'T HAVE THAT!
SO YOU'RE GOING TO DO AWAY WITH US BECAUSE WE'RE GOOD LOOKING?!
SIMPLY PUT-- YES!
WHEN THAT WATER COMES TO A BOIL--
--YOU'RE COOKED!!
WOW! THIS IS TOUGHER THAN HIGH SCHOOL!
PSST! GUYS! I'M HERE TO HELP YOU!
GRETEL! YOU ROCK!
HOW CAN YOU UNLOCK THIS CAGE?!
13

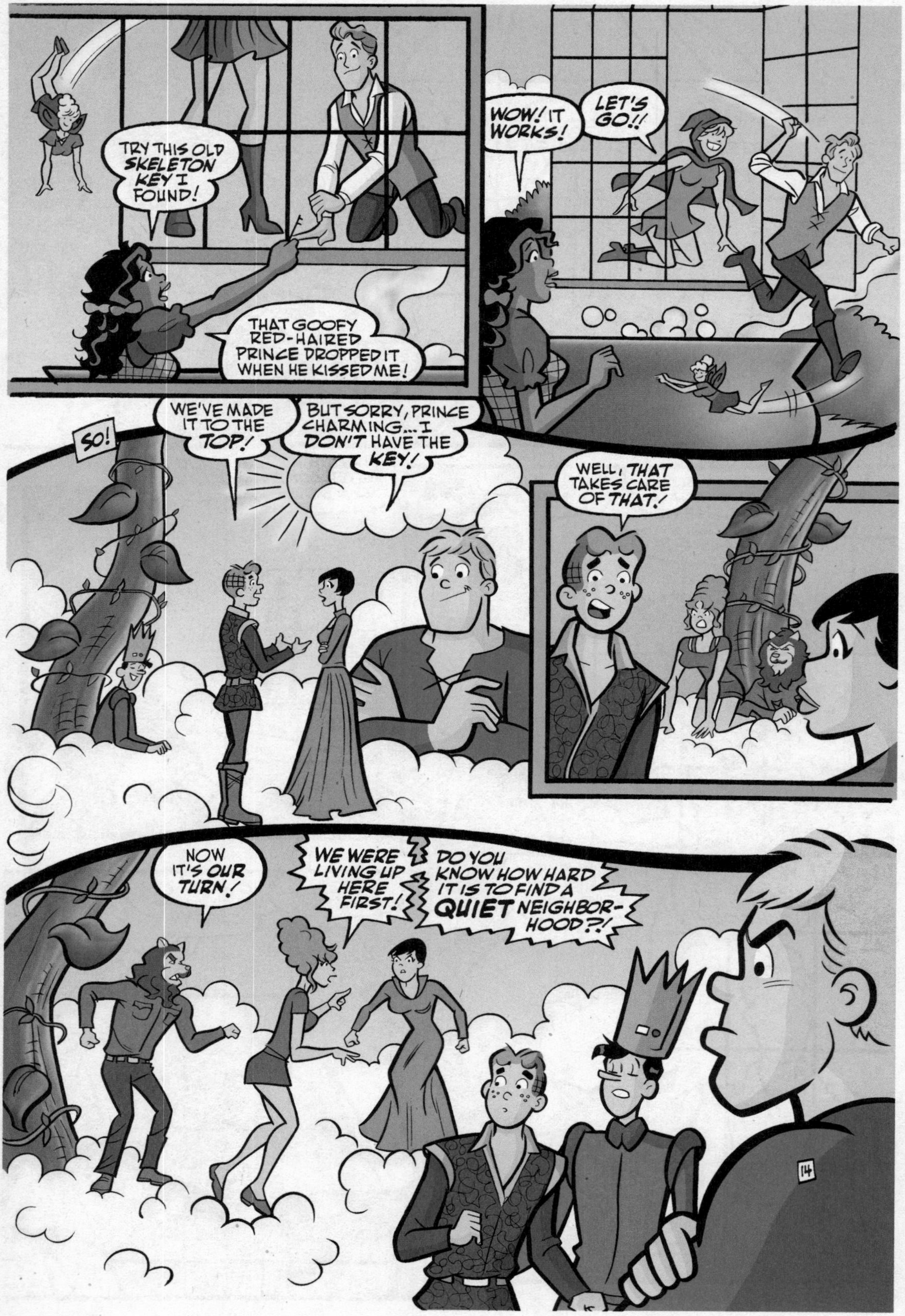
TRY THIS OLD SKELETON KEY I FOUND!
THAT GOOFY RED-HAIRED PRINCE DROPPED IT WHEN HE KISSED ME!
WOW! IT WORKS!
LET'S GO!!
SO!
WE'VE MADE IT TO THE TOP!
BUT SORRY, PRINCE CHARMING... I DON'T HAVE THE KEY!
WELL, THAT TAKES CARE OF THAT.!
NOW IT'S OUR TURN!
WE WERE LIVING UP HERE FIRST!
DO YOU KNOW HOW HARD IT IS TO FIND A QUIET NEIGHBOR-HOOD?!
14

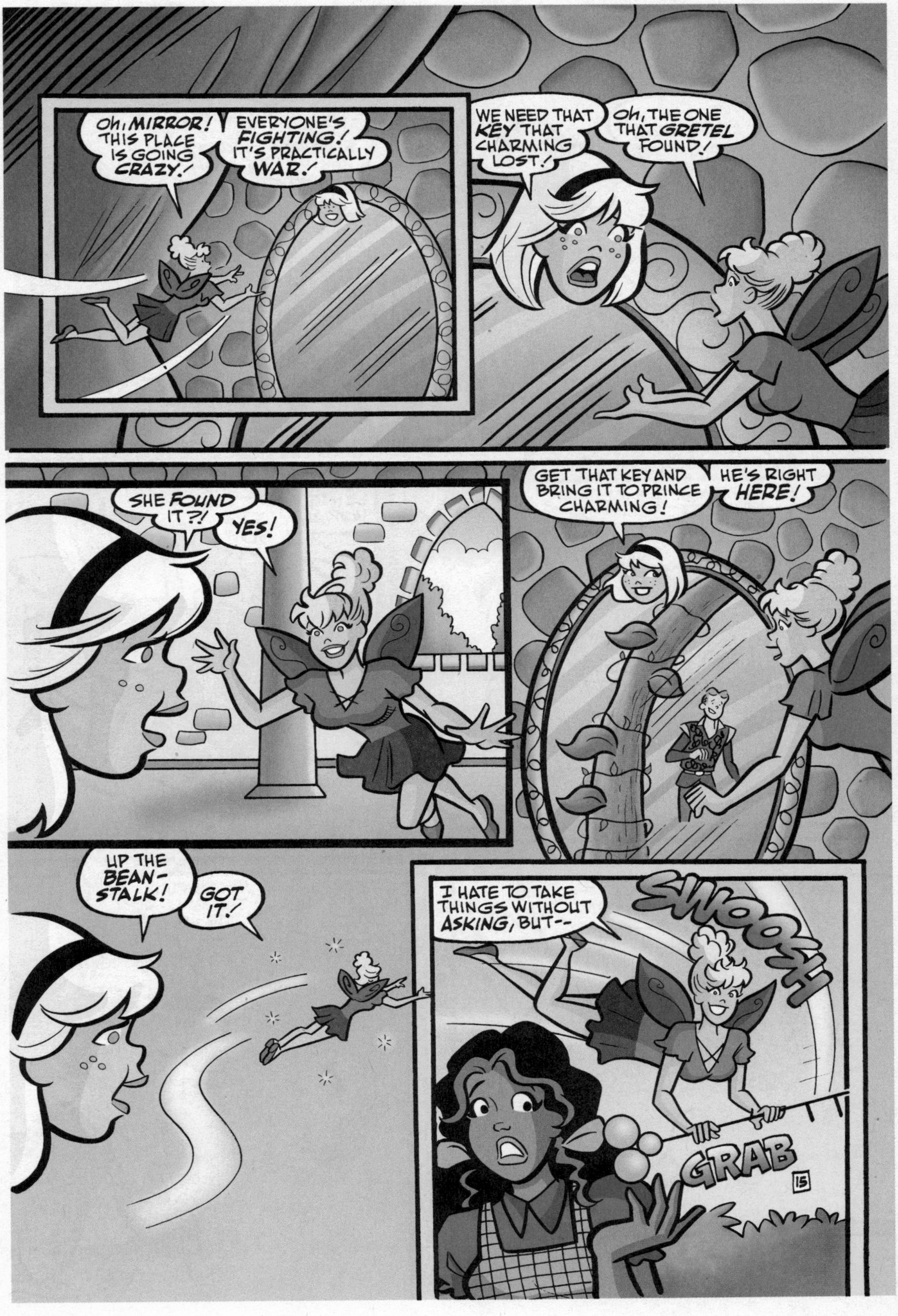

OH, MIRROR! THIS PLACE IS GOING CRAZY!
EVERYONE'S FIGHTING! IT'S PRACTICALLY WAR!
WE NEED THAT KEY THAT CHARMING LOST!
OH, THE ONE THAT GRETEL FOUND!
SHE FOUND IT?!
YES!
GET THAT KEY AND BRING IT TO PRINCE CHARMING!
HE'S RIGHT HERE!
UP THE BEAN-STALK!
GOT IT!
I HATE TO TAKE THINGS WITHOUT ASKING, BUT--
SWOOSH
GRAB
15

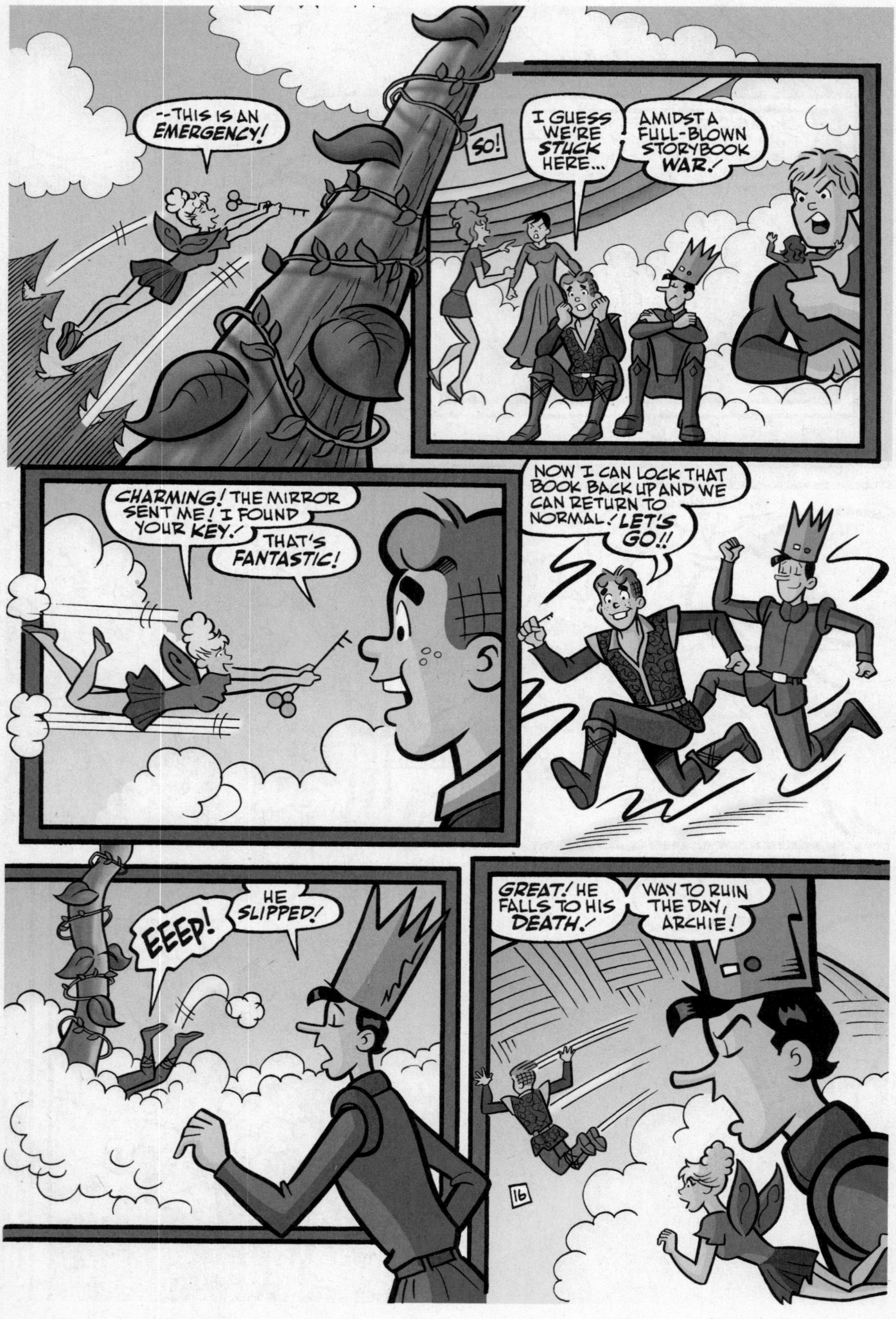
--THIS IS AN EMERGENCY!
SO!
I GUESS WE'RE STUCK HERE...
AMIDST A FULL-BLOWN STORYBOOK WAR!
CHARMING! THE MIRROR SENT ME! I FOUND YOUR KEY!
THAT'S FANTASTIC!
NOW I CAN LOCK THAT BOOK BACK UP AND WE CAN RETURN TO NORMAL! LET'S GO!!
EEEP!
HE SLIPPED!
GREAT! HE FALLS TO HIS DEATH!
WAY TO RUIN THE DAY, ARCHIE!
16

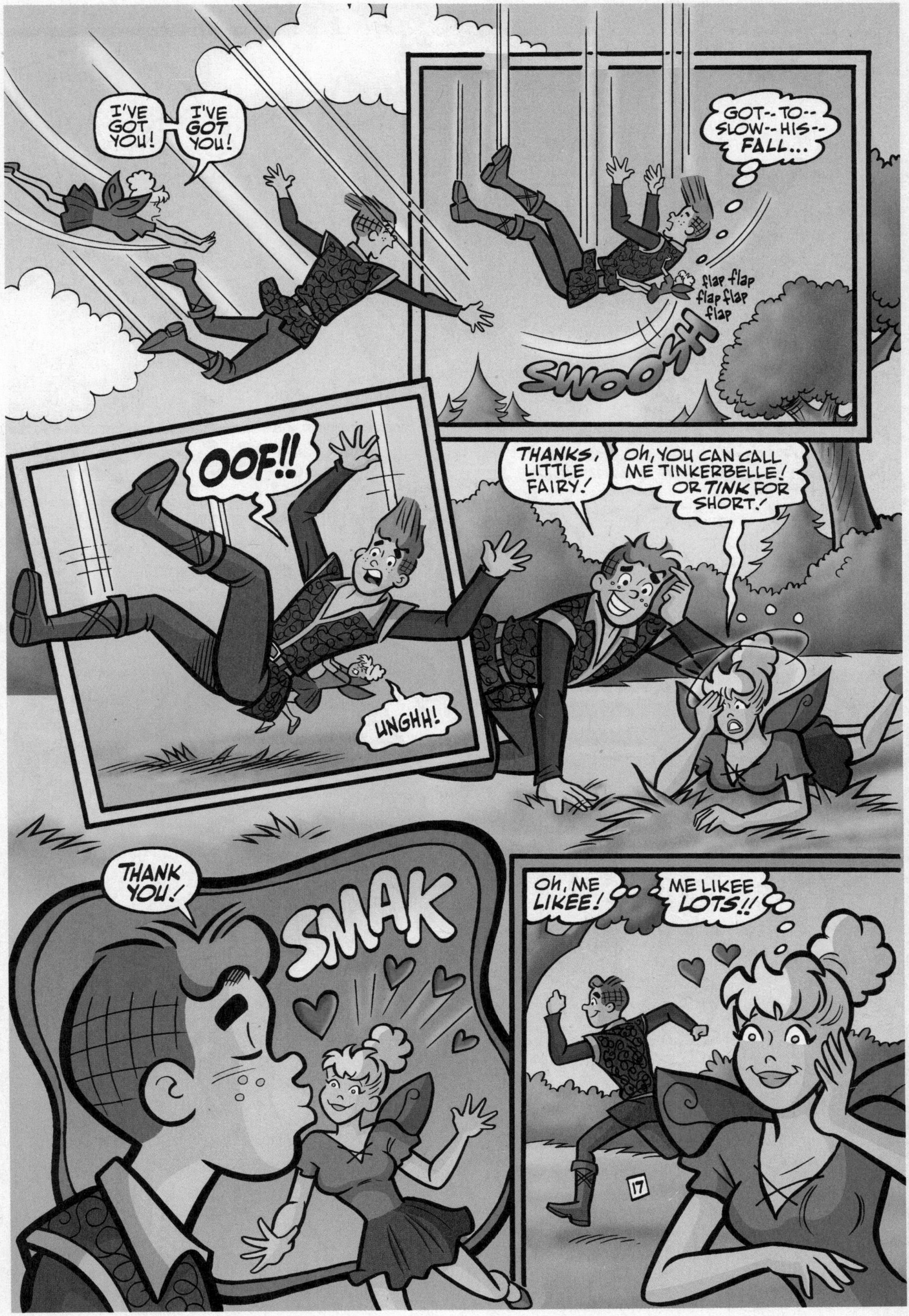

I'VE GOT YOU!
I'VE GOT YOU!
GOT--TO--SLOW--HIS--FALL...
flap flap flap flap flap
SWOOSH
OOF!!
UNGHH!
THANKS, LITTLE FAIRY!
Oh, YOU CAN CALL ME TINKERBELLE! OR TINK FOR SHORT.!
THANK YOU!
SMAK
Oh, ME LIKEE!
ME LIKEE LOTS!!
17

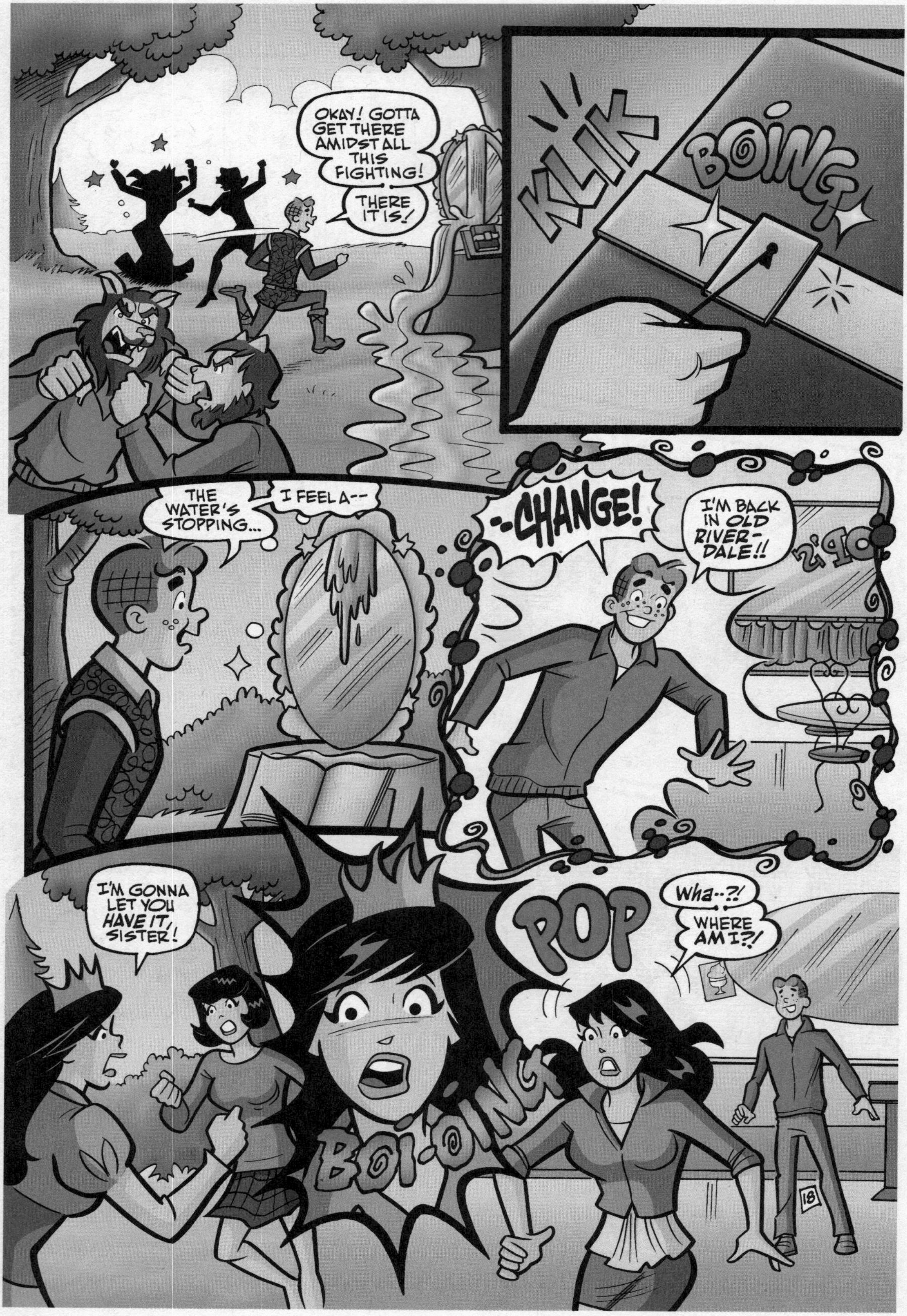
OKAY! GOTTA GET THERE AMIDST ALL THIS FIGHTING!
THERE IT IS!
KLIK
BOING
THE WATER'S STOPPING...
I FEEL A--
--CHANGE!
I'M BACK IN OLD RIVERDALE!!
POP'S
I'M GONNA LET YOU HAVE IT, SISTER!
POP
WHA--?!
WHERE AM I?!
BOI-OING
18

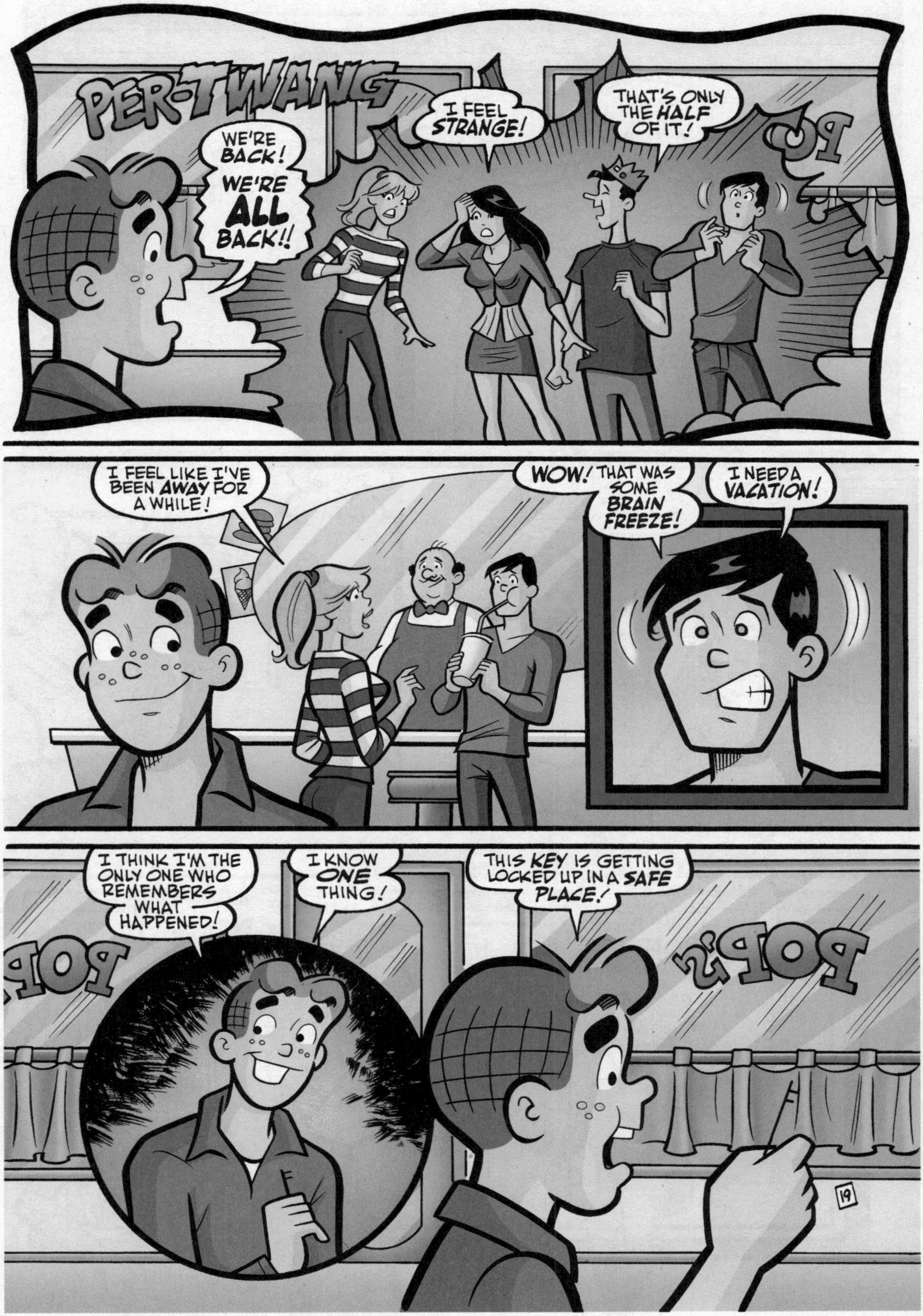
PER-TWANG
WE'RE BACK! WE'RE ALL BACK!!
I FEEL STRANGE!
THAT'S ONLY THE HALF OF IT!
I FEEL LIKE I'VE BEEN AWAY FOR A WHILE!
WOW! THAT WAS SOME BRAIN FREEZE!
I NEED A VACATION!
I THINK I'M THE ONLY ONE WHO REMEMBERS WHAT HAPPENED!
I KNOW ONE THING!
THIS KEY IS GETTING LOCKED UP IN A SAFE PLACE!
POP'S
19

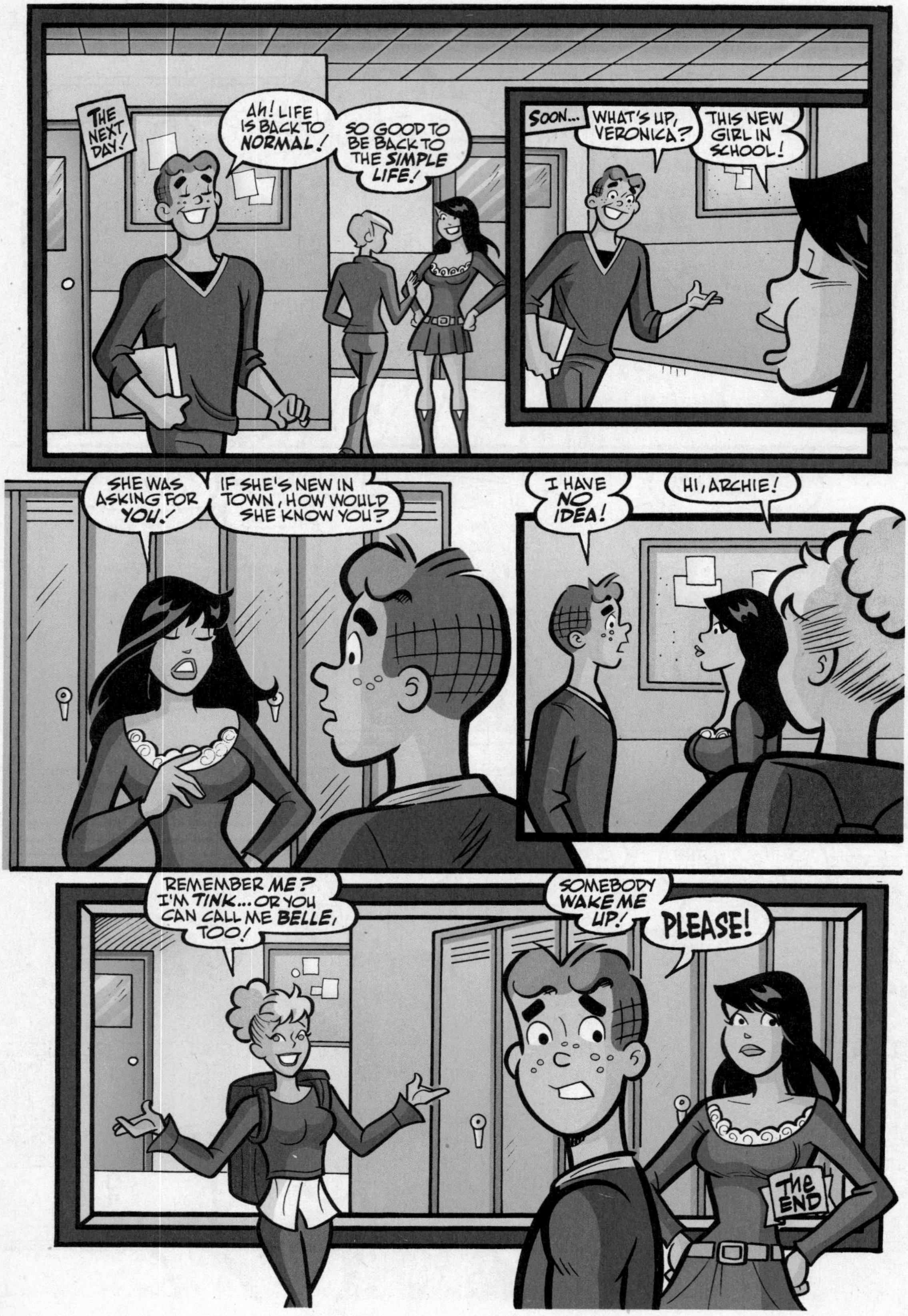
THE NEXT DAY!
Ah! LIFE IS BACK TO NORMAL!
SO GOOD TO BE BACK TO THE SIMPLE LIFE!
SOON...
WHAT'S UP, VERONICA?
THIS NEW GIRL IN SCHOOL!
SHE WAS ASKING FOR YOU!
IF SHE'S NEW IN TOWN, HOW WOULD SHE KNOW YOU?
I HAVE NO IDEA!
HI, ARCHIE!
REMEMBER ME? I'M TINK...OR YOU CAN CALL ME BELLE, TOO!
SOMEBODY WAKE ME UP!
PLEASE!
THE END

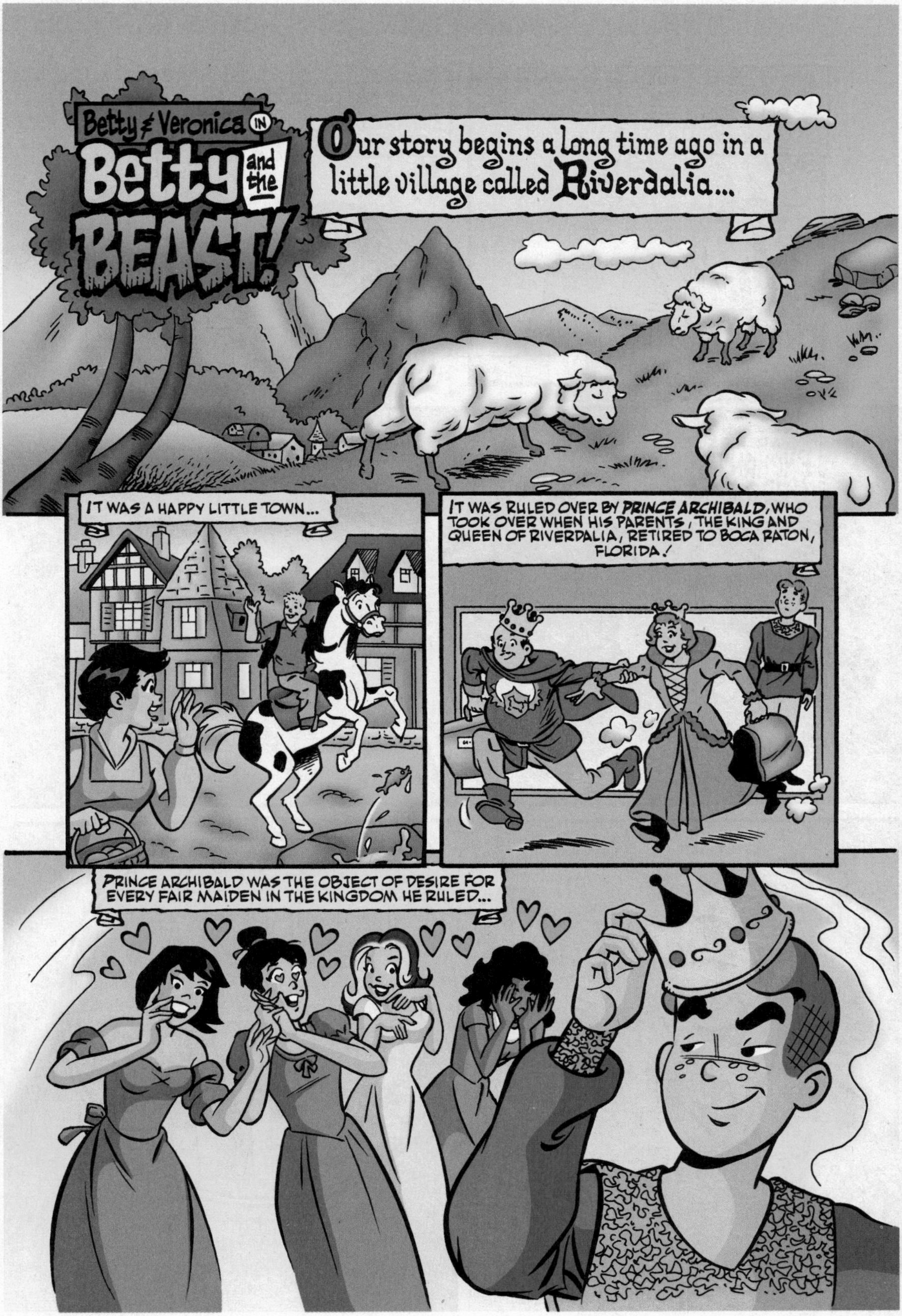
Betty & Veronica IN
Betty and the BEAST!
Our story begins a long time ago in a little village called Riverdalia...
IT WAS A HAPPY LITTLE TOWN...
IT WAS RULED OVER BY PRINCE ARCHIBALD, WHO TOOK OVER WHEN HIS PARENTS, THE KING AND QUEEN OF RIVERDALIA, RETIRED TO BOCA RATON, FLORIDA!
PRINCE ARCHIBALD WAS THE OBJECT OF DESIRE FOR EVERY FAIR MAIDEN IN THE KINGDOM HE RULED...

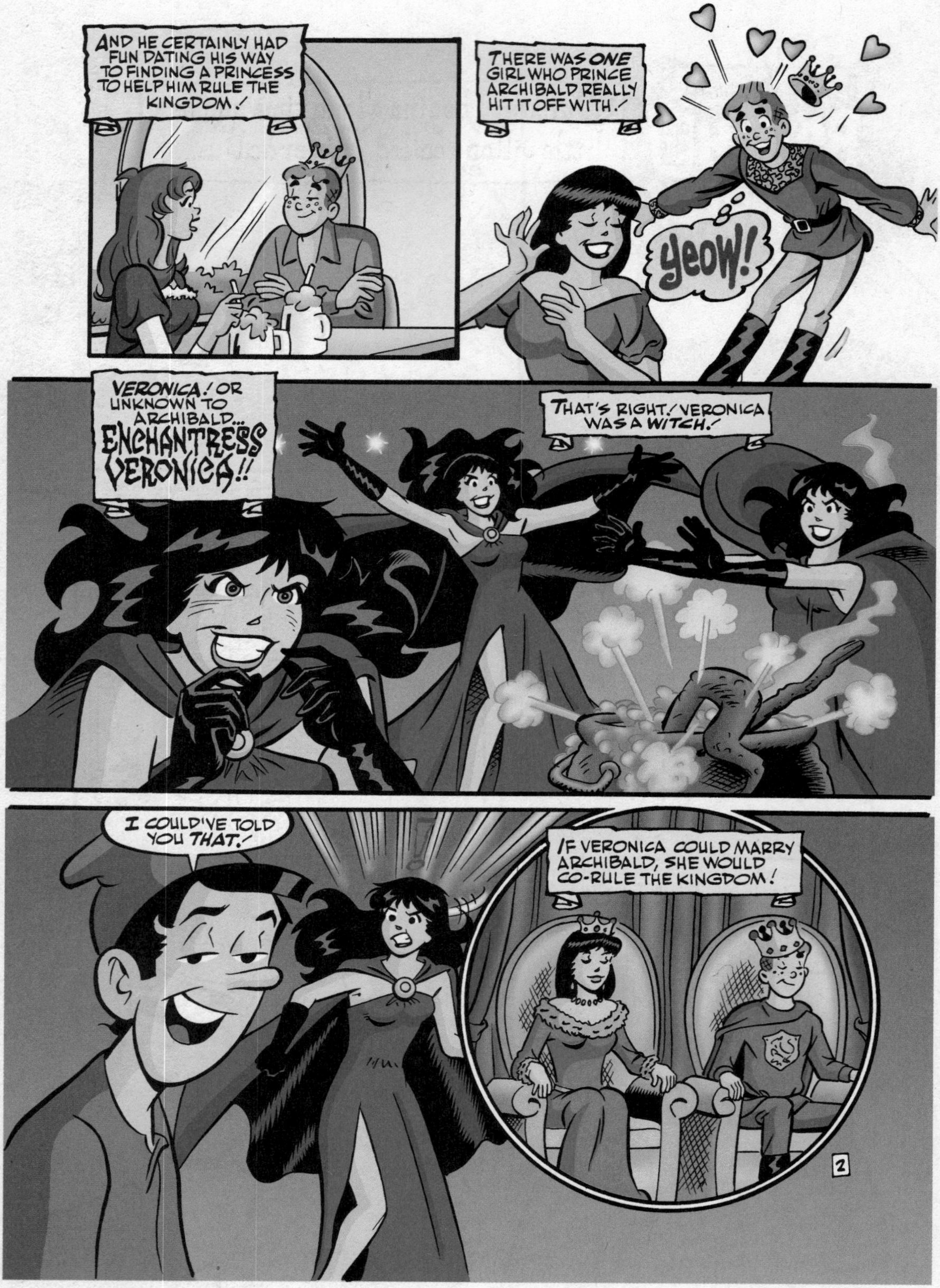
AND HE CERTAINLY HAD FUN DATING HIS WAY TO FINDING A PRINCESS TO HELP HIM RULE THE KINGDOM!
THERE WAS ONE GIRL WHO PRINCE ARCHIBALD REALLY HIT IT OFF WITH!
YEOW!
VERONICA! OR UNKNOWN TO ARCHIBALD... ENCHANTRESS VERONICA!!
THAT'S RIGHT! VERONICA WAS A WITCH!
I COULD'VE TOLD YOU THAT!
IF VERONICA COULD MARRY ARCHIBALD, SHE WOULD CO-RULE THE KINGDOM!
2

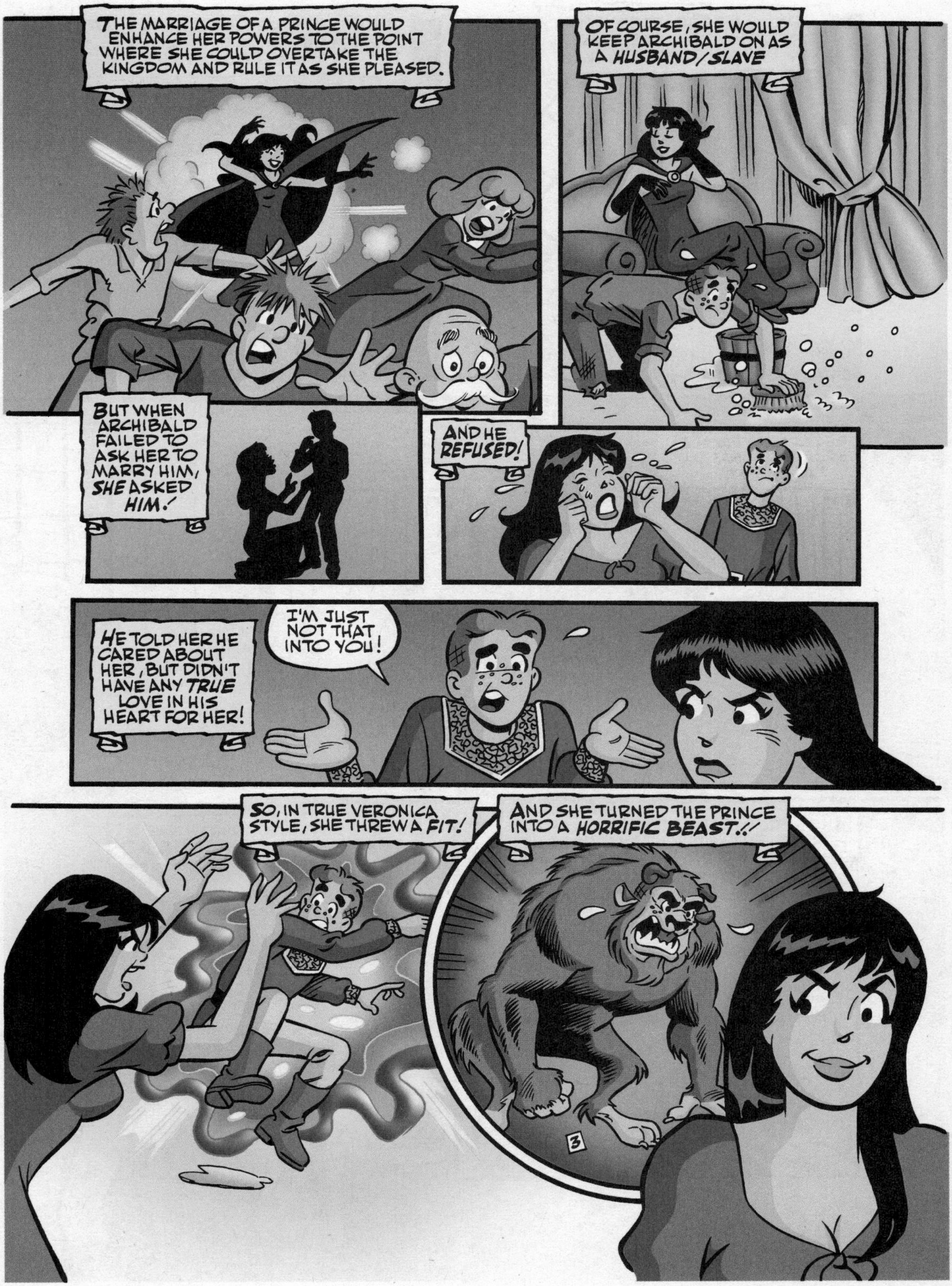
THE MARRIAGE OF A PRINCE WOULD ENHANCE HER POWERS TO THE POINT WHERE SHE COULD OVERTAKE THE KINGDOM AND RULE IT AS SHE PLEASED.
OF COURSE, SHE WOULD KEEP ARCHIBALD ON AS A HUSBAND/SLAVE
BUT WHEN ARCHIBALD FAILED TO ASK HER TO MARRY HIM, SHE ASKED HIM!
AND HE REFUSED!
HE TOLD HER HE CARED ABOUT HER, BUT DIDN'T HAVE ANY TRUE LOVE IN HIS HEART FOR HER!
I'M JUST NOT THAT INTO YOU!
SO, IN TRUE VERONICA STYLE, SHE THREW A FIT!
AND SHE TURNED THE PRINCE INTO A HORRIFIC BEAST!!
3

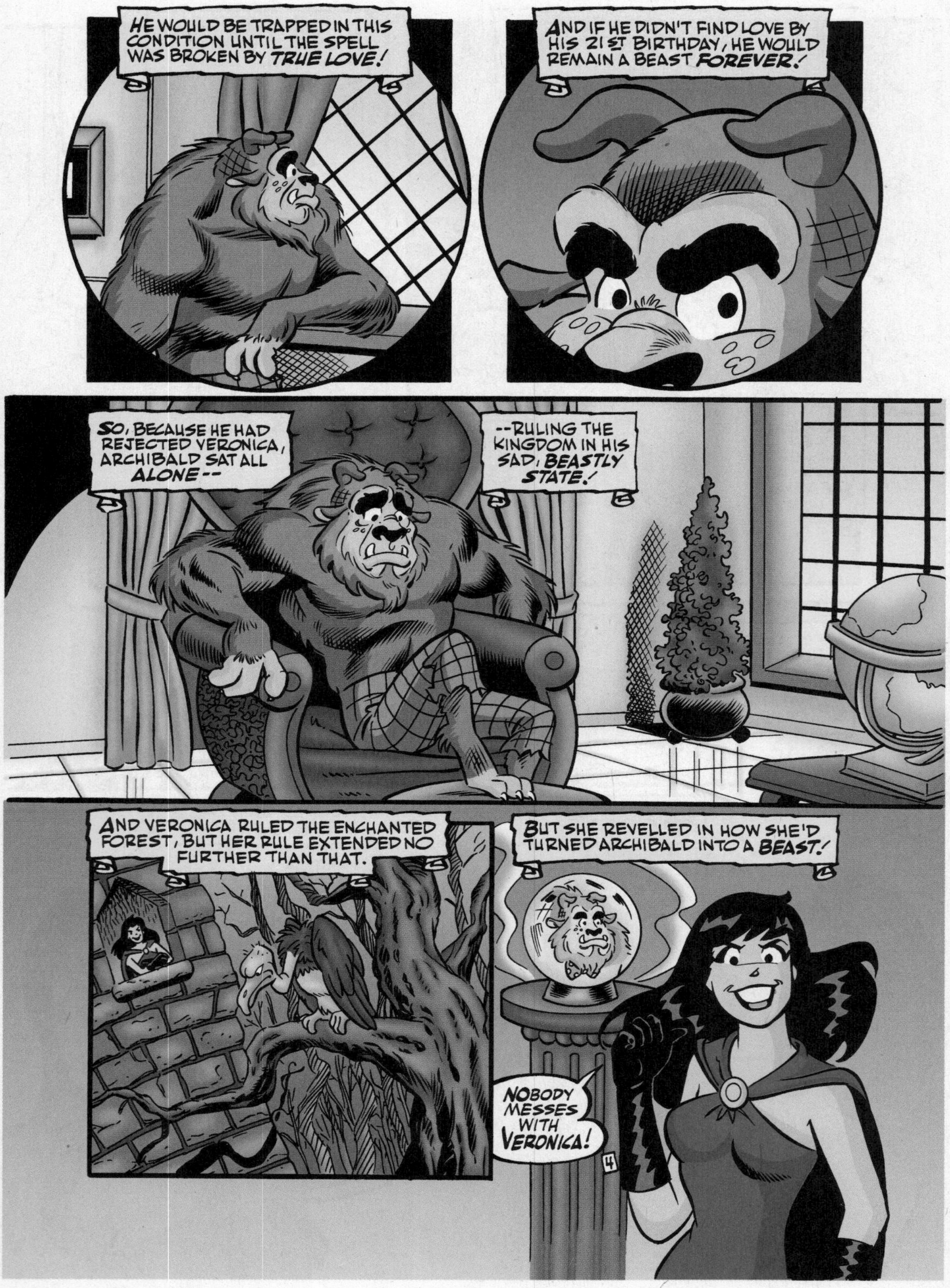
HE WOULD BE TRAPPED IN THIS CONDITION UNTIL THE SPELL WAS BROKEN BY TRUE LOVE!
AND IF HE DIDN'T FIND LOVE BY HIS 21 ST BIRTHDAY, HE WOULD REMAIN A BEAST FOREVER!
SO, BECAUSE HE HAD REJECTED VERONICA, ARCHIBALD SAT ALL ALONE--
--RULING THE KINGDOM IN HIS SAD, BEASTLY STATE!
AND VERONICA RULED THE ENCHANTED FOREST, BUT HER RULE EXTENDED NO FURTHER THAN THAT.
BUT SHE REVELLED IN HOW SHE'D TURNED ARCHIBALD INTO A BEAST!
NOBODY MESSES WITH VERONICA!
4

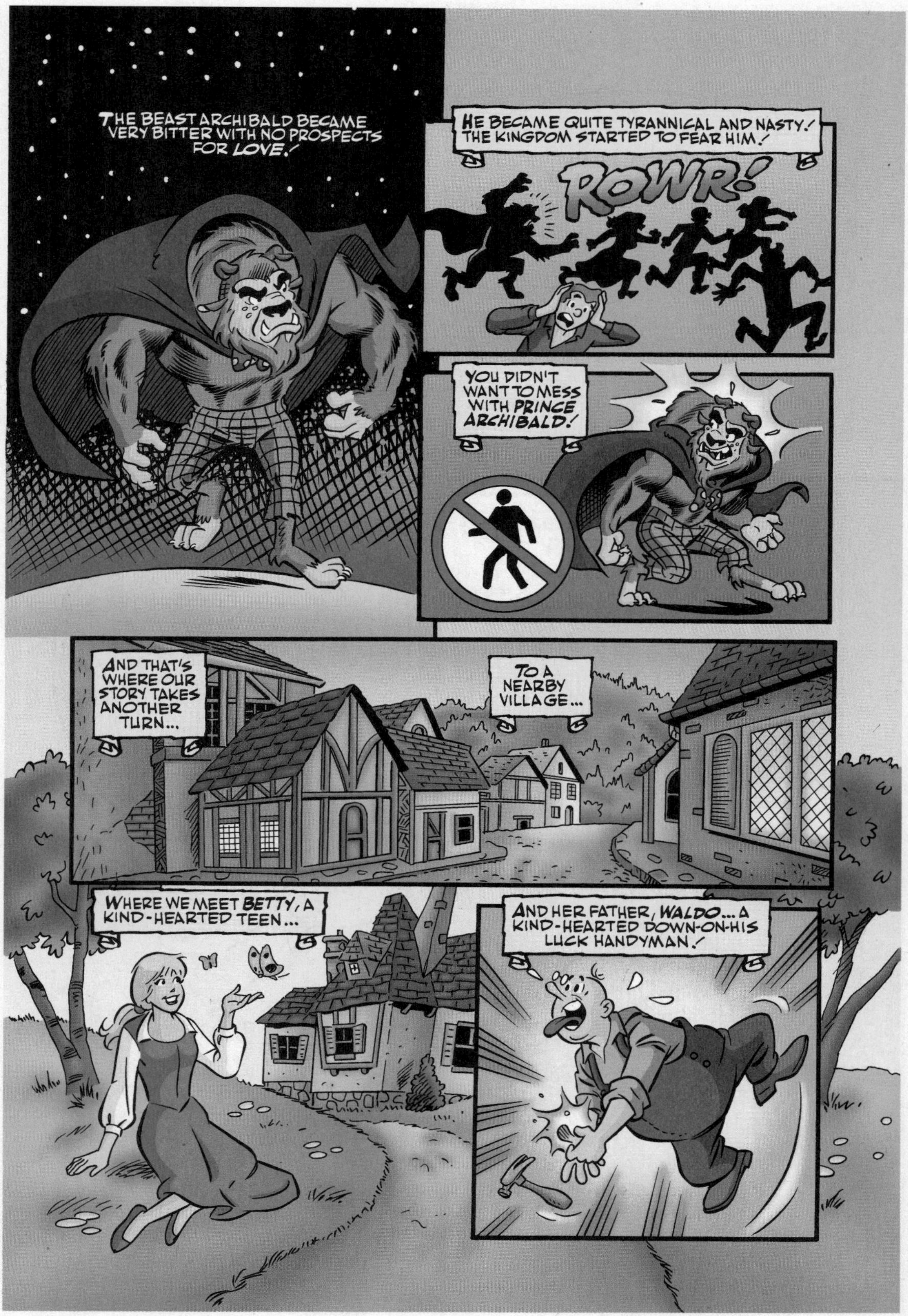
THE BEAST ARCHIBALD BECAME VERY BITTER WITH NO PROSPECTS FOR LOVE!
HE BECAME QUITE TYRANNICAL AND NASTY! THE KINGDOM STARTED TO FEAR HIM!
ROWR!
YOU DIDN'T WANT TO MESS WITH PRINCE ARCHIBALD!
AND THAT'S WHERE OUR STORY TAKES ANOTHER TURN...
TO A NEARBY VILLAGE...
WHERE WE MEET BETTY, A KIND-HEARTED TEEN...
AND HER FATHER, WALDO... A KIND-HEARTED DOWN-ON-HIS LUCK HANDYMAN!

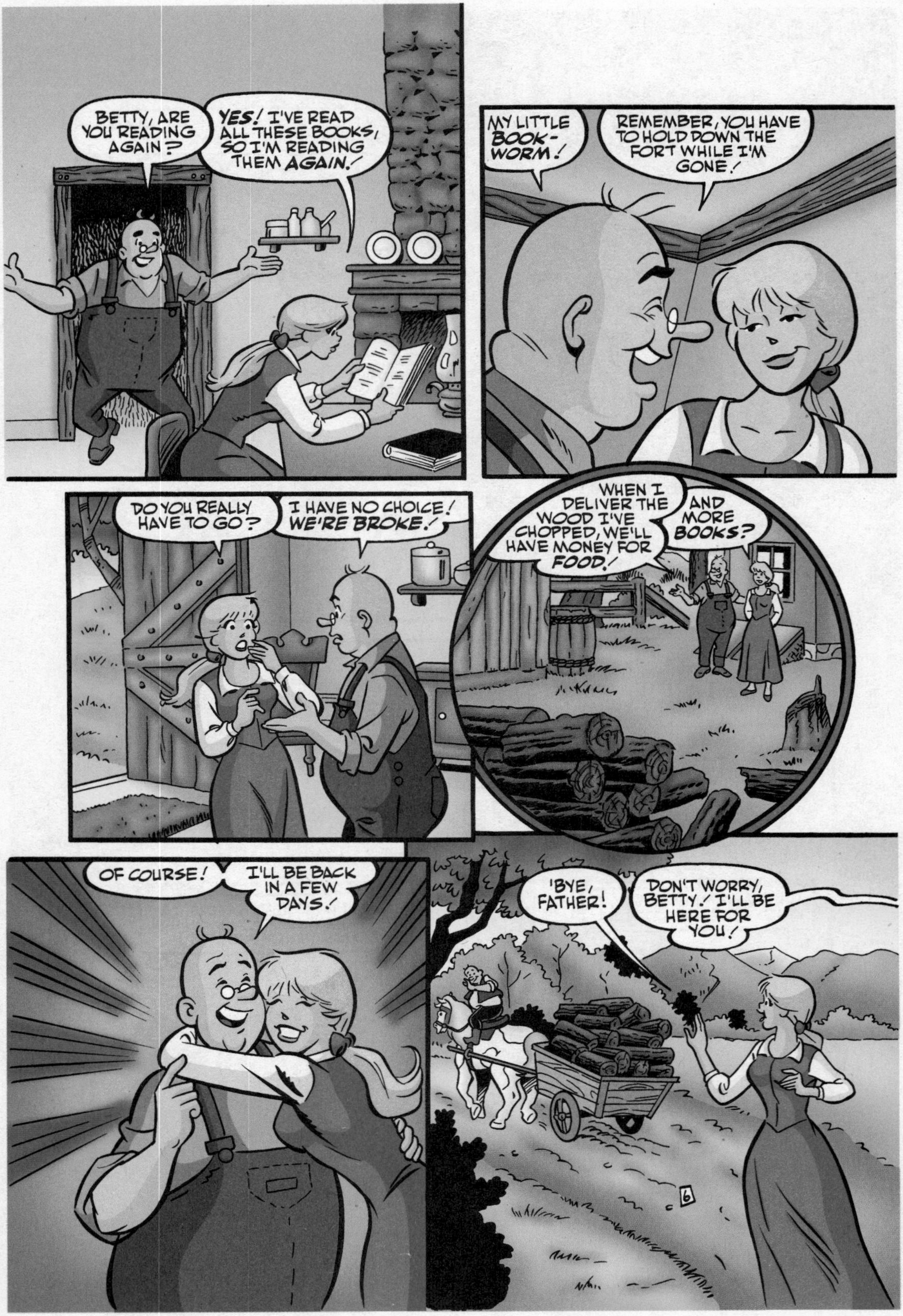
BETTY, ARE YOU READING AGAIN?
YES! I'VE READ ALL THESE BOOKS, SO I'M READING THEM AGAIN!
MY LITTLE BOOK-WORM!
REMEMBER, YOU HAVE TO HOLD DOWN THE FORT WHILE I'M GONE!
DO YOU REALLY HAVE TO GO?
I HAVE NO CHOICE! WE'RE BROKE!
WHEN I DELIVER THE WOOD I'VE CHOPPED, WE'LL HAVE MONEY FOR FOOD!
AND MORE BOOKS?
OF COURSE!
I'LL BE BACK IN A FEW DAYS!
'BYE, FATHER!
DON'T WORRY, BETTY! I'LL BE HERE FOR YOU!
6

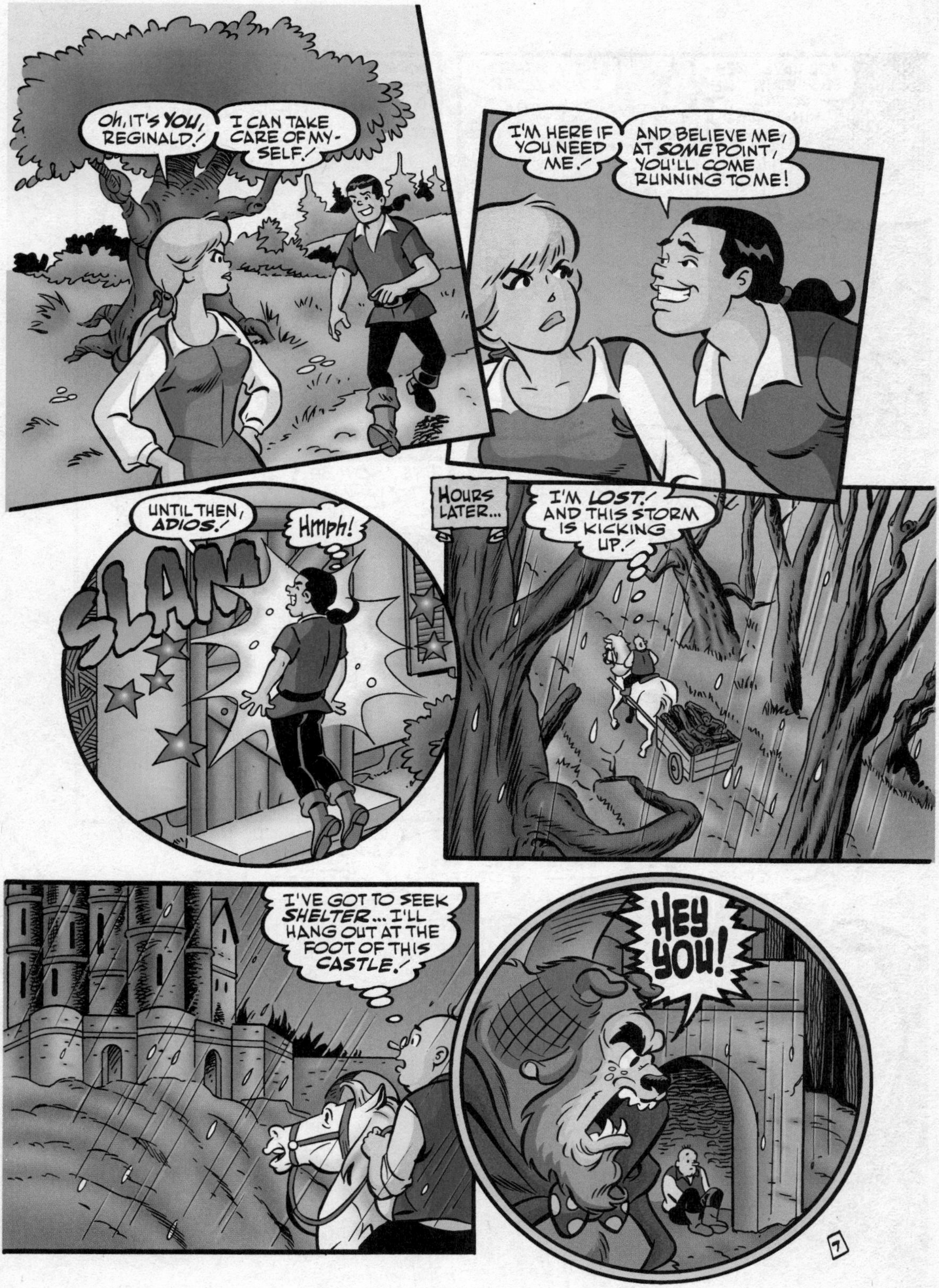
Oh, IT'S YOU, REGINALD!
I CAN TAKE CARE OF MY-SELF!
I'M HERE IF YOU NEED ME.
AND BELIEVE ME, AT SOME POINT, YOU'LL COME RUNNING TO ME!
UNTIL THEN, ADIOS!
Hmph!
SLAM
HOURS LATER...
I'M LOST! AND THIS STORM IS KICKING UP!
I'VE GOT TO SEEK SHELTER... I'LL HANG OUT AT THE FOOT OF THIS CASTLE!
HEY YOU!
7

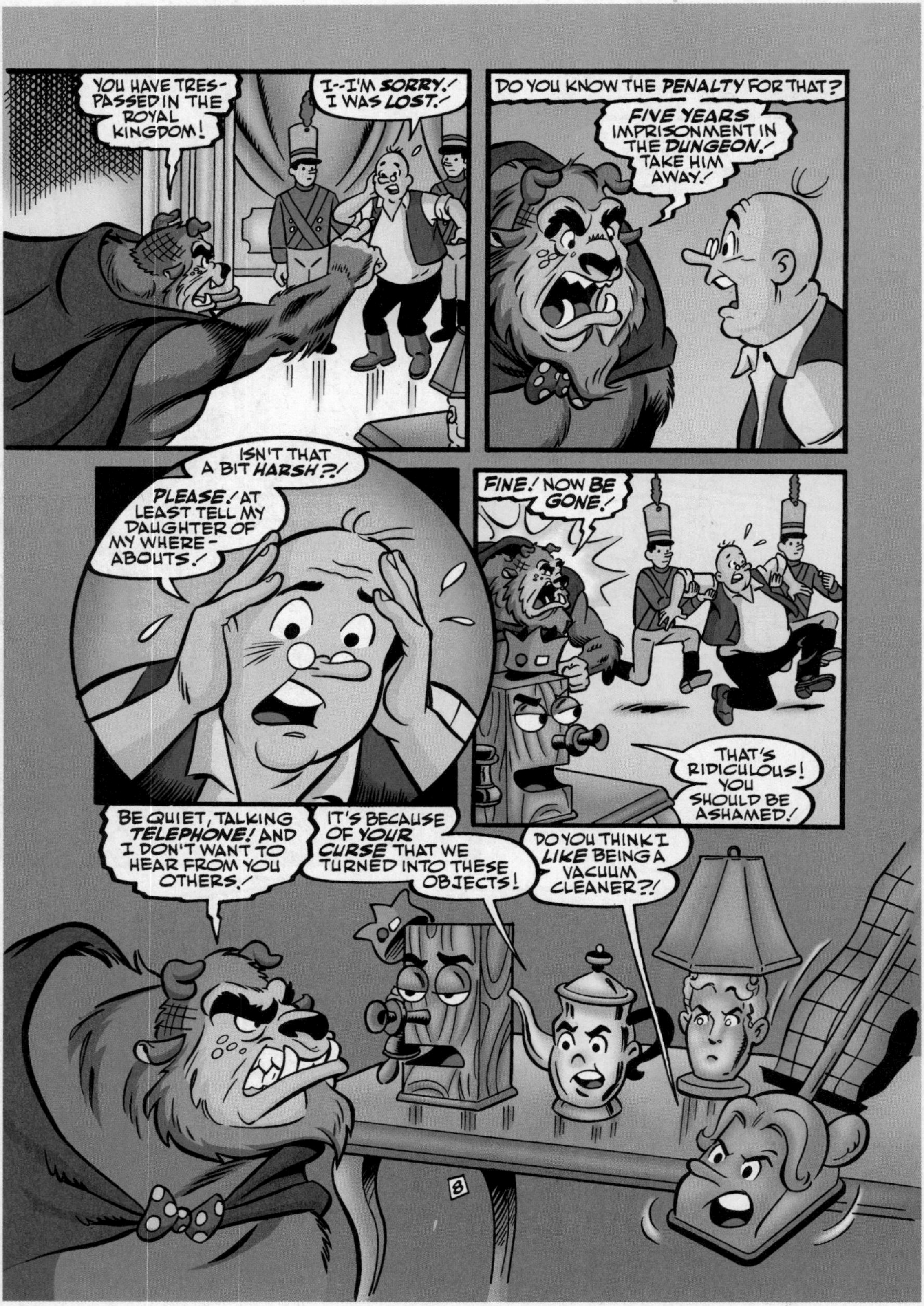
YOU HAVE TRES-PASSED IN THE ROYAL KINGDOM!
I--I'M SORRY! I WAS LOST!
DO YOU KNOW THE PENALTY FOR THAT?
FIVE YEARS IMPRISONMENT IN THE DUNGEON! TAKE HIM AWAY!
ISN'T THAT A BIT HARSH?!
PLEASE! AT LEAST TELL MY DAUGHTER OF MY WHERE-ABOUTS!
FINE! NOW BE GONE!
THAT'S RIDICULOUS! YOU SHOULD BE ASHAMED!
BE QUIET, TALKING TELEPHONE! AND I DON'T WANT TO HEAR FROM YOU OTHERS!
IT'S BECAUSE OF YOUR CURSE THAT WE TURNED INTO THESE OBJECTS!
DO YOU THINK I LIKE BEING A VACUUM CLEANER?!
8

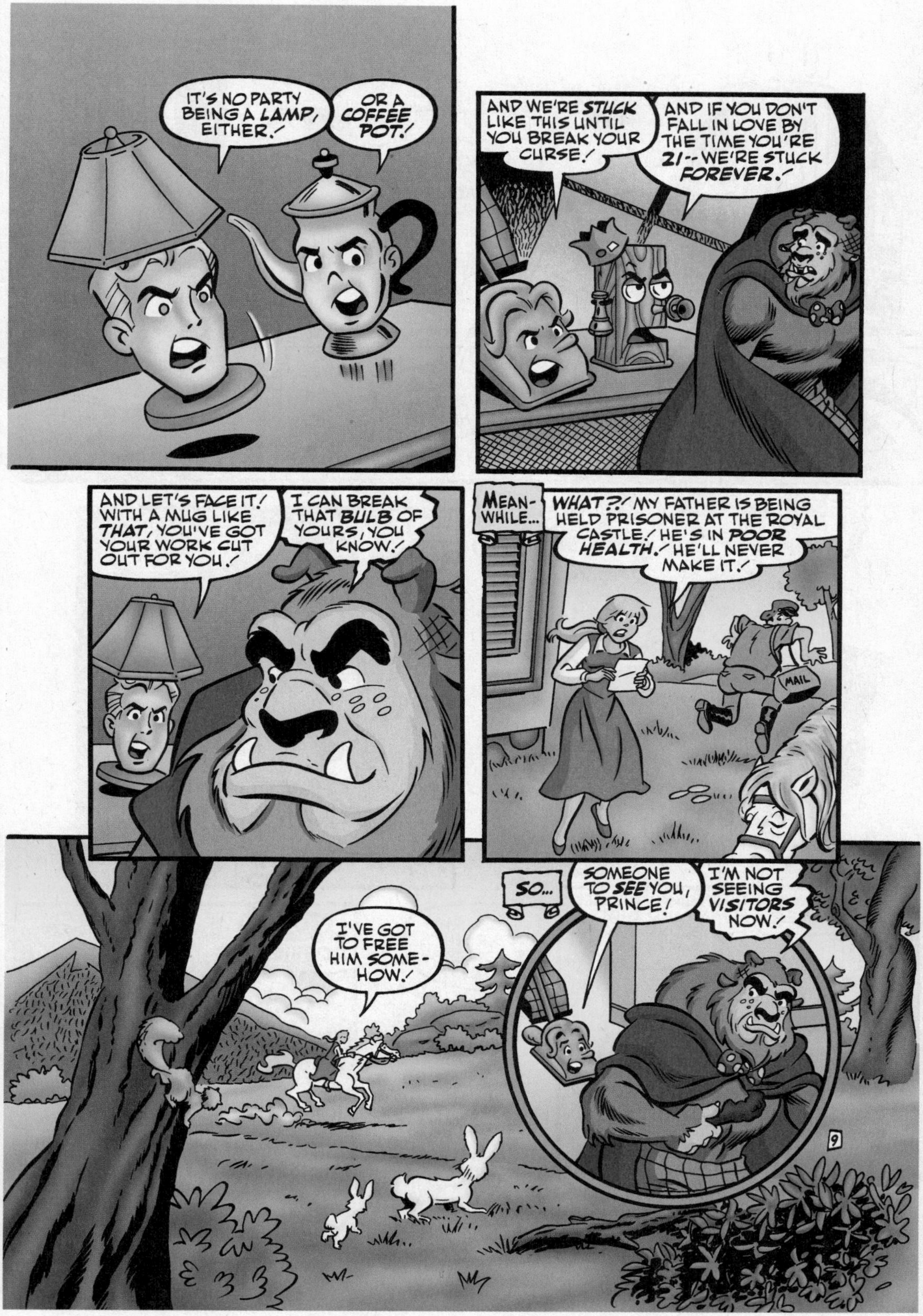
IT'S NO PARTY BEING A LAMP, EITHER.!
OR A COFFEE POT!
AND WE'RE STUCK LIKE THIS UNTIL YOU BREAK YOUR CURSE!
AND IF YOU DON'T FALL IN LOVE BY THE TIME YOU'RE 21-- WE'RE STUCK FOREVER.!
AND LET'S FACE IT! WITH A MUG LIKE THAT, YOU'VE GOT YOUR WORK CUT OUT FOR YOU!
I CAN BREAK THAT BULB OF YOURS, YOU KNOW!
MEAN-WHILE...
WHAT?! MY FATHER IS BEING HELD PRISONER AT THE ROYAL CASTLE! HE'S IN POOR HEALTH! HE'LL NEVER MAKE IT!
MAIL
I'VE GOT TO FREE HIM SOME-HOW!
SO...
SOMEONE TO SEE YOU, PRINCE!
I'M NOT SEEING VISITORS NOW!
9

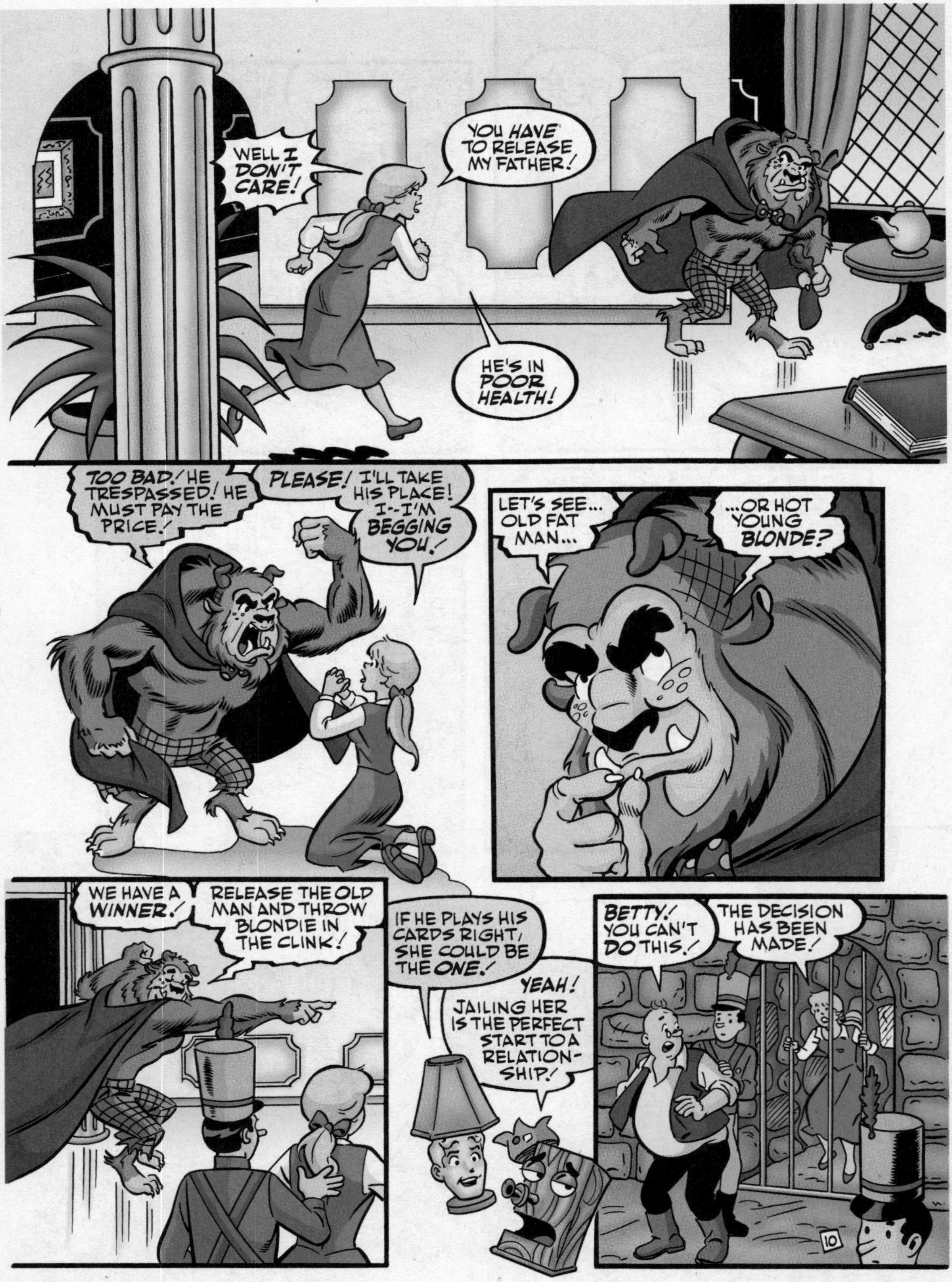
WELL I DON'T CARE!
YOU HAVE TO RELEASE MY FATHER!
HE'S IN POOR HEALTH!
TOO BAD! HE TRESPASSED! HE MUST PAY THE PRICE!
PLEASE! I'LL TAKE HIS PLACE! I--I'M BEGGING YOU!
LET'S SEE... OLD FAT MAN...
...OR HOT YOUNG BLONDE?
WE HAVE A WINNER!
RELEASE THE OLD MAN AND THROW BLONDIE IN THE CLINK!
IF HE PLAYS HIS CARDS RIGHT, SHE COULD BE THE ONE!
YEAH! JAILING HER IS THE PERFECT START TO A RELATION-SHIP!
BETTY! YOU CAN'T DO THIS!
THE DECISION HAS BEEN MADE!
10

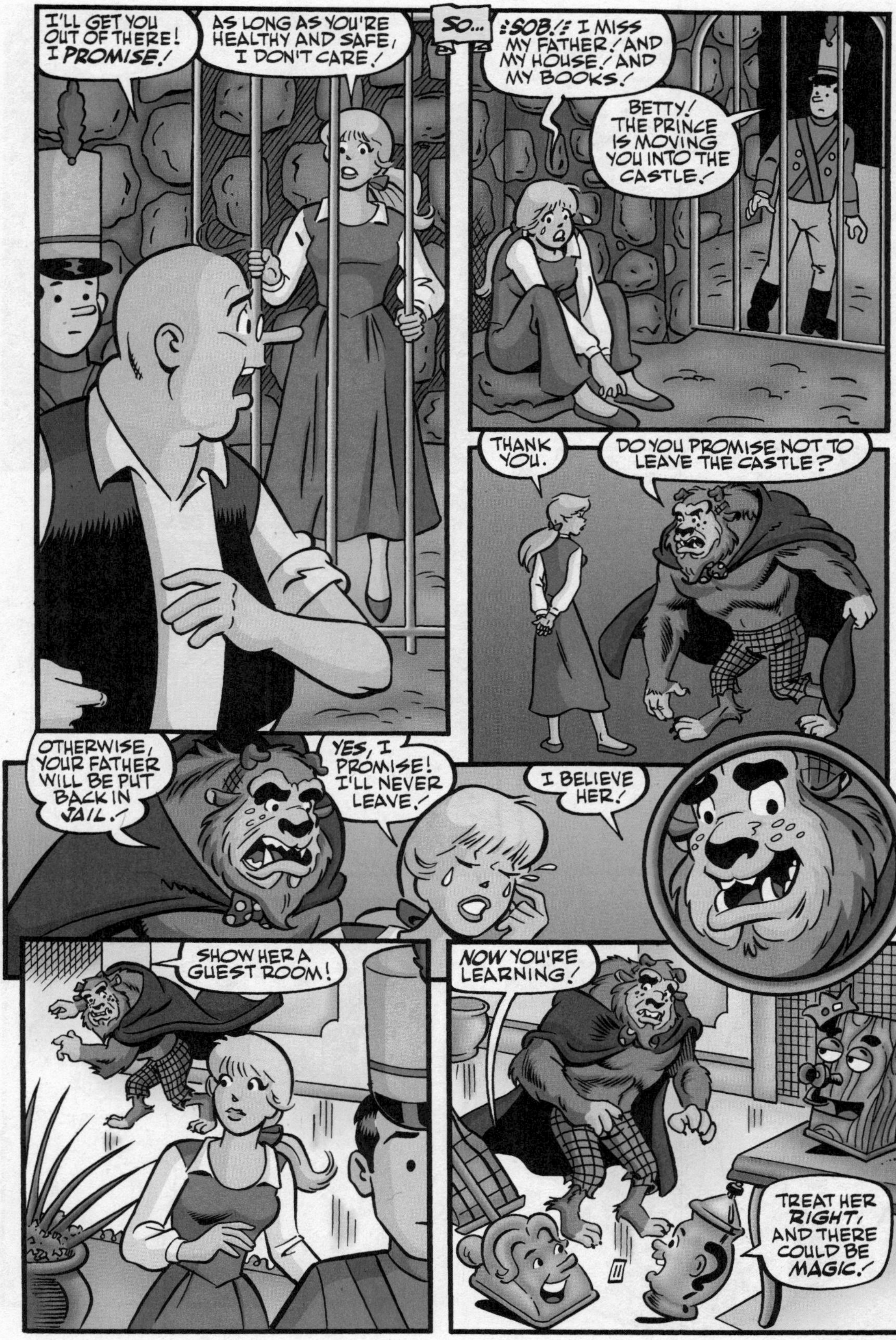
I'LL GET YOU OUT OF THERE! I PROMISE!
AS LONG AS YOU'RE HEALTHY AND SAFE, I DON'T CARE!
SO...
:SOB!: I MISS MY FATHER! AND MY HOUSE! AND MY BOOKS!
BETTY! THE PRINCE IS MOVING YOU INTO THE CASTLE!
THANK YOU.
DO YOU PROMISE NOT TO LEAVE THE CASTLE?
OTHERWISE, YOUR FATHER WILL BE PUT BACK IN JAIL!
YES, I PROMISE! I'LL NEVER LEAVE!
I BELIEVE HER!
SHOW HER A GUEST ROOM!
NOW YOU'RE LEARNING!
TREAT HER RIGHT, AND THERE COULD BE MAGIC!

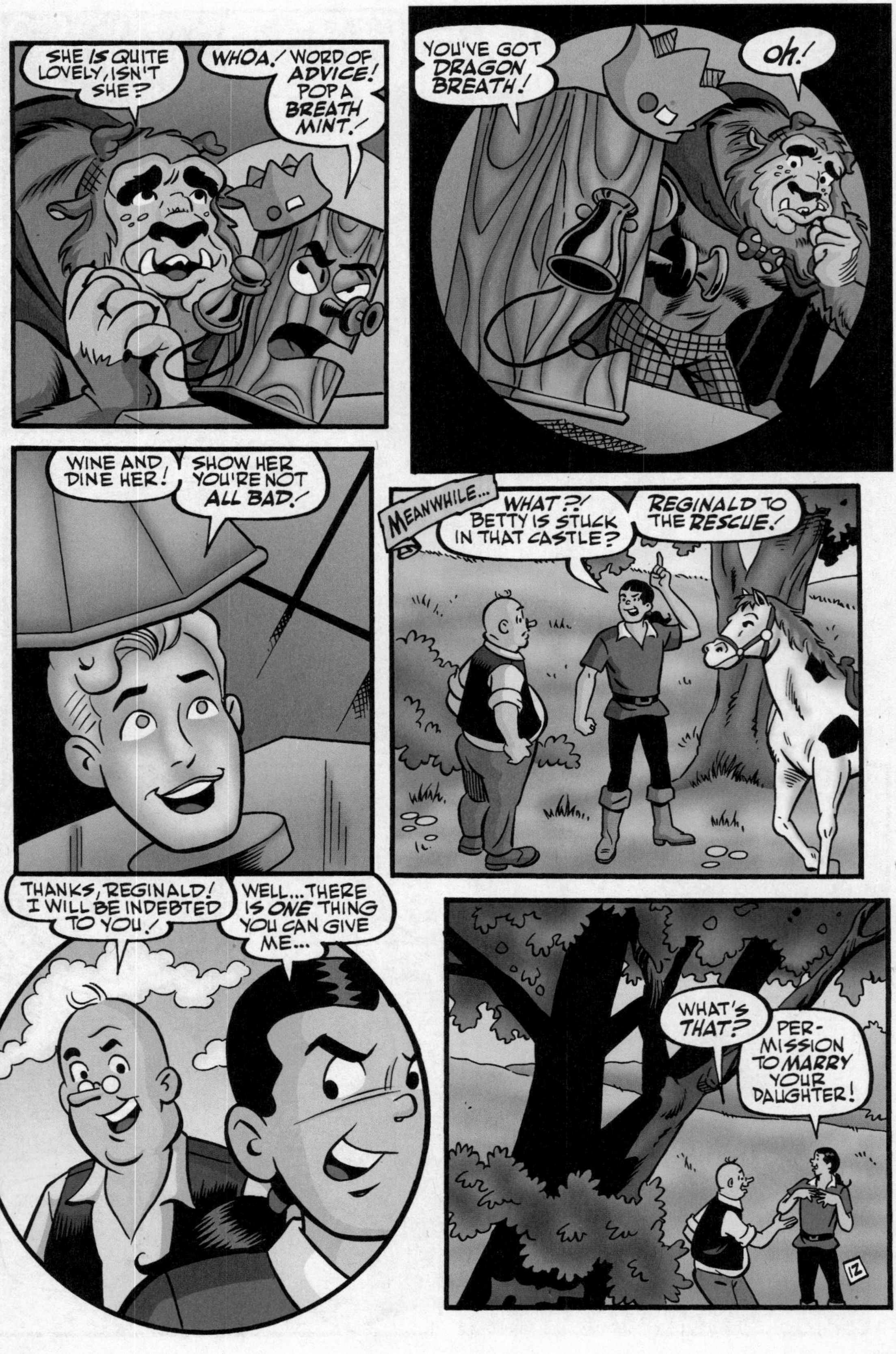
SHE IS QUITE LOVELY, ISN'T SHE?
WHOA! WORD OF ADVICE! POP A BREATH MINT!
YOU'VE GOT DRAGON BREATH!
oh!
WINE AND DINE HER!
SHOW HER YOU'RE NOT ALL BAD!
MEANWHILE...
WHAT?! BETTY IS STUCK IN THAT CASTLE?
REGINALD TO THE RESCUE!
THANKS, REGINALD! I WILL BE INDEBTED TO YOU!
WELL... THERE IS ONE THING YOU CAN GIVE ME...
WHAT'S THAT?
PER-MISSION TO MARRY YOUR DAUGHTER!
12

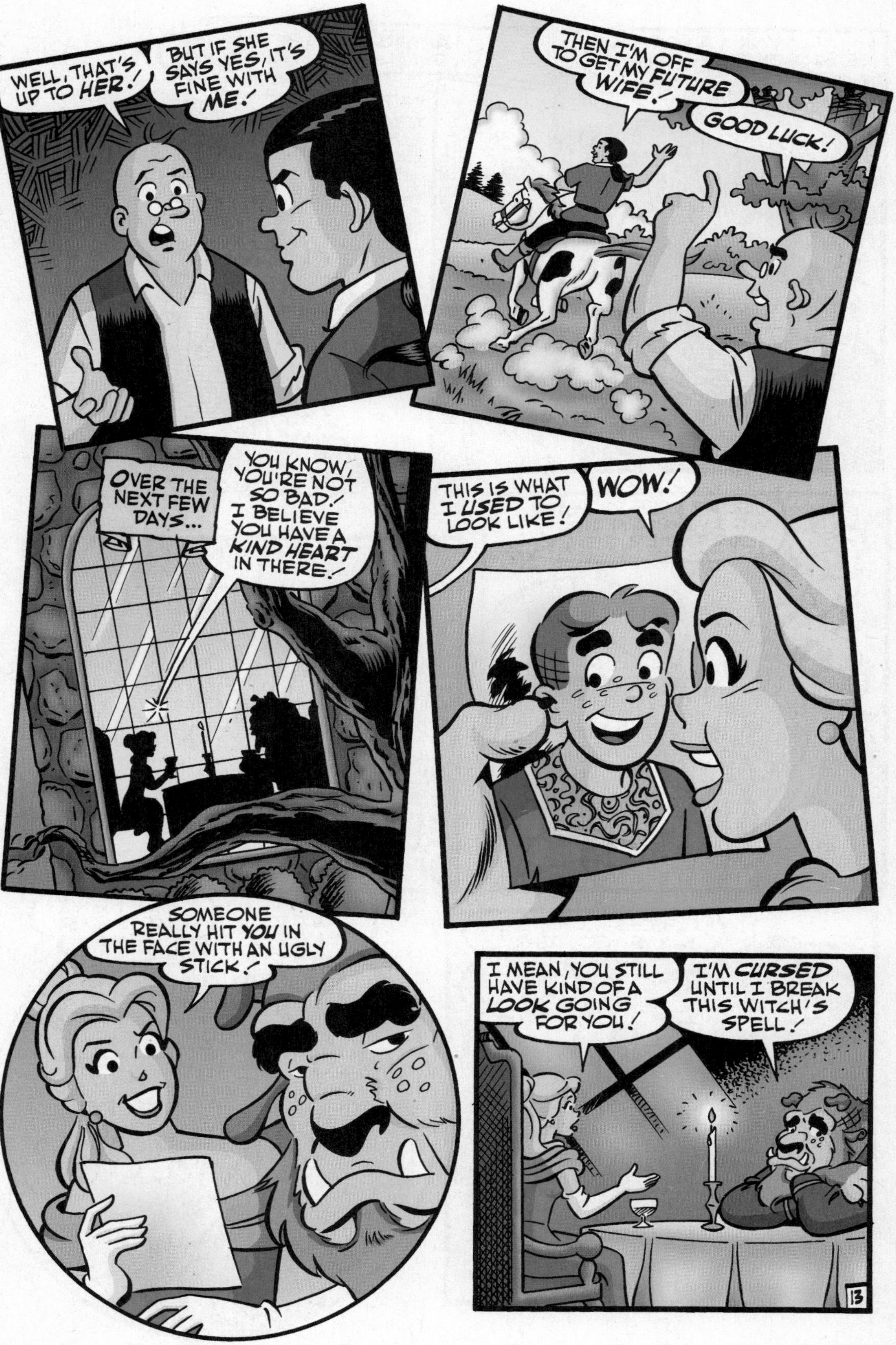
WELL, THAT'S UP TO HER!
BUT IF SHE SAYS YES, IT'S FINE WITH ME!
THEN I'M OFF TO GET MY FUTURE WIFE!
GOOD LUCK!
OVER THE NEXT FEW DAYS...
YOU KNOW, YOU'RE NOT SO BAD! I BELIEVE YOU HAVE A KIND HEART IN THERE!
THIS IS WHAT I USED TO LOOK LIKE!
WOW!
SOMEONE REALLY HIT YOU IN THE FACE WITH AN UGLY STICK!
I MEAN, YOU STILL HAVE KIND OF A LOOK GOING FOR YOU!
I'M CURSED UNTIL I BREAK THIS WITCH'S SPELL!
13

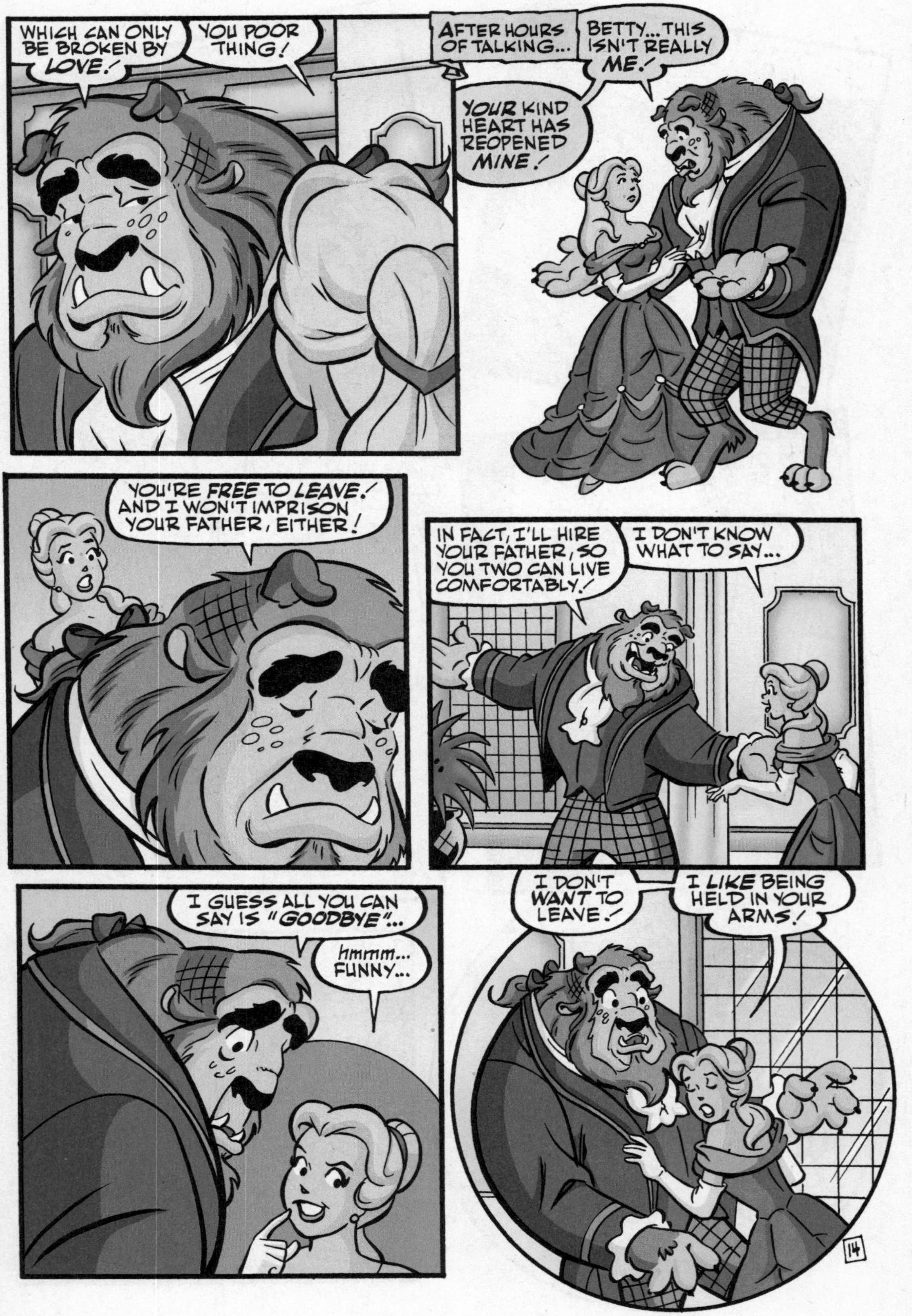
WHICH CAN ONLY BE BROKEN BY LOVE!
YOU POOR THING!
AFTER HOURS OF TALKING...
BETTY...THIS ISN'T REALLY ME!
YOUR KIND HEART HAS REOPENED MINE!
YOU'RE FREE TO LEAVE! AND I WON'T IMPRISON YOUR FATHER, EITHER!
IN FACT, I'LL HIRE YOUR FATHER, SO YOU TWO CAN LIVE COMFORTABLY!
I DON'T KNOW WHAT TO SAY...
I GUESS ALL YOU CAN SAY IS "GOODBYE"...
hmmm... FUNNY...
I DON'T WANT TO LEAVE!
I LIKE BEING HELD IN YOUR ARMS!
14

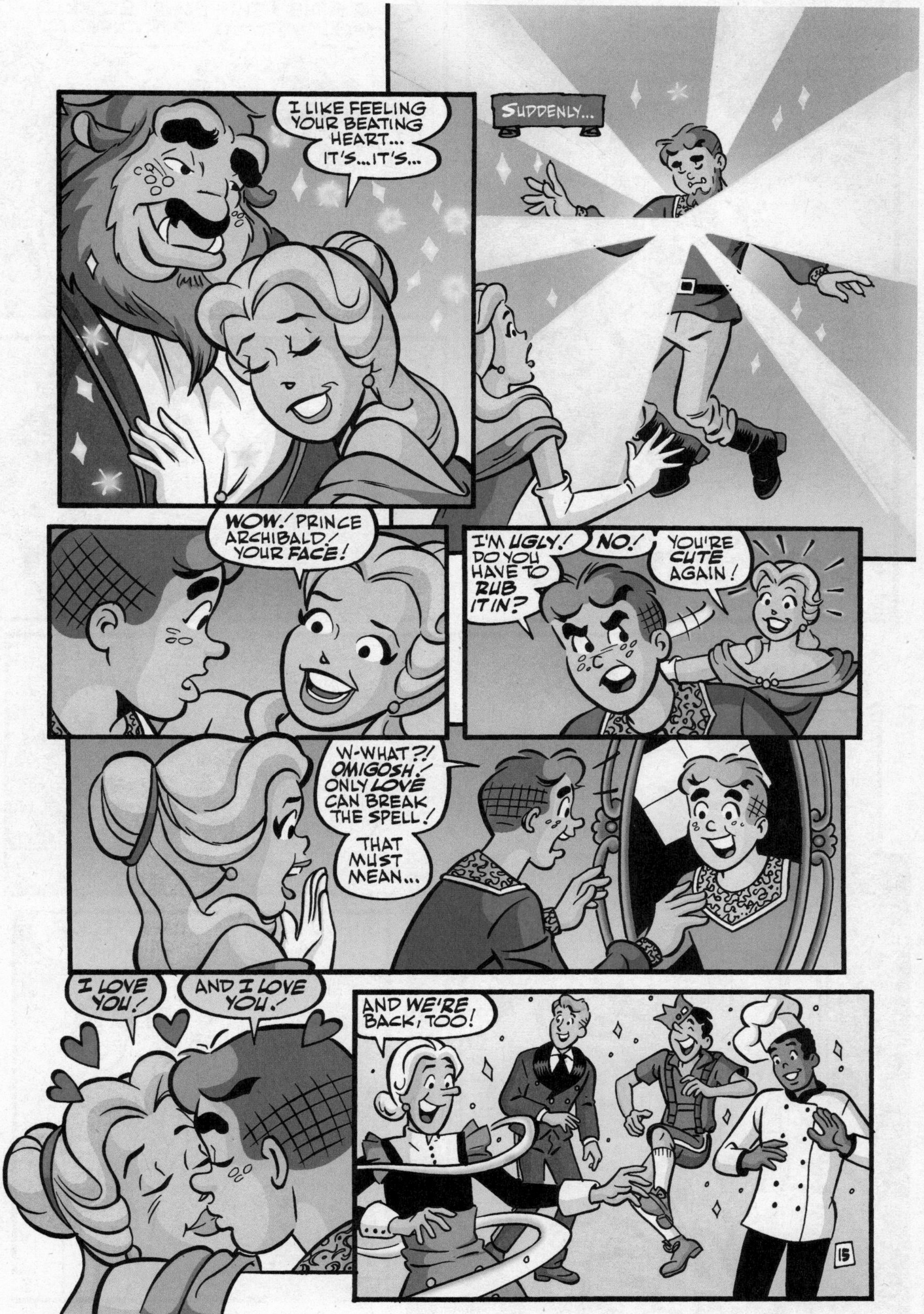
I LIKE FEELING YOUR BEATING HEART... IT'S...IT'S...
SUDDENLY...
WOW! PRINCE ARCHIBALD! YOUR FACE!
I'M UGLY! DO YOU HAVE TO RUB IT IN?
NO!
YOU'RE CUTE AGAIN!
W-WHAT?! OMIGOSH! ONLY LOVE CAN BREAK THE SPELL!
THAT MUST MEAN...
I LOVE YOU!
AND I LOVE YOU!
AND WE'RE BACK, TOO!
15

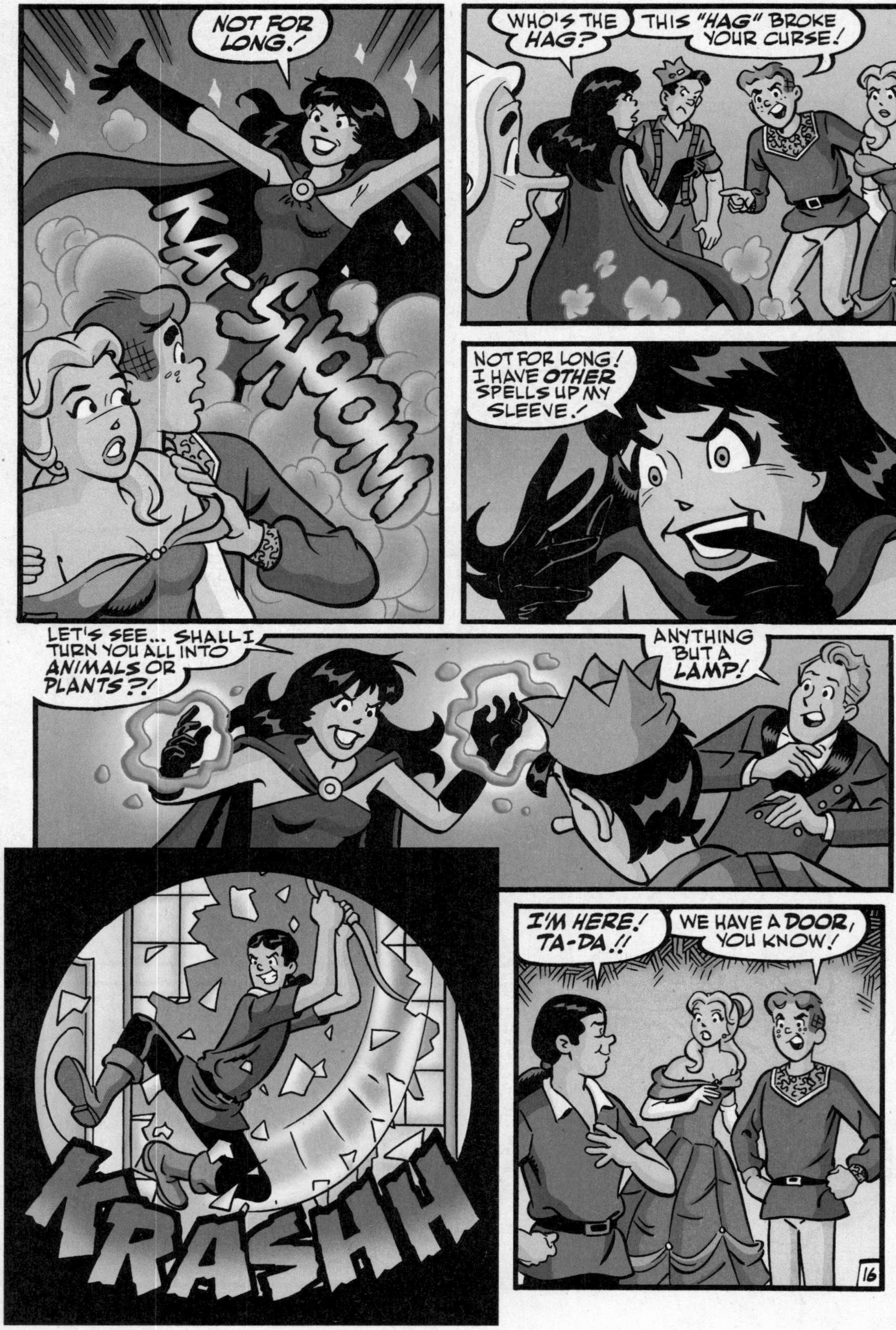
NOT FOR LONG.!
KA-SHOOM
WHO'S THE HAG?
THIS "HAG" BROKE YOUR CURSE!
NOT FOR LONG! I HAVE OTHER SPELLS UP MY SLEEVE.!
LET'S SEE... SHALL I TURN YOU ALL INTO ANIMALS OR PLANTS?!
ANYTHING BUT A LAMP!
KRASHH
I'M HERE! TA-DA!!
WE HAVE A DOOR, YOU KNOW!
16

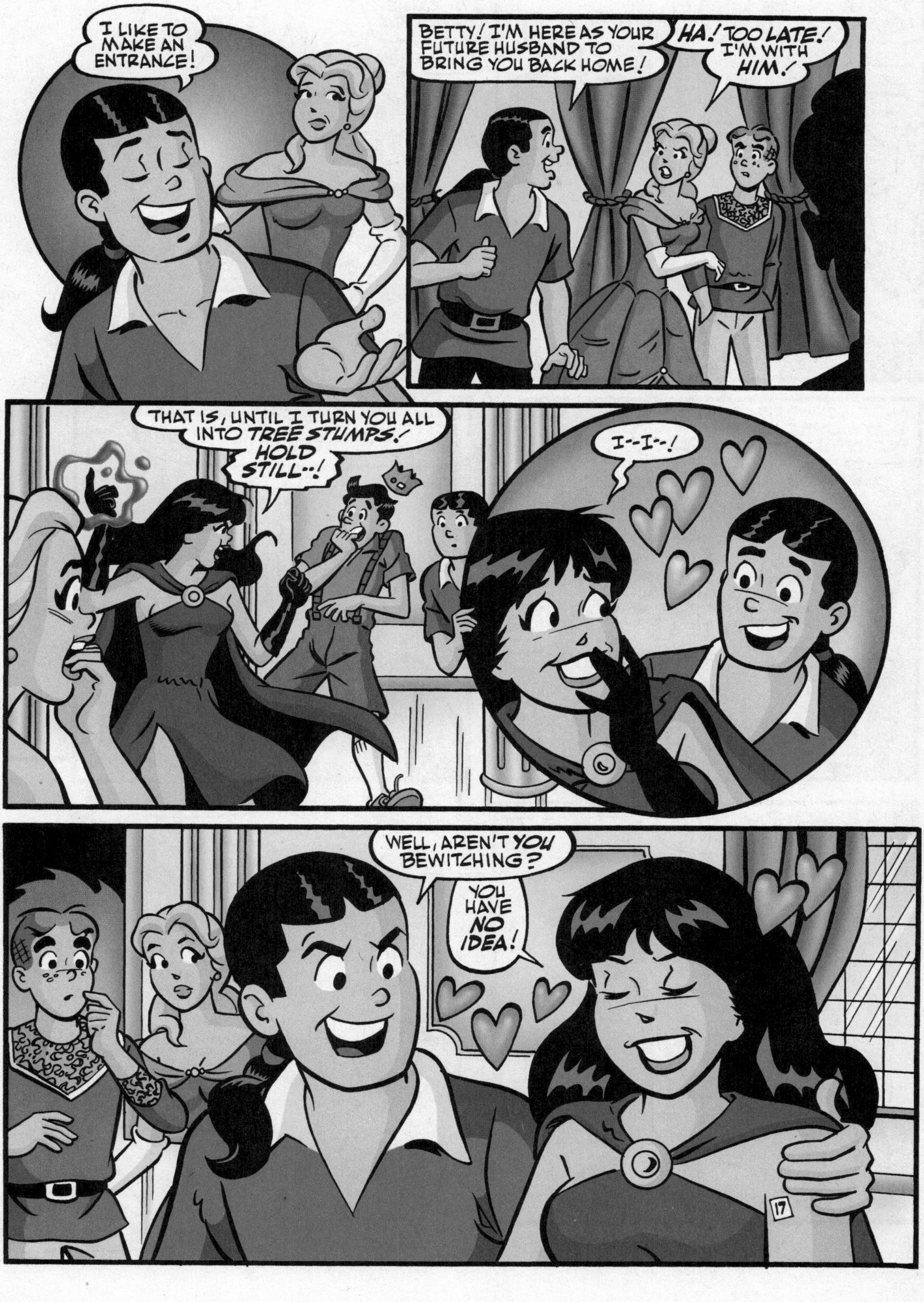

I LIKE TO MAKE AN ENTRANCE!
BETTY! I'M HERE AS YOUR FUTURE HUSBAND TO BRING YOU BACK HOME!
HA! TOO LATE! I'M WITH HIM!
THAT IS, UNTIL I TURN YOU ALL INTO TREE STUMPS!
HOLD STILL--!
I--I--!
WELL, AREN'T YOU BEWITCHING?
YOU HAVE NO IDEA!
17

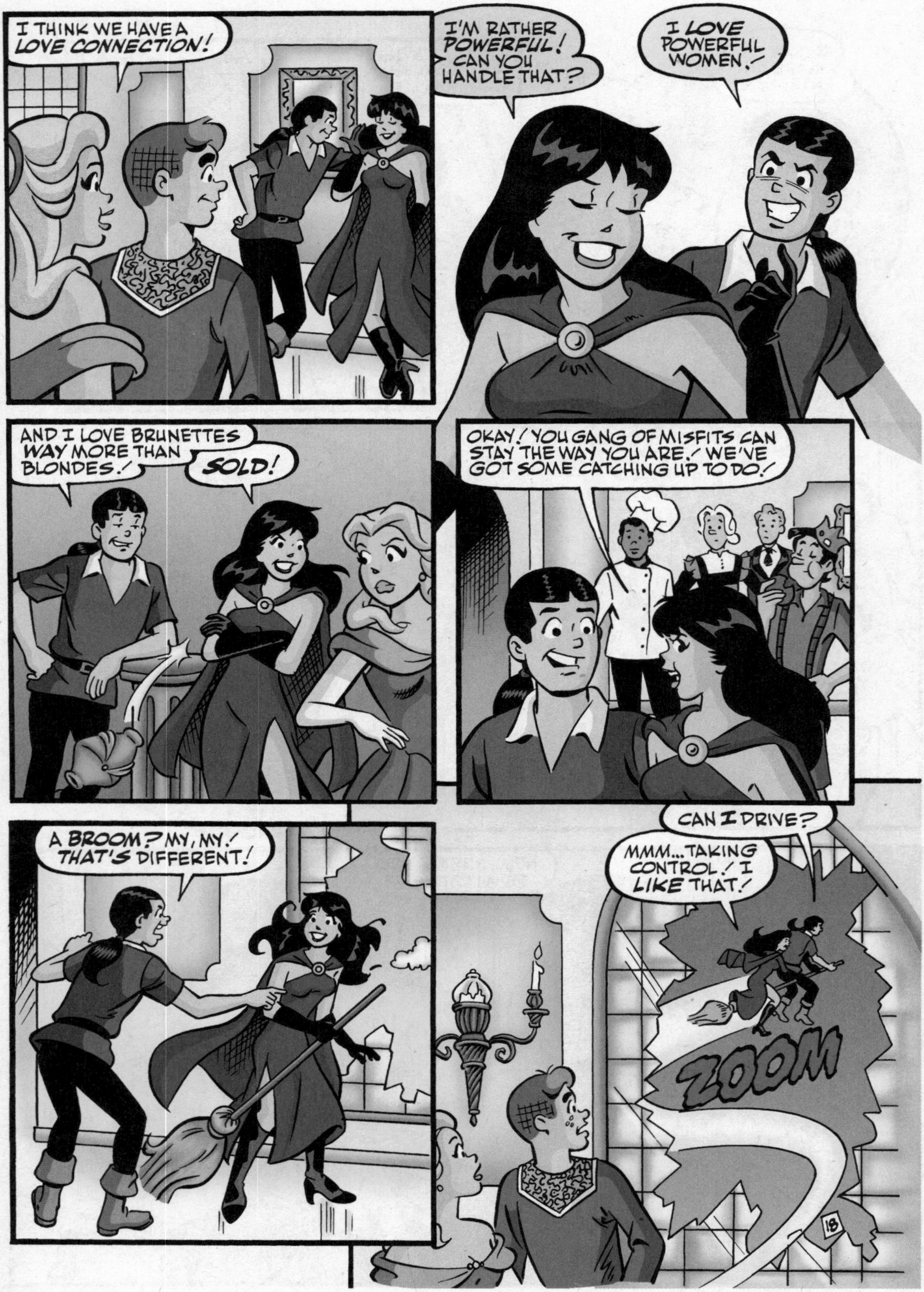
I THINK WE HAVE A LOVE CONNECTION!
I'M RATHER POWERFUL! CAN YOU HANDLE THAT?
I LOVE POWERFUL WOMEN.
AND I LOVE BRUNETTES WAY MORE THAN BLONDES!
SOLD!
OKAY! YOU GANG OF MISFITS CAN STAY THE WAY YOU ARE! WE'VE GOT SOME CATCHING UP TO DO!
A BROOM? MY, MY! THAT'S DIFFERENT!
CAN I DRIVE?
MMM...TAKING CONTROL! I LIKE THAT!
ZOOM
18

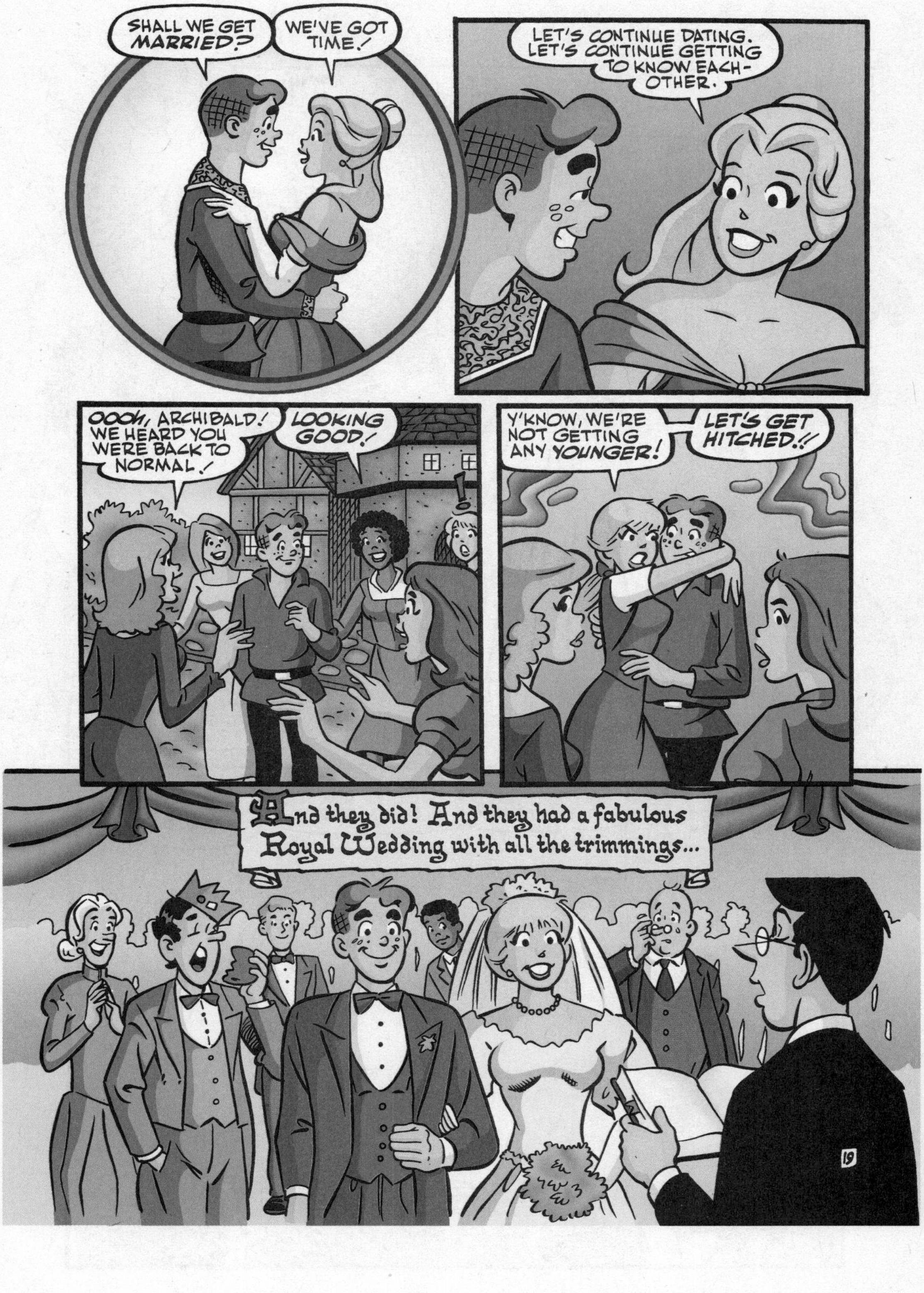

SHALL WE GET MARRIED?
WE'VE GOT TIME!
LET'S CONTINUE DATING. LET'S CONTINUE GETTING TO KNOW EACH-OTHER.
OOOH, ARCHIBALD! WE HEARD YOU WERE BACK TO NORMAL!
LOOKING GOOD!
Y'KNOW, WE'RE NOT GETTING ANY YOUNGER!
LET'S GET HITCHED!!
And they did! And they had a fabulous Royal Wedding with all the trimmings...

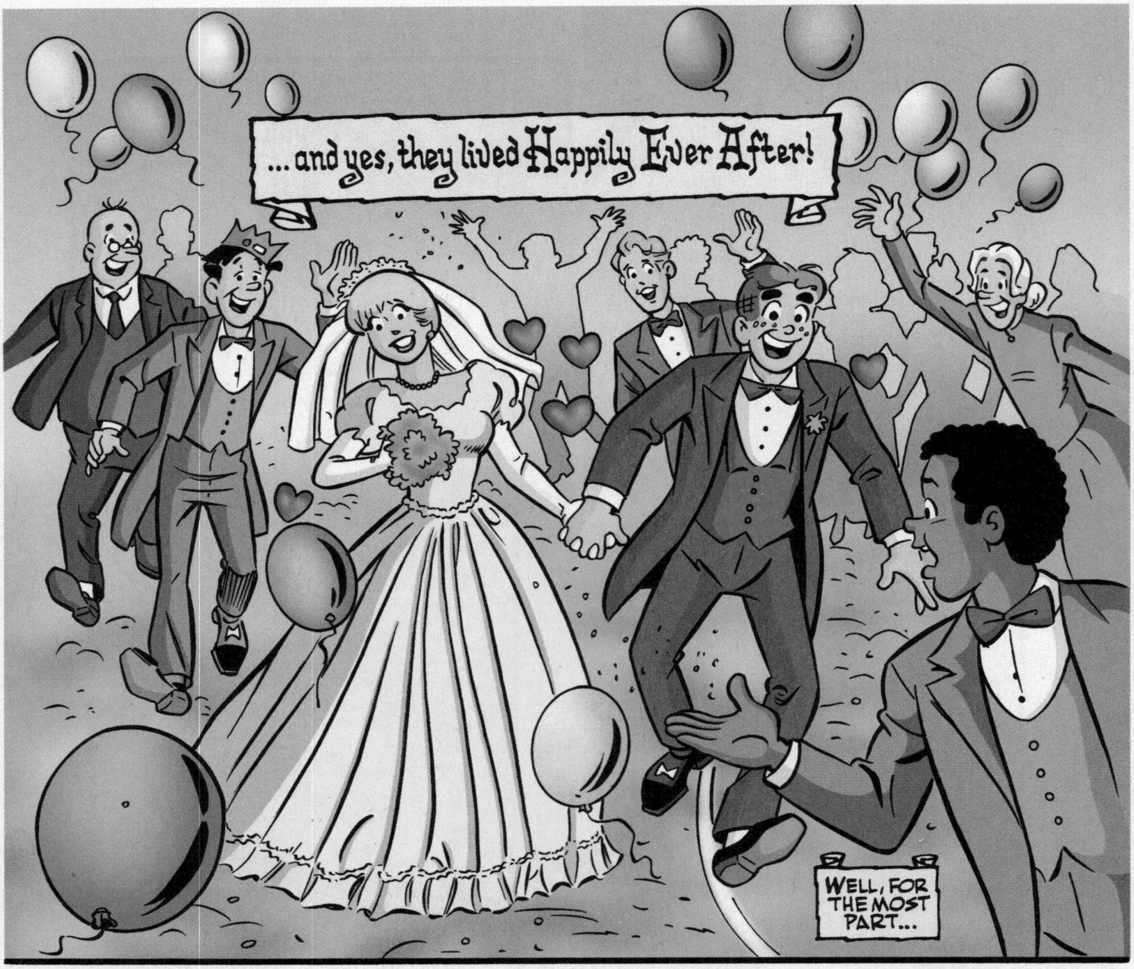
...and yes, they lived Happily Ever After!
WELL, FOR THE MOST PART...

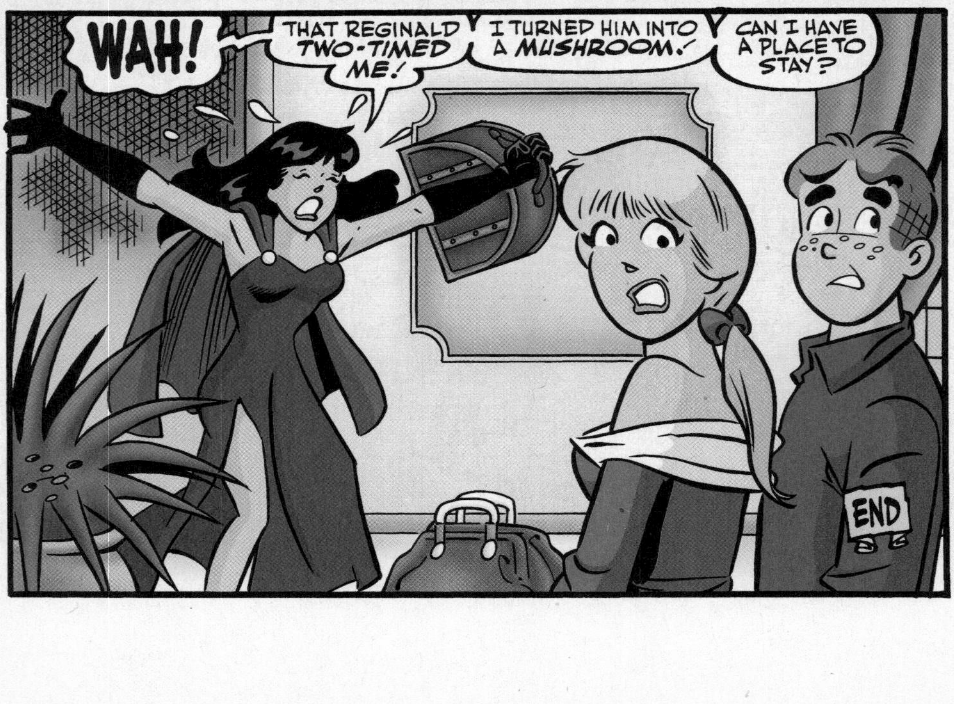
WAH!
THAT REGINALD TWO-TIMED ME!
I TURNED HIM INTO A MUSHROOM!
CAN I HAVE A PLACE TO STAY?
END

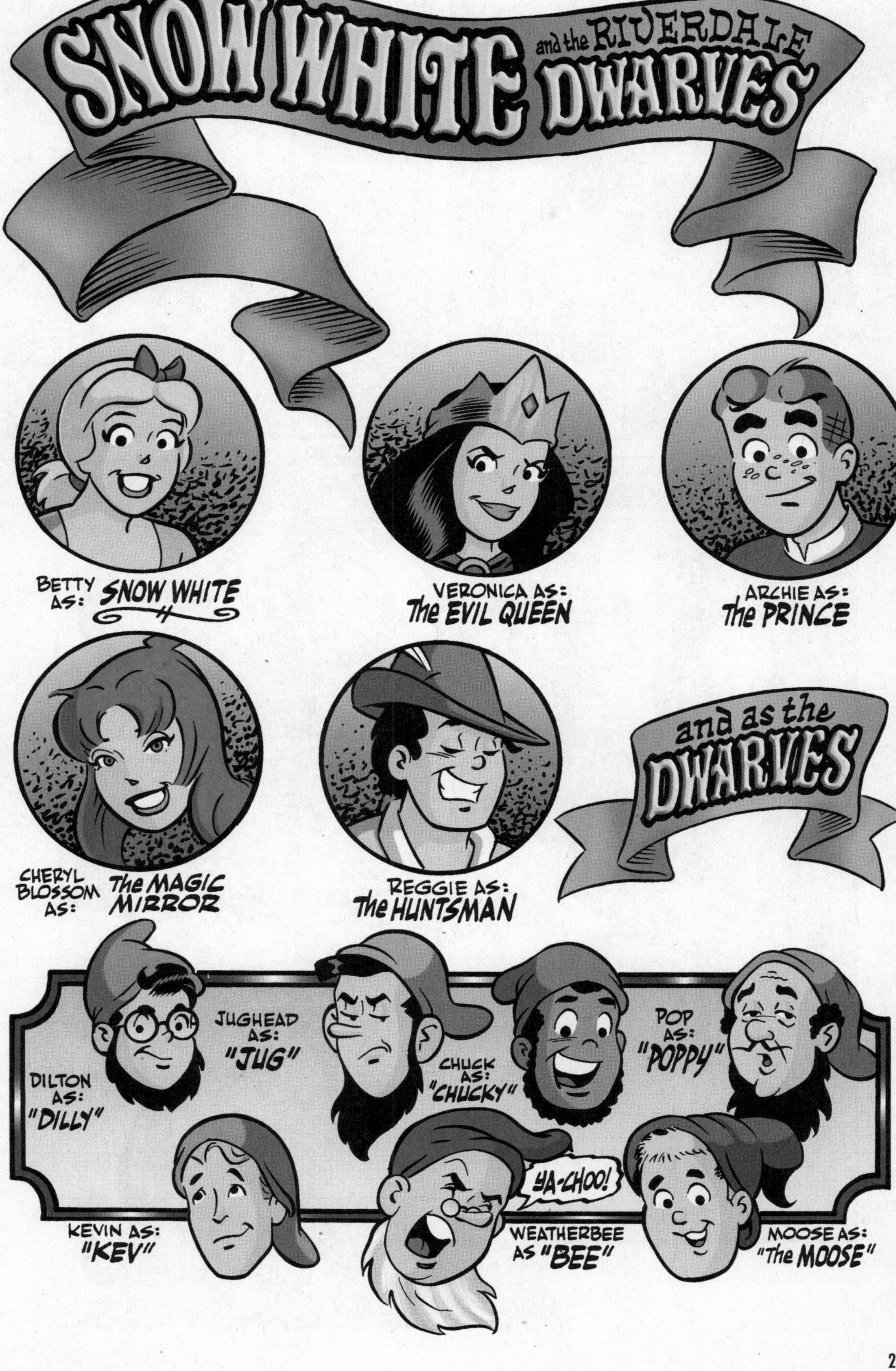
SNOW WHITE and the RIVERDALE DWARVES
BETTY AS: SNOW WHITE
VERONICA AS: The EVIL QUEEN
ARCHIE AS: The PRINCE
CHERYL BLOSSOM AS: The MAGIC MIRROR
REGGIE AS: The HUNTSMAN
and as the DWARVES
DILTON AS: "DILLY"
JUGHEAD AS: "JUG"
CHUCK AS: "CHUCKY"
POP AS: "POPPY"
KEVIN AS: "KEV"
YA-CHOO!
WEATHERBEE AS "BEE"
MOOSE AS: "The MOOSE"

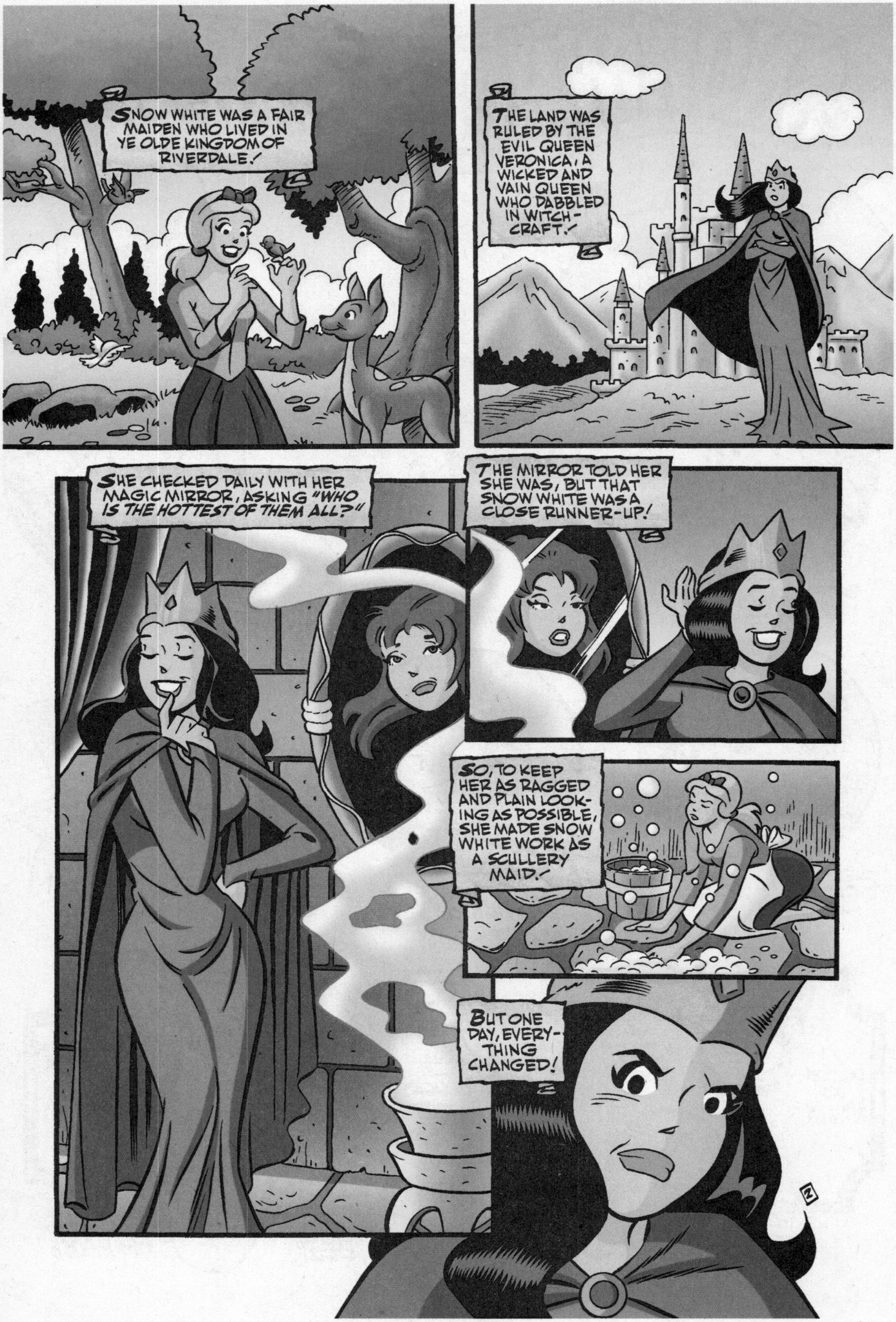
SNOW WHITE WAS A FAIR MAIDEN WHO LIVED IN YE OLDE KINGDOM OF RIVERDALE!
THE LAND WAS RULED BY THE EVIL QUEEN VERONICA, A WICKED AND VAIN QUEEN WHO DABBLED IN WITCH-CRAFT!
SHE CHECKED DAILY WITH HER MAGIC MIRROR, ASKING "WHO IS THE HOTTEST OF THEM ALL?"
THE MIRROR TOLD HER SHE WAS, BUT THAT SNOW WHITE WAS A CLOSE RUNNER-UP!
SO, TO KEEP HER AS RAGGED AND PLAIN LOOKING AS POSSIBLE, SHE MADE SNOW WHITE WORK AS A SCULLERY MAID!
BUT ONE DAY, EVERY-THING CHANGED!

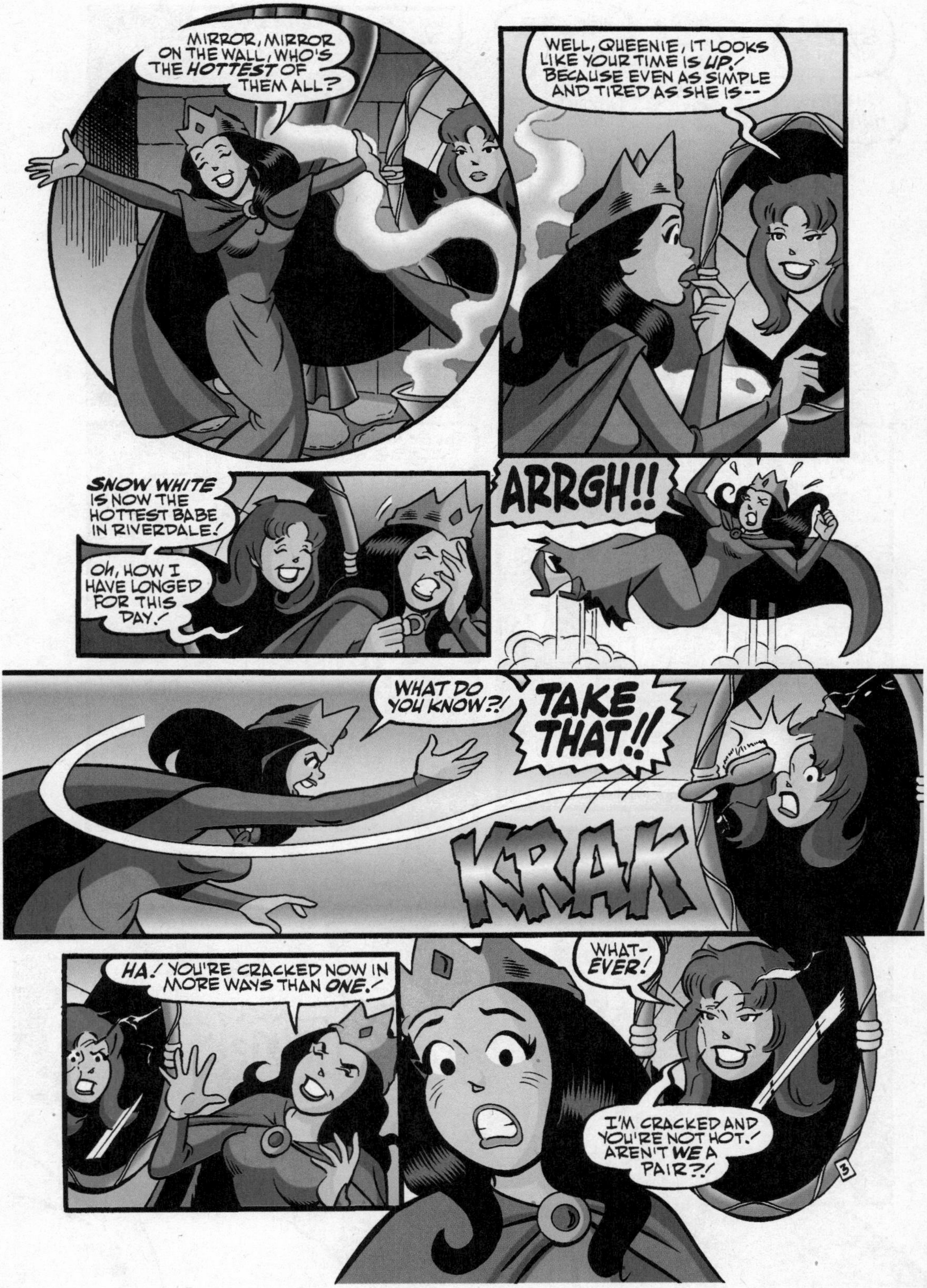
MIRROR, MIRROR ON THE WALL, WHO'S THE HOTTEST OF THEM ALL?
WELL, QUEENIE, IT LOOKS LIKE YOUR TIME IS UP! BECAUSE EVEN AS SIMPLE AND TIRED AS SHE IS--
SNOW WHITE IS NOW THE HOTTEST BABE IN RIVERDALE!
OH, HOW I HAVE LONGED FOR THIS DAY!
ARRGH!!
WHAT DO YOU KNOW?!
TAKE THAT!!
KRAK
HA! YOU'RE CRACKED NOW IN MORE WAYS THAN ONE!
WHAT-EVER!
I'M CRACKED AND YOU'RE NOT HOT! AREN'T WE A PAIR?!
3

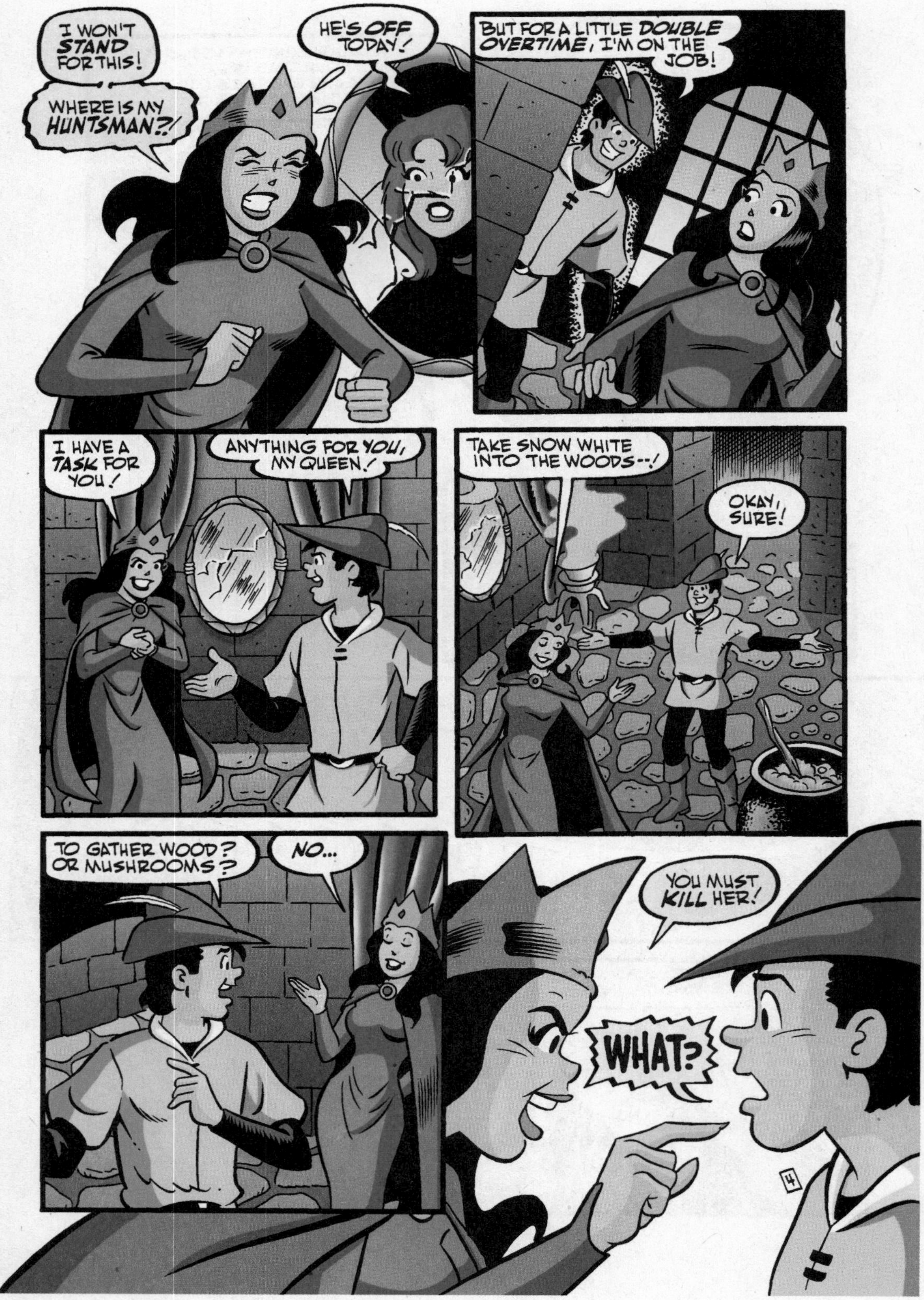
I WON'T STAND FOR THIS!
WHERE IS MY HUNTSMAN?!
HE'S OFF TODAY!
BUT FOR A LITTLE DOUBLE OVERTIME, I'M ON THE JOB!
I HAVE A TASK FOR YOU!
ANYTHING FOR YOU, MY QUEEN!
TAKE SNOW WHITE INTO THE WOODS--!
OKAY, SURE!
TO GATHER WOOD? OR MUSHROOMS?
NO...
YOU MUST KILL HER!
WHAT?
4

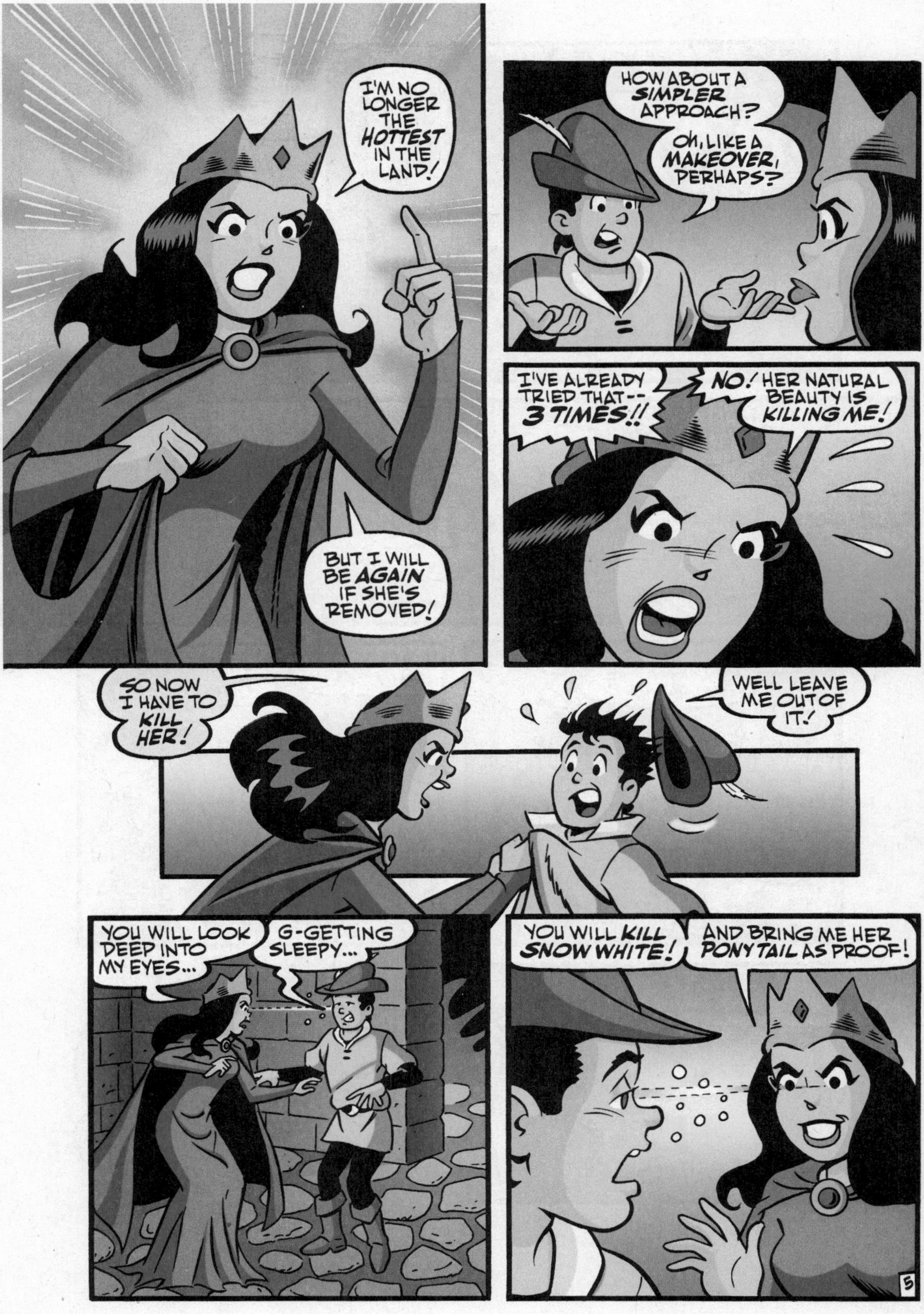
I'M NO LONGER THE HOTTEST IN THE LAND!
BUT I WILL BE AGAIN IF SHE'S REMOVED!
HOW ABOUT A SIMPLER APPROACH?
Oh, LIKE A MAKEOVER, PERHAPS?
I'VE ALREADY TRIED THAT-- 3 TIMES!!
NO! HER NATURAL BEAUTY IS KILLING ME!
SO NOW I HAVE TO KILL HER!
WELL LEAVE ME OUT OF IT!
YOU WILL LOOK DEEP INTO MY EYES...
G-GETTING SLEEPY...
YOU WILL KILL SNOW WHITE!
AND BRING ME HER PONYTAIL AS PROOF!
5

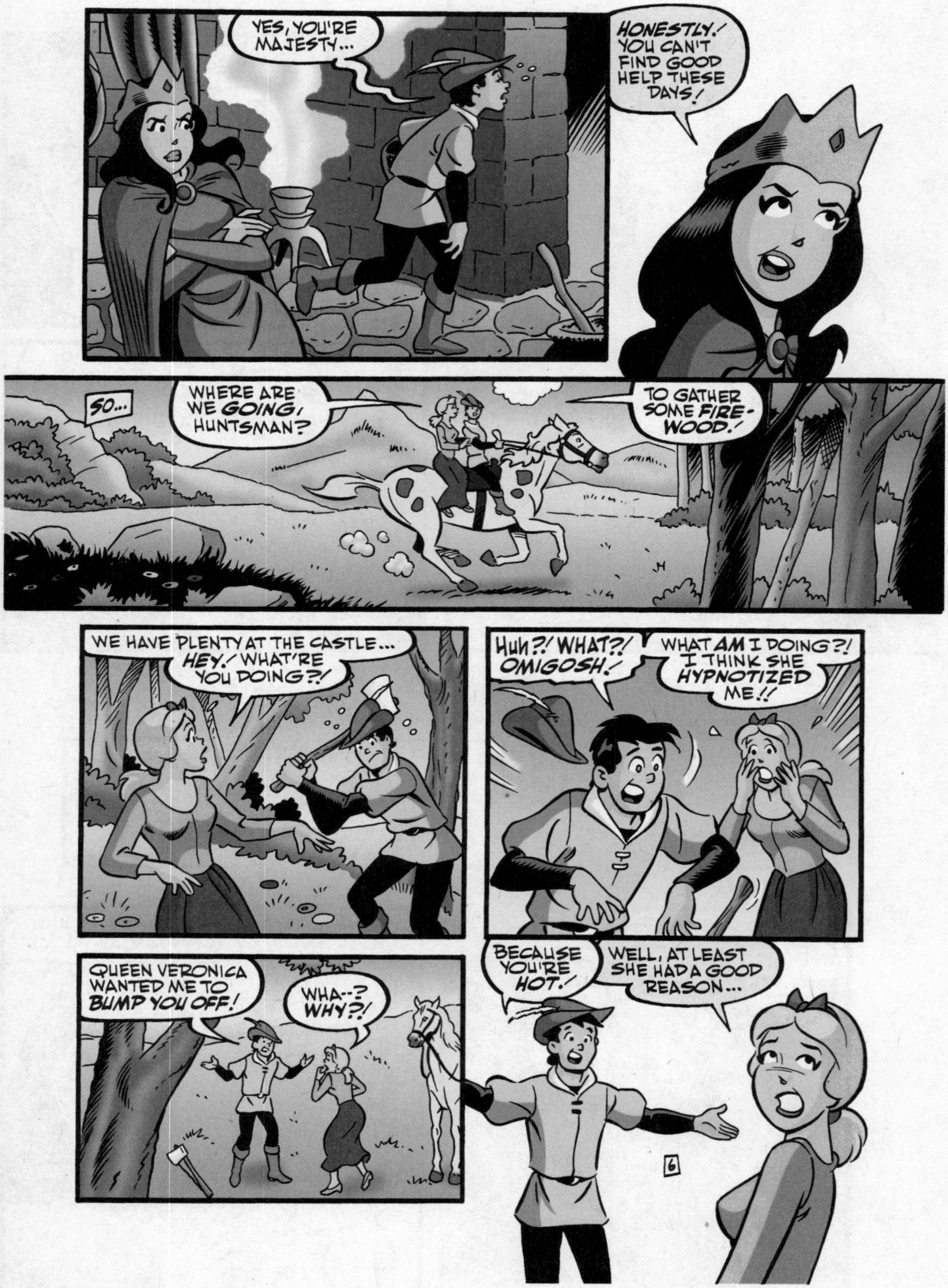
YES, YOU'RE MAJESTY...
HONESTLY! YOU CAN'T FIND GOOD HELP THESE DAYS!
SO...
WHERE ARE WE GOING, HUNTSMAN?
TO GATHER SOME FIRE-WOOD!
WE HAVE PLENTY AT THE CASTLE... HEY! WHAT'RE YOU DOING?!
HUH?! WHAT?! OMIGOSH!
WHAT AM I DOING?! I THINK SHE HYPNOTIZED ME!!
QUEEN VERONICA WANTED ME TO BUMP YOU OFF!
WHA--? WHY?!
BECAUSE YOU'RE HOT!
WELL, AT LEAST SHE HAD A GOOD REASON...
6

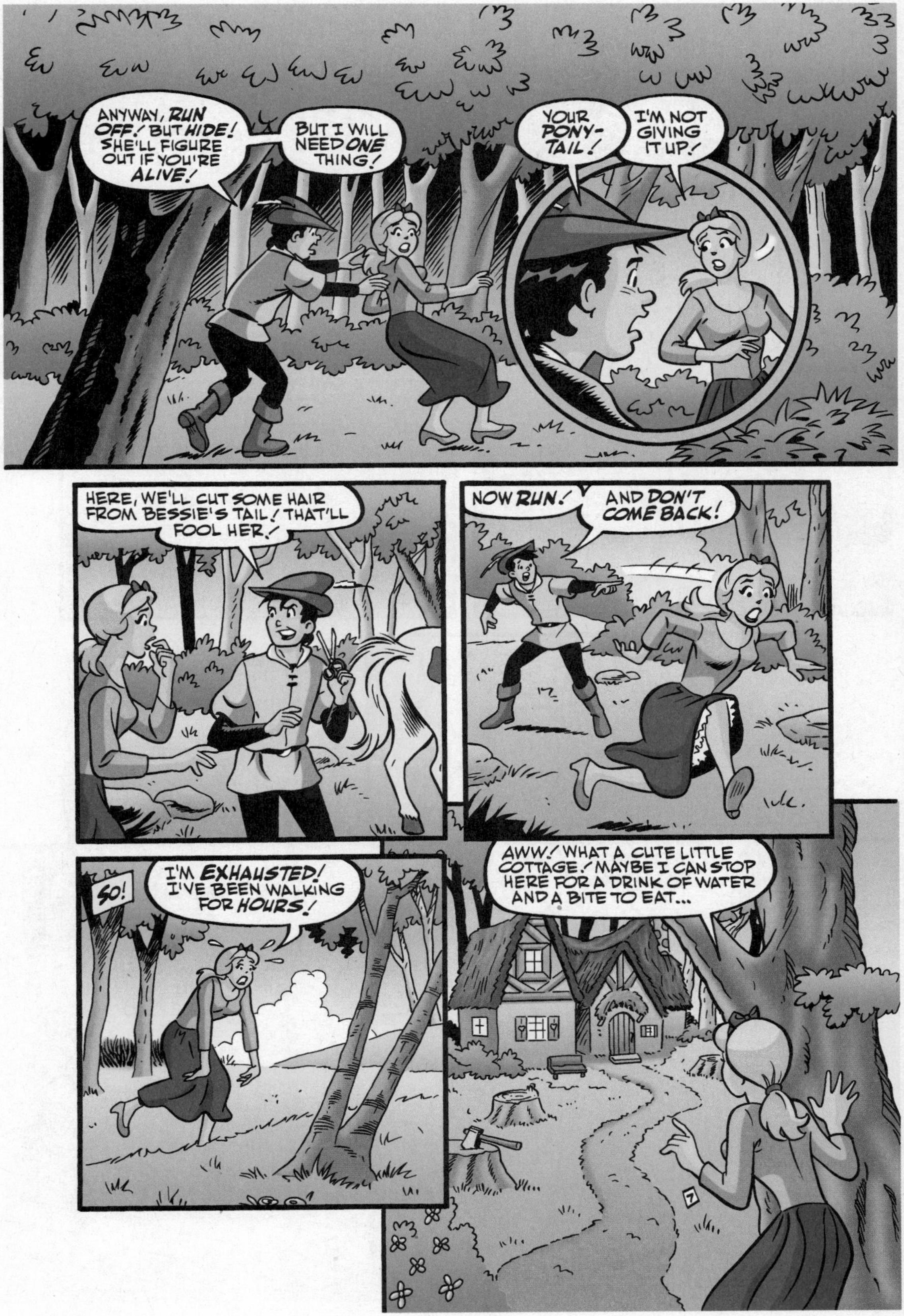
ANYWAY, RUN OFF! BUT HIDE! SHE'LL FIGURE OUT IF YOU'RE ALIVE!
BUT I WILL NEED ONE THING!
YOUR PONY-TAIL!
I'M NOT GIVING IT UP!
HERE, WE'LL CUT SOME HAIR FROM BESSIE'S TAIL! THAT'LL FOOL HER!
NOW RUN!
AND DON'T COME BACK!
SO!
I'M EXHAUSTED! I'VE BEEN WALKING FOR HOURS!
AWW! WHAT A CUTE LITTLE COTTAGE! MAYBE I CAN STOP HERE FOR A DRINK OF WATER AND A BITE TO EAT...
7

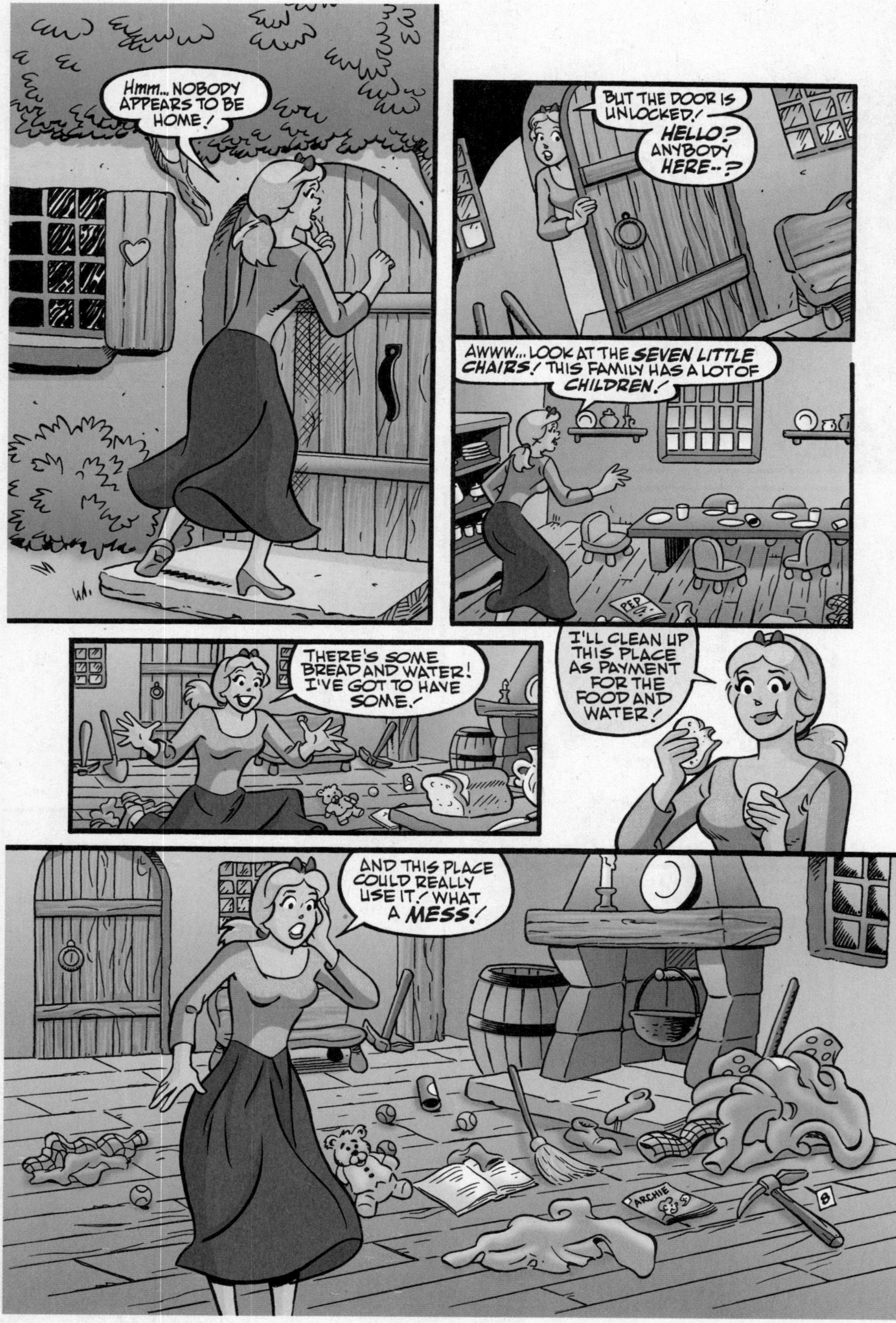
Hmm... NOBODY APPEARS TO BE HOME!
BUT THE DOOR IS UNLOCKED! HELLO? ANYBODY HERE--?
AWWW... LOOK AT THE SEVEN LITTLE CHAIRS! THIS FAMILY HAS A LOT OF CHILDREN!
PEP
THERE'S SOME BREAD AND WATER! I'VE GOT TO HAVE SOME!
I'LL CLEAN UP THIS PLACE AS PAYMENT FOR THE FOOD AND WATER!
AND THIS PLACE COULD REALLY USE IT! WHAT A MESS!
ARCHIE
8

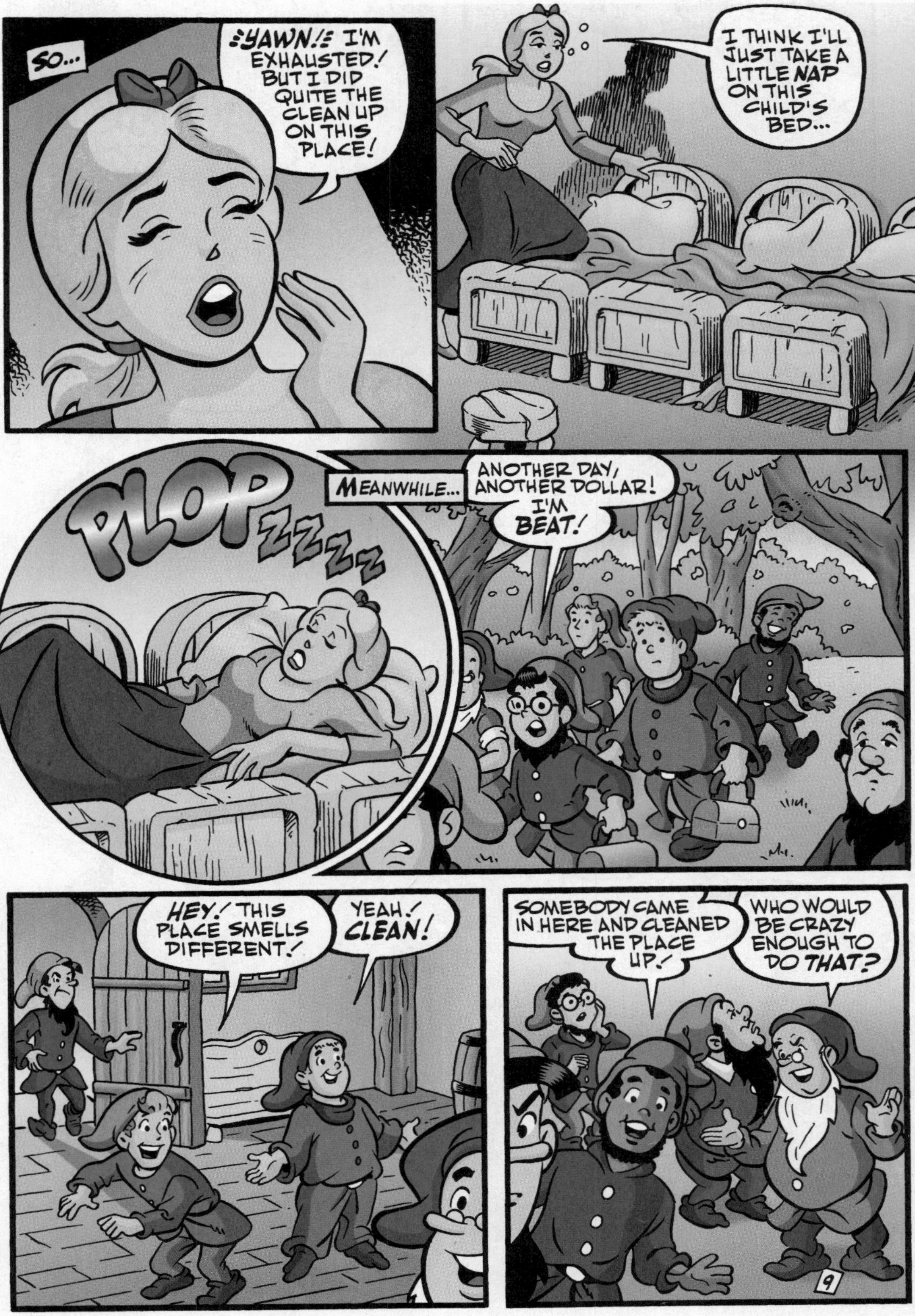
SO...
:YAWN!: I'M EXHAUSTED! BUT I DID QUITE THE CLEAN UP ON THIS PLACE!
I THINK I'LL JUST TAKE A LITTLE NAP ON THIS CHILD'S BED...
PLOP ZZZZ
MEANWHILE...
ANOTHER DAY, ANOTHER DOLLAR! I'M BEAT!
HEY! THIS PLACE SMELLS DIFFERENT!
YEAH! CLEAN!
SOMEBODY CAME IN HERE AND CLEANED THE PLACE UP!
WHO WOULD BE CRAZY ENOUGH TO DO THAT?
9

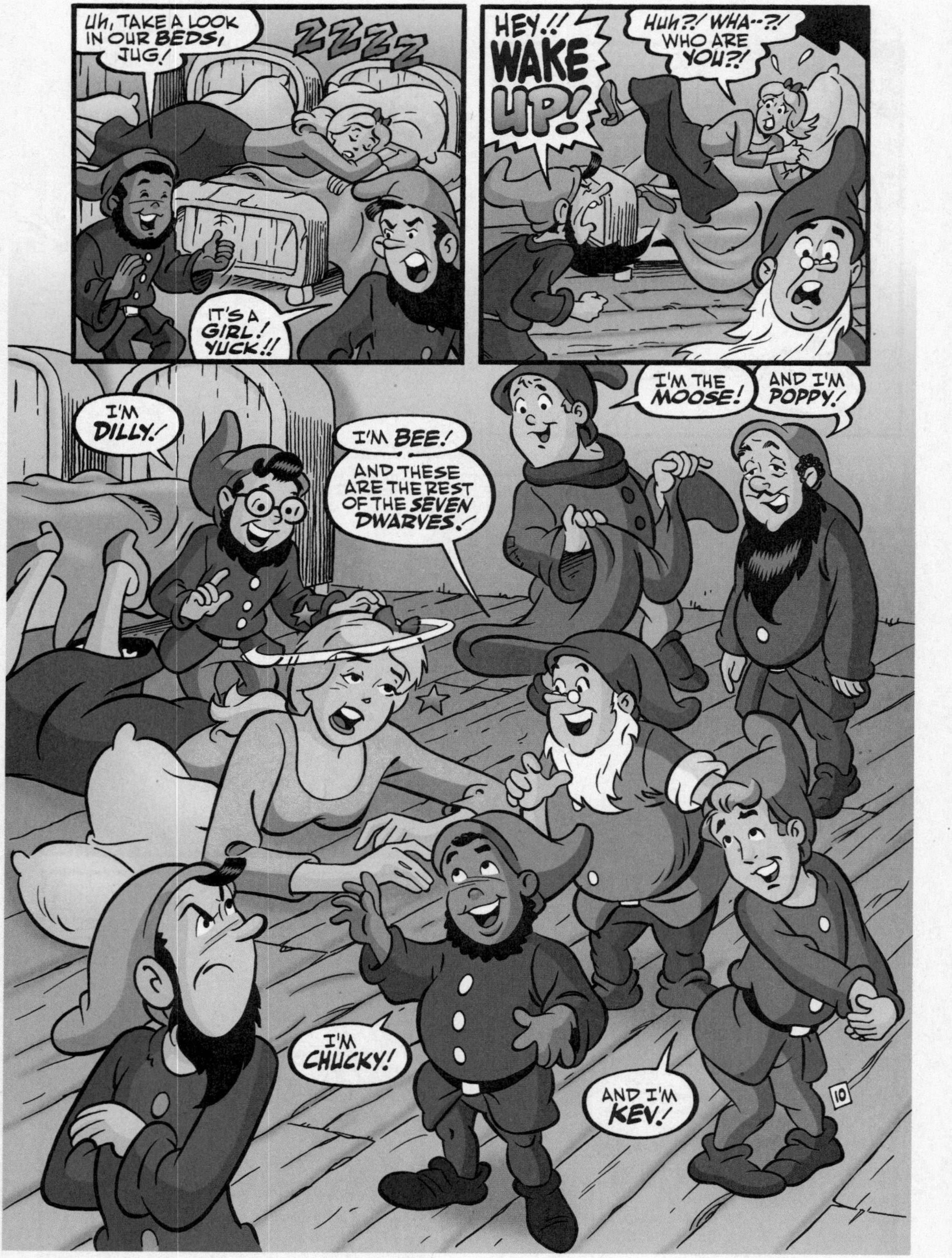
UH, TAKE A LOOK IN OUR BEDS, JUG!
ZZZZZ
IT'S A GIRL! YUCK!!
HEY!! WAKE UP!
HUH?! WHA--?! WHO ARE YOU?!
I'M DILLY!
I'M BEE!
AND THESE ARE THE REST OF THE SEVEN DWARVES!
I'M THE MOOSE!
AND I'M POPPY!
I'M CHUCKY!
AND I'M KEV!
10

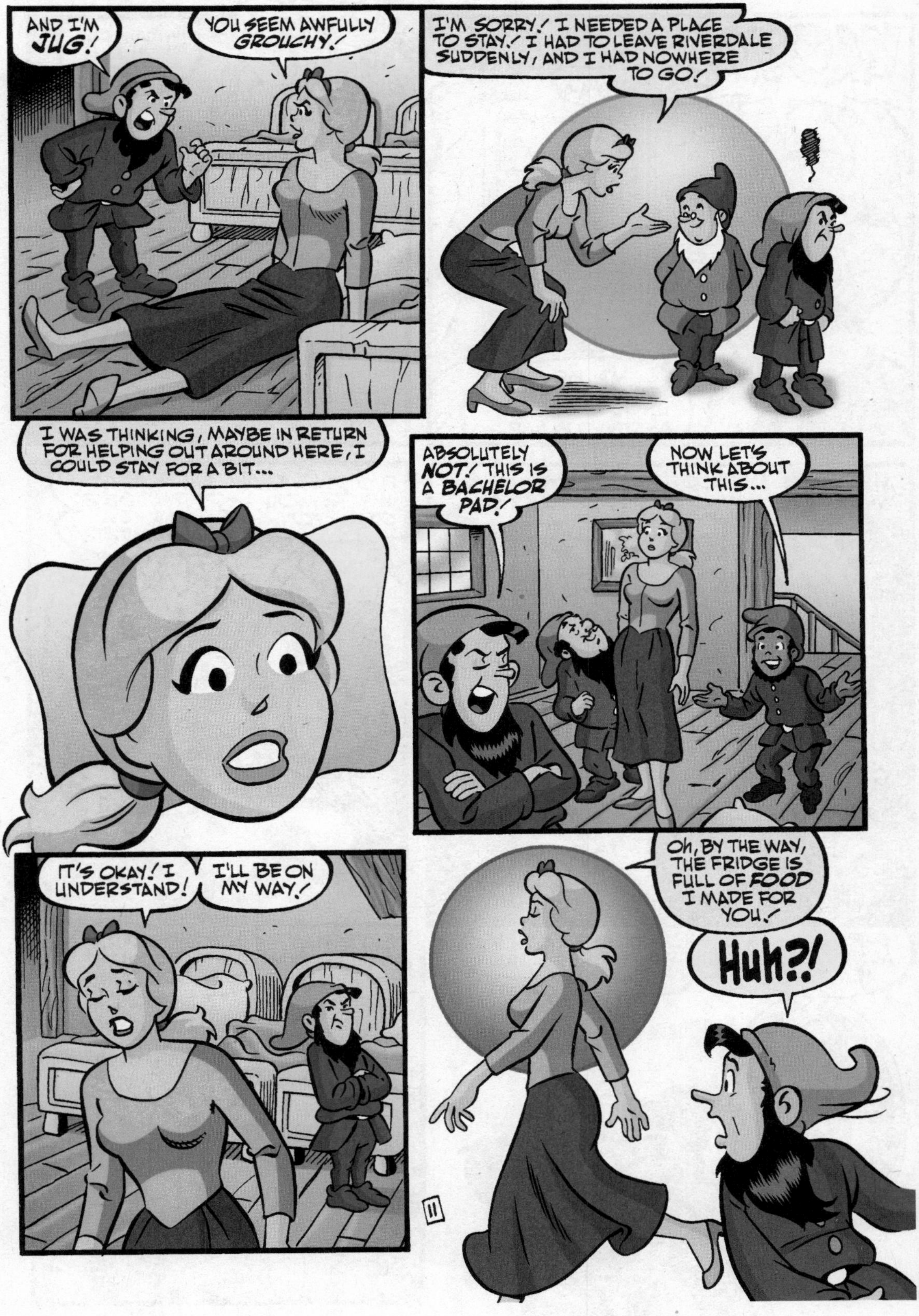
AND I'M JUG!
YOU SEEM AWFULLY GROUCHY!
I'M SORRY! I NEEDED A PLACE TO STAY! I HAD TO LEAVE RIVERDALE SUDDENLY, AND I HAD NOWHERE TO GO!
I WAS THINKING, MAYBE IN RETURN FOR HELPING OUT AROUND HERE, I COULD STAY FOR A BIT...
ABSOLUTELY NOT! THIS IS A BACHELOR PAD!
NOW LET'S THINK ABOUT THIS...
IT'S OKAY! I UNDERSTAND!
I'LL BE ON MY WAY!
Oh, BY THE WAY, THE FRIDGE IS FULL OF FOOD I MADE FOR YOU!
Huh?!
11

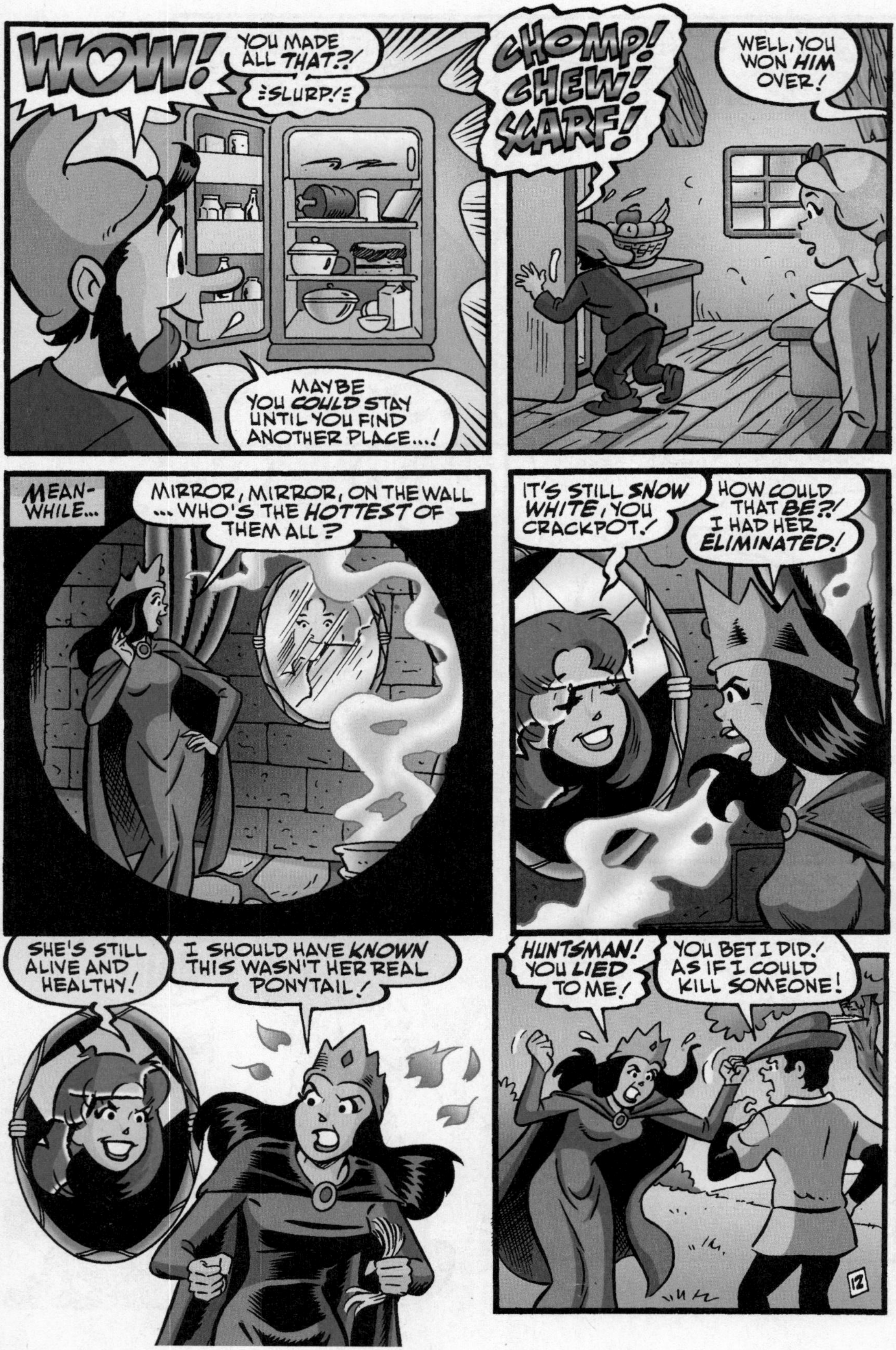
WOW!
YOU MADE ALL THAT?!
:SLURP!:
MAYBE YOU COULD STAY UNTIL YOU FIND ANOTHER PLACE...!
CHOMP! CHEW! SKARF!
WELL, YOU WON HIM OVER!
MEAN-WHILE...
MIRROR, MIRROR, ON THE WALL ... WHO'S THE HOTTEST OF THEM ALL?
IT'S STILL SNOW WHITE, YOU CRACKPOT!
HOW COULD THAT BE?! I HAD HER ELIMINATED!
SHE'S STILL ALIVE AND HEALTHY!
I SHOULD HAVE KNOWN THIS WASN'T HER REAL PONYTAIL!
HUNTSMAN! YOU LIED TO ME!
YOU BET I DID! AS IF I COULD KILL SOMEONE!
12

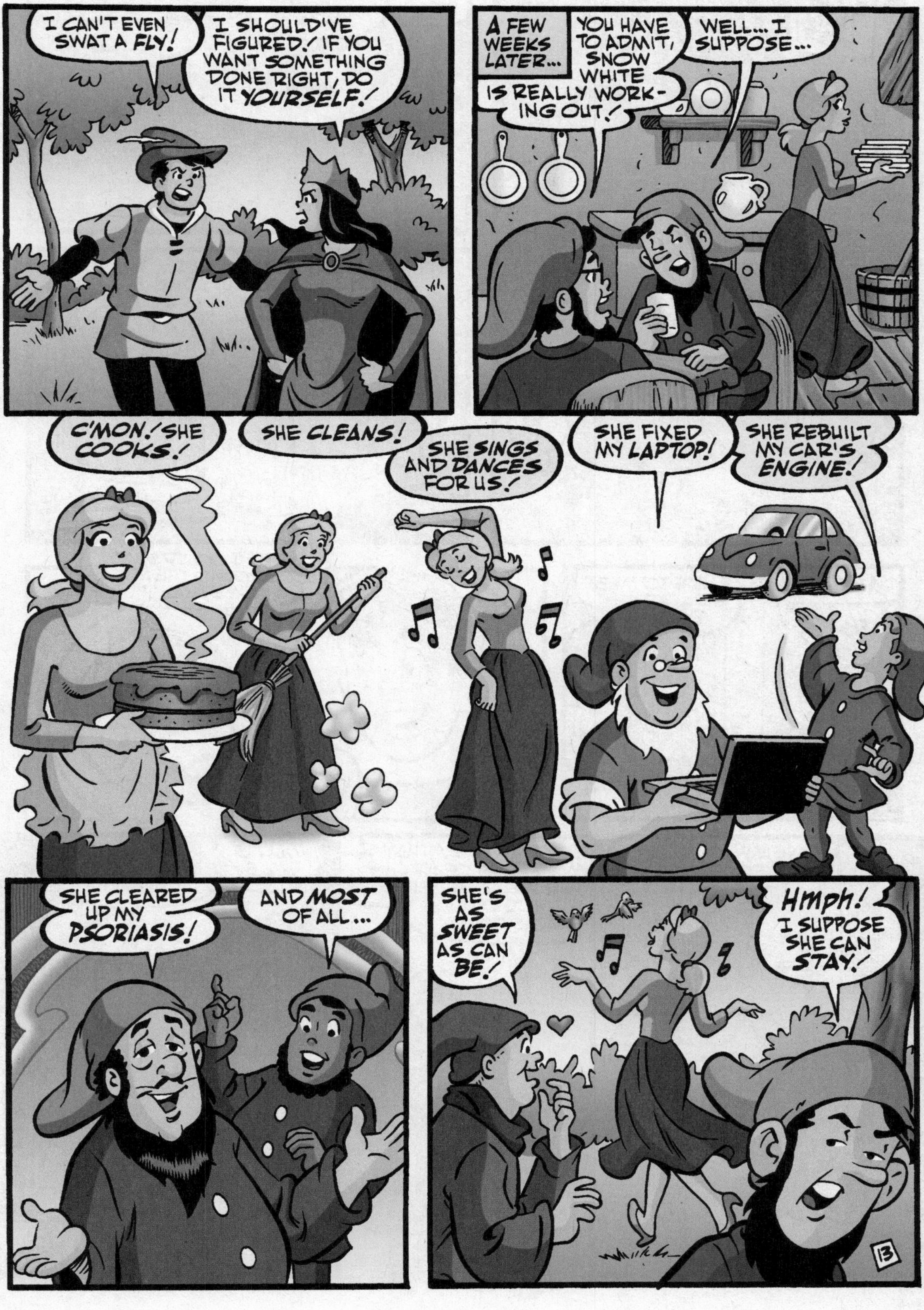
I CAN'T EVEN SWAT A FLY!
I SHOULD'VE FIGURED! IF YOU WANT SOMETHING DONE RIGHT, DO IT YOURSELF!
A FEW WEEKS LATER...
YOU HAVE TO ADMIT, SNOW WHITE IS REALLY WORKING OUT!
WELL... I SUPPOSE...
C'MON! SHE COOKS!
SHE CLEANS!
SHE SINGS AND DANCES FOR US!
SHE FIXED MY LAPTOP!
SHE REBUILT MY CAR'S ENGINE!
SHE CLEARED UP MY PSORIASIS!
AND MOST OF ALL...
SHE'S AS SWEET AS CAN BE!
Hmph! I SUPPOSE SHE CAN STAY!
13

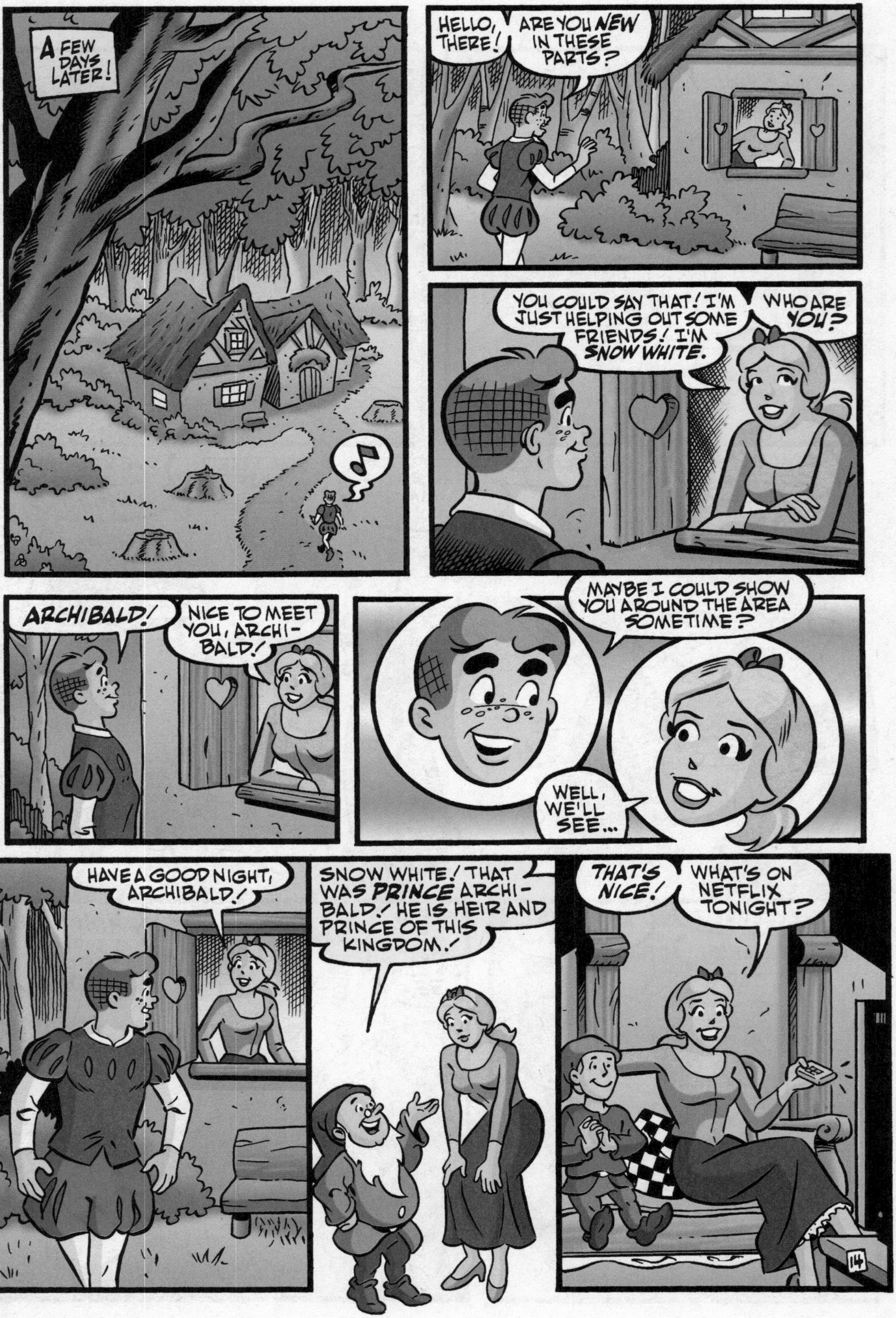
A FEW DAYS LATER!
HELLO, THERE!
ARE YOU NEW IN THESE PARTS?
YOU COULD SAY THAT! I'M JUST HELPING OUT SOME FRIENDS! I'M SNOW WHITE.
WHO ARE YOU?
ARCHIBALD!
NICE TO MEET YOU, ARCHI-BALD!
MAYBE I COULD SHOW YOU AROUND THE AREA SOMETIME?
WELL, WE'LL SEE...
HAVE A GOOD NIGHT, ARCHIBALD!
SNOW WHITE! THAT WAS PRINCE ARCHI-BALD! HE IS HEIR AND PRINCE OF THIS KINGDOM!
THAT'S NICE!
WHAT'S ON NETFLIX TONIGHT?
14

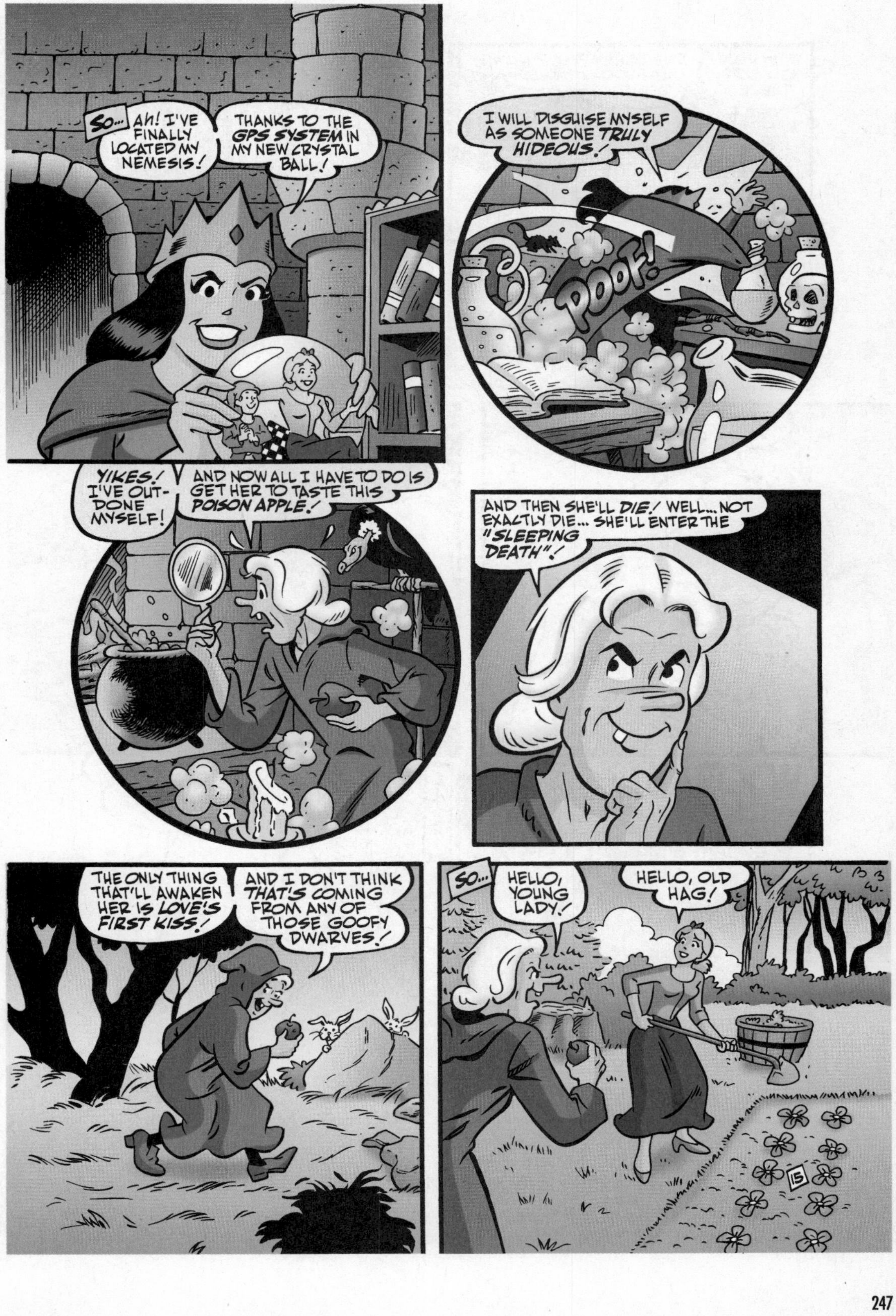
SO...
AH! I'VE FINALLY LOCATED MY NEMESIS!
THANKS TO THE GPS SYSTEM IN MY NEW CRYSTAL BALL!
I WILL DISGUISE MYSELF AS SOMEONE TRULY HIDEOUS!
POOF!
YIKES! I'VE OUT-DONE MYSELF!
AND NOW ALL I HAVE TO DO IS GET HER TO TASTE THIS POISON APPLE!
AND THEN SHE'LL DIE! WELL... NOT EXACTLY DIE... SHE'LL ENTER THE "SLEEPING DEATH"!
THE ONLY THING THAT'LL AWAKEN HER IS LOVE'S FIRST KISS!
AND I DON'T THINK THAT'S COMING FROM ANY OF THOSE GOOFY DWARVES!
SO...
HELLO, YOUNG LADY!
HELLO, OLD HAG!
15

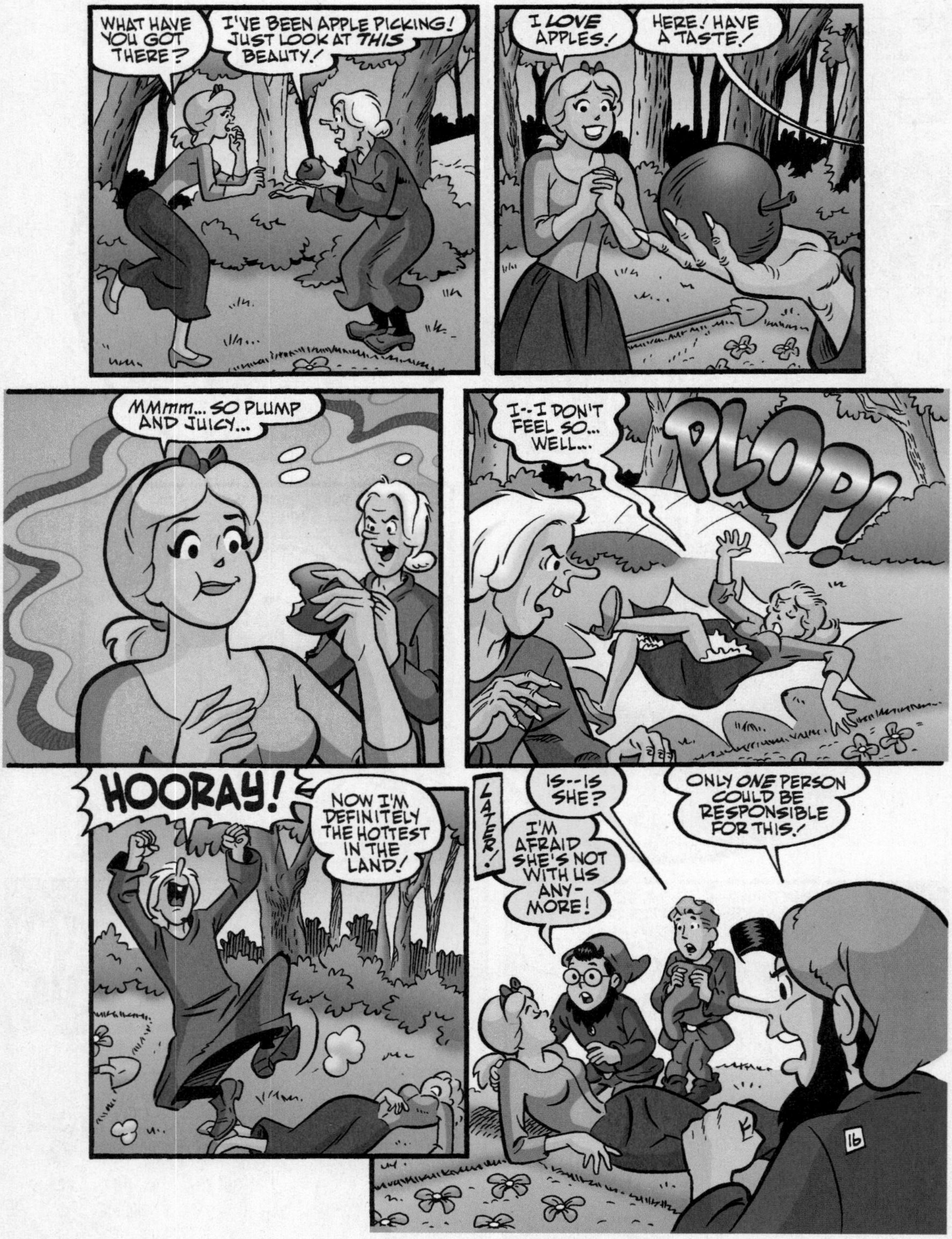
WHAT HAVE YOU GOT THERE?
I'VE BEEN APPLE PICKING! JUST LOOK AT THIS BEAUTY!
I LOVE APPLES!
HERE! HAVE A TASTE!
MMMMM... SO PLUMP AND JUICY...
I--I DON'T FEEL SO... WELL...
PLOP!
HOORAY!
NOW I'M DEFINITELY THE HOTTEST IN THE LAND!
LATER!
IS--IS SHE?
I'M AFRAID SHE'S NOT WITH US ANY-MORE!
ONLY ONE PERSON COULD BE RESPONSIBLE FOR THIS!

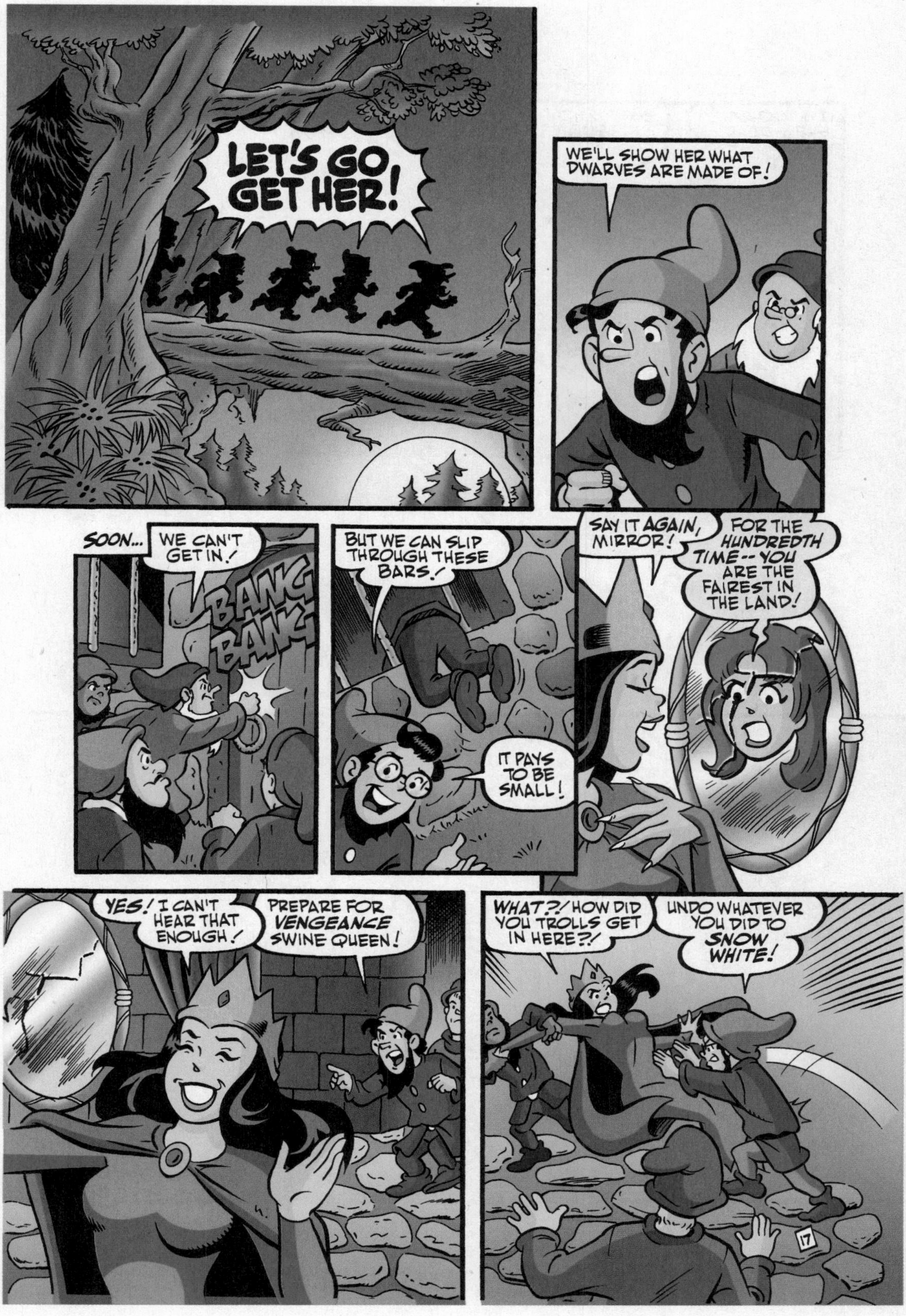
LET'S GO GET HER!
WE'LL SHOW HER WHAT DWARVES ARE MADE OF!
SOON...
WE CAN'T GET IN!
BANG BANG
BUT WE CAN SLIP THROUGH THESE BARS!
IT PAYS TO BE SMALL!
SAY IT AGAIN, MIRROR!
FOR THE HUNDREDTH TIME-- YOU ARE THE FAIREST IN THE LAND!
YES! I CAN'T HEAR THAT ENOUGH!
PREPARE FOR VENGEANCE SWINE QUEEN!
WHAT?! HOW DID YOU TROLLS GET IN HERE?!
UNDO WHATEVER YOU DID TO SNOW WHITE!
17

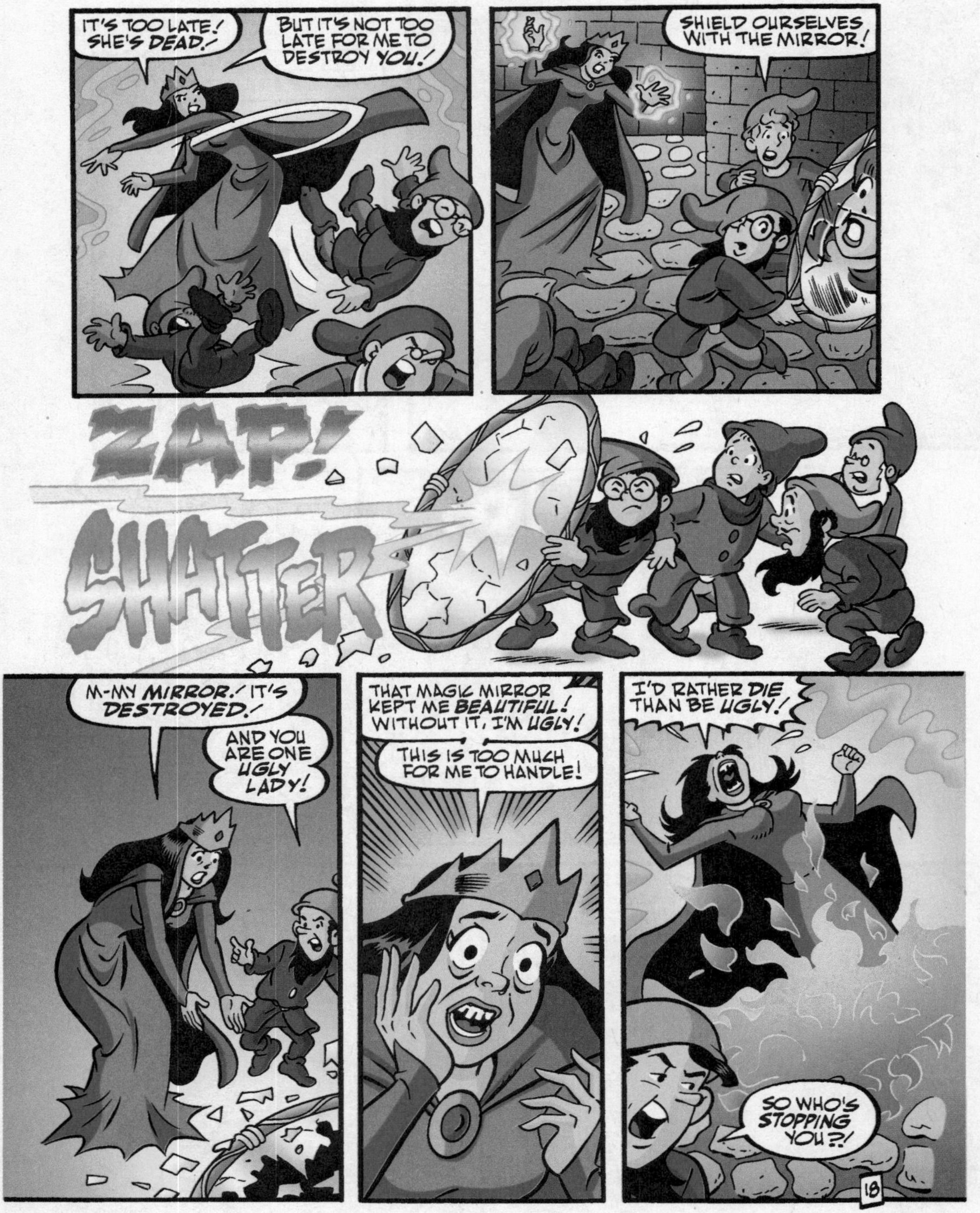
IT'S TOO LATE! SHE'S DEAD!
BUT IT'S NOT TOO LATE FOR ME TO DESTROY YOU!
SHIELD OURSELVES WITH THE MIRROR!
ZAP!
SHATTER
M-MY MIRROR! IT'S DESTROYED!
AND YOU ARE ONE UGLY LADY!
THAT MAGIC MIRROR KEPT ME BEAUTIFUL! WITHOUT IT, I'M UGLY!
THIS IS TOO MUCH FOR ME TO HANDLE!
I'D RATHER DIE THAN BE UGLY!
SO WHO'S STOPPING YOU?!
18

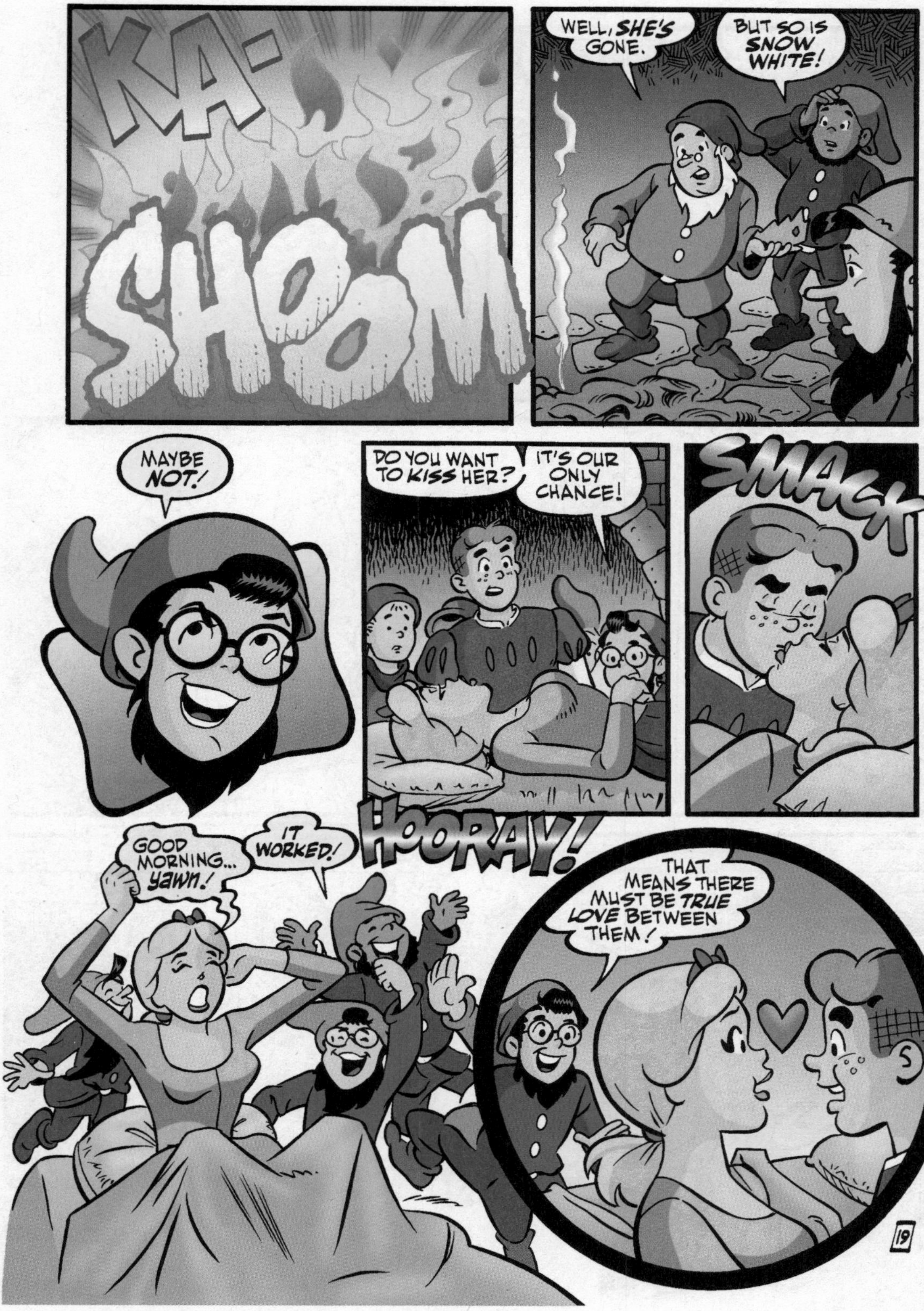
KA-SHOOM
WELL, SHE'S GONE.
BUT SO IS SNOW WHITE!
MAYBE NOT!
DO YOU WANT TO KISS HER?
IT'S OUR ONLY CHANCE!
SMACK
GOOD MORNING... yawn!
IT WORKED!
HOORAY!
THAT MEANS THERE MUST BE TRUE LOVE BETWEEN THEM!
19

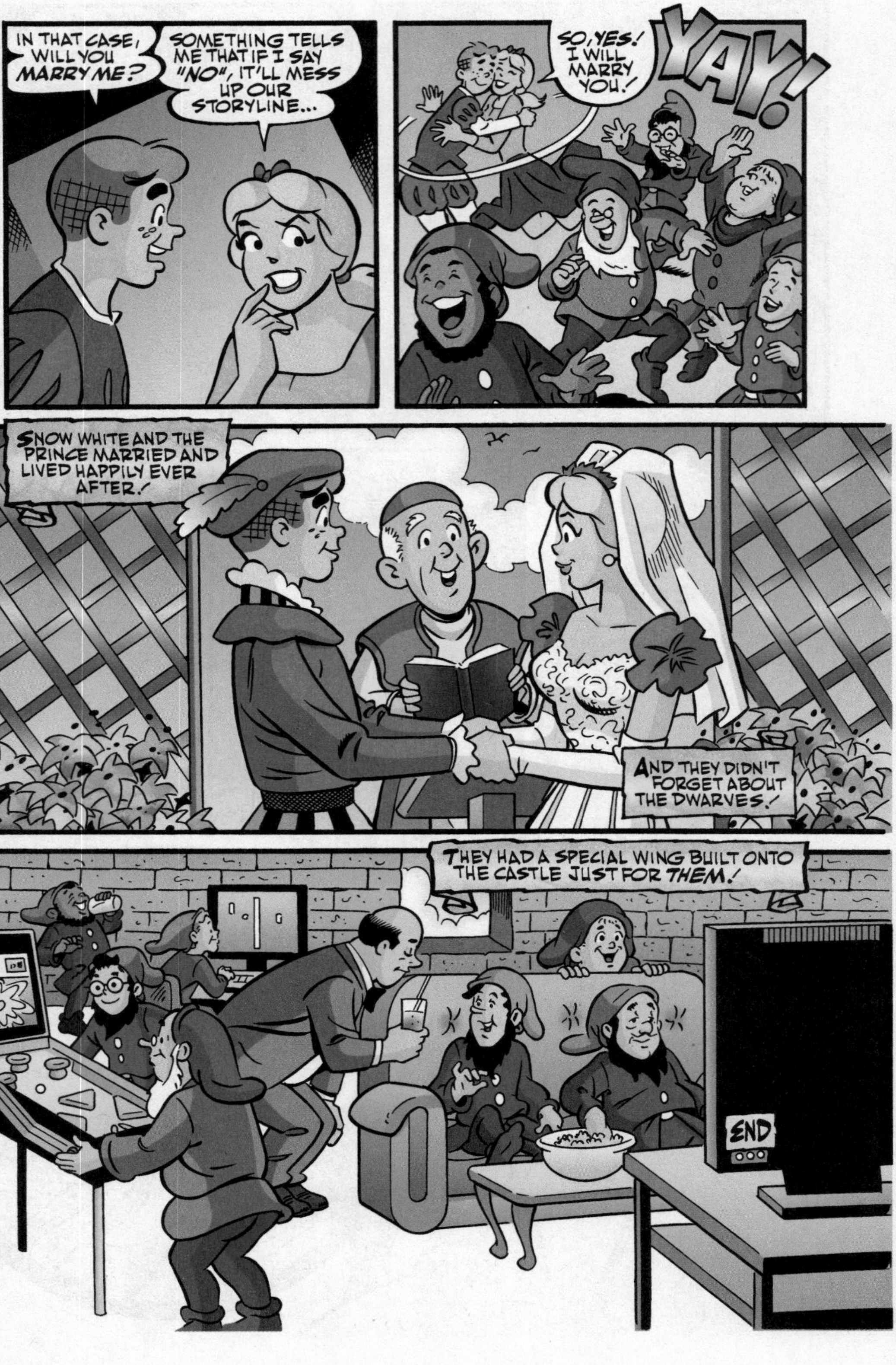
IN THAT CASE, WILL YOU MARRY ME?
SOMETHING TELLS ME THAT IF I SAY "NO", IT'LL MESS UP OUR STORYLINE...
SO, YES! I WILL MARRY YOU!
YAY!
SNOW WHITE AND THE PRINCE MARRIED AND LIVED HAPPILY EVER AFTER!
AND THEY DIDN'T FORGET ABOUT THE DWARVES!
THEY HAD A SPECIAL WING BUILT ONTO THE CASTLE JUST FOR THEM!
END

CHAPTER SIX

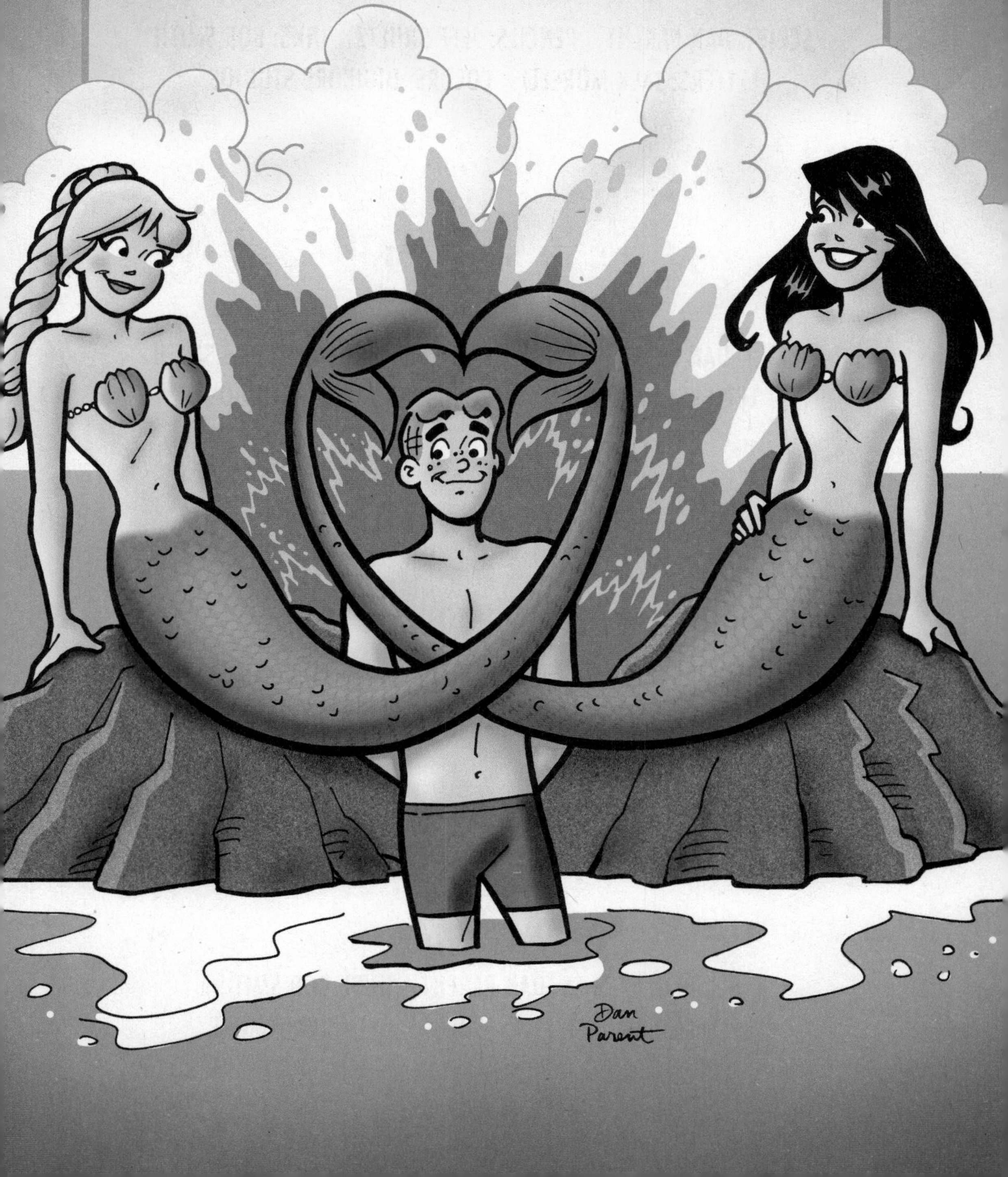
Dan Parent

BETTY & VERONICA IN
LITTLE MERMAIDS
OCTOBER 2013

SCRIPT: DAN PARENT   PENCILS: JEFF SHULTZ   INKS: BOB SMITH
LETTERS: JACK MORELLI   COLORS: DIGIKORE STUDIOS

BETTY & VERONICA IN
REGGIESTILTSKIN
DECEMBER 2013

SCRIPT: DAN PARENT   PENCILS: JEFF SHULTZ   INKS: BOB SMITH
LETTERS: JACK MORELLI   COLORS: DIGIKORE STUDIOS

BETTY & VERONICA IN
THE PRINCESS AND THE PEA-BRAIN
APRIL 2017

SCRIPT & PENCILS: DAN PARENT   INKS: BOB SMITH
LETTERS: JACK MORELLI   COLORS: GLENN WHITMORE

BETTY & VERONICA IN
THUMBLEONICA
MAY 2017

SCRIPT & PENCILS: DAN PARENT   INKS: BOB SMITH
LETTERS: JACK MORELLI   COLORS: GLENN WHITMORE

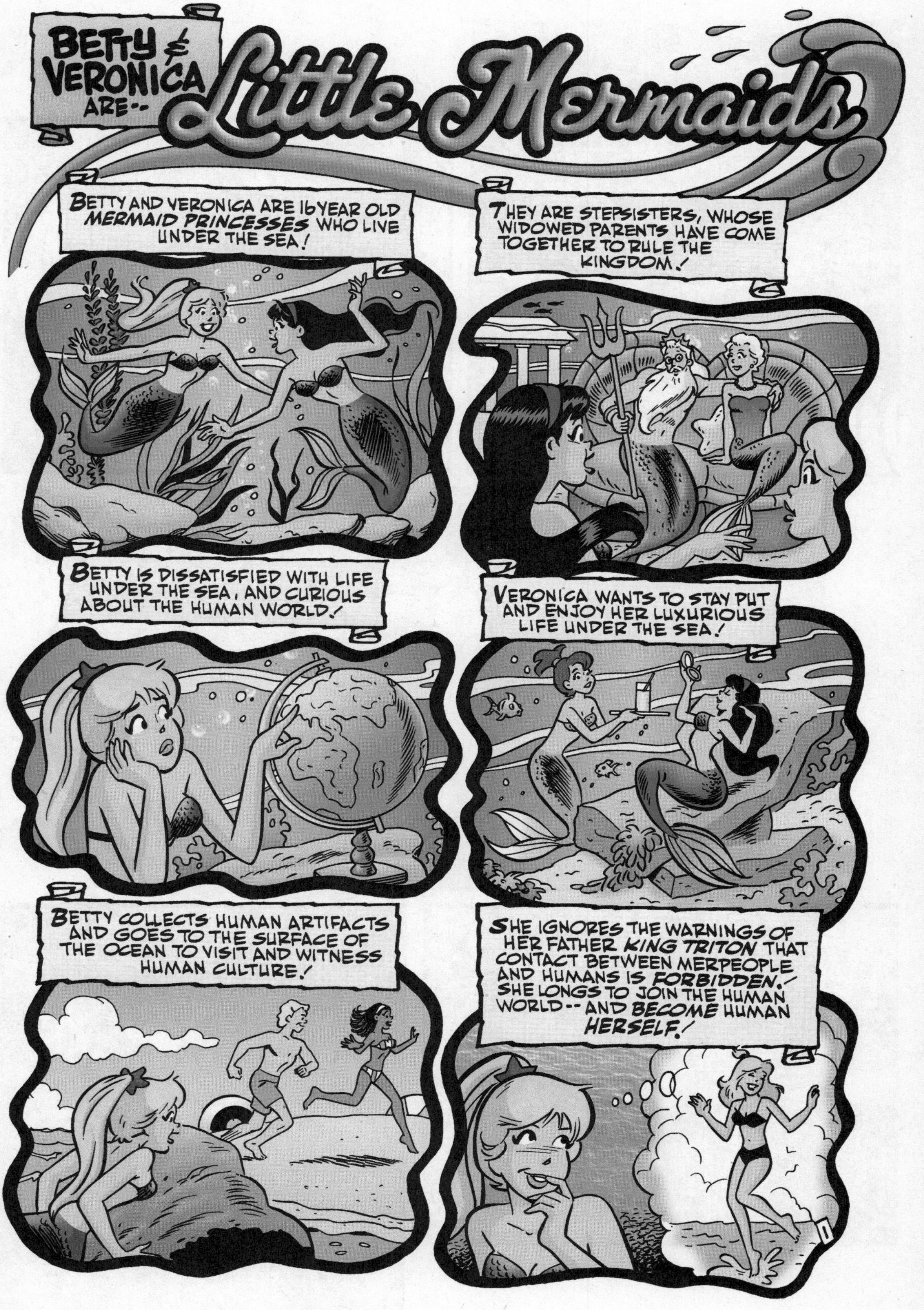
BETTY & VERONICA ARE--
Little Mermaids
BETTY AND VERONICA ARE 16 YEAR OLD MERMAID PRINCESSES WHO LIVE UNDER THE SEA!
THEY ARE STEPSISTERS, WHOSE WIDOWED PARENTS HAVE COME TOGETHER TO RULE THE KINGDOM!
BETTY IS DISSATISFIED WITH LIFE UNDER THE SEA, AND CURIOUS ABOUT THE HUMAN WORLD!
VERONICA WANTS TO STAY PUT AND ENJOY HER LUXURIOUS LIFE UNDER THE SEA!
BETTY COLLECTS HUMAN ARTIFACTS AND GOES TO THE SURFACE OF THE OCEAN TO VISIT AND WITNESS HUMAN CULTURE!
SHE IGNORES THE WARNINGS OF HER FATHER KING TRITON THAT CONTACT BETWEEN MERPEOPLE AND HUMANS IS FORBIDDEN! SHE LONGS TO JOIN THE HUMAN WORLD--AND BECOME HUMAN HERSELF!

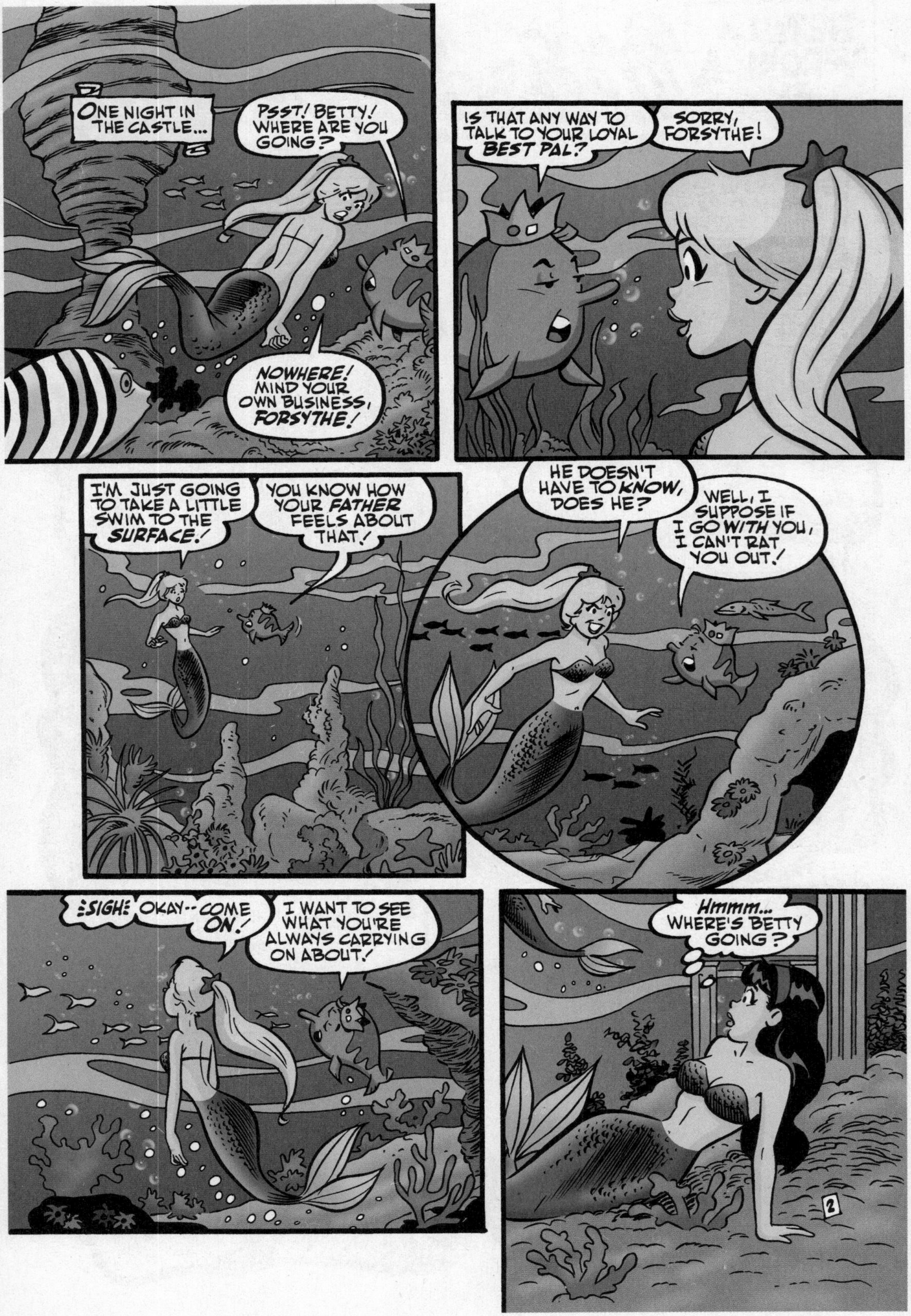
ONE NIGHT IN THE CASTLE...
PSST! BETTY! WHERE ARE YOU GOING?
NOWHERE! MIND YOUR OWN BUSINESS, FORSYTHE!
IS THAT ANY WAY TO TALK TO YOUR LOYAL BEST PAL?
SORRY, FORSYTHE!
I'M JUST GOING TO TAKE A LITTLE SWIM TO THE SURFACE!
YOU KNOW HOW YOUR FATHER FEELS ABOUT THAT!
HE DOESN'T HAVE TO KNOW, DOES HE?
WELL, I SUPPOSE IF I GO WITH YOU, I CAN'T RAT YOU OUT!
SIGH OKAY-- COME ON!
I WANT TO SEE WHAT YOU'RE ALWAYS CARRYING ON ABOUT!
Hmmm... WHERE'S BETTY GOING?
2

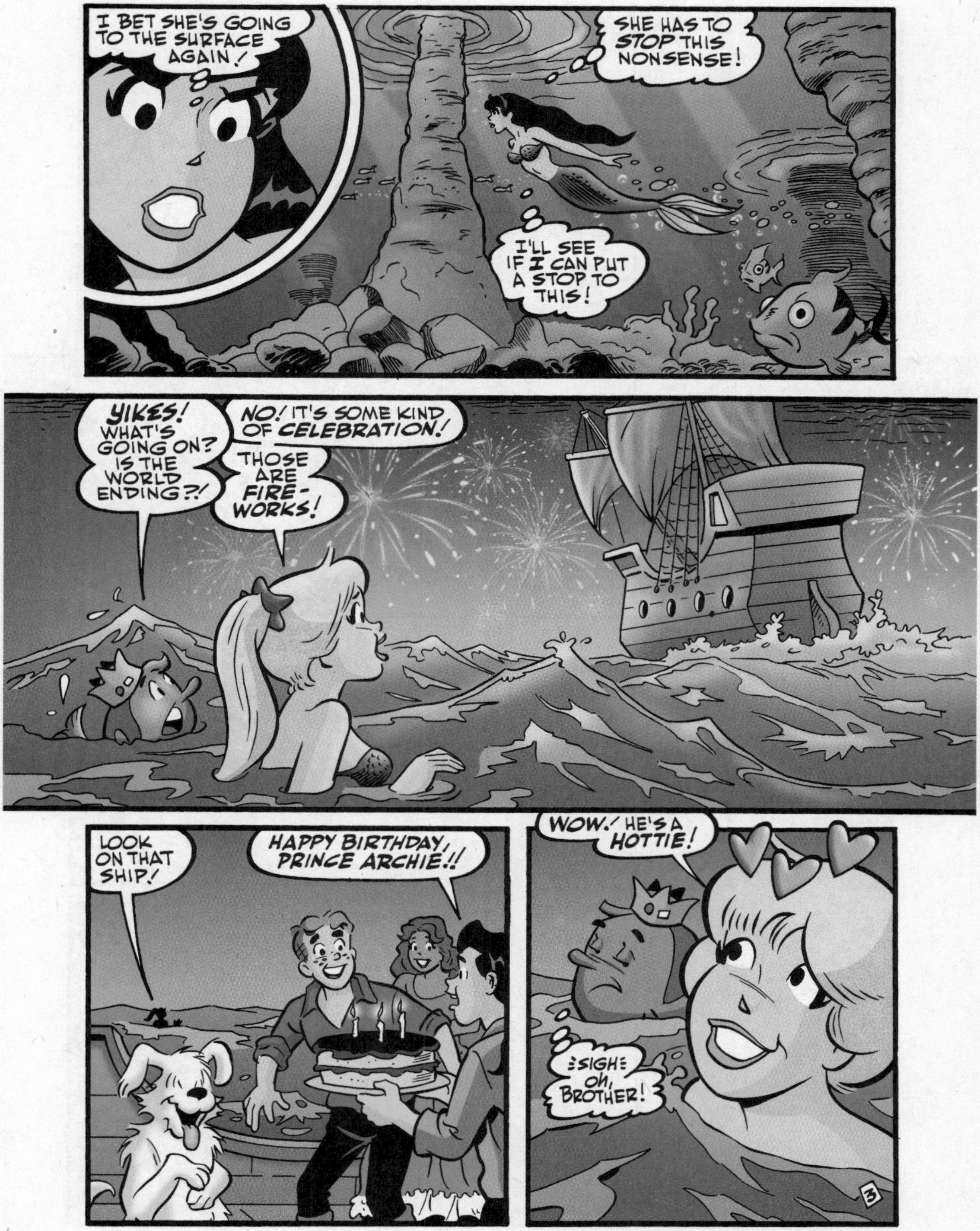
I BET SHE'S GOING TO THE SURFACE AGAIN!
SHE HAS TO STOP THIS NONSENSE!
I'LL SEE IF I CAN PUT A STOP TO THIS!
YIKES! WHAT'S GOING ON? IS THE WORLD ENDING?!
NO! IT'S SOME KIND OF CELEBRATION!
THOSE ARE FIRE-WORKS!
LOOK ON THAT SHIP!
HAPPY BIRTHDAY, PRINCE ARCHIE!!
WOW! HE'S A HOTTIE!
SIGH oh, BROTHER!
3

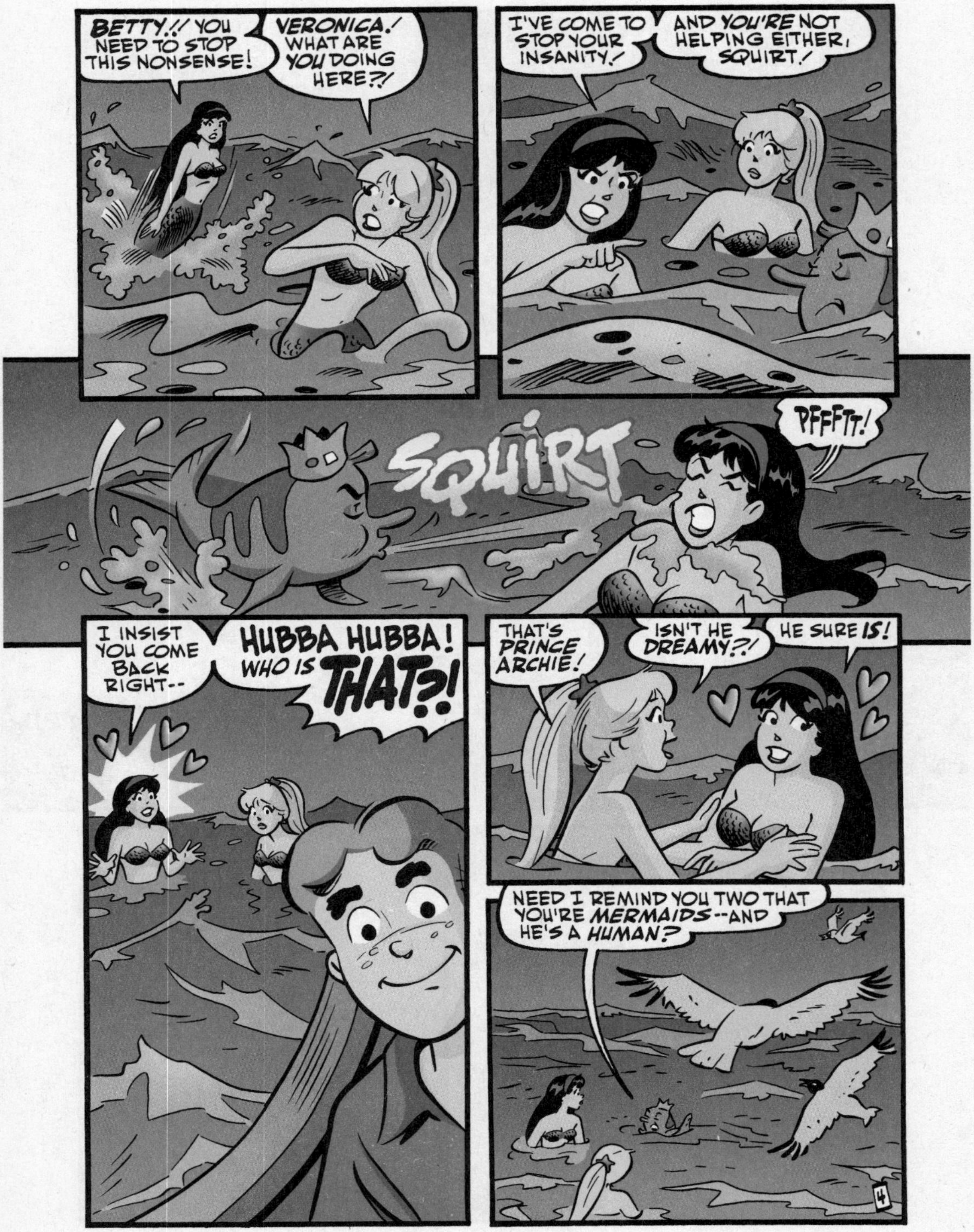

BETTY!! YOU NEED TO STOP THIS NONSENSE!
VERONICA! WHAT ARE YOU DOING HERE?!
I'VE COME TO STOP YOUR INSANITY!
AND YOU'RE NOT HELPING EITHER, SQUIRT!
SQUIRT
PFFFTT!
I INSIST YOU COME BACK RIGHT--
HUBBA HUBBA! WHO IS THAT?!
THAT'S PRINCE ARCHIE!
ISN'T HE DREAMY?!
HE SURE IS!
NEED I REMIND YOU TWO THAT YOU'RE MERMAIDS--AND HE'S A HUMAN?
4

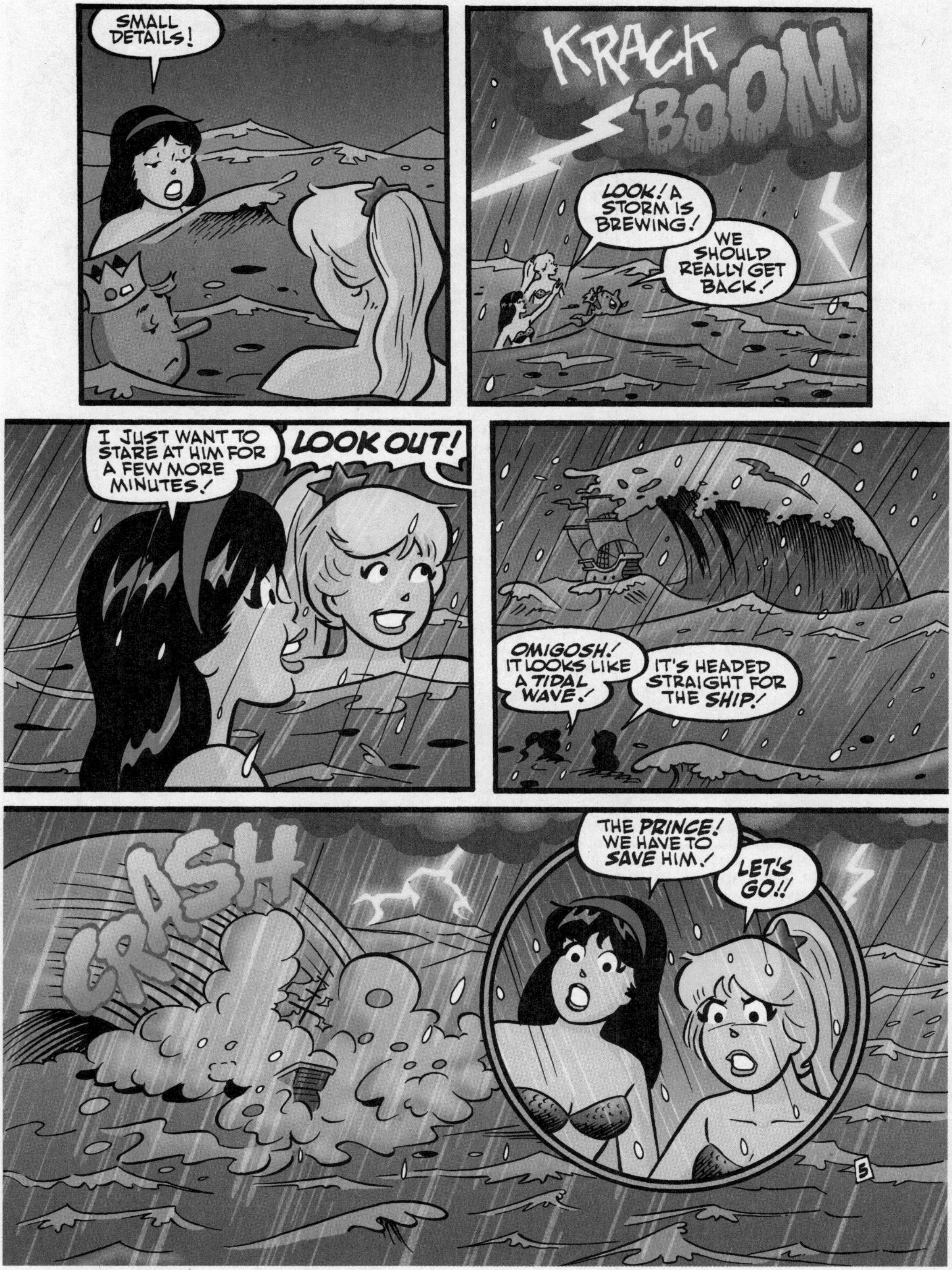
SMALL DETAILS!
KRACK
BOOM
LOOK! A STORM IS BREWING!
WE SHOULD REALLY GET BACK!
I JUST WANT TO STARE AT HIM FOR A FEW MORE MINUTES!
LOOK OUT!
OMIGOSH! IT LOOKS LIKE A TIDAL WAVE!
IT'S HEADED STRAIGHT FOR THE SHIP!
CRASH
THE PRINCE! WE HAVE TO SAVE HIM!
LET'S GO!!
5

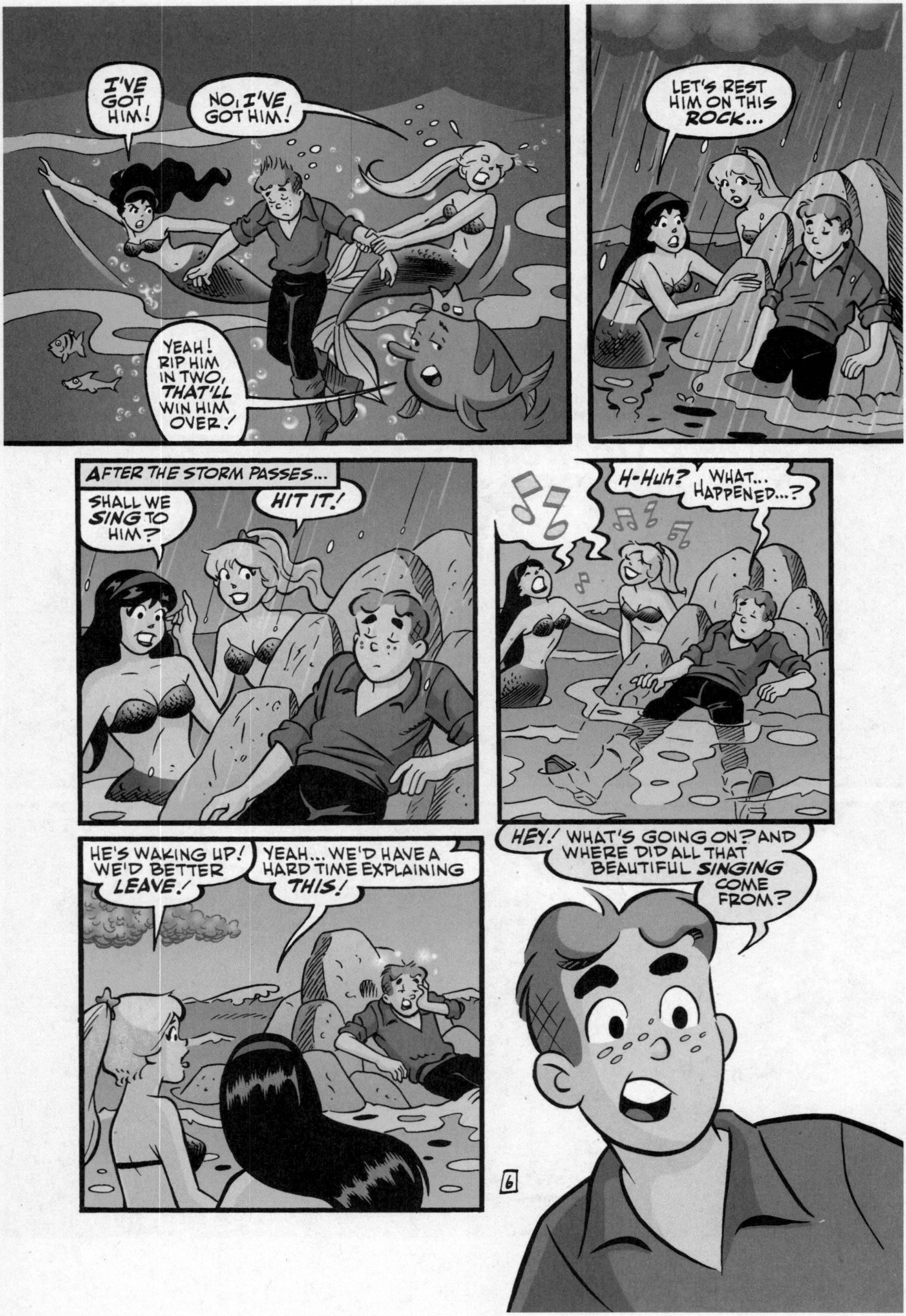
I'VE GOT HIM!
NO, I'VE GOT HIM!
YEAH! RIP HIM IN TWO, THAT'LL WIN HIM OVER!
LET'S REST HIM ON THIS ROCK...
AFTER THE STORM PASSES...
SHALL WE SING TO HIM?
HIT IT!
H-Huh? WHAT... HAPPENED...?
HE'S WAKING UP! WE'D BETTER LEAVE!
YEAH... WE'D HAVE A HARD TIME EXPLAINING THIS!
HEY! WHAT'S GOING ON? AND WHERE DID ALL THAT BEAUTIFUL SINGING COME FROM?
6

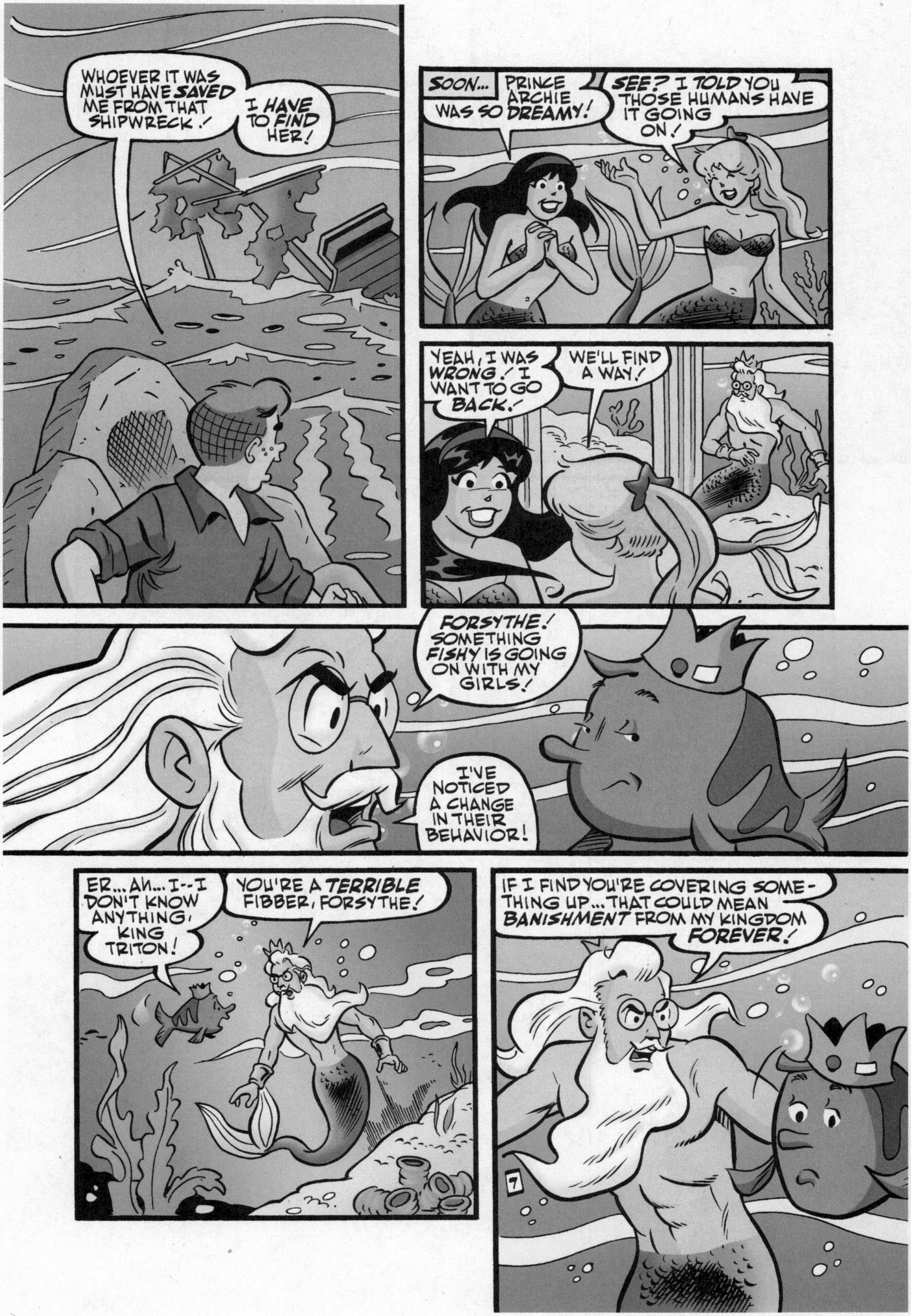
WHOEVER IT WAS MUST HAVE SAVED ME FROM THAT SHIPWRECK!
I HAVE TO FIND HER!
SOON...
PRINCE ARCHIE WAS SO DREAMY!
SEE? I TOLD YOU THOSE HUMANS HAVE IT GOING ON!
YEAH, I WAS WRONG! I WANT TO GO BACK!
WE'LL FIND A WAY!
FORSYTHE! SOMETHING FISHY IS GOING ON WITH MY GIRLS!
I'VE NOTICED A CHANGE IN THEIR BEHAVIOR!
ER... AH... I--I DON'T KNOW ANYTHING, KING TRITON!
YOU'RE A TERRIBLE FIBBER, FORSYTHE!
IF I FIND YOU'RE COVERING SOME-THING UP... THAT COULD MEAN BANISHMENT FROM MY KINGDOM FOREVER!
7

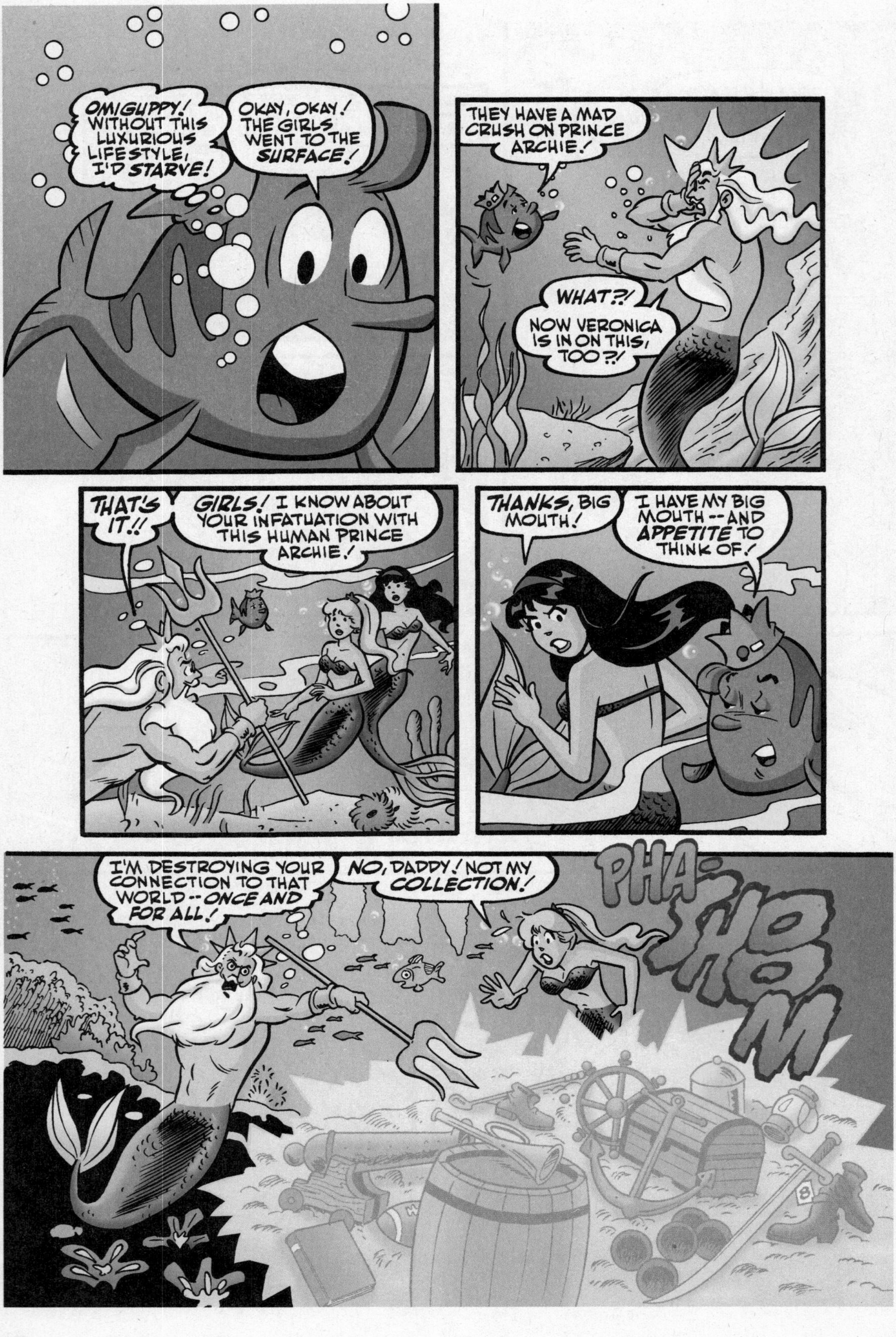
OMIGUPPY! WITHOUT THIS LUXURIOUS LIFESTYLE, I'D STARVE!
OKAY, OKAY! THE GIRLS WENT TO THE SURFACE!
THEY HAVE A MAD CRUSH ON PRINCE ARCHIE!
WHAT?!
NOW VERONICA IS IN ON THIS, TOO?!
THAT'S IT!!
GIRLS! I KNOW ABOUT YOUR INFATUATION WITH THIS HUMAN PRINCE ARCHIE!
THANKS, BIG MOUTH!
I HAVE MY BIG MOUTH -- AND APPETITE TO THINK OF!
I'M DESTROYING YOUR CONNECTION TO THAT WORLD -- ONCE AND FOR ALL!
NO, DADDY! NOT MY COLLECTION!
PHA-HOOM

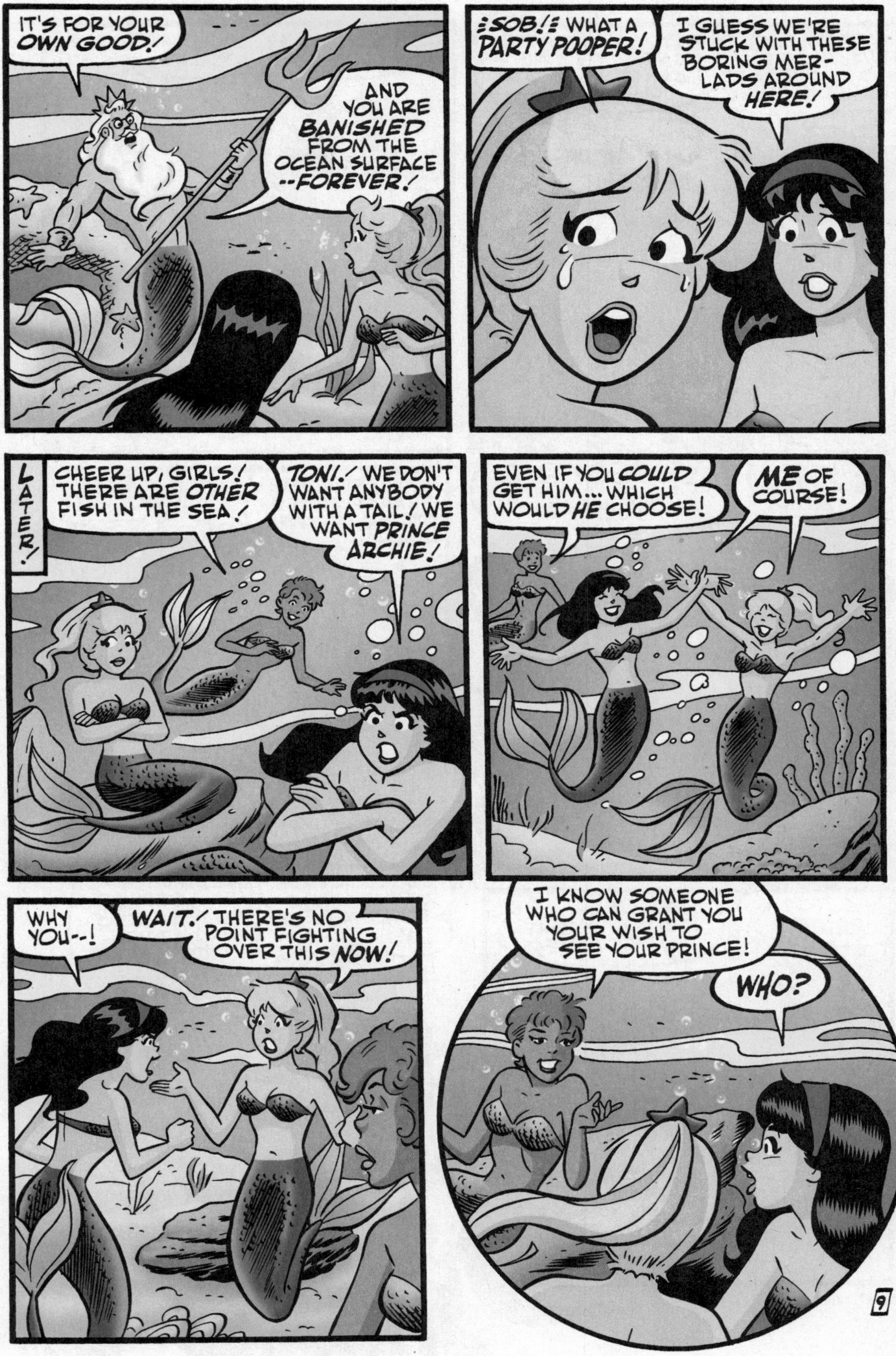
IT'S FOR YOUR OWN GOOD!
AND YOU ARE BANISHED FROM THE OCEAN SURFACE --FOREVER!
:SOB!: WHAT A PARTY POOPER!
I GUESS WE'RE STUCK WITH THESE BORING MER-LADS AROUND HERE!
LATER!
CHEER UP, GIRLS! THERE ARE OTHER FISH IN THE SEA!
TONI! WE DON'T WANT ANYBODY WITH A TAIL! WE WANT PRINCE ARCHIE!
EVEN IF YOU COULD GET HIM... WHICH WOULD HE CHOOSE!
ME OF COURSE!
WHY YOU--!
WAIT! THERE'S NO POINT FIGHTING OVER THIS NOW!
I KNOW SOMEONE WHO CAN GRANT YOU YOUR WISH TO SEE YOUR PRINCE!
WHO?
9

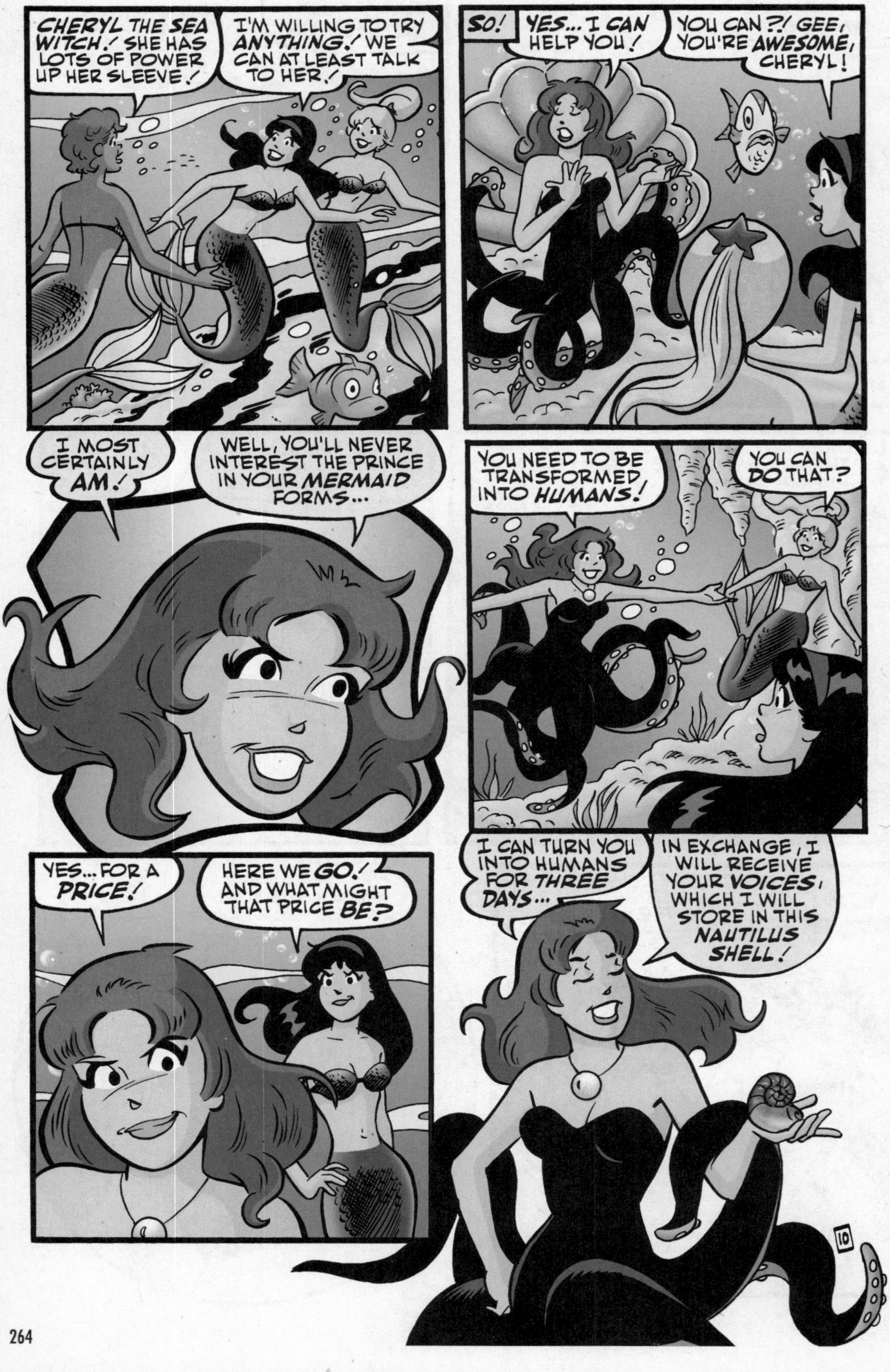
CHERYL THE SEA WITCH! SHE HAS LOTS OF POWER UP HER SLEEVE!
I'M WILLING TO TRY ANYTHING! WE CAN AT LEAST TALK TO HER!
SO!
YES... I CAN HELP YOU!
YOU CAN?! GEE, YOU'RE AWESOME, CHERYL!
I MOST CERTAINLY AM!
WELL, YOU'LL NEVER INTEREST THE PRINCE IN YOUR MERMAID FORMS...
YOU NEED TO BE TRANSFORMED INTO HUMANS!
YOU CAN DO THAT?
YES... FOR A PRICE!
HERE WE GO! AND WHAT MIGHT THAT PRICE BE?
I CAN TURN YOU INTO HUMANS FOR THREE DAYS...
IN EXCHANGE, I WILL RECEIVE YOUR VOICES, WHICH I WILL STORE IN THIS NAUTILUS SHELL!
10

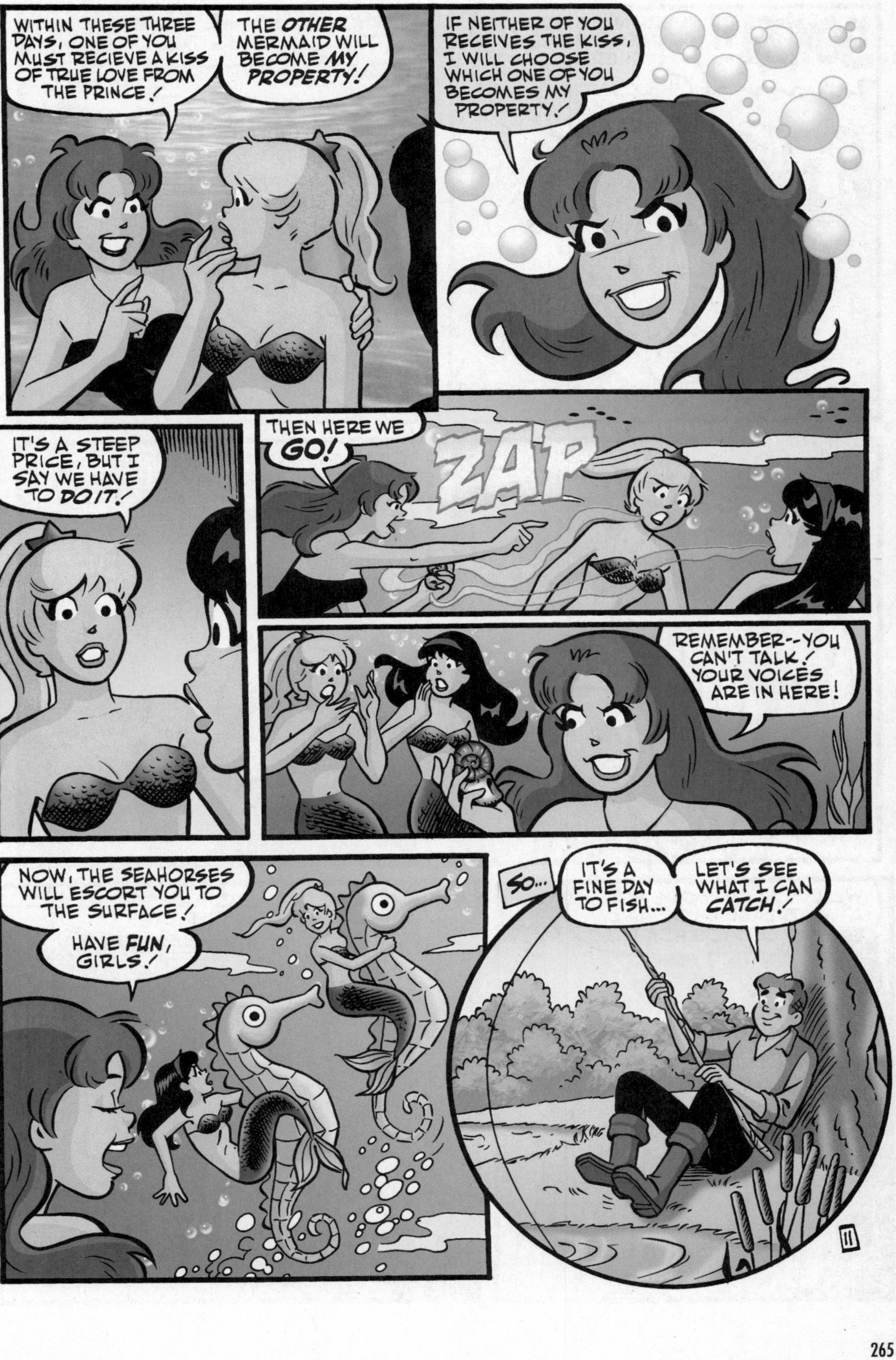
WITHIN THESE THREE DAYS, ONE OF YOU MUST RECIEVE A KISS OF TRUE LOVE FROM THE PRINCE!
THE OTHER MERMAID WILL BECOME MY PROPERTY!
IF NEITHER OF YOU RECEIVES THE KISS, I WILL CHOOSE WHICH ONE OF YOU BECOMES MY PROPERTY!
IT'S A STEEP PRICE, BUT I SAY WE HAVE TO DO IT!
THEN HERE WE GO!
ZAP
REMEMBER--YOU CAN'T TALK! YOUR VOICES ARE IN HERE!
NOW, THE SEAHORSES WILL ESCORT YOU TO THE SURFACE!
HAVE FUN, GIRLS!
SO...
IT'S A FINE DAY TO FISH...
LET'S SEE WHAT I CAN CATCH!
11

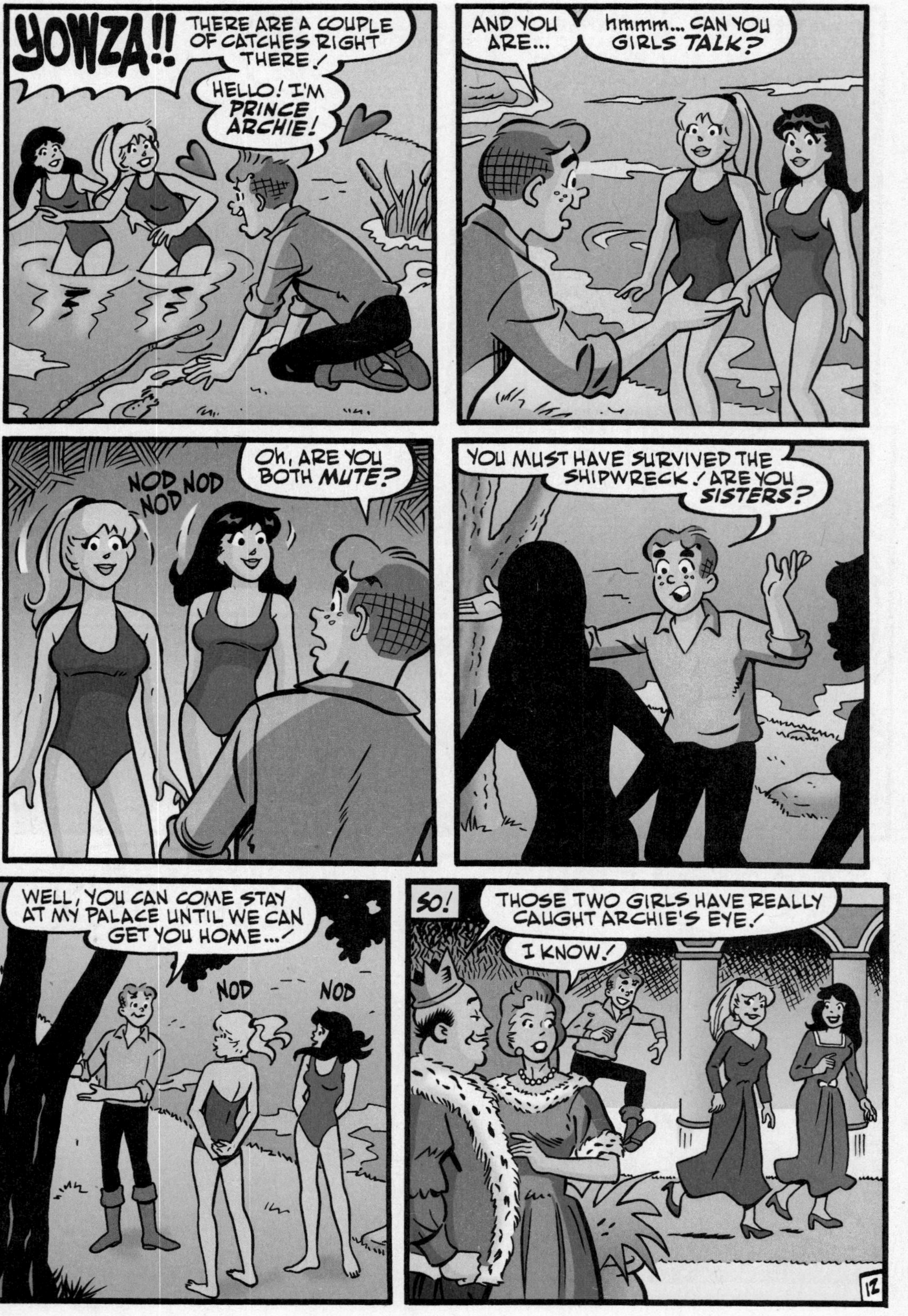
YOWZA!!
THERE ARE A COUPLE OF CATCHES RIGHT THERE!
HELLO! I'M PRINCE ARCHIE!
AND YOU ARE...
hmmm... CAN YOU GIRLS TALK?
NOD NOD NOD
Oh, ARE YOU BOTH MUTE?
YOU MUST HAVE SURVIVED THE SHIPWRECK! ARE YOU SISTERS?
WELL, YOU CAN COME STAY AT MY PALACE UNTIL WE CAN GET YOU HOME...!
NOD
NOD
SO!
THOSE TWO GIRLS HAVE REALLY CAUGHT ARCHIE'S EYE!
I KNOW!
12

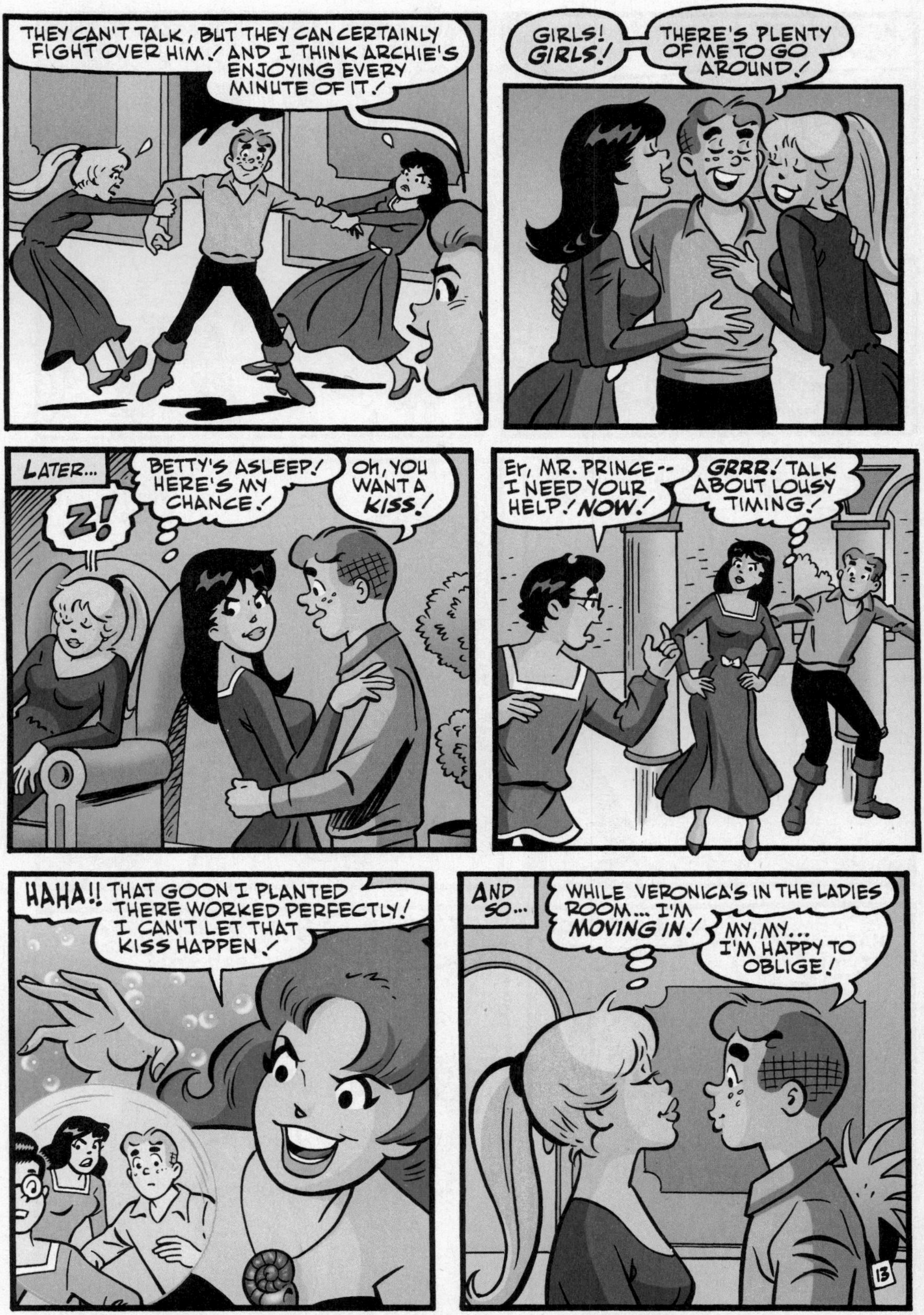
THEY CAN'T TALK, BUT THEY CAN CERTAINLY FIGHT OVER HIM! AND I THINK ARCHIE'S ENJOYING EVERY MINUTE OF IT!
GIRLS! GIRLS!
THERE'S PLENTY OF ME TO GO AROUND!
LATER...
Z!
BETTY'S ASLEEP! HERE'S MY CHANCE!
Oh, YOU WANT A KISS!
Er, MR. PRINCE-- I NEED YOUR HELP! NOW!
GRRR! TALK ABOUT LOUSY TIMING!
HAHA!! THAT GOON I PLANTED THERE WORKED PERFECTLY! I CAN'T LET THAT KISS HAPPEN!
AND SO...
WHILE VERONICA'S IN THE LADIES ROOM... I'M MOVING IN!
MY, MY... I'M HAPPY TO OBLIGE!
13

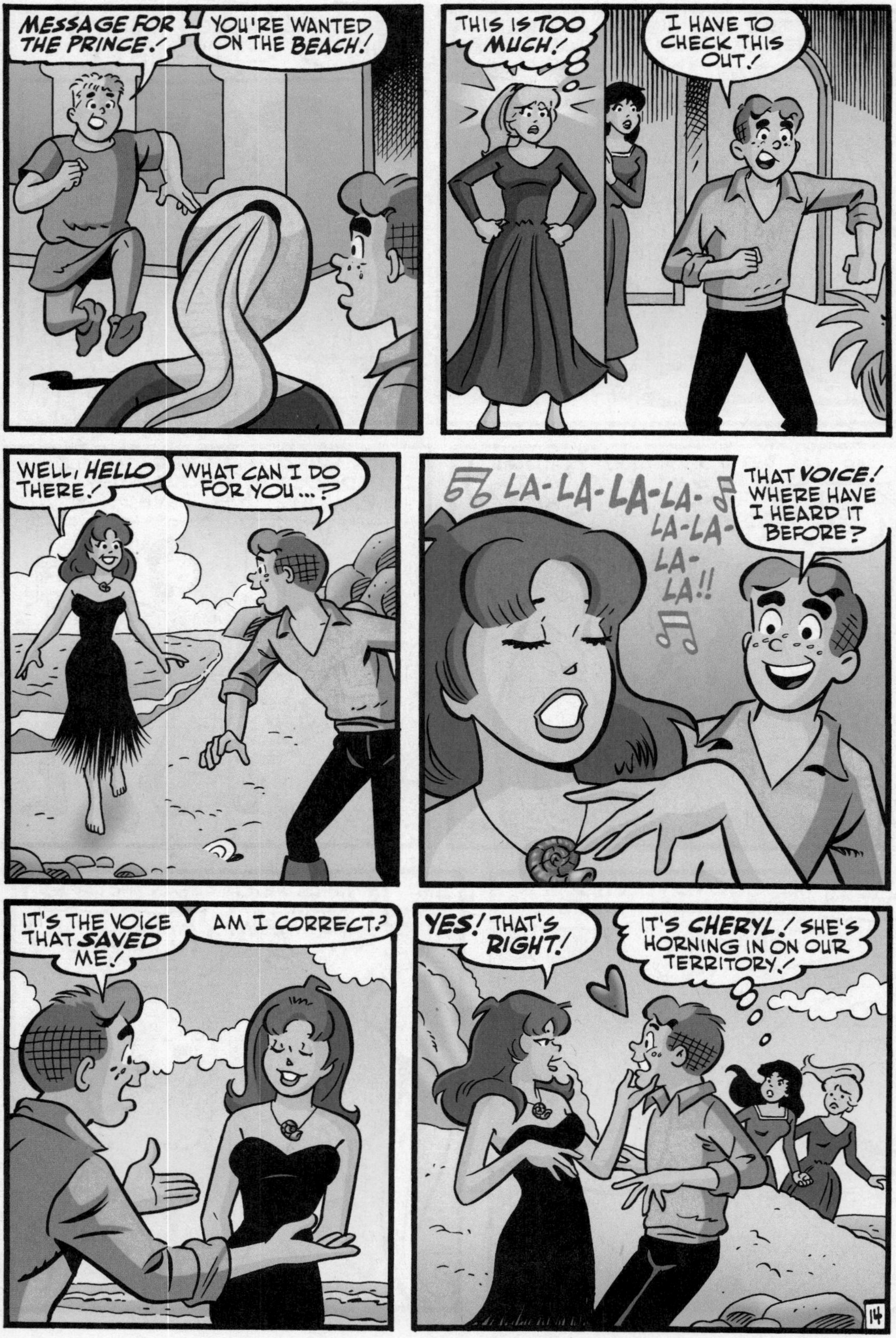
MESSAGE FOR THE PRINCE!
YOU'RE WANTED ON THE BEACH!
THIS IS TOO MUCH!
I HAVE TO CHECK THIS OUT!
WELL, HELLO THERE!
WHAT CAN I DO FOR YOU...?
LA-LA-LA-LA-LA-LA-LA-LA!!
THAT VOICE! WHERE HAVE I HEARD IT BEFORE?
IT'S THE VOICE THAT SAVED ME!
AM I CORRECT?
YES! THAT'S RIGHT!
IT'S CHERYL! SHE'S HORNING IN ON OUR TERRITORY!
14

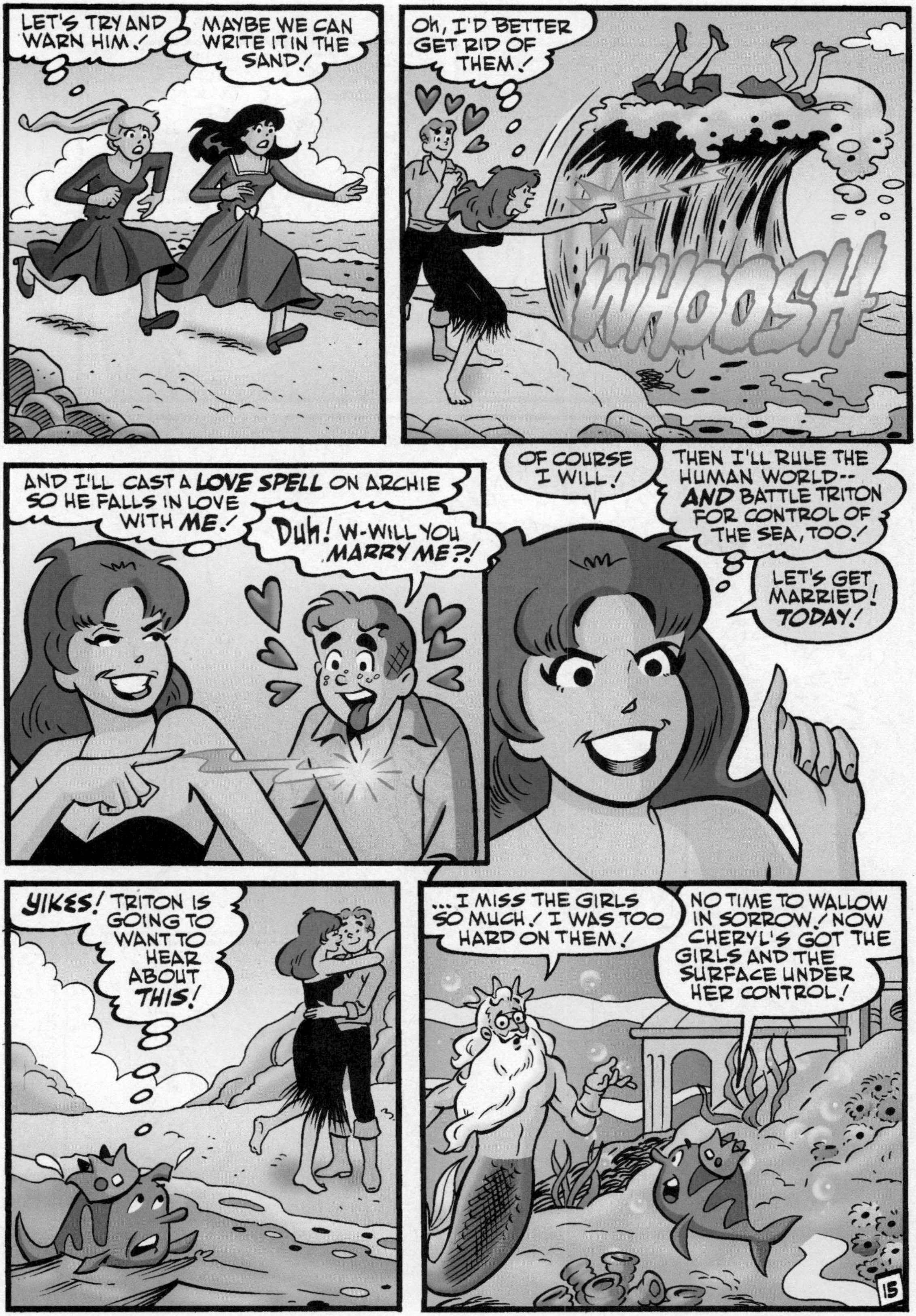

LET'S TRY AND WARN HIM!
MAYBE WE CAN WRITE IT IN THE SAND!
Oh, I'D BETTER GET RID OF THEM!
WHOOSH
AND I'LL CAST A LOVE SPELL ON ARCHIE SO HE FALLS IN LOVE WITH ME!
Duh! W-WILL YOU MARRY ME?!
OF COURSE I WILL!
THEN I'LL RULE THE HUMAN WORLD-- AND BATTLE TRITON FOR CONTROL OF THE SEA, TOO!
LET'S GET MARRIED! TODAY!
YIKES! TRITON IS GOING TO WANT TO HEAR ABOUT THIS!
...I MISS THE GIRLS SO MUCH! I WAS TOO HARD ON THEM!
NO TIME TO WALLOW IN SORROW! NOW CHERYL'S GOT THE GIRLS AND THE SURFACE UNDER HER CONTROL!
15

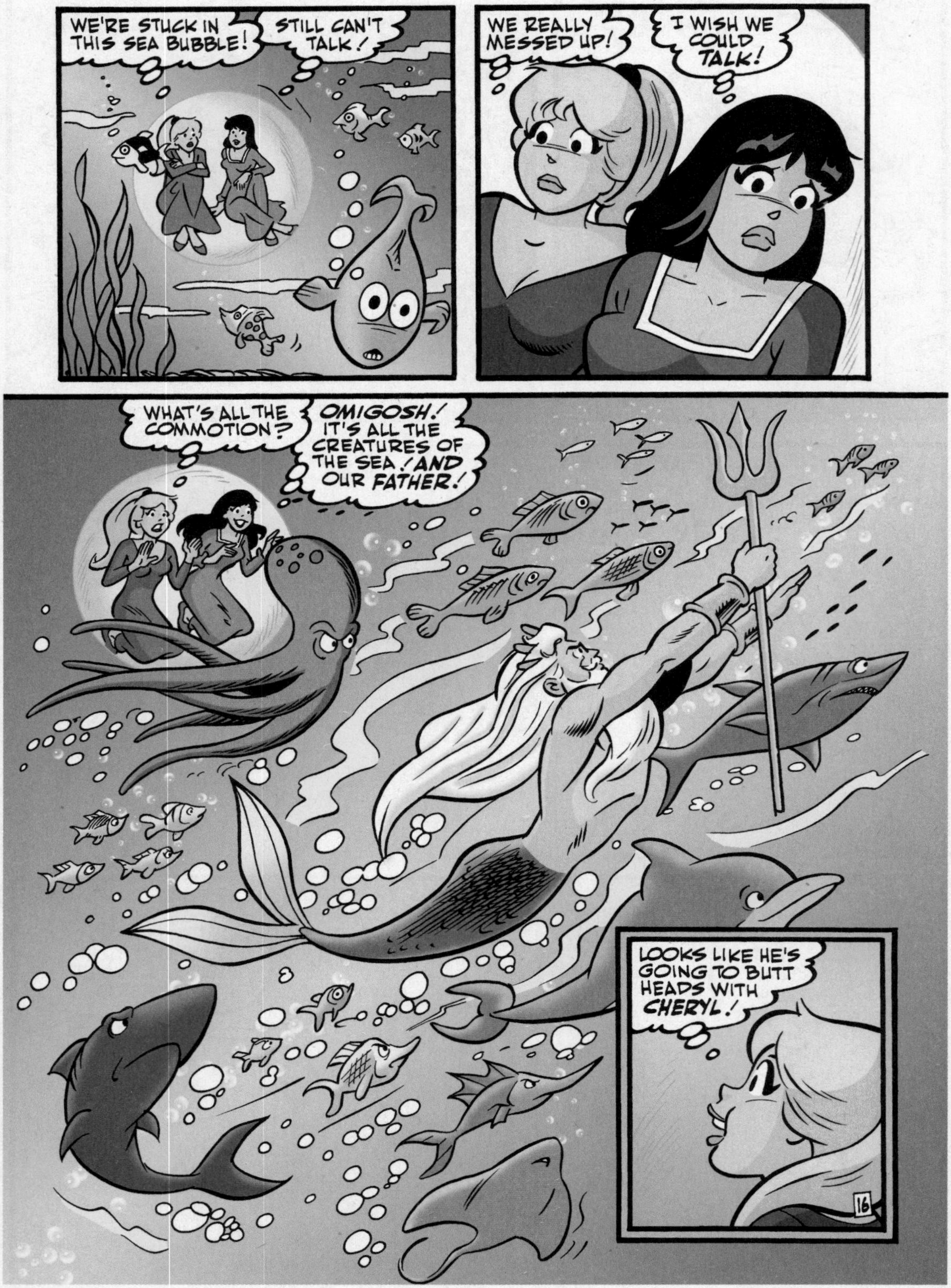
WE'RE STUCK IN THIS SEA BUBBLE!
STILL CAN'T TALK!
WE REALLY MESSED UP!
I WISH WE COULD TALK!
WHAT'S ALL THE COMMOTION?
OMIGOSH! IT'S ALL THE CREATURES OF THE SEA! AND OUR FATHER!
LOOKS LIKE HE'S GOING TO BUTT HEADS WITH CHERYL!
16

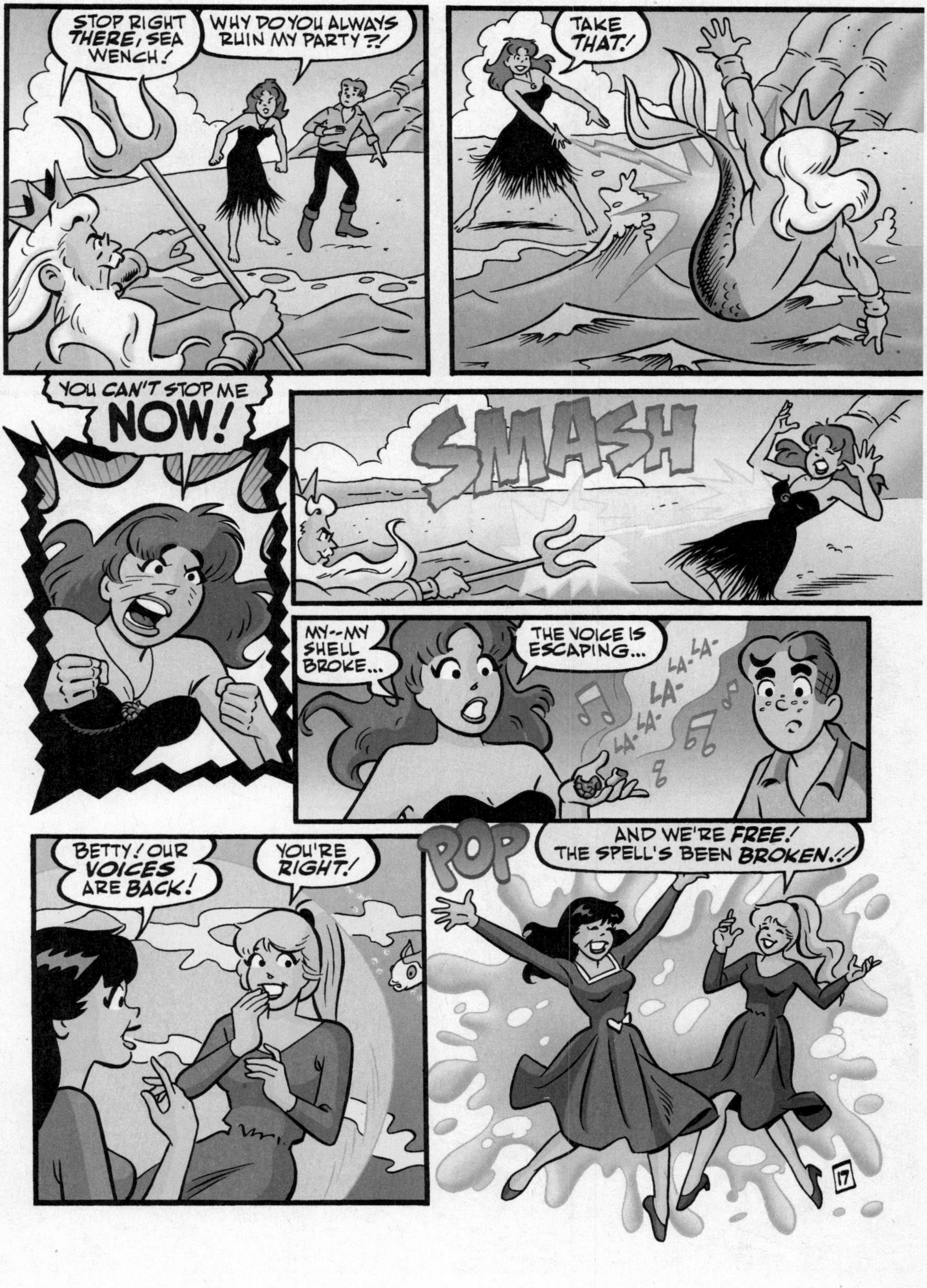

STOP RIGHT THERE, SEA WENCH!
WHY DO YOU ALWAYS RUIN MY PARTY?!
TAKE THAT!
YOU CAN'T STOP ME NOW!
SMASH
MY--MY SHELL BROKE...
THE VOICE IS ESCAPING...
LA-LA-LA-LA-LA-LA-
BETTY! OUR VOICES ARE BACK!
YOU'RE RIGHT!
POP
AND WE'RE FREE! THE SPELL'S BEEN BROKEN!!
17

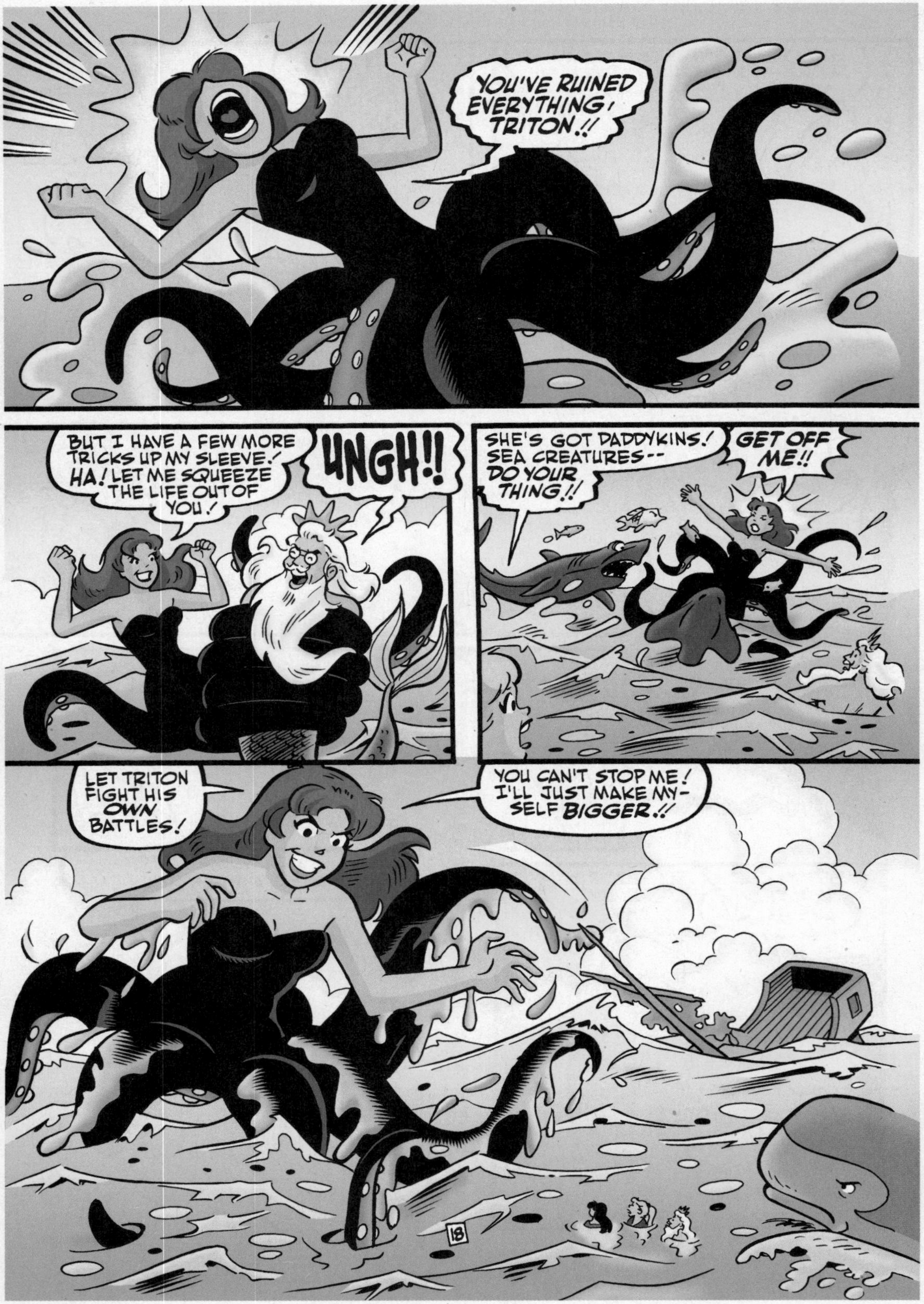
YOU'VE RUINED EVERYTHING, TRITON!!
BUT I HAVE A FEW MORE TRICKS UP MY SLEEVE! HA! LET ME SQUEEZE THE LIFE OUT OF YOU!
UNGH!!
SHE'S GOT DADDYKINS! SEA CREATURES-- DO YOUR THING!!
GET OFF ME!!
LET TRITON FIGHT HIS OWN BATTLES!
YOU CAN'T STOP ME! I'LL JUST MAKE MY-SELF BIGGER!!
18

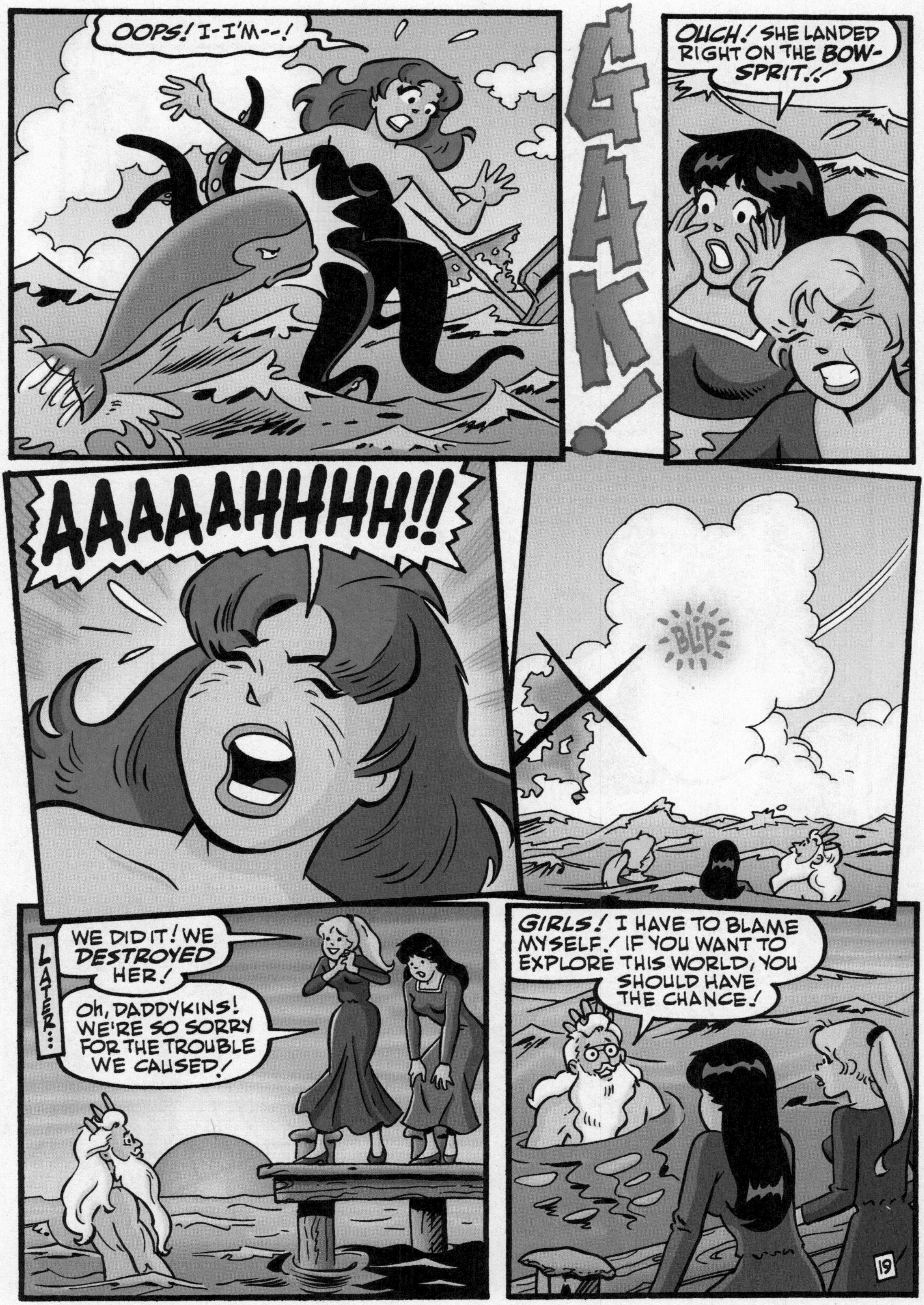
OOPS! I-I'M--!
GAK!
OUCH! SHE LANDED RIGHT ON THE BOW-SPRIT!!
AAAAAHHHH!!
BLIP
LATER...
WE DID IT! WE DESTROYED HER!
OH, DADDYKINS! WE'RE SO SORRY FOR THE TROUBLE WE CAUSED!
GIRLS! I HAVE TO BLAME MYSELF! IF YOU WANT TO EXPLORE THIS WORLD, YOU SHOULD HAVE THE CHANCE!
19

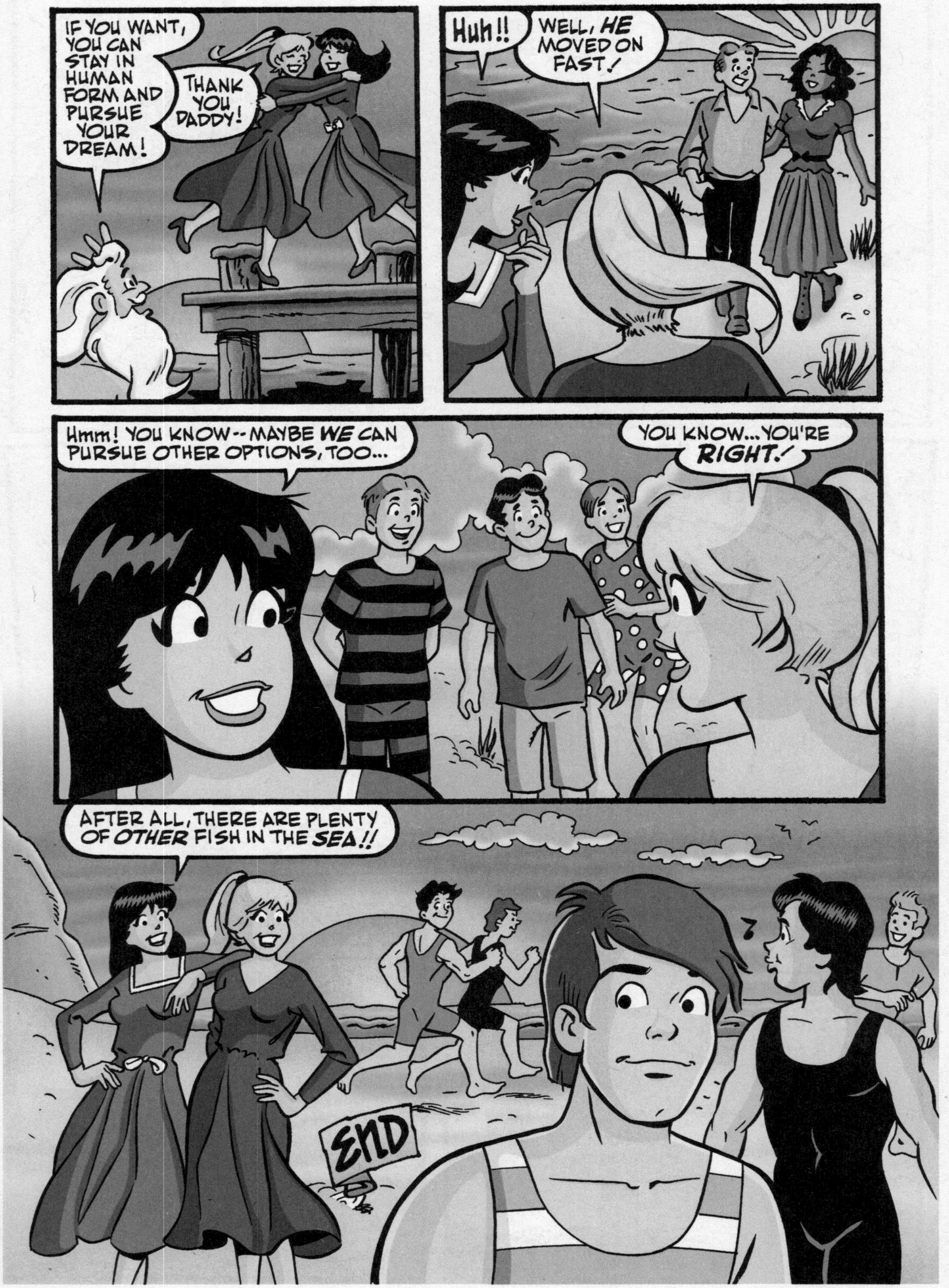
IF YOU WANT, YOU CAN STAY IN HUMAN FORM AND PURSUE YOUR DREAM!
THANK YOU DADDY!
Huh!!
WELL, HE MOVED ON FAST!
Hmm! YOU KNOW--MAYBE WE CAN PURSUE OTHER OPTIONS, TOO...
YOU KNOW...YOU'RE RIGHT!
AFTER ALL, THERE ARE PLENTY OF OTHER FISH IN THE SEA!!
END

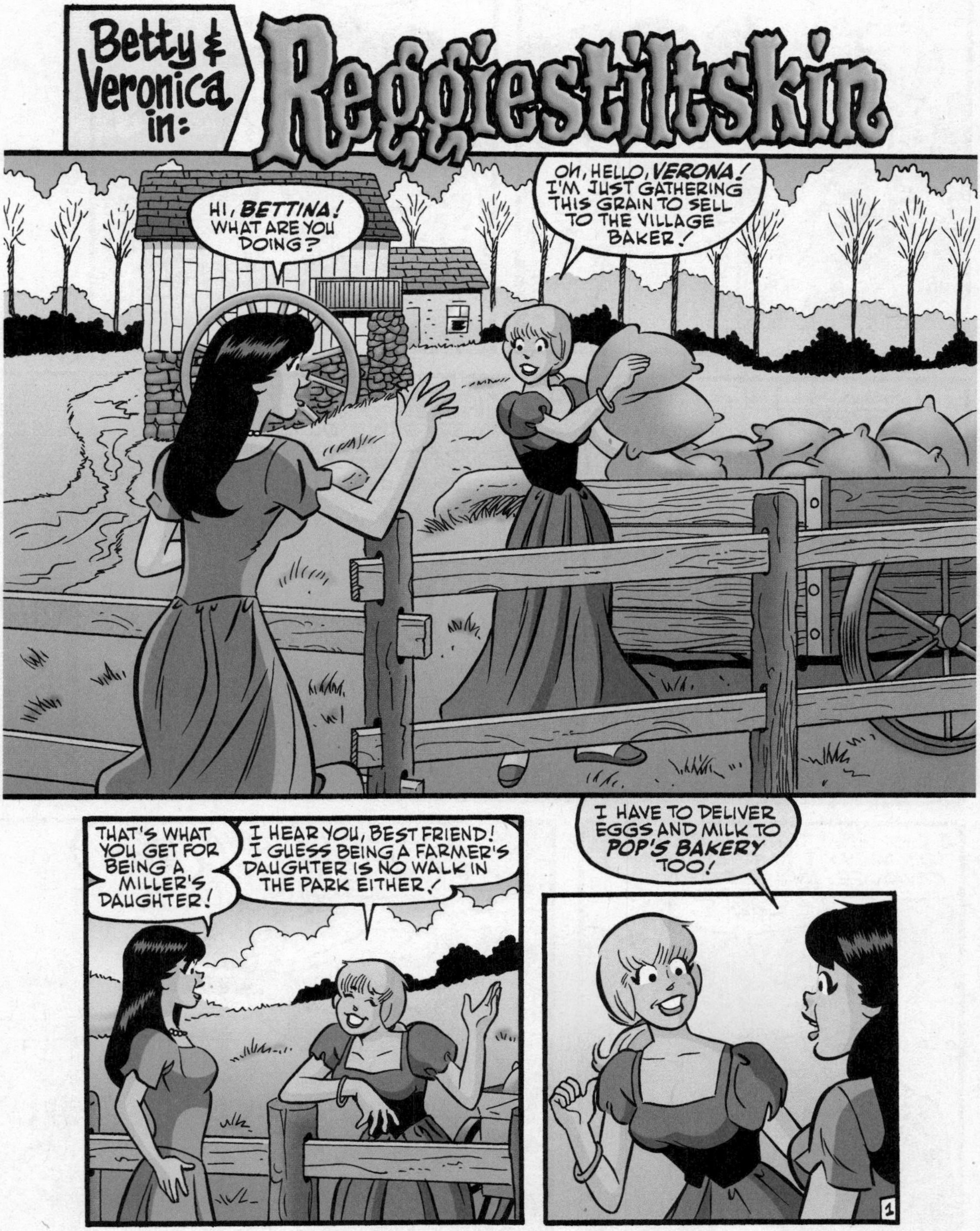
Betty & Veronica in:
Reggiestiltskin
HI, BETTINA! WHAT ARE YOU DOING?
OH, HELLO, VERONA! I'M JUST GATHERING THIS GRAIN TO SELL TO THE VILLAGE BAKER!
THAT'S WHAT YOU GET FOR BEING A MILLER'S DAUGHTER!
I HEAR YOU, BEST FRIEND! I GUESS BEING A FARMER'S DAUGHTER IS NO WALK IN THE PARK EITHER!
I HAVE TO DELIVER EGGS AND MILK TO POP'S BAKERY TOO!
1

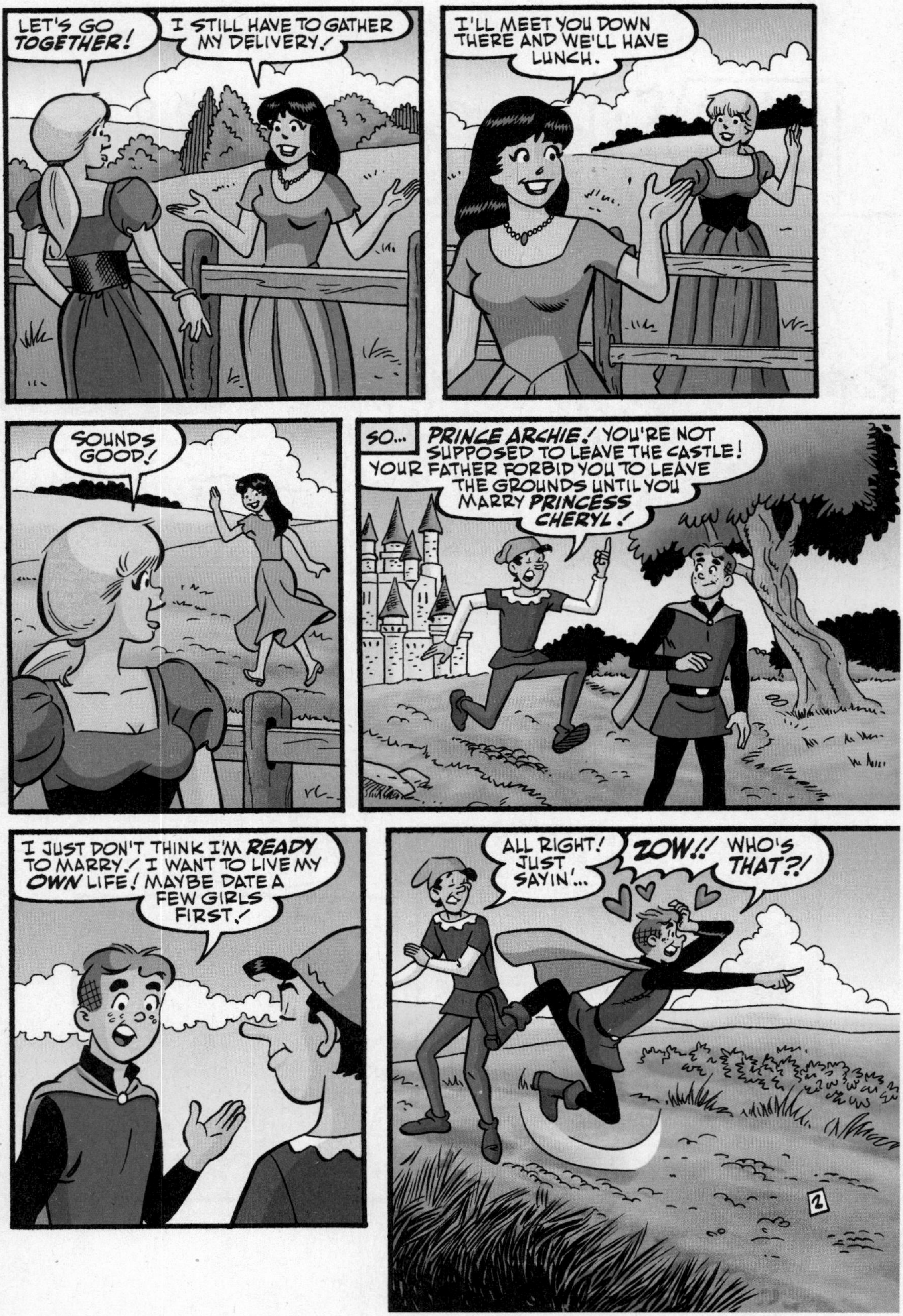
LET'S GO TOGETHER!
I STILL HAVE TO GATHER MY DELIVERY!
I'LL MEET YOU DOWN THERE AND WE'LL HAVE LUNCH.
SOUNDS GOOD!
SO...
PRINCE ARCHIE! YOU'RE NOT SUPPOSED TO LEAVE THE CASTLE! YOUR FATHER FORBID YOU TO LEAVE THE GROUNDS UNTIL YOU MARRY PRINCESS CHERYL!
I JUST DON'T THINK I'M READY TO MARRY! I WANT TO LIVE MY OWN LIFE! MAYBE DATE A FEW GIRLS FIRST!
ALL RIGHT! JUST SAYIN'...
ZOW!! WHO'S THAT?!
2

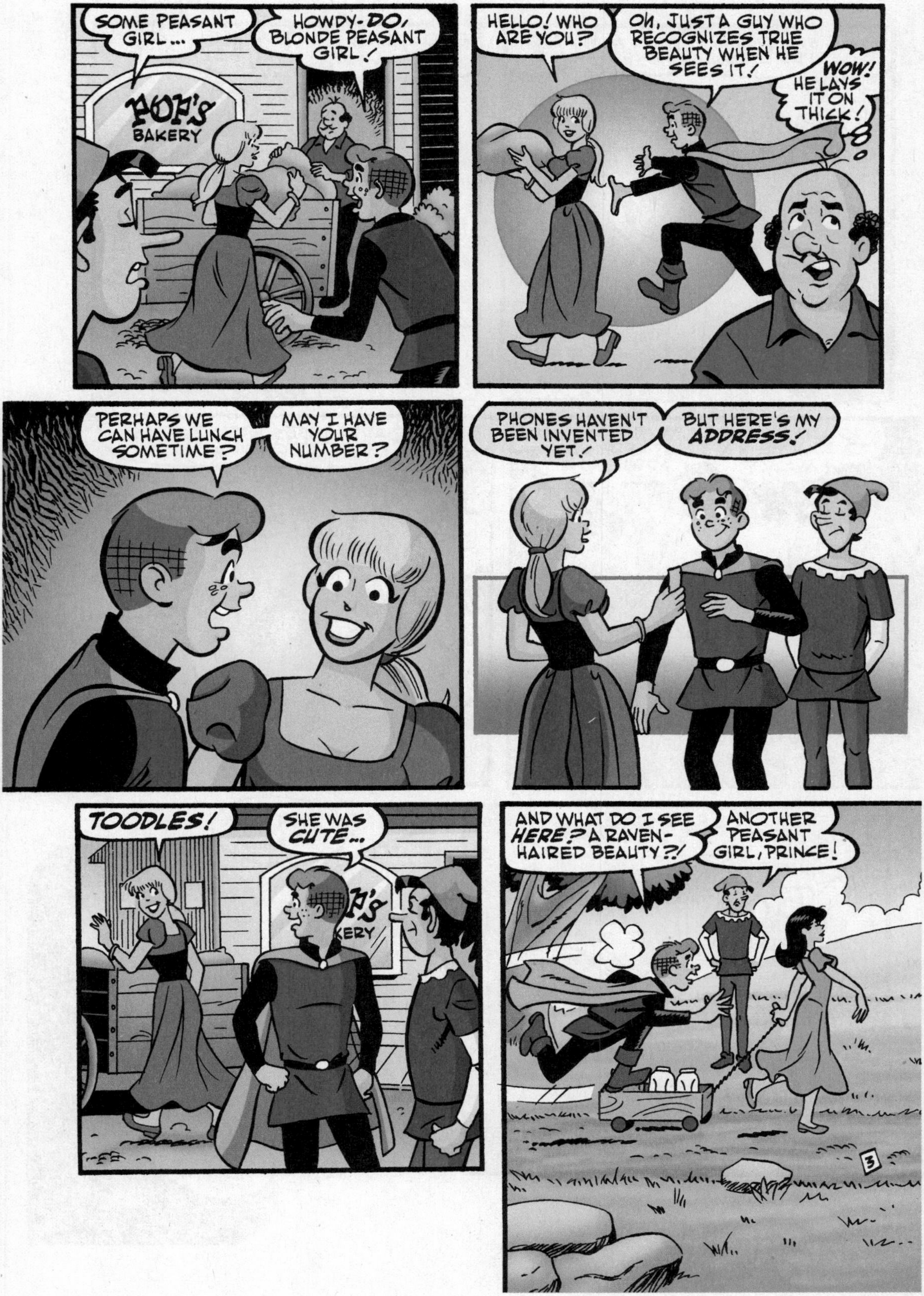

SOME PEASANT GIRL...
HOWDY-DO, BLONDE PEASANT GIRL!
POP'S BAKERY
HELLO! WHO ARE YOU?
OH, JUST A GUY WHO RECOGNIZES TRUE BEAUTY WHEN HE SEES IT!
WOW! HE LAYS IT ON THICK!
PERHAPS WE CAN HAVE LUNCH SOMETIME?
MAY I HAVE YOUR NUMBER?
PHONES HAVEN'T BEEN INVENTED YET!
BUT HERE'S MY ADDRESS!
TOODLES!
SHE WAS CUTE...
AND WHAT DO I SEE HERE? A RAVEN-HAIRED BEAUTY?!
ANOTHER PEASANT GIRL, PRINCE!
3

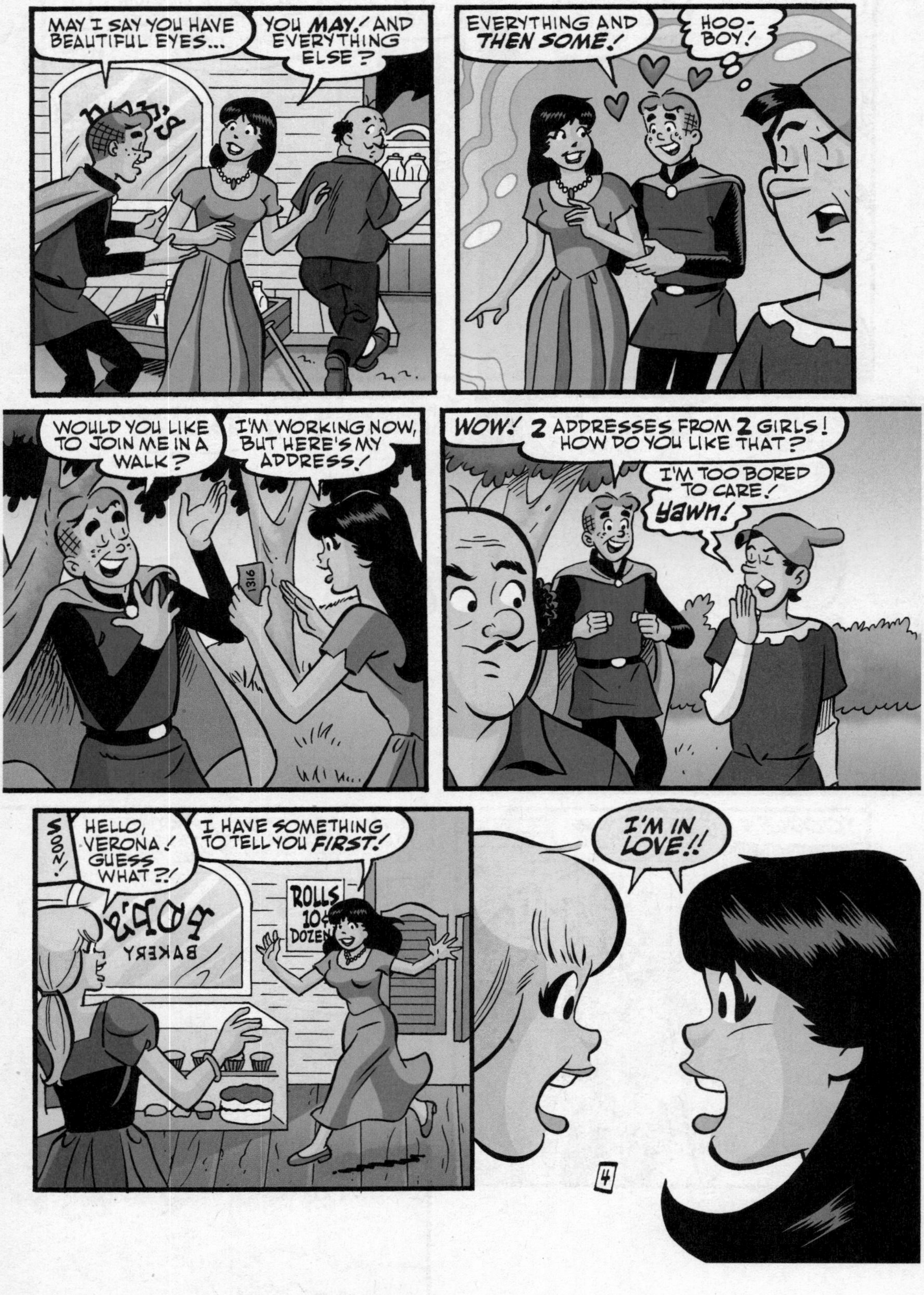
MAY I SAY YOU HAVE BEAUTIFUL EYES...
YOU MAY! AND EVERYTHING ELSE?
EVERYTHING AND THEN SOME!
HOO-BOY!
WOULD YOU LIKE TO JOIN ME IN A WALK?
I'M WORKING NOW, BUT HERE'S MY ADDRESS!
1316
WOW! 2 ADDRESSES FROM 2 GIRLS! HOW DO YOU LIKE THAT?
I'M TOO BORED TO CARE! YAWN!
SOON!
HELLO, VERONA! GUESS WHAT?!
I HAVE SOMETHING TO TELL YOU FIRST!
ROLLS 10¢ DOZEN
POP'S BAKERY
I'M IN LOVE!!
4

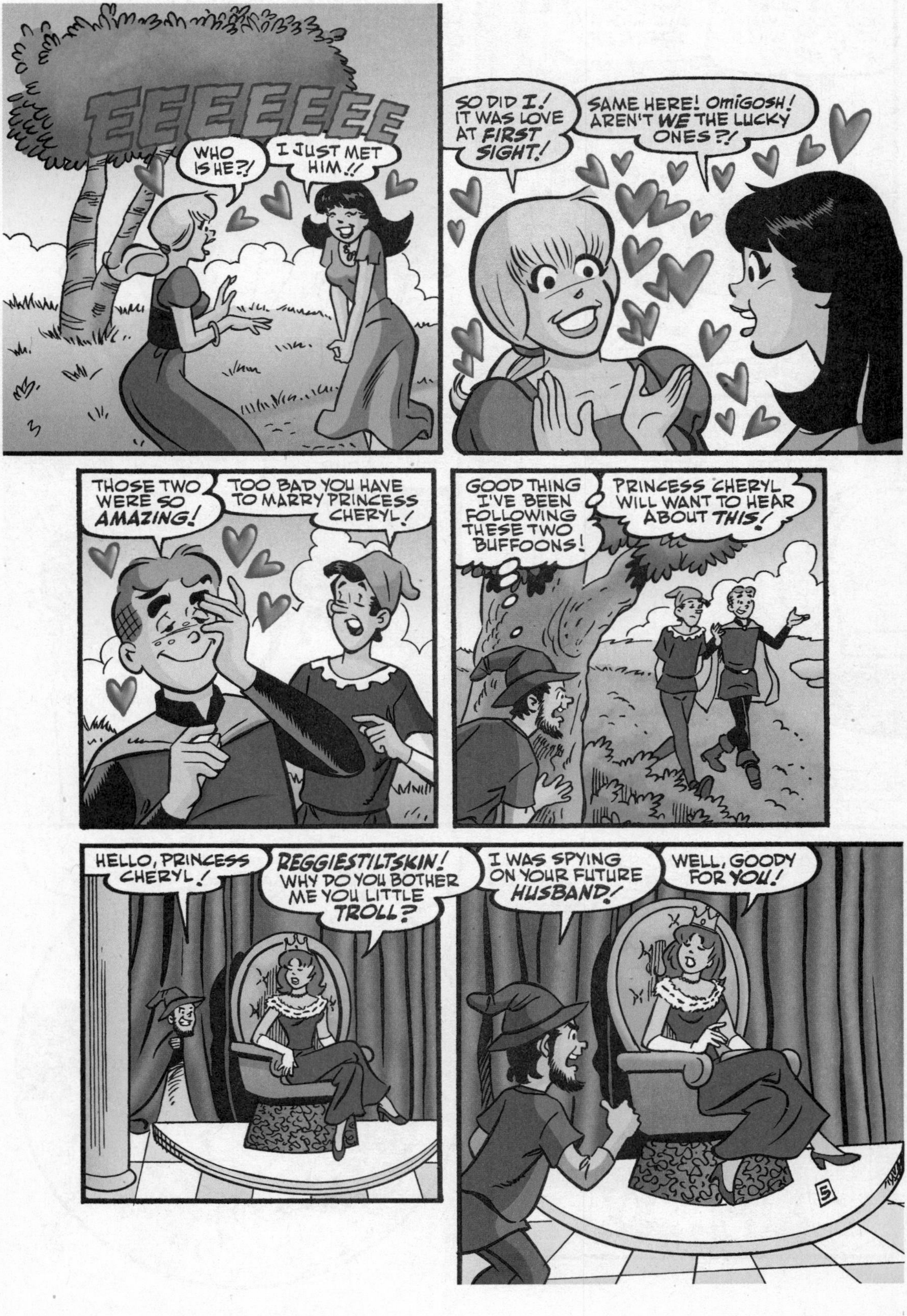
EEEEEEE
WHO IS HE?!
I JUST MET HIM!!
SO DID I! IT WAS LOVE AT FIRST SIGHT!
SAME HERE! OMIGOSH! AREN'T WE THE LUCKY ONES?!
THOSE TWO WERE SO AMAZING!
TOO BAD YOU HAVE TO MARRY PRINCESS CHERYL!
GOOD THING I'VE BEEN FOLLOWING THESE TWO BUFFOONS!
PRINCESS CHERYL WILL WANT TO HEAR ABOUT THIS!
HELLO, PRINCESS CHERYL!
REGGIESTILTSKIN! WHY DO YOU BOTHER ME YOU LITTLE TROLL?
I WAS SPYING ON YOUR FUTURE HUSBAND!
WELL, GOODY FOR YOU!
5

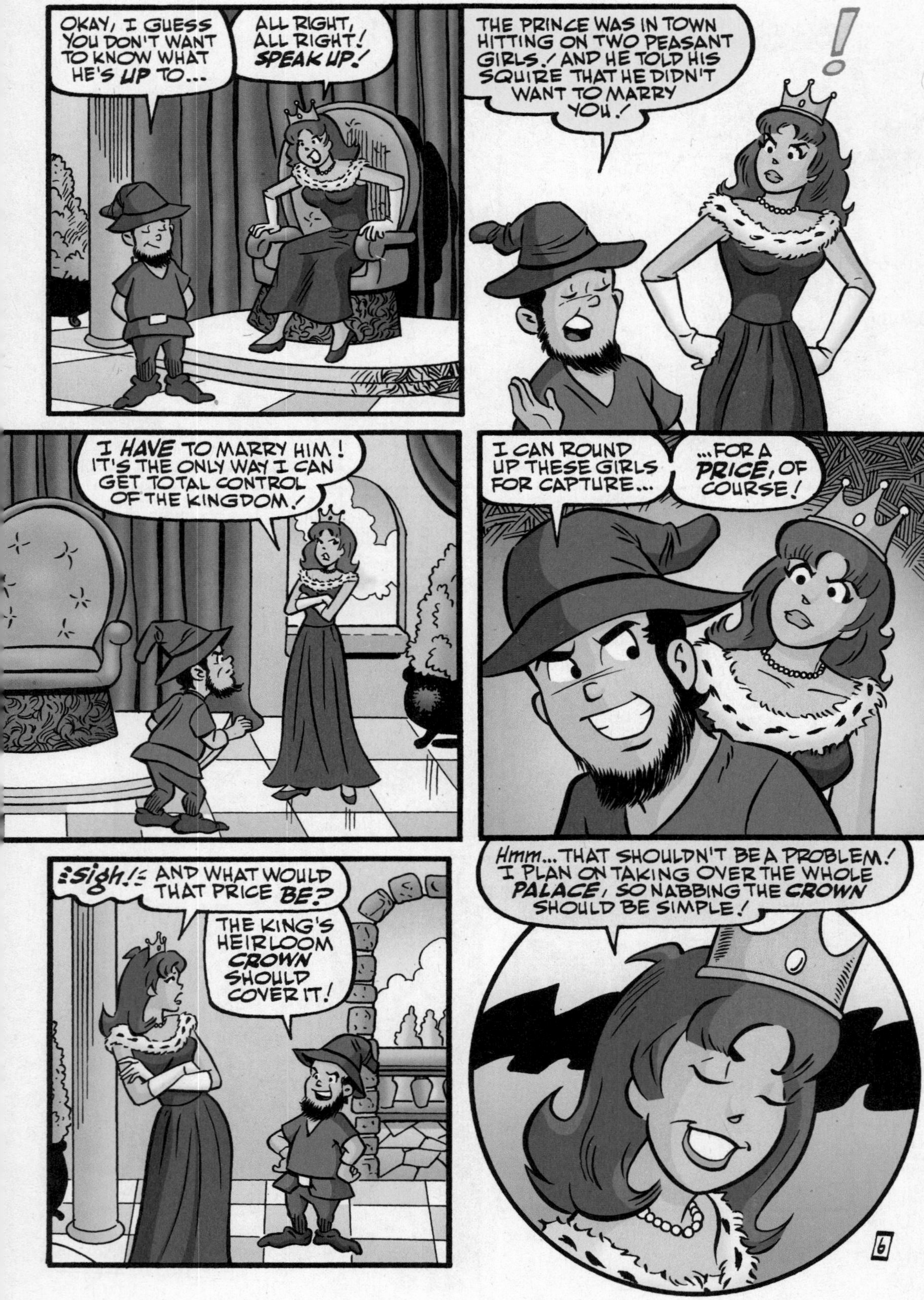
OKAY, I GUESS YOU DON'T WANT TO KNOW WHAT HE'S UP TO...
ALL RIGHT, ALL RIGHT! SPEAK UP!
THE PRINCE WAS IN TOWN HITTING ON TWO PEASANT GIRLS! AND HE TOLD HIS SQUIRE THAT HE DIDN'T WANT TO MARRY YOU!
!
I HAVE TO MARRY HIM! IT'S THE ONLY WAY I CAN GET TOTAL CONTROL OF THE KINGDOM!
I CAN ROUND UP THESE GIRLS FOR CAPTURE...
...FOR A PRICE, OF COURSE!
SIGH!
AND WHAT WOULD THAT PRICE BE?
THE KING'S HEIRLOOM CROWN SHOULD COVER IT!
Hmm... THAT SHOULDN'T BE A PROBLEM! I PLAN ON TAKING OVER THE WHOLE PALACE, SO NABBING THE CROWN SHOULD BE SIMPLE!
6

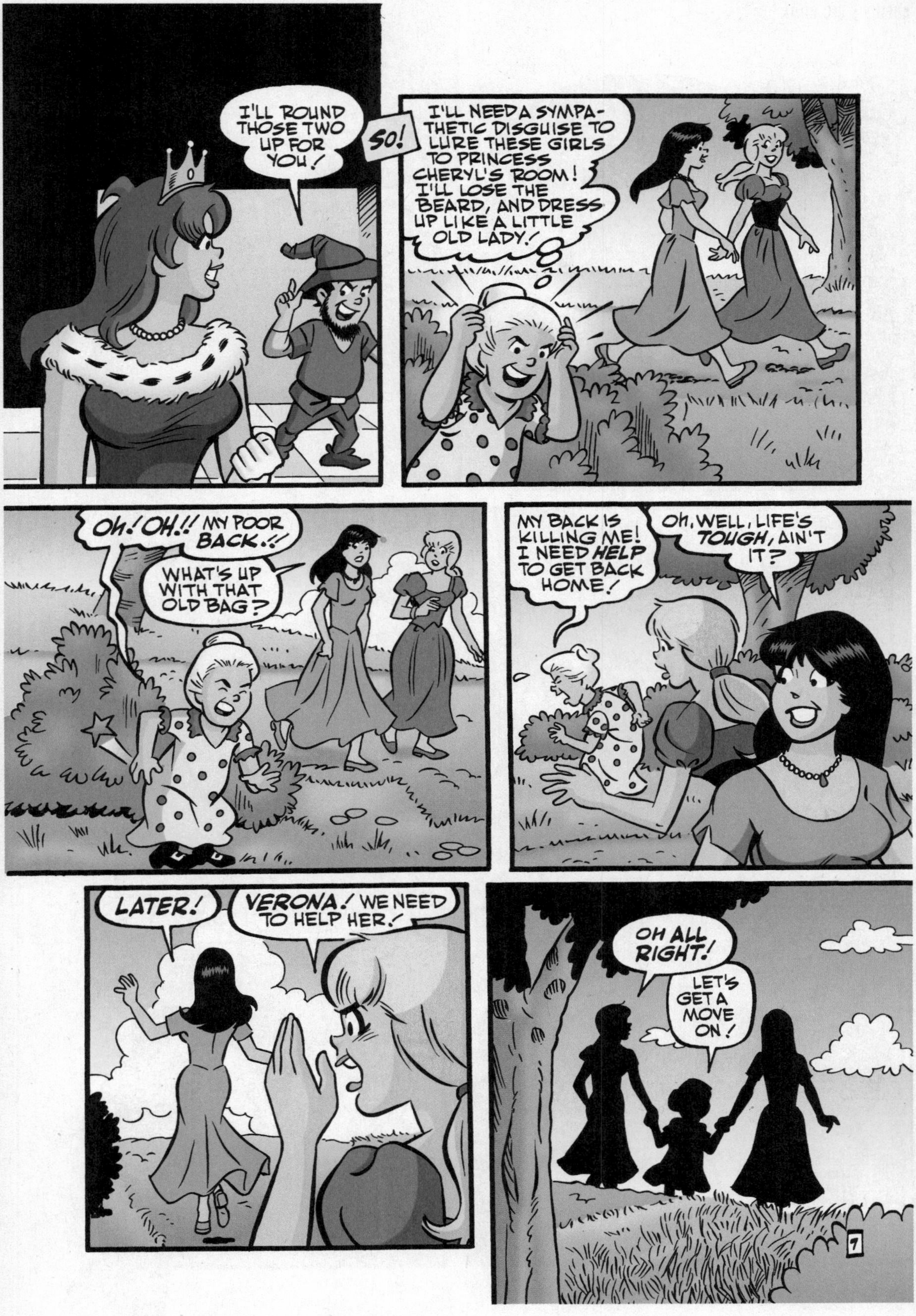
I'LL ROUND THOSE TWO UP FOR YOU!
SO!
I'LL NEED A SYMPATHETIC DISGUISE TO LURE THESE GIRLS TO PRINCESS CHERYL'S ROOM! I'LL LOSE THE BEARD, AND DRESS UP LIKE A LITTLE OLD LADY!
OH! OH!! MY POOR BACK.!!
WHAT'S UP WITH THAT OLD BAG?
MY BACK IS KILLING ME! I NEED HELP TO GET BACK HOME!
OH, WELL, LIFE'S TOUGH, AIN'T IT?
LATER!
VERONA! WE NEED TO HELP HER!
OH ALL RIGHT!
LET'S GET A MOVE ON!
7

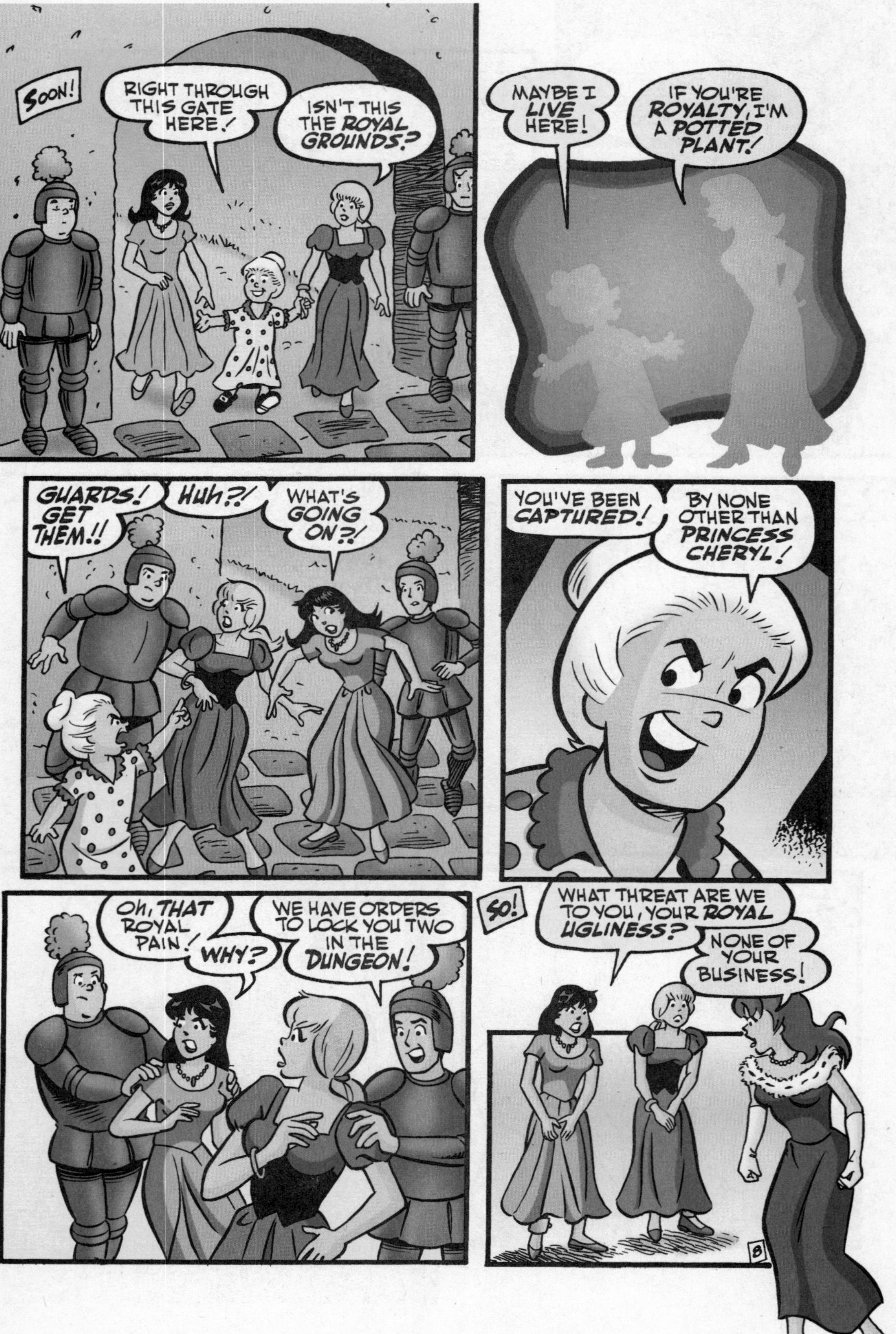
SOON!
RIGHT THROUGH THIS GATE HERE!
ISN'T THIS THE ROYAL GROUNDS?
MAYBE I LIVE HERE!
IF YOU'RE ROYALTY, I'M A POTTED PLANT!
GUARDS! GET THEM!!
HUH?!
WHAT'S GOING ON?!
YOU'VE BEEN CAPTURED!
BY NONE OTHER THAN PRINCESS CHERYL!
OH, THAT ROYAL PAIN!
WHY?
WE HAVE ORDERS TO LOCK YOU TWO IN THE DUNGEON!
SO!
WHAT THREAT ARE WE TO YOU, YOUR ROYAL UGLINESS?
NONE OF YOUR BUSINESS!
8

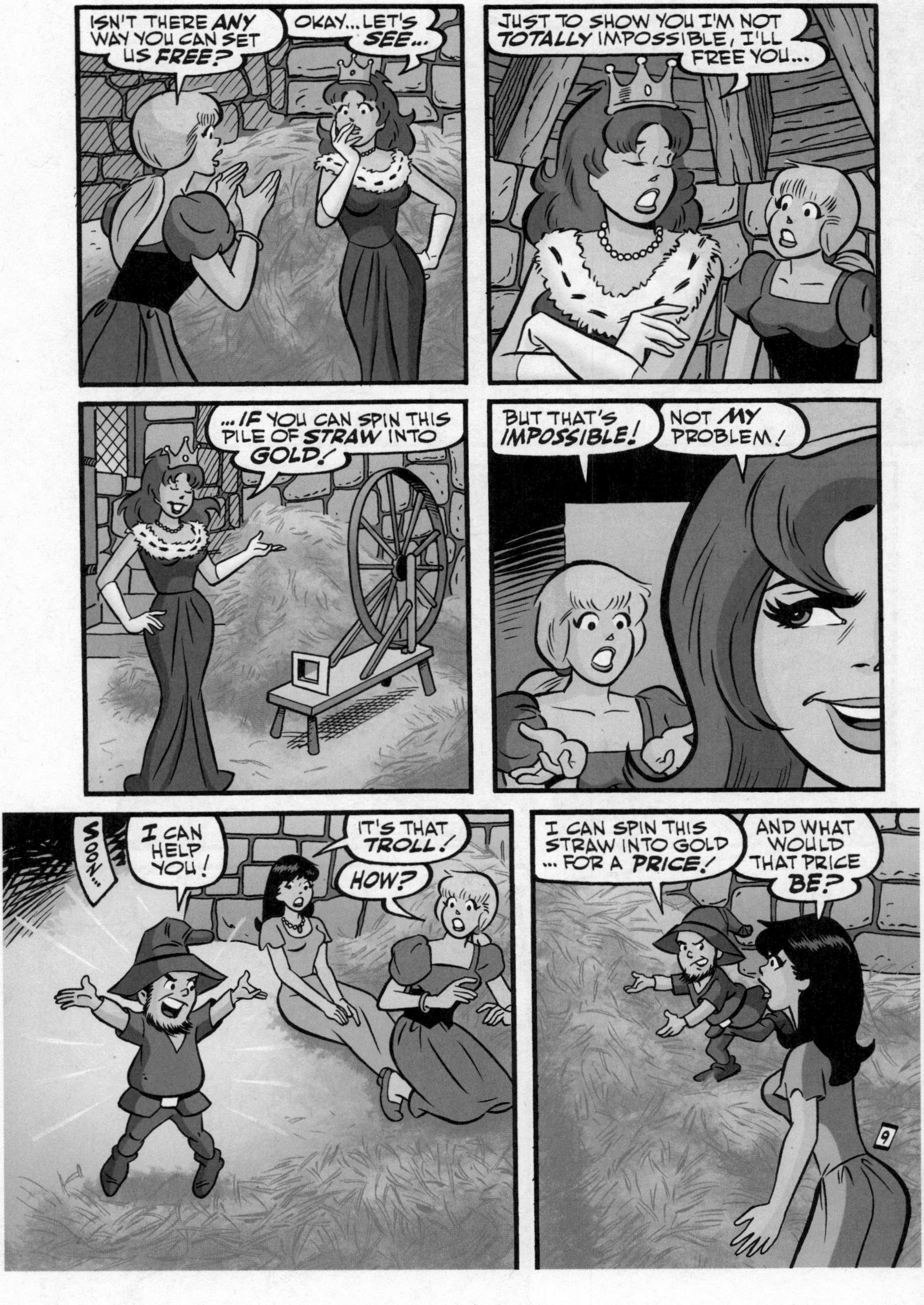
ISN'T THERE ANY WAY YOU CAN SET US FREE?
OKAY... LET'S SEE...
JUST TO SHOW YOU I'M NOT TOTALLY IMPOSSIBLE, I'LL FREE YOU...
...IF YOU CAN SPIN THIS PILE OF STRAW INTO GOLD!
BUT THAT'S IMPOSSIBLE!
NOT MY PROBLEM!
SOON...
I CAN HELP YOU!
IT'S THAT TROLL!
HOW?
I CAN SPIN THIS STRAW INTO GOLD ...FOR A PRICE!
AND WHAT WOULD THAT PRICE BE?
9

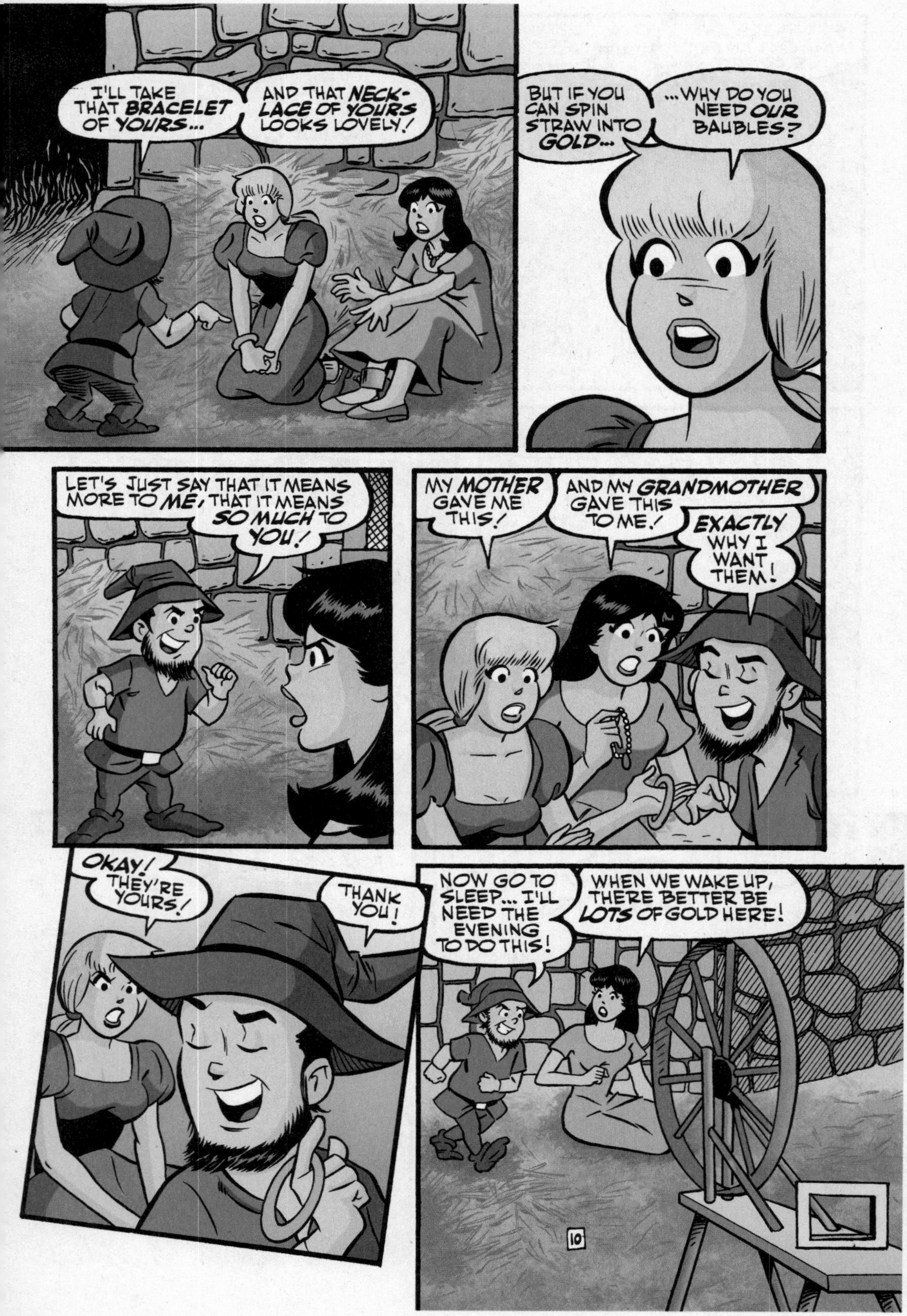
I'LL TAKE THAT BRACELET OF YOURS...
AND THAT NECKLACE OF YOURS LOOKS LOVELY!
BUT IF YOU CAN SPIN STRAW INTO GOLD...
...WHY DO YOU NEED OUR BAUBLES?
LET'S JUST SAY THAT IT MEANS MORE TO ME, THAT IT MEANS SO MUCH TO YOU!
MY MOTHER GAVE ME THIS!
AND MY GRANDMOTHER GAVE THIS TO ME!
EXACTLY WHY I WANT THEM!
OKAY! THEY'RE YOURS!
THANK YOU!
NOW GO TO SLEEP... I'LL NEED THE EVENING TO DO THIS!
WHEN WE WAKE UP, THERE BETTER BE LOTS OF GOLD HERE!
10

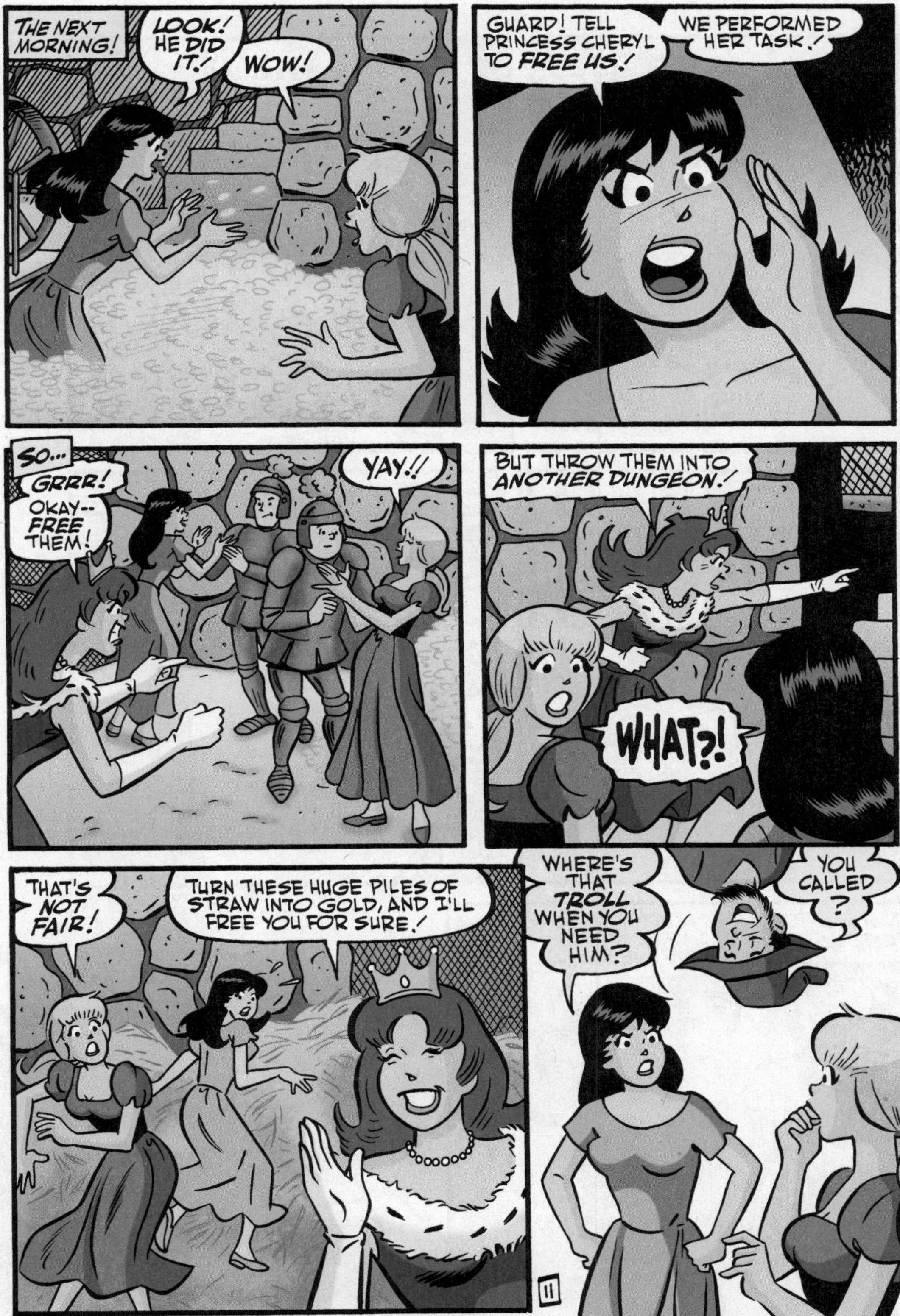
THE NEXT MORNING!
LOOK! HE DID IT!
WOW!
GUARD! TELL PRINCESS CHERYL TO FREE US!
WE PERFORMED HER TASK!
SO...
GRRR!
OKAY-- FREE THEM!
YAY!!
BUT THROW THEM INTO ANOTHER DUNGEON!
WHAT?!
THAT'S NOT FAIR!
TURN THESE HUGE PILES OF STRAW INTO GOLD, AND I'LL FREE YOU FOR SURE!
WHERE'S THAT TROLL WHEN YOU NEED HIM?
YOU CALLED?
11

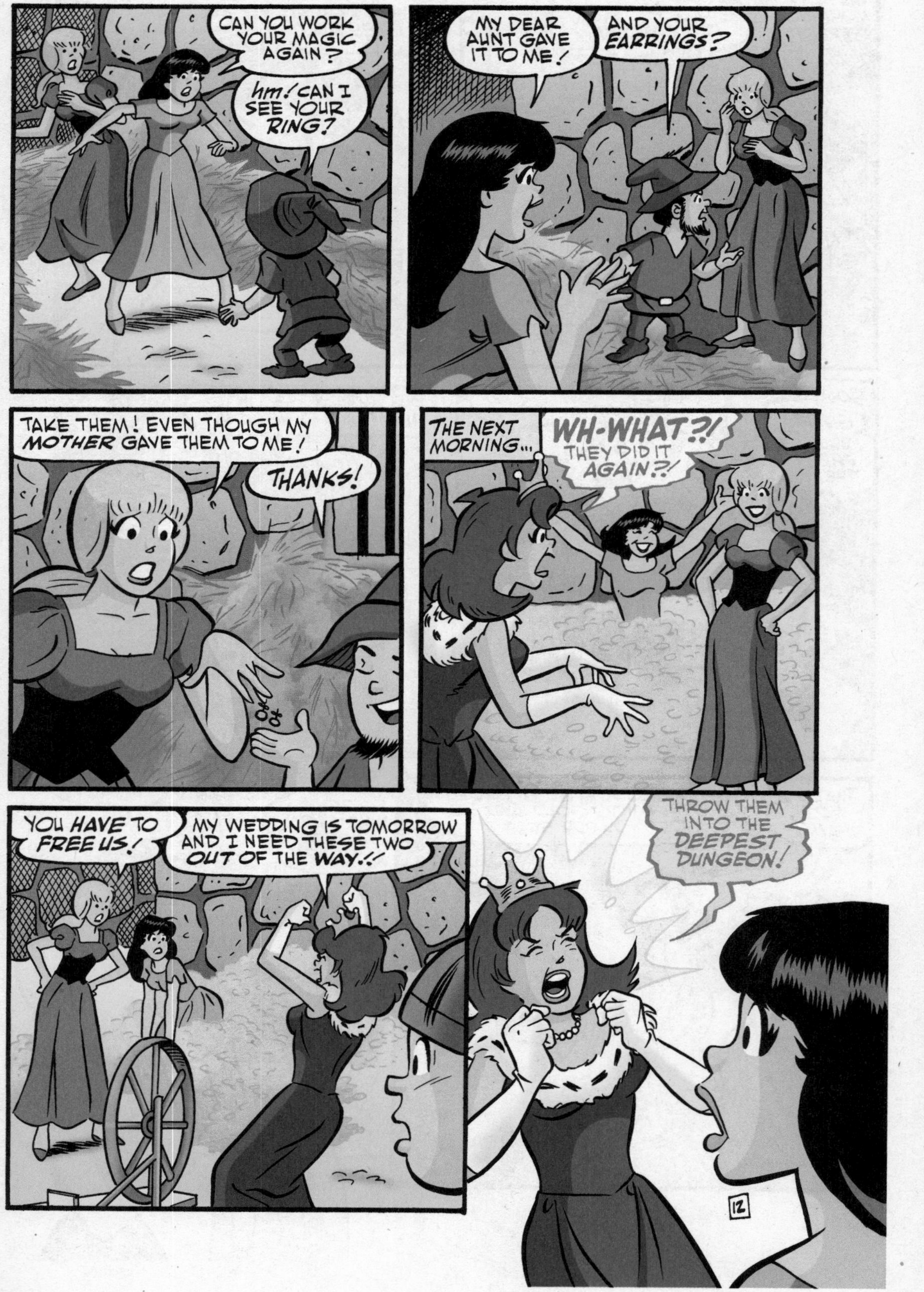
CAN YOU WORK YOUR MAGIC AGAIN?
hm! CAN I SEE YOUR RING?
MY DEAR AUNT GAVE IT TO ME!
AND YOUR EARRINGS?
TAKE THEM! EVEN THOUGH MY MOTHER GAVE THEM TO ME!
THANKS!
THE NEXT MORNING...
WH-WHAT?! THEY DID IT AGAIN?!
YOU HAVE TO FREE US!
MY WEDDING IS TOMORROW AND I NEED THESE TWO OUT OF THE WAY.!!
THROW THEM INTO THE DEEPEST DUNGEON!
12

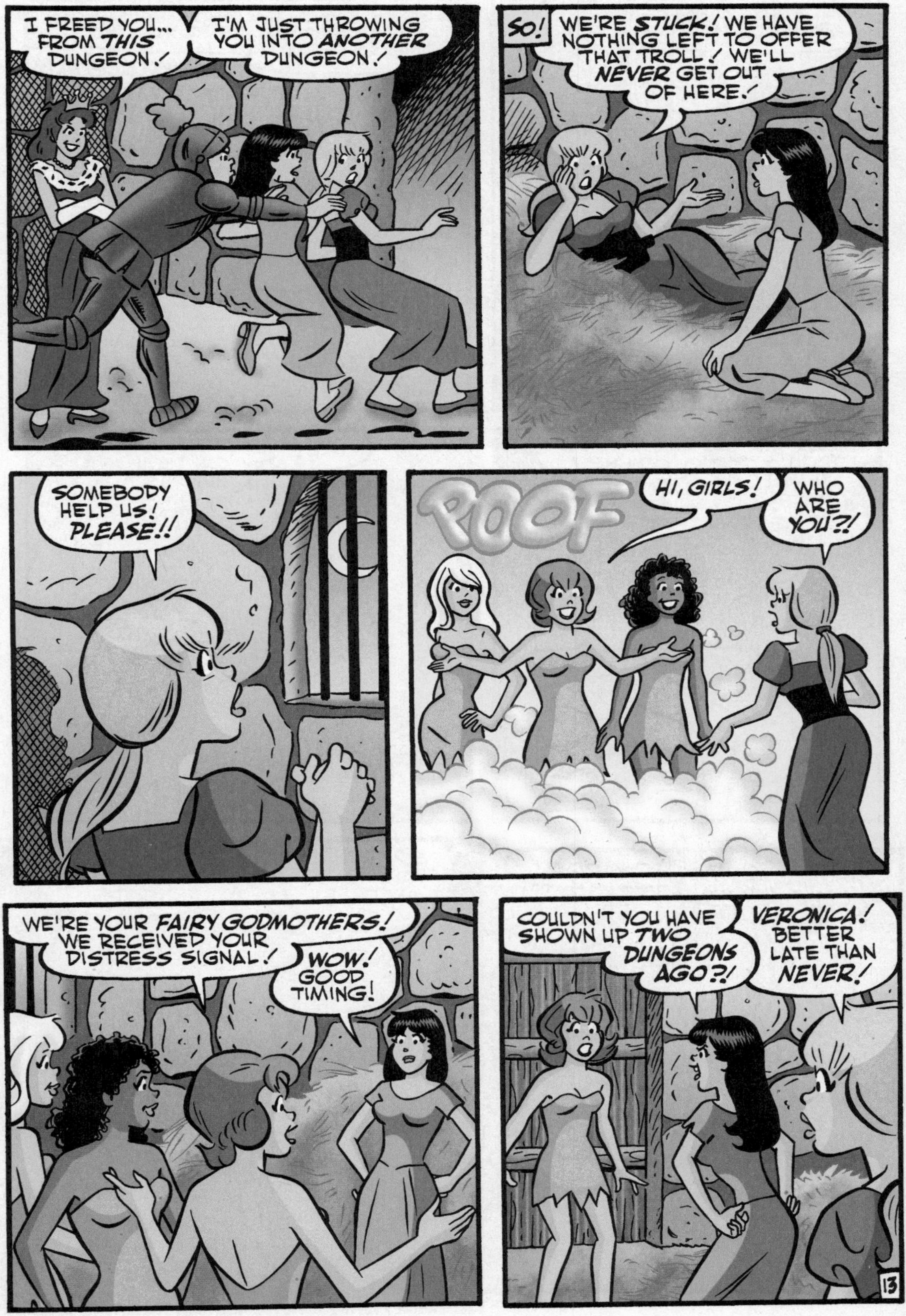
I FREED YOU... FROM THIS DUNGEON!
I'M JUST THROWING YOU INTO ANOTHER DUNGEON!
SO!
WE'RE STUCK! WE HAVE NOTHING LEFT TO OFFER THAT TROLL! WE'LL NEVER GET OUT OF HERE!
SOMEBODY HELP US! PLEASE!!
POOF
HI, GIRLS!
WHO ARE YOU?!
WE'RE YOUR FAIRY GODMOTHERS! WE RECEIVED YOUR DISTRESS SIGNAL!
WOW! GOOD TIMING!
COULDN'T YOU HAVE SHOWN UP TWO DUNGEONS AGO?!
VERONICA! BETTER LATE THAN NEVER!
13

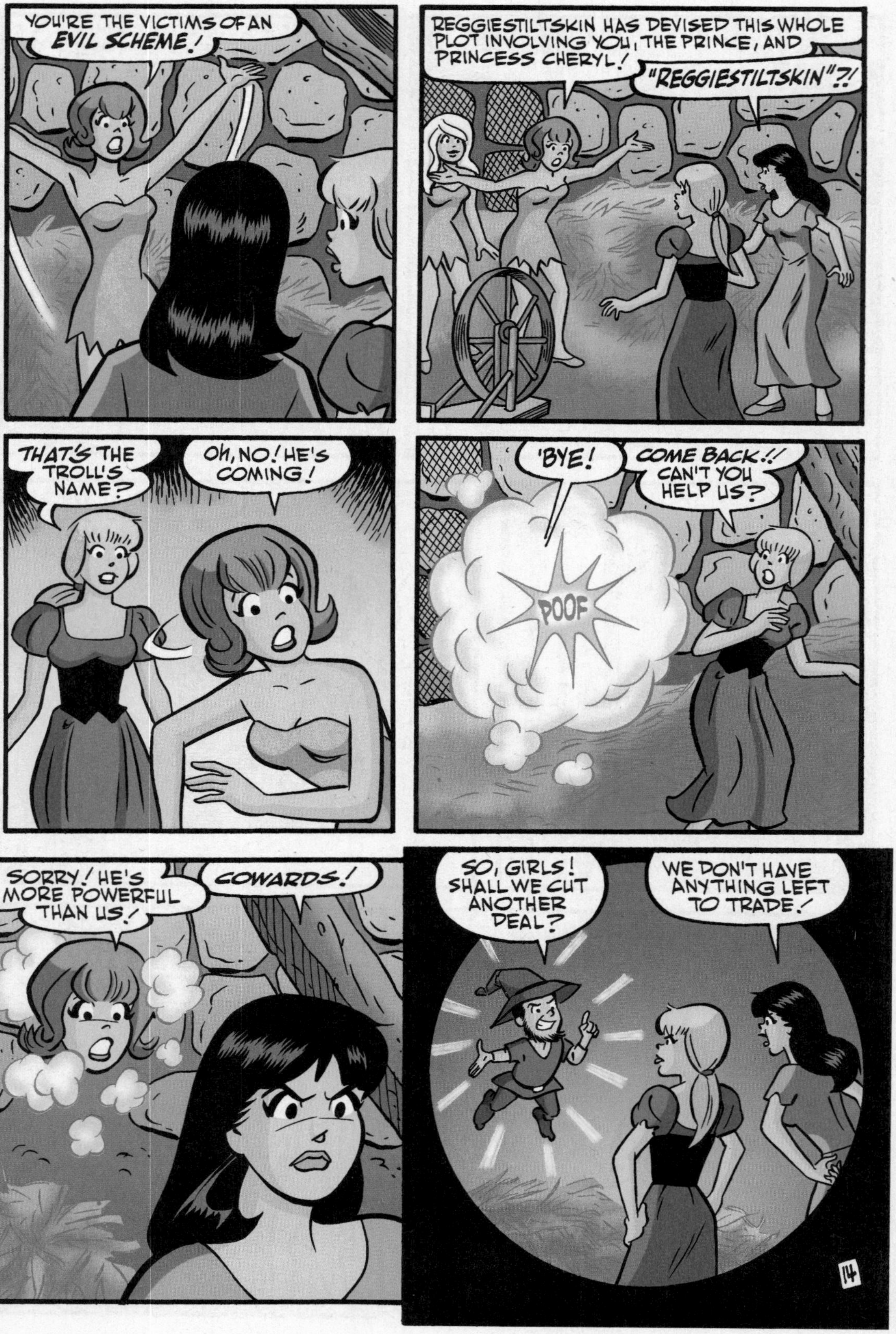
YOU'RE THE VICTIMS OF AN EVIL SCHEME!
REGGIESTILTSKIN HAS DEVISED THIS WHOLE PLOT INVOLVING YOU, THE PRINCE, AND PRINCESS CHERYL!
"REGGIESTILTSKIN"?!
THAT'S THE TROLL'S NAME?
OH, NO! HE'S COMING!
'BYE!
COME BACK!! CAN'T YOU HELP US?
POOF
SORRY! HE'S MORE POWERFUL THAN US!
COWARDS!
SO, GIRLS! SHALL WE CUT ANOTHER DEAL?
WE DON'T HAVE ANYTHING LEFT TO TRADE!
14

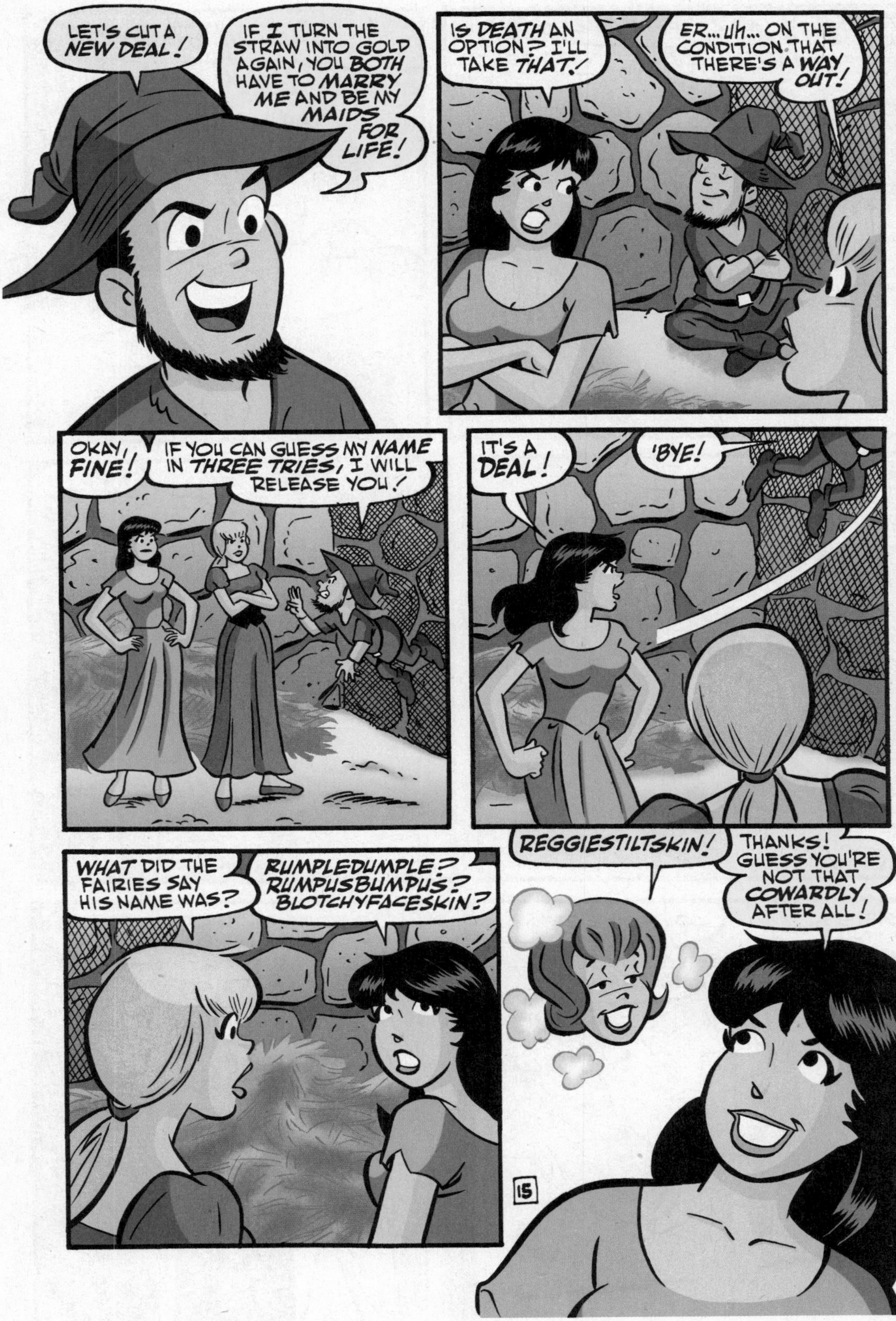

LET'S CUT A NEW DEAL!
IF I TURN THE STRAW INTO GOLD AGAIN, YOU BOTH HAVE TO MARRY ME AND BE MY MAIDS FOR LIFE!
IS DEATH AN OPTION? I'LL TAKE THAT!
ER... UH... ON THE CONDITION THAT THERE'S A WAY OUT!
OKAY, FINE!
IF YOU CAN GUESS MY NAME IN THREE TRIES, I WILL RELEASE YOU!
IT'S A DEAL!
'BYE!
WHAT DID THE FAIRIES SAY HIS NAME WAS?
RUMPLEDUMPLE? RUMPUSBUMPUS? BLOTCHYFACESKIN?
REGGIESTILTSKIN!
THANKS! GUESS YOU'RE NOT THAT COWARDLY AFTER ALL!
15

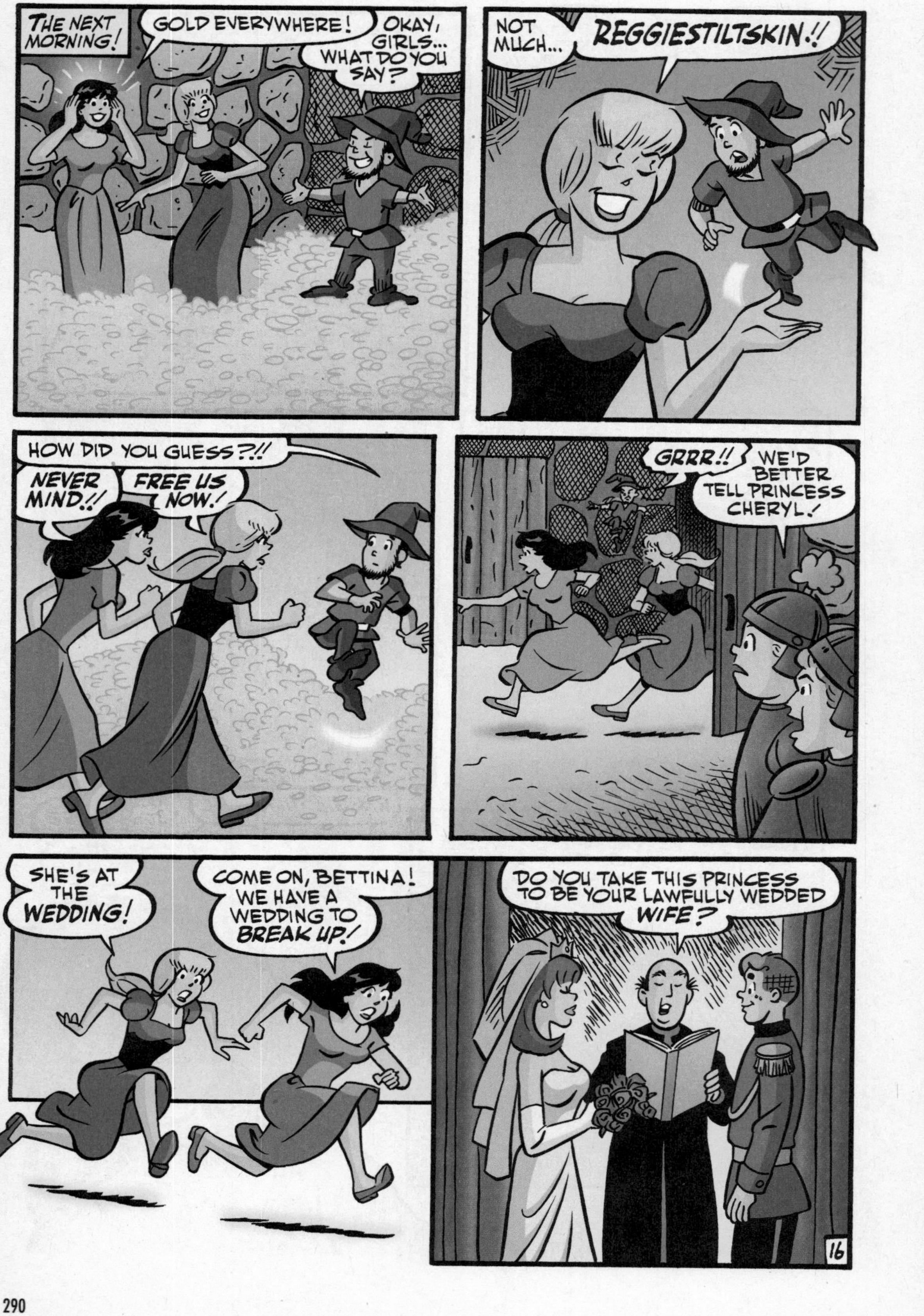
THE NEXT MORNING!
GOLD EVERYWHERE!
OKAY, GIRLS... WHAT DO YOU SAY?
NOT MUCH...
REGGIESTILTSKIN!!
HOW DID YOU GUESS?!!
NEVER MIND!!
FREE US NOW!
GRRR!!
WE'D BETTER TELL PRINCESS CHERYL!
SHE'S AT THE WEDDING!
COME ON, BETTINA! WE HAVE A WEDDING TO BREAK UP!
DO YOU TAKE THIS PRINCESS TO BE YOUR LAWFULLY WEDDED WIFE?
16

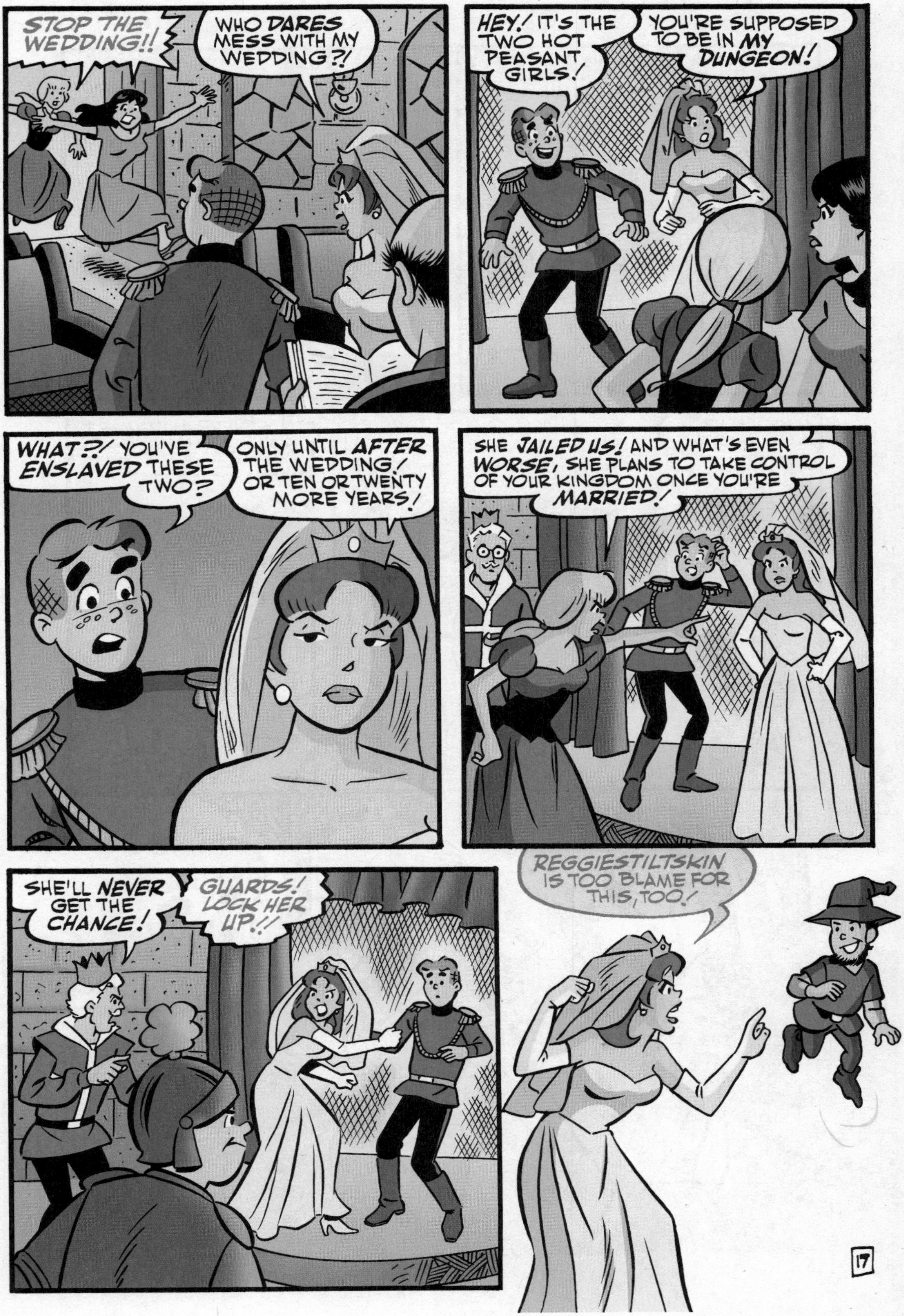
STOP THE WEDDING!!
WHO DARES MESS WITH MY WEDDING?!
HEY! IT'S THE TWO HOT PEASANT GIRLS!
YOU'RE SUPPOSED TO BE IN MY DUNGEON!
WHAT?! YOU'VE ENSLAVED THESE TWO?
ONLY UNTIL AFTER THE WEDDING! OR TEN OR TWENTY MORE YEARS!
SHE JAILED US! AND WHAT'S EVEN WORSE, SHE PLANS TO TAKE CONTROL OF YOUR KINGDOM ONCE YOU'RE MARRIED!
SHE'LL NEVER GET THE CHANCE!
GUARDS! LOCK HER UP!!
REGGIESTILTSKIN IS TOO BLAME FOR THIS, TOO!
17

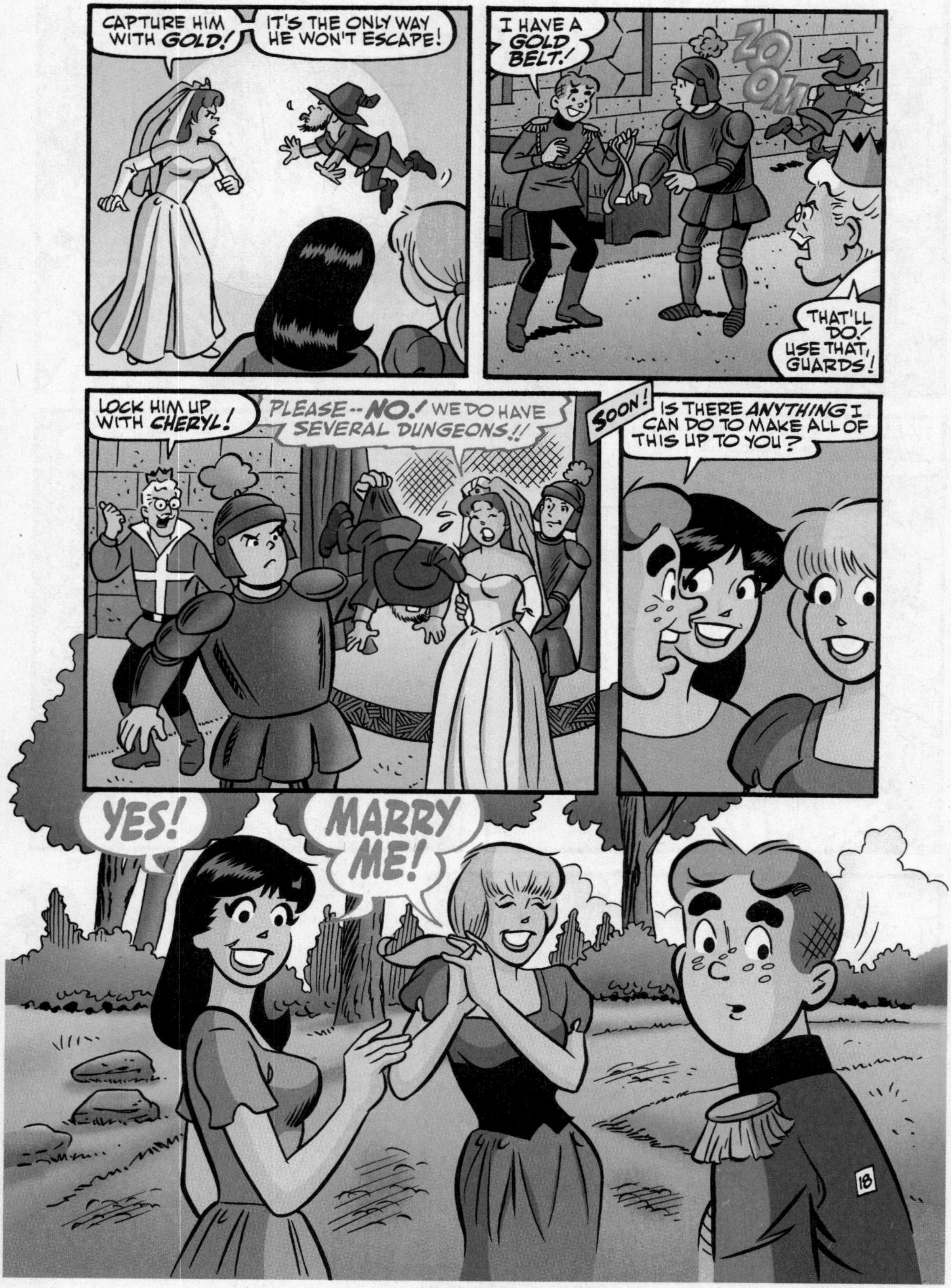
CAPTURE HIM WITH GOLD!
IT'S THE ONLY WAY HE WON'T ESCAPE!
I HAVE A GOLD BELT!
ZOOM
THAT'LL DO! USE THAT, GUARDS!
LOCK HIM UP WITH CHERYL!
PLEASE--NO! WE DO HAVE SEVERAL DUNGEONS!!
SOON!
IS THERE ANYTHING I CAN DO TO MAKE ALL OF THIS UP TO YOU?
YES!
MARRY ME!
18

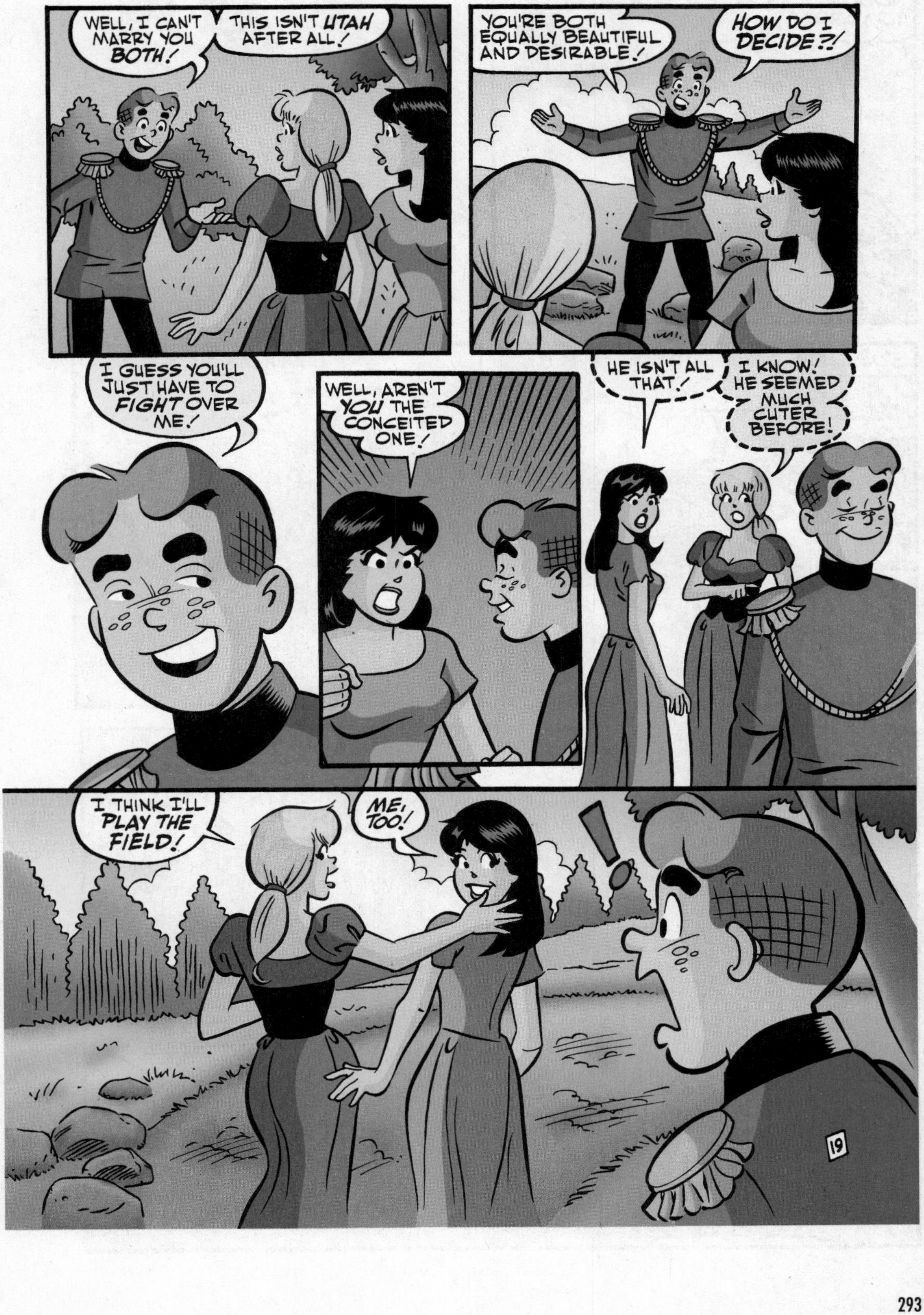
WELL, I CAN'T MARRY YOU BOTH!
THIS ISN'T UTAH AFTER ALL!
YOU'RE BOTH EQUALLY BEAUTIFUL AND DESIRABLE!
HOW DO I DECIDE?!
I GUESS YOU'LL JUST HAVE TO FIGHT OVER ME!
WELL, AREN'T YOU THE CONCEITED ONE!
HE ISN'T ALL THAT!
I KNOW! HE SEEMED MUCH CUTER BEFORE!
I THINK I'LL PLAY THE FIELD!
ME, TOO!
!
19

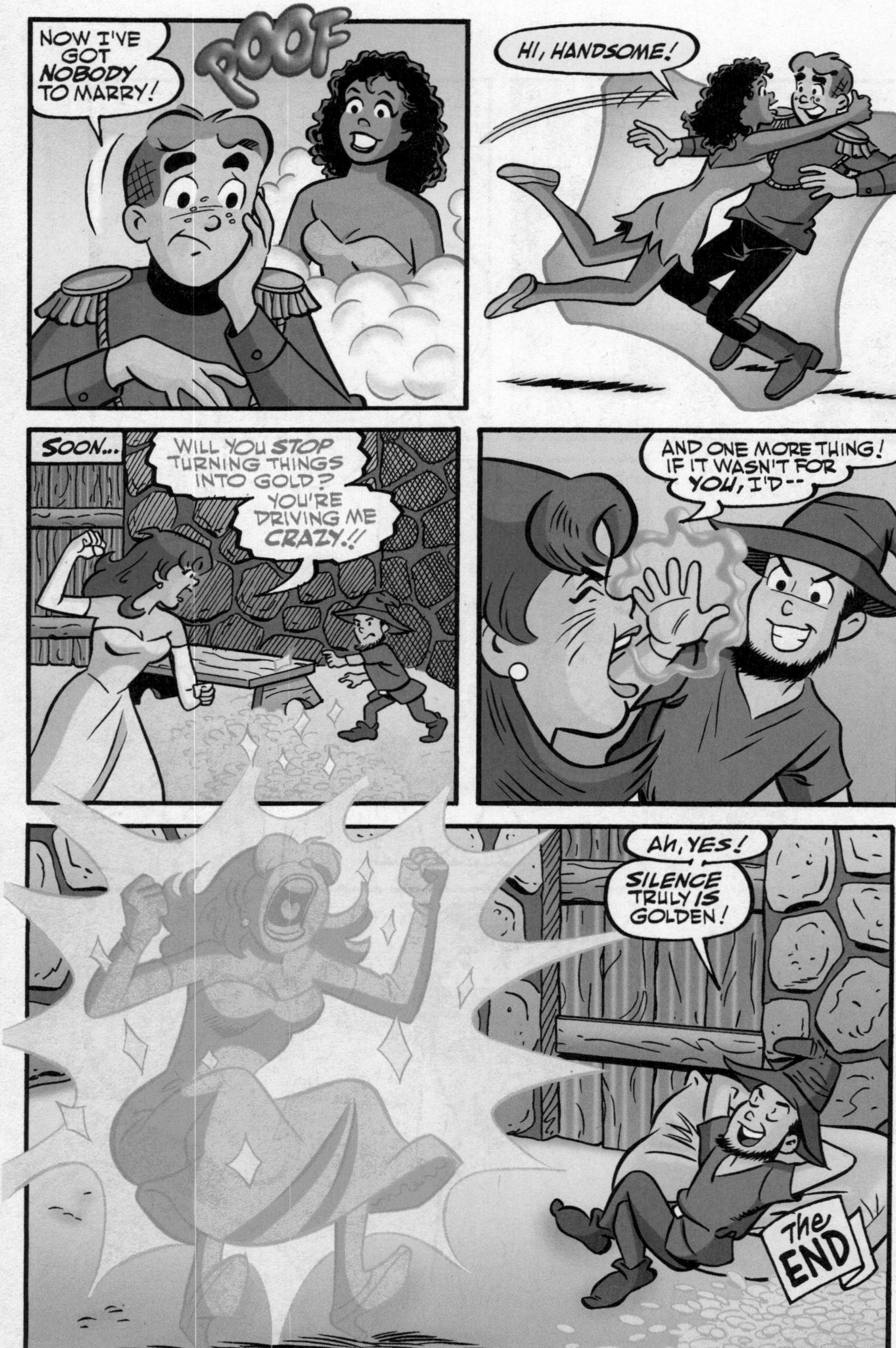
NOW I'VE GOT NOBODY TO MARRY!
POOF
HI, HANDSOME!
SOON...
WILL YOU STOP TURNING THINGS INTO GOLD? YOU'RE DRIVING ME CRAZY!!
AND ONE MORE THING! IF IT WASN'T FOR YOU, I'D--
AH, YES!
SILENCE TRULY IS GOLDEN!
THE END

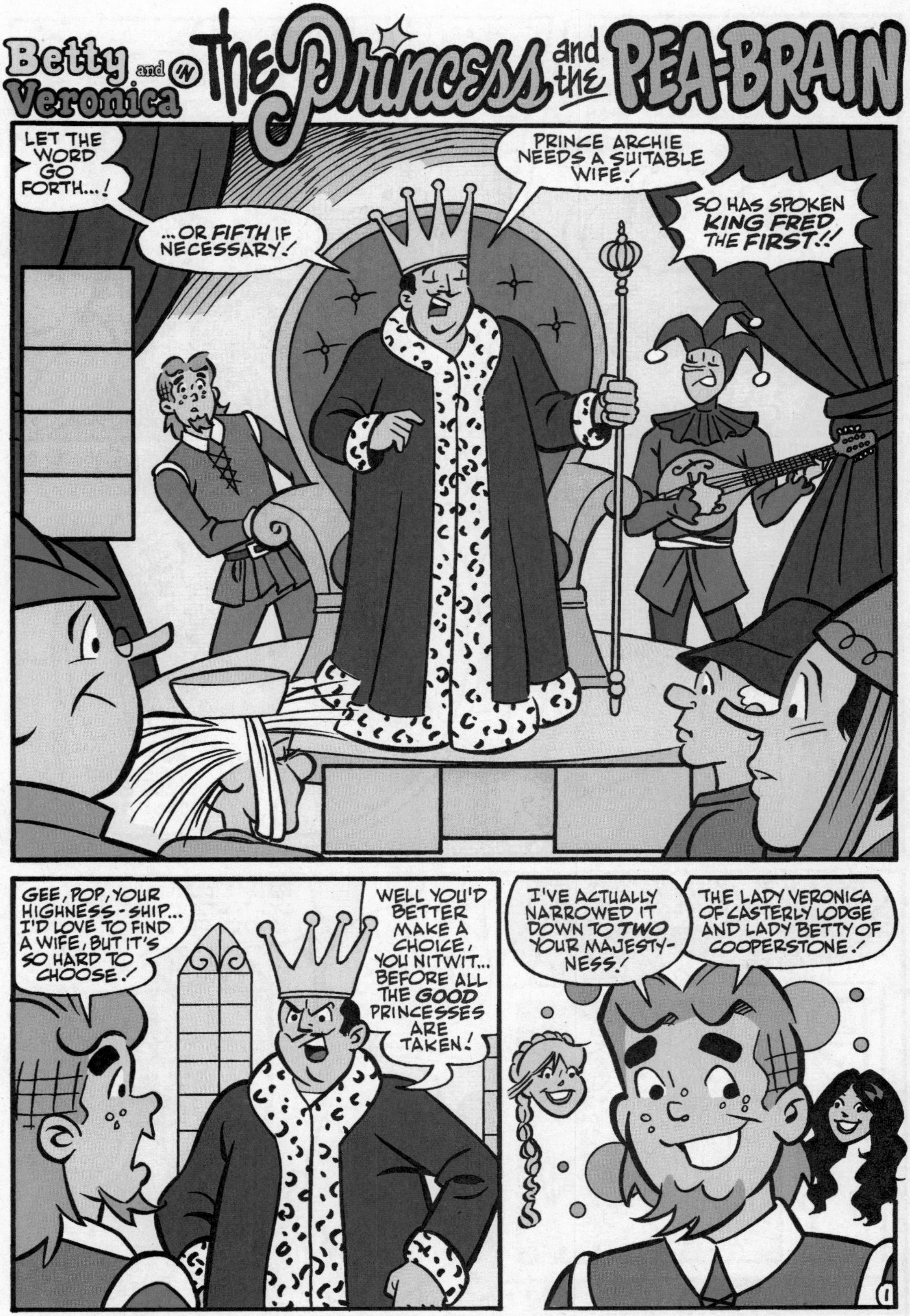
Betty and Veronica in The Princess and the PEA-BRAIN
LET THE WORD GO FORTH...!
...OR FIFTH IF NECESSARY!
PRINCE ARCHIE NEEDS A SUITABLE WIFE!
SO HAS SPOKEN KING FRED THE FIRST!!
GEE, POP, YOUR HIGHNESS-SHIP... I'D LOVE TO FIND A WIFE, BUT IT'S SO HARD TO CHOOSE!
WELL YOU'D BETTER MAKE A CHOICE, YOU NITWIT... BEFORE ALL THE GOOD PRINCESSES ARE TAKEN!
I'VE ACTUALLY NARROWED IT DOWN TO TWO YOUR MAJESTY-NESS!
THE LADY VERONICA OF CASTERLY LODGE AND LADY BETTY OF COOPERSTONE!
1

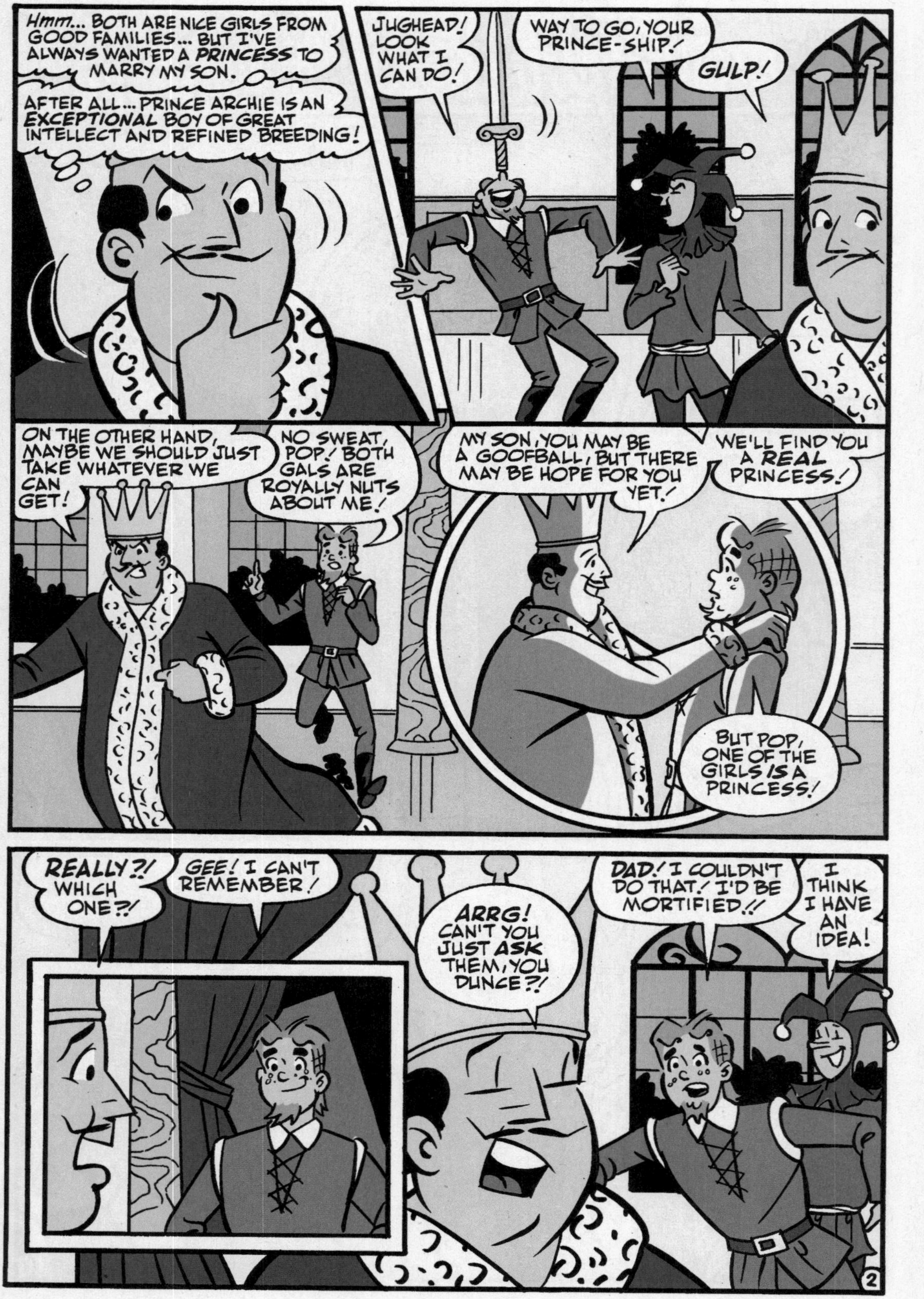
Hmm... BOTH ARE NICE GIRLS FROM GOOD FAMILIES... BUT I'VE ALWAYS WANTED A PRINCESS TO MARRY MY SON.
AFTER ALL... PRINCE ARCHIE IS AN EXCEPTIONAL BOY OF GREAT INTELLECT AND REFINED BREEDING!
JUGHEAD! LOOK WHAT I CAN DO!
WAY TO GO, YOUR PRINCE-SHIP!
GULP!
ON THE OTHER HAND, MAYBE WE SHOULD JUST TAKE WHATEVER WE CAN GET!
NO SWEAT, POP! BOTH GALS ARE ROYALLY NUTS ABOUT ME!
MY SON, YOU MAY BE A GOOFBALL, BUT THERE MAY BE HOPE FOR YOU YET!
WE'LL FIND YOU A REAL PRINCESS!
BUT POP, ONE OF THE GIRLS IS A PRINCESS!
REALLY?! WHICH ONE?!
GEE! I CAN'T REMEMBER!
ARRG! CAN'T YOU JUST ASK THEM, YOU DUNCE?!
DAD! I COULDN'T DO THAT! I'D BE MORTIFIED!!
I THINK I HAVE AN IDEA!
2

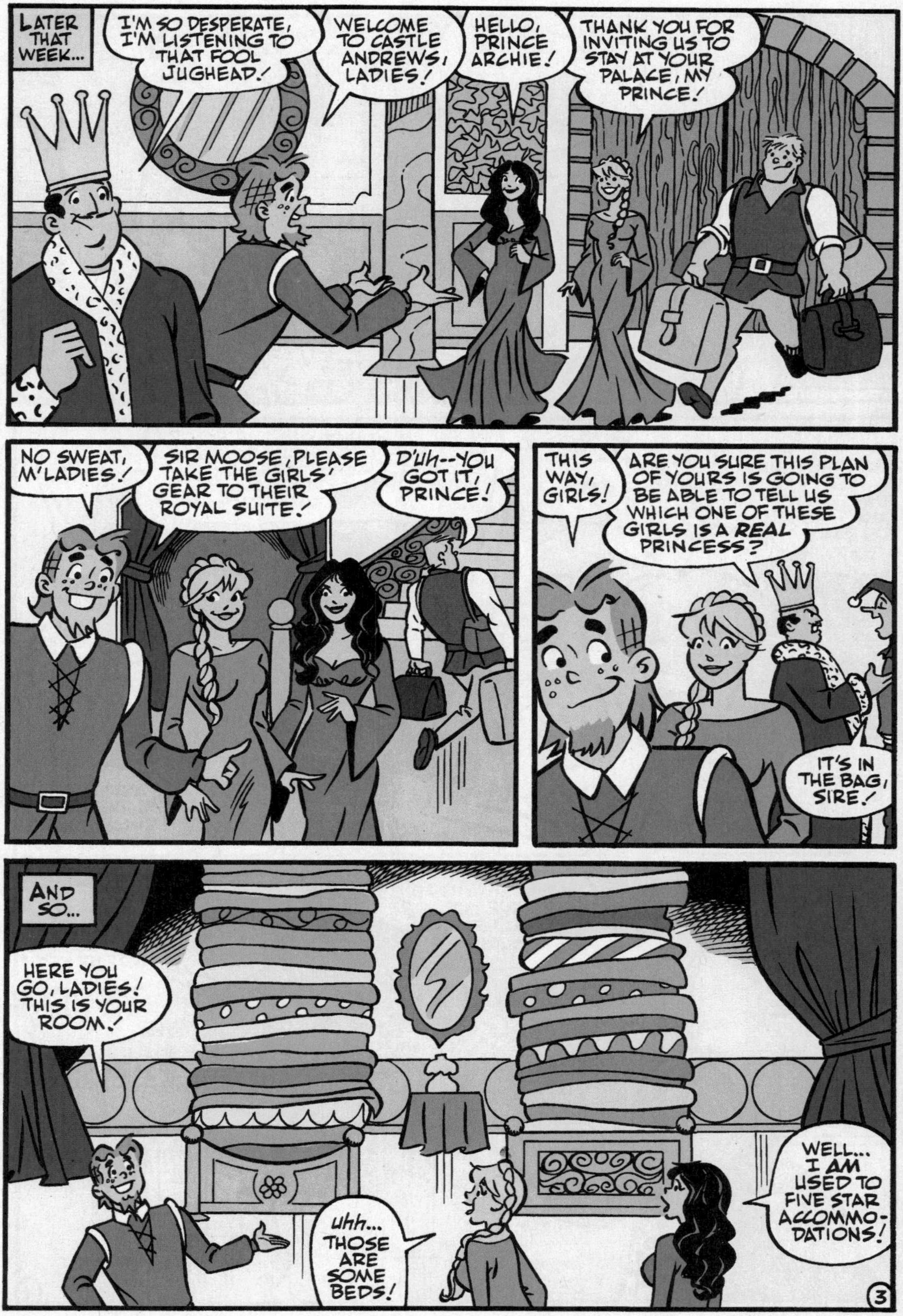
LATER THAT WEEK...
I'M SO DESPERATE, I'M LISTENING TO THAT FOOL JUGHEAD!
WELCOME TO CASTLE ANDREWS, LADIES!
HELLO, PRINCE ARCHIE!
THANK YOU FOR INVITING US TO STAY AT YOUR PALACE, MY PRINCE!
NO SWEAT, M'LADIES!
SIR MOOSE, PLEASE TAKE THE GIRLS' GEAR TO THEIR ROYAL SUITE!
D'UH--YOU GOT IT, PRINCE!
THIS WAY, GIRLS!
ARE YOU SURE THIS PLAN OF YOURS IS GOING TO BE ABLE TO TELL US WHICH ONE OF THESE GIRLS IS A REAL PRINCESS?
IT'S IN THE BAG, SIRE!
AND SO...
HERE YOU GO, LADIES! THIS IS YOUR ROOM!
UHH... THOSE ARE SOME BEDS!
WELL... I AM USED TO FIVE STAR ACCOMMO-DATIONS!
3

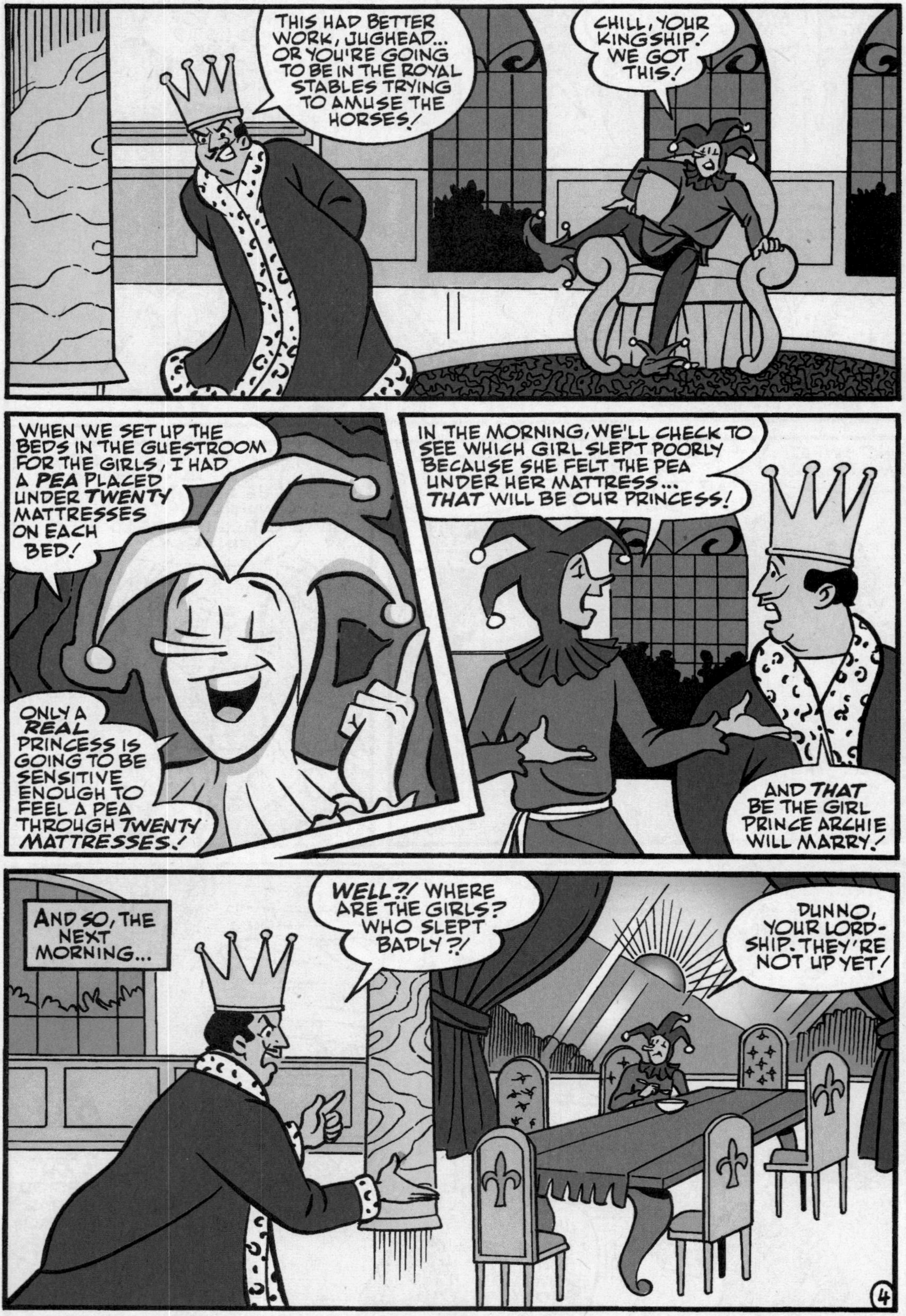
THIS HAD BETTER WORK, JUGHEAD... OR YOU'RE GOING TO BE IN THE ROYAL STABLES TRYING TO AMUSE THE HORSES!
CHILL, YOUR KINGSHIP! WE GOT THIS!
WHEN WE SET UP THE BEDS IN THE GUESTROOM FOR THE GIRLS, I HAD A PEA PLACED UNDER TWENTY MATTRESSES ON EACH BED!
ONLY A REAL PRINCESS IS GOING TO BE SENSITIVE ENOUGH TO FEEL A PEA THROUGH TWENTY MATTRESSES!
IN THE MORNING, WE'LL CHECK TO SEE WHICH GIRL SLEPT POORLY BECAUSE SHE FELT THE PEA UNDER HER MATTRESS... THAT WILL BE OUR PRINCESS!
AND THAT BE THE GIRL PRINCE ARCHIE WILL MARRY!
AND SO, THE NEXT MORNING...
WELL?! WHERE ARE THE GIRLS? WHO SLEPT BADLY?!
DUNNO, YOUR LORD-SHIP. THEY'RE NOT UP YET!
4

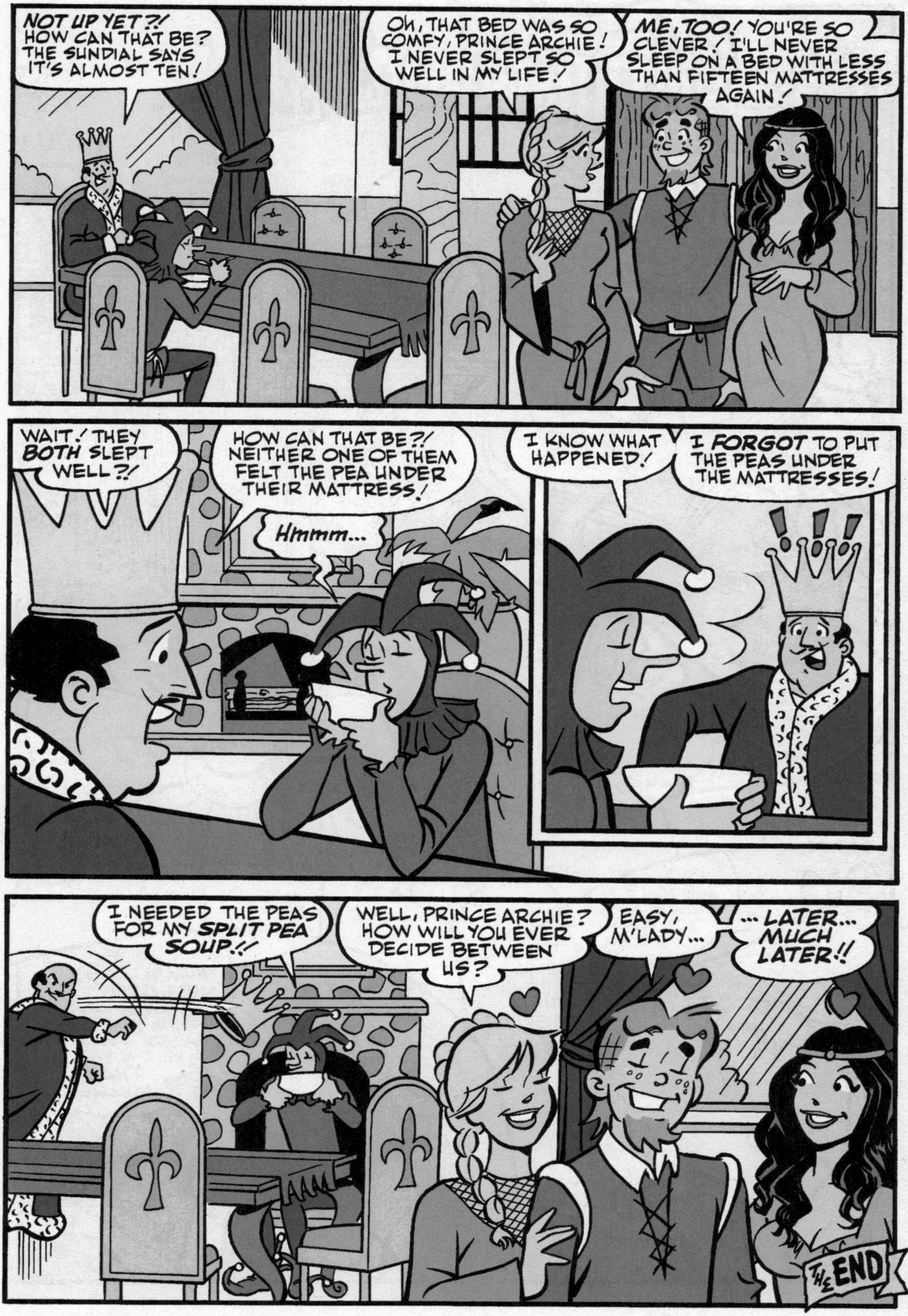
NOT UP YET?! HOW CAN THAT BE? THE SUNDIAL SAYS IT'S ALMOST TEN!
OH, THAT BED WAS SO COMFY, PRINCE ARCHIE! I NEVER SLEPT SO WELL IN MY LIFE!
ME, TOO! YOU'RE SO CLEVER! I'LL NEVER SLEEP ON A BED WITH LESS THAN FIFTEEN MATTRESSES AGAIN!
WAIT! THEY BOTH SLEPT WELL?!
HOW CAN THAT BE?! NEITHER ONE OF THEM FELT THE PEA UNDER THEIR MATTRESS!
Hmmm...
I KNOW WHAT HAPPENED!
I FORGOT TO PUT THE PEAS UNDER THE MATTRESSES!
!!!
I NEEDED THE PEAS FOR MY SPLIT PEA SOUP!!
WELL, PRINCE ARCHIE? HOW WILL YOU EVER DECIDE BETWEEN US?
EASY, M'LADY...
...LATER... MUCH LATER!!
THE END

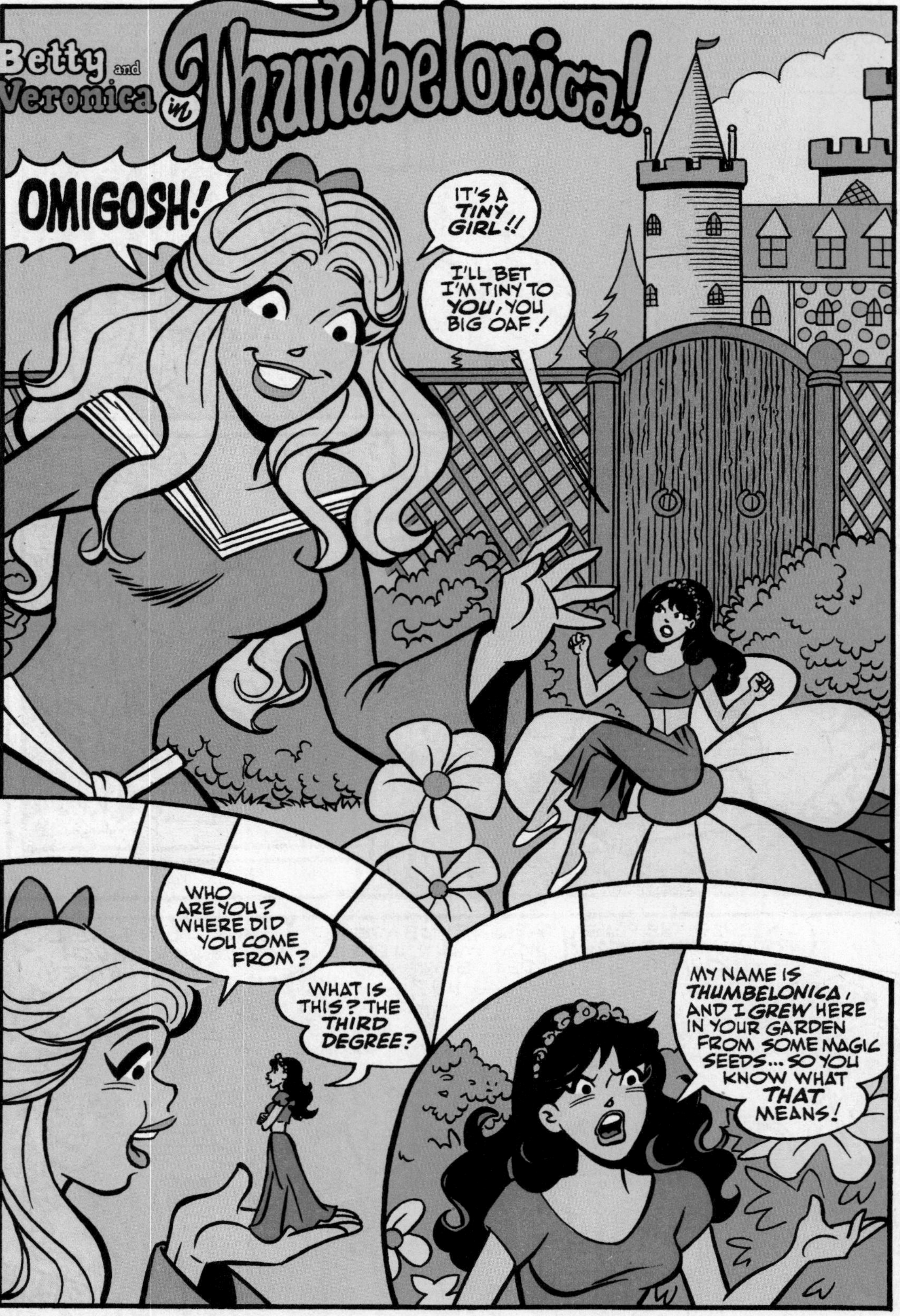
Betty and Veronica in Thumbelonica!
OMIGOSH!
IT'S A TINY GIRL!!
I'LL BET I'M TINY TO YOU, YOU BIG OAF!
WHO ARE YOU? WHERE DID YOU COME FROM?
WHAT IS THIS? THE THIRD DEGREE?
MY NAME IS THUMBELONICA, AND I GREW HERE IN YOUR GARDEN FROM SOME MAGIC SEEDS... SO YOU KNOW WHAT THAT MEANS!

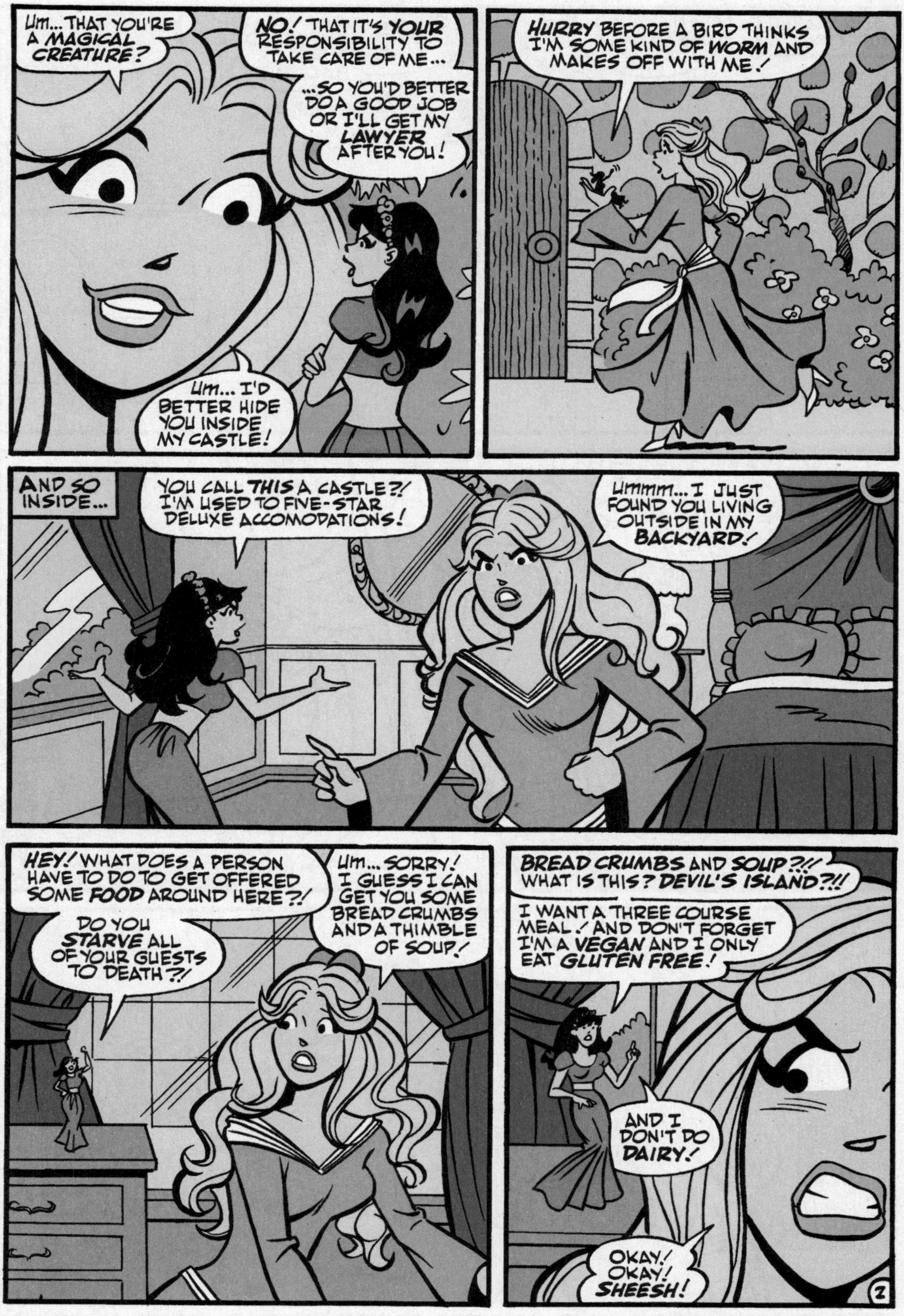
UM... THAT YOU'RE A MAGICAL CREATURE?
NO! THAT IT'S YOUR RESPONSIBILITY TO TAKE CARE OF ME...
...SO YOU'D BETTER DO A GOOD JOB OR I'LL GET MY LAWYER AFTER YOU!
UM... I'D BETTER HIDE YOU INSIDE MY CASTLE!
HURRY BEFORE A BIRD THINKS I'M SOME KIND OF WORM AND MAKES OFF WITH ME!
AND SO INSIDE...
YOU CALL THIS A CASTLE?! I'M USED TO FIVE-STAR DELUXE ACCOMODATIONS!
UMMMM... I JUST FOUND YOU LIVING OUTSIDE IN MY BACKYARD!
HEY! WHAT DOES A PERSON HAVE TO DO TO GET OFFERED SOME FOOD AROUND HERE?!
DO YOU STARVE ALL OF YOUR GUESTS TO DEATH?!
UM... SORRY! I GUESS I CAN GET YOU SOME BREAD CRUMBS AND A THIMBLE OF SOUP!
BREAD CRUMBS AND SOUP?!! WHAT IS THIS? DEVIL'S ISLAND?!!
I WANT A THREE COURSE MEAL! AND DON'T FORGET I'M A VEGAN AND I ONLY EAT GLUTEN FREE!
AND I DON'T DO DAIRY!
OKAY! OKAY! SHEESH!
2

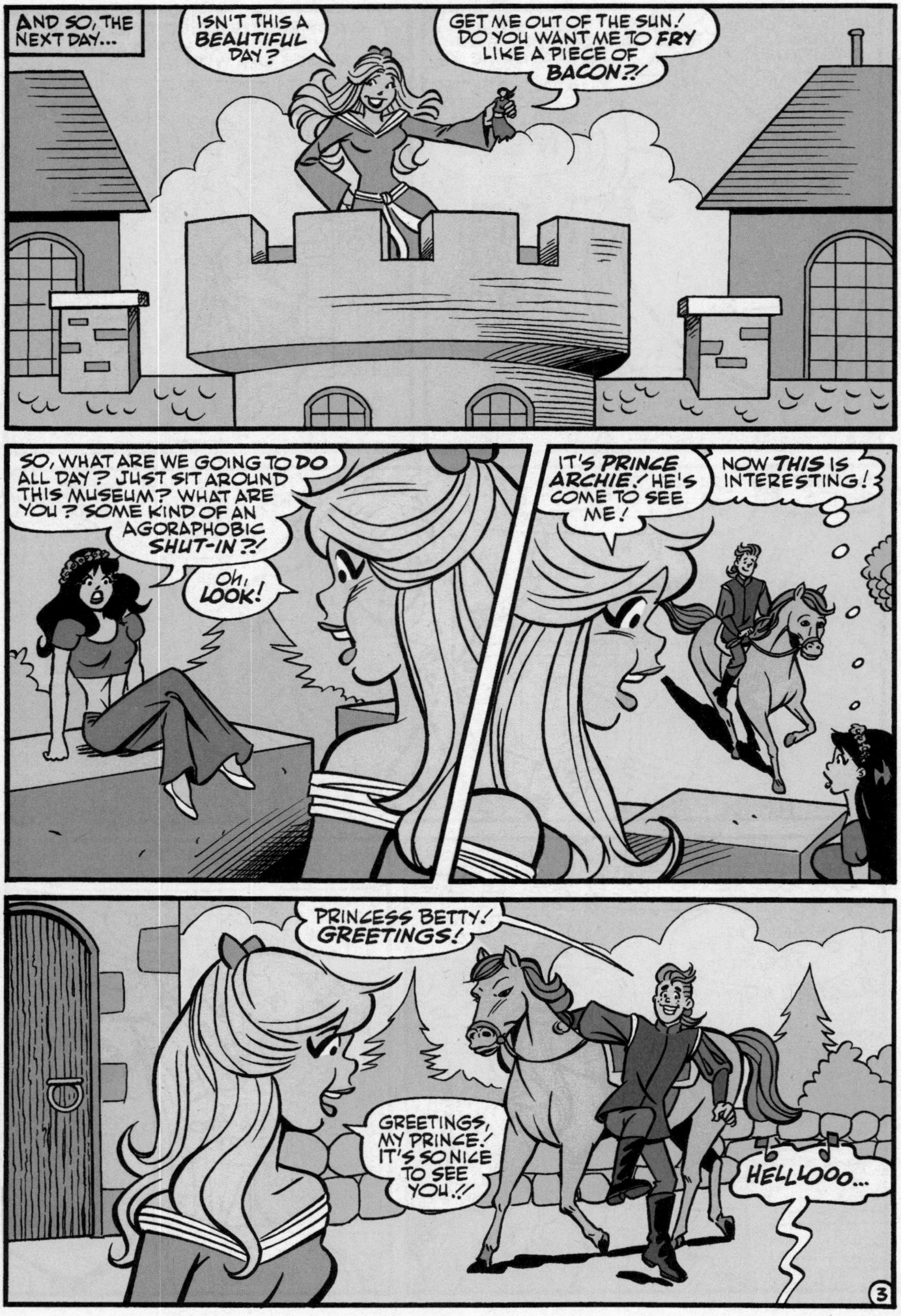
AND SO, THE NEXT DAY...
ISN'T THIS A BEAUTIFUL DAY?
GET ME OUT OF THE SUN! DO YOU WANT ME TO FRY LIKE A PIECE OF BACON?!
SO, WHAT ARE WE GOING TO DO ALL DAY? JUST SIT AROUND THIS MUSEUM? WHAT ARE YOU? SOME KIND OF AN AGORAPHOBIC SHUT-IN?!
Oh, LOOK!
IT'S PRINCE ARCHIE! HE'S COME TO SEE ME!
NOW THIS IS INTERESTING!
PRINCESS BETTY! GREETINGS!
GREETINGS, MY PRINCE! IT'S SO NICE TO SEE YOU!!
HELLOOO...
3

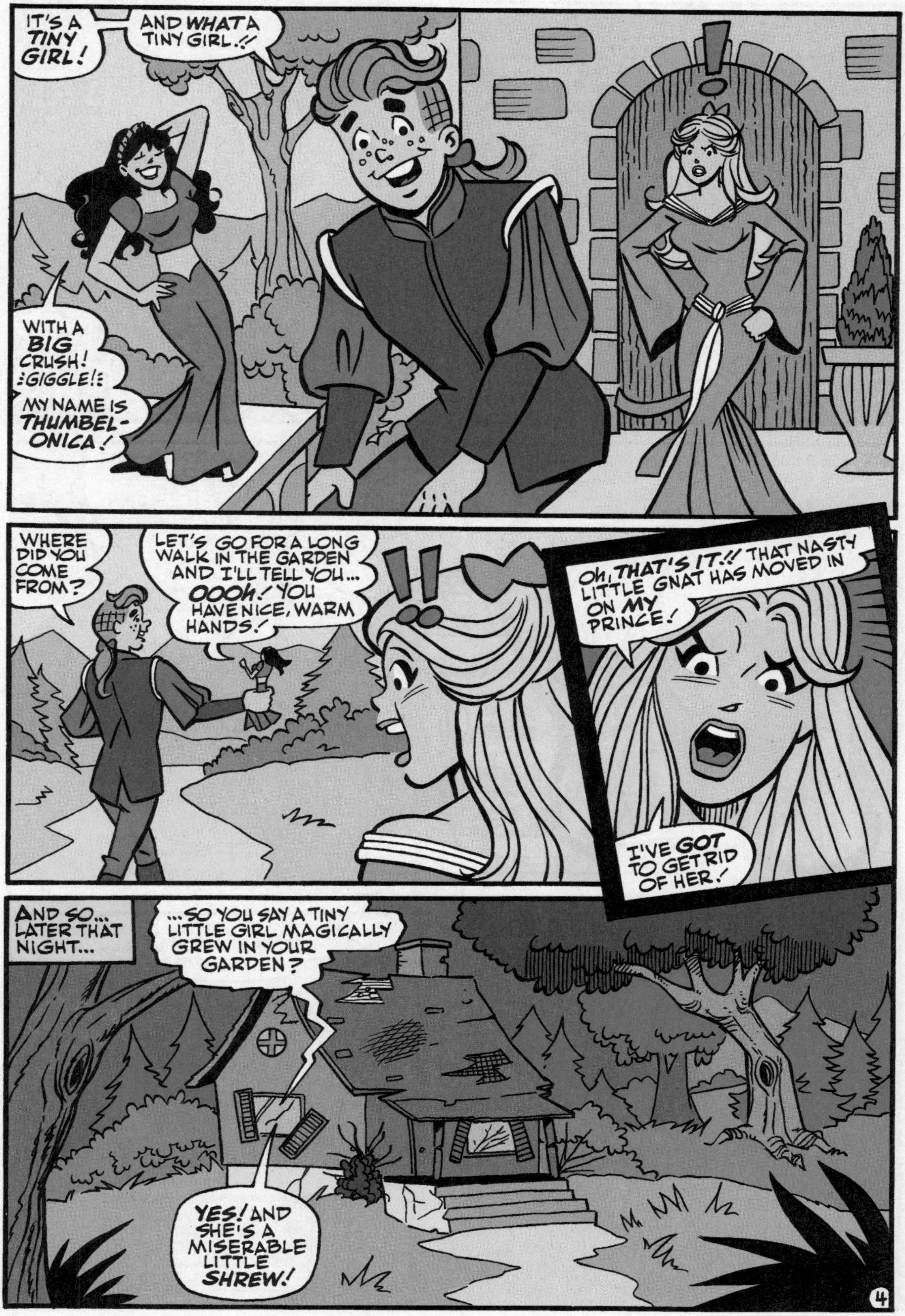
IT'S A TINY GIRL!
AND WHAT A TINY GIRL!!
!
WITH A BIG CRUSH! :GIGGLE!:
MY NAME IS THUMBEL-ONICA!
WHERE DID YOU COME FROM?
LET'S GO FOR A LONG WALK IN THE GARDEN AND I'LL TELL YOU... OOOh! YOU HAVE NICE, WARM HANDS!
!!
Oh, THAT'S IT!! THAT NASTY LITTLE GNAT HAS MOVED IN ON MY PRINCE!
I'VE GOT TO GET RID OF HER!
AND SO... LATER THAT NIGHT...
...SO YOU SAY A TINY LITTLE GIRL MAGICALLY GREW IN YOUR GARDEN?
YES! AND SHE'S A MISERABLE LITTLE SHREW!
4

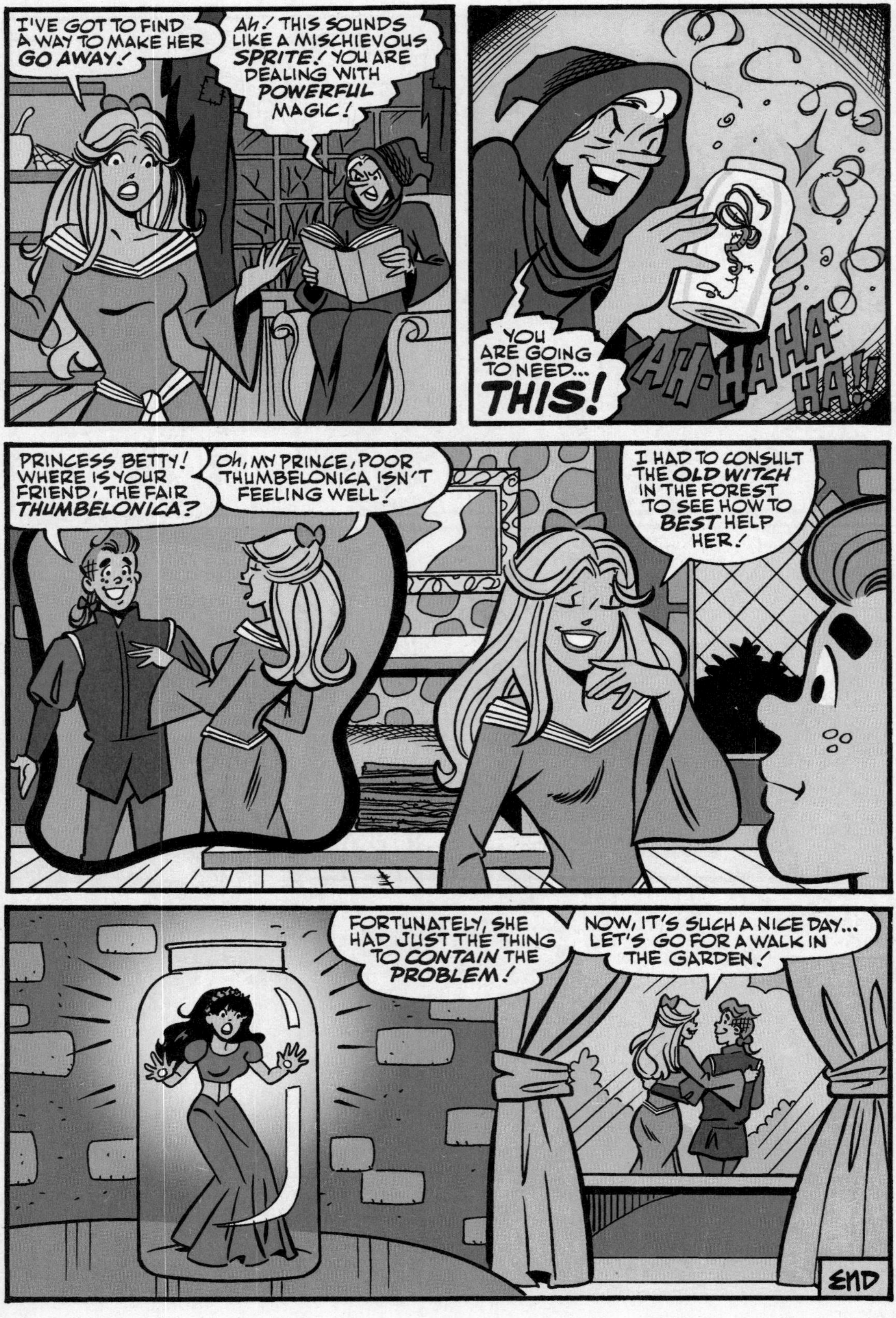
I'VE GOT TO FIND A WAY TO MAKE HER GO AWAY!
Ah! THIS SOUNDS LIKE A MISCHIEVOUS SPRITE! YOU ARE DEALING WITH POWERFUL MAGIC!
YOU ARE GOING TO NEED... THIS!
AH-HAHAHA HA!!
PRINCESS BETTY! WHERE IS YOUR FRIEND, THE FAIR THUMBELONICA?
Oh, MY PRINCE, POOR THUMBELONICA ISN'T FEELING WELL!
I HAD TO CONSULT THE OLD WITCH IN THE FOREST TO SEE HOW TO BEST HELP HER!
FORTUNATELY, SHE HAD JUST THE THING TO CONTAIN THE PROBLEM!
NOW, IT'S SUCH A NICE DAY... LET'S GO FOR A WALK IN THE GARDEN!
END